Copyright 1998 Linda Coleman
Cover Design © 1999 Press-TIGE Publishing

All rights reserved, including the right to reproduce this book
or portions therein in any form whatsoever.

For information address:
Press-Tige Publishing
291 Main Street
Catskill, NY 12414
http://gtesupersite.com/presstige
http://ordercom.com/show1/presstige.htm

First Press-Tige Edition 1999

Printed in the United States of America

ISBN# 1-57532-194-7

NORMANDALE COMMUNITY COLLEGE
LIBRARY
9700 FRANCE AVENUE SOUTH
BLOOMINGTON, MN 55431-4399

Chapter 1—Cassie

January in Minneapolis, Minnesota is like living in a white microcosm, white on the ground, on buildings, roofs, and in the surrounding sky on most days . . . white . . . until one's eyes are blinded by it. And on this particular day in the first month of the year, in the crust of a Minnesota winter, verging on near blizzard conditions, the Mall of America, the largest mall in the world, could barely be seen. It looked as though someone had taken the most humongous blanket in the universe and tossed it over the massive structure . . . a white blanket.

After four hours and twenty-three minutes outside the mall, Cassie Callahan was sensory overloaded with white, despite the sunglasses perched on the bridge of her small, upturned nose.

"Is that someone coming?" She lithely bounced up on her boot soles.

Tightly hugging herself and teeth clattering, Cassie's best friend, Sarie Nelson squinted through the whipping snow. "The abominable snowman, maybe," she replied.

Cassie craned her neck to look closer. "No! It's a moving form, human not mechanical, but I can't tell the sex yet."

Sarie hugged tighter. "What does it matter, Cass? The place is like a tomb today with this damn snow. You're not gonna get any takers. Everyone's in their nice cozy homes, sipping hot chocolate by the fireplace, listening to Peter Cetera on the stereo, and staying warm."

Cassie pulled the homemade stocking cap over her shoulder-length pale blonde hair, then hiked up the collar on her red ski jacket that had seen better days. "Yeah--I heard you," she replied, her sunglasses fastened on the approaching figure. "But I promised myself that I'd push twenty books today and I intend to stay until I do, damn snow or not."

"Twenty? That means you have nineteen to go--or to be more specific, nineteen and a half when you consider you were forced to sell your only sale at half-price."

"The loss was worth it Sar. He promised to read it, and tell his friends . . . That's what I need, notoriety, recognition to my writing style and theme: The tortured man," Cassie replied with dramatic flair.

"What about your tortured friend?" Sarie shivered. "She could have a story or two to tell the world about peddling books with a fantasy-based female who should just give it up!"

Flinging off her sunglasses, Cassie angrily flashed her huge green eyes. "Give it up? Give up my life, my love, my passion, my obsession? Give up my reason for being, my every breath I take, the thud of my every heartbeat, the metabolism of my every cell? Give it up?"

"Yes!"

Cassie threw on her sunglasses and felt the familiar misery. No one understood, not a soul. They all thought her ten years of writing was a joke, a fluke, a passing fancy that they couldn't wait to pass. That is, except her Grandfather Scarpelli.

Despite her inability to achieve success, he still prodded her with his encouragement, verbal and financial. Angelo Scarpelli had kept her afloat in the world of self-publishing, five books total, and all of them she had been forced to sell on the streets of Minneapolis, St. Paul, and Anoka, Minnesota, her hometown. Not a bookstore would touch them, not even the outlandish in downtown Minneapolis.

"Who the hell is Cassie Callahan?"

This was always the question when she imploringly approached a book store owner. She wasn't a Steel, a Krantz, a Collins, a Robbins, so they eyed her suspiciously like she was a nutcase. And 'nutcase' held no impression on the bookshelves.

Thus, at age thirty-one, she was still an obscurity when at twenty-one, she had envisioned great things for herself--fame, glory, immersing herself day in and day out in her passion, her heaven on Earth--but, bit-by-bit the greatness had crumbled away like a worn-out statue.

Yet, like a renovator, she kept picking up the crumbles and plastering them back on with each word she placed on her computer. She had to maintain and avoid the final rubble of defeat. She had to keep writing.

She had to . . .

"Looks like another male, Cass. Maybe if you flap those gorgeous green eyes, he'll get horny enough to put out four bucks for the tortured man," Sarie said sarcastically.

Ignoring her friend's tone, Cassie pulled off her sunglasses, lifted her cap, and fixed a toothy smile on her face. Then she sucked in her breath and waited. Perhaps this was the person who would change her life. Perhaps he would read it, love it, and tell his zillion friends about the artiste, Cassie Callahan. Perhaps, she restively told herself, he would take her away from her mundane, unemotional, and a-intellectual existence, and let her live.

"A little blustery to be outdoors, isn't it girls?"

Cassie scrutinized the man in front of her--middle-aged, glasses coated with snow so he looked devoid of eyes, short, squat, possibly bald as there no hair evident under his Minnesota Viking ski cap. Could he be important? His outward appearances didn't indicate this, though she reminded herself about the adage: *A wolf in sheep's clothing.*

"So whatcha got in the box? Sellin' candy or somethin'?" he asked.

Cassie fixed on the white spectacles and widened her smile. "No sir. I'm selling emotions, gripping, gut-busting emotions."

"Huh?" His mouth made a baffled expression.

Instantly, Cassie reached down and pulled up a book. "This is a male diary of emotions, steaming with suffering, agony . . . maleness . . . I'm sure you could identify, sir, I can tell."

His eyebrows raised his over his glasses. "You can? How?"

"By . . ." Cassie racked her brain for a plausible answer. "By your eyes! They seem endless, much that is unspoken behind the . . . ur. . ." She took a closer look at the snow-covered lenses. "White endless orbs that reek of . . . ah . . . a question!"

"A question?"

"A question that asks, What lies within the deep recesses of the seemingly blankness? It must be more than is evident to the naked eye, much more. Perhaps anguish, pain, excruciating torture . . . a veritable variety of submerged emotions that could be surfaced by reading my masterpiece. It's not only fiction sir, but a guide to disclose your innermost feelings to an unsuspecting world. You'll be a new man for the effort. I promise."

With a gloved hand, he pulled off his glasses to reveal small, pinpoint eyes that directed onto the book, and read.

"The Tarnished Male, by Cassie Callahan." Then looking up at her, "That's you, I take it."

"Yes, sir," she replied with a bright, frozen smile, adding proudly, "This is my fifth published book."

"Hmmm . . ." He raised a gloved hand to his chin and rubbed. "Never heard of you. And you're from the Twin Cities?"

"Anoka, born, bred, and still residing."

More chin rubbing. "How much?"

Cassie broadened her smile. "Seven-fifty, a steal."

"Too much." He began to walk away.

"But sir!" She jumped in front of him and her eyes to grow huge and pleading. "To be a new man is priceless and I offer it to you for a measly seven-fifty."

He sighed heavily. "For seven-fifty, I'll stay my old self." Again he tried to move past.

Again she blocked his movement. "Would you leave your old self behind for six-fifty?"

"Nope, not even for five-fifty," he replied.

"Then five dollars . . . I offer you fulfillment for five lousy bucks."

He paused, then shook his head. "I guess the blankness will have to stay. Sorry Miss." He began to skirt her, but she leapt in his path.

"Okay—Okay . . . four-fifty, a giveaway," she dickered.

Again he thought. "Naw--I was planning on buying Gresham's latest book. I'll put the money towards that and just get pissed off instead of fulfilled."

Desperation gripped her. "Gresham? You'd pass up the chance for self-actualization and discovering a preponderance of new powerful emotions, for *Gresham*?"

For the third time he contemplated. "Yup--seems so," he finally replied.

"Four dollars for a chance at finding your personal Nirvana?" she pressed on.

"I dunno." He ran a gloved finger up and down his red cheeks. "Cassie Callahan, huh?"

She nodded eagerly.

"Anoka, you say?"

Cassie nodded once more.

"All right--what the hell? Two-fifty and you got a deal," he finally conceded.

"Sold!" she exclaimed happily, then watched him pull out his wallet.

"Got change for a twenty?" he asked.

Cassie widened her eyes. She didn't even have change for a five! Hastily she turned to a stiff with cold Sarie. "Please tell me you have change," she said, distressed.

Sarie glared through the whipping snow. "Change? What's that? I live in a plastic world, twenty-two cards strong. You know that."

Frustrated, Cassie turned back to the man. "No change," she told him.

Smiling wryly, he dug in his coat pocket, extracting a handful of coins. "This is all I got, take it or leave it," he said.

Cassie stared down at the nickels, dimes, and pennies lying in the man's palm, and she wondered what to do. Should she take such a massive loss, again and be thankful that her book was getting into the mainstream? Her hand inched closer to the money, and soon the coins rested in her palm. "Enjoy the book, sir, and may all of life's fulfillment touch you from the first word," she said, experiencing the same disheartening feeling that always pervaded when her work of art was undervalued by a non-appreciative public.

"Yeah--I may take a gander at it, after I get done with Gresham . . ."

****

Interstate-35W North was coated with two inches of fresh snow and an underlay of ice. Never having been a skillful winter driver, Cassie tried to maneuver her seven-year-old Toyota down the icy low-trafficked lanes. Sarie had her shoulder harness tightly pulled across her, and despite the warmth of the car, was still shivering, this time in fear.

"Easy does it, Cass. I'm in no hurry to get back to Anoka."

Cassie fixed her eyes directly above the steering column. "I'm in a bit of a hurry . . . Kyle you know," she replied.

"He'll have a bird," Sarie said knowingly. "Four dollars and ninety cents in five hours . . . he'll have a bird all right."

"Four dollars and ninety-one cents," Cassie corrected with a wince. Her husband Kyle would have an 'ostrich' when he learned of her take for the day. They only lived on his used car salesman salary, and his monthly gross was hit and miss, depending on the demand for used cars. He constantly harped on her to find a real job to supplement the family's meager income. But she didn't have time—writing took up most of her time. So far she had held him off, although that it wouldn't last forever. One of these days he would crack her.

"And then there's Kristi, Cass," Sarie spoke on. "You gotta think of her future, college and a prestigious job to match her brain . . ."

The snow had lightened up a bit, and Cassie assumed a more relaxed driver's stance. Leave it to Sarie to fill her with guilt, she thought. Kristi, her precocious ten-year-old, had fared okay so far, despite the fact she went without more times than not. It was only Grandpa Scarpelli's and her parent's generosity that prevented Kristi from being classified as an underprivileged child. She knew she should find that job for her child's sake, but every time the notion grew serious, she was hit by the sense of being on the verge of something big, and the writing took precedence.

"You're a smart woman, Cass, always have been. I can still hear your valedictorian speech in high school. I needed a dictionary to decipher it, but it was good, damn good."

Cassie peeked at the her friend. The black hair was layered to perfection, the face made up like a model despite the snow she had been exposed to, and her nails, each an immaculate two inches long and painted without a mar. The only flaw was Sarie's figure. She had always been on the chubby side, despite she worked out three times a week at a gym and owned a treadmill. Yet, she was successful, Cassie thought. Sarie had taken a C-average in college and propelled it into a thriving real estate career. Although, Sarie's life had changed drastically, they remained best friends, each doing anything for the other. Thus, Sarie's willingness to give up another Saturday to peddle books, despite Sarie's hatred of the activity.

"And Kyle feels ignored, I know," Sarie continued on.

Seeking Out Harry

Damn! Cassie pushed deeper into the accelerator. She knew her husband constantly made pleas to Sarie. "Talk some sense into Cassie. Make her see she's ruining our life . . ." And statements to that effect.

It was him, Kyle Matthew Callahan, who was her greatest driving force to write. Writing was her means to escape the biggest disappointment in her life: Her twelve-year marriage, brought about because she had thrown away her inhibitions and allowed one of the star jocks in high school to have her in the back of a van, then have her again, and again, until she got pregnant from a defective condom, she always figured. They hastily married under her strict, Italian Catholic family's eyes, and two months later she had a miscarriage. She wanted to divorce him then and there; the incompatibility was blaring. Yet she was Catholic, and the mere notion was unthinkable. So she was stuck with a man who provided her no psychological, emotional, or intellectual connection . . . and the physical aspect had long become tedious, as well. The only positive to come out of the union was Kristi.

She loved her daughter. The little girl's wit and intellect delighted her. "She's just like you," many of her family and acquaintances always said. But Kristi cringed with the comparison. The girl said she wanted to be like her friends' mothers and not nothing like her own. Kristi didn't understand the writing—she called it 'doodling' and likened her mother to a daydreamer, an unproductive entity in her focused, structured mind. Thus, in Kristi's thinking, her mother had no worth, except to make chocolate chip cookies when she had the proclivity, and get the dirt stains out of blue jeans. Far from a modern mother, in Kristi's estimation.

"I see the exit up ahead, Cass." Sarie pulled a hairbrush from her shoulder bag and smoothed out her hair strands until they gleamed.

Cassie pumped her brakes to decelerate then cautiously slid into the right lane. Once the car was righted, she again peeked at her friend. Conversely, she felt like a drenched rag, a piece of crud, and total personal disaster rolled into one. She slid her gaze to the rearview mirror, and glanced. Writing sixteen hours a day had taken its toll. Her face looked gaunt and skin dull. She never even bothered with make up anymore; although people told her she looked beautiful nonetheless. Her naturally pale blonde hair, inherited from her Swedish mother, had lost its luster, as did her huge green eyes, acquired from her Grandpa Scarpelli. She was a mess! In more ways than appearance, she was an absolute mess.

Yet . . . she couldn't give it up.

"You're pretty quiet, Cass. Trying to figure out a confabulation to tell that gorgeous husband of yours?" Sarie smiled deviously.

Gorgeous? Ugh! Cassie restrained the impulse to make a face. Sarie had always had a soft spot for Kyle. He had been her heartthrob in high school, ever since he scored three touchdowns to win the football conference title their junior year. But Kyle never even gave her a nod. He liked his woman slim, and he always said that Sarie needed to lose a good thirty pounds, most of it from her behind. Yet he always cried to Sarie; Sarie's better than a mother, Kyle said. *And could she cook.* Sarie would make a gourmet chef groan.

"You didn't answer my question, Cass."

Cassie drove up the exit to Anoka. "No confabulations. I'll just evade him, as usual."

"How can you evade a man like Kyle? He's six feet four inches of perfect maleness. And he's hardly changed all these years."

"Except for his beer gut, receding hairline, and a mouth that complains at a rate of hundred twenty rpms," Cassie replied with bitterness.

"A tiny gut, and a bit more forehead, otherwise, he's sexier than he was in high school."

"Says you."

"No Cass, says every woman in Anoka under the age of a hundred."

It was futile! Sarie would never see the truth behind the man.

Sarie undid her shoulder harness then reached in the back seat to grab one of Cassie's books. She gave it a firm shake. "The tortured male . . . that's your own husband. Did you base the book on him?"

Cassie sniffed. "You've got to be kidding, Sar. Kyle hasn't even a hundredth inch of depth as Cyrano, my protagonist."

"Cyrano?" Sarie broke down in laughter.

Immediately, Cassie's defense mechanisms sprang forth. "What's so funny? Cyrano is a highly distinguished name for a man with an outward distinguished appearance, though in actuality, he's highly agonized from an incestuous relationship with Zelda, an older cousin twice removed who lured him into a closet with a Mr. Goodbar. Didn't you read it? You promised me you would, Sarie."

"Zelda? Mr. Goodbar? Oh Cass . . ." Sarie laughed harder.

Cassie gunned the accelerator, not caring if the car spun. This was a prime example of the support she got from the people nearest and dearest, she thought angrily. She had studied, taken correspondence courses, and wrote until she was blue in the face--and it *had* gotten better. She *knew* she had improved regardless of what anyone thought. She tried to be so literary and creative, it oozed with every sentence she wrote. She twisted cliches' as well as plots, and created conflict that kept her at the edge of her seat while she wrote.

And I'm getting closer to the edge with each book . . .

"Okay--I'll admit I didn't read the whole thing. I only made it to the second page, Cass."

"Thanks a lot!" Cassie spewed.

"I tried, Cass, believe me, but your words . . . I need a thesaurus, and your symbolism is so complicated, it takes the pleasure out of reading. There! I've said it."

Cassie felt a surge of fury. "Maybe it's just too sophisticated for a palate that finds the funny papers intriguing!"

"Insults won't change my mind, Cass, in fact make me more adamant when I say that the comics are more intriguing than that crud you write about," Sarie retorted back.

How dare her! A woman who had a stack of romance novels and magazines in one corner of her bedroom to compensate for her loveless, sexless life. No wonder she had no appreciation for finer literature. Sarie's literary mind was the equivalent of Jell-O, Cassie seethed. And her incessant television watching . . . She squealed like a half-baked idiot over any male actor with a little hair on his chest or had a semblance of bulge in his pants. That's her definition of literary!

"Why can't you speak in plain English or pick normal names like John, Mary, or Sam or make your setting small town America, instead of Timbuktu?

Seeking Out Harry

And why can't you just tell a story instead of placing a bunch of sentences on a merry-go-round so one's brain twirls?" Sarie sighed deeply. "I just think you can't, and that's the problem. You don't have the ability to write for the average Joe. So. . . . a career in medical assisting may be a brighter future for you."

Cassie's insides twisted with rage. "And I suppose Kyle put you up to that one!"

"Well . . . he did get some pamphlets from the technical college."

"Screw him!"

"And that seems to be another problem."

"What?" The Toyota almost veered off the road, and Cassie quickly swerved. She took several calming breaths after the near disaster. What had Kyle told her? Was nothing sacred between them? That jackass!

"He's a vital man, Cass. He has more urgent needs than most men."

"How the would you know?"

Sarie caressed her hair between her fingers. "From high school of course. Kyle was an animal. Don't you remember? Locker rooms, behind bleachers, in janitorial closets . . . pure animal that man."

Oh barf! Couldn't Sarie get off the high school mode where Kyle was concerned? He was no longer super jock, rather super jerk. Couldn't she see that? Couldn't anyone see that?

She made a sharp turn and the car did a half-spin. Undaunted in her wrath, Cassie quickly straightened out the car and kept going at a comparable speed. "So you're saying I should fall at Kyle's feet because he's a physical attraction?" she asked through the grit of her teeth.

"Like any other warm-blooded, living, breathing female," was Sarie's emphatic response.

"The primary trait." Cassie nodded knowingly. "But what about the secondary and tertiary traits? Aren't those equally important?"

"Huh?" Sarie gave her a blank look.

"The inner traits which touch a woman to the core, fulfill her, tantalizes her senses to the point that the only word that exudes from her brain is *wow*, those types of attributes."

"You're making as much sense as The Tarnished Male . . ."

"Intelligence, talent, sensitivity, creative artistry, compassion, fire . . . all adding up to a magnetism that makes a woman's insides curl." Cassie's body engulfed in intense longing.

Sarie let out a rip-roaring giggle. "Sounds like a fag to me, Cass."

It would! Sarie only rated men from the waist down. She was sex-starved, plain and simple. But that lost its luster without the other traits. Sarie could never see this—she'd never been able to see this. Sarie had a cock for a brain.

"Two more blocks to go." Sarie gagged on her laughter.

"Laugh! I don't care. We'll see who laughs last once I get my big break."

Sarie laughed harder. "Five books you had to publish yourself at a cost of thousands of dollars that's long gone and you'll never inherit, because not even an agent would give you the time of day for your creative works that they call garbage and beyond repair. I read every letter. Remember? I think there's a message for you, Cass, but you aren't heeding it."

The cruel bluntness washed over Cassie. It was bad enough that total strangers discouraged her without a friend doing the same. In fact, her parents, older sister, and assorted relatives from her father's large extended family were just as merciless. Get a job--waitress, store clerk, fast-food counter person, anything--to help Poor Kyle. They all thought he was the best thing since Warren Moon, every single one of them . . . except her Grandfather Scarpelli. He saw Kyle for what he really was and likewise, saw her immense unhappiness. She never hid it from the old man. Angelo Scarpelli may be purely Italian, but he was her grandfather first, in the true blood-tied sense of the word. That's why he helped her despite Kyle's disdain of her chosen career. It was his way of giving her a bit of victory amid the air of stifling negativism around her. And Angelo Scarpelli would do anything to make her, his most kindred relative, happy.

"Here's my house, still upright, despite the foot of snow on the roof," Sarie said cheerfully while undoing her shoulder harness.

"How about dinner at my house? My Nona sent over homemade ravioli and sausage," Cassie invited, despite her anger. She figured she owed something to Sarie for the last six miserable hours.

"Sounds delish, but fattening, and you know my perpetual diet," Sarie swung her booted feet out the passenger door and into a pile of fresh snow. "Anyway, I wanna watch the reruns of *Knot's Landing*, and you always give me dirty looks when I turn on the teevee."

"Suit yourself." Cassie was relieved at the refusal. This way she didn't have to suffer the sight of Sarie and Kyle in their conspiratorial huddles, mapping out their strategies, with her the target of their battle plans. "Operation Cassie." Get her back to the world of normal . . . whatever normal was.

Shifting the car into drive, Cassie slid past four more houses until she reached her own . . .

****

The lights in the Callahan's two-story forty year old home were dimmed to the point that is was questionable if any inhabitants were present in the house.

Kyle's on his cost-saving mission again, Cassie thought scornfully as her worn leather boots cracked over the icy walkway. The air had turned bitter cold and the wind had kicked up. A shiver ran through her and she hastened her gait to the front door. Once inside, a sudden warmth hit her. She smelled the burning pitch of the wood stove was on full blast. *Wood's much cheaper than gas* . . . Kyle's constant touts rattled her brain. Never mind the asphyxia or pungent odor that touched the very pit of one's stomach.

Cassie peeled off her winter gear and casually tossed the items in the small coat closet. She looked left to right. No one was in immediate sight, and she flooded with relief. Perhaps she could take pause and twist the confabulation that Sarie had suggested.

Kyle had no idea about abstract, she thought, slyly. Things had to be spelled out in black and white for comprehension. He had graduated eight hundred and twenty-two in a class of eight hundred twenty-four, and this fact had vexed her every moment of their married life. It was near impossible for her to converse with such a stubborn brain when her own was so nimble. She may as well have been married to a stone wall.

Cassie deliberately climbed the stairs. She would go to her Land of Peace, Contentment and Serenity, the decrepit walk-up attic, her writing abode. It was cluttered, stifling hot, and smelled like a mold-infested refrigerator. Yet an *artiste* must suffer for success, she constantly reinforced, thus discounted the small discomforts and enjoyed the solitude of the room.

"Stop Cass!"

Promptly halting, she widened her eyes in alarming surprise. He had spotted her! And her without a confabulation sitting in her brain to dupe him. Now she had to face his putdowns, scoldings, recriminations, and less than objective attitude—she had to face them all. Again.

"I know you heard me, Cass."

The low, snarly voice penetrated her brain once more, and ever-so-slowly she turned her head to peer down. There stood the big hulk, his eyes spewing brown fire. Minuscule drops of sweat dotted his forehead, and his white T-shirt was moist and clingy. She wished he would figure out the house was too damn hot and ease up on his Paul Bunyan act with the wood stove.

"Did you bring home enough to pay the electric bill like you promised?" Kyle demanded.

Confabulate! She commanded herself. And as she did, she emitted a light, elongated laugh while her five foot five, lanky frame descended the stairs.

"Well . . . ?" he demanded again.

Cassie cut her noise. A contrivance hadn't even tickled her brain. "It depends."

"What the hell does it depend on?"

"The bill total," she blurted. "Does it equal price of a four-slice toaster or a bottle of shampoo?" She mumbled her last word.

His eyes flashed suspiciously. "What is this crap? Toaster? Shampoo? Try canister vacuum with attachments and a year's supply of bags, then I think we got it covered!"

"How quaint, vacuum cleaners and electric bills. There must be a metaphor of comparison somewhere. Let me think . . ."

"Think my ass! I want cold hard moola," Kyle sneered.

"Moola . . . what a provincial way to describe one of life's necessities. So profound, so prone to thought provocation, so. . . ."

"Cut the shit, Cass. It ain't gonna work this time," he warned.

Cassie saw his insistence and knew her lack of prefabrication was her downfall. She could usually get around him with her glib, agile tongue given a minute degree of preparation. But why she hadn't done it today, she had no clue. Maybe she was just tired of the lies, or maybe, just maybe, Kyle was smartening up in his advancing age. The final notion was so bizarre, it almost frightening, she thought.

"So spill it Cass. How much?"

"Guess!"

"For Christ's sakes Cass, I'm in no mood for games. I have over seventeen hundred dollars worth of bills to pay this month and I'm short a couple hundred."

"A bank loan! Or perhaps you could ask your father for a . . ."

"Forget it Cass!" Kyle angered. "I'm into the old man for a good five thou already and all the bankers pull their shades when they see me comin'."

"So. . . . " she burst with brightness. "What will you do this month?"

He ran a hand, frustrated, through his thinning light brown hair. "*What?* How the hell do I know *what* anymore?"

"*What?*. . .a philosophical question whose answer has infinite possibilities."

"Huh?"

"Perhaps you should curl up in your recliner with a beer and a football game, and come up with as many endless answers as your brain will allow. Then you can go from there, sort out the plausible from the ridiculous, jiggle pros and cons, until the one correct, shining answer beams in all its glory, and *that* will guide your course."

He gave her a blank look.

"Digest my words dear Kyle in between your harmonious belches and I assure you that the answer to *what* will eventually materialize." *Maybe in your second life,* she added silently. "Now I must start supper . . . Nona's ravioli and sausage . . . and because of your diligent contemplative efforts, I'll even toss in those baking powder biscuits that you're so fond of."

She took a light skirt past him.

"Huh?"

Without turning she lifted a hand. "Ta-da . . . happy thinking . . ."

****

A pig has nothing on him, Cassie thought, watching Kyle slobber down her grandmother's homemade Italian sausage like they were pretzel sticks and biscuits like they were *Fruit Loops*.

The three, her, Kyle, and Kristi, sat at the kitchen table. Per usual, Kristi dartingly looked from one parent to the other. She never seemed to know what to say to either parent. Or perhaps the grotesque sight to the side of her has stunned her into silence, Cassie thought, glancing up now and then at the inquisitive face.

"Great chow. Your granny's a genius with the food." Kyle's cheeks jutted with each word.

Ad nauseam . . . Cassie shifted from the stomach-turning sight and focused her eyes on Kristi. She was the image of her father, same hair color, eyes, and physique. She could see little of herself in the small face. Only Kristi's mind gave credence that Cassie took part in her conception. Her daughter was the smartest girl in the fourth grade class, much as Cassie herself had been.

"How's your dinner, honey?" Cassie questioned with a smile.

Kristi paused to think. This was her normal stance when a question was posed to her. The girl's answers were never of the impulsive sort. "I liken it to Italian take-out," she finally replied.

"Take-out? It's homemade or homegrown Kristi, right down to spinach in the ravioli shells," Cassie protested.

"Maybe so." Kristi fastened a calculating look on her. "Yet you didn't cook it yourself and it came from another place, the Scarpelli kitchen to be exact."

"So? I made the biscuits," Cassie defended.

Kristi plucked up a baking powder biscuit and wrinkled her nose in disgust."Eighty-nine generic cents for a can of preservatives that by now have probably built up to toxic proportions in my system," she complained.

"Huh?" Kyle looked baffled as he stuffed a seventh biscuit into his mouth.

Cassie glanced at him, then rolled her eyes back to her daughter. "Generic, *Pillsbury*, what's the difference?"

"Speaking of *what* . . ." Kyle said with a full mouth.

"Freshness, naturalness . . . a bread machine," Kristi replied with great aplomb.

"What?" Cassie suspiciously narrowed her eyes. Kristi was always full of grandiose ideas garnered from who knows where.

"I needa talk to you about *what*, Cass," Kyle sharply interjected.

"Heather's mom makes homemade bread in their machine all the time, *and* she works sixty hours a week, buyer for *Casual Corners*, brings in forty-five thousand a year, Heather brags. The honey nut bread melts in my mouth." Kristi leveled an accusing glare on Cassie.

The familiar guilt assailed her, as it had ever since Kristi was cognizant enough to realize her deprivation in relation to other children. The revelation hit in her fifth year of life, and since then, the precocious Kristi hadn't let up. Peer pressure was horrible in the schools, Cassie knew.

"We can't afford such an extravagance," she mumbled.

"Ask Nono," Kristi said without a flinch.

Frustrated, Cassie slammed a ravioli into her mouth and chewed. Her grandfather had already shelled out a small fortune on her self-publishing efforts so she had a chance to get her name out to the public when no one else would touch her. It was his investment in her, he always said. Then he concluded with the statement that he had faith in her. Her hard work wouldn't be for nothing, he told her.

Now, she saw all his thousands of invested dollars floating away and cumulatively landing in a fiery inferno. Did she dare ask for more to appease her daughter, yet again? No, she finally decided. Kristi needed to learn that the true richness of life didn't include expensive material possessions, rather deeper entities.

"Nono's given us enough," Cassie said decisively.

"That's for sure." Kyle waved his fork at her. "Eighteen thousand five hundred seventy-five much-needed dollars from the old man that are *nada*."

"It could have financed a lucrative career in gymnastics for me, or expanded my mind with a tour of New England, or England for that matter," Kristi sulked.

"He gave it to me!" Cassie argued.

"And *me* is all-important!" Kyle thrust his fork down in the middle of his third helping of ravioli. "I'm telling you Cass, this shit has to end! Ten years of pure hell."

"I'm outa here." Kristi stood, grabbed her plate and utensils, and plopped them into the sink. "Did I mention a dishwasher would be nice too?" she retorted before exiting the kitchen.

Oooh! Cassie's mind shrieked. She couldn't deal with any of it. Her mind was already congested with story after story that never quit spinning even if she was doing a hundred other things at once. And the need to get the words down on paper burned inside her like a perpetual torch. Medical assisting? She wouldn't last a day. Her creative juices would defeat her the moment she stuck a card in a time clock. Writing was her destination, her *fait accompli*.

"Now we discuss *what*." Kyle sat back in his chair and tenderly patted his paunch.

What next? She jittered while trying to rustle together her weary brain cells. There had to be a way to amass victory on this subject. But what? She asked herself repeatedly while trying to ignore the exact quality of Kyle's gaze.

"How much today, Cass? And I don't wanna hear any bullshit."

She gulped. He had her cornered unless she could concoct a parody on the word bullshit, otherwise he left her little room for witticism--or *bullshit*, as the case may be . . .

"I'm waiting dammit." He tapped his fork atop a ravioli, reducing it to a mushy pulp.

A limp laugh emitted from her. "Quite an artistic piece you're making on your plate . . . the *Pillsbury* doughboy caught in a snowblower perhaps?"

"Shut!" Kyle tossed down his fork. "How much? Forty? Forty-five? Maybe fifty so half the electric bill is covered?"

"Ah . . . Actually, the snow storm was a bit of a hindrance."

"How much of a hindrance?" His big teeth bared at her.

"Actually, I procured a tad under forty dollars," she replied.

"Thirty-nine? I'll take it."

"Not quite--lower the anti a little."

"Thirty-eight!"

"I'm afraid, you're ice cold. Try again."

Kyle lowered the anti, dollar by dollar, until he reached twenty.

"You're getting warmer," she enthused.

"Spare my breath," Kyle said irritably. "Toss me the number that'll make me boiling hot."

"How does fifteen dollars sound?"

"Like I wanna wring your neck, but I'll take it anyway."

Cassie nervously shifted on the garish aqua-hued flower-patterned, mismatched from the rest around the table. Perhaps Sarie would make up the ten dollar and nine cent deficit of her lie. *No.* Sarie had made it perfectly clear that she would help Cassie finance a dress, or a bottle of cologne, or a sexy negligee so she could rekindle her marriage, but her writing taboo. Sarie viewed it as plain wrong,

"Well I'm waiting . . ." Kyle thrust his big meaty palm under her nose.

"Okay!" The sight of the wet, clumsy extremity made her insides coil with repugnance. "I collected an Abe Lincoln . . . well nearly."

Kyle's eyes popped with angry disbelief. "Five bucks for six fuckin' hours? Per hour that's . . ." He paused to calculate.

Exasperated, Cassie raised her eyes to the ceiling. The figuring took painfully long and she thought that hell would convert to an iceberg before the answer came to him. "How does eighty-three cents an hour grab you? Or to be more specific, eighty-three point infinite three cents per hellish hour."

"Eighty-three *cents*? Hell! Kristi makes more babysitting. A ten-year-old kid makes more than an able-bodied supposedly mature woman!"

Cassie winced. "I tried, but The Tarnished Man didn't spark people's curiosity today."

"Oh really!" His massive form lifted from the chair and he stormed out of the kitchen, returning minutes later pushing a large cardboard box.

Not again. Cassie's eyes locked onto the familiar box, worn out from all of Kyle's draggings. She felt her crusted over wounds open one-by-one.

He pulled out a book and shook it at her. "The Plastic Male! A goddamn fag who daydreams about the private parts of male mannequins!" Kyle tossed it on the floor and extracted another book. "And this! The Castrated Male about another fag who daydreams what it would be like to lose his cock!" That book he disgustedly pitched against a cupboard. "Oh, this one I love, The Male Artiste. The guy's got a name no one can pronounce and the whole book consists of him fluttering his gentle fingers over a goddamn canvass so he can create a masterpiece of the perfect male which, in reality, is his mind's vision of himself. Shit! The thing might as well been written in Swahili!"

Plain English is Swahili to you! Cassie thought angrily, wishing she had the nerve to insult him with her mind's utterances so she could hurt him as much as he was hurting her.

"The Male Server!" He flung this book like he wanted to hit her with it. "The story of a waiter. The fairy has fuckin' fantasies about the food the regular male customers eat."

"He's mentally tortured. And I worked my brain overtime to twist food into human attributes so the true degree of his insanity would come across to the reader!" Cassie's eyes moistened with tears. "The self-publisher thought the concept was brilliant!"

"That's no surprise! A whiff of a few thousand dollars will make anyone lie like a son of a bee!" Kyle spat, then reached back down into the box and pulled out her latest book. "And we go from bad to worst . . . The Tarnished Male, a homo who suffers throughout the whole book because of a goddamn candy bar!"

"It's much deeper than that." The tears streamed down her cheeks.

"Deeper? Why not try Chinese. And why so many fags? I swear you got fags on the brain, Cass." He flung the book back into the box, making a loud crack.

"They aren't fags!"

"They all sound like fags to me!"

They would! Kyle was the premiere Minnesota man—tunnel-visioned, opinionated, and always right, she thought with utter contempt. Any man who didn't chug beer, play sports, or show his sexual prowess in bed at least three times a week, was a fag in his opinion.

She loathed the predictability.

She loathed him.

"Why this crud, Cass? Huh?" He gritted his teeth so hard they shook.

She thrust out of her chair to clear the table of dishes. Everything seemed to be collapsing on her, her dreams, hopes, plans, aspirations, everything. She was on the verge. Every sense in her body keenly felt this. If only she kept on, made herself better, more prolific . . .

"You have no talent for this line of work," Kyle said in his cruel, blunt tone. "Face up to it, and do something productive. For instance Medical Assisting. I have pamphlets for you to . . ."

"Just leave, Kyle." Her hand shook as she picked up the dishes and placed them into the sink. It was all too much for her at the moment. The familiar restlessness was overwhelming. She needed to quickly wash the dishes then escape to her safe haven. Another story burned—her stomach knotted with the anticipation.

He gave an abrupt nod. "Just leave the five on the table in the hall. It'll buy a cheap six-pack at least." He turned and charged out of the kitchen.

"Damn him!" She filled the sink with soapy water and added the dishes. Looking around the kitchen, she saw the scattered books. She quickly moved forward to picked them up, lovingly stroking the multicolored covers before placing them back into the box. It was *her*, between the pages. But no one could see it. They might as well slap her face, she thought, miserably. Every bit of her heart and soul went into every sentence she wrote, a piece of Cassie

Callahan intricately woven into each book. Would anyone in her immediate world ever understand?

With care, she closed the box then returned to the sink, letting her thoughts drift amid the gentle waves of her mind. She tried to will a story to form while she drizzled water into the glasses and onto the plates. But only the digs she had heard that day, emerged.

"Why not normal names, normal settings, normal stories, normal..."
Sarie's comments rumbled through her head.
"I need a thesaurus, and your symbolism..."

Perhaps she *should* tone it down a bit, she thought, gliding the wash rag across the knives and forks. Perhaps her meanings were so Byzantine, that they were only interpreted by her.

"Swahili! Chinese!"

Repulsion sprung on her face. Yet... maybe Kyle was the norm--although the mere idea was a horror. What lie beyond Minnesota men? She had no clue, as she had never left Minnesota except for a short jaunt to the Apple Festival in Bayfield, Wisconsin in her teenage years, and the men there appeared to be cut out of the same mold. Ugh! Could fifty million Kyles inhabit this country? The possible nightmare had never crossed her mind in all her thirty-one years. But now, the possibility confronted her.

"Why fags? You have fags on the brain, Cass..."

She slowly ran the silverware under the warm faucet stream. Maybe all fifty million would interpret her tortured men as crossing the line of manliness as did her husband, she pondered, her motions slowing. And maybe a good half of them couldn't divide six into five dollars, quick as a wink. And maybe a quarter of the half graduated at the same class rank as Kyle. Maybe... Cassie slapped the silverware into the drying slot and hastily wiped her hands on a Muslim dishtowel.

"Yes!"

And she rushed out of the kitchen...

****

At ten past eleven at night, there was a tap on the locked attic door.

On impulse, Cassie wanted to yell, "Go away." But she thought that maybe it was Kristi, needing something, so she forced herself away from her immersing work to unlock the door.

It was Kyle wearing that familiar smile and gleam in his eyes.

Has it only been twice this week? Cassie groaned inwardly.

"Gettin' late, Cass." He raised his eyebrows, suggestively.

"Um... it's like this... I'm starting a new book, a humdinger."

"Shit." He glowered down at her. "Who the hell is this new tortured man? A school janitor who fantasizes about the jocks?"

She bristled. "No. This is your every day tortured man, a Minnesota man, in fact, so you should approve."

"A Minnesota man? No way, Cass."

"Okay!" she spat in bitter tones. "A Minnesota man with a twist. He's well traveled and worldly, so the word fag never even crosses his vocabulary. He's like no one else... different... perhaps an hallucination for Minnesota, yet that's the setting I chose."

Kyle let out a long throaty laugh. "Won't work, Cass. Men from Minnesota don't give a pisser's shit about torture. You're wasting you time, Cass. It'll never sell, not a one."

"Says you!'

"Says me and every male in a five-state region, maybe ten-state," he touted with authority.

"Go to bed!" Cassie placed a hand on the doorknob. How dare him do this to her again!

Kyle put a foot to the door to keep it open. Again the familiar smile played on his lips. "So how about a little fornication? You look pretty good to me, still the most beautiful girl in Anoka."

She sniffed loudly. How dare him emphatically!

"Got some new condoms . . . fruit flavored."

Oh gross! She wanted to puke at the mind's picture of a pink condom on Kyle's cock.

"Strawberry . . . your favorite fruit," he said huskily, leaning closer to her.

She thrust back. "No thank you. I've had my allotment of fruit for today."

An ugly snarl twisted on his lips as he pulled away from her. "Fine!" He angrily tossed his arms into the air. "It's the story of my fuckin' life! Go ahead! Spend all your time with Rufus, Sinclair, Cyrano, and all those other fairies you've concocted. Go ahead! See if I care!"

"Harry," she replied quietly.

Momentarily, he was taken aback. "Harry?"

"My new book character . . . Harry Hannigan."

"Well what do you know . . . a fag with a normal name."

"Get out!" Cassie tried with all her might to push the door closed on him. "I'll show you." Her teeth gritted with determination. "Harry Hannigan *will* be an enigma, yet all of America will know and love him nonetheless. I'll show you, dammit! I'll show everyone . . ."

Chapter 2—Jack

The large suites atop a once-decadent pink Spanish-style hotel on Hollywood Boulevard in Los Angeles held a dual purpose: Offices of EMAX Studios, and its sound stage which took up one large suite. It was here, where they made their premiere skin flicks . . . in excess of five hundred million dollars a year, premiere.

Rud Hanna, the gruff, no-nonsense studio owner, stood on the sidelines. His bulging eyes, reminiscent of a goiter, shifted back and forth in an exacting manner, taking in every movement that was occurring on the stage. He had hired the best for this production—cinematographers, sound men, set designers, director, and the cast, especially the cast, the cream of erotica, money-makers *extraordinaire*, most of the money he pocketed.

He licked his lips, not at the gorgeous nude female bodies—he was immune after seventeen years in the business and having such bodies inhabit his bed on most nights—rather, it was the sensual, mesmerizing sex acts that were occurring on the large king-sized bed, on the floor, and against the false wall of the simulated bedroom. A stiff bulge formed in his crotch that he didn't attempt to restrain. It was an omen, he thought deliciously. Every male who watched the 'skin' would respond like him—money in the bank, sure shit.

The female stars had bodies lithe and firm as racehorses. And the male star . . . What could he say? The man oozed dark handsome maleness and his intense piercing eyes emblazoned on film like a pair of sharp daggers. Rud's tongue rolled around his mouth, licking away the increased saliva. And a million-dollar cock, the man's claim to fame. If that cock was cut off tomorrow, the man would be through in Hollywood. That cock . . . it was sheer Da Vinci.

And he'd gone out of his way to keep that cock happy and satisfied.

Coke, pot, well-endowed women who performed every perversion, and a decent salary which he wouldn't otherwise have. The man was a beggar in Hollywood . . . talent with no offers, drive without an outlet, obsession minus a stage to feed it . . . so Rud had provided it all, and now he had the man's ass bundled up tightly, until he unbundled the ass and tossed it on the street.

When?

When he decided, that's when.

His crotch throbbed when the man rammed his prized part into the vagina of the moaning, writhing female spread out on the bed. He moved like a Brahma bull, his solid leg muscles rippling with each thrust, and his body shiny moist from the sweat of his usual superior effort. He was made for the 'skins', Rud told himself, his teeth gritting against the orgasm that wanted to burst inside his pants. From the day he was born, that cock was destined for X-rated greatness.

A lusty scream surged through the sound stage as the female star's orgasm hit and, like a madwoman, she dug her long claw-like fingernails into the man's sinewy shoulders.

Wetness flooded Rud's pants, yet he stood rooted, unable to remove his eyes from the scene, until the man's savage moan rocked the sound stage and, as if hit by a bullet, he collapsed atop the female star.

"Cut!"

****

Jack Torelli forced himself off the female star then the large circular bed which he had performed on more times that he could remember. Every bone and muscle ached and his head throbbed from the large hit of coke he snorted prior to the scene.

Ever-so-gently, he straightened his body to his full six-foot two-inch height. A dull pain was concentrated in his groin area and he gazed down. His cock throbbed, and a mixture of semen and perspiration ran down his inner thighs. Sweat was coated his body and his skin felt furnace hot. But inside, the familiar frosty cold permeated to his very core. That's why he snorted Coke-- it minimized the chill.

"Oh Jack . . ."

A breathy voice spoke below him. His eyes glazed from a lack of sleep, Jack looked down. The French actress that Rud Hanna hired for this 'skin', gyrated amongst the satiny sheets like her orgasm was still hitting her. Jack's facial muscles tensed up as he stared. He thought of his mother, of his sisters, and the sight below repulsed him. Bile slowly moved up his gullet until it settled in his mouth. He had done it again, though each time after, he swore he wouldn't. And now he swore again. *No more skins.*

She popped up and balanced on firmly planted elbows. "You give Celeste another tumble, eh Jack?" she asked in a raunchy French accent.

"No," he replied bitterly.

Her body curved upward so he could gain a better view of her forty two-inch bust, that, according to Rud Hanna, lent to more European hard-ons than Bardot had created in her heyday. Conversely, the sight of the fake bosoms made Jack's own cock drop limply.

"I bring some Coke, finest in the world, from the most succulent coca plants in Columbia. I am . . . ur . . . personal friends with one of the drug kings."

The notion was tempting. He thrived on prime coke, not for its addictive properties, rather its numbing effect. And he felt a great need for that numbing effect. But he said nothing.

"I even bring the finest Puerto Rico rum. I hear you like a little rum with your coke . . . ur . . . one of the other girls told me."

He clenched his jaw, not liking his preferences so widely known. *Yet you brought it on yourself, Torelli.* On the surface, he had publicly flaunted his lifestyle while at the same time silently smacking himself for the words. Why the discrepancy? The farce? He didn't know exactly, but figured it had to do with his life taking such a devastating turn, so all that was left was the attitude: *What the hell?*

"Finest coke and rum. What do you say? Tonight?" she purred.

While vacillating, Jack pierced his dark eyes into the woman. Was she worth an intrusion on his much-needed solitude after his gut-wrenching day? Was the coke? The rum? Was any of it worth it when he placed the three within his broader scope? His inner voice screamed out a resounding 'No'. But . . . "What the hell?" he replied, the habitual apathy overcoming. He never listened to his inner voice anyway. Why start now when soothing 'numb' was in his future?

She snaked closer and her hands ran up and down his thighs. "What time Jack?"

The sensation made him stiffen with revulsion, and the bile sat clumped in his throat Her hands slowly moved to his cock. He made no move to stop her. After all, his cock was public property and she *was* a member of the public, wasn't she? Why not just let every hand of the world touch it? One hand, a billion hands . . . What difference did it make? Either way, it spelled absolute degradation.

"Eight? Eight-thirty? Or maybe nine-ish?" One hand cupped and massaged his balls, while the other stroked his velvety shaft.

"Just give me an hour warning. The office has my unlisted number," he mumbled.

Her hands flew from his groin and she leapt off the bed, jiggling to his side. Lifting on the balls of her feet, she reached up to caressed his cheek with her tongue and lips. The bile clump shot to the forefront of his mouth and Jack closed his eyes—her assault seemed endless. Finally, she pulled back, and brandished a toothy smile, revealing badly capped teeth.

"I'll call, Cherie." Breasts flapping and ass wiggling provocatively, she disappeared behind the set.

The cheek felt drenched with her saliva, but Jack made no move to wipe it away. Instead he tried desperately to make himself insensible to the sensation. It was good practice for what lie ahead once the light of day disappeared. More degradation and self-destruction, more self-destruction and degradation . . . the new clockwork orange pattern of his life.

But it hadn't always been like that.

Jack tightly shut his eyes. He refused to think of *what was*—his resignation of that part of his life was complete. *What is*, the glaring, miserable reality of his existence was enough for his fragile psyche to handle.

"Mr. Torelli."

He opened his eyes to see a young man dressed West Hollywood casual, standing beside him, holding out a robe in one hand and a plastic bag in the other.

Jack grabbed the robe and slid it over his shoulders without tying it, then he eyed the plastic bag—the contents were unmistakable.

"Gift from Mr. Hanna for another great job." The young man thrust out the bag to Jack.

His gaze fixed onto the ultra-fine particles of weed, a gift that brought him a half an inch closer to total destruction. Rud must have peed in his pants big time, Jack thought cynically.

"Looks like choice stuff, Mr. Torelli," the young man commented.

Making no move to take the bag, Jack studied the young face before him. "How old are you, kid?"

"Twenty-one . . . and you're from New York, right? I kin hear it."

Jack ignored the last statement and focused on the first. "Whatcha doin' here, kid? You got no business in a hellhole like this. Find a decent job, why don't you."

"Minimum wage on the Strip? No thank you," the young man replied adamantly.

"To what end kid, huh?" Jack questioned.

The young man's mouth broke into a wide grin and his eyes held a very familiar glow. "I wanna break into the business and this'll help me. I wanna be a star like you, Mr. Torelli."

Jack crumpled at the innocent words. He saw himself at twenty-one, willing to do anything and anyhow to get his foot in the acting business. It was a human-eat-human world, and any minuscule shred helped. And if one was bit, it was a lifelong affliction, only cured by acting, and more acting, any type, any set, and means, *any*. "I understand kid. End of discussion." He snatched the plastic bag, turned, and headed for his dressing room . . .

****

A few drops of rain fell, chilling further the fifty-degree temperature on the late afternoon January day. Jack shivered while tossing his shoulder bag into the back seat of his 1992 black Corvette convertible, still in mint condition from his reverent care. Despite the light precipitation, he decided to keep the top down for the ride home.

He pulled out of the parking area reserved for studio personnel and turned east onto Sunset Boulevard, heading for home. The raindrops felt like sparks as they hit his face, but Jack welcomed the sensation. It felt clean and rejuvenating, as if he was being bathed of the filth he had endured for the last seven and half hours. At least he could perceive that to be the case. It was these minute, innocuous delusions which cropped up now and then, that maintained his tiny semblance of self-worth. Otherwise, he may as well be covered up in a deep dark hole.

Decency . . . just a tiny bit was imperative.

The Corvette zoomed past Sunset Strip, a mecca of shoddy buildings, mangy and trashy people, and sleazy establishments that sold sexual dreams, visual or tactile. He saw a hooker every forty feet, hanging out of doorways or perched against parking meters. Several gangs of bald black leathered men and women sporting lethal looking chains dotted the scape now and then. And interspersed were the hollow-faced junkies and a couple dressed-to-the-nines pimps. It was ugly, damn ugly, Jack thought, turning his gaze forward. Suddenly his eye caught something.

EROTICA! TORELLI IN CAVEMAN CUTIES!

Oh Christ! Jack wanted to sink through the car floor even though he was totally anonymous to anybody else. *But not to myself.* He gunned the accelerator so he could quickly pass the humiliation. Granted, he had seen it before, shimmering in all its neon glory on signs gracing some of the sleaziest movie establishments in L.A. Yet, he could never be nonchalant of what he had actually done. Those inner voices . . . Why didn't he listen? If he had, the once-proud name of Torelli would be erased from the sign, replaced by the name of some other hard-up actor who performed his craft amid the smut so he had a craft to perform.

That's my excuse.

"Was it a cop out? The easy way out? Or. . . . the coward's way out?"

The last question gripped him with shame. All Torelli men were men, and the word 'coward' had no place in his ingrained context of things. Suddenly, he felt his insides playing a never-ending tug-o-war—origin versus actuality, actuality versus origin. The two concepts tugged and pulled constantly, neither ever landing in the muck, rather both still in the game, continually torturing him.

He shifted the car into a higher gear and pressed his foot deeper into the gas pedal until the Corvette was parked outside the old, but well-kept stucco building that housed his one-bed-room apartment. He thought he could probably afford better—his salary was rising with his notoriety as the 'Prince of the Skins'—yet he preferred the obscurity. The area was quiet and devoid of many 'Hollywood types', so he had solace as well as privacy to his conduct of his chosen lifestyle without any interference.

After affectionately making sure his prized car was tucked in for the night, Jack hoisted his shoulder bag out of the back seat and moved up the rutted cement walkway with greenish-brown grass sprouting from the crevices. Despite this hideous sight, the rest of the grounds were maintained to perfection—lawn and hedges trimmed, the fronds of two medium sized palm trees, green and lush, and red and yellow poppies along the entire perimeter of the building. "It's beautiful," he muttered, and for a brief moment he was touched with another whisper of decency.

The whisper evaporated, however, once he stepped inside his apartment. Empty and half-filled rum bottles scattered the living room, a couple partially smoked joints hung from an ashtray overloaded with slim brown cigarette butts from the two women who had romped in his bed the night previous. And then there was all the sex toys, a necessity along with the coke and rum, so he could raise it. Without the camera shining on him, it was harder than hell, and he needed all the help he could get.

Humiliation seized him. It was the origin versus actuality again. In truth, he hated the women who invaded his apartment once the sun set. They gave him nothing, not even physical pleasure. So why? He didn't know why . . . why he kept inviting them or prowling after them on the streets, at parties, in restaurants, bars, and at rare times on the sound stage; though, as a rule, he avoided the 'skin' actresses like the plague. They only added to his guilt by being a physical reminder of it.

Am I losing my maleness?

All the signs seemed to be pointing to that direction, and now he shivered in fright at this possibility. If that were the case, he might as well crawl into that hole and cover himself with dirt until he asphyxiated. All Torelli men were the height of maleness. To lose such would mean he was no longer a Torelli, sure death for him.

He carried this sobering though as he walked into his bedroom. The place was a mess. Clothes, dirty and clean were strewn in corners and poked out from under the bed, bottles of exotic sex oils, some opened, littered the two bedside tables, his king-size bed was covered in a tangle of bedclothes, heavy metal CD's were stacked haphazardly by the stereo, and dust, one inch thick, frosted the tops of the furniture.

Then he fastened his eyes on the plastic object lying near a flattened pillow. It was his anal stimulater, his primary security that his manliness wouldn't betray him. A cynical laugh emerged out of him. What would his fans say? Him, 'Mr. Cock Magnificent', needing a dildo to get his rocks off. It was too ironic for believability, which suited him just fine. He had no desire for the greatest secret of his life to be revealed to a world beyond his bedroom. The woman never knew, or at least he assumed that to be the case. He made it seem like a game, and they participated willingly, without question. Although, like a predator, he waited for the question to crop up.

How would he answer it?

Kick the woman out on her ass--that's how he planned to answer it.

Foregoing any tidying up, Jack deposited his shoulder bag in the middle of the floor and headed for the small kitchen to get something to eat. He opened the refrigerator to check the contents, and he scowled. Not much for food. But he wasn't much of a shopper, except for the array of expensive clothes from Rodeo Drive and exclusive West Hollywood shops. He had to maintain his image. It wasn't copacetic to appear down-on-one's-luck from a superficial vantage. That would lead to rumors, to ridicule, to rejection. One might as well put a gun to one's head if the latter occurred. To be accepted was part of the big Hollywood Game, and that meant big houses, big cars, big parts, big studios, big names . . .

He rustled through the moldy fruit, vegetables, and wrapped packages. Although the rest had eluded him, he told himself that he still had a big name without thinking about *how* he got it. It was too painful after his once renowned, acclaimed, respected career in Hollywood. Then, he had been on top of the world, big on the outside and inside. Now, he tried like hell to maintain the magnitude of his outer appearance to compensate for the negligible inner appearance. It was just a fucking game, a game getting harder to play each year. He wasn't getting any younger, thirty-eight in another eight months, and the competition was fierce.

Jack placed his pickings on the wooden counter. He grabbed a knife from the drawer and began cutting until a large triple decker sandwich sat in front of him—lettuce, tomatoes, Swiss cheese, proscuitto, plump baloney, a dab of mayonnaise, horseradish, and a wallop of French mustard. He unscrewed the cap off a bottle of Perier, and guzzled between giant, hungry mouthfuls.

As he stood at the counter and ate, he thought that perhaps he should make time to go grocery shopping tomorrow. His diet was shitty, and he had lost some weight over the past year, though he tried like mad to maintain his physique by working out with a personal trainer three mornings a week. Rud Hanna's white popping eyes devoured his physique as if it were adorned with jewels--or more likely dollar signs. Jack thought. Yet, he knew that a loss of his physique meant the loss of Rud Hanna and the final 'big' in his life. So he had to hold on, keeping his outward appearances perfect, no matter the increasing difficulty—he had to hold tight.

The last bit of sandwich devoured, and the last drop of Perier drunk, Jack disposed of the bottle and did a hit-and-miss cleaning job before walking into the living room, a futile decorating effort in art nouveau. The room lines attempted whiplash, though it was less than striking, and the pink drenched painting of *Isolde* on the wall looked like the cheap copy. Then, the sprinkling of vases and figurines, neither exotic nor decadent, were a conglomeration of cheap pieces that looked like they were bought at an East L.A. flea market. Yet, the apartment had come furnished, a bounty of sorts, Jack recalled now. He had sold his house with the contents to boost the price so he could fabulously maintain his exterior when he was out and about. His abode was secondary. Looking and acting accomplished and successful . . . that's what it was all about.

Jack sat in the Barcelona style chair, the leather worn and crusty. He reached in the back pants pocket and pulled out the gift from Rud Hanna. First-rate weed, he thought, letting the fine particles caress his fingers. The feathery sensation made his anticipation rise, and he hastily lifted his fingers out of the bag. He located a package of cigarette papers on the mahogany table next to the chair and expertly rolled two joints. Before lighting one, he got up to rustle through the scattered rum bottles strewn on the floor until he found one that was relatively full. He guzzled immediately, telling himself he needed to be ultra-numb for what lie ahead

The grass tasted mellow. Leave it to Rud to get the best, he thought while the drug slowly clouded his brain. The studio owner was a millionaire many times over from his ruthless exploitation of human meat. Rud was like a scrutinizing butcher, his eyes able to pick up every inch of a human form, disregarding even the minutest flaw, and only choosing the prime cuts. He prided himself on this ability, though he himself looked like a pregnant cat and had an ostrich stance for a walk. And those eyes . . . they made Jack crawl.

Yet, Rud needed no beautiful outward appearance—he was 'big' regardless. And 'big' got him the best of everything. If it didn't, Rud would just take it—young boys, young girls, anything he could stick his substandard cock into. He was near an enuch, or so Jack had heard at the numerous parties he attended, also attended by women who had one time inhabited the studio owner's amatory bedroom. Jack let out an amused laugh at this revelation. Then he pictured Rud with a pants full while the whites of his eyes jutted out at the erotic scenes occurring on the set. Rud was such a slime, he was coated with the shit . . .

A ringing phone penetrated Jack's foggy brain.

"Cherie . . ." a voice purred on the other end of the line.

Shit . . . the word echoed through his head. "Yeah?" he mumbled.

"I be there in an hour, Jack."

"Whatever . . . you know where to find me."

Dazedly, he hung up.

Without delay, his hand skirted the floor for another rum bottle. Next, with a jittery hand he lit the second joint then sucked deeply, then sucked deeply again, then he kept sucking, interspersed with healthy gulps of rum. He only had an hour to enter the Land of Oblivion . . .

****

Dressed in a silver spangled brassiere, an open white silk shirt and white skin-tight Gibeau jeans, and her dyed rust-colored hair a mass of unruly waves, the French actress contorted seductively as she stood outside Jack's apartment.

Though a haze, he watched her nondescript brown eyes slowly move from his head to his bare feet. She had a more scrutinizing eye than Rud Hanna, his fogged brain thought, though it bothered him none. He had lost most of his sensibilities after the second joint and half-pint of rum.

Her collagen injected lips coursed into a enchanted smile. "So you invite me in, Jack?"

Saying nothing, he opened the door wider and he saw the deep cleavage of her breasts when she sashayed past him. Without delay, she whipped off her silk shirt and jeans to reveal the silver spangled bikini panties that matched her bra.

"You like Jack?" She strutted around like she was the most glorious creature on Earth.

He fastened on the silver gleam, and felt dizzy. Even so, his eyes roamed, taking in her gently muscled arms, flat stomach, and firm, shapely legs that seemed endless. Then he fastened on her face--thick pancake foundation, deep maroon-hued cheeks and lips, dark-lined eyebrows, thick eyeliner above and below her eyes, and a generous painting of dark navy eye shadow on her lids. Quickly, he lowered his eyes. It was too flagrant to view. So he wouldn't.

He'd get so corked on the promised coke and booze that her face would blur from his consciousness.

"I wear it just for you, Jack," she said in a silky voice while moving closer to him.

"Where's the coke and rum," he asked quickly?

She halted. With a devious smile, she moved to the brown leather couch where she had deposited her oversized white *Gucci* bag. She extracted a tiny vial filled with white powder and a half-pint of pure Puerto Rican rum, holding up both items to him.

"That's it?" He was disbelieving of the paltry quantity of each that she dared produce. It went against his scheme of things, and he wouldn't tolerate it. "Get dressed and get out."

Her face fell. "But Cherie . . . both are splendid, I promise."

Skeptical, Jack stayed rooted while he examined the two items. Finally, he held out his hand. "Okay--gimme the rum," he conceded.

Like a lithe Siamese, she moved closer, and he instinctively stepped back. "Fuck! Just hand it to me," he ordered between clenched teeth.

Looking miffed, she paused and stretched her arm out until the small bottle was in his hand. Then she stepped back, her face sulky while she watched him.

Jack clumsily unscrewed the bottle cap then placed the rim to his lips. He drank liberally until only half of the clear liquid remained. While lowering the bottle, he gazed at her face, noticing the maroon-coated lips were petulant. But that's all he could distinctively make out; the rest of her looked like a silver fog. So he lifted the bottle and drank again until every drop of the magic brew had touched his tongue.

"You like, Jack?" she asked in a eager tone.

He tossed the bottle onto the floor and took a few steps towards the silver gleam. "Yeah, I like. Make me a line of coke and I see if I like again."

So she made him a small line, and he snorted. Then she made him a longer line and he snorted again. When he was through his insides pounded, and only the dull silver danced before his bleary eyes.

"Bedroom's somewhere around here," he said vaguely, feeling his body move on its own volition.

He peeled off his clothes when his bare feet touched the familiar ultra-shaggy carpeting in his bedroom. Once he determined his nakedness, he fell onto the bed, belly down. Soon thereafter, a pair of velvety hands caressed his back and buttocks.

"I make you feel so good, Cherie . . ."

He hazily felt the slow up and down massage of her fingertips as his backside was swathed in oils. A slight throb sat in his groin while the rest of him stayed numb. It was a satisfying state.

With darted motions, her tongue licked away the oils, and the pressure in his groin grew a little stronger. Then the feel of her tongue ceased, replaced by the sensation of her fake collagen lips on the small of his back. The groin pressure disappeared and his cock went limp.

"For Christ's sakes stop it." He thrust his head upward to see the shine of silver before his eyes. "Take that silver shit off, dammit. Now!" He had no desire to see any of her.

The silver faded away, and she snaked across his backside. Her furry triangle ran up and down against his buttocks and a touch of pressure returned, but it wasn't enough, not by a long shot. So he flipped around, tossing her off to the side of him.

"Do me," he commanded.

"First a kiss, Cherie, and then . . ."

"No!" His voice roared and echoed. "No lips . . . anywhere. You understand?"

Wordlessly, her mouth moved down to his groin. Carefully she grabbed his cock between her teeth and her tongue licked up and down his shaft, first gently, then with more frenzied motions. Her hand cupped his balls, and the pads of her fingers pressed and circled in an undulating fashion. He felt a bit more pressure between his legs.

"You are magnificent, Cherie."

The breathy words pierced his brain, and the bit of pressure evaporated. "Shut up, dammit! Not a word. Ever!"

Promptly, the sensation of tongue against cock resumed, and Jack let his mind float with the sensation. Then came the feeling of the luxurious oils penetrating his shaft and balls, followed by renewed tongue maneuvers on the surface of his oily cock. He felt a bit harder, then harder, although he was a far-cry.

So he grabbed her wild head mane and flipped her on her back, finding the humongous breasts and sucking her nipples until he thought he would gag from the sound of her grating moans. He spit out the nipple and next found her cunt and he darted finger, then tongue, then finger, out of her vagina. Her taste nauseated him. But he continued on, as he felt even harder and thought perhaps . . .

"I love it, Cherie . . . Don't stop."

Damn! It was as if his cock had been punctured by the heavily breathing voice. It was useless! The bitch couldn't make him. So . . . "Reach under the pillow. Now!"

Her high-pitched laughter peeled through his ears. "A dildo! I haven't seen one since I . . ."

"Shut that mouth!" he ordered, unable to stop the humiliation that seeped into his coke-soaked brain. The sensation made him angry, yet he spoke with a low tone. "Now we're gonna have some real fun . . . and games."

She made an excited noise.

"Gimme that thing." Acting like the white plastic was inconsequential, he ordered her to turn. Her rust hair flew into his face while she gleefully flipped onto her stomach. Moments later, he held the vibrating object in her anus amid her loud mirthful squeals.

His hand shook, not only from the intense vibration, but from the anticipation that he was next. Soon his groin would explode with his maleness. He couldn't wait!

He clicked off the machine. "My turn." He nonchalantly lifted his buttocks into the air. Only seconds elapsed before he felt a rocking sensation inside him, heating up his groin until it scorched. His balls tightened up and the rigidity of his penis intensified.

"Touch me," he commanded, and soon the vibration was accompanied by the feel of her hand moving up and down his shaft and her fingers pressing deeply into his balls.

Now he was ready.

Seeking Out Harry

In a split-second he had her on her back and his penis ramming into her, forcefully thrusting, willing his drug washed brain to produce. Finally he felt a warm surge course through his shaft and out. He had done it . . . once more.

He rolled off of her and moved far away from where she lay writhing like a crazy woman, moaning French words intermingled with American obscenities. He tried to blank out the moans while he lay turned away from her.

Her noise came to a leisurely halt and her body pushed up against him. The sensation made him smolder with intense repugnance.

"Again Cherie . . . ?"

"Get out," he hissed lowly.

"But Cherie, the little dildo . . .

Snarling fiercely, he leapt into a sitting position. "Out! And never come back!"

Her eyes widened with terror, she inched away.

"And leave the coke," he added in a sneer.

She dressed hastily. "I see you tomorrow, Cherie?. . .Rude says we have redoes."

"What do you think?" Jack replied tensely and left it at that. Then he watched until the glisten of silver disappeared.

He gently pushed the side of his face into the pillow and a shiver went through him. The inner frostiness was worse than usual, much worse, and the vast loneliness slowly settled.

He was alone with nobody or nothing, except a shaking piece of plastic to give him some semblance of warmth. What had he become? It was supposed to be different. His father always told him that if he acted like a man, the riches of the world would fall at his feet.

He had.

But where were the riches, Pop? Where, Pop? Where?

Chapter 3—Cassie

Outside the solitary, paint chipped attic window, there was the constant drip of rapidly melting icicles. The Minnesota winter was slowly-but-surely disappearing with the passing days of March; except for a precipitous snowstorm now and then which fluxed quick as a wink when exposed to the gradually warming sun.

Except for the growing heat of the attic, Cassie Callahan welcomed Spring. It meant starting anew, and in terms of her chosen profession, she told herself that's what she was doing.

Writing had suddenly become a new challenging adventure. She took ten years of nearly constant writing, her vast vocabulary, her solid technical knowledge, her immense imagination and creativity with words, and propelled this into a more simplistic writing style that would be understood by a spectrum of IQ's.

Think Kyle!

The words guided her when twisting sentences, names of characters, establishing backgrounds, conflicts, and the dialogue which seemed to flow naturally for the first time in ten years. The manuscript was built for her husband's comprehension, yet still contained the rich detail and intricately woven plot that she prided herself on. It had been a challenge all right.

Cassie turned from her McIntosh and sighed with satisfaction. Another chapter done—that made twelve. Now came her least favorite part: Revision. A cut here, slash there—she despised it.

Despite her immense love of the story, to revise over and over was mundane—she wanted to move on and find out what happened next; it was blistering inside her. But . . . that wasn't her way. She revised as she went, and told herself she *was not* to change ten years of disciplined habits, even though this was the most riveting story that had ever come out of her.

And it was riveting to the point of frightening.

Once she established a psychological profile of her main character, her mind set off like a firecracker, and the words rushed out of her in a steady stream like they had never done before. She could barely pry herself away from the keyboard. On many days she would work for eighteen, nineteen hours a day with only short enough breaks to see how her family was faring, and on several nights, she just sacked out on the makeshift bed in the attic, obtaining a few hours of sleep, then bouncing off the cot, bright, chipper, and raring to go. She had never felt so obsessed.

Furthermore, the book invaded her dreams, making her sleep fitful. Scene after scene, dialogue, and her mind's vision of the characters filled her head all night long, so when she woke up, she felt as if she had never left her manuscript for even a moment.

The obsession was destructive, she well knew. Her lanky frame had become lankier, as many days she forgot to eat except for a morsel here, a tidbit there. Then her hair looked like a tangled mess of split-end disaster, and her face held the pallor of indoor seclusion. Her family too seemingly suffering, if she could judge such by their ceaseless complaints--overdramatized in her estimate. They weren't suffering totally.

She always took Sunday off from her writing. On that day, she flew around like a hurricane, cleaning, doing eons of laundry, cooking a variety of dishes for the next six days, the freezer to oven sort, and catching up on phone calls to Sarie and the Scarpelli family. Plus, she spent quality time with Kristi, which the ten-year-old begrudgingly accepted, and she gave Kyle his one night of sex, as difficult as that was.

She hated Sundays!

And tomorrow was Sunday.

She tangled her stringy blonde hair between her fingers while thoughts of her one forced day away from her passion twisted her insides with restlessness. Could she leave 'Harry'? Could she leave the man of her innermost emotions in favor of dust, laundry detergent, and tuna casseroles? Could she? Would Kyle accept meat loaf six times in a week? Or his permanent pressed slacks not so perfectly creased? Or a half-assed version of Madonna in bed? Would he, so she could have a few precious hours with her Harry on Sunday?

Harry . . .

Just the name shot delicious shivers up and down her spine, sent her heart pounding, and made her breaths pant. 'Harry' was pure male in the physical and powerful sense of the word, yet so sensitively male in all other aspects. He was a beautiful man inside and out, but *oh so* such an enigma that the challenge of him was exhilarating!

And he was Minnesotan, born and bred . . .

That fact still boggled her mind, tickled her funny bone, constantly played on her common sense, and she wondered now, as she had wondered on umpteenth occasions, if some publisher would get her on the realism factor. He or she might, if they had ever perchance ended up in Minnesota, she reasoned. Yet, despite her reservations, she had kept her home state as the setting. She felt comfortable with it—the familiar gave her a great sense of security.

"Cass! Open up!"

She shifted her eyes back and forth. Was she hallucinating?

"C'mon Cass!"

"Sarie?" she whispered with caution.

"I know you're in there, Cass. Let me in!" The insistent knocking rattled the wooden door.

"I demand entrance into the Bastille!"

It was only Saturday, her last free day to be creative before submerging into monotonous.

Why Sarie? Why?

"I've got my ram rod, and I'm prepared to use it!"

Oh damn! The frustration of it all, the utter, all-consuming frustration!

"I'm warning you, Cass. I got it positioned at the door and I'm ready to ram . . ."

Leave me alone!

"One . . . two . . . three . . . three and a half . . ."

"All right!" Cassie charged to the door and promptly unlocked it.

"Oh my god, Cass . . ."

Cassie squinted so her eyes adjusted to the sudden surge of light. When her vision was clear, she looked at Sarie. Her friend's face was mortified.

"You look like a corpse, and maybe I'm being too optimistic," Sarie said, distressed.

"What?" She had no idea what Sarie was babbling about.

"Your hair, your beautiful hair, and your eyes, your beautiful eyes and your skin . . . you've lost that subtle Italian darkness, and, oh . . . your freckles are pale. I've never seen pale freckles."

Cassie rubbed a hand over one cheek, then the other. Besides a dry feeling from a lack of humidity in the attic, she couldn't understand the reason for the big show Sarie was putting on. So what if she looked a little untidy? If it didn't bother her, why should Sarie care?

Without invitation, Sarie swung past her into the attic. Sarie's eyes darted around, growing more disgusted with each turn. "My god! It's worse than the Bastille," she breathed out.

"I don't remember you ever going to the Bastille," Cassie challenged.

"I've seen pictures, Cass. *I do* sell real estate. Remember?"

The comparison eluded her, but Cassie didn't challenge and just let Sarie release all her 'attic insults'.

". . .And Poor Kyle. The man is beside himself with your . . . your self-imposed exile!"

"How is he beside himself?"

"Lonely . . . the man is drowning in loneliness, and his sex life . . . it tears my heart out to think about such a vital, sexy, needy . . ."

"Cut it, Sar!" Cassie snapped. How dare she bring up such a private thing because of her sex-stud delusions about Kyle! If she only knew . . . Harry . . . Kyle couldn't even come a thousandth of an inch close to her Harry.

"Someone has to be blunt, Cass. You're throwing it all away on an impossible dream."

The biting words hurt, and Cassie couldn't hide it. Eighteen, nineteen hours a day for an *impossible dream?* How crass after all her sacrifice. *Why not just smack my face, Sarie?*

"And little Kristi . . . she comes to my house for cookies like a beggar! She's just a child. She needs her cookie fix!"

Another smack. Using her child as a weapon of guilt. Kristi could barely tolerate being around her worthless, unproductive mother just because she didn't go out into the work world for sixty hours a week, bring home a forty-five thousand dollar a year salary, or made honey nut bread. *My God!* What was happening to her life?

"And your tortured man . . . it's a joke, Cass. Five failed books! And you have the audacity to start a sixth one, and put everyone through more hell than you ever have!" Sarie waved a firm arm at the computer. "I could smash it! Kyle could smash it! And your folks . . . your mother's been crying. Crying! Because she thinks that you've lost your mind and may do something drastic like cut off your ear like that mad writer from the olden days!"

"Artist," Cassie corrected. "Toulouse-Lautrec, deformed, debauched, the ultimate tortured man."

"Tortured? Why don't you look into your own bedroom? There lies the ultimate tortured man!"

"I don't care!" Cassie blurted, then she wanted to cut off her tongue. How could she be so truthful? She was so damn unhappy, but to actually indicate this to someone . . . she had never . . . only to her grandfather . . . otherwise never . . .

"You don't, huh?"

Cautiously, Cassie lifted her eyes and saw Sarie's dark glare. What could she say to take the words back? And . . . did she really want to take back the words? So she said nothing and positioned herself in front of her computer. She lifted her fingers and took a typing pose.

She felt Sarie's hefty form directly behind her, but she commanded herself to stay as she was. *Don't turn around . . . defeat . . . to turn around is defeat.*

"So you choose to ignore all the problems and misery that you've caused with this insane behavior. Is that is, Cass?"

Cassie trembled. Never before had she so stoutly held her ground. But Harry . . . The mind's picture made her strong. *Faith!* She had unyielding faith in 'Harry'.

"All right, Cass. It's everyone for themselves, I'm warning you. You've made your choice."

Yeah--you're right, Cassie silently concurred. She had made her decision ten years ago, had taken the plunge, dared to chase a dream, and now there was no escape. No utterances could ever sway her path. She was too hooked, a slave to the written word, an addict who needed her fix, day in and day out or else she felt like she would crack from restiveness.

She was too long gone.

Sarie angrily stomped out of the attic and slammed the door.

And she dug into the tedious task of revising . . .

****

At 6:30 A.M. the next morning, Cassie shut off her computer. She had been up most of the night, revising Chapter Twelve. It was three-quarters done, and perhaps, just perhaps, she could squeeze in a few extra hours on this hectic Sunday to finish it, so Chapter Thirteen could begin on Monday. The words scalded her insides, and she felt an intense need to release them.

God! She couldn't wait until Monday.

Cassie dragged herself of the attic. Once out the door, she suddenly felt weary—her lust vanished-- and the nearly three months she was behind on her sleep collapsed on her like a ton of boulders. At the same time her insides jittered, and she gritted her teeth to maintain.

It was Sunday, she reminded.

No Harry on Sunday.

A half-hour later, showered and her hair thrown up with a clip, she was behind the wheel of her rusty flaming red Toyota, headed for the twenty-four-hour grocery store to stock-up on food for the week . . . and her jitters had uncomfortably escalated . . .

****

"Another Pop Tart, Kristi?" Cassie asked in a harried tone while she raced around with a moistened rag, cleaning cupboards, appliances, and dark finger smudges off the kitchen walls.

"No thanks. Generic's not sitting well," Kristi replied, then flashed a devilish grin, "How about an omelet--Swiss cheese, bacon, mushrooms, onions--and a croissant with homemade raspberry jam? That's Heather's favorite breakfast. Her mother makes it every Sunday."

Feeling the guilt cave in on her, Cassie slowed her wiping motions. "I need every egg I've got for meatloaf, and the rest . . . except for the onions, I'm afraid

Linda Coleman

you're outa luck."

"It figures. Deprivation runs rampant in this house," Kristi said with a sulk.

"I'm sorry." Cassie went back to her cleaning, but the task had lost its frenzy. She was losing her daughter by her own hand, she well knew. She had created the deprivation with her stubborn, selfish dream. Yet that verge . . . it was getting stronger.

"As for our quality time today, forget it," Kristi added. "Heather's mother is taking us to Maplewood Mall, shopping, lunch, video games . . . I'll be gone all day."

With a resigned drop of her hand, Cassie halted the rag's motion. "Sounds like fun. Have a good time," she cracked out, then lifted the rag and furiously moved it across the refrigerator.

Deprivation, emotional not financial, was familiar to her. Her own mother had dished it out in large measures, and Cassie had decisively sworn years ago that in no way would Kristi Anne-Marie Callahan suffer the same fate. It was very *Un*-Italian not to place your family at the center of one's universe. This belief was constantly expounded forcefully, emphatically and, in a heavy Italian accent, by a large, powerful Angelo Scarpelli, the designated family head.

And there was a bounty of Scarpelli family in Anoka, Minnesota.

****

The onslaught began in the late 1920's when Angelo and his three brothers exited the boat at Ellis Island and headed Northwest, until they landed in the Minneapolis/St. Paul metropolis.

They were a boisterous, feisty lot. All four married pure Italian girls and immediately went about procreating pure Italian families. At the same time, the brothers took their meager inheritance from a deceased father and purchased a small glass factory. The business expanded as quickly as the four families, and when two decades had passed, all the brothers were quite rich.

So when Cassandra Caroline Scarpelli, middle named after the much beloved president's daughter, came along in 1962, her family was in the upper echelons of the upper-middle class.

Her mother June, a stoic, severe, but breathtakingly beautiful Swede, and her father Arturo, 'Art', Italian in looks but more quiet in demeanor, shunned the glass business, and started their own: an investment firm in downtown Anoka. The venture was an eighty hour a week proposition, thus Cassie and her sister Meg, eight years older, were relegated to carefully picked housekeepers and sitters, all as stern and disciplining as her mother.

When June Scarpelli dictated something, she viewed it as an indisputable fact. "Cassandra's too big of a name for such a skinny little thing. So we'll call you Sandy."

So she was Sandy, until the name nearly choked her.

Though quite painfully alone in her immediate family life, beyond it, she tried to put her hurt aside to become a happy-go-lucky free spirit. She intensively studied people and things, and could accurately, imitate what she saw as well as describe it prolifically on paper.

She wasn't a Sandy.

Her mind constantly questioned, What if? How come? Why this instead of that? Does Sophia Loren have a nose job? A 'Sandy'? No way!

Books amazed her, especially the outlandish and thought-provoking. Dr.

Suess never held much charm. She read the entire of *War and Peace* at age eight and slyly digested the words of *Forever Amber* at age nine. The love scenes made her blush, and descriptions of the handsome, suave Lords and Dukes curled her toes. She loved it and for a time, envisioned herself as the brazen Amber, so determined, so cunning, so bewitching, so oozing with allurement, so, so, so. A 'Sandy' wouldn't be cocky enough to read Amber, let alone adopt her lifestyle as her own.

'Sandy' was definitely out

She deliciously grasped life, every morsel. She secretly adored George McGovern, though her staunchly Democratic family claimed he was a hippie, and for the first time voted Republican. And with high-intensity curiosity, she snuck into the movie *In the Heat of the Night*, on the pretense that a family emergency had occurred and she needed to find her brother. She had never seen such large breasts before, and wondered if they were real, and wondered what size bra cup would cover such bosoms, and wondered if she would ever be fortunate enough to get that big, and wondered and wondered . . . A 'Sandy' would never wonder, merely accept. In fact, a 'Sandy' would be too perfectly perky to lie about an emergency or a brother.

A Sandy? Absolutely not!

"Sandy!"

Her mother's exact voice pierced the core of her twelve-year-old person and her cowardice punctured. The farce was over!

"My name is Cassie!" She stubbornly stomped her foot for emphasis.

"Sandy!"

"Cassie!"

The debate went on, and on, and on . . . And finally it ended two months later.

"Let her be Cassie, June," Grandfather Scarpelli commanded in his heavy Italian accent.

"But she's twelve-years-old, Nono. She's been 'Sandy' for twelve years." Her mother argued, though her voice lacked its usual confidence. Grandpa Scarpelli had that effect. He was built like a bear and had a roaring voice to match. Not many dared challenge him.

"She's Cassie!" he decreed, then in more gentle tones added, "And to me, she's Cassina."

So from that point on, she was 'Cassina' to Grandpa Scarpelli and 'Cassie' to the rest of the world . . . except to her mother who, on assorted occasions when angry or frustrated, would obstinately yell out "Sandy." June Scarpelli wasn't an easy loser, a major attribute of her success as a businesswoman. Though conversely, she was too self-involved, unloving, and rigid to ever be a halfway decent mother. And her father Arturo, totally enamored with the gorgeous, classy Swede, went along with whatever she wanted.

The scenario in his oldest son's home was so blatantly *Un*-Italian, it rattled Angelo Scarpelli's moral and belief system, and the old man butted heads with both parents to try to bring about a change so his *very* Italian conscience was soothed.

"You must stay home and care for Cassina and Meggie, June," he said decisively.

"That's impossible, Nono. I have a thriving business to run and Art and I are talking about expanding into the suburbs. Scarpelli Investment Services can't manage without me . . . my clients." June said in a tone that would freeze an ice cube.

"But Cassina is still a little girl." He paused to brandish his lovely smile on Cassie which she identically returned. She adored the way his lips turned up, and had been studying the motion for years so she too could smile with such radiance. Then his smile faded when turning to the apathetic eighteen-year-old, contorted like a pretzel on the carpeted floor. "And Meggie . . ." He could say no more—the answer was obvious.

Cassie glanced at her older sister, turned-off, tuned-out, long, straight, stringy, grease-caked blonde hair, clad in filthy jeans and a Vietnam War army surplus jacket that looked like it could stand up on its own, and constantly doing Yoga.

"Hey, don't sweat it, Nono. It doesn't bother me," Meg interjected listlessly.

Her statement was true. Meg didn't care about her parents' constant absences, she welcomed them. It gave her the freedom to drink, smoke pot, and have sex with boys, Cassie knew. Furthermore, Meg had skipped out of half her senior year at Anoka High School and was barely passing--Cassie knew this too.

Out of inquisitiveness, she had raided her sister's bedroom and found drug paraphernalia, empty booze bottles, birth-control pills, hidden report cards, and the most tantalizing, Meg's diary. It was juicy despite the massive amount of spelling and grammatical errors which Cassie itched to correct. But, she forced restraint so her covert activities weren't discovered.

"You have no direction, Meggie, no guidance, no discipline, and that is not right," Angelo Scarpelli argued.

Dazedly, Meg promptly responded. "Negative Nono. I got big plans . . . waitress in a coffeehouse on Lyndale where I can read the poems I'm gonna write in the attic apartment I'm gonna rent."

Poems? Cassie thought with humor and disbelief. Meg didn't even have a handle on the English language and her sentence structure was right out of Kindergarten. *Poems?* When she spelled penis, *p-e-e-n-u-s?*

"Rent?" Angelo's green eyes flashed furiously. For even one of his family members, no matter how bizarre, to suggest they were leaving Anoka, no matter the short distance, was unthinkable to him.

Art Scarpelli finally pried open his lips to cut in. "Meg just needs to find herself, Pop, and it's best she does it away from home." And June gave a stiff, emphatic nod of agreement.

Cassie looked from parent to parent and saw the evasiveness in their eyes. Meg was a humiliation, not productive for business or impressive to their fancy clients, thus was expendable. They had business on the brain--business, business, business--and their kids were secondary, decorations to spruce up their image. Meg wasn't a very aesthetic decoration.

"Bullshit!" Angelo Scarpelli roared so loud the walls shook.

"No debate, Nono. I'm eighteen. I kin join the Israeli Army if I want." Meg peered over her horn-rimmed glasses that her perfect vision didn't need.

"The hell you will!" Angelo's voice rushed through the room like white water rapids. "You're a Catholic girl. A Catholic girl has no place in Israel with those kinds of men. You will marry a Catholic man, preferably full Italian, but I will accept half!"

Meg let out a low stolid laugh. "You're on LSD, Nono. I like my men light, blonde, with hair as long as mine, and worshipers of the Yoga of Force."

So a battle ensued: Dark versus light, and Catholic versus Brahma and atman.

Looking like he'd been through the War of Bafflement, Angelo Scarpelli threw up his hands with vexation, said "Ai-yi-yi," then shifted back onto Cassie.

"And my little Cassina . . ." he began with much affection. "She had no love, no attention, no tender motherly care . . ." His eyes grew moist with the tears of his ever-present powerful emotions. "So smart, so talented . . . her beautiful stories and poems . . ."

An inflamed June Scarpelli leapt to her feet. "Are you saying I don't love my daughter?"

Art Scarpelli also stood, and placed a comfortably palm on the small of his wife's back, then slowly, with circular motions, rubbed. The gentle curve of her father's hand mesmerized Cassie, especially when she saw the palm inch closer, and closer to her mother's buttocks.

"Yes! That is what I am implying!" Angelo swiped an arm at the parental pair.

"That's not fair, Pop! June is a good mother," Art defended with a hint of tentativeness. Challenging his father had been taboo since birth, and old habits were tough to break.

So the second battle ensued: Good mother versus bad mother, and the Italian versus Swedish way of raising children.

When this dispute finally ended, her grandfather looked like he had been frozen by an ice gun. June Scarpelli had shaken him up, badly. And ultimately, the old man gave up, especially when seeing that nothing would change. Meg rented an attic apartment in a grimy area near Lyndale Avenue, and SIS expanded, prospered, and became a hundred hour a week proposition. Thus the old man took Cassie into his own hands and became her surrogate parent.

Life grew more delicious amid the warm, comforting, always stimulating environment of her grandparents' hundred-year-old two-story home. The abode was nothing fancy, despite her grandfather's wealth. It had been the place where he and Grandma Scarpelli started their married life, then subsequently raised five sons—he refused to move.

A wide, pillared porch encompassed the front of the house, and apple, plum, and cherry trees dotted the front and sides of the yard. It was great fun to shake the trees when her grandparents weren't looking, procuring all the fruit she wanted. And she would wonder what it would be like to live life so primitively, among the fruit trees only, sucking on the juiciness when she desired, otherwise merely romping in the sweet-smelling grass, studying the colors and configurations of the sky, and feeling the warm, whipping breezes against her skin, as she would need no clothes in such a world, just paper and pen so she could describe every sense.

Oh what a glorious vision!

The back yard too was an intrigue and she felt like *Alice in Wonderland* with her explorations. Vegetable and flower gardens fruitfully abounded and were rapt with olfactory and mouth-watering aromas. There were strawberries, raspberries, and the forbidden blackberries. No human hand could touch those except Angelo, as he used these to make his rich, pungent wine.

His distillation, recipe, and hiding place were secrets . . . or so he thought.

The clandestine wine-making operation led to her great curiosity. It must be a magic elixir, she thought. After all, he fretted over each little berry that popped out. So she searched for weeks, in the front yard, back yard, upstairs, downstairs, in every closet, on every shelf, until she ended up in the darkened, dank, stonewalled cellar, that made her nose burn with its mustiness. Yet, despite her terror of what she likened to a black cave, she creaked down the shaky wooden stairs. Her mind saw a mouse with each step, and grisly faces on every wall stone, yet her inquisitiveness was sizzling. She cautiously peeked into the dark enclosures that peppered the moist cellar, and even found the nerves to open the bolted cold room . . . but all she saw was rows upon rows of Mason jars filled with her grandmother's homemade delights . . . no wine in sight.

"Now where?" she asked herself while leaning against the damp stone wall.

And promptly her body caved in.

The stone was loose! She leapt from the wall, fearful she had disturbed a sleeping shrew or perhaps a person as small as *Thumbelina* who would fly into a rage at her intrusion.

Then as if in slow motion, a large stone plummeted from the wall to the ground, and she held her breath while her eyes widened. Then they widened even more. Then they felt like they would fly out of their sockets.

The dark liquid gently swayed in the Mason jars making the glass glisten in hypnotizing fashion. Ever-so-mincingly, she shuffled forward until she faced the magic elixir. She looked left and right, then, with great care, snaked her hand into the hole where the stone once sat.

When the bottle rested in her hand, she felt like Adam about to taste the forbidden fruit. Should she taste? Should she resist? Should she . . . ?

"Cassina!"

The distant sound shook her brain out of its vacillation. Uh-oh . . . Nona!

She stuffed the bottle back into the hole, then, with a grunt and heft, she boosted the stone and managed to put it back in place. With stone secure, she stepped back and shifted her eyes to and fro, memorizing its proximity. She would try again, she knew—her curiosity was *red-hot*.

And it stayed red-hot, through grade-school, through junior-high graduation . . . She was declared the best student, the best artist, and to her utmost pleasure, the best writer.

Her poems won citations, and her stories awards, even a fifty-dollar savings bond from the Anoka Weekly Shopper, a local paper. She proudly framed her first published literary endeavor on the wall of her bedroom in the Angelo Scarpelli home where she stayed more than not. She doubted that her parents even knew she was a missing child. They only made an appearance when they could be on public display--school plays, concerts, school Open Houses-- otherwise it was like living with no parents. This fact greatly saddened Angelo Scarpelli, though he said little. He wasn't one to fight losing battles, rather passionately attack those things which he could change. Her affection needs were an example. He poured every ounce of fiery Italian love on her to the point, he regarded her as his little girl.

That designation suited Cassie fine. She madly loved her grandfather.

They were kindred spirits down to their matching green eyes, the only two mutants in the family possessing such an intriguing, unusual eye color.

"We inherited our eye shade from a distant relative who was a leprechaun," he would chuckle, followed by his fanciful, weaving tales of the green little men who had inhabited the Italian countryside of his boyhood home, a hop and a skip from Rome.

And in his prudent, infinite wisdom, he encouraged her greatest love . . . writing.

"You're a special girl, Cassina. God has given you a very special gift . . . the gift of wonder and words. Don't refuse the gift Cassina. Accept it, embrace it to your fullest, and you will be a success in the most important things in life."

"What are the most important things, Nono?"

"Maturity and experience, Cassina. Only those two things will give you the answer."

So she sought both. Her grandfather was the smartest man she knew, and every word that came from his mouth, she viewed as pure gold.

When it came time for her to start senior high, her parents finally made a nudge in her life, insisting she attend a private school. They viewed massive Anoka High School as contributing to the downfall of her sister Meg who had now taken her army jacket and poetry writing to San Francisco to live in sin with her Minneapolis boyfriend Todd, light, blonde, hair down to his shoulders, and a premiere Yoga contortionist. Anyway, the children of all their fancy friends went to private schools and they needed to have something to talk about in social situations.

The notion was disgusting. Private school? It was so blase'. Hundreds of same sex students parading around in identical uniforms, all mental clones of one another . . . where was the spice? She would suffocate from sensory monotony, Cassie told herself.

Maybe a 'Sandy' would jump at the chance.

But a Cassie? *Pleeese* . . .

On this issue, Angelo Scarpelli stomped a heavy foot. His Cassina wasn't going anywhere. She would stay put in Anoka under his protective Italian wing. And if the two dared to take her away, he would cut off his son's inheritance, stone cold.

Likewise, the private school issue stopped stone cold.

So she got her 'spice' . . . a variety of individuals, experiences up the ying-yang. Spicy hot!

It was on her first day of senior high that she met Sarie Nelson. Despite the intellectual desert between them and the fact that they looked like a pair of mismatches, they were glued to each other, discovering the pleasures of teenager-hood and the hidden mysteries of adulthood.

Sarie knew plenty. She read every trashy book and magazine that came along, and she had a sure-fire entrance to the local X-rated theater. She bribed the old projectionist with her scrumptious fudge brownies or crunchy, chock-full-of-nuts chocolate chip cookies, and he always gave them prime seats in his little cubbyhole.

Was that the way a naked man *really* looked? She wondered, her eyes locked onto the movie screen. And was sex always so intense? So *thrashing*? She wondered about this obsessively, and pictures of herself thrashing so mightily filled her daydreams as well as her night dreams. She had to know.

So she began dating all types . . . smart, dumb, winners, losers . . . they all bored her. She would drain them dry of thoughts, feelings, anything, that would help her experience and mature, then she would heartlessly fling them back where they came from. And as for the thrashing sex-- she never got past kissing and innocent fondling. Just those activities seemed tedious. She was waiting for her Prince Ivanhoe, her Lawrence of Arabia, her Sean Connery . .

"We must be the only two virgins in Anoka High School," Sarie bemoaned for zillionth time in their senior year.

Absorbed in the book *Catch--22*, Cassie barely heard her.

"Face it Cass. We're like two runabout motors, whirring and chugging, and shaking, ready to take off, only to find we're on dry land."

What . . . The paperback fell to her lap. The figurative comparison was luscious! A creative masterpiece, she thought, just able to picture herself as a quivering motor. *Sarie?* The girl didn't have an imaginative bone in her body. *Yet* . . . "That was absolutely beautiful, Sar, like a well-orchestrated melody. Do you mind if I use it in my writing? Of course I'll give you credit in my acknowledgments."

"Huh?" Sarie placed her chubby hands on her abundant hips. "I'm horny as hell and you talk about acknowledgments . . . whatever they are!"

"It's a 'thank you', alms to friends."

"Humph!" Sarie sniffed. "I need the real thing. X-rated movies just don't cut it anymore. I'm ready to attack the old projectionist out of sheer desperation."

Could he even *thrash* with his arthritis? Cassie wondered.

"Well Cass . . . ?" Sarie flipped her black curly head. "What's our next step?"

Having no conclusive answer, Cassie gave a light shrug of her shoulders. "Improvise Sar. You still have that blown up picture of Kyle Callahan on your closet door . . ."

If ever an ominous warning was given, it was on that day. *Stay clear, Cass . . . Back off. . . . Keep twenty paces away from that blown-up picture* . . .

But her head had been too full of wonder that day to heed any of them.

He was the stereotypical jock: Big, beer-guzzling, bragging, brainless. Yet he was the premiere jock at Anoka High School and girls fell at his feet. In fact, all of Anoka honored him for his prowess on a football field, the basketball court, and the baseball diamond. He was "Mr. Sports" in Anoka during their junior and senior years of high school.

And Kyle Callahan played it to the hilt.

"Cassie, isn't it?"

She looked up from her locker rummaging to see Sarie's poster brought to life, standing above her. The shock rendered her speechless

"I'm Kyle . . . Kyle Callahan . . . in your Government class?"

How could she forget? His class speech on 'The Effects of Communism on the Western World' had nearly put her in a coma with his feeble attempts at reading it.

"So you wanna go out? Maybe movie? Burger? Seven o'clock okay?".

He had a confident air and physically, looked like an Irish God. Those muscles . . . She wondered what it would be like to be caught up in them. Would she *thrash*?

"Or seven-thirty if you *gotta* study."

"Seven's just fine," she heard herself stammer.

Those stammering words rushed through her brain over and over, for weeks, months, years. Three little words . . . they had ruined her life.

To discover she was pregnant by a man she could barely tolerate, let alone love, was total devastation. Her entire world collapsed. She had garnered a full academic ride to the University of Minnesota, and she planned to learn all she could about writing plus experience a wonderful new world. She had no desire to give up such pleasures for Kyle Callahan.

So why the sex in the first place?

The question kept her wondering, and in her mind she analytically retraced the progression of their torrid relationship. Each time she came up with the same answer: He was hooked on her "bod' and she, his. She thrashed a little, and him . . . a helluva lot.

She knew this wasn't enough to sustain her, so came her announcement that she wouldn't marry Kyle Callahan, rather raise her child alone.

How *Un*-Italian!

The announcement caused a family uprising. Every family member who could walk or crawl got involved in the gigantic controversy: Disgrace versus more disgrace. Clucking, reproaching voices, half-Italian, half-English, surrounded her, especially those of her parents.

"You will not humiliate this family, Cassandra! If you get married within the next month, no one will know. We can hide the horrid truth!" Her mother pressed in never-ending fashion, primarily fearing what her friends would say.

"Well maybe I'll just abort the humiliation!" she finally spat out from sheer nerves.

The cumulative gasp was so deafening it could be heard in a two-hundred mile radius, followed by an assortment of slews all adding up to one thing. Sinner!

Kyle was no better. He bombarded her with reasons as to why they should get married. But what did his pleas *really* mean? Plainly, he wanted her bod in his bed every night so he could thrash like a wild man. He didn't care about her mind--he ignored her mind. He was too busy bragging about himself. The notion of being hooked up with such a man forever, was unbearable.

"Cassina, we need to talk, just you and me," her grandfather said late one night when the controversy had reached a summit.

She lie in bed, unable to sleep for the fifth night in a row. It couldn't be good for her baby, she knew. The sound of his familiar gentle voice soothed her, and maybe if she listened to the tone long enough, she'd be lulled into a badly needed sleep. So, she agreed to the talk.

He quietly spoke about his beliefs regarding family and children, ones she had heard for most of her nineteen years. Then he followed this with all the reasons that she needed to do the right thing for the child she carried. It took top priority, he said. To be without a father was a horrible fate for a child.

"But I don't love him, Nono. He's not right for me, I swear," she sobbed.

After pausing to absorb her words, Angelo Scarpelli gave a resigned nod. "Nevertheless Cassina, he's the father, and in the least you owe your child that."

"I won't be happy, Nono. I won't have my experiences, my chance at maturity, my . . . writing . . . I won't have my dream."

"That's no true, Cassina. Write. You don't need fancy schooling. You've been touched by the golden quill of God. Motherhood . . . it's a wonderful experience," he argued wisely.

His words rolled around her head in the proceeding days, and she finally convinced herself she could have marriage, motherhood, and the golden quill.

And as for love? Perhaps it would come in time. Perhaps her and Kyle's minds would eventually merge and they could find some satisfactory communicating level. *Perhaps* . . . she wondered, and wondered, until the wondering stopped and she walked down the "Aisle of Discontent and Lost Dreams" amid what seemed like a million smiling Scarpelli faces . . .

****

Except for mine . . . She glided the washrag over the already clean refrigerator.

"Cassie . . ."

She jarred her gaze upward. Kyle leaned against the jamb of the kitchen entrance. He had that smile and eye glint. Her eyes darted to the wall clock. *My God, it's barely twelve noon.*

"I thought since the kid was gone, we could start our game of fornication a little early today. My middle's pumpin' babe."

So what else is new? His middle had been *pumpin'* since birth, she thought, repulsed.

"Bathtub . . . bathroom floor . . . bedroom floor . . . I got the whole route planned," he said with nauseating confidence.

That'll take all of five minutes, her brain screamed, able to feel the chill she would experience at every pit stop. He had no care of her satisfaction. His pumpin' middle took precedence over everything else. She loathed his pumpin' middle!

"My pants are full as we speak." He ogled her like she was a baking powder biscuit.

Oooh . . . She wanted to violently barf. If she was cut off at the waist tomorrow, Kyle Callahan would be packed and out the door.

"Ten minutes . . . bathtub . . . be there. Let's make some heat."

With a devilish smile, Kyle lifted from the door jamb and sauntered away with the same walk he had once used when triumphantly walking off a football field.

The sight sickened her. *This* was her reality. No matter how many hours she spent in the attic trying to deny it--this was it. And her only means out of it was fulfillment of her dream--and that wasn't even a sure thing. Perhaps if would take another ten years, or another. What would be left of her? *Working like hell* . . . it was her only defense to prevent such a frightening eventually.

And Harry . . .

With every breath she took, with every beat of her heart, with every metabolism of her
cells . . . she had to work better than hell, ultra-careful revisions, flying like a super cyclone on Sundays, whatever it took, to make the world feel the wonder of 'Harry'.

The passion and determination made her feel better for what she must endure. She bore up to satisfy a promise and appease a one-track minded man with a *pumpin' middle.*

Chapter 4—Jack

The day was unusually steamy for late March in Los Angeles. Blessed with a day off from the never-ending world of 'skin flick' production, Jack Torelli took advantage of the crystal clear day and scorching sun to rejuvenate his tan in a natural manner. For the last couple months, he had utilized tanning salons to maintain his darkly handsome skin, so he projected onto the screen, all that his faithful followers expected of him--regardless of the probable nature of the followers.

Fans were fans, money in the bank, job security, 'perpetuators' of one's star status. They kept egos fed when one's table was otherwise empty, and boosted esteems with their appreciation of the talent presented, no matter the specifics of the talent.

Yes, he would bake like a tortilla on flat stone for his fans, because his Hollywood psyche literally screamed out for all of the above, and to lose even one was paramount to a rapid, merciless death in the fabled town. *Yes, he would bake to perfection.*

His padded lounger was flanked on four sides by tall redwood walls which shielded him from view except for the planes flying in and out of LAX. Without specifying his reasons, he had talked the landlord into allowing him to have carpenters build the enclosure onto the existing balcony so his privacy was maintained.

Flipping on his back, he evenly applied coconut oil over his naked body until his muscled form gleamed with the slick solution. He needed no other protection. It was his fortune to possess naturally dark skin which never burned, no matter how long he partook of the sun's rays.

With faint admiration, he glided his eyes down the length of his body to make sure the oil covered every inch. *It still looks good,* he told himself with a large measure of relief. His looks had always been his stock-in-trade, his golden key to the Hollywood gates. In years past, he had been compared to a Roman prince, an Italian god, referred to as a "superstud" and more benignly, a "Hollywood Heartthrob." But over the last five years since he started doing "skins," the names had been less than flattering; the press had been cruelly mocking, behind his back initially, though now they minced no words to his face.

He was a curiosity. Why? Was the most frequently asked question of him. Why the drastic career switch, Jack? Why, Jack, when you had halfway decent acting talent? Why the smut, Jack? His earlier self-regard deflated as the questions painfully muddled his mind. He flopped his head back onto the lounger, letting the sun to soothe him into much-needed settled state. Life had been hell. Three of his 'skins' were released almost simultaneously and Rud Hanna's insisted that he get out and about to socially promote the trio, This meant more women, so more booze and coke, so more stilted sex. He felt the toll of his increasingly destructive lifestyle, and that was fucking frightening. Keenly, he felt like his time was running out.

With this sobering thought, he clenched his eyes shut. If the baneful end struck tomorrow, what would his obituary say? He wondered, gruesomely.

It would give a stunning list of all his "skin flicks" and conveniently omit his most proud roles, he thought bitterly. He could just visualize the media's sensitive treatment of his career. The trades and major networks would terminate his life in the gutter, perhaps even show segments of his X-rated movie career on television, precluding them with a warning. *Yeah . . . he could just visualize the media circus with the body of Jack Torelli in the center ring.*

And his funeral . . . Who would come? He figured not many of the industry people. Most likely they would just throw up their hands and say "No loss," even Rud Hanna. The studio owner may grieve for an hour or two, then merely look in the wings and find a hundred, maybe a thousand, Jack Torellis waiting like predators.

Although his family would congregate en masse, he told himself. They would all feel a great obligatory need to pray for the sinner. He could just picture his grandmother, wailing like a wild woman while she threw herself over his coffin, and his mother wouldn't be much calmer. Suicide . . . that's the way they would view his untimely demise. He had brought it on himself with his lifestyle, a slow death at his own hands, a catastrophic event in the Catholic doctrine.

"A coward's way out," he muttered, anguish gripping him when remembering the root of the words.

The quote came from the old Irish priest who taught the Catechism classes he had faithfully attended as a youth. The four words represented the priest's definition of suicide. Though now, he also remembered the spiel that proceeded the definition.

"It takes greater courage to face life . . . The measure of a true man . . . "

Nervously, he shifted his body position on the lounger. In pitiless fashion, the nagging origin versus actuality analogy tugged at his conscience, though he tried like hell to *un*-tug it. But the hold seemed tighter than usual, and he figured his grisly thoughts had contributed to this. So he tried to concentrate on the glorious warmth the sun created, and willed his mind to go blank.

Stubbornly, it wouldn't.

****

Continual strident voices and pungent, tantalizing aromas were the two best ways to characterize the rollicking Torelli home.

Located in the Lower East Side of Manhattan in Little Italy, the building with living space above, had been in the Torelli family for two generations, since family patriarch, Paulo Torelli left Venice with his wife Margareta and their three children, and landed in New York in 1922.

Selling a piece of land inherited from an uncle, Paulo took the fairly generous proceeds and his bricklaying ability to the Land Paved with Gold Streets. Though once he got there, he discovered life was far from the easy. The land sale proceeds bought the two story building a block east of Mulberry Street close to Old St. Patrick's Cathedral and allowed him to start a one-man business. But maintaining the building, even with his skilled trade, was a hardship, one that never let up until the day he retired from bricklaying in 1956. At that point, he decided to turn the house over to his son Carlo, a plumber and oldest of his now eight children. In Torelli procreating fashion, Carlo already had nine children, and his wife Marianna expecting her tenth soon.

They named him Jack Anthony Torelli.

Being the youngest, the bambino, of the over abundant family had its ups and down. His parents, four sisters, and five brothers gave Jack most of the affection, but he also took most of the knocks the wild bunch doled out. And to be the smallest trapped in this untamed environment was no easy proposition. He learned from an early age, that he had to "toughen up" to survive.

He was always bragged upon as being the '"pretty boy" of the family. He had the large size of his mother's side of the family, and he possessed the dark skin and thick wavy black hair of his father and brothers. But his eyes were a mystery, according to his mother. They were sharp like a black arrow point, she always said, and his sisters teased that his eyes went through them as if he could see their underwear.

"Jacko's going to be a politician; he's an *incantatore*, a charmer," his grandmother, Margareta frequently said in half-American, half-Italian, as neither grandparent had completely adopted the English language.

Other family members, seemingly hundreds, would also predict his future. He would be a lawyer, a doctor, a college professor, a businessman, an army general . . . and on, and on, each, in clairvoyant fashion, declaring he would be a success. And most certainly it was he who would cross the Torelli family line, and go to college.

It was a big mouthful for a young kid to swallow. To be the shining hope of his family seemed to be an awesome responsibility, one he felt for all the years of his youth.

So from the first day he started school, he tried to excel at everything, schoolwork, music, art, sports . . . anything that confronted him . . . And, ultimately acting confronted him.

"Jack you will play Romeo. You have that look," Sister Genevieve, his fourth-grade teacher said decisively. So if he had any reservations, he didn't dare voice them.

Instead he put his usual superior effort to the task and began to tediously learn his lines while everyone in his immediate family wanted to help with the prompting. At some point, the tedium evaporated and he found he enjoyed the activity, especially when he discovered he could ham it up with his voice and gestures. It was great fun!

On the night of the production, the auditorium at the Catholic school was brimmed with Torellis—his debut had been the talk of the family for weeks. And once he strutted onto the stage, and the single camera light shone on him, and he saw silhouettes of the audience, and he heard the wild hoots and clangorous applause, he felt the *sheer* thrill.

He was hooked.

From then on, he volunteered for every grade school play the grade school, even if it just meant painting scenery or working behind the stage. But he hated the latter. He'd intensely stare at the stage performers and wish it were him up there instead. *I could be better*, he always thought of the male lead who seemed to be reading his lines, rather than acting them.

The summer after sixth-grade graduation, he went about building a stage from scrap lumber in the tiny back yard, to his older siblings' amusement. Once the flimsy structure was done, he charmed friends and family members into being in his plays, all of which he wrote, starred, and directed. The cost of admission was only a quarter, but as his reputation for "cute plays" spread among the communal neighborhood, he collected a lot of quarters; although his stash dwindled quickly when the other Torelli children demanded payment for their acting contributions.

Since he had done most of the work, he strongly protested. But it was for *not*. They just beat the money out of him. Yet, he retained enough money to frequent the neighborhood movie theater where he could study and dream while chewing on ju-jubees. Once in the confines of the bedroom he shared with two of his brothers, he recreated the male lead in front of the small, tarnished wall mirror. He felt powerful with each word he spoke, especially when they sounded exactly like what he had heard come from the movie screen. And the thrill was ever-present.

In between his movies and plays, he attended summer religious classes at Old St. Patrick's Cathedral where his family worshiped every Sunday, and hung out with his gang of friends, all full Italian heritage like him.

The religious classes made him think; though generally quite somber in this environment, he questioned little and merely listened to the soothing brogue of Father O'Malley expound the responsibilities of the Catholic male. Like all else he learned in his life, he took the words to heart and became an exemplary student of Catholicism . . . alter boy, church choir, living by the Commandments that the old priest hammered into their heads. He was so diligent, his family began adding "priest" to their lists of possible future careers for him.

But he saw this prediction as laughable. Despite the fact he was only twelve, he had a great itch to experience beyond his sheltered neighborhood, and even more sheltering family. A priest wouldn't cut it. Experience, he figured, was vital for creating a richness to his characters, and making the treasured words spring more convincingly from his lips. Even at this age, he knew what his future course would be, and thought it wise for his family to rip up their list for good.

He was none of the above.

In the meantime however, he thoroughly enjoyed the bustling neighborhood around him. He and his friends would cruise Mulberry Street, *Via San Gennaro* to his grandfather, and there, they would linger at the shop windows, whiffing the fresh pastas and breads, and salivating over vast varieties of homemade cheeses and exotic sausages. None of them ever had any money to buy the treats, as they all came from large, lower middle-class families, and there was no extra money to freely toss out to the kids.

Despite the lack of funds, life was rich and full in the convivial, primarily Italian neighborhood. Sensory deprivation was never a problem. The boisterous, insistent sounds of a thousand Italian voices filtered through the air, and everyone knew and watched out for each other. One was never alone, rather constantly surrounded by young and old alike, all partaking in whatever event happened to be going on that day, such as a stick ball game.

Stick ball, much like baseball except for the use of a stick instead of a bat, was Jack's favorite sport. He was a star player, garnering much neighborhood respect for his athletic prowess. Mostly the games were conducted on quiet, low-trafficked streets, but on occasion, he and his team would sneak across the Bowery to spacious Sara Delano Roosevelt Park where they could really stretch out and play. Regardless of the location, after every game the team would converge on the Torelli kitchen where an abundantly generous Marianna Torelli stuffed them with mouth-watering homemade spaghetti and bread.

The majority of food in the Torelli house was homemade, much of it grown in the piecemeal gardens to the side and back of the building. Tomato plants sprouted everywhere, even on the front and back porches and Italian pole beans and fat peas climbed up on vines alongside the building. Then there was the lettuce patch full of rich green iceberg lettuce and endive, and carrots, radishes, and potatoes hid under the rich soil that Margareta Torelli had carefully cultivated ever since she and Paulo moved into the building. And there were fruit bushes-- raspberries, blueberries, strawberries--in the backyard, cumulatively giving off an enticing odor.

The Torelli children constantly filched the fruit and vegetables, though if caught, they would get a slap to the head, or shoe to the behind by an irate Marianna Torelli. She needed the food for canning to feed their *da porco*, their piggish, little mouths, she would yell with her fringed Italian accent. In fact, she took little monkey business from any of them. There were too many of them to take any *rifiuto*, any garbage, she would shriek after a perceived misdeed, then followed this with a resounding smack.

Jack got his share of his mother's rage, but many times it wasn't justified. Being the youngest he got blamed for plenty whether he was guilty or not, but Marianna never listened to his pleaded explanations, and whacked him anyway. This only heightened when he was in junior high and started paying attention to the fairer sex. The brothers, close in age to each other, had a similar look about them, and snoopy neighbors would confuse the Torelli boys, blabbing to Marianna that Jack was kissing so and so in broad daylight, when it was actually his brother Stephano, 'Steve', who was the offender. Naturally, Steve didn't dispute this, and let Jack take his mother's punishment for such *depravare*, perverted, behavior.

"You are to show *rispetto*, show respect, for girls!" Marianna emphatically told her sons, and if she considered a girl too *tristo*, too wicked, the boys were read the riot act if they went near such a type. They were only to take out decent girls, she would say, and this sentiment was echoed by an equally fiery Carlo Torelli, who protected his own five daughters' virginity like an vigilant, eagle-eyed sentry. He refused to have a *prostituta*, a whore in his house, Carlo fiercely told his sons, and if they dared bring such a woman into his midst they would be *miscuglio*, they would be mincemeat.

The passion behind the message wasn't lost on any of the sons. Yet all five were carefully sneaky, and took turns at the girls with so-called 'reputations', including Jack. He discovered he liked women as well as the necking, and as he got older, the sex. Though committing the act nudged plenty on his conscience, as many times he heard the calm, Irish brogue in his head, followed by his mother's voice, telling him he must save himself for his virgin bride, followed by his father hollering *prostituta!* And after, he would feel plenty guilty with the play of voices lingering in his brain for days. He was still an altar boy, and sang tenor in the church choir, though with the breaking of the commandments, he felt like a hypocrite and this was plaguing. He continued to have that great desire to excel.

At the highly structured Catholic high school all the Torellis attended, or had attended, he was a top student in every subject, especially math and science, and all the priests and nuns were pushing him towards a career as a doctor or engineer. In fact, they helped him garner college scholarships with these professions in mind. Soon his parents, and the multitude of Torelli family members learned of this wonderful coup, and they broke out the *vino*.

He silently took in all the hullabaloo, not disputing any of them, though inside he felt like a confused mess. On one hand, he wanted to please everyone like always, and on the other, he was unable to deny his destiny.

The acting bug had never left him, rather intensified all through junior high and high school. He tried out for every play, and more times than not, garnered the lead. His bent seemed to be the Shakespearean type actor, and he constantly envisioned himself doing this kind of serious acting off-Broadway, or even on Broadway.

The neighborhood acclaimed his acting ability, including the entire Torelli family who never missed a stage performance. Yet, it was referred to as "Jacko's hobby" or "Jacko's little plays"—no one took it seriously. After all, *no one* chose acting as a *real* job. It wasn't a man's job, and to be a man was paramount in the Torelli family. It was expected, Carlo perpetually touted.

"To be a man is to do what is right in life. A true man finds the courage to stay on that right track, no matter the hardship. To take the easy way is the coward's way, not a man's way," he told his sons while they sat together on the front porch, smoking cigarettes and sipping dry wine, as they did on most Sunday nights when if was forbidden for any of them leave their home.

As he puffed and sipped, Jack let his father's words settle over him, and he felt more confused than ever as to what to do. High school graduation was looming. He was the Torellis' last hope. None of his numerous cousins, or his five brothers had opted for college, rather, followed normal Torelli tradition and chosen a variety of trades. His four sisters didn't even do that. They worked at minimum wage jobs until, marrying men also in the trades.

So he was it, the one with the brains and the opportunity. What next?

Those two months before graduation he vacillated back and forth, trying to determine what was the right thing to do while "proud" statements surrounded him. Finally, he snapped from the pressure and went to Fordham University in New York City on a full scholarship.

He tried, but he was restless. The classes bored him and more times than not, he skipped them to head for Times Square, so he could feel close to his first love. Whenever he scraped together enough money, he bought a cheap ticket to a Broadway show, then intensely watch the stage like he had done in his youth, and wish to be the male lead, or even an extra, any part, just let him be on that glorious, inviting stage. He felt it beckoning.

Ultimately, his grades reflected his lack of school attendance and the scholarship was rescinded. He gnawed more, this time nervously, wondering how he would explain the first failure of his life to his pride-filled family who always spouted about "Jacko the great surgeon" or "Jacko the engineer who, with his math brain, would put a man on Mars.".

To tell the truth was terrifying. So he said nothing, leaving Fordham and getting two jobs, waiter by day and bouncer at a Manhattan club, at night. He rented a room in a dive hotel, and saved every possible penny so he could go to acting school.

Although he allowed his family to believe he was still in college and doing splendidly.

The truth came out eventually, but he didn't tell it, rather a priest from his old high school, friends with the Fordham University administrator who had helped arrange the scholarship. "How's Jack Torelli doing?" the priest asked his friend. And the truth was revealed. Then it was revealed to his parents, then to his entire family, and finally to him when he paid a visit home.

Initially, they let him tout about his illustrious college career. Then suddenly he was confronted by his parents, who spat "Liar" at him, until he crumpled from the intense shame.

"You've disgraced us, Jacko!" Marianna said furiously.

"A coward Jacko . . . not a man. . . . a coward!" Paulo spat in his face.

He felt the sting of his father's words and the wetness of his spit, and wanted to die where he stood. The moment was horrible, as if his entire nineteen years of life caved on top of him like a sham. After all he had done to excel and this is what he was left with: *A coward*. It was devastating and unbearable.

Unable to face the accusing looks, he fled the warm, secure home that had been the center of his world all of his life. Painfully, he stayed away for a year, no contact or explanations.

The year away from his family was horrible. He constantly felt a frightening loneliness, even though he was establishing a circle of friends, the majority aspiring actors like himself. He moved to an apartment in Soho with a couple of these friends and they all attended The Actor's Institute by day and he worked at night as a bartender in a halfway decent club in Lower Manhattan. The pay and tips kept him afloat, and with his darkly handsome looks, he was pursued by a variety of women from all walks of life.

These females were a much more sophisticated breed than the ones who inhabited his old neighborhood, so at first he felt unsure, not knowing how to converse with such types. But as his confidence grew, so did his courage, and soon he was having several relationships, none particularly special. Although, the play of voices remained in his head where women were concerned, no matter the type, and he treated each with *rispetto*, as his mother had dictated.

The acting classes kept his thrill vigorously kicking. A constant excitement was with him when he found himself on stage, portraying a patchwork of characters. All the teachers heartily praised him. He had excelled once more. Yet, without his family, he felt afloat and craved that sense of community again. The loneliness was gradually eating away bits of him. But try as he might, he couldn't find the courage to take that trip to Mott Street to rectify his wrong.

Finally, after thirteen months elapsed, Mott Street came to him.

Ever since the day he had departed his home, his father had frantically tried to locate him. Carlo Torelli finally did, and humbly showed up outside Jack's apartment.

"You're our bambino, Jacko. We can't leave it like this," his father pleaded.

He noticed his father looked grayer and had a deeper web of wrinkles. Guilt washed over him. Had he caused it? . "Come in, Pop."

Once seated, he haltingly confessed what he had been doing with his life, then sat back and listened to his father's startled responses.

"You're such a smart boy, Jacko . . . Acting?"

"It's all I ever wanted, Pop. You gotta understand . . ." He spoke with a passion that had never come out of him before, and Carlo Torelli couldn't help but notice the undeniable change that had over his once, so-compliant youngest child. ". . .And I'll never give up the stage, Pop. I'll shrivel up and die if I hafta give it up."

It took awhile for Carlo to digest all the heartfelt emotion, but finally he nodded. "You must do what is right, Jacko. You have my blessing," he replied with some tentativeness.

His eyes flooded with tears at his father's affirmation, and they hugged tightly to seal his renewed, much-coveted status as a Torelli. Then, all the family embraced him likewise like he hadn't been gone for even a second. His life had been richly blessed once more, and this reflected in his acting. He was a dynamo!

Lead roles in the plays at the Institute dropped into his lap . . . Shakespeare, Tennessee Williams, Faulkner . . . a miscellany of juicy, stimulating characters that taxed his acting ability. He joined a summer stock company that traveled New England, and the next summer another, one that went farther west, Cincinnati, Indianapolis, and ending in Chicago. The travel sparked him, and he stared with awe and exhilaration at life beyond Mott Street. He could just feel the well-roundedness of his person beginning to start its course to full circle. It was a wonderful, deliciously innocent time in his life.

When he returned from his travels, a letter awaited him. He, Jack Torelli, had been invited to join the American Academy of Dramatic Arts, an acting school on whose alumnus were Oscar, Emmy, and Tony winners. He thought it to be the greatest honor of his twenty-one years.

He worked and studied like hell, soaking up every bit of acting knowledge he could from the teachers, and alumnus, famous and not so famous, that had been invited to speak to the students. He had stars in his eyes that grew more luminescent with each passing day. He couldn't wait to hit the lights beyond the classroom and seriously pursue the career all his teachers predicted he would have.

He got his first nudge when he was two months short of his twenty-second birthday, garnering a part in an off-Broadway play, a parody on Communism. He played a richly charactered inmate in the Gulag who was ultimately sent to Siberia. The role was great fun—he could ham it up to the limit, and he found he liked comedic roles.

All of his immediate family, now at forty members and rapidly growing, came to the production. Few understood the abstract quality of the play, but they all liked his portrayal, and even admitted to laughing wildly when his character insulted the Gulag chief.

"I can see the talent, Jacko," Carlo said in quiet tones, and his brothers and sisters more heartily echoed these sentiments.

"I hope you're going to church on Sundays, Jacko," Marianna said tearfully while her potently emotional, abundant person clung to him.

"Sure Mom." Guilt consumed him, and briefly, the richly Irish brogue coursed his mind like a denouncement. But he didn't reverse the lie, rather allowed his family to believe he was a still a steadfast Catholic boy who could have been a priest if he had the proclivity.

In truth, his life was slipping away from the Catholic doctrine more and more. The women came and went, the sex was more kinky, and the play of voices grew dimmer. He drank more, not the mellow dry wine of his youth, but harder liquor that his mother always preached against, and pot became a daily ritual. He experimented with speed and hallucinogens, but there he drew the line. He refused to have destructive drugs mess with his dream. He knew he needed all his faculties to compete in the tough, cutthroat environment he had chosen to inhabit.

And the stars grew brighter and brighter.

After his first off-Broadway role, he garnered more varied roles; although, light comedy seemed to be his forte, and soon he was sought out for these roles. A "Neil Simon-type" actor, he was called by critics. And fortunately, in 1980, when he was twenty-four, the world of acting was bombarded with these types of roles.

He had acquired a minor role in a Broadway play, his first big break, and he gave the role everything he had. It was grueling, several shows a day, little food or sleep, a major indoctrination into what lie ahead. But he loved every minute despite the hardship. The moment he walked onto that glorious stage--felt the lights, the audience's presence, the set surrounding him--the words magnificently poured from his lips, his gestures sparked, and he felt the *sheer* thrill.

He emphatically told himself, it was the only world he ever wanted and would never be satisfied with less. So he garnered more roles, appropriate to his forte, on Broadway and off—his name was becoming recognizable in New York. Finally, at age twenty-six, he hit the big time, a prime role in Neil Simon's *Brighton Beach Memoirs*. His portrayal was well-reviewed by critics, some major, and it was like the match that touched the dynamite keg.

Television miniseries based on novels were picking up major steam in Hollywood and producers looked for new, exciting unknowns to star in them. All the major television networks were heralding several of these types of productions in the year 1983, a monumental, life-altering year for Jack Torelli.

It was a novelization for television, and he was asked to come to Hollywood to audition for the role of a sexy race car driver who had a secret death wish. Upon reading the script, he found the role a more serious than he was used to portraying, and wondered if he could carry it out admirably. *Yet to make it to Hollywood.* It was like a lifelong dream come true, especially when he was stirred with remembrances of his incessant movie watching as a youth.

Finally, he agreed to the audition . . . and he was offered the role . . . and he retained a Hollywood agent named Harv Wellson . . . and he moved away from the city of his birth.

Hollywood was everything he had ever imagined, and much more. The people were curious as well as exciting, the night life was an enticing adventure, and the *warmth* . . . he loved the sun's brilliance day in and day out. Although it *was* exceedingly difficult to leave his family and stable of friends. When by himself, the familiar frightening loneliness would grip, and it gripped even tighter after a year, and a second miniseries role passed. The fabled city, though enrapturing, was void of true loyalty, and his once adhering trust in human nature began to slowly sink. He became a harder, more cynical man.

Despite, he grew addicted to the world, effortlessly, it seemed.

The sex was more kinky, the drugs more plentiful, and the night life tantalizing to every sense. He couldn't imagine being without it. So he stayed and starred in more miniseries, had guest spots in several television series, and even a couple significant roles in movies that were highly acclaimed. Jack Torelli was an up-and-coming star, several voices in Hollywood said.

But his personal life was a desert covered with shit.

When he inched towards to his thirtieth birthday he began to take closer stock at his life, and he discovered he only had his acting, no other meaningful entities. He began to fantasize about his old existence on Mott Street, the stability, the ever-present feeling that one belonged, the warming sensation of a family's embrace, the unconditional love for one another.

Suddenly, he wanted that back. So he went out to seek it.

Gloria Moran was a fairly familiar face, who graced makeup ads in magazines, and on billboards. He met her at a party, and they clicked it off, a quip here, a quip there, and they landed in bed. She was exotically beautiful, sultry eyes, rich dark brown hair, a perfect well-endowed figure, and she was a temptress in the sack . . . so he married her in Las Vegas, only telling his family after the act had been committed.

Highly upset, his parents refused to accept his letters and calls for a good three months. But in usual Torelli forgiving fashion, they ceased their snub and begrudgingly agreed to his offer of plane tickets to California so they could meet his wife.

They only had a ten minute conversation with he and Gloria, before standing up to leave. An hour later he received a terse, emotion-packed phone call.

"That *prostituta* is never to cross my front door!" Carlo raged while the sounds of his mother's heart-wrenching wails filled the background.

Unable to face the words and sounds, he hung up the phone, and crumbled with intense shame mixed with raw disappointment. He had let them down again.

From that point on, the marriage went downhill, mainly due to him. He resumed his nightlife and women, and left Gloria alone, more and more. None of it hurt him. He had discovered he had little feeling for his wife beyond the physical. The only hurt was his father's stinging words and his mind's sounds of his mother's cries. He couldn't bear it--the misery-filled sound, the emasculating words--he couldn't bear it. And less than ten months to the day he said "I do" in Vegas, he and Gloria were divorced.

But his career flourished . . . for another eighteen months it flourished.

He had a major role a Neil Simon movie, a lesser role in a Vietnam War drama, an even lesser role, playing a dashing rogue, in a historical miniseries, a minute role as an advertising piranha in a made-for-television movie, a more minute role as a suave socialite in a another television movie, a guest starring role on a nighttime soap opera, a lesser guest starring role on a police show, a part on a medical drama, a lesser part on a dramatic legal series, a bit part on a comedy, a walk-on at the end of a comedy . . . and then it dried up.

"Torelli looks like hell most of the time.". . ."Late for filmings" . . ."Bad news.". . ."Has talent, but. . ."

He felt every sling like a slap in the face. So, he had a few problems? He never, *never,* let it influence his acting. That was his first priority. They all had to see that.

But not a reputable producer saw beyond what was in their direct vision, a hardcore. Virulent man who had lost his humor and appealing, gorgeous dark innocence that had once so plainly magnified on the screen. And he was barely pushing thirty-two. Sad but true, the story of a Hollywood casualty . . . *se le vive.*

He thought he would go raving mad with the turned backs. Suddenly, no one would touch him. Like a puff of smoke, it was gone. How could it be? After all the hard work to pursue the only dream he ever wanted, how could this, in anyone's wildest imaginings, be happening? It couldn't. He wouldn't let it. *His superior effort* . . . No way in hell, would he let this happen . . .

"Harv, you gotta get me something. I'm losing my frickin' mind," he pleaded to Harv Wellson, his casual social acquaintance and agent.

Harv rustled the papers on his desk, a sure-fire sign that he was anxious. "No can do, Jack. I've tried, believe me. But your reputation smells like a stink bomb. Why with your talent? I don't got a goddamn clue, except to say they're all treating your name like dirt. It's like a goddamn conspiracy amongst the big boys. Hands-off Torelli."

His body convulsed with desperation and anger. "What big boys? Who?"

"All of 'em it seems, Hayes, Moreau, Isle . . . particularly Isle."

"Fuckers!" Jack exploded at the names representing the miniseries magnates, especially the last. He was the man who gave him his first break in Hollywood, and for the producer to rebuff him after the asshole had lured him to the Hollywood in the first place . . . He wanted to kill the venerable Michael Isle.

Harv shuffled again. "There is an offer from a small-potatoes television producer who's been inquiring about you for a television series for cable."

"Who?" he demanded, and Harv gave an unfamiliar name. "Never heard of him."

"He's new in the business. High imagination sort, kinda nouveau boob-tube."

With Harv's desk antics, he immediately grew suspicious. "What kinda 'nouveau'?"

"A detective show, somewhat comical in . . . ur . . . a serious sense."

"What the hell . . . ?"

"View it as an experiment with you the guinea pig who may make television history if this thing flies. You could be develop a new mode of acting, and it pays ten thous' an hour segment."

"Ten thous'? That's goddamn crap, Harv!"

Harv's only response was a spread of his hands.

He read the message loud and clear. "So beggars can't be choosy, huh?"

The hands spread again.

Desperate, he signed the contract to do ten segments of *Clay Slade*, an ultra-low budget television series that had brain dead writers, and a certifiable nut for a producer. It was garbage. The dialogue was etched in crap and as humorous as a graveyard. Yet every day he stepped onto the set, trying to salvage 'crap' with his acting talent. Even a thousand percent effort didn't help. The script was an impossibility that Olivier couldn't resuscitate. And the action scenes . . . stilted, contrived, no spontaneity, no element of surprise . . . They may as well have hired mechanical men.

Still, he did get one significant, earthshattering thing out of the series.

For two episodes, the filming went to the Bahamas, and it was there he met Sheeny Delancey, a native of the Grand Bahamas, hired by the producer to do a walk-on for *Clay Slade*. At the lowest point in his life, personal and professional, he was sparked by the sight of the energetic Sheeny strutting past him. He almost forgot his lines.

Four hours later, he got her into bed where her high energy continued, and he felt like he had been given a mega-dose of vitamins. She was good medicine at that time, and he was reluctant to let go of that good feeling. So he talked her into coming back to Hollywood with him.

They lived together in his Bel-Air home, until the old guilt began to gnaw—where it came from, he didn't know—but the play of voices grew stronger that they had in years.

So, he married her.

It was the biggest mistake of his entire life.

She was a closet coke-head.

The addiction almost ruined him financially.

They divorced after only six months of marriage.

. . .And *Clay Slade* was axed from the cable network after only five episodes.

He was finally through in Hollywood . . .

"Go back to New York, Jack. Broadway, off-Broadway, even summer stock. Your reputation may still be intact there," Harv Wellson urged.

"How?" he trembled out.

"I doubt if *Clay Slade* made it that far."

It made it. His brothers still laughed about the hokey television series, and his parents said the show filled the old neighborhood with much humor.

"New York, Jack . . . New York."

He felt too filthy to return to New York. "I can't. I gotta stay in Hollywood." Harv began to furiously shuffle papers.

Mesmerized, he watched the action and waited for the next bomb to fall.

"There is an option to keep you here, Jack. But . . . I'm a little reluctant . . ."

"What," he asked, desperation crawling all over him.

"A producer and studio owner who . . . actually admired your work on *Clay Slade*."

"Who?" He anxiously leaned over Harv's desk. "Who is he?"

"A guy named Hanna . . . Rud Hanna . . ."

****

After the first movie was released, Carlo Torelli called him less than a man . . . *And I haven't seen or spoken to him since* . . .

Rare tears rolled down Jack;'s face, neck and chest, mixing with the coconut oil, while the frightening loneliness pervaded.

The shining hope . . . *Damn.* He wanted to die.

He slowly raised from the lounger into a sitting position. Deliberately, he ran his eyes over his body, every inch. *No white lines.* But he wasn't satisfied. He felt too numb to feel anything except the unending self-loathing which started the day he signed the contract on Rud's desk.

But he thought it was useless to dwell on this fate. There was only a small concentration of power in Hollywood, the rest of them beggars. He was the premiere beggar--that fact was irrevocable.

Sighing out his resignation, he stood. A distant motorized sound hit his ears, and he lifted his eyes upward, hooding them with his hand, when the sun's glare threatened to blind him. The silver glint of a plane flashed directly above him. Immediately, he formed a mind's picture of the passengers looking down at his nakedness, perhaps gasping, perhaps laughing, but all gawking. He stayed rooted so they all could get a free show.

Then suddenly, he felt impulsive.

"This is Torelli!" he yelled ferociously, at the top of his lungs. Then emotions overtaking, he yelled some more. "Torelli! The black sheep! *Pecora nera!* Castrated! *Castrare!* You hear me? *Castrare . . . !*"

His voice echoed through the gently swaying palm trees in the front yard, long after the plane had disappeared. And then, he quieted.

There was another party to attend, he silently reminded. All the slime of Hollywood expected his presence. *And Rud* . . . it was part of the package deal. He couldn't afford to piss off Rud. The *sheer* thrill was still addicting.

His eyes shook forward. He was still 'The Prince of the Skins', he thought, girding himself. And having this fact in mind, he took long strides to prepare for his royal subjects.

Chapter 5—Cassie

"You must stop this nonsense, Cassandra."

Why doesn't she just call me "Sandy," and be done with it? Cassie thought with irritation, watching her severe, be speckled mother briskly write behind her huge mahogany desk that looked like it cost more than Kyle's yearly salary.

"It isn't healthy. You . . ." Gazing up, June Scarpelli peered over her glasses, and shot an exact look across her desk. " Look terrible. Your hair, skin, and Lord . . . you're as skinny as hell!"

Jealous mother? Cassie thought deliciously, noticing that 'Old June' had put on a few pounds in the derriere'. It must be grating at her perfect person.

"And Kyle, poor man . . . He looks like hell too."

Poor man, my ass. Cassie wanted to vomit at the nauseating sympathy. It was more than "The Freezer Nymph" ever showed for one of her kids, she thought disdainfully.

"Then there's poor little Kristi . . ." June's facial muscles grew so rigid, Cassie thought they would crack from the tenseness. "I had to sent my housekeeper shopping with the unfortunate child, so she could acquire a summer wardrobe. And then she cried to Art about summer soccer, summer camp, and a New England tour with other students . . . My God Cassandra, can't you afford anything for my granddaughter?"

Yeah, she screamed silently. Those housekeepers *were* great shoppers. I have first hand knowledge. Remember mother?

"The writing must stop, now!" June obstinately smacked a fist onto the desktop.

Cassie felt diverting. *Oh*, to battle with the chronic loser, June Scarpelli—she loved it!

"No, Mother!"

"Yes!"

"No!"

"You will!"

"I won't!'

Pulling off her glasses, June methodically rubbed the bridge of her nose.

"Does that mean 'uncle'?" Cassie asked with glee.

"No uncle!"

"Yes uncle!"

"Damn!" June's rubbing resumed.

Silent laughter shook Cassie. *Victory one thousand five hundred twelve* .

June austerely straightened her stance, patted her pale blonde hair bun, and folded her hands in front of her. Cassie thought her mother could frostbite an entire army with that look.

"I talked to an acquaintance, a friend of a friend of a book publisher in Minneapolis, Cassandra, and the chances of you, without a name, getting published is less than five percent. Five percent Cassandra. Think about it. You're destroying your life for a lousy five percent."

She widened her eyes in wonderment. "Can I have his name? A

recommendation from the friend of a friend? Can I?"

"Not on your life!"

Startled by the roar across the desk, Cassie jumped back in her chair, muted.

"I will not in any way, shape, or form, support your pipe dream!" June said with total decisiveness. Then a brief look of smugness cross her face.

Curious about the look, Cassie leaned closer. "What is this *really* about Mother?"

"I have no idea what you're talking about, Cassandra," June replied without a flinch.

Picking up on a subtle evasiveness, she grew more curious. "I mean, you drag me down here so we can have lunch at a nice restaurant--so you said--and I find myself being brutally attacked by your tongue. What gives?"

June's stiff posture jittered a bit, Cassie noticed. *She was up to something, all right.*

"Meg!" June burst out. "Your sister is doing quite well at the insurance agency, I hear. She'll pass the million mark in sales soon.'"

Big deal! She thought with disgust. She could hardly tolerate the hippie turned super-yuppie. Meg had been a much more real person when she was contorted on the floor than now. In fact, Meg was becoming the clone of "Mrs. Arctic Circle."

"And Todd, a wonderful businessman. The two service stations are prospering, and his three car washes . . ."

She couldn't resist making a face. A Kyle with a bank account . . . that was the only way to describe Meg's loudmouthed husband. What a family!

"Actually, they've been attending some of the same parties your father and I attend, and my friends are enamored with them. A child to be proud of."

Bingo! "And perchance, what do your enamored friends say about me?"

"Well . . ."

She saw the ever-so-slightly nervous shifting that could be interpreted as a wee tug at her mother's conscience, followed by a harshly clearing throat, providing her mother a moment to think of a way to skirt and sugarcoat a tiny bit.

"Indeed, there is a minute amount of controversy about you . . . mainly about your hermit status in that dreadful attic. It seems . . ." June paused to emit another grating sound from her throat, "Your neighbors have been talking . . . a little that is . . . about a ghostly light that burns in your attic all day and night and the story has spread . . . a bit, mind you."

Highly amused, Cassie flopped back into her into her chair and let out a rip-roaring laugh. "How quaint. The witch in the attic stirring her cauldron, night and day, concocting diabolical brew after diabolical brew. Perhaps I'll use the plot for a juvenile story."

"I fail to see the humor is such humiliation, Cassandra!"

Cassie stopped her laugh to the quick. "Yours or mine, Mother, huh?"

"That's beside the point!"

June gave a shifty turn of her face, and the entire truth was revealed to Cassie. "And what will your *enamored* friends say when I sell a book?" Cassie posed.

June shot her icy blue gaze across the desk. "You will never sell a book, Cassandra! Face reality! You have no talent!"

The cruel words said so cooly and with certainty, and coming from a woman who was supposed to be a significant member of her immediate family, stung horribly. It wasn't necessarily surprising, she told herself, rather generically shocking that a mother, no matter the type of mother, would be so calculating and defeating towards her child. Was there not even an ounce of love? She questioned of herself, then promptly answered. *No, there couldn't be.*

Cassie stood up and forced her head to lift high despite the sudden feeling that she was a stretch of vast deserted desert. "I'm not hungry anymore, Mother. Perhaps, one of your *enamored* friends will join you for lunch, instead . . ."

****

The pain helps a bit, Cassie told herself a few hours later while her fingers flew over the computer keys. She was writing a particularly emotion-packed scene in Chapter twenty and all the bitter feelings her mother had swirled up, reflected in the manuscript. She could feel Harry's own bitterness with each word, sentence, and paragraph she composed.

Perhaps June Scarpelli *was* turning into a productive cathartic, she thought cynically, Although her mother's sure prediction of failure had heightened her desperation. She *must* make Harry shine so his character clutched the reader's feelings. *Revise perfectly . . . make every word glitter.* She kept on with the mental boosts, as she was the only one to give them to herself.

It was getting tougher. *Oh God*, she was exhausted, shifting right brain to left, back and forth, like a pendulum, for eighteen, nineteen hours a day. *Oh God, it was so exhausting.*

But like an addict, needing his fix and passionately craving that thrilling moment, she had to find the inner fortitude to go on. *The words . . . they're your Hercules, Cass.*

And she typed on . . .

She saw double, and felt a persistent throb in her back, shoulders, neck, and forehead, and sensed the heaviness of her swollen feet and ankles, and drenched in sweat from the heat of the late May sun, and gnawed with hunger pangs--still she typed on until hitting the period key for the millionth time, it seemed.

Another chapter, *fini!*

She felt jubilant. There were only four more. *Only.*

Now for the revisions . . . *Yes Cass! No Cass, no arguments!*

With efforts concentrated, she began the most grueling task, staying focused until hearing a knock at the attic door, followed by a whiny yell.

"Mom!"

She leapt from her chair. Her daughter needed her! That, took precedence, she told herself firmly. Then she firmly told herself again while unlocking and the attic door.

Peering downward, she saw the little face, cherubic despite its petulant quality, and the mousy brown, child-fine hair, pulled back with a fancy white clip to match her slimming, and obviously costly shorts and buttoned down knit shirt, and she took in the white crew socks and spanking white, evidently new *Nikes*, and delighted with the sight of the childlike monotony, as she swung an air-light *Spalding* tennis racket jacketed in red leather, and, *oh my*, her ears twinkled with a pair of tiny pearl earrings. When did Kristi get her ears pierced? She wondered.

"I'm starving after my tennis lesson. Aren't you ever going to make supper?" Kristi gave an exasperated raise of her eyes.

"Tennis lesson? Where? How . . . ?"

Next came an exasperated noise. "Grandpa and Grandma, *of course*. They said such training was vital for me so that I become a well-rounded, socially adept person."

The intellectual, superior tone, sounded a *titch* more superior than usual, Cassie thought. In fact, if she didn't know better, she would have thought a pint-sized June Scarpelli had just spoken. "Supper? Where's your father? He usually . . .

"He's not coming home for supper, again," Kristi cut in. "He called and said he had cars to sell. Anyway, he said he was tired of putting food from the freezer to the oven."

Yeah, how tiring! She thought sarcastically, wishing she had the nerve to call the used car lot and give Kyle a piece of her mind. But she didn't dare. Their marriage was becoming more strained by the day and Kyle was touchy. She thought it best to leave him to his cars this one time and make supper herself.

Giving her computer one last longing look, she shut the attic door, and told her trembling body to 'Cool it'. Her lips shivered into a smile. "C'mon honey--supper beckons . . ."

****

"Scalloped potatoes and generic, loaded with everything but meat, hot dogs, again?"

Cassie tried to ignore the complaint as she placed the casserole dish on the worn wicker trivet in the middle of the kitchen table. Then she followed this with a plate of tomatoes and a decorative tin full of canned crescent rolls. She thought the tin to be a colorful touch to Kristi's and her rare meal together, as was the milk she had laced with both chocolate and strawberry syrup. All was ready and looked wonderful, she determined. Then feeling quite accomplished, she proudly sat down on the multi-striped brown and gold kitchen chair, mismatched from the other chairs circling the table.

"So how was school today, honey?" she asked absently, spooning out potatoes, sans the anemic looking hot dogs chunks, onto her plate.

"School was over three days ago, *Mother*," Kristi replied with utter annoyance.

"Oh yeah--I forgot." She speared a tomato slice with her fork and felt stupid, or perhaps reminiscent. It was a question her mother would have asked, and her answering in like fashion. The similarity made her body tremble with a discomfiting dread.

"But don't worry about me being alone." Kristi wrinkled her nose at the potato and hot dog conglomeration. "Grandpa paid my soccer fee and he scribbled out a check for that girl's camp in Wisconsin, and he even said he'd pay the fee for that New England tour if . . ." Kristi's lips twisted into a pout. "I harass you into dimming that damn attic light--his words."

"Oh, really?" Cassie replied through the grit of her teeth. How dare her father use a child for his own gains! Although, she knew her father was merely playing his customary puppet role.

The sexually enticing June Scarpelli had struck again, she acridly told herself.

"*Verbatim*, he said the light was a goddamn embarrassment . . . the talk of the town, he muttered like a growly dog, thinking I didn't hear. But I did. What did he mean?"

When seeing the brown eyes twinkle quizzically, Cassie burned with anger over the fact that her parents would involve her child in such smut. Now it was she who had to try to explain the unexplainable small-mindedness.

"It's a symptom, Kristi."

"A symptom?"

"Like an illness . . . an illness highly prevalent in this part of the country."

"Does the illness have a name. Mom?"

She looks ready to burst out of her high-quality polyester knit shorts, Cassie thought, wondering how to answer. Perhaps, she could come up with a metaphorically colorful name that would tantalize the child, or maybe, in horror-movie fashion concoct a deliciously gory term. But, she had no such figurative ability in the kitchen, it seemed. Only the attic set her mind into a creative whir. Thus, she was forced to be utterly mundane.

"The illness could have several names," she finally replied.

"What are they? What are they?"

"For one . . . boredom . . . having nothing else productive to do except eyeball the activities of other people. Which, brings us to our second name . . . snoopiness, the compelling need and desire to delve into the lives of others, because their own lives are devoid of anything stimulating except months of monotonous white, followed by a wisp of a break, followed by more white."

"Huh?"

"And then we have the name 'communication compulsivist', at sword's point, to chat incessantly on the telephone, on the streets, in the grocery store, at the health spa, on the cross-country ski trails . . . anywhere a mouth can flap like a broken shoe sole. Finally . . . we have 'voyeur', a sickly and drawing need to stare at a dim white light!"

"Oh . . ." Kristi said slowly.

Thank God. For once the child looked baffled, she thought with relief. She had no desire for Kristi to get mixed up in the hoopla. In fact, she thought it prudent that Kristi escape Anoka for the majority of the summer. After all, people were out and about more so the poor child was bound to catch wind of the community controversy over her mother's erratic behavior. Her insides twined in ire. *Damn all of them!*

"Fairly decent tomatoes, Mom." Kristi slowly munched around the pale red periphery. Then she just *had to* add, "Heather's mother grows their own tomatoes, cute little cherry ones in pots that she puts on their tri-level deck—makes their halogen deck lights glow red."

How thrilling! Cassie raised her frustration to the ceiling. She hankered for Kristi to see that life was composed of more wondrous things than tri-level decks, halogen lights, and . . .

Ugh! . . .cherry tomatoes. She loathed the superficiality.

"Well . . ." Kristi bounced out of her chair. "Back to peer pressure and social climbing."

Cassie studied the small face. *Does she really mean that? Or is she spoofing? Oh my poor indoctrinated child . . . Damn you, June!*

"Oh! Sarie gave me a plateful of homemade carrot cake with real cream cheese frosting. She said I looked sugar-deprived. You can have a piece if you want," Kristi offered.

Carrot cake? Cassie seethed inwardly. It was Kyle's favorite dessert, and she figured it was Sarie's way of pouring more motherly sympathy on the constantly whimpering jackass. Some friend! She wouldn't even eat a crumb of the cake, reeking of misplaced compassion. Thank you!

"You know . . ." Kristi stopped at the kitchen opening. "Sarie's getting fat. I wanted to ask her why, but figured she wouldn't appreciate the question."

That's for sure, Cassie thought with disgust. Now, it meant that Sarie was stuck alone on her king-size *Sealy Posturpedic* with only her extensive videotape collection of Miami Vice reruns to keep her orgasms coming. She felt a maliciously gleeful. It served Sarie right for making that damn carrot cake, and *pissing her off!*

"But I do wonder why, Mom. Sarie always seems so obsessed with bodily perfection."

Cassie urged her lips into a bright smile."Perhaps her treadmill is on the fritz, or her health club membership ran out, or maybe, no matter the disbelief, she finally said, 'To hell with it'."

Kristi let out a mirthful childish giggle. "Sure Mom . . ." She heard Kristi's giggle long after her daughter's chubby form disappeared from view.

She felt a surge of happiness at Kristi's delightful noise and, feeling like the child who had romped among her grandparents' fruit bushes, she lithely bounced about the kitchen while cleaning up the remains from dinner.

It had to help!

Chapter Twenty-One was filled with Harry's beatitude, and she would spill out all her glorious feelings onto her beloved character. So she told herself that this time, *this one time*, the revisions on Chapter Twenty could wait.

****

May undramatically slipped into June, and the days grew hotter. Kristi was off to the southern part of Minnesota with her soccer team, participating in a three-day tournament, and Kyle was working.

Her brow bathed in sweat, Cassie diligently tapped on the computer and tried not to think of the growing misery of her marital existence. However, it was tough not to have Kyle's apathy seep into her brain. He had even stopped bugging her on Sundays and pathed no routes for them.

She kept telling herself she was relieved—it was a scenario she had desired for years. But was she? Truly? When she added Kristi to the scenario? It was a scenario she had created with her obsession--she knew that--yet she was powerless to stop. Kyle *could* have sympathized, even a little, with her powerlessness, couldn't he? For the sake of their child, couldn't he?

Unable to stop it, her mind drifted with the wise, gentle voice of her Grandpa Scarpelli, telling her the paramount *importante* of two-parent families, words he had emphasized over the years when he saw her growing unhappiness with her marriage. She always took the words to heart and maintained within her home despite her overwhelming sadness, dissatisfaction, frustration, anger, and every other emotion Kyle seemed to bring out in her.

Yet, it was so unfair.

Within, she carried an undefinable urgent, decades-long, restive *something* that needed a very special outlet for expression. And Kyle Callahan or Anoka, Minnesota wasn't it. It they had been, she reasoned now, that something would have left her years ago. Even at that moment the *something* blistered inside her.

She paused to bask in that resplendent *something*. It was a sensation that would immensely help her go on. Despite the horrendous fatigue, aching joints, and the sun's merciless rays, it was a prod, a catalyst, a blotter of discomforts, an all-encompassing verging sensation. It would keep her super-glued to the computer, eighteen, nineteen hours a day, despite everything.

Feeling that *something* nudge, Cassie placed fingers to keys and typed as if her life depended on it. The end was looming. *Two more chapters.* Her wonderful Harry's story was coming to a close. *Yet.* Again she paused. There was more story than she could tell, and she wondered . . .

Yes! A sequel!

The familiar excitement-charged spark rushed through her. She couldn't wait to write her Harry's story beyond the story.

Oh glory! To again be with the most wonderful, dynamic, intellectually-stimulating man in the world was totally enticing. He thrilled her, made her body tingle with his magnetism, and his *oh so* satisfying hands, making a woman feel like the most desirous, beautiful creature in the world. And *his* body . . . it turned a woman's hands into the most satisfying as well.

Oh to find such a man . . .

Filled to her brim with the wonder of 'Harry', and having no other mind's space for any sad, defeating thoughts, Cassie industriously went back to her noble task.

Keep revising . . . Chapter Twenty-Two was almost in the can!

And then she could get some much-needed food and satisfy the SOS signals her stomach was giving off . . .

****

Hours later, Cassie crept down to the darkened kitchen and flipped on the light. The round white wall clock read ten minutes past eleven p.m., and she startled. Had it been seventeen hours already? She questioned herself on her workday. Actually, it only felt like half that or less, she thought, letting out a laugh. *I'm hooked all right.*

Finding the activity pleasurable, she still laughed when digging in the refrigerator for sandwich makings. *I must be a bit punchy,* she thought, pulling out a mushy tomato, leaf of lettuce, brown-dotted along the periphery, and packages of generic baloney and yellow American cheese. Then she stacked a sandwich.

"Well . . . the hermit emerges from her black hole."

Jolted by the sound of another human voice, she spun around. A sneering Kyle stood in the kitchen entrance. *Shoot! Why did I listen to my stomach?*

"Christ Almighty," he sneered again.

Cassie felt naked while his scrutinizing gaze ran up and down her person.

"You look like a goddamn mess. Shit! I barely recognize you, what's left of you. Looks like you're back to a twenty-eight triple A bra cup."

She tightly crossed herself. *He's shallow and self-possessed,* she tried to told herself, to ease the bite of his assessment.

"Fuck! A skeleton would be repulsed getting in bed with you!" he spat angrily, taking a few steps forward.

"Stay back, Kyle. I wanna be left alone," she said as firmly as she could.

He sent a glare across the kitchen. "What the hell does that mean? I'm your husband for Christ's sakes!"

She shivered despite the closed-up stifling warmth of the house. The truth was bubbling inside her--she could feel it--a horrible unsettling sensation that she was at a crossroads. "I. . .I just don't want anyone near me, messing my mind, that's all."

"Why dammit?" he demanded.

Courage, Cass, she pleaded silently. But her self pleas were useless. All she could hear in her head was the guilt-producing chorus of Italian voices like she had heard fifteen years ago when she announced she wouldn't marry Kyle Callahan.

"A father, it's the least you can give your child . . ."

Now the gentle, reasoned voice consumed her mind. Even Angelo Scarpelli, her greatest ally in the world, would condemn her if she succumbed to the fevered self-pleas. She would be an outcast! Not a single Scarpelli past or present had ever dared breath the word *divorce*.

"Answer me, Cassie!"

She saw intensity on his face. Never had she seen Kyle Callahan so intense. "Ah . . . the flu! I feel horrendous, itchy throat, heated forehead, stomach has butterflies. I don't want you to catch my horrible disease." She sputtered.

Promptly, he took a giant step back. "Why didn't you say that in the first place? Dammit! I'm probably exposed to your crud now!" His eyes darted around and fastened on the counter top. "I thought you had a stomachache. How the hell can you eat that with a stomachache?"

She slowly turned to see the dry looking sandwich. What now? She frantically asked herself. "Ah . . . I made it for you!" Instantly she wanted to kick herself for being so obtuse. The response was about as believable as saying there was a Santa Claus.

"Bullshit!" Kyle shouted. "I believe that about as much as I believe there's a Santa Claus!"

Oh no! Our minds are on the same wavelength. I'm deteriorating badly.

"You're to explain that sandwich, now, Cass!"

A nervous laugh shook out of her. "Explain? Not much to explain . . . two pieces of generic baloney, a piece of plastic generic cheese, a slice of squishy tomato, and a lettuce leaf with only a whisper of green, on generic Wonder Bread. That's all."

"Damn you, Cass." Kyle looked ready to explode. Then without warning he settled down. "You know, I don't give a shit why that sandwich is there, and I don't give a shit if you feel like crap. I. . .just don't give a shit any more."

Nor have I ever.

Kyle stormed out of the kitchen. Now what? She asked herself. The marriage was over, yet neither had the nerve to end it. It was one big mess! She yearned to escape, and briefly she diddled with this notion. But ultimately, she acquired a mind's picture of Kristi. She possessed no such nerve, wish as she might.

Leaving the sandwich untouched, she dragged out of the kitchen and told herself to move towards the stairs, towards her only escape.

On the way she heard heavy footsteps followed by the slam of the front door.

And she kept moving . . .

****

June drifted away, one day seemingly like the next, except for the temperature and humidity that climbed daily. Mosquitos were abundant outside and in, as were woodticks—June was their prime month in Minnesota. And everything baked in this pseudo-tropical jungle, grass, houses, people . .

It was Sunday.

Kristi was at neighboring White Bear Lake, swimming and picnicking with her friend, Heather, and her family. Kyle was gone, as he had been for most of the time since that night in the kitchen. And Cassie was revising like a woman possessed.

The Life and Times of Harry Hannigan, her chosen title for the manuscript, was finally completed. And like she had done for the past three weeks, she was slicing and slashing what her careful pen had missed during her first chapter revisions. It was tough. The sweat trickled down her face in constant streams, despite her near nude state and the small metal fan that blew directly on her, and she experienced the intense, constant fatigue of monotony plus the ever-present multi-area body aches that made her feel like a chronic arthritic.

Yet, she had to make it perfect—these words constantly pounded into her head. She thought the manuscript to be much more than the best writing of her life, or the work which had truly disciplined her to her chosen career, or brought out of feelings, emotions, and the wonder, she hadn't felt in years, or had strengthened her resolve to pursue, regardless, or made her sacrifice beyond human endurance . . .

It's my shot at life again, and I'm so damn desperate.

With this thought in mind, she felt that familiar drive to excel. She had it in her. She knew it. Though to what ultimate life summit? *No clue.*

For hours, morning into afternoon, afternoon into night, she kept cutting, adding, on page after page, in scene after scene, chapter after chapter. It had to flow perfectly . . . it had to transition perfectly . . . Show don't tell . . . feel the life of Harry; feel his outside, his inside, his true wonder. Feel!

Darkness streamed through the attic window, and Cassie basked in the greater effectiveness of the fan. She scrupulously read the final scene in Chapter Twenty-Four, her last chapter, then reread, and read a third, fourth time. It was paramount, she told herself. Not only did she have to show, in as few carefully chosen words as possible, the culmination of Harry's life alteration, but end it so the reader nearly salivated, *begged,* for a sequel. So she read it again, and again, then she slowly coursed back in her chair to pause in reflection, and loosely recall, in sequence, the story from start to finish . . .

****

Growing up in the far reaches of Northeastern Minnesota, near the Canadian border, outside of a town where logging was the primary industry, Harry Hannigan came from a poor family, yet he was rich with the wonder of his surroundings, the stately woods, the wild flowers, the strawberries and blueberries which grew in abundance between the trees, the animals, large and small, and the real people who inhabited his community.

He was particularly close to his grandfather, a burly, former logger who filled Harry with stories of places beyond the tiny, rustic community. And Harry, a very smart boy by nature, would dream of these places, and silently vow to see every one.

Seeking Out Harry

When he was nine, his grandfather died suddenly, and the death swirled up emotions that would never leave Harry. Just a year later, his father died in a logging accident, leaving he and his mother alone and with few resources.

The pair moved to a small city, three hours due south where employment opportunities were better for Harry's unskilled mother. Though life in the city was even more poverty-stricken, Harry made an abundance of friends, young and old, including a soccer coach who encouraged the young boy to play the sport. Harry did, and his potential shone almost immediately. The coach took Harry under his wing, became a surrogate father, and he made Harry even greater, one of the best soccer player in Minnesota by the time he was eighteen.

On full soccer scholarship, he attended the local university. With his keen mind, he majored in Finance as well as pursued, and was pursued, by many women. His sexual prowess emerged, as did the brilliance of his soccer. He was named top player in the Division II college conference during his two last years of college, and offers to join semi-pro teams, streamed.

Always vigorously hard working herself, his mother wanted him to find a job upon college graduation—she viewed soccer as merely fun, nothing substantial. But he couldn't give it up, yet, as the sport hadn't burned out of him. He was physically intact, and most importantly, he wanted to travel to the places his grandfather had talked about, and being on a team that coursed the United States would give him that opportunity.

So he played soccer, traveled, played more soccer, and out of his environmental element, his life slowly swirled into the gutter, woman, drugs, fights, run-ins with the law, a rape charge that was dropped, but garnered much publicity, drug and alcohol rehabilitation, in and out, in and out, and finally termination of his semi-pro contract.

He was strung-out, slovenly, ruined man at age twenty-eight.

For months he wandered, homeless, friendless, stealing money for drugs and booze, and he wondered a lot, and yearned for those sweet-smelling woods of his youth.

Finally, he was rescued by the man who started his soccer career, and for a brief moment, the man became a surrogate father again. He brought Harry to Minneapolis, fed him, nurtured him, and committed him to a drug and alcohol rehabilitation facility.

There, he healed physically with the help of a beautiful, compassionate therapist whom he fell in love with, and wanted to marry once he got his life together. But she died suddenly in a car accident, and he was devastated once more. He wanted that coke and booze so bad, and almost regressed, if not for a tour of her apartment. The tour changed his life. He found her writings, a hobby he didn't know she had, and her words touched his very core. He knew she would want him to go on, kick his addictions, and bring his life back up to a functional level. So he did . . . but he never forgot her.

With the help of psychiatrists who saw the true brilliance of Harry beyond his problems, he acquired a job at a stock brokerage under a special program for reformed junkies. He was watched like a hawk—no one trusted him. He felt alone and many times wanted to relapse, but would just read the gentle words of his former love and realize that he wasn't truly alone. Finally, upon realizing Harry's business astuteness and productivity, the suspiciousness slowly subsided, and Harry was accepted into the Minneapolis financial and social community. From that point, there was no stopping him; the writings were his driving force.

By age thirty-eight, he was a millionaire, and he opened his own stock brokerage firm, then he expanded, and ultimately diversified, until by age forty-five he had a small empire and a life of tortured female relationships. He was passionate and fiery about business, but these traits came out as being hard and forceful when he was with women. He showed little affection, little respect—he fervently missed the woman he had once loved so wholly.

And then came Courtney, a focused stockbroker, who was lovely with a kind, warm nature about her. He fell in love with her, but the life's suffering he had sustained, created roadblock after roadblock which he desperately tried to skirt around so he could give Courtney a wonderful type of love. Ultimately, after much duress, he triumphantly crossed the boundary . . . and he had Courtney, as well as an empire . . .

****

And what did that really mean to him? Cassie asked herself as she chomped on a pencil, a bad habit she had acquired of late. Would he feel like a general who won the greatest battle of the world? Or would he feel as powerful as a rainmaker? Was it greatness? Was it power? Or . . . She found herself chomping furiously. Would he merely feel human again? Wasn't that the greatest triumph of life, after all? She chewed the pencil to a pulp. *Yes!* Her fingers furiously flew across the computer keys, and she revised, and revised, a two-page scene for a like number of hours, until she felt it, with every pore of her being. *She felt it!*

Her own triumph bounding, she flew back in her chair. "Yippeeee . . . !" she yelled at the top of her lungs until the sound bounced from attic wall to attic wall. It was done!

Then, without warning, the sheer weariness of the last six months toppled on her. She ran her hand over her pale blonde hair. It felt like an oily hornet's nest, and her skin oozed of dryness and grime. Feeling a little frightened, she moved her eyes down the front of her body. *I am skinny, dreadfully so.* It was three meals a day and malted milks until they were coming out of her ears, she firmly told herself.

But for now, the total exhaustion of her body took precedence. Tomorrow she would sleep a little later, then try to pull everything together, self and manuscript, she thought. Once painstakingly done, Harry Two beckoned.

And she held this final thought while crawling onto the well-worn cot with grayed bedclothes in a darkened corner of the attic. Unable to resist the messages her body was giving off, she promptly allowed her eyes to drift shut.

Chapter 6—Cassie

The fireworks, parades and red, white, and blue had disappeared five weeks ago, and the Twin Cities was blistering hot, with ninety percent humidity on most days, unless it was muggy and overcast, then it was "take shelter," a tornado watch or warning.
What a lovely place to live.
Biting sarcasm was the primary emotion as Cassie, dripping wet from head to toe and her f newly-trimmed hair hanging in moist threads, hoisted up the boxed and bound manuscript into her arms en route to the Anoka Post Office.
It had been quite an effort, she recalled while dragging along.
Upon completion of her manuscript, she swallowed her reservations and went to Angelo Scarpelli. She needed help in the financial department, she told him. It was a bit costly to get one's book off the ground, she said. Then she held her breath and waited.

****

"Self-publishing?" He eyed her suspiciously.
"No more of that, Nono," she hastily reassured. "I'm going the legitimate route this time, and pray it takes me where I wanna go. I. . .finally have a little courage behind me."
Slowly he poured, letting the blackberry wine drip into a glass set in front of her while his face was full of contemplation. In a corner of the kitchen, a gray-haired, petite Madelaina Scarpelli, her grandmother, was quietly mixing ravioli stuffing and trying to remain unobtrusive. She shifted her eyes from grandparent to grandparent, unnerved by the everlasting silence. So to settle her jitters, she grabbed the wine glass and guzzled the bitter liquid. It burned. And for a fleeting moment she wished she had thrown a piece of dynamite into that hole in the cellar wall when she was twelve.
"Easy Cassina, sip the wine. Sip . . ."
Relieved to finally hear the gentle Italian voice, she slowed her guzzling. It tasted no better, despite. Although, she curled her lips up in a smile that signaled the wine was the most supreme elixir in the world--the way her grandfather defined the awful stuff.
"Okay . . . tell me what you need the money for, Cassina," he finally said.
While forcing herself to sip, she talked about query letters to literary agents, copies of her manuscript, postage, and the need for a few more supplies . . . paper, ink cartridges, diskettes . . .
His gray bushy eyebrows knitted in confusion. "But Cassina, that is *le piccino patata*," he said. "It's small potatoes, and surely Kyle can afford to pay such a meager amount."
She nearly choked on the wine, but she tried her damndest to minimize the response. She *couldn't* tell him. "Ah . . . Kyle's a bit strapped for funds this month, used car desert, so to speak."
To her near gag, her grandfather slowly refilled her wine glass, then again grew endlessly quiet. Finally, she saw him precisely narrow his green eyes directly at her.

"I want the truth, Cassina."

Damn! Now, she had no choice. He'd see through every confabulation she tried to weave. Yet, she made her voice nonchalant. "Okay, Nono--I'll come clean. It's primarily the same old thing. You know . . . lack of karma with Kyle."

"Hmmm . . ."

He thoughtfully rubbed him firm Roman jaw without altering in his gaze on her. "That isn't what I hear, Cassina. The gossip . . ."

She hastily jumped in. "They're tales of imbeciles. They have no idea about the true nature of things and concoct stories based on a measly white light. Small-minded, Nono, that's all."

"And is the state of your marriage *romanzo*, a tale too?"

She picked up the wine glass and guzzled again. "We're having a wee bit more problems," she hedged, and his green eyes bore into her like a pair of sabers. "Maybe a hint more than I just indicated, and . . .

The slam of He slammed his fist on the tabletop. "Why Cassina?" he roared.

She felt terrified. Never had she seen such fire in his eyes. "It's Harry," she blurted out.

"Harry?" His roar grew ferocious. "Harry who? I break him in two."

"Wasted effort, Nono." She let out a nervous laugh. "Harry is . . ." She gulped, knowing how her answer would sit with the level headed man. "My book character."

Looking like he had been struck by a bolt of lightening, he quickly ran a hand over his thick gray hair. "You *devastore*, you destroy, your marriage for *Uomo Invisibile?*"

The invisible man . . . what a quaint way to describe Harry, she thought anxiously, as her grandfather always lapsed into primarily Italian when he was raging mad.

"I pay you close to twenty thousand dollars, Cassina, so you stay happy!" he angered.

"I know." She nodded until her head hung. "And I appreciate all your support, Nono. You, it seems, have been the only one. But . . . I'm still not happy, granted I've tried."

"Ai-yi-yi!" he said with sheer vexation, guzzling his wine too. "I will talk to, Kyle. Make him understand about your need to write, and maybe . . .

"No!" she burst out more intensely than she intended. *Where had it come from?*

"What do you mean, 'No'?" he demanded with a passionate fire.

"Ah . . . it may be a tad bit too late, Nono. You see, Kyle and I . . . ur . . . haven't been what you could call, connubial."

"No *sesso*?" he exploded.

She let out a tinkly laugh. "No sex, not even a nudge."

"Christ almighty!"

Ever-so-cautiously, she inched her eyes to her highly religious grandmother and saw the pain on the old wizened face. She wondered what was going through the beloved woman's mind at this moment. Then, on second thought, decided she didn't want to know.

"What does this mean, Cassina?"

She had no definitive answer. It was probably the most confusing aspect of her life, she thought. So she shrugged and feigned flippancy. "I guess it means I live a nun's existence with only my writing to keep me warm at night."

He narrowed his eyes. "You will stay in the marriage?"

"Absolutely! Kristi, you know . . ."

He languidly sipped his wine while his sharp gaze studied her face. "All right," he said at last. "I will invest in you again. Say . . . five hundred dollars."

She felt joyful! "That's wonderful, Nono, thank you, *Grazie* . . ."

****

And the money had been the pad to help me launch 'Harry' from the attic . . .

She pushed in the heavy glass door to the post office, then hefted her manuscript through the opening. She was trying the literary agent route again; although after seventy-five query letters sent out, only three literary agents had requested to see her entire manuscript. The rest had rejected her idea outright. Now, she pulled the third manuscript through the door, knowing it may be a month's waiting game before she heard a reply. Yet, she felt hopeful. Someone out there had to be touched by Harry, she kept telling herself.

While making her way to the counter, she felt the 'sneaky gape', as she called it. Shifting her eyes to the left, she saw two middle-aged women peeking up and snickering at her. Wishing she had the immaturity to stick out her tongue, she lifted her head and sauntered past the two. Busybodies! As if she didn't have enough problems, the snoopy populace of Anoka seemed hellbent on creating more, she thought angrily.

Why should they give a damn? She wondered, even though the answer was crystal clear. Not only was 'Scarpelli' a big name in Anoka, but the name Kyle Callahan was as well.

All because of a dim attic light.

She couldn't believe it!

Cassie boosted the box onto the counter. "I wanna to send this to Denver, first-class," she told the man behind the counter. "After you weigh it, I need that same amount in stamps for possible return postage."

"Huh?" he asked, looking amused.

The response perturbed her. Every time she mailed out a manuscript they acted like she was speaking in Japanese. Taking a deep, calming breath, she repeated her request.

"So . . . should I weigh the return postage with the box?"

"No!" She thought she would scream. "Weigh the box, write down how much it costs to send it, then I will tell you to get me that same amount in return postage, stick it the corner of the box I haven't bound, then adios to the Rocky Mountain state. Capisce?"

"Nope--but I'll do it anyway," he laughed.

Damn, what a feeble mind! It seemed like *nobody* cooperated with her efforts. It was like a conspiracy to wear her down and defeat her. *And Art and June Scarpelli were in the crux of it.* Her parents hadn't let up on her writing, and they had strongly taken Kyle's side in this matter. *Poor Kyle this, poor Kyle that* . . . she wanted to vomit until she was dry.

"I wrote down the total . . . *Ms. Callahan.*"

She saw the gleam in his highly diverting eyes. Yet, she peeked at the total, and chose to ignore his look. "So give me fifteen dollars and seventy cents in return postage, please."

"Quite a few stamps." He leisurely tipped his chin to the box. "What you got in there?"

She gasped. "How dare you inquire about such a private matter . . . a member of the United States Government workforce. Is there no sanctity?"

"Just looks interesting, that's all," he said, then turned to get her postage.

A rectangular box that held five hundred sheets of computer paper . . . some thrill! It sure didn't take much to entice the citizens of her hometown. Suddenly, she heard a loud laugh behind her and whipped around. A man about her age hooted like a senile owl. *Oh yuk!* It was one of Kyle's beer-guzzling beer buddies.

"Mailing out your witch's charms to Transylvania, Cassie?" he joked loudly.

She threw a high-pitched laugh back at him. "No! I'm sending ultra-strong wooden spikes to kill the vampires . . . wonderful sideline business." She spun back around to see the broadly smiling face of the postal employee. *Oh Lord, the dizziness of it all!*

"That'll be $31.40, check or cash."

She rummaged for her checkbook, and scribbled as fast as she could. "Thank you!" She slapped the check on the counter. "You've been a fine help." Forcing her head high, she took brisk strides out of the post office.

A surge of heat blasted her face the moment she stepped outside the glass doors, and she grew listless. The implications had stung worse than she would ever admit. She envisioned herself on a deserted island with only her computer and endless supplies of everything else. The idea was tempting. But there would be no Kristi. And promptly the vision disintegrated. She was stuck. No debate. *I'm as stuck as a stamp on my package.*

The futility made her even feel even more deflated as she moved towards the rusted flaming red parked Toyota.

****

"Eerie," Cassie muttered when she stood in the tiny foyer of her home. All the shades were drawn to block out the sun's heat. Yet it felt stifling, and she wished they could afford central air conditioning. *Wishful thinking.* High speed fans barely fit into the Callahan budget.

Instinctively, she headed for the stairs, then firmly reminded herself that she was on a bit of a hiatus to rejuvenate--hard as that was. Her body needed a major reconstruction job, and she intended to do that before assaulting it again with 'Harry Two'.

So instead, she headed for the kitchen to make her malt and a frozen loaded with everything-including-mega-calories pizza which she forced herself to eat daily, despite her penchant for plain cheese pizza. When she passed the old wooden hutch, she paused, spotting a framed school picture of Kristi. Lovingly, she picked up the frame and delicately traced around her daughter's face.

She missed the precocious little face and voice. Kristi had been absent for most of the summer and now was in New England on tour of five states. Only one postcard, a picture of the Old North Church in Boston, containing a brief three lines, graced the front of the refrigerator. It was as if Kristi had forgotten about her mother when she had promised to write at least twice a week. But all she had gotten was one lousy postcard with three lines that said Kristi was having a good time on four separate occasions. What was going on in Kristi's mind, she wondered now?

Deciding that the answer to her question wasn't good, she hurtfully placed the picture back on the hutch and scurried to the kitchen. *I'm a lousy mother, no doubt,* she told herself while gathering the ingredients for her malt. Then she stuck the pizza in the oven without preheating it. Self-directed anger consumed her. She had vowed never to be such a mother, and she had become one, nevertheless. How *horrible* to be a June.

Tears sprung to her eyes while she blended her chocolate, banana, and strawberry ice cream malt—she loathed vanilla ice cream. *Too blase'*. As the thick mixture spun in the blender, she thought of her mother's constant badgering over the past few weeks, badgering echoed by her equally nauseating sister, Meg. Then add to this, Sarie's evasiveness. Why? She had no idea.

She had made several attempts to call Sarie but always got her answering machine and no return calls. It was barely believable, that her friend would turn on her after what they had meant to each other. *Yet Sarie had.* And more sadness gripped her. It was *so* terrible to feel so alone in one's immediate world.

Awhile later, she miserably chewed her pizza interspersed with slurping absently on her malt, and enumerated all the woes of her life. *All because of my poor 'Harry'.*

Suddenly she jumped. The front door slammed, followed by heavy footsteps heading in her direction. She recognized the footsteps. *Oh god, not again.*

"Cassie!"

She slapped down her pizza on the paper plate, thrust down her malt in a plastic cup smeared with pictures of Donald Duck, and fastened her eyes on the kitchen entrance. Moments later, Kyle's large bulk charged through. He looked livid as he shook something at her.

"How dare you spend my money after the hell you've put me through!"

It was a checkbook, she determined, and she wrinkled her brow in confusion.

"Don't give me that 'dumb-blonde' look! Twenty-five dollars at a beauty shop, and *shit*, another forty-eight dollars at a place called *The Body Shop!*"

"What?" She angrily lunged forward in her chair. "*I* put five hundred dollars in that account, a gift from my Nono!"

"No! it's a gift to me for all the years you sat on your lazy ass and contributed nothing to this family, except your crap!"

"You can't have that money--it's mine," she protested hotly.

"Well regardless, I'm takin' it!" Kyle said decisively, then added, "I got expenses, and you're gonna contribute to them."

"What expenses?" she demanded.

He began hedging, and she steadily stared at him. It wasn't often that the 'big mouth' didn't have an instant answer for everything. Desperation hit her, sensing that something was horribly wrong, and because of it, she would lose her precious manuscript money.

"Tell me Kyle. Are we in financial trouble, are we?"

Again, he hedged, and terror filled her. Where they losing the house? Their cars? What? He looked ready to croak.

"Just expenses," he muttered at last, not elaborating, but she saw the sudden pallor of his skin and slump of his shoulders.

She spoke uneasily. "I need that money, Kyle. My book . . ."

His eyes glared with rage. "Don't you dare mention that piece of shit! It's what's caused my problem . . . all my problems!" His shoulders collapsed further.

Briefly, she felt piteous. She had never seen Kyle look so defeated. Perhaps he's ready to cry 'uncle', she panicked. *Kristi . . . and oh god, Nono!*

"I. . .just don't know what to do," he mumbled almost to himself.

She was afraid to ask, but knew she had no choice now. The crossroads could come at that very moment, she told herself. "What exactly are you trying to say?"

He raised his face and just stared at her, his eyes moving across her face, her body, for a long time, before he finally spoke. "I. . .Jeez! . . .I don't know . . . I . . ." He twisted around and raced away from the kitchen. Soon thereafter, she heard the front door shut.

What in the world . . . ?

Cassie fastened her eyes on the kitchen opening while eating the remains of her cold pizza and sucking up the rest of her warm malt. Why the sudden change in him? What did it mean? *What . . . ?*

****

"A bacon and feta cheese quiche' Cassandra. I had Cook whip it up for you." June Scarpelli held out a small casserole. A stiff expensively suited Art Scarpelli stood at her side.

Leaning on the frame of her open front door, Cassie blinked her eyes. She felt spent after hours of trying to interpret Kyle's bizarre behavior, and the last thing she wanted was a rare, impromptu visit by her elusive parents.

"Aren't you going to invite us in, Cassandra?" her mother asked as graciously as her 'polar bear' persona would allow.

No! She wanted to shriek. But she had no moxie to voice her thoughts out loud. "Come in, by all means." She tried to be as gracious as her mother had been.

The two stepped into the foyer and immediately eyeballed the house.

"My lord, Cassandra, it's like a sauna in here. Don't you have air . . . ?"

The remark delighted her. "I have plenty of air, Mother. As you notice, I'm not gagging, or blue in color."

June Scarpelli tensely pursed her lips. "It's unhealthy to have such a hot house," she said pointedly. "And Kristi . . ."

"She's not here, courtesy of Father's generosity, and yours too, I presume."

"Yeah." Art Scarpelli finally loosened his tongue. "Remember all those postcards she sent June? Concord . . . Lexington . . . Providence . . . Montpelier . . . Trenton . . ."

"Not Boston?" Cassie's insides miserably crumbled at this news.

"Take the quiche', Cassandra, and stick it in your microwave for warming." June thrust the casserole dish at her.

Cassie grabbed the casserole, wanting to pitch it at her mother for stealing her daughter. "Is it oven-safe as well?" she quipped to hide her intense hurt.

"If you must, but set it on 'high'. Your father and I are pressed for time."

Oh hell, dinner guests! She couldn't believe it. They had barely shown up for the last thirty-one years and now, when she was at her lowest point . . .

"We need to talk anyway, Cassandra."

Seeking Out Harry

"Talk?"

"I think by now you know the subject by rote, Cassie," Art Scarpelli said sternly.

She sighed heavily. "Of course, Father . . . verbatim . . . in my sleep, verbatim . . ."

****

"I do believe Cook outdid herself," June commented without the usual litheness such words would demand.

Cassie picked out the bacon pieces from her quiche' and popped them into her mouth. She hated eggs, and was convinced, her mother knew this when she chose a quiche' as her offering.

"Better eat, Cassie. You're not getting any fatter," Art said sharply.

Cassie looked at her father. She saw much of her grandfather in him. Yet, the wonderful inner qualities her grandfather possessed, had eluded his oldest son. He was like such a *nothing* in her life. "I'll try, Father." But she kept picking.

"Unusual collection of kitchen chairs." June slightly creased her nose at the fuschia patterned chair beneath her.

Cassie creased up her nose as well. "I like variety, Mother, a virtual rummage-sale addict. They push out their old kitchen chairs when they see me coming."

"Really . . ." June made an obvious swallow of distaste. "I'll have to keep that in mind if we have an old chair or two, Cassandra."

As if I would take your chairs! She would rather sit on the floor than take anything from the child kidnapper, she furiously told herself.

"Do you, perchance, have anything for dessert, Cassandra? *You know your father likes dessert after his meals.*"

Now how the hell would I know that? She wanted to let out a scream, but instead forced a perky smile. "I have a scrumptious box of generic 'Cool pops'. Father can suck while he bitches."

June drew in a sharp gasp, then hastily ate her quiche' without comment.

"So Father . . . can I get you a cherry or lime?" Cassie retorted, feeling victorious with her mother's easy surrender. "Or maybe *blah* orange suits you better . . ."

Art uneasily loosened his shirt collar. "No dessert, Cassie. But talk is essential."

"So talk—tell me what a horrible person I am—talk." She suddenly had no care about deportment, parental respect, or the screwed-up feelings she had for these two. She only cared that she was fed up with their hidden agenda intrusions in her life . . . and now they had used these same agendas on her precious Kristi. *I despise them!*

"You have to snap out of this destructive obsession of yours," Art began.

"What destruction obsession? I have no destructive obsession."

"Denial," June said like a foremost expert. "You need a psychologist, Cassandra. I have a list of names . . .

"What?" Cassie leapt to her feet. "Are you crazy?"

"Settle down, Cassie, there's no need for violence," Art said with shaky insistence.

"Violence? Standing is violence?" she seethed out, unable to believe the kick the duo were on now.

"Easy Art . . ." June cautioned, turning to her husband. "Remember what the doctor said . . . don't attack her obsession."

"What doctor?" Cassie moved closer to her mother.

"A friend of a friend, Cassandra."

"Oh of course!" Cassie spat out. "How stupid of me to even ask!"

"Kyle is beside himself, Cassie. I saw him recently and he looked a mess. You must stop torturing that poor man with your . . . idiosyncracies," Art said.

"And then his financial difficulty . . ." June sympathized. "Our banker friend happened to mention that he was forced to turn down Kyle for a loan . . . poor risk."

"Loan?" Cassie quaked.

"Second mortgage on the house, our friend happened to mention," Art replied.

My god! Cassie's hysteria rapidly rose. *Are we to lose everything? Be homeless? Cast at the mercy of Art and June Scarpelli? Nooo . . .* She couldn't bear it, and needed to sit back down, her legs like jelly.

"Now back to the doctor." June shot a direct look at Cassie. "We're willing to pay such a cost, your father and I."

"Forget it, Mother!"

"Think about Kristi," June kept on as if she hadn't heard the her. "You can't be a good mother with this . . . this problem that's afflicted you."

The blunt, hypocritical words said with such superiority, fueled the bitterness she had carried longer than she could remember. "Perhaps I had no role model, Mother. Perhaps . . . you should look in a tarnished mirror."

"How could you, Cassie!" Without delay, Art placed a comforting arm around a rigid, numbed June.

Cassie's anger rose with the sight of the totally enamored duo. It was typical, and had contributed much to her lifelong misery. "Perhaps you should look in the same mirror Father."

"Tacete!" he shouted.

For a fleeting moment, having thought that her grandfather told her to 'Shut up', she clamped her lips closed.

"She's your Mama, for Christ's sakes. *Your Mama!"* Art furiously flashed his dark eyes across the table. "And I'm your Papa!"

What a time for his Italian conscience to suddenly pop up, she thought with hurt and indignation. And now as a result, hers had popped up as well. *Damn him!*

"I'm sorry," she muttered.

Art gave an emphatic nod of his head and hugged June tighter. The loving gesture so easily dispensed on her mother made Cassie's insides grate familiarly. The view was so hard to swallow, a bitter pill she had never really swallowed in all of her thirty-one years.

"Now back to your writing obsession . . ." Art started in more calmly. "It has led to you leading an unsavory . . . ur . . . Bohemian lifestyle that doesn't . . . ah . . . sit well in the community where you *have* to live."

"And where you two have to live as well, I presume," she quipped.

June jumped in instantly. "That's beside the point, Cassandra!"

Isn't it always . . . besides the point when it is the point?

"Your mother's right, Cassie, we're talking about *you*."

She saw the refined shift of her father's dark eyes and, in much-interpreted fashion, she knew his paternal conscience was giving him a jab. But the effect was temporal. In short order, the austere quality returned to his eyes.

"The writing is a sickness. You must see that and try to cure it, Cassie."

"And what if my book sells, huh?"

Art sadly shook his head. "It's a delusion, Cassie, a symptom of your illness. It will never happen. You have no knack for such a career. Haven't you discovered this in *ten years*?"

She felt the collapse of her spirit like rocks slowly cascading down a mountainside. How could he be so cruel? She wondered. After all her hard work, suffering, and show of great determination, how could he be so *callous* for his own gain? It inconceivable that she had spurned from the two before her!

"You *must* face reality, Cassandra. *No one* wants your scribblings," June said icily.

Scribblings? She wanted to drop to the floor and scream like a madwoman, then beat her fist against the chipped tile, followed by pulling out every hair strand by its root. The absolute, unequivocal sheer gall!

"Here's a list of qualified names." June pushed a piece of paper across the table.

Cassie forced her eyes to the names written out in her mother's precise script. A slow, fulminating tremor rolled through her, then finally went off like a stick of TNT. She grabbed the paper, ripping it to confetti. "Please leave--I'm quite tired at the moment."

Horrified, the parental pair hastily stood and stared down like she was a frightening loony.

"Just return the casserole at your convenience," June said nervously.

Like a pair of scared bunnies, the parental duo scampered out of the kitchen. Moments later, Cassie heard the quick close of the front door.

She felt like she had been brutally attacked by a pair of rabid dogs. The pain was *so* stinging, and she paused to let it absorb. Then she slowly stood. The urge to flail was gone, replaced by another equally strong urge. She *couldn't* give into it.

So she began to walk forward.

Harry Two beckoned . . .

****

During the next week, Cassie again was holed up in the attic, horribly stifling as it was, pounding on the computer keys eighteen, nineteen hours a day. And all her carefully-nurtured rejuvenation efforts appeared for *not*.

Brushing away an oily, wet hair strand from her face, Cassie's fingers moved to computer cursor keys. She cursed up, then slowly down, rereading the last paragraph she had just completed. With a loud tortured groan, she hastily blocked out and deleted.

Then she paused to rack her brain.

Damn--why is it so tough?

She knew what she wanted to say, yet explicitly was the problem.'Simply', she had covered, but colorful and figurative were hidden somewhere beneath the layers of her other unshakable thoughts.

Kyle was one . . .

The *why* of his bizarre behavior bedeviled her. He hadn't returned since their confrontation in the kitchen; although she *had* tried to get to the root of the problem.

Calls to the used car lot remained unanswered, however, the voice at the other end of the line assured her that Kyle had gotten the message. Then, when her insides knotted with foreboding, she had called the bank that held their home mortgage to check on its status. All was well, she was told. The same held true for the loan companies that had financed their two cars and the company of their one seldom-used major credit card.

Why then?

Her mind ran amok with every possible personal tragedy . . .

Closet boozer? Sly junkie? Compulsive gambler? A terminal illness? A Mafia hit man?

Her imaginings had been endless, all spelling financial doom.

And if that wasn't enough suffering . . . *Kristi* . . .

Her daughter hadn't written since Boston, while her parents had received four more postcards--or so they boastfully said. Now she gritted her teeth as the word *kidnappers* pounded her head like a riveting jackhammer.

Where Kristi was concerned their hidden agenda was *so* blatant, she angrily told herself. They wanted to create a miniature June Scarpelli for egotistical and socially effective reasons. She could just hear her mother's *enamored* friend 'ooh' and 'ah' over the popsicle—Kristi Anne-Marie Callahan.

Barfarama!

Then her inner anger uncomfortably dissipated and an uneasy lump formed in her throat.

Nono . . .

For the first time ever, even her grandfather had been on her case. "Have you had any nibbles on your book yet, Cassina?" he constantly asked. And when she gave him a negative, he always decisively followed this with, "No more self-publishing dollars, in fact no more book money, *periodo!*"

Periodo . . . The end of a sentence, the beginning of womanhood, the end of a century, the beginning . . . she could think of no other beginnings, only ends.

The end of our decade-long fruitful, if less than lucrative, financial liaison.

But she feared it was the end of much more than that, and the possibility gnawed her with sheer terror

Oh god, gruesome thoughts be gone.

Without delay, she turned back to the tortuous paragraph. She had to find her creative flair again. Suddenly 'Harry Two' had become as vital as the first book. Her life was more tangled than ever, therefore required drastic actions to remedy it.

'Harry Two' had to be *more than* perfect . . .

****

"Damn!" Hours later, Cassie pounded a gentle fist onto her computer keys so a variety of characters appeared on the screen. She examined her creative burst. "Hmmm . . . looks better than what I've done so far." And with this revelation, she pounded again.

Ten pages in twelve hours must be an all-time low record, she thought, utterly frustrated. She could feel the story was inside of her ready to burst its bounds. But those bounds remained steadfast. There was no steady stream—there was no stream at all—just mind-labored activity resulting in nothing.

This must be what they call writer's block, she thought with disbelief, never imagining that such an affliction would strike *her*. It was an impossible!

Her mind constantly whirred and spewed. And she *had* placed her horde of problems on the back burner. So why wasn't her mind whirring and spewing? She wondered somewhat desperately. What if I've lost it? What if June Scarpelli's 'scribblings theory' is correct? What if--. *Oh god!* It was too hair-raising to question!

She sprung from her chair, gazing helplessly around and wondering what could be done to cure such a terminal disease.

Maybe a massive dose of carbohydrates?
Maybe standing on my head for an hour or so?
Maybe meditation, chanting 'Harry' over and over?
She took several calming breaths in slow succession.
Maybe a tad bit of a respite . . .

Telling herself to settle down-- *all is not lost*--she took careful steps out of the attic, then more careful steps down the stairs so her now serene mental balance was maintained. She stood in the center of the living room, and greatly appreciated the slightly less stifling air that greeted her.

Now what? She wondered, perfectly calm. Moving her head left to right in slow, deliberate fashion, she finally fastened on the worn-out couch with a paisley throw. Was that pattern too eye-twirling to promote total relaxation? She wondered.

No--it's quite hypnotizing, she decided.

Cassie gently lowered onto the couch then draped limply. She intently stared at the green and blue hued paisley, until green and blue spots danced before her eyes. In fact, she couldn't remove her eyes from the cross-eyed effect. Was her mind clearing somewhat? She asked herself, concentrating her efforts on her state of her mind. Ultimately, she concluded the answer was difficult to determine with the preponderance of green and blue in the background. So she held her stare, willing her mind to blaze with a glowing *nothing*.

Engrossed in her activity, she never heard the front door open nor was cognizant of a figure at the living room entrance until a distant-sounding voice penetrated her ears.

"Cass, it's me."

Her mind drifting like ocean waves, she leisurely raised her head to the sound. A tad cross-eyed at first, she had difficulty focusing, but soon a face came into her view. Suddenly she felt joyous. "Sarie?"

"We needa talk, Cass," Sarie said with quiet decisiveness.

"Sure." Cassie lifted her into a sitting position and smiled brightly. "I'll make some cof . . ." Her smile slowly converted into a gape. "Sarie . . . When? How . . . ?"

Sarie moved her expanded bulk deeper into the living room. "When? About five months ago, according to the doctor's estimate. And how? Do you needa ask?"

The shock was so numbing, Cassie clutched the couch arm for support. "Who? Is it that building contractor who you were eyeing? Or . . . that shoe salesman with the hairy chest who made your feet tingle? Or . . ."

"Neither," Sarie quickly cut in. "This man, unfortunately, is married and a father."

"Oh no, Sarie." Cassie felt every ounce of her best friend's woes.

"But he's promised to get a divorce."

"Is that a wise solution, Sar? I mean, forcing a split of this man's family?"

Sarie's nod was emphatic. "Yeah--his wife is spoiled and selfish with no feelings for him, and he's pretty unhappy. I love him and know I can make him happy."

"Does this man love you, Sar?"

With an evasive veer of her eyes, Sarie didn't answer.

"He doesn't?" Cassie cried out. "Don't do it, Sar. Raise your child alone, I'll help you. Just don't fall into such an inescapable trap . . ."

"Like you did, Cass?"

Cassie twisted her head to the left. Kyle's form filled the living room entrance.

"I know you never loved me," Kyle began painfully. "You were too good for me. I knew that too." His voice shook into a staccato of words. "Cassie Scarpelli . . . so smart, so talented, so beautiful, so rich, so inaccessible' . . . I knew from day one, that I wasn't worthy of you."

Cassie's eyes blurred with tears. "Kyle, please don't . . ."

"So I closed my eyes to all of it . . . your refusal to get a job, your slipshod care of me and Kristi, your obsessive illness . . . because I loved you and woulda done anything to keep you in a marriage that I know damn well you never wanted. But that's over. I. . .can't take another minute of it. I'm tired of appeasing you."

"No god." Cassie felt an explosion of tears as her head twisted from Kyle to Sarie and back again, until the truth soaked through her head. "Sarie, no."

Briefly, a pain-filled expression crossed Sarie's eyes, then they settled into cold impassivity. "Kyle needs what I can provide."

"What?" Cassie shrieked, feeling a frightening hysteria. "What can you provide? *Friend!*"

"Appeasement . . . Kyle can experience the other side of the coin for a change."

Cassie pivoted her gaze to Kyle. "And I suppose you'll take it?" she panted. "Go ahead! Ruin another woman's life! Damn you! Go ahead!"

"I will!" he angrily flared back. "Anything's better than living in a goddamn tomb!"

Diverting her eyes to Sarie, Cassie saw the intense hurt at the cruel thoughtless words, that she, Cassie had suffered all these years. She shifted her gaze unable to look at history repeating itself.

"I've retained an attorney in Anoka. You'll be getting a letter," Kyle trembled out.

"Get out!" Cassie screamed at him. "Both of you!" She glared at Sarie. "Damn you! Damn you both . . . !"

Chapter 7 — Jack

"Pretty hot, huh Jack?" Harv Wellson twirled his vodka martini at a long-legged, bustie, provocatively clad female, entertaining a group of men attired in Rodeo Drive casual.

Feeling hemmed in from the crowded party at the Chateau Monet Hotel in West Hollywood, Jack Torelli tossed down his double bourbon on the rocks and asked the bartender for another before responding to his agent.

He turned to view the woman in question. In usual fashion, he eyed her from toe to head, lingering on her top and bottom girth. "She's all right," he replied at last, shifting back to the bar to get his drink.

"Cm'on Jack," Harv chuckled. "You gettin' picky in your old age?"

Jack sipped and shrugged. "Maybe just sick and tired of the goddamn monotony."

"Monotony? Her?" Harv asked, incredulous. "My poker's hot even at this distance."

Shit! A female dog would get your poker hot, Jack thought, irritated as the mellow bourbon coursed down his throat. The good booze was the best part of the party, otherwise it *sucked*. The personalities, though different, were clones of one another. *Dress and act to impress people you don't even like* One big fucking game. And he wasn't in the mood to play—not tonight. "You read that script from Rud?" Harv questioned.

"Yeah." He wished Harv hadn't brought it up. It was the main reason for his foul mood.

"So . . . ?"

"So what?" Jack took a hefty gulp. "It's all the same shit regardless of the supposed decadence of this production," he said with biting sarcasm.

"Jack . . ." Harv placated. "It's gonna gross millions if you can pull it off the way Rud envisions. The writing if fuckin' brilliant according to him."

"Brilliant?" Jack tensed up with disbelief. "You call that total depravity, *brilliant*? My god man . . . I grunt like an animal for ninety fucking minutes. Not a lousy word of English. *Nada!*" He drained the glass, promptly asking for a refill.

"But the sex scenes . . . they'll make you an even bigger star, Jack."

"Yeah--I'll be the most famous 'cock' in the world . . . some star status," he muttered bitterly. "The quality offers should pour in."

Harv slammed his glass on the bar top. "What's the matter with you? It's money in the bank. A job in Hollywood. That's what I thought you fuckin' wanted, Jack. But lately . . ."

"Forget it, Harv." Jack stiffened to gain control of his burning anger. He couldn't afford to ruffle Harv's feathers, with ingratitude. The agent stood between Hollywood and obscurity, and he needed Harv Wellson to stay in his ball court. "You know I'll give it my best shot, Harv."

"That's better." Harv patted the back of Jack's white *Armani* blazer.

The amiable action made him bristle. *And how much is Rud paying you to utter those words, huh Harv?* He shrugged the jacket and hid the true resentment he felt towards the oily man. Harv's eyes were small and wide-set, and his grandfather had always told him to beware of men with those kind of eyes. So, he kept that bit of information in the forefront of his mind when in the agent's company. *"Averlo con qualcuno,* Jacko, knife in the back."

"Looks like the natives are gettin' kinda restless," Harv commented.

Fourth drink in hand, Jack swung around and leaned against the bar. His eyes moved around the room. A few couples were hot and heavy, and others seductively danced to Van Halen. Then came the groups . . . ambitious females who had weaseled an invitation and were playing up to the male who may hold a golden key; then the 'already' actresses, some from the 'skins', others bit players in television or movies, clawing to hang onto what they had or clawing for more at these parties; actors, no big names but recognizable faces, and; a few directors and producers of no big significance . . . *same old, same old.* In the corners were the coke snorters, trying to be unobtrusive yet starkly visible. And the smell of pot suffocated the air.

"Looks the fuckin' same to me," he finally muttered. *One big fucking show starring plastic people.*

"You should snort some coke, Jack. You're damn uptight tonight," Harv said, perturbed.

Jack turned back to the bar and hung over it. "Ignore me. I'm just a little ansy lately."

"How so?" Concerned, Harv moved closer to him.

Jack sucked on his drink, wondering how to answer when there was no conclusive answer. "I dunno. Maybe I need a vacation or something."

"You're gettin' one, pal, remember? *Jungle Love* is going on location in the Caribbean, small island in the Caymans."

With further reference to the touchy subject, Jack's tension exploded. "That's no fuckin' vacation! It's a goddamn torture chamber! Don't you the hell understand?" He slowly massaged his forehead. Why his sudden rebellion? He wondered. He had always played the lamb being led to slaughter. No explicit answer, except, *I'm damn ansy.*

"Take it easy, Jack," Harv soothed. "I retract my earlier statement . . . maybe you better lay off the coke for a while. It might be gettin' to you. You're not yourself, boy."

Hell, I haven't been myself for more years than I can remember.

He rubbed away the throb in his forehead. He was nearly thirty-eight years old, twenty-six months shy of forty, and this was all he had: A shame-filled existence filled with plastic people. Sudden fear sprouted in his gut. How long before he didn't even have that? It couldn't last forever. 'Skins' thrived on new, young meat. He *had* to stay young.

"Well *lookee,*" Harv laughed. "Miss Gorgeous is eyeballing you, Jack."

Feeling desperation grip, he veered around and his gaze landed smack into the long-legged fox Harv had raved about. She gave a slow, inviting smile which he didn't return. Rather, he intensely stared at her until she sauntered in his direction.

"She'll settle your balls, boy," Harv hooted with amusement.

His stare fixed on the heavily made up face and bouncy blonde hair streaked with black roots, Jack didn't respond. She'd say her name, he'd say his, she'd simper that she knew, then move closer to him and he'd take inventory of her body then look a little bit appreciative. She'd run a hand down his jacket sleeve, and ask, "Wanna fuck?"

Seeking Out Harry

My pseudo-trip into manliness is looming . . . and he turned quickly, going against his party policy and asking the bartender for a triple rum, Then he shifted around again.

"Hi, I'm Debra . . ."

****

Good shit. Jack sat propped up in his bed, eyes forward, sucking sluggishly on a joint.

He felt an eager hand stroke his crotch. The sensation sent his insides into a broiling rage. "Hands off," he warned in a menacing tone, not altering his gaze.

"No more?" she questioned.

The ripe smoke bathed his nostrils, and he ignored her. It was almost as satisfying as the smells in that Mott Street kitchen, fragrant with tomatoes, spices, and the yeasty odor of freshly baked bread, he thought with bitter sadness. And he let those smells consume him.

"I've done some acting, you know," She dotted her fingertips on his arm hairs.

The smell vanished, and his ire exploded at the cruel intrusion. "I said hands off, dammit!"

She promptly lifted her fingers. "I heard about *Jungle Love* . . . the talk of the party . . . Everyone said it would make 'skin' history. Is that true?"

"Shut up," he growled, wanting to wring her neck for referring to his humiliation when he felt relaxed for the first time in days.

" Female bit parts still need filling, I hear," she spoke on, totally ignorant to his mood.

"So? Who the fuck cares?"

She let out a tinkly laugh. "I do--it could boost my career."

"What career?" he scoffed.

She quickly defended the point. "I've done roles for Kiss Productions and Stan Downs."

Jack laughed cynically. "They're gutter producers . . . low quality smut." He felt a boost to his self-worth. Rud Hanna *was* the best. Not everyone got a shot with Rud.

More defense. "Well at least it's better than waitress-*ing* in a West Hollywood club."

"At least that's decent."

The sound of her strident, amused laugh grated his ears with irritation, and he stared more intensely at the wall across from the bed. He wanted to smack her for her flagrant behavior that did nothing except *piss him off*. Was there no one who could make him feel good?

"You're joking. Right, Jack?"

He inhaled deeply. "Yeah--big joke."

"So . . ." The nipples of her implants skirted his arm, and concurrently, his body tightened. "Can you maybe put a tiny bug in Mr. Hanna's ear for me, huh?"

Like hell I will. He had finished playing years ago. No gratis sex . . . *just sex.*

"Not even a microscopic bug," he mumbled.

"But Jack . . ." She snaked closer until her cold, plastic nipples grazed his cheek. "I can be great. I have moves. Mr. Hanna will be impressed. You won't be sorry for telling . . .

"Get out!" he snarled at the white stucco of the wall.

"Please Jack. I need this chance. My career . . . it's stagnant . . . I need .

"Out!" He angrily spun towards her. "Get out now before I kill you!"

Her eyes glazed with fear, she backed away from him, and he felt his tenseness ease.

He tried to block out the sounds of her dressing, the hair combing, the click of her compact . . . He just wanted her gone . . . *from my hell on earth* . . . gone.

"Debra DaMont . . . do you think you'll remember?" she asked cautiously.

"Not even in my head," he replied flatly, then, not knowing why, he added with an undertone of passionate shivering, *"Addio."*

"What?"

Goodbye forever, he answered silently, feeling the frightening loneliness. And the mellow smoke curled up his nostrils.

And the dots of white stucco danced merrily in front of his hazy eyes.

****

Days, then weeks, passed, and soon it was the end of October. The International Fest of Masks and the Los Angeles Poetry Festival were history. For another year. And the set of *Jungle Love* was ready to move to the Grand Cayman Islands in the Caribbean.

Treating the production like a twenty-four-carat flawless diamond, Rud Hanna had scrupulously seen to every minute detail, including sending a large pre-production crew to prepare the location in Cayman Brac, a small island eighty miles northeast of the Grand Caymans, and pour the place with advanced publicity so there wasn't a, native or tourist, who didn't know they were coming. The movie was his prized baby, and everybody in Hollywood, famous or otherwise, knew this fact.

Now, gathered in his large but unremarkable office, were three times the normal size production crew to go over the final details so there were no fuck-ups.

Twirling an unlit panatella in his mouth, Rud's buggy eyes scanned the gathering. Low life scum, most of them, he thought of the derelict-looking group. Suddenly the sight angered him, and he thrust forward in his leather chair, whipping the panatella from his mouth.

"Clean up, all of you!" He slowly moved a stiff, meaty finger around the room. "I want some class with this production. You're up for public scrutiny, so in the least, you can look like you gotta pot to piss in."

An uncomfortable silence settled in the room while the crew took sneaky glances at one another, then back at the man who had given most of them their big chance. It was quite a coup to work on the much publicized *Jungle Love*.

"Now . . ." Rud stuck the panatella back in his mouth. "I want this tastefully done." And he chomped. "Every scene is to read like pure European erotica."

"Taste how, Rud?" the Director demanded. "All we have to work with is a jungle hut, a vine, a stream, and a half-assed canoe. I wouldn't call that European ambiance."

Rud let out a raspy laugh. "Why the taste of cock and pussy, what do you think, Doug?"

A low humorous titter circled the office, and the bodies relaxed.

"I want Torelli turned into a savage animal with every move," Rud continued thoughtfully. "That cock is to be the center of focus." He veered towards the head cinematographer and his eyes bugged in a threatening manner. "Not boobs, pussy . . . *cock!*"

"Got it, Rud," the man replied.

Rud brushed a speck of dust off his otherwise immaculate black *Armani* suit—he had a closet full. It was the only men's shop on Rodeo Drive that he patronized. Not even the trendy shops on Melrose or the chic sophisticated European shops in Sunset Plaza held any appeal. His image blared *Armani*. "And . . ." He sharply shifted to his production assistant. "I want Torelli kept happy . . . you know how."

"Don't worry, Rud. I know it by rote," the assistant replied.

Rud twisted the cigar from one side of his mouth to the other. He suddenly remembered something he had heard several months back, and he broke out in amused laughter. "And you better pack that plastic 'something', just in case our star forgets his."

The production assistant laughed as well. "It's in my bags as we speak, Rud."

"Good!" Rud slapped the panatella to his desktop. "I want double and triple checks on those props." He again skirted around his finger at the group. "The same goes for the costumes."

Loud laughter filled the office.

"Regardless of the irony of that statement," Rud said more casually to befit the sudden levity in the environment. "And clean up!" he concluded in a thunder.

****

His office was cleared of bodies, Rud let the panatella roll around his tongue while he pondered his great production. Though the price tag was quadruple his usual film budget, the total cost was low by industry standards--especially when the potential return was figured into the equation. He would make a virtual killing on his 'grand baby'. *Greenbacks raining from heaven.*

He insisted on it.

Then in a flash, his eyes grew serious. That little plastic 'something' had touched his remembrance. *"Cherie, Torelli has this charming leetle dildo . . ."* He could hear the French slut's words as if she was speaking them now.

Despite his earlier amusement, in reality *the leetle dildo* had led to a small amount of suffering, primarily directed towards the life's aspect that led to his greatest suffering—his pocketbook. Could Torelli maintain? He wondered, chomping furiously.

Probably no.

He had seen it many times over the last seventeen years: The failing porn star. It was inevitable, he told himself. After all, how much wild pussy could a body take without feeling the effects? Then add the pot, coke, and booze needed to maintain . . . and in Torelli's case, he could also add, *mechanics to raise it*. Torelli was failing, miserably, *sure shit.*

So what now? Like a frenzied chipmunk he gnawed the panatella while solution after solution ran through his mind. Ultimately, he could come up with only one solution.

He would let Jack Torelli peak with *Jungle Love*, then let him slowly course down the hill until he reached rock bottom. It was a well-used, effective method, Rud thought.

Although he did have one regret.

That cock!

He wished he could cut it off and transplant it on a male star fifteen years younger.

Then he'd be rolling in dough for years to come . . . *sure shit.*

****

The fiery sounds of Chopin piano music flowed from the *Sony* stereo system. Despite the superbness, Jack Torelli angrily tossed clothes and essentials into his black *Cardin* luggage.

That fucker, Rud!

He threw and slapped.

God damn him!

He slapped and threw.

Then he paused in his rampage to step back and survey the suitcase contents.

Did Rud want to check his clothes like a fussy mother sending her kid to camp? He wondered sarcastically. Maybe he should call Rud and tell him he was ready for inspection. His lips cascaded into a sneer when the hoarse voice of Rud Hanna filled his head.

"I want you on brilliant display, Jack, like a Hollywood peacock . . . most expensive clothes, a little tight in the crotch to get the voyeurs' juices going, and just the right shirts to display that magnificent chest. Remember . . . that place is loaded with American tourists who go back home and put down dough at their local porn theaters, and I want them salivating over your balls so they put that dough on the right movie. And . . . a few pair of sexy swim trunks wouldn't hurt. You know . . . the type that gives full dimension of your greatest physical trait. We'll get you on the beach a few times for display. And . . . get a haircut, a stylist type. Forget the shave. I want you looking primitive . . ."

It was Rud's usual lack of mincing words, Jack thought bitterly. He wished he could jam a 'Hollywood peacock' up Rud Hanna's ass. But . . . he had no choice but to graciously comply, lest he wanted to experience one of the studio owner's means of revenge for bad little porn stars. Rud was full of them, including months' long suspensions so one was forced to come back begging to him. Rud loved the humiliation.

No outright begging, Torelli.

No way would he resort to this with Rud Hanna unless he wanted to feel totally emasculated. He had to play the game so it lasted. *Otherwise, I'm a dead man. . .*

With this final dark thought, he resumed packing, paused momentarily to let the glorious sound of Chopin bathe his ears, then he bent over his suitcase, and abided . . .

****

In the ensuing days, the cast and crew of *Jungle Love* baked in the strong Caribbean sun of Cayman Brac, the smallest of the Cayman Islands. The set was on an isolated part of the island, and hired police patrolled the perimeter. No one was allowed five hundred feet near the filming. Yet the native inhabitants congregated, hoping to get a glimpse of the American movie stars.

"Dirty up that canoe, dammit! I want *real.* How many times do I have to tell you idiots!" Rud Hanna's yelled at a group of assistant set designers, hoisting a canoe into the small stream, on whose bank most of the filming was being done.

Clad in a thin robe, Jack disgustedly watched the proceedings from a distance. All he had heard for the past two days was Rud's gruff voice yelling about 'real' as if he was filming a prime epic. *It was trash.* The script, the phony props, the actresses looking like they'd been made-up and bewigged for a 1920's movie, and him . . . looking like Johnny Weismuller, minus the loincloth, which irked him.

He was a *cock*--that's it.

"Keep your groin to the camera at all times, Jack," was all Rud seemed to say to him, as well as the Director, and the group of cinematographers, most of whom acted like they were fresh out of school. The fifty bucks he had dropped for his 'stylish haircut' was wasted money for all it had been filmed. *Rud's grand baby . . . it was one big joke.*

"Jack get the hell over here! We're ready for the big fish scene," Rud commanded like an owner calling his pet.

Jack seethed. *Big scene, my ass.* He angrily charged over to the stream. *The scene is shit, pure, unadulterated shit!*

When he reached the stream's edge, he was handed a fake mushy fish by one of the assistant directors. "Here's your breakfast, Mr. Torelli," the young man joked.

Resisting the urge to vomit, Jake looked down at the shiny fins and round staring eyes, and he cursed the stupid writer who wrote such asinine crap into the script. Now, because of this extra little ditty, he would look like an absolute fool. He could just read the Hollywood trades humorously slamming Torelli and his fish.

"Off with the robe Jack, then stick these in your cheeks."

The Director held out two blood capsules, and the bile crept up Jack's throat. Regardless, he thrust off his robe, feeling the blistering sun beat down on his bare skin, and he plucked the capsules, placing them in his chops.

"Okay cameras, get ready to go!" the Director shouted, then turning back to Jack, "I want you to look crazed, white of the eyes predominant, then you know what to do, and once done, I want you to gaze left and right like a caged animal . . . this is your big scene. Remember that."

Big scene . . . fuck! He figured they might as well write RIP on his forehead, because his reputation would be as 'dead as a duck' when the Hollywood press got through with him.

"Keep that groin facing the camera, Jack," Rud Hanna reminded.

Shit! Why doesn't he just cut me off at the middle and be done with it?

The blood capsules and the fish in his hand sat like emetics. *Hell!* When he crazily looked left and right he may be looking for the crapper.

"Okay, Jack . . . Action!"

Gathering every nerve he possessed, he lifted the fish to his mouth. Then gathering more nerves, he bit into the gruesome mushiness until it was sawed in half. A sticky substance drizzled out of his mouth. Not wanting to repeat such a horror, he made his face as crazy as he could, glanced left and right, then right and left for good measure.

"Cut! . . .That's a print!"

Jack thrust the fish to the ground and rapidly swiped his mouth with the back of his hand. He didn't know whether to feel relieved or scream with sheer vexation.

"Okay, ten minute break for Jack to get cleaned up, then he takes the dive . . ."

****

Still nauseated ten minutes later, Jack again stood at the stream's edge and stared down at the clear rippling water. Now, he had to dive for the fish, he had just demolished with his jaws.

Dead fake fish number two floated atop the water's surface. This one looked grosser than the first. He told himself to be thankful that Rud didn't extend *real* to this scene.

"Okay Jack . . ." the Director began. "All you gotta do is give us a stunning dive, then come up with the fish between your teeth."

That's all? He asked himself, incredulous, watching the fish sway back and forth on top of the water. *Shit!* With calculation, he tried to judge the maneuver so his mouth landed up on the fish. And after a few moments, he silently cussed again.

"Let's get this on the first take, Jack . . ."

. . .It took twelve takes before he triumphantly held the fish between his teeth.

Red-hot with anger, he spit out the fish and stormed out of the water. Once he stood, dripping, on the bank, he crazily glanced left and right. Now he *would* kill that fucking writer!

"Break for lunch!" one of the assistant directors hollered.

Lunch, my ass. I'm lucky if I'll ever be able to eat again . . .

****

"Jack, get set for the canoe scene," the Director said an hour and a half later.

Jack forced his gaze to the stream. A muddied canoe rocked back and forth ten feet from shore. Languidly stretched in it was a relatively famous porn actress from Czechoslovakia, sporting a curly golden wig down to her bare ass. She's huge, he thought with a small measure of awe. Her super pumped up breasts were the largest he'd ever seen, let alone diddled with.

"Okay Jack . . ." the Director placed a firm hand on his shoulder, and Jack stiffened from the intrusive sensation. The man tipped his sharp chin to the stream. "I want you to wildly glance left to right until you fasten on the canoe. Then you look like an animal who's found his mate. With haste, you do another stunning dive, this time landing inches from the canoe. You lift up into it, and attack Nadia like she's a wild animal attacking you. Need I say more . . . ?"

Hell no, do you ever? He felt the strong urge to pounce on the slimy snake standing far too close to him for his comfortable liking.

"Cameras ready . . . Action!"

Telling himself, that no way was he going to do twelve takes again, he rustled all his determination and effort together, and made a clean precision dive . . .

****

The brilliant pink/orange dawn was rising above the turquoise Caribbean Sea. Jack took in the beautiful sight while he stood at the window of his bungalow, smoking a joint containing fine quality weed, courtesy of Rud Hanna.

Best pot, best coke, best rum, best women . . . Rud had been bountiful during the ten days they had been on Cayman Brac, he recalled, savoring the mellow pot.

I wonder why the over generosity?

Although providing him with little amounts of each over the years, Rud, cheap by nature except for where himself was concerned, had never been so abundant with the gifts. It was suspicious as it lacked any of Rud's obvious agendas.

But why question?

No way would Rud answer.

Emitting a heavy sigh, Jack took one last toke then stamped out the joint in the aqua tortoise shell ashtray purchased in a shop on the island. He ran a finger over the ashtray's smooth surface as thought back to his purchase, and a rare smile cracked on his lips.

The owner of the shop, a native, with a Jamaican accent, gave him a detailed explanation about the shell. It had come from a local turtle farm, the small energetic man said, then proceeded this with a description of the fine art of harvesting turtles for exportable items.

Fascinated by this previously unknown information, Jack listened closely, questioned a bit, then listened some more, thoroughly enjoying what he considered the first decent, normal, conversation he had experienced in years.

And I felt good. It was the best part of this entire fucking trip.

He lifted his fingers from the shell. The familiar frigid chill coursed through him despite the tropical mugginess seeping through the walls of the bungalow. He had concluded that Rud's prized movie royally sucked, and if he had been an observer looking in, he would be in hysterical laughter. But he wasn't . . . so it was far from a laughing matter. He feared the response, even by hardcore porn goers, to the sheer depravity laced with the total hokiness of Rud's grand baby.

But he had no choice but to keep playing the game Rud dictated, he thought, gazing at the gentle sea waves. He felt no sense of relaxing calm like the brochures promised, rather felt dread about what lie ahead—publicity, parties, escorting the barely tolerable, freakish-looking Nadia around town, lying through his teeth about the virtues of the film—yet, in slaughtered lamb fashion, he would do all of the above, because to refuse was lethal.

And now, it's time to go home to pay the piper.

After one last look at the sea, and a lingering look at the tortoise shell ashtray, Jack turned from the window, paused to scratch the itchiness out of his balls then made his way to the wicker and bamboo wardrobe. It was time to pack, he reminded. Precisely at nine a.m., the boat would leave for George Town on Grand Cayman where he *would* be a Hollywood peacock . . .

****

Docked at the marina in Cayman Brac, the large chartered boat was taking on the loads of production equipment and luggage, when Jack, dressed to kill and sporting opaque sunglasses, exited the repainted pea green Volkswagon, circa 1970's. He tipped the driver twenty dollars to the man's effusive delight, and Jack's as well.

He boosted his carry-on bag over his shoulder, hung his garment bag over his right arm, and with his left hand, held the pull-up handle on his suitcase. Then he headed for the boat.

When reaching the anchored vessel, he saw most of the cast and crew had arrived. He was greeted by a few voices and Nadia promptly tossed him a seductive kiss. He ignored it, wishing the barely verbal woman would evaporate back to Czechoslovakia. A couple other of the women who had graced his bed for a few hours gave him eager, inviting smiles, and he briefly focused his shades on them without any other acknowledgment.

"Jack . . ." Rud Hanna boomed as if they were best friends.

Jack's body tightened more with each step the studio owner took towards him. When Rud stood in front of him, a streak of fury shot through him like a rocket.

"Looking good, Jack, damn good," Rud commented.

Through his shades, he watched the buggy eyes roam up and down his body and cunningly linger on his crotch. He felt like a filthy piece of meat despite his bright expensive attire.

"Pure peacock, Jack. Just what I asked for." Rud wore a broad, superior grin. "Should get me a few bucks, sure shit."

Unable to view the gaping, mocking face, he lowered his sunglasses. "Glad you're pleased, Rud." He felt the excruciating choke of each word.

"Guess they're ready for us to board. It's Grand Cayman or bust, eh?"

He slightly lifted his glasses and saw the 'dare me' curve of Rud's mouth that usually brought about immediate compliance. And he told himself, *I'm no different. Hollywood beggar of the highest magnitude . . . and the fucker damn well knows it.*

"Shall we, Jack?"

Hoisting his luggage, he gave a slight nod, and like the proverbial lamb, followed Rud Hanna to the boat . . .

****

The lovely island of Cayman Brac gently faded into the distance.

Insisting on solitude, Jack leaned over the wooden deck rail of the boat and intensely stared at the slowly vanishing island. A few voices were in the background, but no one dared interrupt his quiet—he had made that clear to anyone who tried. He wanted to see nothing in his mind but the island he had resided on for ten days. He needed no reminders of the rest of it.

It's beautiful, he thought, bathing in the foreign emotion his assessment had produced. He needed more beauty in his life, he thought. It gave him a bit of warmth amid the frigidity. Now he clutched that warmth like a life raft. So he could feel it a longer. *Just a little longer . . . Please.*

"Whatcha looking at, Jack?"

He felt too paralyzed to turn and view those eyes.

"What's the big attraction? Looks like just fuckin' boring water to me, Jack."

Go away! He heard his mind's scream. But as usual where Rud was concerned, he willed his body to calm so he could respond civilly. "Guess I'm just staring at the fuckin' water."

Rud let out a hoarse chuckle. "Must be bored. Maybe you need a little side dish of Nadia."

"No!" he replied too forcefully, so he covered it up with a nervous laugh. "I mean, I'm not in the mood."

"Yeah, Jack--I see your point. She's a little too spontaneous for your liking."

He saw a strange look cross Rud's face. Was it jeering? He wondered. Suddenly a pit of trepidation formed in his stomach. "What do you mean, Rud?"

"I mean nothing, just a play on words. Well . . ." Rud jovially slapped his back. "Like I said earlier, you look like a pretty peacock, an Argus type . . . you know . . . the ones with the gold erectile train adorned with all the eyes."

In customary 'Rud Hanna' fashion, the implication was obvious, and Jack merely stared back at the man that he hated with the purest of hate. And so badly he wanted to add, *But on the inside he's like a fourteenth century Argus peacock roasted in his own plumage . . .*

"Onto Grand Cayman. Big things, Jack. My advice is to enjoy it for all the hell it's worth." Rud gave another slap then left Jack to his peace.

Shit! I swear he wanted to slap my cock instead.

Jack watched the pregnant-like figure lumber away. *Fuck you Rud!* And he spun around to face the Caribbean Sea again. All that remained of Cayman Brac, was black land and the dark silhouettes of the majestic palm trees. With renewed intensity, he fixed his eyes on the vision until the last bit of black was near extinction.

No more quaint, energetic men or turtle farms.

It had all felt so good, no matter how fleeting or fictional, it had felt amazingly good.

He doubted he would ever forget that.

"*Arrivederci,*" he whispered to the last speck of black. "Goodbye for now."

Chapter 8—Cassie

Salvation Army bells were on every corner, and colorful, luminescent lights glowed on windows, buildings and leafless trees. Merry voices filled the air and gold, silver and red peeked above shopping bags. Three inches of snow covered the ground and the days' highs hovered around a tolerable thirty. It was a cheery time in Minnesota. And Cassie Callahan had recently turned thirty-two.

Happy birthday, Merry Christmas, Bah humbug with a capital 'B'.

Everything was going wrong with her life, Cassie thought in the confines of the attic, laboriously eeking out another scene in Chapter Ten of 'Harry Two'. She carefully read the last paragraph she had written, then silently assessed that all her horrific misery seemed to pour into every sentence.

Oh God! The mere thought of what she would soon face made her feel like she was going stark-raving crazy. And unable to stop the flow of events, again, the nightmare she had been living, replayed in her mind . . .

"Stupido!"

Her Nono's yell echoed through her ears, along with the vision of his shaking, angry fist at the house four door away where Kyle and Sarie had cruelly set up housekeeping.

They might as well pick up a mud ball and rub it in my face.

The love nest was the major talk of Anoka, and the worst of it was that nobody, it seemed, faulted Kyle. It was *her* fault for driving the poor man into the arms of another woman. Of course, there was no sympathy directed to the fact that the other woman had been her best friend. Instead, most found this quite amusing . . . except for her family.

"You've totally disgraced the Scarpelli family name, Cassandra. Your father and I can barely hold up our heads, and the business . . . your antics have hurt it."

"You need psychological help immediately, Cassie, before we're forced out of town from total humiliation. Your mother and I will pay *anything*."

Now her eyes stung with tears. The duo hadn't helped, not one iota. In fact, they had hurt her beyond belief.

"Don't you blame Mother, Cassie!" Wearing a monastic black pantsuit and loafers, her sister, Meg, had screeched this in her high-pitched voice. "She's only doing what's right for an innocent, impressionable child!"

"You're divorced, you're jobless, you're slovenly, you're with an obsessive disorder that precludes normal functioning . . . you're unfit!" Todd, her conservatively dressed, uptight brother-in-law had inhumanely added.

Unfit? And, *oh lord*, they were winning . . .

"I will speak on your behalf, Cassina," Angelo Scarpelli reassured. "I will make the judge see what that *animale* did to you." He fiercely snarled for a moment. "And I will make him understand your need to write, as well as your love for Kristi."

"But Nono . . . one person against their hundred who think I'm the reincarnation of *One Flew Over the Cuckoo's Nest.*"

"You're Kristi's Mama, and that is the most *importante*," he said with firm conviction.

"Even Kristi's court guardian hates me, Nono. She got a hold of a couple of my self-published books, and she kept asking me from twenty feet away if I really had such a dark, perverted view of the male anatomy."

"Perverso or not, you still her Mama . . ."

"And that lawyer you hired Nono, he's so . . . how should I say it? . . . unenlightened."

"He's the best!" Angelo emphasized. "He used to work with Humberto Humphrey!"

"But he thinks writers drunkenly swing from chandeliers and live on the Moulins Rouge."

"You are her Mama! No worry about nosy guardians and *un avocado asino*, jackass lawyers. Kristi will be home with you, Cassina . . ."

No Nono, it seems without hope. A warm stream of tears coursed down her cheeks. And, it seemed as if her parents were completely deaf to her pleas for understanding and mercy . . .

"Kristi needs me, Mother . . ."

"No! Kristi neither needs a mentally absent mother, or a . . . a . . .

"Vitaiolo!" her father snarled between clenched teeth.

"Yes--a playboy, for a father," her mother finished, adding point blank, "Anyway, Kristi has no desire to live with either of you, after this . . . this . . ."

"Scandalo de sesso," her father said in a hiss.

"Yes--sex scandal. We insist our granddaughter grow up decently, Cassandra."

"Decent?" Cassie shrieked. "*I* grew up in that environment, remember?"

"What are you implying, Cassandra?"

"You know exactly what I'm implying, Mother."

"Shut up, Cassie," her father warned.

" No--you *Tacete*, Father!" she yelled back at him. "You two have the utter nerve to talk about absent!" And then she felt All her inner bitterness gathered, then came to a sudden explosion. "I refuse to have Kristi grow up on an iceberg, only warmed by a few rare words of Italian and the body heat you two create with your Antony and Cleopatra act!"

"Cassandra!" June sucked in a startled gasp.

"And furthermore, I doubly refuse to have you turn my child into the clone of Princess Anne just so all your friends are *enamored!*"

"That is beside the point!"

"It *is* the point, Mother! The entire point of my life where you're concerned, and you damn well know it!"

"Are you saying I never loved you, Cassandra, are you?" Her mother stood up and a tense quake shook through her body.

Fed up with the pseudo-maternal conscience, she stood as well. "Yeah--that's without a doubt or hint of apology, what I'm saying to you. Mother!"

"How dare you, Cassie!" Art predictably placed a tight grasp around June.

"How dare, I?" Cassie drew back her anger then let it rip. "How dare *you* gather lies for evidence, woo the Twin Cities legal community, and turn my daughter against me, just so your friends are *enamored!"*

"That's not true, Cassie. We're your parents for Christ's sakes."

"Don't you mean Mama and Papa, Father?" she asked directly, stunning her father into temporary silence. *"Allucinazione!"*

"Hallucination? What do you mean, Cassie?" her father asked nervously.

"You know precisely what I mean, Father," she challenged.

He swallowed his obvious anxiety. "No, I don't know, Cassie."

"Okay--if you need me to spell it out . . . you two ain't Angelo and Madelaina Scarpelli, not even close. And add to that list . . . Ozzie and Harriet, Jim and Margaret, Ward and June, Lucy and Ricky . . .

. . .And they haven't spoken to me since."

Cassie absently tapped a finger on her computer key, and more tears formed when she thought about Kristi who hadn't been home since coming back from New England. Kristi refused. She claimed her parents' behavior had made everyone laugh at her, even Heather. So it was best she stay in her grandparents' house where she could hide.

Her child had sounded so miserable, she thought about the last phone call, a month ago, that she had with Kristi . . .

"No Mom--I feel funny coming back to that house. Like . . . a murder or something was committed there. It gives me the creeps."

"What if I move?" Cassie desperately asked.

There was a pause. "It wouldn't work, Mom. If I lived with you, maybe the kids would say that I'm a ghoul too . . . sorry."

She crumbled at the words, but she tried to mask it for her child's sake. "I understand."

"Are . . . you still doodling by any chance?" Kristi asked in a small tentative voice.

"Yeah--I'm still doodling." And she crumpled some more.

"Do you think that's wise . . . considering . . . ?"

"It's wise for me, Kristi, an essential, in fact."

"So I've heard . . . Grandpa calls is a mental illness. Is it a mental illness, Mom?"

The inquisitiveness and charming voice tone made unwanted tears of longing flow. "No, honey. It's a passion, like your soccer. Could you live without soccer?"

"Isn't that beside the point?"

"No Kristi, that *is* the point. There's a definite difference."

"How's that?"

"Besides the point, means one isn't facing the truth. *Is* the point, means one bravely confronts the truth about themselves and moves on from there. Like soccer . . . you admit you have a passion and can't live without it, so you give it your all. My doodling't the same thing."

A longer pause. "I understand, but I better explain it to Grandma. I don't think she understands."

"You do that," Cassie replied in embittered tones.

"Um . . . Dad called me yesterday. He wants to see me, but Grandpa said a long string of Italian words when he found out. And . . . I just can't see him, Mom. What he did . . ." She made a disgusted sound. "It's so yucky . . . I mean, Sarie?"

"Yeah--the carrot cake with real cream cheese frosting isn't gonna help her now."

"But Dad sounded so sad and I felt weird having to tell him no," Kristi continued on. "And then there's you . . ."

"Me?"

Kristi spoke in a low, secretive tone. "Grandma and Grandpa don't even allow your name to be mentioned in the house. Grandpa keeps calling you *Ingrato* . . . Is that a dirty word, Mom?"

Ungrateful, my foot. "Yeah, Kristi. In Grandpa's case, it's a filthy word." *After all those years I kowtowed . . .*

"And he yells that you're now invisible to him, and I heard Uncle Tomo, Uncle Vince, Uncle Emilio, and Uncle Roberto say the same thing. What does 'invisible' mean, Mom?"

She wanted to pound and maul all of them. "It means that I never have to be neither cutthroat nor bloodhound when the will is read. I can just stay on the sidelines, watch the proceedings, and laugh my head off."

"Huh?"

"Forget it, honey. Your mother doesn't care. She'll show them all."

"How you gonna do that, Mom?" Kristi asked excitedly.

"Just watch me . . ."

. . .*And so now it's twenty hours of 'Harry Two' and it's gotta be perfect beyond comprehension.*

Cassie felt the acute rise of her desperation.

All three manuscripts she had sent out were rejected on a variety of grounds, primarily the fact that the three agencies did think they could convince a book editor to publish the manuscript. Although all three encouraged her writing-- and one said she had seen potential. But her agency pushed nonfiction manuscripts.

Yet, the agent *had* seen potential.

The highly satisfying words kept her going, including finding the courage to send out more query letters to literary agents, and risk further rejection on a manuscript that was her heart and soul. It was tough to have that combination rejected--every letter back took a bite.

Yet she must remain brave, despite all the heartache, she told herself.

She *had* to triumph.

It's my only hope . . .

She squared her jaw and placed fingers to computer keys. She *would* master this chapter, she thought with a bit of her old determination. She *wasn't* going to wring her hands and wait for the ax to fall.

****

Christmas passed without fanfare, except for a quiet dinner with her grandparents on the day after Christmas, as her family refused to come to the traditional celebration at the elder Scarpellis' home if 'the Invisible Woman' showed up. And New Years' Eve was worse—an invisible party and glass of champagne. Cassie was even too broke to buy a bottle of *Ripple*. She had never felt so desperate or lonely, despite her brave front of disconcern as to what the *Famiglia* Scarpelli thought of her.

And now she wanted to scream from sheer exasperation. She was in a fancy law office in St. Paul, watching the old heavily wrinkled face of her lawyer contort while he read her file in painstakingly slow fashion.

"Hmmmm . . ." he hummed, then read some more.

Hurry up! I gotta get home to Chapter Thirteen. It's thronging through me like an orgasm.

She wanted to scream her thoughts at him, but told herself, *forget it.* The old guy would need an interpretation.

"Miss Callahan . . ." he said at last, looking at her above his tri-focals. "After going through your file . . ." He looked back down at the file and read again.

She agitated in the chair. Damn! Don't lawyers have a retirement age, like eighty or something?

"All right Miss Callahan . . .

Frustrated, she cut in. "*Ms* . . . I'm *Ms*. Callahan. Miss is antiquated and objectionable. I've told you, and told you."

He gave a weary nod of his head. "Ms. Callahan . . . Pardon my lack of memory."

"You're pardoned, again. Now you said you had a small thing to discuss with me, and I'm in a bit of a hurry, so . . ."

"A psychiatrist. I think you need an evaluation by one," he popped out.

"What?" She stiffened in anger. "Whose side are you on, sir?"

"I'm on yours, Ms. Callahan, that's why I find such an evaluation imperative to your case. A clean mental bill of health from a reputable doctor will go a long way in minimizing the damaging evidence your parents have accumulated, as well as the testimony of over one hundred witnesses they have listed as willing to testify against you. Even a priest . . ."

"Priest?" She widened her eyes, unable to believe such news. "That's ridiculous!" I. . . haven't been to church for over a year so how could a priest even know about me?"

His well-lined lips squished in frustration. "Apparently that's the problem, Ms. Callahan. The Father claims that you've been a faithful church goer all your life, and now something must be horribly wrong with you because of your abstention," he explained.

"Oh no . . ." She wanted to cry where she sat, just able to hear the kindly, warm Irish tinged voice of Father Patrick, soothing the judge's ears with all his concern over the 'crazy Cassie Callahan' who had suddenly been touched by the devil.

"And to add insult to injury, your father now teaches a preschool Catechism class."

She whirled from the sudden dizziness. "My father teaches catechism . . . to preschoolers? I think I need a stiff drink . . . and even maybe a chandelier to go with it."

"They're a wily bunch, Ms. Callahan, and we need all the ammunition we can gather to fight them, so . . . will you see a psychiatrist?"

Damn! It's like saying 'uncle' to June.

She vacillated back and forth, wondering if there was another course she could take to win the battle for Kristi.

"Angelo has already agreed to pay for such a consultation," he interrupted her thoughts.

"Nono? My Nono *wants* me to see a shrink?" she asked in total disbelief. It was like the ultimate betrayal.

He spoke in a grand-fatherly tone. "Don't take it as an insult Ms. Callahan. It's just that Angelo is very cognizant of all the schemes going on within your family, and he feels you may need some help to strengthen your case."

A large slice of her hope deflated with the answer. "But . . . I'm the Mama . . ."

****

"Name?"

"Cassie Caroline Scarpelli Callahan."

"What's the date?"

"February second, nineteen hundred and ninety-four."

"Where are you?"

On a lumpy bed in the middle of hell with an overpriced nincompoop stoking the flames around me.

"Where Cassie?"

"On a cozy bed in a lovely office with a brilliant, and may I say handsome, doctor leaning over me." Cassie flashed a brilliant smile, figuring a little flattery may go a long way in court.

"And I hear that you write . . ."

"Why yes--I've been a writer for ten years . . . fiction . . . primarily male protagonists . . . the tortured male psyche is my forte . . . fascinating subject."

He paused to write a few notes, then his eyes fastened on her like suction cups. "Why tortured males?"

Why? She had never thought about this before. So she racked her brain for a reason, but nothing definitive would come to her. The obscurity tickled her. "You know Doctor, I have no idea why. Isn't that odd, after ten years?"

"Yes--quite." He wrote some more. "So . . . my information says that you spend several hours a day writing about such males."

"Eighteen to nineteen hours. Stamina, huh?" she replied with much pride.

He loudly cleared his throat. "I also hear that you're divorced as of three months ago."

She seared with anger at the mention of Kyle. "In actuality, it should have been twelve years ago, Doctor, after I had a miscarriage. Kyle and I were like oil and water."

"Tell me about the problems in your marriage . . ."

Grateful that someone would finally listen, she haltingly enumerated all the marital problems. When she concluded, she felt tense with bitterness.

"You're saying there were severe sexual problems, Cassie?"

"Yes . . ." She halted only briefly. "The mere thought sickened me."

"So . . . did you ever fantasize about these tortured males?"

Did I? She wondered. Thoughts of 'Harry' filled her mind, and pleasurable body responses followed. "Yes--no doubt," she finally replied in a haze of glorious sensations.

"And you fantasized while you wrote, eighteen, nineteen hours a day . . . ?"

Immediately, she snapped out of her highly personal thoughts. "Of course! How can one write without fantasizing? A fictional writer is creating a fictional world."

"Uh-huh . . ." And he wrote some more.

"What are you jotting down, if I may ask?" Cassie questioned.

He ignored her question. "So can you specifically tell me about these tortured males . . . ?"

Thrilled that he had asked her a question that no one ever asked her, she boastfully described, in colorful detail, the protagonists of her first five self-published books, purposely ignoring 'Harry'--'Harry' was too deliciously private to disclose to anyone, quite yet.

". . .And Cyrano saw his female torturer, diabolically and with a swing to her hand, hold up an unwrapped Mr. Goodbar, and his body writhed in tortured spasm after spasm. Then, she took a slow, erotic bite, and make lewd tongue movements as she savored the silky, nutty, and succulent chocolate. And he felt a horrific pain in the center of his head, the ultimate tortuous sensation. He falls to his knees and begs her over and over to stop her action, but she plays deaf to his pleas, and continues to eat the symbolic candy bar. Finally the pain overcomes him and he collapses, dead—his torture has finally and forever ceased. The end . . . Did you like my tortured men, Doctor?"

Not interrupting his furious writing, he made no comment.

"You know, Doctor, I really enjoyed telling such an avid listener about my books. In fact, I feel better than I have in days. Perhaps if we both put our brains together, we could come up with the reason why I find the tortured male so scintillating. I think the discovery would be fun. Are you game?" she asked excitedly.

He stopped his writing and locked his intense gaze on her. "Most definitely, Cassie . . ."

****

The beginning of March approached quickly, if not quietly, and on the fourth day, Cassie found herself by her grandfather's side, standing in the Anoka County Courthouse in front of a courtroom with the words **Family Court** on the closed double doors.

She stared at the words and felt terror assaulted her. "I'm so afraid, Nono," she whispered.

Angelo Scarpelli wrapped an arm around her shoulders. "It will be okay, Cassina. Only God can determine the course now."

"Yeah--I hope he's looking down at Earth, eleven years past, and seeing a thrilled Cassie Callahan lovingly holding her new baby girl, because that's all I've been able to see myself for the past twenty-four hours." Her eyes misted with tears.

"None of that, Cassina," Angelo soothed. "You must be a brave girl."

Be brave, she firmly told herself, despite that she only felt a tiny amount of courage. What little she had evaporated bit-by-bit over the past month with her family's bombardment of her character, compounded with their refusal to let her have physical contact with Kristi, and further compounded by seventeen outright rejections of her manuscript out of the twenty-one queries she had sent to literary agents. Only one agent requested to see her complete manuscript.

"We're not taking on any new authors at this time . . . We only work with established authors . . . Your idea didn't grab me . . . Theme sounds too well-used . . . We only work with specific genres and your idea is questionable . . . We only deal in literary fiction . . . I pass . . . I pass . . . I pass . . ."

She thought her head would explode from all the excuses why the plot of *The Life and Times of Harry Hannigan* stunk. She felt disheartened. She had hoped to be able to tell the judge that a few literary agents were interested in her work, so he wouldn't view her as an unproductive entity like she knew her parents would emphasize. But it didn't happen, she thought, resigned, so now her vulnerability was bared without a shred of defense, except . . . *I have a passion.*

"We better take our seats, Cassina. It's no good being late," Angelo said quietly. Then with arm around Cassie, he led her into the courtroom.

Upon entering the room, she saw a sea of familiar faces, some staring at her. *My god, they look like a pack of hungry wolves,* she thought, tightly gripping her grandfather's arms.

"Ignore them, Cassina," Angelo whispered down as he urged her along.

She tried to do as her grandfather asked, but the eyes seemed to glue onto her brain, each pair holding the same message: Unfit!

"Forget the faces, Cassina."

Taking a few calming breaths, she absently straightened the conservative two-piece black suit her grandfather had purchased for her, then patted the french roll that had taken her two hours to get just right. She held up her head as far as she could and felt the wobble of her legs as she walked to the front of the courtroom, neither gazing left nor right the entire way.

Her lawyer stood behind a long table, and held a hand out to her. He looks even more decrepit today, she thought, and her already shaky nerves shook more.

"Let me get your chair, Miss Callahan," he said in courtly fashion.

"*Ms* . . ." she hissed nervously.

"I apologize, Ms Callahan. I always seem to forget," he said with genuine apology.

Damn! I really had to hear that now! And frustration added to her many other emotions. She forced her body to bend at the middle and her buttocks touched the hard wooden seat. *This is really it . . . my baby . . . this is it . . .* And she felt the prod of tears behind her eyeballs.

Be brave, Cass. For Kristi's sake, be brave.

She turned and saw the comforting face of Angelo Scarpelli staring back at her. The sight greatly pacified her jitteriness and she forced a shaky smile in return.

Then she saw the exact, icy blue eyes of June Scarpelli fastened on her. She fastened her eyes back on her mother, wanting to claw at those eyes for all the infractions past and present.

Damn you, June for creating this misery in the first place.

"Eyes forward Ms. Callahan. The judge is entering the courtroom," her lawyer informed in a hushed tone.

Cassie forced her gaze from her mother and shifted to a man with a heavily-creased though kindly face, looking only slightly younger than her attorney.

"All rise for His Honor, Judge Harvey Kline," the bailiff called out into the courtroom.

Jeez! She stood on even wobblier legs. It's Moulins Rouge, chandeliers, and Miss for sure . . . Can't anything go right?

"Please be seated," the judge directed after he sat. "This court comes to order in the child custody case of Scarpelli versus Callahan . . ." ****

"So what is your point with the little white light, Mr. Johnson?" the judge wearily asked two hours later, after hearing witness after witness talk about the light in Cassie's attic.

Cassie's old neighbor replied immediately. "It's strange, that's all. It's like something *real funny* was going on in that attic."

"And can you be more specific as to what exactly was going on in that attic to come to such a conclusion?" the judge questioned on.

"Never saw. It's tough to peep into an attic," the neighbor replied.

"And illegal, may I add." The judge turned to the court. "I find the topic of the little white light irrelevant to this case, as the testimony has all been vague and purely subjective. Thus, I propose we strike any testimony which refers to such light, and cease from introducing any further witnesses who expound on this topic."

"But your honor . . ." The Scarpelli lawyer immediately objected. "A large share of our case involves the number of hours Mrs. Callahan maintained a near-hermit like status in that attic which would preclude her from properly caring for her daughter."

The judge looked point blank at the lawyer. "Be that as it may, since no one knows exactly what went on in that attic, or even if Mrs. Callahan was actually there in a hermit-like state, as you call it, the evidence is purely hypothetical. So, objection overruled." He turned to the court reporter. "Strike out all the testimony from the last forty or so witnesses."

Oh joy! Cassie happily clutched her widely smiling attorney's arm.

"Now that we've settled that, you may call you next witness," the judge directed the Scarpelli attorney.

"I'd like to call the child's grandmother, June Scarpelli . . ."

****

Cassie felt like an animal needing to attack while listening to her mother's cruel, calculating putdowns.

". . .So, Mrs. Scarpelli, you're implying that your daughter actually became violent when you confronted her about her writing?" the judge closely questioned.

"Most definitely," June replied.

"Would you describe these violent behaviors you witnessed?"

"Absolutely!" June glared at Cassie. "She screeched that I didn't love her, nor her father either, and said we were using her for our own gain . . . after all we did for her."

The judge gave a tired sigh. "Mrs. Scarpelli, I don't qualify a screech as violent."

June lost a shred of composure. "It was her look . . . like . . ." And her eyes directed at Cassie. "A look like she's wearing now. Like . . . she wants to fly over the table and claw me."

Instantly, Cassie forced her lips into a bright smile and focused this square on the judge. He gave a slight smile in return.

"Mrs. Scarpelli." He turned back to June. "I see no violence in your daughter's face, so if you could be more specific?"

June grew visibly more nervous. "It's just that she wouldn't listen to her father and I. We told her, and told her, that she *must* give up the writing for her own good, and she refused . . . after we told her that she must."

The judge lifted his glasses and rubbed the bridge of his nose. "So in essence you're peeved because your thirty-two-year-old daughter wouldn't do as you say. Am I correct?"

"No--that's isn't solely it!" June disputed hotly. "She doesn't do anything fruitful with her life. She merely taps on a computer all day to no end, and the money she's wasted . . . the woman has no talent, and yet she continues ruining lives, including her own. To me it's nuts. I'm fully convinced she been mentally ill for years."

"Are you a psychiatrist, Mrs. Scarpelli, to make such a serious accusation?"

"I'm her mother!" June flashed her frosty eyes at the judge. "A mother is more astute than a psychiatrist for God's sakes."

"You didn't answer my question, Mrs. Scarpelli."

I love it! Cassie thought delightfully. She would send the judge a dozen roses for making June sweat like a pig and croak like a frog. It was the best entertainment she had in her whole life.

"Don't you, a man of distinction, think that a person writing all day, day in and day out, is crazy?" June asked weakly.

"I'm not on the witness stand, Mrs. Scarpelli." The judge glanced at Cassie. "But if you're asking me personally, I find it no more obsessive than one who devotes their life to art, music, business . . . a variety of things."

He's brilliant! He stabbed the witch right in the throat, Cassie thought with more delight.

Then, her delight only heightened when her father, uncles, aunts, cousins took the stand and the judge crushed every single damaging testimony. She began to plan all the things that she and Kristi would do together once they were reunited.

". . .Mr. Scarpelli, that's ridiculous!" The judge fisted the top of his desk. "You have no proof that the box she mailed at the post office contained . . ." The judge hoarsely cleared this throat. "Vampire-killing spikes."

Cassie broke out in silent, gleeful laughter.

"The Postmaster said so," her Uncle Vince challenged.

"Next, I suppose you're going to tell me that the Postmaster has X-ray eyes."

"Well . . ."

The judge turned to the Scarpelli lawyer. "I'm done with this witness and any others that dare mention that stupid box again."

The uncomfortably pulled at his shirt collar. "That's all of our witnesses."

"Good," the judge muttered then he checked his notes. "We'll hear from the child's court guardian Mrs. Jacobsen . . . ?"

****

"Mrs. Jacobsen, I've told you over and over, the lack of a job does not make a mother unfit, and . . ." The judge looked over his glasses to check his notes. "I have a notation here that states the child's great-grandfather has agreed to pay over and above what the father sends in child support." He glanced over at Cassie's attorney who stood immediately.

"Yes, that's true your Honor. Mr. Angelo Scarpelli will take over financial support of both, so child and mother can stay together until such a time the mother can independently support the child herself."

Cassie veered around and gave her grandfather a bright, grateful smile.

"I love you, Cassina," he mouthed to her.

"Me, too, you, Nono," she mouthed back, then feeling triumphant she tossed a like look in the direction of her parents who, to her utmost satisfaction, looked absolutely nauseous.

". . .But her writings, your Honor, they are . . . how should I say it?. . .quite vivid and bizarre. I've brought along a couple of her books for you to review." Mrs. Jacobsen, Kristi's legal advocate, handed the judge two of Cassie's self-published books.

Totally frustrated, the judge slapped the books down on his desk. "Mrs. Jacobsen, bizarre and vivid are *your* assessments, and even if it's *my* assessment as well, that has no relevance. It would be like saying Mozart is a lousy father because you aren't partial to a symphony he wrote."

"Your honor . . . her descriptions of males are perverted and skewed. I think you need to consider this in terms of influencing an impressionable child," the woman argued.

"All right! I'll review the books, but I warn you Mrs. Jacobsen, that you need to have more conclusive evidence than two books to establish parental unfitness in Mrs. Callahan."

So she expounded on the wonderful traits of Mr. and Mrs. Arturo Scarpelli and compared these to Cassie's less luxuriant lifestyle.

". . .And the child indicates that she desires to stay with the Scarpellis," she concluded.

"I object to that last statement." Cassie's attorney flew out of his seat. "The minor child, and I emphasize minor, is only eleven years old, and lives in an environment hostile towards her mother, as we have seen today. So perhaps the child is confused as to what she really wants."

"Good point, Mr. Helgeson." The judge turned back to the guardian ad lidin. "Have you investigated this possibility?"

"Yes, your Honor," she promptly responded. "The child definitely doesn't want to return home and risk gossip to herself, she tells me."

"Gossip?" He looked perturbed. "Maybe someone should just shoot out that little white light," he muttered.

Oh, he's a gem, Cassie thought, barely able to control the laughter bubbling inside her. She decided that the trial was turning out to be much more fun than she imagined. And in relaxed fashion, she planned how she would redo Kristi's bedroom.

"You may step down, Mrs. Jacobsen, and I will refer to you again if need be." The judge gave a halfhearted wave of his hand. Then he turned to Cassie's lawyer. "I trust, Mr. Helgesen, that you don't have any witnesses that specialize in fairy tales . . ."

****

"So you're telling me, Mr. Scarpelli, that your family made diabolical plans against Mrs. Callahan?"

Angelo snarled at the Scarpelli section of the courtroom. "Yes--I hear them in my living room at Christmas when they think I'm in the cellar getting my blackberry wine."

"And what did they say, Mr. Scarpelli?"

"They say that Cassina is evil." He flashed fiery green eyes. "And they say that they find a way to run her out of town so she no longer embarrasses them."

Cassie felt pangs of hurt shoot through her. *Her own family?*

"How did they propose to do this, Mr. Scarpelli?"

"With pressure," Angelo sizzled. "They plan to make Cassina crack so she leave Anoka."

"What type of pressure, sir?"

"Bocca da grosso," Angelo replied, "Their big mouths. They plan ways to make other people use their big mouths also, to wear down my Cassina."

"Do you have a more specific reason than embarrassment as to why they would do such a thing, Mr. Scarpelli?"

"Pecora nera," he hissed at the Scarpelli group. "Black sheep. They call my Cassina this. They say she's invisible to all of them."

The judge paused to rustle through his papers. "This is all interesting, Mr.

Scarpelli, but all it implies is the family's hostility towards Mrs.Callahan, and as her attorney pointed out, we've already seen much of that here today. I see it as having little bearing on this custody hearing."

Angelo tossed a tender look at Cassie, then he turned a plea to the judge. "She's Kristi's Mama and she love the girl. Kristi belongs with her Mama. There should be no other arguments."

"But unfortunately there are, Mr. Scarpelli." The judge sighed heavily. "So I have to take into account all of them, no matter . . ." He loudly cleared his throat. "The outrageous aspect of the arguments."

"I *comprendere*, Your *Onore*," Angelo replied, but his face indicated that he didn't understand any of it.

"You my step down, Mr. Scarpelli . . . Now if we may hear from Ms. Callahan . . ."

****

I feel like an aristocrat in a 1790's French court with the impoverished masses watching.

Cassie eyed all the contemptuous looks from the Scarpelli side of the courtroom.

"So you've made no money thus far from your writing, Ms. Callahan?" the judge questioned.

"I've made some," she replied. "Well . . . actually a pittance, but I'm hopeful."

The judge peered over his glasses and read a piece of paper in front of him. "Your attorney has provided me with a sworn affidavit from an Associate Professor of English at the University of Minnesota which states that ten years is not an unrealistic time frame for a serious writer to establish himself/herself, and that a full-hearted attempt does take several hours a day. So, it seems that according to this expert, you're not out of the ordinary."

The encouraging words gratified her. "Thank you, Your Honor. Gracie."

"But . . . I do have a concern about the child's welfare in lieu of your need to put so many hours into your work so your success is possible," he firmly told her.

"Yes I know," she rapidly responded. "But understand, Your Honor, there were circumstances inside that house which made me to write maniacally."

"And they were . . ."

Feeling unnerved by what she must reveal, she shifted to the belligerent faces in the Scarpelli section, then to her grandfather who was smiled assuredly. Finally, she lowered her eyes to waxed tile floor. "It was my marriage. I. . . couldn't stand to be around my husband, so . . . writing was my refuge. But now, with my main problem gone. I feel that I can more easily break away from my work and give Kristi the quality time that she needs. I love my daughter very much." Her voice shook with all the emotions she felt for her beloved child.

"All right Ms. Callahan . . ." the judge began with gentleness. "I think I've heard enough of your testimony. You may step down."

Avoiding the snarling faces of her family, she descended the stairs and took hasty steps back to her seat. Once sitting, she felt the gentle reassuring pat of her grandfather on the back of her wool-blend suit coat.

The briefly glanced around the courtroom. "The information in front of me states that we are scheduled to hear from a Doctor Peter Pederson."

Shuffling around, Cassie saw the distinguished form of her psychiatrist make his way to the front of the courtroom. She smiled at the sight. He *was* a wonderful, highly insightful man, she thought . . . and also quite helpful, she silently added when thinking how he had worked so diligently to help her understand her attraction to the tortured male.

"Dr. Pederson . . ." the judge started while perusing some papers. "I see here that you've been a psychiatrist in the Twin Cities area for twenty-two years."

"Yes, Your Honor."

"And I see that your specialty is obsessive disorders. In fact, you have conducted much research in this area," the judge continued on.

"Yes--I've worked extensively with the University of Minnesota School of Medicine on projects involving the root of obsessive disorders, and I've had several articles printed in a variety of medical journals, including *The New England Journal of Medicine*," the doctor replied.

"And I see that Mrs. Callahan has been a patient of yours . . . ?"

"I've seen her a total of five times over the last month," the doctor replied, then explained further. "Initially, it was for a psychiatric evaluation per request of her attorney, but after that initial evaluation, we found it necessary to keep going with the therapy."

"And why was that?"

"Mrs. Callahan requested more visits so that she could come to a more greater understanding about her obsession, and I concurred after reviewing the notes I made at that initial evaluation."

"Obsession?" the judge asked closely. "Would you please expound on that statement."

"Simply . . . it's her writings," the doctor replied.

What? Cassie filled with total disbelief. He had *never* voiced such a thing to her, she panicked. Then this feeling grew when seeing the judge intensely crinkle his brows, as if highly interested in the doctor's words.

". . .And it's not the writing, per say. From first-hand experience I understand the tedium of writing, and the hours it involves to do this effectively. Rather, it's the contents of her writing. It seems to have a universal theme of male submission and a need to punish and torture the male with her words, as if she's punishing something more tangible in her life, a person for instance."

"A person?"

"Like a husband, or . . . a father."

Unable to take anymore of the unjust assessment, she leapt to her feet. "Liar! We were just doing it for fun, for my enlightenment to make me a better writer!" she cried out.

"Sit down, Ms Callahan!" the judge ordered in a strict tone.

The gentle yet firm hand of her attorney pulled her back down into her seat. She experienced a numbing sensation, like a nightmare swirled around her with no means to wake up.

"And why would you conclude that these two tangibles were possible roots to her obsession?" the judge questioned.

"Her husband is obvious," the doctor replied. "She felt forced into the marriage, then felt impotent to escape. This impotence created many resentful feeling in her, that she couldn't voice outright, so she wrote them down in magnified fashion. It was her way of punishing her husband for placing her in such an inescapable trap."

"Damn you!" Cassie flew up again, feeling the vulnerability of his words, especially when voiced in front of such a highly critical audience.

"I'm warning you, Ms. Callahan. You are to remain quietly seated," the judge said in a firm, pointed voice.

Oh god . . . So badly, she wanted be back in her attic where there was no probing judgement of her. She sat back down and raised her hand to her brow to hide her vincible emotions from those around her.

"Go on, Doctor Pederson," the judge directed.

The doctor continued on. "And I've gathered from our talks, that Mrs. Callahan harbors quite a bit of animosity towards her father, as well. She refers to him as a 'Pompous ass frozen into submission', an 'Italian caricature', and most interesting, an 'Overaged Romeo with a penchant for Swedes'." He gave a light, amused laugh. "Mrs. Callahan does have a colorful way of expressing herself."

"And have you determined what she means by her colorful expressions, Doctor?"

"Vaguely, Your Honor, but I need more time to come to a specific conclusion, which is the case with such deep-seated obsessive origins," the doctor replied.

Deep-seated? Am I really that crazy? She felt none of the craziness the doctor was indicating. It was just her, *Cassie,* like she'd always been from day one. Couldn't he see that?

"So what is your conclusion at this point, Doctor?"

"Mrs. Callahan has an obsessive mental disorder of unclear origin, that needs to be vigorously treated on an outpatient basis, but may need inpatient if it worsens."

"Worsens?" the judge probed.

"Many times the individual may display dangerous tendencies to protect the sanctity of the obsession, if threatened. And . . ." He gazed out at the Scarpelli side. "With all the negative feelings I've heard expressed since I've arrived here, I would say that the chances of this happening are quite high. Though . . ." He turned back to the judge. "Mrs. Callahan is not at this point so extensive outpatient should suffice."

"Are you crazy?" Cassie took a third leap to her feet. Is he mad? Outpatient? Inpatient when she felt perfectly normal? "I'm not one of your laboratory rats, Doctor. I'm me! Cassie! Do you hear me? Me!"

"Ms. Callahan!" The judge gave an insistent pound of his gavel.

The noise made her clamp her lips together.

"I will expel you from this court, if I hear one more interruption. Do you understand?"

"But I need to defend myself, against this . . . this quack!" she insisted back.

"Sit! Now!" he commanded in a no-argument tone.

She felt the urge of her attorney's hand as it grabbed her jacket sleeve, and she angrily thrust her bottom back onto the chair. As she did, an intensifying panic consumed her. The judge was eating up every cockeyed word—she just knew it.

"So in terms of this case, Doctor, what is your expert assessment?" the judge asked.

The psychiatrist paused only briefly. "My opinion is that Mrs. Callahan needs extensive therapy and should not tackle the rigors of motherhood until she's better."

No! Her mind screamed, feeling like she was viewing the courtroom in slow motion. She drifted her eyes to the Scarpelli side and saw the scoffing, jubilant faces. And then, feeling like pieces of a ruined building were dropping around her, she viewed her mother's face. It looked cooly victorious, as if she, Cassie, had said 'uncle' a thousand times.

The sight was intolerable.

And shortly thereafter she felt the spin of her surroundings . . .

****

All the shades in the house were pulled, dust coated the furniture, the carpet was dotted with small bits of debris, uneaten food was scattered along the kitchen counter, and Cassie was still asking, *Why?*

"Cassina, I bring your mail."

Sitting cross-legged on the living room carpet, Cassie raised her eyes when hearing the comforting voice. Her vocal cords felt paralyzed.

"It's been two-an-a-half weeks since you get the judge's decision. You need to snap out of it, Cassina," Angelo Scarpelli pleaded.

"Why did you force me to go to him, Nono?" she whispered.

"Dolente," he replied. "I'm sorry. We had no idea he would turn on you Cassina. Mr. Helgesen say that his report only said your writing wasn't *Occeessione*."

Obsession! She wanted to rip the word to bits.

"And Mr. Helgesen says we can appeal, Cassina, after . . ." He hung a sorrowful head. "You get the psychiatric help the judge ordered before you can see Kristi."

"I won't," she said woodenly, feeling nothing except the void of immeasurable loss.

"You must, Cassina. The judge say so. You must do it for Kristi."

"No . . . not after . . ." The tears started again and she couldn't finish.

Angelo tossed the mail on the end table and encircled her in his large arms. "Please Cassina . . . you must find the strength to do the right thing."

Her tears flowed harder. She hated his insistence on this matter. "Do you think I'm crazy too? Do you Nono? Do you?"

"No, Cassina," he replied immediately. "But the judge . . ."

"He doesn't know me. Me, Nono! There's a difference. I wish you could understand that," she sobbed with utter misery.

"I cannot *comprendere* . . . your child, Cassina, your child . . ."

"So you're saying that you don't like me."

"I no say any such thing, Cassina. What kind of *nonsenso* do you spew?"

"You'll let those vultures get a hold of me, and change me. Is that what you want, Nono?"

"They are Doctors, Cassina," he spoke soothingly. "They do not change; they help."

She angrily untangled herself from her grandfather's arms. "So you think I *do* need help, a brand new Cassie Callahan, because that'll be the pay off, Nono."

He spoke with an underlying impatience. "What pay off? I see no pay off except getting little Kristi home where she belongs."

"The pay off is my mode of survival in the world. All will be lost . . . I'll be lost."

"I don't know what you say, Cassina."

She saw the confused shake of his head, and a horrible sadness filled her. He was the closest person in her life right now, and if he didn't understand . .

"I get your mail, Cassina." Angelo quietly moved to the end table and scooped up the letters. He squatted in front of her and held out the stack.

She pushed his hand away. "You open them, Nono. I have no strength."

With a nod, he slowly opened each envelope. Silently, he stuffed every bill in his jacket pocket. The junk mail, he ripped in half and tossed into a pile on the carpet. The store ads he stacked into a small pile to the side of him. And then she saw the familiar gold envelope, her body crumpling at just the sight. Regardless, she fixed on her grandfather as he opened the envelope.

He read quickly, then she saw the slump of his shoulders. "They say 'no', Cassina."

She felt the bitter weight of his words. "*Why* this time?" she half-cried, half-demanded. "Tell my why 'Harry' stinks this time!"

Angelo looked down at the letter. "They say that your story idea has merit, but their client load is filled at present."

"Filled? That's a new slap in the face!" she seethed with acrimony. "Is there no place for Cassie Callahan?" Tears exploded on her cheeks.

He fastened a tentative look on her. "There's another one, Cassina." He nodded down at the second gold envelope. "Maybe we should save it for another day."

"Maybe we should just rip it up!" she yelled. "Go ahead, Nono. Its junk mail anyway!"

"No Cassina, I cannot do that." Without delay, he slid open the top of the envelope and paused. "Are you sure this won't upset you?"

"Upset me?" She screeched. "How could this ever upset me when every bit of my heart and soul is eaten away by eleven years of 'no'? They might as well just send a carving knife in those envelopes and be done with it!"

"I will save it." Angelo began to stuff the gold envelope into his pocket.

His action inflamed her. "No! You will open it, read it, then cut out the last of my heart!"

Nodding with resignation, Angelo pulled out a white letter three pages long.

What the . . . She blinked, thinking her eyes were deceiving her.

"Cassina . . ." Angelo breathed out. "It's from a man in Chicago. He say he read *The Life and Times of Harry Hannigan*." Angelo looked up at her. "Did you send this man your book?"

She grabbed the stapled letter, and felt the shake of her body while reading the header. "It must be the fourth manuscript I sent out in December. I forgot all about it with the hoopla."

"He likes it Cassina, very much, he likes it."

Oh-my-god. She forced herself to read. He had been trying to get a hold of her by phone, it said. But he never received an answer. It must have been recently, she thought. She had refused to answer the phone in her desire not to talk to anyone.

"He thinks the manuscript has potential with revision. Oh Nono! He's having an editor carefully go through it so I have some direction. And then, he wants to see it again." She felt the emotional tremble of her voice as she said the coveted words.

"What are the other papers, Cassina?"

Quivers coursed down her fingers, while she looked at the other two pages. "The first is agency guidelines for submission of manuscripts and . . ." She quickly down the third sheet, and a spark of joy touched her. "It's a sample contract that the literary agency sends out to its clients. Oh Nono, I wish it was real."

He tenderly grasped her shoulders between his hands. "Well then make it real, Cassina."

She was warmed by the encouraging words. "I'll give it my best shot, Nono, I swear. I'll do anything and everything not to blow this chance."

He gave the shoulders a small squeeze. "Now tell me . . . who is this man?"

"Quickly, she moved her eyes down the cover letter. "His name is Ferris Mitchell, and . . . he says to call him at my earliest convenience . . ."

Chapter 9—Jack

Legendary Sunset Boulevard, the few blocks parallel to Hollywood Boulevard which geographically, and in a figurative sense, terminated into the limits of Hollywood was packed with tourists, taking pictures with their 35 mm's or video cameras, and carefully looking around, possibly with the hope of catching a glimpse of a famous face.

In a well-kept colonnaded building, close to KTLA, the television station made famous by Gene Autry, with the geodesic roof of the Pacific Cinerama Dome in view, Jack Torelli stood looking out the expansive window in Harv Wellson's office, drifting his eyes to the people in flashy Bermuda shorts, tropical patterned shirts, and various colors of tennis shoes, as they passed below his gaze. They look so damn corny, he thought, aliens from another world.

"I'm ready to talk now, Jack," Harv said.

Jack turned and saw Harv hastily collecting papers from his desktop. Were those legitimate television and movie contracts? He wondered, stabbed with envy at the mere possibility. But he decided not to ask, and made his way to the padded armchair across from Harv's desk.

"Sit Jack. Can I get you something? Coffee maybe?"

How about a saber to cut my throat, and avoid the pussyfooting.

But he didn't say it.

Like it or not, he still needed Harv, now in the worst way.

"I read the trades this morning." Harv gave an amused chuckle. "They can't seem to get off their 'fish' jokes, huh Jack?"

Jack felt the broil of his anger. "Yeah--those goddamn maggots have a one-track mind."

"No doubt. *Jungle Love* has been the highest grossing porn film ever made and that fact attracts the maggots like flies." Harv settled his slight frame back in the chair that looked bigger than him. "You should be proud, Jack. You made film history."

Yeah--proud as hell, he thought cynically, thinking back to his four months of hell since the film's release. It had been crack after crack, humiliating article after article, all focusing on one thing. And now, he thought he should just cut the damn thing off and hang it up for the world to see, laugh at, and interview, because that's what it's finally come to after Rud's "grand baby."

"You're famous, Jack. You should be basking."

"Oh yeah?" He bore his dark eyes into Harv. "Then why didn't I get the lead in Rud's new production. Huh?"

Without delay, Harv shuffled the papers that he had moments ago straightened.

Feeling like a predator, Jack just waited.

Finally the sound of paper rustling ceased. "From what Rud tells me, he just needed a more youthful face for that part—view it as a creative decision," Harv replied.

"Creative? Is that a goddamn joke?" he flared angrily, then reminded himself to play it 'cooler' despite his desperation. "C'mon Harv, what kinda 'creative' is needed for that smut?"

Harv shrugged. "Rud seems to think there's a creative aspect."

"Yeah--he would," Jack muttered, while scene after scene of *Jungle Love* replayed in his head. *That* was a shining example of Rud Hanna's creativity, he thought, wanting to puke at the injustice. The 'skin' had made Rud the 'King of porns' while truly talented producers didn't get one-tenth the publicity for their efforts. The injustice of Hollywood: *Money gotcha everything.*

"Anyway Jack, I don't know what you're beefing about. Your role is pretty decent size," Harv reasoned. "It'll pay the bills and get you a few necessities.'

Jack burned with intense resentment at all the evasive answers he was getting from Rud, Harv, all of them. This was his third secondary role since returning from the Cayman Islands, and the little 'gifts', that Rud had so once easily dispensed, were tapering off. He strongly sensed that something horrible was happening and it was damn scary. "What's going on, Harv?"

"Going on?" Harv's hand crept to the paper pile and began to shuffle. "Nuthin's going on, Jack. It's . . . just the roles cropping up in Rud's stable. Guess they all need an actor a little bit younger. Nothing personal."

The hell it isn't . . . He drifted his eyes down his front. Where had he gone wrong when he went to the gym faithfully, roasted in the sun like a plucked chicken, and kept his skin taut with a variety of creams and oils? *I'm only thirty-eight for Christ sakes.* And he told himself this wasn't happening to him. *Calm down.* He was blowing a few lousy roles out of proportion. "Yeah, nothing personal, Harv," he finally said. "You said you needed to see me about something?"

"Yeah, Jack" Harv quit shuffling and resumed his leisurely chair pose. "Rud has a few more requests."

"Requests?" He could barely get the word out.

A smile played on Harv's lips. "Actually I view it as a pleasurable request. It's Nadia. She's back in the country to do a layout for Male magazine. And Rud wants you two out in public. You know . . . a little perception of Jungle Love, or . . . the real thing if you have the proclivity."

Shit! He inwardly raged at just a mind's picture of the freakish Czech birdbrain. It was bad enough that he had spent nearly a month after Cayman Brac, escorting her all over town to promote Rud's grand baby. She was like a Doberman in heat, and he had to will away every ounce of disgust to portray the public role Rud expected of him to portray with the actress. Now Rud wanted it again, probably to squeeze out a little more stash out of his grand baby, Jack figured.

"Rud said to tell you he made reservations at Le Ivie' for eight o'clock tonight."

"It figures. Put me on display where all of Hollywood haunts."

Harv slid a piece of paper across the desk. "Here's the hotel where the bimbo is hangin' her bra. Rud said to get there a few minutes early. Maybe some reporters on the premises, he said."

He snatched the paper off the desk and read it. "The Beverly Hills Manor . . . looks like Rud loosened the pocketbook for his little Czech dish," he said with caustic bitterness.

"You know, Rud . . . drop a few thousand and reap back millions. That's why he lives at the foot of Bel-Air and the rest of us make do on the fringes. Rud makes prudent investments."

Investments with human blood as the ante, don't you mean, Harv?

And he told himself he hated Rud Hanna with more virulence than he had ever felt for another man in his. But even more so, he hated himself for capitulating to the bastard.

"And Rud said that you know what to do to gain the most exposure. Right, Jack?"

He gave a strained nod of his head.

Harv nervously checked his Rolex. "Getting a little cozy with such a fox, isn't such a horrible request, Jack. Rud says you don't have to lay it on that thick, just enough to get a few tongues wagging. Try to show a little class, Rud says."

"Rud says . . ." Jack leveled his gaze across the desk. "You sound like his PR man, Harv," he said with a hint of flippancy to make it sound like the joke it was far from being.

Instantly, Harv began reshuffling the papers in front of him.

****

I hope this is early enough for Rud, a tuxedo-clad Jack thought with raging anger when, at twenty minutes after seven, he knocked on the door of Bungalow Number Five at the Beverly Hills Manor. Almost instantaneously, the door swung open.

"Darling . . ."

He stared at the garish female form. Then, as was customary, he languidly moved his gaze in a vertical direction. Her dyed blonde hair was pinned up with several showy clips and her eye makeup blared like a neon sign. She wore an expensive silver spangled dress that barely covered her bottom and even more skimpily, covered her massive bosoms. Her long legs terminated in a pair of silver heels with straps that encircled her ankles. P.T. Barnum would have loved her for his Oddity Museum, Jack thought.

"Aren't you going to greet me, Jack?" she asked in crude, broken English.

"Hi," He pushed past her into the bungalow.

"A drink Jack? I had some rum and ice sent up."

The words made him burn with anger, and he thought her an idiot for saying them. He never drank rum in public. Never! Couldn't she figure that out? "No drink." He hissed.

"Perhaps champagne? A little wine . . . ?"

"This isn't a social visit," he replied coldly. "Let's get the hell outa here and start the show so we can end it."

Her lips seductively curved into a faint smile, she made her way up to him. She raised her long, silver-painted fingernails, and delicately brushed them against his coat sleeve. "So you already pant for the end with Nadia, eh Jack?"

The feel of her finger through his jacket felt like sharp knives, and he jerked his arm out of her reach. "No" he breathed out. "I want no part of you that's outa the public's eye. I've had my unfortunate fill of you."

"But Jack . . ." She inched closer until her huge implanted bosom pressed against the breast of his suit jacket.

Possessing the strong sense that his jacket was being coated with filth, he clamped his eyelids together to block out the degrading sensation. "Get away from me," he said in a barely controllable voice.

"You like it, Jack, I can tell." She pressed deeper.

The limp condition of his cock penetrated his brain. He felt an icy cold in the core of his tux pants, as if his naked groin was stretched out on an ice patch with the word *enuch* written on it. "Stop it!" he raged. "Stop it, now!" He pushed her away from him then charged to the door. "I'm leaving with or without you. Capisce?"

A light amused smile touched her lips. "I capisce, Jack, really I do." And then she dashed to a table to get her silver purse.

He turned from the sight of her, and let total misery consume at his body's continued treachery. What if it never ended? He thought desperately. I'm only thirty-eight years old.

What the hell next?

"I'm ready for our show, Jack."

He lifted his gaze to see Nadia expectantly looking up at him. He saw deep purple hue of her eyelids and the preponderance of black around of her eyes that nearly masked the light brown color. So damn gaudy, he thought. Then he shifted his gaze across the rest of her, and repulsion settled in his gut. Plastic woman, not even an ounce of substance, he told himself.

But why should I care when I've never cared before?

Yet he did, and he had no explanation *why*.

"You have a pale look to your face? Are you feeling ill, Jack?"

He let out a low cynical laugh. "Yeah--I feel sicker than hell, if you give a shit."

"Aspirin?"

A harsher cynical laugh. "If only it were that easy." Jack flung out the door and took long strides to the elevator without waiting for her . . .

****

The cooly elegant Le Ivie' restaurant in Hollywood seemed to be the main watering hole for celebrities as well as tourists who stood at the front entrance, waiting for a table, only to be snubbed by the management.

Highly visible in a centralized booth, Jack wanted to evaporate. Ever since arriving with the loud, outrageous-looking Nadia, he felt the gawks and amused whispers to the point of overwhelming humiliation. He anxiously drank a bourbon, desiring to drown in it.

Without warning, he again felt the seductive pressure of Nadia's body against him. He wanted to pounce on her for the continued outlandish display that hadn't quit since they had confronted a group of reporters outside of the Beverly Hills Manor, courtesy of Rud Hanna, he had no doubt. "Smile Jack. Rude expects it," she breathed into his ear.

"Rude expects." He mimicked her Czech accent. "That's all I've heard come out of you. Just get off it for a good ten minutes so I can take a breather, huh?" And then to make his point he scooted away from her and leaned over his drink.

The bourbon glided down his gullet like silk. He relished the mellow, warm, sensation, offsetting the inner chill that hadn't abated since Nadia's display in her bungalow. Go away, he silently pleaded, especially when feeling the chill concentrate in his crotch.

"To be your own man, no matter the price, is the hallmark of a man, Jacko."

He felt the mental pound of his father's words, and this was followed by a sensation of cold as if a thousand ice picks where puncturing him at once, a thousand accusing Torelli fingers.

Without hesitation, he hand motioned their waiter. The mocking faces openly or covertly stared at him. He wanted to lower his head and hide, but the need for the bourbon was greater so he held his pose and looked like he didn't give a shit. The faces of legitimate producers hit his vision, producers he had once worked within better times when Jack Torelli had talent. Their faces said that he was a disgusting joke, and he was stung with a deep hurt, despite his facial attempts to show otherwise. Then, his gaze fell on the booths of legitimate stars and saw the jeering in their eyes. *They* had something better, *clean,* while *Ha-Ha*, he was up to his ass in dirt. And he made more insistent hand signals to the waiter.

"Do you need something, Mr. Torelli?" the waiter asked graciously.

"I need another bourbon, triple this time."

Once the fresh drink sat before him, he resumed his hunched position and sipped, trying to block it all out--Rud Hanna, Nadia, the faces, and the frost glazing his insides.

Then he felt the seductive pressure again. "Your ten minutes are up, Jack . . ."

****

The fettuccine and clams stuck like mush to the roof of his mouth.

Jack tried to swallow the food while Nadia's oversexed body snaked up his sides like she was in the throes of sex. It was the best show in town, he thought miserably, peeking up at the faces that now weren't even being covert in their voyeurism.

"Can't you let me eat," he hissed under his breath at her?

"But Jack, Rude say . . ."

"I don't give a pisser's shit what Rude say!" he yelled louder than intended, and the general noise of the restaurant quieted. He lowered his eyes to white and pink concoction in front of him, and wished it would devour him instead. "Just cool it until I get done eating," he hushed.

"If you insist, Jack," she replied, miffed.

He peeked to his left. Nadia daintily played with her crabmeat salad, placing a tidbit in her mouth now and then, while her seductive smile circled the restaurant like she was the greatest thing on earth. Drifting his eyes down, he saw the subtle gyrations of her body as if openly inviting every man in the restaurant to take a poke.

Revolted by her public display, he returned to his food, deciding to finish it pronto, so he could escape this nightmare. He would be the talk of the town tomorrow—he knew, sure as day.

Fuck you, Rud!

Forgetting his 'Hollywood manners', he slopped down the food between healthy gulps of bourbon. It tastes like bitter shit, *every bite*, but he kept slopping . . .

****

"Well Jack . . . long time no see . . . in person, I mean."

The familiar voice rattled Jack's brain with dread, and he kept his eyes on his plate.

"And who do we have here?" the voice questioned.

He heard Nadia's playful giggle followed by a low male laugh, and the sound made his insides cringe. The inevitable was upon him, he knew. The man wasn't one to snub.

"How are you, Mike?" Jack raised his eyes slowly to absorb the figure little-by-little. He saw the sturdy, medium-sized physique clad in a silk black tuxedo, and the speckled red and white bow tie, looking out-of-place from the rest of the suit, but it was utterly typical of the man. He always wore one piece of clothing that made him stand out to magnify his attitude about himself.

He ascended his eyes to the firm angular chin, always tensed up slightly, and the hawk-like nose, falsely giving him an aristocratic air. Finally came the squinty eyes, as black as his thick dyed hair, without a strand of gray although the producer was firmly in his fifties.

"I came over to congratulate you, Jack. I had no idea that you were such a wonderful fisherman," he said pompously with a large measure of scoffing.

Jack raged inwardly, hating the familiar tone, indicating to the world that he was a notch above. *And the biting words were pure Michael Isle.* Yet he forced a smile.

"I'm glad I made such an impact, Mike."

Nadia jutted out her chest so it expanded over half the table. "So you've seen my great movie, Mr. Isle . . . ?"

"Yes, my dear." Michael Isle peeked at Jack. "Wouldn't be a party without it."

"Undoubtedly," Jack muttered angrily.

"I've seen a few of your miniseries, Mr. Isle . . . dubbed in Czech of course." Nadia's breasts moved as if they had a life of their own.

"Oh yes . . ." Michael let out a malicious chuckle. "My particular favorite was Wind and Fire . . . had a dandy race car scene where the driver lost control and ended up rolling until he ultimately smashed into a wall, his career ended." Another malicious chuckle. "Or to be more specific his life ended. *Morte*, as the Romans say."

I'll kill him. Jack stiffened to repress every murderous feeling. "What do you know . . . that's my favorite too," he replied tightly.

"Not surprising," The producer fastened an exact gaze on Jack. "After all, one's peak is always the most memorable, isn't it now?"

Jack wanted to grab the gaudy bow tie and choke him. But he told himself he would *really* be *Morte* if he tried such a stunt. "Yeah, memorable as hell," he muttered.

"And you, my dear." Michael turned a bright smile on Nadia. "Your canoe scene was memorable as well."

Nadia giggled pleasurably.

"I especially liked the part where that animal slid up from the water and attacked you. The grunts, growls, and screams were pure acting magic."

Another giggle escaped Nadia, and Jack wanted to strangle her too.

"So . . ." Michael leisurely turned back to Jack. "I hear you two are an item of sorts. How appropriate, Tarzan and Jane sans the charming jungle costumes. What a unique way to twist a truly great epic series. I tell you . . . Johnny Weismuller must be doing flip-flops in his grave."

"And Chita too," Nadia purred, looking like she wanted to devour the producer.

Damn her! Now he really wanted to choke her for her idiotic mouth. To Michael Isle's delight, she had fallen right into his trap of degradation.

"Well . . ." Michael absently glanced at his watch. "I better get back to my table. People are waiting, you know."

Good! Get back to your flunkies!

Yet, Jack smiled. "It was nice talking to you, Mike. Maybe I'll see you around."

"Possibly . . . but not likely." Michael's face held a superior quality. "Busy, you know. The world of television miniseries never quits with all the wonderful books potentials out there. And you know me . . ." He gave a low laugh. "I get my hands on every one."

Or take 'em like a greedy octopus, Jack thought, having heard about the producer's methods. Except for being legitimate, Michael Isle and Rud Hanna had a lot in common. *But I don't think the sonofabitch would appreciate the comparison.*

"And you, my dear . . ." Michael casually shifted to Nadia. "That scene on the bed of bamboo will set forever in my mind. Your . . ." His gaze inched to the humongous breasts, clearly outlined through the silver spangles. "Antics were awe-inspiring."

And you can't wait to try them out, you goddamn hypocrite, Jack thought acridly, knowing about the producer's penchant which he hid in a glow of classy elegance that was the best acting in town.

"Maybe we watch the film together and Nadia give you her interpretation." She suggested.

"Perhaps, my dear." Michael tried to sound cooly gracious, but Jack could just picture the two together. And then, as quickly as he had popped up, Michael Isle was gone.

"Important man." Nadia locked on the retreating figure.

"Yeah." Jack also eyed the back of the silk black tuxedo. "It's amazing how the messages in one's mind can be so convincing."

"What?" She curiously shifted to him.

"Forget it." Jack pierced his eyes into her. "You wouldn't get it anyway." He turned to his fettuccine, stuffing the lukewarm tangled mass into his mouth. His body felt frigid . . . *damn frigid.*

Jack knew what he needed, and needed fast.

"Hurry up and finish eating," he hissed at Nadia. "I wanna get this show on the road . . ."

****

Next morning, the gold star-studded Hollywood Walk of Fame on Hollywood Boulevard was packed with tourists when Jack pulled his Corvette into the EMAX parking lot. His eyes hidden under black opaque sunglasses, he dragged out of the Corvette and reeled slightly when upright. His head felt like a zillion cotton balls were packed inside and his throat was parched, despite consuming a gallon of mineral water. He silently cursed himself.

How the hell could you capitulate to the cunning witch?

Everything—Rud, Michael Isle, his cold body—collapsed on him at once. In response, he allowed Nadia to do her worst after the rum, the coke, the pot, and his white plastic friend, the only friend that took the chill away for a little while.

Now he hated himself for letting it happen when he told himself it wouldn't.

He paused to let the sun bask his face. The natural warmth without pretense . . . it was the most positive aspect of Hollywood, he thought. Reluctantly, he turned from the sun and directed his sunglasses towards the pink Spanish-style hotel.

It had a 1920's era artsy facade with its black cast-iron balconies circling every window; except for the top floor where the windows were barred like a prison. The sight churned his stomach with disgust. The bars stood out from the rest of the place, openly advertising what it truly was without a doubt.

And Rud never beats around the bush, Jack thought, shuffling forward like a condemned man heading for the dungeon where he would be tortured and lose another chunk of himself . . . a chunk of his manhood.

Damn you, Jacko . . .

****

Rud Hanna's plain but functional office was filled with the top brass of EMAX studios. The group, starkly contrasted from Rud in an immaculate tan *Armani* suit, was stretched out on a couple well-worn Duncan Phyfe sofas, drinking coffee out of styrofoam cups and munching on *Dunkin' Donuts*.

Unlit panatella in mouth, Rud was perched like a king behind his desk, eyes bugged at the entrance and lips moist with anticipation. "Next!" he bellowed to the production assistant.

Stuffing the last of a custard donut into his mouth, the assistant moved to the entrance door and called out a name. A young man no more than twenty-five, wearing a thin robe, walked into the office. His body grew terror-stiff while he looked at the nonchalant, munching faces.

With calculation, Rud examined the young man's face. The kid was dark—skin, hair, and eyes, looking hungry despite their fear. The final sight pleasured him. His business thrived on both of the looks. The face held an innocent, sensual quality that would take years to toughen. In the meantime, he envisioned the 'skins' . . . oversexed women ravishing innocence. He loved it.

"Ever do any acting, kid?" Rud finally asked.

The young man tentatively approached Rud's desk. He held out a piece of paper neatly folded in business fashion. "My acting credits, Mr. Hanna."

Chomping furiously on the panatella, Rud snatched the paper and sat back in his chair. He quickly scanned the typed resume'. He wanted to laugh. It was so typical.

Rud turned to the face across from his desk, and his own broke out in a smile. "You even had a part on Broadway, huh kid?"

"Yes, a bit part two years ago before I came to Hollywood," the young man replied with a heavy New England accent.

Rud smiled broader, deciding not to even ask the kid why he came to L.A. He knew the answer by rote. "Twenty-six, huh? Looks like you could pass for twenty or even the young one, nine . . . that's a positive quality kid."

A nervous smile crossed the young man's lips.

"So . . ." Rud pulled the panatella from his mouth. "Let's shed the robe and take a look at the rest of you."

The young man's eyes jittered to and fro while he positioned himself directly in Rud's view. The group of men, lazily eating donuts while staring at him, made him hesitant.

"C'mon kid . . . donuts are standard fare around here," Rud said point blank.

Nodding, he shook the robe off his shoulders and onto the floor. Instinctively, his arms encircled his upper body.

Rud rolled the panatella around his tongue while his eyes took in every feature so no flaw was missed. He felt a surge of excitement. The cock was magnificent, almost as much as the one he revered, he thought in awe, just able to see the greenbacks stacking up to the sky. Rud decided the rest of him wasn't bad either, except for his size. The kid wasn't as large as . . . and he lacked the muscles. Easy to rectify, Rud told himself. With all the artificial means, it was *damn easy.*

But that cock!

"You got an agent, kid?"

Eyes slightly dropping, the young man shook his head.

"No takers, huh?"

Another shake.

Rud plucked the panatella out from between his lips and leaned across the desk. "That's okay, kid. I don't like the bastards anyway." He couldn't help smiling at the nervous face. "You can throw the robe back on and wait in the next room. We'll let you know."

Once the door closed, a low laugh ascend from Rud's bowels. "He's gonna be squeamish, but he's perfect," he said to the group. Then he suddenly twisted his head towards the production assistant. "You get him set up, Pero, a snort or two of the prime to kill those jitters, followed by a size forty to zap the rest of his inhibitions. But nothing too heavy. I wanna see that innocence on film. And . . . make sure he signs a contract. Tell him agent Rud Hanna will take him on as a client." He thrust the squishy panatella into his mouth and chomped while his mind whirred with pictures of his new acquisition on the sound stage, making him a pile of dough.

"Yup . . ." He chomped so hard, the slime of his saliva dribbled out of the sides of his mouths. "I do believe gentlemen, that I've found my new Torelli . . "

****

"Cut!"

The cameras on the sound stage of EMAX Studio came to a slow halt, and gradually the room filled with primarily male voices.

Feeling the strain of his muscles, Jack carefully lifted from the actress. She was new, one of the ponies in Rud's new stable of young stars, he thought bitterly, gazing down at the face that looked no older that eighteen.

The sight sickened him.

"That was great, Mr. Torelli." She bounced off the bed like she had just taken a siesta.

She looked natural, free from the wear and tear, without implants or dyed hair, and she was firm without even trying, Jack silently assessed. And then he wondered . . .

"Jack . . . call me Jack," he invited suddenly.

"Carly."

"You like pizza, Carly?"

Her eyes lit up. "I like anything. I practically live at *Tail-o'-the-Pup.*"

He wished he could smile at the spontaneous response, but he felt too much self-revulsion to feel anything else. "I could get you a pizza after we're done shooting."

"You want to buy me a pizza?"

"Any kind you want." He took in every innocent curve of her face. "Even anchovies."

She wrinkled her nose. "They sound horrible."

He couldn't help the tiny crack of his lips. "Then, no anchovies."

"Sure," she nervously bounced in place. "If you wanna be seen with a lousy bit player..."

Watching the familiar jitteriness, he felt even more sickened. For Christ's sakes, Rud, she's just a kid! His mind yelled.

"I'll see you later... gotta go... need some fortification," her voice shook out.

He slid the robe over his shoulders while watching the youthful figure wiggle off the set. Guilt flooded through him. *What's happening to you, Torelli.* And for a moment, he thought about running after her and telling her to forget it. But the cold sensation was stronger than ever, and he knew that wasn't an option.

To be a man for only one night... No, it wasn't even a remote option.

"Hey Jack."

He spun around to see the movie's director standing next to him.

"Go in the back room and take a big hit, man. You were sluggish with that ripe tomato. She had you out-distanced. The next one is even riper. Doesn't look good on the camera," the director said more like an order than request. Then, with a quick pat, he was gone.

Initially, the command made him seethe with anger until the implication penetrated, then a feeling of fright gripped him. The camera doesn't lie. It was the first thing an actor learned in Acting 101, and now, suddenly, he was faced with another major problem—his body's treachery was extending. How long? He wondered, thinking about Carly.

No--it can't be an option. Not now...

****

The pizza parlor in West Hollywood off Sunset Boulevard near the Roxy and Whiskey AU Go Go, and a mile from Jack's apartment, was neither trendy nor exclusive, rather small, non-descript, and filled with biker types. Although despite the restaurant's obscurity, Jack had dubbed their pizza some of the best he ever ate.

"I was a 'smack' baby, so my future was mapped out from birth." Carly ripped off pieces of pepperoni and popped them into her mouth. "So this was *the* career choice for me unless I wanted to waitress somewhere like this. And of course, the supply is endless."

Jack slowly chewed his pizza while he listened to the girl flippantly describe a heartbreaking life. Which was bound to get even more heartbreaking, he thought, stabbed with guilt.

"It's not so bad." She drizzled a string of mozzarella into her mouth. "I get smack and a little money, and all I gotta do is my favorite activity. Sounds like a chic life, huh?"

Speeding up his eating, he didn't respond. He had no desire to get caught up in the tragedy of her life. He had one agenda, and one agenda only.

"So, what got you into the 'skins'?" She boldly tossed her wild brown curls.

The question took him off-guard. Everybody in Hollywood knew why the once famous Jack Torelli ended up in Rud Hanna's stable. "My business, kid," he replied simply.

"I'll respect that... so... I s'ppose you wanna fuck."

Jack saw a knowing smile play on her lips. "Sure--why not?" He tried to be nonchalant despite the trepidation compressing his gut. This *had to* work... if young meat didn't do it . . .

"My place is slum status, but if you don't mind . . ."

"No," he said quickly. "My place is only a mile away."

She popped the last piece of pizza into her mouth and washed it down with the remains of her root beer. "Lead me a mile, Jack . . ."

****

A half-hour later, Jack watched Carly shake like a belly-dancer while she took in the sights of his apartment like it was the Palace at Versailles.

"This is *tooo* . . . funky. I'm gonna need a double load to cope," she jittered, cocking her head from side-to-side at the abstract picture of Marilyn Monroe in his living room.

"Take it easy, kid. It's not that great." It was tough to watch her 'smack attack'. The sight only intensified his guilt.

"And that vase . . . makes my eyeballs twirl. I never seen such bright red before."

"Settle down, kid, you're making me jumpy too," he said, irritated.

She began to undo her clothes, tossing each piece willy-nilly around the living room until she stood naked in the center of the room. "Cm'on, Jack. I'm ready to fly in this heavenly place."

For what seemed like forever, he stared at the young body shaking from head to toe. Suddenly he filled with self-revulsion. She's like a sick little girl, his mind berated in horror at how low he had nearly sunk for his own self-satisfaction.

"Get dressed, Carly, no fun and games tonight," he trembled, wondering how long it had been since he had uttered such unselfish words. He couldn't even remember.

"No," she whined. "I wanna fuck the big star, Jack Torelli."

"No way, kid. You need major help."

She began bouncing around the room like she hadn't heard him. "And this statue thing! Looks like a pair of cats doin' it!"

"I said to get dressed, kid."

"And the bottom of this lamp looks like two fat snakes doin' it!"

"What's the matter with you, kid?" Jack asked more than nervously, seeing the bright red flush of her cheeks and clear glaze over her eyes.

"I wanna do it too!" She jumped hyperkinetic from couch to chair and back again.

"I said to get dressed, Carly, right now!" he yelled.

"No! I won't!" she shouted like a petulant child.

"When did you take that smack?" he demanded, moving closer to her.

Lips pouting, she thrust out her forearms. He saw the needle tracks under the carefully applied skin makeup. "When I went into your kitchen to peek. I liked the karma," she sassed.

"You stupid kid!" he yelled right at her.

"Look who's talking!" she yelled back at him. "I don't see you mincing on the coke!"

"Why you little . . ." He lunged forward, wanting to slap her brazen little mouth. But he stopped cold when getting a closer look. A fine tremor racked her whole body and her head twirled like her neck was unstable. And her face . . . it didn't look right, almost zombified, in fact. He was suddenly filled with fear.

"I'm taking you to a hospital, kid. You don't look too well."

"No!" she bounded off the couch. "I'm not going back to that place with the snoopy, grabby doctors!"

"What place, Carly? Tell me?" he asked in frantic tones.

"That place I left!" She screamed so loud the walls shivered. "Now fuck me dammit!"

"Where did you leave? Runaway? Did you run away?"

"I gotta wee-wee." She agitated like a penned animal.

The sight set off warning bells inside him. "How old are you?"

"What do you care?" she answered anxiously.

He pressed closer to her. "How old, I asked?"

"Nineteen."

"Bullshit!"

"Then I'm eighteen." She jittered a look left and right.

"Liar . . . how old?"

She hugged herself and screamed. "Sixteen! Who the hell cares?"

"Christ Almighty!"

"Don't tell Mr. Hanna, Jack. You promise? He thinks I'm twenty."

"The hell I won't!" he raged at her. But of it was self-directed. *I screwed a sixteen-year-old in living color . . . !*

"I'll do anything if you don't tell, Jack." Her shivering body moved nearer to him. "The smack . . . you know I need it."

"I'm taking you to a hospital, Carly. Now get dressed and no mouth," he said as firmly as his shaky insides would allow.

"But I'll die there, Jack," she whined like a small child.

He shook his head at her. "No kid, you'll die if you don't go. At least this gives you a chance. I gotta give you this chance."

"Can I go wee-wee first?" she whimpered.

"Take your clothes, kid, the bathroom's next to the kitchen . . ."

Impatiently standing by the front door, Jack held his Corvette keys ready to leave, but Carly hadn't emerged from the bathroom yet.

"Cm'on kid!" he yelled. "I don't got all night!"

He heard no reply, so he yelled again, then again.

"Shit!" He stormed up to the locked bathroom door and pounded on it. "Get out here, Carly! You don't gotta look like Madonna for Christ's sakes!"

There was no reply, so he placed an ear to the door. He heard nothing. Suddenly his whole body collapsed in terror.

"Carly!" he yelled and pounded until he was in a total panic. "I'm breaking down the door! Now!" With all his strength, he heaved against the door until it flew open. He stopped cold.

Jesus H. Christ . . .

He stared at the naked form on the floor. Beside it was an empty needle and syringe. Feeling the numbed shock of his body, he inched forward until standing over her. His legs wobbled as he squatted to her side. He willed himself to grab her limp arm and his fingers trembled from base to tip as he felt for a pulse. Unable to detect one, he frantically moved his fingers over her wrist. No thump. It was as still as the rest of her.

He dropped her arm and placed an ear to her open mouth—he could hear nor feel anything. A disbelieving horror gripped as he forced himself upright.

I can't deal with this . . . I can't . . . I can't.

He gripped the walls as he made his way out of the bathroom. When outside, his eyes drifted to the phone and he tottered towards it. He jittered the receiver to his ear, then shook a finger to the number panel. It took several attempts to get the number right, but finally the ring of the phone perforated his numbness.

And then the familiar voice did likewise.

"Harv . . . I need help . . . my apartment . . . dead . . . dead kid . . ."

Chapter 10—Cassie

It was two days short of the Fourth of July and the sounds of firecrackers permeated the attic continuously, unnerving to a greater degree, an already frantic Cassie Callahan who sat in a collapsed state at her computer

At least it's soothingly cool.

A portable air conditioner, courtesy of Angelo Scarpelli, now graced the attic so Cassie could work on her manuscript without feeling like a damp dish rag. She greatly appreciated the gesture as it seemed like she had no time to pause for even sweating.

Revising has reached a new level.

She hastily reread the last scene she had just revised for what seemed like the umpteenth time, and felt desperation seep through her. Will Ferris Mitchell like it or tell me it's too distant again? More desperation. Does it show Harry's point of view? She paused to read the entire scene again. Did I feel the plot moving along? She wasn't sure, so she read it yet again.

I feel something, but I don't know if it's what I'm supposed to feel.
Will Ferris feel something different?

And she racked her brain for the answer. Finally, frustrated, she deleted the entire scene.

Oh damn. I wish I had him on my desk via closed circuit TV

She gently fingered the crown of her head, feeling every minute of her twenty, twenty-one hour writing days. Life had become computer hell. She heard the tap of the keys in her scant sleep, while she chewed on her meager meals, when she bobbed her head under the shower, *and now*. And the worst, was the proud feeling she always felt when mailing her newly revised manuscript to Ferris Mitchell in Chicago, only to have it returned ten days later with more revisions needed. It sure zaps one's pride in the bud, she thought. And even worse, was the fact that it had yet to hit the hands of a publisher where, she feared, it would be *tap-tap* all over again.

Who in the hell was the idiot who said that writing was glamorous?
...*Me, that's who.*

Letting out a tortured groan, she placed fingers to keys.
Can I stand it? Ready ... Set ... Go!

A split-second later, the *tap-tap* tapped through her ears like Bo Jangles ...

****

"Now I feel it. Most definitely, I feel it," she said with conviction, three hours later after rereading the revised scene six times. Then she paused. *But will Ferris feel it?*

Cassie gnawed about this. Even if he feels it, will he think it's tight enough? She picked up a pencil and gnawed some more. *He always says you're an adverb disaster area ...*

She reviewed the scene yet again and this time, counted all her adverbs. Twelve for two-and-a-half pages. Is that too many? *I wonder what's the standard number of adverbs per page ... ? Maybe I better cut a few ... under ten per three pages.*

She reduced the adverb count to nine. "Now I can feel both 'Harry' and the tightness," she said to the four walls of the attic, and a sense of accomplishment surged through her. "Only thirty-two more scenes to revise. Oh joy!"

Deciding that she had earned a bit of a break, she exited the attic and headed for the kitchen to make a high-carbohydrate snack so her brain could tick for another eight hours or so.

While she stuck two large potatoes in her microwave, also a gift from her grandfather, Cassie thought about her life as it sat now. She had much gratitude for the concentrated effort her writing now demanded as it had taken her mind off most of the heavy-duty emotional events that surrounded her.

And there had been plenty.

Tears stung her eyes as her mind flooded with the most emotional event of all . . .

****

"Don't you love me anymore, Mom?" Kristi's teary voice said through the phone line during one of her 'sneaky' calls home.

The question shredded her heart with guilt. "Of course, honey. I love you very much."

"Why are you being so stubborn, then? Grandpa says I'll be here 'til hell freezes over, because you'll never admit to your mental illness. Is that true, Mom?"

The nerve to say such things in front of an innocent child! She wanted to maul her insensitive parents. "I don't have a mental illness, Kristi. Grandpa is wrong. I. . .just can't go to a psychiatrist. I'm . . . afraid what they'll do to me."

"But I can't see you until you go to a psychiatrist." Kristi's tears accelerated.

"I'm hoping there's another way, honey."

"What?"

"I don't wanna say, yet. But I swear, your mother's got another solution in the back of her mind. It may take a while though."

"How long?" her little voice pleaded.

" I don't know for sure. Are they treating you all right?"

There was a pause. "I like the housekeeper. She practices soccer with me."

"Yeah," Cassie agreed. "I always liked the housekeeper too."

"I miss you, Mom."

"And I more than miss you."

"Living on the other side of the fence isn't all it's cracked up to be," Kristi said sadly. "Even a thousand trips to New England wouldn't help."

"I know . . . I lived through it. Remember?"

****

Tears streamed down her cheeks while removing the soft baked potatoes from the microwave. Harry *had* to score, she thought with desperation. She had promised her daughter salvation and it was imperative she fulfill that promise.

But unfortunately, others hadn't seen the method to my madness . . .

****

"Cassina, I beg you. It's been nearly four months since you got the judge's order. You must comply. Your child needs you," Angelo Scarpelli harped constantly.

"No! I need all my faculties as they are, no interference, no scrambling, so I can get Kristi back home," she replied adamantly.

"What does that mean, Cassina, what?"

"It means, I plan to use my writing as the way to get my daughter back."

Looking totally frustrated, he shook his head. "I still no *compredere.*".

"What's there to understand, Nono? I put may nose even closer to the grindstone and try to find success with my writing. Then I dare anyone to call me mentally ill, even that judge in traitor's clothing."

"But Cassina, writing? It could take another eleven years."

"No," she said with determination. "I can't let that happen, or even think about that possibility. I. . .gotta make 'Harry' a literary perfection. I know I can."

"See reason, Cassina, please . . ."

She firmly shook her head. No shrink would ever make her the topic of an article in the *New England Journal of Medicine*. "Ferris says 'Harry' has the potential to be a wonderful character if I dig beneath the excessive words to find him, and he says my writing voice will be delightful if I better learn how to technically present it for commercial value. So I plan to dig and learn 'til my brain paralyzes into a permanent state."

"This is crazy, Cassina. You're a Mama," Angelo said with tears in his eyes.

"I know." Tears also glinted her eyes. "But I feel in my heart, that this is the right thing to do for all of us."

"Dolente," he said. "I'm sorry, Cassina, but I still no *compredere* . . ."

****

And so he keeps harping . . .

She slathered the baked potatoes with canned chili, sour cream, and shredded generic cheese. She had heard, *and heard*, every reason in the English and Italian language why she *must* see the helpful doctor. She felt like a building that was being erected higher and higher with guilt-filled bricks. He could really lay it on, she thought, bringing her snack to the table.

Then, to add insult to injury . . .

She plopped down in the hot-pink, black dotted kitchen chair and directed her irritation on the cracked ceiling. Her old attorney hadn't been much better with his steady phone calls.

He's chomping at the bit to appeal when there's nothing appealing to appeal . . .

****

"Miss Callahan . . . this behavior is ridiculous. We can win the next custody battle if you show some cooperation."

"Its Ms.! Capital M, small s, period. It's been the proper way to address a single woman for a good twenty years," she replied with bare control.

"I'm sorry, Ms. Callahan, truly I am," he said graciously. "But it's this appeal . . . it's making me more than a little nervous."

"Well rip it up then. No use putting any added strain on your ticker. I would hate to be responsible for . . . never mind . . . there will be no appeal for the time being."

"I beg you Ms. Callahan . . ."

****

And he kept begging until I told him the Moulins Rouge beckons, and hung up.

She tossed large pieces of potato into her mouth and chewed quickly. All of her recollections had made her more desperate. *You gotta get back to Harry.*

Suddenly her chewing stopped cold. *That baby's wail again.* It echoed through her brain off and on ever since she had seen the heart-pounding sight from her front yard, and then was cruelly confronted by it . . .

****

The hose nozzle she used to sprinkle the lawn, suddenly felt like a hundred-pound boulder when seeing a heavier-than-ever Sarie push a stroller past her house. Such insensitivity!

"Hi Cass," Sarie had the nerve to say.

Pretending deafness as well as nonchalance, Cassie kept sprinkling in a manner similar to one lightly sprinkling donuts.

"I said 'Hi', Cass," Sarie had the brash to repeat, then even had the greater brash, to stop by her badly-in-need-of-paint, picket fence.

She sprinkled a little less lightly.

"Don't you wanna see my baby?"

My god. Just stab me in the heart, Sarie.

"His name is Kyle Junior."

And that's even worse. Yuk!

"He's only five months old and already over thirty pounds." Sarie gave a nervous laugh. "Kyle says he's gonna make a football player out of him."

That's all the world needs is another . . . and the mere thought of seeing that 'strut' seventeen years hence, walking off a football field, made her haphazardly swish the hose nozzle across the already saturated lawn.

"Have you see Kristi?" Sarie anxiously popped out.

Cassie abruptly halted her hose antics and let the sadness grip. *It's the most vulnerable thing she could say to me.*

"Kyle hasn't seen her either, though he's tried, but your father . . ."

How dare she call him my father. He's invisible to me too!

"Kyle's talking about going to court to obtain visitation rights, despite . . . Kristi's refusal to see him," Sarie said with much woe.

Do you blame her? She's at that impressionable age. She thinks sex is gross.

And then she heard the baby's loud wail, followed by Sarie's comforting noises.

"Guess I better go, Cass. The baby's hungry, per usual. It was nice talking to you again."

****

I bet he gnaws on baking powder biscuits instead of teething biscuits!

Cassie stuffed potato skins in her mouth, hating herself for resenting an innocent baby. But it was like a physical reminder of Sarie's great betrayal, and she couldn't help it. She wished they would move, or she could move, but neither had the financial resources, she knew. Sarie had lost her job with the real estate firm after all the hullabaloo--so her parents had touted in superior fashion like Sarie deserved it. But Kyle retained his job at the used car lot--or so her parents had screamed, believing that 'Kyle too' should have been given the ax. None of them had fared well. Every point of the infamous triangle had paid a huge price.

Kristi . . .

Her daughter had paid right along with them, she thought with desolation while raising from the chair. *Back to the drawing board.* She *had* to rescue Kristi from June Scarpelli's prison.

I just have to . . .

****

In the final days of August and into the early part of September when the trees were already shredding their leaves, indicating an early winter, Cassie was a basket case while waiting for word on her fourth newly revised manuscript.

In between gnashing her teeth, she worked on 'Harry Two', as she always did during the tense waiting period.

And I've been careful as hell.

She spent all her time going over her already completed fourteen chapters, closely scrutinizing each word, paragraph, and scene, then using her newly acquired knowledge from her many editings to take out every bug, so the tap-tap was minimized with this manuscript.

If the first ever sold to a publisher, she reminded herself.

Despite, she stayed diligent, avoided too many adverbs or fluttery descriptions, and only used narration when it couldn't be shown. Show don't tell. Tell only when it can't be shown, and SHOW as much as possible.

Now, as she reviewed a paragraph, she felt the ever-present flutter of her brain with just the activity. Her right brain commanded her to show while her left brain commanded her to show in a technically correct, tight manner. Oh, it was dizzying!

"With a lithe to his step, and the signed contract in his hand, Harry walked out of the bank. He felt the resplendent warmth of the midday sun on his face. It's an omen, he thought. And now, no one can step on Harry Hannigan . . ." Cassie paused to wonder. Would 'Harry' have a lithe step? She stuck the pencil between her lips and contemplated this question.

The ring of her desk phone nudged her from her thoughts.

Damn! If it's old Mr. Helgesen, I'm gonna pretend I'm the tipsy French maid.

She angrily plucked up the receiver. *"Oui?"*

There was a pause. "Cassie Callahan?" a familiar voice asked, and she widened her eyes.

"Ferris?" she asked cautiously.

"Yes, it's Ferris . . . Ferris Mitchell."

As if I know another Ferris, except for a ferris wheel.

"How are you, Ferris," she jittered?

"I read your revised manuscript, and I gotta say it's getting damn good."

"Really?" She felt the *boom* of her heart against her T-shirt. Then reminding herself to 'play it cool', "I mean, I'm happy you like it."

"I more than like it. That 'Harry' . . . he could be quite a grabber."

The *boom* stopped cold. "Could be?"

"He's got to drive the plot more. The emotions you've created in him are wonderfully powerful. Use those emotions to bring Harry's story from start to finish."

"Haven't I done that? And done that? And . . ."

"Well . . ." He hedged. "Not to its potential, and with this book, I want to see potential."

Seeking Out Harry

"Can you elaborate?" she barely was able to sqeak out.

"Nope--I never elaborate on gut responses."

His damn gut. I wish I could find a way to put the tap-tap in it for an hour or so.

"So I'm sending the manuscript out today with my suggestions."

"And as usual, I'll be waiting with bated breath." She couldn't help the creep of her tongue from between her lips.

"Any questions, Cassie?"

Quickly, she thrust her tongue back into her mouth. "Since you asked, I do have a teensy question irrelevant to this manuscript, if you don't mind . . . ?"

"Go ahead--ask," he invited.

"It's like this . . . Harry has just taken over his second bank, after months of negotiations that have churned up hard feelings and made him a few enemies. So on the day he finally has the signed contract in his hand, would he walk with a lithe to his step?"

He answered immediately. "I dunno, Cassie. You didn't tell me how Harry was feeling at that moment. Angry? Fed up? Triumphant over his enemies? Had a bunion on his foot? What?"

"What?'"

"You know 'Harry' so well. Get into his head, and think! How would Harry Hannigan, at this point in his life, after all the changes he's made, feel and react to this situation. Understand?"

"Yeah--I capeche," she replied, then silently added, *But it's easier said than done no matter how well I know Harry.*

"So get cracking on those revisions. I'm getting anxious to see the finished result."

"You are?" She felt the *boom* again.

"You can do it, Cassie . . ."

Minutes later, Cassie furiously chomped on her pencil while digesting Ferris Mitchell's words. She looked at the computer screen, then digested some more. Finally, she placed fingers to keys, deleted the paragraph, and started over . . .

*

Despite the animosity, the new foes made, and even the sense that a foot bunion was beginning, he victoriously clutched the contract and felt a lithe to his step as he walked out of the bank. The resplendent rays of the midday sun touched his face. It was exhilarating! An omen! He wanted to exclaim to the world. And now, he thought with the sheer joy of a well-deserved triumph, No one in the universe could ever step on Harry Hannigan . . .

*

Yes! I can feel it!

****

Damn! I can't feel a thing.

Numbed with fatigue, Cassie drifted her eyes to the calendar tacked on a rough, saw-hewed wall of the attic. It had been three weeks since she had received her manuscript back.

Thankfully, the revisions hadn't been *too* horribly extensive, and she did have a better grasp on what Ferris Mitchell was asking of her. In fact, it was starting to even come a little naturally. And it was even getting to be a little challenging fun, she admitted to herself. Even better, it was almost ready to be sent back to him.

That must be my revision record.

Yet to get to this point had been a trial. Not only did she look like a personal disaster area that the finest salon in the world couldn't rejuvenate, but she decided that old Mr. Helgesen's body was in far better shape than hers. And then her eating habits . . . she figured *Betty Crocker* would croak and the *Pillsbury* dough boy would blow up.

Ah the price of success . . . Was it worth aged skin, brown hair where blonde used to sit, flabby muscles, emaciation, and destruction of American institutions?

Damn tootin' it is!

And with a determined grit to her teeth, she began to type. The manuscript *would be* mailed out by the end of the week. And then she'd worry about cleaning up the wrack and ruin . . .

****

Four hours elapsed, and Cassie was well into her revisions, telling herself to ignore the sharp, burning sensation that ran down her neck.

And I can add chiropractor to my list of 'dos' after Friday.

A light knock came to the attic door, and she startled.

"Cassina!"

She rushed to the door and opened it. Angelo Scarpelli came into her blurred vision, and next to him was a long, wide box.

"You look terrible, Cassina," he breathed out.

"It's the price of success, Nono," she said flippantly.

He let out with a long string of Italian phrases of which she only caught bits.

"I don't care if I look like Mussolini's mother, or Mussolini for that matter. This manuscript will get out by Friday, Nono."

"This is *logorato!*" he yelled directly at her.

"Crazy or not, Nono, this manuscript hits the mail by eight a.m. Friday morning."

"Ai-yi-yi." He pursed a tight, stubborn look at her. "I have your Nona cook you a seven-course meal *which* you will eat, Cassina."

"Only after Friday, Nono," she said firmly, then nodded at the box. "What's that?"

"*Salvazione*, Cassina," he replied. "Salvation, Cassina."

She twisted her head and read the box. "You bought me a treadmill?"

"A little treadmill so you can get some *escercizio.*"

Exercise? What a quaint idea. But only after Friday.

"I put it right by your desk so there will be no *scusa,*" he said definitively.

Oh, I'll have plenty of excuses up until Friday, she thought just as definitively, helping her grandfather get the box into the attic . . .

****

"So, Cassina . . ." Angelo Scarpelli said an hour later after putting together the treadmill. "Have you thought any more about the judge?"

Cassie eyes scurried across the paragraph she had just finished. "I've thought plenty about him, Nono. But I don't wanna repeat my thoughts in mixed company."

"Quit making light, Cassina. This is serious business," he pleaded. "Little Kristi always looks so sad, so lost. I cannot stand it."

Damn! He's piling up the bricks again.

"She no happy. I can tell, Cassina."

Feeling the guilty weight of his words, she turned from her computer. "Well maybe you should talk to your son about letting Kristi visit her me."

Angelo sadly shook his head. "Arturo is like a mule. He insist that you hurt his business and reputation, and he want to punish you, Cassina."

"It's sick, Nono!" she flared angrily. "He's using my child to punish me. Now you tell me what kind of Papa, *or* Grandpapa, would do that?"

"I fail with Arturo." Tears misted his eyes. "I don't know how, but I fail miserably."

Cassie leapt from her chair to comfort him. "It isn't you, Nono. He probably would have been all right if he hadn't fallen into Swedish territory. That was his downfall, believe me."

"Yes." A slow stream of tears ran down his cheeks. "June is a cold-hearted woman. She ruin Meggie, and she try to ruin you too."

"Yeah, Nono. She tried to ruin me by forcing the psychiatrist issue. My mother wanted the 'helping doctor' to turn me into a clone of her. Do you want another Meg, Nono? Another June? Or do you want Cassina like she's always been?"

"But little Kristi . . ."

"I won't be any good to my daughter any other way than I am now. *This* is the Cassie Callahan that Kristi loves, and I won't give her any less just to appease the judge, that nutty shrink, *or* my mother. And I refuse to risk my career with such a mind-altering experience. I have a right to be me. It's my most basic right."

"Just one little visit and the judge may . . .

"No! I'm not mentally ill, only damn passionate, and I like it that way. I dare anyone to take my passion away from me. I'll fight it with every ounce of will and strength that I've got. And . . ." Cassie felt the familiar painful sting to her conscience. "I won't sacrifice that, not even for my own daughter." She collapsed into sobs.

He tenderly stroked her hair. "I try to understand, Cassina, but no good. She's your child. Your *passione* is secondary. It just isn't right."

"It's right for me, selfish or not. I. . .can't lose myself, Nono. I *have* to cope, more now than ever. I. . .can't have anyone messing with my coping mechanisms. I just can't." She fell, sobbing, against his strong shoulder.

He patted, caressed, and finally spoke resignedly. "Me and your Nona will bring over a seven-course dinner . . . on Friday."

****

Dramatically carved out pumpkins dotted door stoops, leaf piles were aplenty, and what leaves were left on the trees glowed with Autumn brilliance. It was one of the most beautiful times in Minnesota—the glorious color burst before the monotonous white. And Minnesotans let their eyes relish the vision.

Is it still October?

Cassie skirted her eyes over the wall calendar while she briskly walked on her treadmill.

Good! I still have a few more days to prepare the haunted house for tricksters.

And she slowed her steps to plan her booby traps for this year.

Diabolical plan in mind, she jumped off her treadmill. She felt wonderful!

Furthermore, the exercise cleared her head so she could tackle 'Harry Two' with a vengeance.

Positioning herself at her computer, she continued her review of the existing chapters and found herself more confidently making changes. In fact, she was amazed at how her writing insecurities were vanishing with the total feel of 'Harry' inside her. It was satisfying to create a character by the feel of him rather than by distant events surrounding him.

And I want readers to feel the same wonder of 'Harry' as I do.

So she would create the *feel*, not by racking her brain but by letting the wonder flow out of her, and onto the computer screen in a technically correct, tight manner. She loved it! The new relaxed mode had brought her writing to a new level--she could tell.

The ring of the phone interrupted her immersion.

Damn! I swear if it's another tele-operator . . .

"Hello!" she snapped.

There was a pause. "Cassie Callahan?"

She felt horrified. "Ferris . . . how are you?"

"Fine, Cassie. I read your manuscript and I think it's ready to go."

Her mouth went agape. He said it as if telling her the time of day.

"I'm sending you an agency contract so we can try to push 'Harry'."

"A. . .A real contract, not a sample?" She tried to let the shock settle.

"Of course a real one, Cassie," he replied.

"Wait a minute . . ." She dropped the receiver and let out a rip-roaring squeal. Then she retrieved the receiver. "Why that's wonderful, Ferris."

"Don't get too excited. I still have to interest an editor, but my gut feeling . . ."

"What is it saying? Tell me!"

"Nope--I never discuss my gut feelings."

I only go by instinct, she silently finished for him. *Damn that gut!*

"And I need you to send a glossy of yourself, something nice," he spoke on.

She gazed down at herself and wanted to cry. "I suppose a Halloween picture won't do."

His laugh came through the line.

It's no joke, Ferris, believe me.

"No, Cassie, send me a doozy."

She shook a disparaging head. "What else should I do?"

"The only thing you can do . . . wait . . ."

****

The Thanksgiving turkey was just a carcass and the jingly sound of *Jingle Bells* could be heard in stores, restaurants, and schools. Blizzards and sub-zero temperatures were the fare this Minnesota winter, and a full six-months of the white stuff appeared to be in the offing. So it was time to hibernate, stretch out, and relax--nothing else could be done.

Wait . . . Wait . . . Wait . . .

Cassie's mind spewed the word repeatedly while she burned off her jitters on the treadmill.

At least I've firmed up a little. Now I'm a skeleton with muscles.

The timer on the treadmill indicated she was done, so she bounced off the track, and made her way out of the attic to the bathroom. She turned on the faucets to the old clawed bathtub, tossed in aromatic bath salts, then let them blend with the running water while she rushed to the sink. There she cleansed her face with herb cleanser, following this with an herb mask.

She threw off her clothes, then stepped into the steamy tub. She slid down and shut her eyelids, promoting total relaxation so her skin could benefit from the luxurious experience.

What a trial to look beautiful!

Yet, she had no choice when Ferris asked for a glossy. She needed a major overhaul or he would get a doozy all right. So she screamed 'Help' to Angelo Scarpelli, who happily financed her transformation so a photography studio could snap a 'doozy'. His only condition was that she keep it up and never look like Mussolini's mother again, she recalled . . .

"You will be my beautiful Cassina once more, not this . . . this *refugee!*"

"Okay Nono--I'll give it my best shot. I'll fight the urge to work on 'Harry Two' for a couple hours a day, even if it kills me."

"And you will eat . . . six meals a day in your case. I have your Nona send over a freezer-full of pastas, and you are to eat it!" he commanded.

"I'll eat until it's coming out of my ears, Nono."

"And your lovely blonde hair . . . I want to see it blonde!"

"I'll wash it daily, two times a day, if you insist."

"And your lovely skin . . . I don't want it looking like the skin of a fish!"

"I'll treat it like a baby's bottom. No quick once over with Ivory Soap, I promise."

"And your eyes . . . I want to see that beautiful green sparkle again."

"I'll sleep five hours a night if I have to, I swear."

"Okay! I pay to make you *bello* again, beautiful again," he finally agreed.

. . .And the glossies didn't turn out half bad.

She even sent one to Kristi in an envelope without a return address. On the back of the photo she wrote, *This is the image of Cassie Callahan from now on.* And below that, she had post-scripted, *Hold on, help is coming.* But she hadn't elaborated to her daughter. She didn't want to get Kristi's hopes up, only to have to shoot them down. And the same applied to herself, she thought. Everything was so ify, it was tough enough to stay calm, let alone plan a future.

So she tried to maintain, keeping indirect contact with Kristi the best she could, doing what Ferris Mitchell and her grandfather dictated, and in between, she worked on 'Harry Two', now seventeen chapters rich--and she was pleased. The plot was straightforward, fast-paced, and 'Harry' glistened like a newly minted dime.

It's the best writing I've ever done.

And just the thought that even better writing may one day be on the horizon made a prickle of goose bumps creep up her arms despite the warmth engulfing her. And she told herself to lavish in the awesome sensation and dream of better times . . .

****

Feeling refreshed and beautiful after her bath and skin regime, Cassie fluffed out her new wildly layered shoulder-length hair, and headed towards the refrigerator to get one of her Nona's pasta dishes. She opened the small top freezer of her fifteen-year-old *Frigidaire* and vacillated over her selections.

I think . . . it's gnocchi again.

She snatched out the container filled with her favorite Italian dish and popped it in the microwave. Then she cut a slice of her Nona's homemade Italian bread, buttered it, and chewed on the crusty slice while waiting for her gnocchi to heat up.

The jingle of the kitchen telephone interrupted her chewing.

No! I don't want any vinyl siding or triple glaze windows!

She stormed to the phone and flung the receiver off the hook.

"What now?" she demanded.

A low laugh filled the line. "This has *got* to be Cassie Callahan."

Oh no! Just cut my tongue out . . . "Ferris! How are you?"

"My gut was right, Cassie."

She suddenly felt the dizzying whir of the kitchen and grabbed the counter for support.

"Your gut?" she squeaked out.

"Got a taker in New York. He loves 'Harry', with editing that is."

Oh, his blessed gut.

"He'll be getting in touch with you about the editing, and I'll let you know about the contractual aspects."

"A real publishing contract?" she trembled out, feeling such a clog of inner emotions, she couldn't separate any of them.

"It won't be a sample, Cassie," he laughed.

"You mean I did it? I *really* did it?" Her face exploded in tears.

"You did it all right. You're an *author*-to be."

She felt the weight of nearly two years of continuous work collapse on top of her, and the impact belied an upright position. Her buttocks hit the kitchen floor, and she stared, feeling nothing except for wetness flooding her cheeks, chin, and neck.

"And I sent your bio information along with the manuscript. Cute glossy, by the way. I've never seen such big green eyes before. Should look stunning on a book jacket, and you better clear your calendar over the next few months, may be busy, Cassie . . . Cassie? . . .Are you on the line, Cassie . . . ?"

Chapter 11—Jack

Her name was Carly Giraldi, a sixteen-year-old foster child from Elko, Nevada, who had been on heroin since age ten, and in and out of treatment since age eleven. A year ago, she ran away from a treatment facility near Reno and came to L.A . . .
   Child corruptor . . .

The words sizzled like a hot brand on Jack Torelli's brain, in his daymares, nightmares, every moment it had seemed, for the past six months. Despite the attempts of EMAX studios to cover up the tragedy, minimize the civil trial, and maximize Carly Giraldi's existing problems, the press had made moral mincemeat out of him, squeezing out every little sordid detail for all it was worth. And that was just the outside effects.

Inside, what little was left of him prior to the tragedy, has been eaten away bit-by-bit.

His psyche crumbled more each day even though he lived in a new environment, a rented house on La Brea as it had been impossible to stay in the apartment with that bathroom. Every time his vision fell onto the room, his mind would conjure up the grisly picture and a convulsion of tremors would promptly commence. He needed a solitary place where he could settle his mind down enough to begin dealing with the horrific event.

The media circus that ensued, however, precluded much serenity. The story, in their minds, was Hollywood juicy: Naked minor female found dead of a heroin overdose in famous thirty-eight year old porn star's apartment. The implications were obvious regardless of the fact that the L.A. County Coroner ruled it as an intentional suicide and that she didn't have recent intercourse. Nonetheless, the fact she was a minor in *his* apartment, his ultimate aims towards the teenager questionable with his reputation, brought about a civil trial where he was convicted of corrupting a minor, and given a ten thousand-dollar fine plus a hand slap for his immorality.

The press loved it. The conviction was just one more way for them to make Jack Torelli a sleazy pariah in the Hollywood community.

And ten days after New Years, almost six months to the day that Carly Giraldi had been found dead, one of the trades had run an article about the child-corruptor, Jack Torelli.

On that particular day, Jack stood at the sliding glass door in his LaBrea home and stared out at the preponderance of rocks in his back yard. All he saw however, was a wild, strung-out, sick little girl with a wondrous childlike nature despite her immense problems. He *had* tried to do the noble thing, he kept telling himself. Despite, the only picture that would stick in his mind was the initial trap he had set and the bed on the sound-stage where he had committed statutory rape.

But that last bit of information would reside in the private hell of my mind.

The day after the event, EMAX studios went on a slicing frenzy, destroying every inch of film containing Carly Giraldi plus shredding evidence of employment, and threatening the existing stable of stars into silence about the underage teenager. A paranoid Rud Hanna had used all his power to keep the event as hush-hush as possible so not an ounce of recrimination fell on him.

Rud hired the best attorneys for his main star, paid big bucks to Realtors and movers to quickly get 'his star' out of the painful environment, provided media spokesmen who blew up the dirt on the unfortunate teenage girl, and kept 'his star' well-stocked with top quality coke and pot during the initial trying period.

God damn you, Rud.

Jack fixed his gaze on the hundred feet of rock where grass should be. He had convinced himself that Rud Hanna knew all along about the minor status of the girl, even though Carly had indicated otherwise. Thus, was the reason for the studio owner's maniacal cover-up, shedding piles of dough which was a highly uncharacteristic for the man--except in the case of his 'grand baby', of course. And he constantly asked himself, *Who else? How many others? How many more times have I committed statutory rape?* The questions had led to much torture. He hadn't sunk that low, he tried to pound into his culpable-ridden brain. In the name of desperation, he had carried out a multitude of shameful things in his life. *But fucking little girls . . . ?*

"You gotta come to, Jack. Get the damn thing out of your mind."

Jack refused to alter his gaze and view his keeper. Rud had paid Harv Wellson plenty to keep the incriminating Jack Torelli quiet. Rud was well aware of his star's deteriorating mental state, and he feared the truth may be spilled to a Hollywood psychiatrist. Thus, the need for a watchdog. "Maybe I don't want the damn thing outa my mind, Harv."

"Jack . . . it's been three months since the conviction--*minor conviction*, no fucking worse than a traffic ticket--and the kid was dead anyway with her addiction. So why the funeral act?"

Traffic ticket? Fuck you, Harv. She was a little girl, not a Hollywood dispensable.

"Rud says that everything's clean at the studio, and he's got a juicy movie coming up that needs Jack Torelli as the star," Harv pressed.

"Clean?" Jack turned his face part ways. "How many fake ID's did he have to buy, huh? And how many papers did he have to alter? Huh Harv?" He turned the rest of the way to level a piercing gaze at the agent. "Sixteen is sixteen no matter how many trumped up ID's says otherwise. Capeche?" He swung around and refastened his eyes on the back yard.

"Jack . . ." Harv said in a jittery tone. "Rud says they've tightened up employment. They're more careful, believe me."

Believe you? The voice of Rud Hanna? He wanted to rage. But he didn't dare. Despite everything, he still had that passion, needed that thrill—it was only temporarily blunted, he figured.

"Rud wants to know what he can do to get you back into the mainstream, Jack."

"To fuckin' leave me be," he replied, barely controlled.

"How about a few gorgeous women to blur the edge?" Harv offered.

"No," he trembled angrily. "Sluts are the last kind of help I need."

"But it's been six months, Jack. You must be as tense as a wire."

He could feel his shriveled up manhood. It had been lost on that bathroom floor, and he possessed no strength to regain the carefully induced little he had. It just seemed too tedious.

"You're a mess, Jack. I can see it from. Take a snort, boy, and try to calm down."

"No," he snarled while the shrieking words of a child rolled through his head.

"I don't see you mincing on the coke . . ."

"Cm'on Jack . . ." A shaky laugh emitted from Harv. "That's ridiculous. A little bit of the shit goes a long way to do a great job."

He filled with bitter cynicism. "I bet Rud says, huh?"

"Jeez, Jack," Harv began nervously. "You've been in the business for five years. You know what needs to be done."

"Verbatim . . . Porn 101."

"So what's your beef?"

Who the hell knows? Who the hell knows anything?

"Maybe you should just read the script, Jack. It may get your juices pumping."

"And maybe I should just leave." He flung around and snarled. "Maybe I should just get away from the public massacre that no one can stop, the conviction that's eating away at me, the slime, you, and especially from what 'Rud says'!"

"Where?" Harv jittered cautiously. "Up the coast?"

"Sure," he replied with heavy sarcasm. "Up the coast is probably delighting in this Hollywood tidbit. I can just see what life would be like 'up the coast'."

"Not, New York . . ."

Jack felt his insides rip apart. His family *must have* heard, and knowing this had devoured his soul. He was merely Jack, *not Jacko*, just Jack, as he knew that he would never be a Torelli again in any sense but the legal sense. His journey into hell had turned unforgivable.

"Well Jack? Do you need a few days in the 'Big Apple'?"

"No," he trembled. "Far away from New York. I don't belong there anymore, Harv. I'm in Hollywood for life."

"Where then, Jack? Rud will pay--I know this. Anywhere you want."

"Cayman Brac . . . I wanna go to Cayman Brac," he said, despite hating to take charity from Rud Hanna. But he had no choice. Six months of unemployment had taken a *real* heavy toll on his bank account. *Anyway*, he silently justified, Rud owed him plenty for creating the problem in the first place and ruining the minuscule shred of decency he had so tightly hung onto.

****

Green feathery babusso palm fronds swayed, and their tall woody stems mildly bent, in the balmy sea breeze that blew across the golden sand. The secluded beach, directly outside of Jack's sequestered bungalow in Cotton Tree Bay, was located on the other side of the island from where *Jungle Love* was filmed. He needed no reminders—he just needed peace.

Cayman Brac had been like a sanctuary.

He stared at the turquoise sea through black opaque shades, relishing the feel of the heated sand penetrating the bottom of his light shorts and the glorious sun rays that beat down on his bare back and neck.

I could stay here forever and be content.

The revelation startled him. Only Hollywood ever held his absolute contentment despite everything. Yet here . . . he could leave all the degradation behind and pretend.

In fact in the last four days, he had pretended a lot. The tranquility of the island seemed to bring out thoughts of his childhood on Mott Street which he analyzed to the point he heard the play of lost moral voices. As a result, he kept asking *why*, tacked onto every conceivable question that applied to his present life. To every question, cropped up the same answer:

It wasn't supposed to be like this.

But the *how* to change any of it now, was beyond his ability to figure out. He was in a hole of his own making long before the porn, he told himself. As a result of the latter, the hole was getting deeper while conversely, the means to escape getting more remote.

He had no clue how to make the ascent.

The tropical breeze faintly caressed his hair and face as he watched the turquoise waves flow and retract. He felt like he was ascending a little here, in Cayman Brac, while Carly Giraldi, the EMAX sound-stage, Rud Hanna, and Harv Wellson were left at the bottom of the hole.

It was a comforting illusion.

"Mr. Jack . . ."

The upbeat voice surprised him, and he swung around. There stood Julio, his acquaintance from the turtle shell shop. He curled up his lips in a slight smile of greeting. "What do you got there, Julio?" He tipped his chin towards the bright orange and red turtle shell clutched in one of the small, dark-skinned man's hands.

"For you, Mr. Jack. She's a beauty from Las Tortugas, the turtle farm west of here." Julio held out the shell.

Jack took the shell and examined it. "I can't take this Julio. You could sell it and make a good piece of dough." He pushed the shell back at the man.

Julio made no move to take it. "But I give to you, Mr. Jack. In Cay-Brac, a gift from a friend is not refused."

Touched by the designation, Jack pulled the shell back. "Thanks--it's beautiful."

"I have more from Las Tortugas, some bigger than this, but not as magnificent. I save the most magnificent for my America friend. But you come to see the rest, yes, Mr. Jack?"

"Maybe tomorrow," he replied, feeling too spent for the trek into town.

"But that's no good. Tomorrow may be too late. My best shells may be bought."

After the thoughtful gift, Jack saw no gracious way out of the invitation. "Okay, Julio, a quick peek," he conceded.

"Good Mr. Jack, you will like."

Jack stood, brushing off his shorts, smoothing his fingers through his wind-blown hair, and touching his four-day-old facial stubble. "Let's take a look at those turtle shells . . ."

****

The business district of Cayman Brac was an intermingle of quaint bamboo and rattan structures, and more modern architecture. The streets bore few American tourists who tended to favor the two larger islands in the trio, and that was fine with Jack. He preferred to see the unpretentious, innocent black native faces as they tended to probe little and instead, thrived on small talk which held no threat to him.

". . .And in ancient Hinduism they preach eight hundred one uses for the palm," Julio concluded while his hand reverently waved at the majestic trees.

Seeking Out Harry

Jack gazed at the willowy deep-green fronds moving in tune to the breaths of wind, and a soothing peace settle over him. The regal palms were like a wall of protection around the beauty, not allowing anything ugly or spoiling to enter the perfect world.

"How do they use the palm tree on Cay-Brac?" he questioned.

"We cook with the palm oil. It is extracted locally. I show you where one day."

"Maybe," Jack muttered, then he picked up his stride.

Julio ran to keep up with the much longer legs. "I take you to Las Tortugas too. You see how the turtle shell is made."

This time he didn't reply at all, rather accelerated his gait more. He felt barely the strength to look at a few turtle shells let alone watch the entire process of turtle farming.

When they reached Julio's tiny shop, the small man proudly escorted Jack through the front door as if he was entering the Taj Mahal. Hanging on every wall and atop the counters were turtle shells of various sizes, decoration, and utility. Behind the counter sat a wizened, hollow-eyed woman, much blacker than Julio. Julio's mother, Jack knew. He gave her a brief nod which she returned with a smile lacking many teeth.

"My Ma watch the shop." Julio let out a high rippling laugh, as if the notion was tickling.

The sound was so delightful, Jack curled up his lips in amusement.

"You make money, Ma?" Another rippling laugh that his mother joined as if her son had made the world's funniest joke.

Jack felt silent laughter bubble upward at the hilarity of the combined sound.

"Make the cowcod soup, Ma. I show Mr. Jack the new turtle shells," Julio directed with a casual wave of his hand. The old woman, about four feet ten inches hunched, scurried into the back of the shop where both lived.

Julio led Jack over to shells. In his glib manner, he told the story behind each of them as if he had a personal acquaintance with the turtles.

Jack smoothed a hand over each shell surface. It felt like lightly jagged satin. *Soothing.*

"You like turtle shell, huh Mr. Jack?"

"Yeah--I like," he replied, wanting to drown in the sensation.

"I take you to Las Tortugas and you meet the turtles," Julio insisted.

"Maybe later, Julio."

"Tomorrow is best. They prime turtles tomorrow, and you meet Miz Mattie."

Jack halted his strokes. "Who's Miz Mattie?"

"She widow lady who own Las Tortugas. She puts charm over each turtle."

Jack felt the amused shake of his shoulders. "Charms? Like spells?"

Julio bore a serious face. "Yes. Miz Mattie is voodoo lady."

"Voodoo?" Jack's laughter burst forth, and the strange sound startled him. "Like shrunken heads? That voodoo?"

"No shrunken heads. Miz Mattie only use charms to help people, including turtles," Julio replied with a stoic face, then added, "She tell your future. Miz Mattie always right."

"No," Jack replied immediately. "No future, Julio, but . . . I'll go to the farm with you to see those turtle charms. I'm kinda curious now."

"Good--I have Ma watch the shop." Then came another round of high rippling laughter.

****

The next morning, Jack was up to see the brilliant sun rise above the pink hued horizon. He tossed on a pair of shorts and walked to the beach take a brief swim. The warm water engulfed him like a refreshing blanket with each powerful arm stroke. When satisfied that his muscles were adequately exercised, he exited the water and laid on the already heated sand where he basked fine velvet grains and watched the sunset culminate

He had slept well. Nearly eight hours, he calculated. *Must be a record.*

Sleep hadn't come easy over the last six months with Carly Giraldi's death, the humiliating trial, the mass of paparazzi always surrounding him, and his own private torture. And then were the financial woes—they were huge. He couldn't bring himself to return to EMAX Studios, so he feared with the long abstinence, his usual superior effort would be far from . . . *maybe nothing.* Perhaps with all he had been through, his body's treachery was complete.

Then what?

Where next?

Without even an ounce of analysis, *he knew* without a doubt. *No Hollywood--no life.*

Don't think about that, not here. Enjoy that final bright light, he told himself.

He bounded upright and his feet pounded into the hot sand back to the bungalow. Once inside, he stripped off his shorts and headed for the enclosed, open-air shower, making the water as hot as it would get. He had to get rid of the chill, he thought. The sensation was incongruent with the wondrous paradise where he had temporarily found himself.

He *wouldn't* do anything except pretend in Cayman-Brac.

As soon as the chill began to abate, he soaped himself and his hair, his fingers stroking the long shagginess of the strands. But he felt unconcerned, rather told himself, it was a way to be someone new, another means to pretend. After showering he put on a fresh pair of shorts then debated about a shirt. Finally, he tossed on a light short-sleeved shirt without buttoning it. Looking into the tortoise shell wall mirror, he examined the weedy black facial stubble, and he debated again. *To hell with it.*

Feeling the hungry rumble of his stomach, he grabbed a couple pieces of bread from the small kitchenette counter. He briefly eyed the toaster, then ignored it, spreading the two pieces of bread with the tart kiwi jam he had purchased in a Cayman-Brac grocery. Between chews, he took generous gulps of mineral water, wishing for a moment that it was rum. But no. . . . a mind's picture of a naked Carly Giraldi on his bathroom floor flashed with vividness, and he told himself he would gag on rum.

He crammed down the bread, tossed on his sunglasses and hurried out the door. The sun's rays were sublime, he thought, letting them bathe his face for a few moments before taking brisk strides so he could see some turtles . .

****

Julio chattered during the entire bumpy five-mile jeep ride to Las Tortugas, the turtle farm, located in the southwest tip of the island in White Bay near the Marina. Deep in thought, Jack gave brief responses, otherwise just listened to Julio's usual fact-filled conversation.

"You see how the bluff keeps sinking, Mr. Jack? West it sinks and East it rises until you hit a steep cliff, end of Cay-Brac. I take you to the cliff someday."

Seeking Out Harry

"Sure Julio." Jack fastened his shades on the coconut palms and lush palmetto bushes while the stiff salty smell of sea water curled up his nostrils. One quick look, he told himself, suddenly feeling in no mood to see anyone or anything, and just longing to get back to his secluded beach where he could let his deepest thoughts surface.

"And I take you to Bat Cave too, early in the morning when the bats sleep so we can see them on the ceiling. You will like that, eh Mr. Jack?"

"Yeah, as long as they're sleeping." A slight smile cracked on his lips.

"See that big house over there?" Julio pointed to the right and the jeep veered.

Jack shifted his sunglasses in the direction of Julio's finger and saw a what looked like a clapboard styled house of three levels with a wide pillared porch in front. The house was white, but even from his vantage, he could see the streaks of wood under the paint.

"That's Miz Mattie's house. And this is Las Tortugas."

Jack turned to the left. A large sign read **Las Tortugas, The Beautiful World of Turtles,** and colorful turtle paintings formed the sign's background. "Who did the paintings?" he inquired.

"Miz Mattie paint. She once painted in Paris until she meet Mr. Claret, then she move to Cay-Brac to help him with turtle farm." Julio maneuvered the jeep over the rocky dirt road.

"Who's Mr. Claret?"

"He Miz Mattie's dead husband. He was third generation turtle farmer, once a rich man, but American ban on turtle products in 1978 ruin him, and he die poor."

Now he whiffed the sea water co-mingled with a reptile odor. "So how come this place is still open if he was ruined, Julio?"

"They opened farm to tourists to make a little money, supply turtle meat and shell products to our local market, and do conservation with the ridley turtle so maybe America government reconsider some day."

"It sounds tough," was all he could think of to reply.

"Miz Mattie tough lady. She make this place survive after Mr. Claret die and still help people with her charms too," Julio said, then pointed to his left and the jeep careened. "There is the turtle hatcheries and pools where turtles live."

"Yeah--I can tell." Jack creased his nose.

"And over there by the processing house stands Miz Mattie . . ."

****

"Miz Mattie!" Julio called out when had and Jack were about fifty feet from the structure where they butchered the turtles.

Jack's smelled the sea, reptile, and now the pungence of blood. Suddenly, he acquired a mind's picture of a dead Carly Giraldi lying on his bathroom floor, and told himself that no way would he go into that building.

"Julio! Who do you got with you, Julio?" a female voice questioned.

Upon hearing the brisk voice with a hint of French culture, Jack swallowed hard to rid himself of his disgust. The infamous Miz Mattie, he told himself, suddenly interested to meet the painter turned turtle farmer and voodoo woman.

"This is Mr. Jack from America . . . Mr. Jack, this is Miz Mattie Claret," Julio introduced.

In familiar fashion, he moved his eyes from bottom to top, seeing a thin body clad in shorts and tank top, her arms and legs a honey brown. He lifted his gaze to her face and saw the distinct Negroid features tattooed into a determined, self-possessed fiftiesh facade. Her face looked leathery and creases lined her forehead, but it was her eyes that were the most grabbing. They raised stunningly at the corners and were a mesmerizing midnight blue color.

"How do you do," he finally said, thrusting out his hand?

She stepped closer and slowly grasped his hand with hers.

He assessed her to be a hard worker by the rough texture of her hand, yet he couldn't help noticing the graceful long willowiness of her thin fingers as they encircled his.

"Mr. Jack who?" she asked directly.

The question startled him. She was the first person on the island to ask his last names, a custom he greatly appreciate. "Tyler . . . Jack Tyler," he lied, then looked at her and suddenly felt uneasy. *Those eyes* . . . they were fastened on him as if they could see his very soul.

"Tyler, eh?" Her cheeks grew taut while probing him. He felt his nerves pull with the closest scrutinization he had ever been under. Finally her cheeks grew limp. "Good old American name . . . Tyler."

He shifted his shades and gave a brief nod in response.

"So . . . I take it your mother was an Italiano," she said without a flinch.

He felt the familiar pain grip his insides. "Yeah . . . mother."

"I could tell. I knew many Italianos when I lived in Europe. They have a distinctive flavor about them."

"Really?" He wished he could will his legs to run at top speed, in the opposite direction, from her oppressive gaze and abrupt manner.

"In fact I painted a few. Italian men brought out my passion as an artist. There was much beyond their physical appearance . . . Do you not agree, Jack Tyler?"

An uneasy knot twisted in his gut with the puncture of her blue eyes. *What is she seeing?*

"Well? Do you see the accuracy of my assessment?" she pressed.

He shook his head until his sunglasses were focused on the sandy ground. "I don't know. I never knew an Italian male who was an artist's model."

"I was making a general statement, Jack Tyler, which you purposely avoided."

Christ Almighty . . . Now fear too twisted in his gut. "If you say so," he mumbled.

"Miz Mattie," Julio interrupted. "We would to tour the farm. Could you be our guide?"

No! Jack's mind yelled out. Never in his whole life had he felt so much fear as he did of the small woman standing before him.

"I would be proud to show Jack Tyler my farm," she replied in more gracious tones.

The softer sound was so surprising, he lifted his shades to her. Her lips bore a pleasant smile. *But those eyes* . . . they looked back at him as if they could see his inner workings. "Fine," he said, not knowing how to get out of the tour now.

"We start at the beach so Jack Tyler can see where my divers catch the turtles . . ."

****

Mattie Claret gave a comprehensive tour, from the catching the ridley turtles to the harvesting of new turtles so the farm could release most back into the sea to hold extinction at bay. Interspersed with her explanations was much stimulating, intelligent dialogue which touched something in Jack that he hadn't felt for longer than he could remember. Drawn by her witty manner, he began to loosen up and ask questions, though avoided direct view of her eyes.

The tour terminated at the large turtle pools where the ridly turtles gracefully swam with their long flippers while their red crowned heads bobbed in the aqua sea water. Their shells looked like crushed velvet as the water glided over them and Jack couldn't help reaching out his hand to stroke the splendid hardness.

"You have a way with the turtles, Jack Tyler." Mattie silently crept up behind him.

His nerves bolted at her sudden presence. "They're gentle animals despite the fire in their eyes," he replied, refusing to turn and meet her gaze.

"Yes . . ." She leaned over to glide her fingers across the turtle shell. "They are gentle giants, my men, much like Mr. Claret was. It's a wonderful trait in the male species, one that is masked all too often, in the name of what? I do not know." She pivoted her face towards him.

He keenly felt the bore of her eyes, though she was a good three feet away. "I don't know either." His hand strokes intensified.

He saw the fluid lift of her fingers from the shell, then sensed her small body moving closer to him. "Perhaps it is beneficial to discover what you do not know, Jack Tyler."

Suddenly paranoid, his protective mechanisms snapped. "What do you mean?" He spun to face her. "What the hell do you want from me?"

"A worker who has telepathy with my turtles."

"Worker?"

"Yes." Her cheek muscles grew taut. "I offer you a job here, Jack Tyler, for as long as you want, a day, a week, a month . . ."

"Are you kidding? I'd never work in that . . . that butcher house." He nodded at the building which processed the turtles.

"You will never cross the threshold of that butcher house, Jack Tyler." Her voice shook with tenseness. "It is not for the unaccustomed eyes and . . . it is *definitely* not for you."

Seeing the fiery blue passion of her stare, he uneasily shifted his shades back to the pool. "I didn't come to Cay-Brac for a job."

"No, you did not. But to work among the beautiful turtles can give one a peace and calm like nothing else can."

Jesus . . . He panicked at her voice tone. *How did she know that? How?* It was like her eyes had voyeured into the deepest recesses of his mind.

"You will be the keeper of the pools. You will keep my turtles healthy and content."

"No--I don't wanna job." He heard the quiver of his words.

She moved nearer to him. "Your face says that you do, despite what your mouth claims."

Unable to bear any more of her frankness, he bounded upward. "Thanks for the tour Mrs. Claret," he said abruptly, then took long strides away from her.

"You will be back, Jack Tyler!" she called after him.

When turtles the hell fly . . .

****

Over the next couple days, Jack lost much of his tranquil feeling, replaced by a restlessness he couldn't shake. His sleep had been fitful, and instead of lying on the beach, he paced it. He tried to swim off his high anxiety and even broke down and smoked a couple joints. But he couldn't calm down. His mind was consumed . . . not with his personal Hollywood woes, or his childhood, or his fears of obscurity . . . *those blue eyes* . . . they seemed to follow him everywhere.

And those damn turtles . . .

The satiny feel of the shells suddenly seemed built into his fingertips so he felt little else; although he had rubbed his fingers in the sand until raw and showered obsessively, digging his fingertips into the soap bar. Despite, the satiny sensation lingered. It was like his senses were luring him back to the turtle pools and Mattie Claret who stirred his insides with terror.

By the third morning since he had stormed away from Las Tortugas, he felt so skittish, he could barely get a cup of herb tea to his lips, a comb through his hair, and his teeth clattered as he brushed them. It was no use, he finally conceded, hastily ridding his hand of the toothbrush. His option was either to take the first plane or boat out of Cayman Brac and escape back to Hollywood, or succumb to his senses.

What should I do?

Neither option was ideal. So it boiled down to choosing the lesser of the two evils, he told himself. In Hollywood, he would be forced to eventually resume his past life--if he could, that is. And if he couldn't, he would have to face much that was unbearable. At Las Tortugas he had to deal with a pair of eyes that seemed to see everything so pretense was impossible. Yet, she was an interesting person if one discounted the eyes. And the turtles . . . his fingertips were broiling with their touch. And he kept vacillating until he stopped his mind's indecision.

There is truly no question.

****

"You look winded, Jack Tyler."

Sweating and breathing heavily, Jack bent at the middle to gain control of himself.

"To run seven miles in this heat shows a truly anxious man," Mattie Claret said, amused.

"I. . .needed to . . . run off a lot of excess energy," he replied between heavy breaths.

"Restless, Jack Tyler?"

He elevated his head to see the surety in the blue eyes. "Yeah--restless as hell. Is that what you wanted to hear?"

She glazed her graceful fingers over the severe black/gray hair bun. "I think you need some special water, Jack Tyler--to take away the heat in your body, that is."

"Yeah," he heaved. "Water would be good."

"Follow me, Jack Tyler . . ."

After letting out a few more hard pants, he straightened himself and forced his cramped legs to walk across the sandy ground to the three-story house.

The wooden steps to the porch wobbled when he stepped onto them. He

Seeking Out Harry

noted several loose planks. "You need a carpenter, Mrs. Claret." He commented, bouncing on a particularly loose plank.

She gave slight lift of her shoulders. "It will have to do for another year," she replied, then opened the front door. "Come into my home, Jack Tyler."

He eyed the peeling house paint and splintered door frame while he made his way to the front entrance. She needs a crew of carpenters, he thought, stepping into the hot, musky-smelling house. And central air too, he added silently, wondering how she slept in such stifling conditions.

"This is the lower level of my house. I never use the upper two levels," she explained while her arm flowed out like a prima ballerina.

Trying to ignore the sudden burst of perspiration from the heated air, Jack walked deeper into the house and gazed around. There were doll-like figures everywhere, on tables, on walls, and standing on the floors, some so simplistic and abstract, it looked like a two-year-old made them. "What are all those?" he questioned.

"My dolls." She picked one up and gently caressed it. "I've collected these for years, even before I came to Cayman-Brac as a twenty-one-year-old bride."

He too picked up a doll, determining it was made of wax. "I've never seen dolls like this."

"The one you're holding symbolizes marriage." She took the doll from his hand and caressed it lovingly. "My mother gave that to me on my wedding day, and it sat in the bedroom I shared with my husband for twenty years."

"That's a long time." The longevity was beyond his comprehension.

She tenderly placed down the doll, then stiffened her face up at him. "It may be hard for you to understand, Jack Tyler, but my husband was my entire world and it would have been thirty years if he had survived the storm. To have someone like that is what life is truly about." With an abrupt raise of her arm, she motioned him to follow her.

How did she know it was hard for me to understand?

"Come Jack Tyler. You need water . . ."

****

While feeling a hot itch under his clothes, Jack stared down at the steaming bowl of liquid on the old frayed rattan kitchen table. "This is the water you promised, Mrs. Claret?"

"It's the special water that I promised, called mannish water, a Jamaican delicacy. My mother was Jamaican." She walked to the table with her own bowl.

"Mannish?" The steam particles hit his already over heated face. "Water?"

Her blue eyes shone with sagacity. "It is a potent water. Jamaican culture says it puts hair on men's chests and women's chins, takes away a cold, cures infertility, and . . . impotence."

What? Terror hit him like a boulder.

"At least that's what Jamaican folklore says, Jack Tyler." She spooned the hot liquid into her mouth. "I ate gallons throughout my married life, hoping to provide Mr. Claret with a child." Her eyes grew sad and thoughtful. "But I never could, hard as I tried."

His appetite dampened, he just stared down at the soup while seeing vision after vision of the stilted sex life he had so once carefully orchestrated for success.

"Eat up, Jack Tyler. One never knows about folklore."

137

Jack mincingly picked up the silver spoon and dipped it into the dirty-looking water. He held the spoon by his mouth for several moments before finding the courage to put the cold silver between his lips. He gagged at the strong sweet and salty taste.

"You'll get used to it, Jack Tyler. Just keep eating slowly."

He couldn't think of any way to get out of eating the soup, so he tightly held his facial muscles with each spoonful. When the bowl was three-quarters empty, he placed down his spoon, unable to force down another drop. "What's in this stuff?" he choked out.

"Bananas, yams, pepper, white rum and the head and feet of goat," she replied pointblank.

Bile rushed up his gullet like a roaring flood, and he fisted his mouth while he frantically looked around.

"The back door, Jack Tyler," Mattie said casually while slurping her soup.

He raced to the back door, then out, just making it to the back yard before he lost every drop of his 'mannish water'.

****

In the ensuing weeks, life took on the peace and calm that Mattie Claret had promised. Jack spent his days at the turtle pools, feeding the ridley turtles fish, mollusks, crustaceans, and various sea plants, changing the pool water from the large barrels of sea water that workers dragged in from the Caribbean, giving each turtle attention with his hands and voice, and answering questions for the few tourists who paid to view the pools.

It was hot, hard work that taxed his body. But he felt stronger for the effort and sustained much satisfaction from doing honest work; although, he tried not to think about the fact that 'honest' was easy being Jack Tyler in a pressure-free environment, and things wouldn't be quite the same in Hollywood. Yet, the grueling work kept his mind off his other problems and for that he felt much gratitude towards the woman who had offered such to him.

For convenience sake--or so he told himself--he had moved out of the bungalow and into a small hut behind the main house. It was the height of primitive, possessing neither running water nor electricity, and he was forced to shower in the area where they spray cleaned the turtles. For the first time in his life he lit kerosene lamps and slept on a lumpy mattress. But the absolute serenity made up for any discomforts.

Every meal he quietly ate with Mattie Claret; although she hadn't offered him any more mannish water after his disastrous first exposure. She cooked food that was easy on his palate, serving Jamaican delicacies like curry goat only rarely. And she would fill his ears with tales of turtles and life with Mr. Claret, and avoided any further inferences about his person. She also took him on a tour of her doll collection, telling him the significance of each and inviting him to handle her treasures.

To pay for his keep, he repaired her porch. Being unaccustomed, it was tough at first. But eventually the carpentry skills, learned in his youth, returned, and he reinforced planks like a pro.

Some nights Mattie invited over friends and he was always asked to join them. The evenings were filled with laughter, jokes, stimulating conversations, and he was always questioned extensively by the eager minds. Did Americans live as wildly as they had heard? Was there really so much crime? Did American television actually have fifty different channels? Was America really so sexually promiscuous . . . ?

There was no denying the last question always rattled him, as he was afraid he would inadvertently show too much first-hand knowledge with the answer. So he mumbled a few carefully chosen words then changed the subject.

On occasion, one of Mattie's friends would bring a guitar and play everything from sacred music to reggae while the rest of the group surrounded the musician. "Would you like to dance, Jack Tyler?" Mattie would coyly ask.

He always agreed, knowing from their meal talks that Mr. Claret had been a wonderful dancer, and Mattie missed this.

"You dance nearly as well as Mr. Claret, Jack Tyler," she complimented while swaying gracefully, her eyes tightly shut.

Jack figured she was pretending that he was Mr. Claret, so he gave her that illusion and kept silent during their dances.

As weeks turned into a month he had become quite used to the leisurely lifestyle, and thrived within it. It was so decent, more decent than he ever expected to live, and this fact alone hiked up his scanty self-worth. He felt reluctant to leave such a coup in his life. Perhaps he would never go back, he started to think, as this action would avoid much heartache. After all, he no longer looked like Jack Torelli. His hair was so long, he pulled it back in a short ponytail and his face was full of stubble which he made no move to alter.

It would be so damn easy.

On one particular morning, he was cleaning out the turtle pools, using a long-handled net, and thinking deeply about his possible escape from decadence, when Mattie confidently strolled up to the pool, as she did every morning. Without a word to him, she held her special turtle doll over the ridley while mumbling words in Jamaican, then did the same at the rest of the pools. When done, she held the doll lovingly close to her chest and briskly walked off without glance.

Curious as to the why of her snubbing behavior, he watched her strode off and saw her disappear into a thicket of the coconut palms. The sight sparked his curiosity more and he found work impossible, his eyes constantly drifting to the thicket and wondering. Finally, after three hours had passed, he tossed down the net and headed for the thicket. He spotted her in a clearing that was evidently manmade, and the sight stopped the crunch of his feet on the bushes.

She was dressed in a flowing robe of expensive quality, perhaps Oriental silk, he thought, and her hair was free of the usual bun, and hanging loosely down her back. She sat gracefully in a chair with pallet and brush, and in front of her was a canvass that her long willowy fingers were brushing over. Her face held a passionate, fiery quality that made the blue eyes flash with brilliance. He thought the total picture breathtaking, and he felt drawn to it.

"I've been waiting for you, Jack Tyler," she said without lifting her eyes from the canvass.

The assured words made him stop cold. "Why were you waiting?"

"I felt the burn of your inquiry," she replied matter-of-fact.

"How?" His insides trembled. It had been weeks since she had acted so mysterious.

She ignored the question, and dotted the paintbrush against the canvass. "Come sit by me, Jack Tyler, and watch me carry out my passion."

Unsure, he hesitated, until again taking in the entire sight of her. It was magnificent! And his feet shuffled forward when his brain said otherwise. When at her side, he sat on the ground. Curious, he drifted his eyes to the canvass and the exaggerated bright colors of the ridley turtle reflected back. The near-perfect detail amazed him. "It's beautiful, Mattie. I can almost feel the strength of the fins, like the turtle could migrate around the world with such power."

Mattie briefly stopped her brushstrokes to gaze lovingly at her work. "Yes--I put much into my turtle paintings. They're like an eternal gift to Mr. Claret who's own passion was the majestic ridley." Her luminous eyes suddenly bored into him. "Everyone has a passion in life. A person without a passion is dead, do you not agree, Jack Tyler?"

What is she getting at? He nervously shuffled his bottom on the sand.

"One cannot deny his passion no matter how hard he tries to do it. It's like a burning imprint, indelible, and to ignore that print in the height of deceit, and eventually makes a person wither and die, Jack Tyler."

"What?" he breathed out, terror gripping him. "Why are you saying these things to me?"

Lithely, she dabbed the canvass as if she hadn't heard him. "Perhaps I never told you, but my real name is Matte', a name created by my French father who was a wine grower in the Bordeaux. My constantly joyful mother, a black Jamaican, thought the name too formal so secretly she called me Mattie until I was old enough to call myself that name."

Jack kept silent.

"As a child, I romped among the grapevines on the banks of the Gironde River. As I grew older, I painted both. Then, when I was nineteen, I left the grapes and went to Paris to study my passion. It was in a Paris art gallery where I met dark, handsome Mr. Claret, and he wooed me, promising me my passion if I came to Cayman Brac. So I succumbed and he made me this private studio among the palms, and raved about every picture." Her eyes cascaded into sadness. "Because he loved me, Jack Tyler. And to truly love one, is to love their passion as well."

He shivered at the words that seemed to come from the deepest bases of her heart. It was a female emotion that was foreign to him, thus frightening as hell.

"To find a person who loves your passion as much as you, is a truly rare, wondrous thing, one worth searching for, Jack Tyler."

"I don't understand Mattie," he said in a desperate whisper.

She stared with thought at her picture. "I know, Jack Tyler. You understand little, though need so much."

A helpless feeling engulfed him. He felt totally naked before this woman and impotent to cover himself. "How do you know this, Mattie?" he pleaded.

With dainty strokes she dabbed the brilliant pink hued horizon, backgrounding the turtle. "I have the gift, Jack Tyler."

"What gift?"

"The gift of introspection, of people, animals, myself . . ."

"Like a psychic?" he questioned.

A light amused laugh escaped her. "No, nothing quite so contrived or superfluous. I inherited the gift from my Jamaican grandmother, my mother said. She would laugh and say nothing was ever sacred around me."

He was unable to remove his stare from her. Never in his life had he believed such hokey things and jested about the psychics clustered in Hollywood. Yet, he couldn't explain the alluring strangeness of Miz Mattie Claret. She was nothing like the flamboyant psychics he had ever seen.

"You do not believe me, Jack Tyler. Your mind pictures other clairvoyants and you think it is fake," she said without a flinch.

Automatically, his arms encircled his chest, wanting to hide himself from the probing eyes that didn't have to look at him to discover the truth. What else did she know? All of it? *Oh god, not all of it.* He leapt to his feet while still holding himself. "I gotta get back to the turtles," he told her. Then without waiting for an answer, he took off at a clip.

****

Night settled over the placid Caribbean Sea, when hours later, Jack lay on his lumpy cot, staring out the single window in his tiny residence. He thought about the beautiful artist in the clearing. The picture had firmly sat in his mind all day, especially when sitting at the kitchen table eating red snapper and French crepes, while the vision, looking like she always did, ate likewise. He felt uncomfortable during supper, trying his damndest not to stare at her. He was certain Miz Mattie Claret knew his every dark, dirty secret. So now, his mind screamed at him to escape though his body dictated otherwise, and he couldn't move a muscle towards his luggage.

The sudden crackle of a palmetto bush, jarred Jack from his thoughts. He turned an ear to the sound. It came nearer, then nearer, until he jumped when his door flew open. He stared. The form of Mattie Claret, identical to how she appeared in the clearing, gracefully moved towards him like a dream scape. She stopped and hung over him, and he saw she clutched two dolls to her chest. He fixed his gaze on her eyes, glistening a glorious blue in the darkness, and his body exploded into tremors.

"You have given me much, Jack Tyler, a trip to my wondrous past. You are like a young Mr. Claret," she said in a soft soothing voice.

"What do you want, Mattie?" he trembled out.

"I desire to give you something back for what you have given to me." With feathery motions, she lowered to the cot and she began to undress him.

"What?" His entire body shook. "What's going on?"

Without a word, she placed one doll to each side of him, then with her long, willowy fingers began to caress his penis and balls while speaking soft Jamaican words.

The total sense was glorious, more glorious than he had ever felt in his entire life, and he felt his hardness culminate quickly. He wanted to scream with sheer ecstasy— the treachery had seemed to evaporate like a puff of smoke. "I need to touch you too," he cried out, desperate to experience the consummation of this miracle with the woman who had created it.

"No, Jack Tyler. I will bring you to your end without offering myself. I cannot be adulterous to Mr. Claret. Never," she whispered softly as her hand strokes became more urgent, until he heard a loud pleasurable moan escape him and his orgasm hit like a keg of dynamite. It had been years, a decade perhaps, since he had felt such absolute satisfaction of his body.

"Mattie." He reached his arms out to her, wanting to ground her body against his own for what she had given him. And he desired to feel it over, and over, and . . .

"No, Jack Tyler. Save your arms for the woman who will make you feel like this time and time again . . . in the city of your sadness."

"No . . ." An intense quiver rocked his throat. "There's no such woman there, Mattie, None. I. . .could never leave here now. I. . .could never leave you."

"You must leave, Jack Tyler. You cannot hide from your passion forever. You have to go back, and make it better, more meaningful."

"That's impossible, Mattie. There's no way, now. How? *How?*"

Her eyes languidly drifted across his face. "With love, Jack Tyler. That's what you are most needy for, a love like the one between me and Mr. Claret."

"Where in the hell would I ever find . . . ?"

"It will be hard," she cut in. "I see much difficulty ahead for you. But your inner body nearly glows in its need for a love such as this. You are a special man, Jack Tyler, a beautiful man inside and out, like my Mr. Claret."

"No Mattie." He violently shook his head. "I'm not, believe me. I don't deserve such a love. I wouldn't know what to do with it. I'd muck it up, sure as hell."

"Thus comes the difficulty, Jack Tyler," she said with absolute conviction.

"What kind of difficulty, Mattie? I don't understand. You're scaring me."

"Good. You need to be scared, Jack Tyler. It will make you more careful with your next move," she stressed.

"What is my next course, dammit?" he cried out.

"A renewal of yourself. We have some fine barbers in Cay-Brac. And then a plane back to your passion."

"No." He felt an urgent pressure behind his eyes. "Don't make me go, Mattie. I need the turtles, and I need you. I can't leave Cay-Brac and go back to that jungle."

Her eyes grew fiery. "You *will* go back and be a man. You *will* go back and find your passion and love. You *will* go back! And you *will not* hide behind the gates of Las Tortugas and wither. I love you as a friend, Jack Tyler, and I will not allow such a fate to come to you."

The pressure erupted, and tears filled his eyes. He hadn't felt the warm wetness on his cheeks for as long as he could remember.

"Cry, Jack Tyler. It will help for what is ahead. Cry. And Mattie will hold you . . ."

****

The Gerrard Smith Airport at the southwest tip of Cayman Brac was fairly empty of passengers when two days later, Jack, sporting a fresh shave and hair cut, dressed in a casual *Armani* jacket and blue jeans, dark shades over his eyes and carry-on bag over his shoulder, stood next to Julio who had driven him to the airport. He bounced with restiveness while watching for Mattie Claret to arrive. She had promised to see him off, but was yet to arrive and his small plane was scheduled to leave in fifteen minutes.

"Miz Mattie come, Mr. Jack. Miz Mattie true to her word," Julio assured.

"Maybe that old rattletrap truck of hers broke down," he muttered anxiously, having a desirous need to see the woman who had greatly impacted his life with honest, gentle concern, much insight, and the giving of a greatly coveted gift.

"There's Miz Mattie!" Julio excitedly pointed to the airport entrance door.

Jack quickly shifted his sunglasses. The small familiar form struggled through the door while carrying something in her hand. "Mattie!" Jack rushed forward to help her. "What do you have, Mattie?" he asked the moment he was facing her.

"A special goodbye gift for my friend, Jack Tyler." She held out a white-clothed rectangle. "It is a reminder of the ridley and the woman who tends them for Mr. Claret."

He undid the cloth to reveal the picture she was painting that day in the clearing, and his mind filled with the vision of the beautiful fifty-year-old artist whose face couldn't deny her passion. "It's beautiful, Mattie. I'll cherish it always."

"And this . . ."

She held out the wax doll, the one he had admired when first seeing her house. It was the one that had sat in her bedroom for twenty years. "I can't take this, Mattie . . . you and Mr. Claret, this doll."

"Take it, Jack Tyler. Perhaps it will someday bring you as much happiness in love as Mr. Claret and I felt." She encircled her willowy fingers around his arms. "At least the doll will give you hope, Jack . . . *Torelli*." Her French accent slid over the last word.

Was he surprised? Even though he had know her just a little over six weeks, she, better than anyone else on the face of the earth, knew him. It forever bound them in a very special way. He carefully placed the doll in the pocket of his jacket. "Thanks for another injection of hope, Mattie." He reached down and planted his lips on her forehead. The touch felt sweet on his lips, and a gentle warmth filled him. *And thank you for that too, Mattie . . .*

****

Jack fixed his shades out the plane window, watching the figures of Julio and Mattie grow smaller as the plane taxied. Then they disappeared when the plane soared into the sky and skirted the outline of Cayman Brac. He squished his glasses against the window when Las Tortugas came into view, then squished deeper when seeing the dots of the turtle pools. Do they miss me? He wondered. Do they miss me as much as I miss them? Then the turtle farm slowly vanished and he felt like a hungry man when taking in the waving palms, the golden sands, the delicate sea waves rolling onto the beaches . . . and he kept hungering until Cayman Brac was a mere speck.

Now the pretense was gone, he woodenly told himself.

He settled back into the seat, and his mind whirred with frightening resignation.

What next . . . ?

Chapter 12—Cassie

Oh Kristi...

Tears ran beneath Cassie's small, circular sunglasses. The pain of indecision and the fear of what lie ahead attacked her on a Northwest jet heading for New York City.

The editor from Starburst Publishing, handling her book, had commanded her presence in New York, at her expense except for transportation. They had much to discuss, he said in a snooty English accent. For how long? He wouldn't specify.

"We're rushing your book through publication," he said.

Why? He cagily wouldn't specify this either.

He only said, "Get yourself to New York City by Wednesday, April fourth because we have a meeting set up with the front-line people promoting her book."

So here I am, frightened, uncertain, and guilty as hell.

"When are you coming back, Mom?"

Kristi's small, terrified voice rattled her mind. Although her daughter never saw her, just knowing that she, Cassie, was a phone call away had provided much comfort. Now, suddenly, Kristi didn't even have that.

"Don't go, Mom. I'm scared with all this stuff happening so fast."

She knew how her daughter felt. After making the few obligatory editorial changes requested by John LaLiberte, her editor at Starburst, he sliced the rest. According to him, it was ready to go. And he was *thrilled* with 'Harry', the only specific she could get out of him.

"Stay Mom. I think Grandma and Grandpa are relenting a little."

Oh sure! Cassie gritted of her teeth with thoughts of her parents' drop in hostility.

"Did you *really* sell one of your books to a reputable publisher?" her snoopy mother asked over the phone.

"Read the Anoka Weekly Shopper, Mother, if you don't believe me," she replied.

"I *did* read the article and I *didn't* believe it, so I called," June replied coldly.

"Just a *little* publisher, Mother, to coincide with your opinion of me," she said before slamming down the phone, unwilling to get sucked into her mother's cat-and-mouse game.

Then, came her father's phone call. "Maybe you'll sell a few hundred copies and finally make a little money," he said to her.

"A few hundred?" Her reply was soaked in sarcasm. "Aren't you optimistic, Father?"

"Maybe," he said. "But you can hope that for once you make enough to live on."

Again she slammed down the phone, and told herself she could be buried ten feet in the ground, *and still*, she wouldn't talk to them.

At least that article in the local paper was somewhat of a blessing. Speculation about the 'little white light' had suddenly subsided, as did the gawking looks, replaced by curious gawking looks. Anything for a thrill, she told herself, just able to hear the chatter in the grocery stores and malls about 'The Famous Cassie Callahan' before she had even sold one book. Her endeavor would be blown up into a major bestseller by the time she returned from New York, she figured.

"Ignore them, Cassina, and concentrate on your second 'Harry'. You are on a roll . . ."

Her tears slowed when the warm, soothing voice filled her head. Her grandfather had been *so* supportive, not only financing her trip to New York but taking her to a local St. Paul mall for a whole new wardrobe. "You need to look like a New Yorker," he told her, and she wondered *why*. Wouldn't they be satisfied with Cassie Callahan as she was? Or did they really expect a sophisticated other? The answers had plagued her, and she felt damn scared. She had barely been out of Minnesota in her entire thirty-three years. Could she even be a sophisticated other?

But this is what you wanted, Cass.

Yes, to finally sell a book after twelve years had been a thrill, a rollcoaster of emotions, a great relief, ammunition to fight an influential family . . .

But you never thought it would be this way, Cass.

In her visions, she had seen herself as the creative deprived *artiste*, Cassie Callahan, living with Kristi in their old house and she in her attic, turning out book after book, making a decent living doing what she loved and earning enough to support her daughter without depending on her grandfather's handouts. But now everyone seemed so insistent, including her literary agent Ferris Mitchell who was coming to the meeting at Starburst Publications on Friday.

"Big doings, Cassie," Ferris said on one of his infrequent phone calls.

"What big doings?" she asked.

"They got huge plans for you."

"What huge plans?"

"A lot, kiddo, but I'll be there to make sure they don't take advantage of you . . ."

Advantage? Ever since Ferris's phone call, the word pounded her brain with terror.

Why? She now wondered. Why the vagueness? What were they going to do to her?

Oh god! I'm too young and green for advantage. Help . . . !

Gripped with panic, she suddenly wished the plane would make an emergency landing so she could escape the confines and hightail it back to the Twin Cities, hide in her attic, and hope the bigwigs forgot about her.

Over two years, Cass . . .

She heard the insistent voice of reason. Two years of starvation, stupor, filth, loss after loss, enough emotions to fill the Anoka water tank, the constant tap-tap, just so 'Harry' could fly.

Wasn't that worth a little advantage?

"Yeah," she replied softly. Then she made herself exhale out all her anxiety.

Suddenly, she sucked it back in when feeling the thump of the plane. Never having flown before, she feared the aircraft had crashed. *But no* . . . the soothing voice of the pilot said they had just landed at La Guardia Airport in New York City. Blowing out all her nervous air again, she peered out the window and saw the plane cruise by a sign that said **Welcome to the Big Apple**, and next to it a picture of, what looked like, a red delicious. So far it looks harmless, she thought. And then the plane came to a slow, shrieking halt, and she rapidly pulled her breath back in.

Oh god, I hate this . . .

****

I love it!

Two-and-a-half hours later, with thoughts of 'bigwigs' and 'advantage' placed on the back burner, Cassie viewed Manhattan from the window of the limousine sent by Starburst Publications. She widened her eyes with every familiar building name she saw. She was really in the mainstream! After thirty-three years, *really!*

"Oh my goodness!" she yelped. "There's *NBC* . . . Willard Scott! I adore him!"

The old chauffeur gave a low chuckle in response.

"Do you know, that once he interviewed a retired *Citicorp* banker from my community that had just turned one hundred and still cross-country skied?" she told the uniformed man.

"Sounds like memorable interview," the man laughed.

"It was to me," she agreed. "Besides Willard, an occasional Letterman when I need a lift, and the video *Schindler's List* once, I hate television. I view it as a scourge on society. It takes the mind away from better things. What do you think?"

"I don't think that'll be a popular opinion in these parts," he replied with a *very* distinct New York accent.

Thrilled by the accent, she drew closer to him. "I love your accent! Could you talk some more? Perhaps describe some of the sights. This is my first trip to New York, you see . . ."

"I couldn't tell, M'am," he laughed again. Then he obliged her request and pointed out sights while the limousine slowly moved down the congested streets and avenues.

"I adore it, Sir! I just know I'm going to love New York!"

****

"I hate New York," Cassie softly bemoaned when next morning, dressed in one of her new two-piece suits, hair twisted into a french roll, and her fingernails nearly nubs, she sat in the back seat of a limousine, taking her to Starburst Publications on Park Avenue.

She ate a solitary supper and lonely breakfast in the hotel restaurant; although her tongue restlessly wanted to wag. But no one would listen to it wag, rather they were abrupt when she tried to strike up a conversation. The same held true for the hotel staff, so gracious yet so cold. She never felt so alone. *And her room* . . . an overpriced mausoleum. Anxious to hear another human voice, she even resorted to turning on the television, settling on a channel with Italian as the primary language. Her ears only picked up half of the conversations. *But oh the comfort . . .*

The limousine maneuvered up to the curb and the driver informed her that they had arrived at Starburst. She turned to the window. A busy courtyard was filled with various restaurants, shops, and colorfully umbrellad tables in front of a tall building with the words **Starburst Publications Inc.** emblazoned at the top.

Seeking Out Harry

Oh lord, this isn't really happening to me.

The back door thrust open, and the chauffeur stiffly stood off to the side, waiting for her to exit. She wanted to grab the door out of his grasp, shut it quick and bolt it. *Courage, Cass.* The inner voice gave her the nerve to dig into her purse for a tip. But to her dismay, all she had left was two dollars from the traveler's check she had cashed at breakfast. *Oh well . . .* She stepped out the door and handed the chauffeur the two bills. "Thank you, Sir. It was a lovely ride."

He snatched the two bills then fixed a dirty look directly on her.

She mustered all her bravery and slunk past the glaring face.

The look of things to come, I fear . . .

****

"Mr. LaLiberte said that you are to go immediately to his office," the receptionist said after Cassie announced herself. "He's waiting for you."

"Really?" Cassie looked around the massive area with people rushing back and forth, then she returned a blank look to the receptionist.

"Is there a problem, Ms. Callahan?" The receptionist asked with irritation.

"Is . . . Mr. LaLiberte's office in the near vicinity?"

The woman raised an eyebrow. "Tenth floor, elevators, left. Do you need an escort?"

"No." She directed her eyes to the left and saw several elevators. "Ah . . ."

"Yes?" the receptionist cut in with impatience.

"Do all those elevators take me to Mr. LaLiberte's office or just one in particular?"

"Oh for goodness sakes!" The receptionist plucked up the phone and spoke a few words. "A security person will escort you, Ms. Callahan," she informed, hanging up.

Off to a great start, she thought helplessly while watching an unsmiling security guard move towards her. *And she's not even a bigwig . . . just a witch.*

****

"Mr. LaLiberte has been waiting for you, Ms Callahan," the editor's secretary fretted when Cassie stood in front of her.

"Well you see . . ."

"Come along, Ms. Callahan, everybody's waiting." The woman grabbed her arm and pulled her forward.

"Everybody? Who's everybody?"

The secretary ignored the question and merely thrust Cassie through a double door, then closed it behind her. Her eyes widened in correspondence with the rapid fluttering in her stomach.

My god . . . all the eyes look like they want to devour me.

"Cassie . . ."

At the sound of the familiar voice, sudden gratitude rushed through her. "Ferris? Where are you?" She sifted her eyes through the sea of faces, until seeing a widely smiling one. "Ferris?" she asked cautiously, then exhaled a big breath when seeing him stand and motion with his hand. Looking left and right, she skirted around the chairs and said multitudes of "I beg your pardons" before making it to her agent's side.

"It's nice to finally meet you in person, Cassie." Ferris thrust out a hand.

"It's so wonderful to see you," she jittered, taking the hand and giving a firm shake. "You're much younger than I pictured, Ferris."

"And you look exactly like your picture, Cassie," he said graciously.
"Yes she does."
She spun her head towards the cultured English accent. A light-featured man with creases at the corners of his blue eyes and a tall air of confidence stood behind a large antique desk.

"I believe we've talked on the phone also, Ms. Callahan," he said with a courtly politeness.

Cassie gulped at the formidibility that seemed to ooze out of him. "Mr. LaLiberte . . ." Telling her wobbly to 'walk', she moved up to his desk. Then she commanded her shaking arm to swing forward. "It's nice to meet you." She felt a set of powerful fingers curl around her hand.

"Ms. Callahan . . ."

She saw the scrutiny of his stare, and felt about as sophisticated as a schoolgirl. "I. . . wanna thank you for appreciating 'Harry'," was all she could think of to say.

"That isn't hard to do, Ms. Callahan. He's quite a strong character, and I want to commend you for the obvious pains you went through to create him."

"Yeah, my body ached with one pain after another, and still does if the truth be known," she blurted out, and immediately wanted to crawl in a hole for her hokey impulsiveness.

Silently, he raised an eyebrow. She felt the pull of her nerves with the look. He was probably reading the word *Minnesota*, most certainly written all over her, she figured.

"Please have a seat next to Mr. Mitchell," John LaLiberte invited.

With a nod, more shiver than downward thrust, she turned. Immediately, she saw the vast sea of visual scrutiny. Eyes down, she moved to the vacant chair next to Ferris Mitchell.

"Well, Ms. Callahan . . ." John LaLiberte settled back in his chair. "I'm happy to report that *The Life and Time of Harry Hannigan* has been copy edited and is now ready for the designers."

"Yeah--it was the copy editor who called me once at home. He said that according to his magnifying glass on a map of Minneapolis, I boo-boo'd with a street name I used in the manuscript." She gave a jittery laugh. "I told him who was I to argue with his magnifying glass."

Again, John LaLiberte raised an eyebrow at her.

Shut up, Cass. Pretend those lips are glued for once in your life.

"Interesting," he droaned, then continued on. "I told the designers two weeks max to get the book's format in shape so it can be typesetted, and a limited amount printed in six weeks."

"Six weeks . . ." she breathed out before she could stop herself. "Really? I mean *really*?" It was *too much*. Her Harry in print in six weeks? She had no idea that book publishing worked so quickly. It was awe-inspiring!

"Yes . . ." John eyed her with a curious gleam. "I'll have our head of Marketing and Distribution, Mr. Lawrence, tell you the plan, Ms. Callahan."

Bubbling with excitement, she whipped her head around to the man in question. A nerve-filled gulp hit the back of her throat. His spectacles reflected a shine that punctured right through her.

"Ms. Callahan . . ." Mr. Lawrence began slowly like a judge ready to pronounce a sentence. "We plan to take this book along carefully, a limited market to begin with, New York, Los Angeles, and the center of the Midwest where we believe 'Harry' will have high appeal. We want to build a slow steam, then hopefully the explosion will occur."

"Explosion?" she shook out.

"A reverberating effect, so to speak, Ms. Callahan," he replied. "From the Midwest, the book's momentum will spread to each coast, and we have a bestseller."

The shock hit like an crashing boulder. "Bestseller? *Me?*"

"We chose *The Life and Times of Harry Hannigan* to be our next bestseller," John LaLiberte cut in.

"How?" She twisted her head towards the editor. "How in the world could you ever do that? I mean the public . . . you can't put a gun to their head to buy it, after all."

"We have many guns to sway a book buying public, Ms. Callahan," he replied without expounding. "In essence, we have chosen you to be our next best-selling author."

"What?" she heaved in disbelief. "You can do that?"

His blue eyes drift up, down, and across her like she was a beef roast in an inspection bin. "Fresh face, innocent quality with those big eyes, writes an emotion-packed plot containing a flawless male protagonist, from a 'macho' area of the country, who's as sympathetic as hell with all his juicy inner conflicts that build from one to the other until he tastes victory . . . I think the female 'a-literary' aficionadoes will eat it up, don't you Ms. Callahan?"

Cassie saw a third raise of his eyebrow and thought, *now my shock's complete.* Could he really make her a best-selling author? Could they? And the mere possibility sent her insides into spasms of jittery anticipation. "If you say so, Mr. LaLiberte," she managed to squeak out.

"That's the spirit, Ms. Callahan, " he enthused, then waved a hand in the air. "Ms. Arugo is head of our art department. Her crew has designed the book cover for 'Harry'."

"Oh my . . ." Cassie happily swerved around. An abrupt visual jar stopped her head movement. She could just feel the cosmopolitan 'cool' of the woman, and in contrast, felt like a dirty speck on the woman's immaculate black silk suit.

"This will be the book cover for *The Life and Times of Harry Hannigan*," Ms. Aruba said point blank, holding up a dummy copy of a book cover.

Oh yuk!

Cassie moved her eyes over the cover, but could find nothing that grabbed her attraction. Yet, the woman's face was aloof and appraising, and she shuddered at the thought of challenging that look. *Oh hell, what's a book cover?* "It's . . . quite interesting, Ms. Aruba."

"And on the back . . ." the woman continued. "We place a picture of you, dressed casually, perhaps some quaint bib overalls, designer of course, set in some woodsy area to simulate the Minnesota setting, down-to-earth sort of photo."

Where's the pigtails and hay straw? Disgust filled her. Her first book . . . her first exposure to America . . . *and this* is what they come up with?

"The naive, provincial author." John LaLiberte said in a cool, calm manner. She turned back to him and repressed the face she wanted to make.

"So innocuous in appearance, yet possessing much fire behind it all . . . I envision that a hungry book-buying America will literally ingest you, Ms. Callahan," he concluded.

Injest? My god! What are they proposing? She turned her helpless feelings onto Ferris Mitchell. He returned with a reassuring smile.

"It's just a metaphor, Cassie. You wanna sell books don't you?" Ferris fastened an exact gaze on her.

She gave a slight bob of her head.

"Good! Because you gotta understand that we're just not selling your book, but an image. And America loves their images . . . gravitates to them . . . and that translates into big money. Do you understand now, Cassie?"

"Somewhat, Ferris, but what if it isn't me? For instance the bib overalls . . . I do own a pair, I admit, but I usually wear them when my knees are in the muck."

"But it *is* you, Ms. Callahan," John LaLiberte interrupted. "We've all studied your glossy extensively, and this is what we see. Pictures don't lie, Ms. Callahan."

She protested weakly. "But, I wore a silk blouse for that picture, and my hair . . ."

"Speaking of hair . . ." A precise male voice broke into the conversation. "That lopsided bun in the back of her head has to go," he finished.

Instinctively, she raised her hand to the back of her head and gently padded her fingers against the french roll to detect any curvature to it.

"This is Curt Farchmin, Ms. Callahan. He's Head of the Publicity Department," John LaLiberte introduced.

All these 'heads' around me and mine in the middle of a platter. She brimmed with sheer terror while rotating her head towards this new face. A hefty dose of rigidity jabbed her when their eyes impacted. The Curt Farchmin's lips were stiff straight and his cheeks quavered with tenseness as he stared back at her. She felt like a bug under a dirty rock that he had accidently uncovered.

"No stabs at sophistication, Ms. Callahan," he said abruptly. "*We* will determine the degree and amount of sophistication that you present to the public."

"You will?" Her voice barely projected above a whisper.

"Designer clothes without the Via Condotti look, and void of any Soho," Curt Farchmin said factually, and she felt the 'numb' of dumbstruck hit her brain. "And that hair . . ." He spoke like he wanted to barf. "You *will* go to a reputable hair stylist, and have those wild layers, that nearly reeked Greenwich Village in that glossy, toned down into a more manageable hairdo."

Feeling like she had just been assaulted by a Chinese general, she turned back to Ferris Mitchell and made her face pleading. He gave a quick pat to her shoulder.

"Just listen to the man, Cassie. You wanna sell books don't you? The image, Cassie. That's what it's about."

She was afraid to ask. "And the talent . . . ?"

"Hell you got that," Ferris replied. "But sometimes . . . that's not enough-- if you want to sell a few million books, that is. Sad but true, it takes a little more than talent, Cassie."

"Image," she mumbled, feeling like the big rock of reality had just pounded her.

"The creation of an entire image—book and author—America loves it," Ferris replied with another quick pat which, in actuality, felt like a 'wallop' knocking out the last semblance of a woman named "Cassie Callahan."

"And tomorrow, you *will* work with Curt. He'll tell you our expectations of you in the promotion of this book," John LaLiberte said with the dictation of a father.

No god . . . She took a peek at the Head of Publicity, so frostily suave, a perfectionist in style, so intolerable of the slightest flaw, so terrifying, she wanted to scream. "Tomorrow sounds lovely," she muttered, wondering what 'Curt' would do if she showed up in her muck-covered bib overalls. *The thought is just* too *horrifying.*

"Now . . ." John boosted forward in his chair and his sharp blue eyes met hers. "There's a slight matter about your contract with us," he said in a voice suddenly coated with graciousness.

"And what would that be, Mr. LaLiberte?"

"A small part that you omitted to agree to, which I'm sure you'll consent us to addendum," His thin, aristocratic lips cracked with a smile.

Cassie gave him a blank look.

He let out a low laugh and spread his hands in nonchalance. "You neglected to give us, or your agency, the television and/or movie rights to 'Harry'."

"The neglect was intentional, Mr. LaLiberte," she replied, then watched his pleasant face evaporate, replaced with a more ironclad look than even Curt Farchmin possessed. "You see . . . I personally oppose those two mediums and refuse to ever have any of my books smeared all over them." She saw his face grow even more exacting. "I believe writing is an art that shouldn't be flagrantly altered for monetary benefit."

Several exhaled noises of exasperation burst out around her, and she thought, *That limo driver yesterday was right on. My opinion is as popular as my hairdo.*

"Cassie . . ." Ferris Mitchell jumped in. "I've told you, and told you, that won't fly. Money Cassie . . . it could mean a helluva lot more money."

"No," she replied, needing to hold on to a wee bit of control, especially with such a ingrained belief. "I will not agree to movies and/or television." She could feel John LaLiberte's hostility from where she sat, and she lowered her eyes so she didn't have to view it.

"Maybe she just needs a little time, John," Ferris Mitchell placated the editor. "You know . . . a little time in New York could change her mind."

I won't change my mind. But she decided not to voice her thoughts. She was already enough of a "naughty little girl."

"Perhaps," John LaLiberte said brusquely while Cassie felt the steely bore of his gaze. "The smell of money *can* be enticing."

She made no comment. The *feel* of his look precluded anything except for sheer fright.

"And you *will* work with one of Curt's underlings tomorrow to establish an appropriate biography . . ." John LaLiberte continued on acidly.

And any moment, 'I will' succumb to my nausea . . .

****

Next morning, Cassie silently fretted with the air of a roused chicken in the back seat of the limousine headed for Starburst Publishing.

Do I look like Via Condotti? Or Soho? Or Greenwich Village? Whatever any of it means? She wondered while doing appraising her black knit two piece suit, short skirt and double-breasted military jacket, which she had decided upon after changing umpteenth times since four in the morning. She couldn't sleep.

The evening had been a repeat of her night before, alone and more scared than ever after being thrust into 'shark infested waters'. *And no one to talk to, not even my computer.* That was the absolute worse. She had vacillated about venturing out of her room and exploring Manhattan a little, but every time her hand touched the doorknob, all her grandfather's dire warnings about New York City socked her, and in fear, she backed away from the door.

I'm so miserable. Kristi . . . Nono. She could hardly bear the mind's picture of her loved ones. Yet, no matter how absolutely terrifying the thought of a bestseller had become, she viewed the torture worth it if it meant she could rescue her daughter. The money was tempting, and she began wondering if she could accumulate enough to give the powerful Scarpelli pair the fight of their lives. But it would take time. How long could Kristi hold on? She asked herself. She had no answer, nor alternative option, except to see a psychiatrist, and *that* wasn't an option.

Out of the corner of her eye, she saw the limousine approach the familiar skyscraper, and her body 'jumped to. Get ready for inspection, Cass, she told herself with more nerves than not. Quickly, she raised a hand to tame down her hair layers so she would look like anything except Greenwich Village . . . *whatever that implied.*

Minutes later she slid her black nylon'd legs terminating in black crisscross heels out of the limousine door and onto the pavement. Proudly, she handed the chauffeur a ten-dollar bill.

. . .And, she slunk by the little less dirty look . . .

****

"Mr. Farchmin is impatiently expecting you," a woman snipped when Cassie walked through the doors of the Publicity Department with security guard in tow. "Come along, Ms. Callahan." With insistent grip, the woman grabbed Cassie's arm and pushed her through the door of an office, *so huge*, she figured it was the size of the entire lower level of her home. And the faces . . . they were more assessing than the ones she had encountered the day before. Terrified, yet knowing the inevitability, she slowly moved her eyes to the colossal desk in front of a large open-air window. It was empty! *I thought he was waiting impatiently.*

"Take a seat, Ms. Callahan," a male voice directed.

She turned to see a smile fixed on her. The sight was so shocking, her knees wobbled. "Curt should be here any moment . . . client problems."

"Thank you," Cassie mumbled, too numb to smile back. She sat in the first empty chair she saw, as far away from the desk as possible. While crossing one leg over the other and smoothing her skirt over her thighs, she felt the sensation of eyes on her. Mustering all her courage, she lifted her gaze to see the "sneak peeks" everyone in the room was taking like she was a Martian who had just landed in their publicity department.

My god . . . I must reek of Greenwich Village.

She turned her head, and patted down her hair, wishing her hand held a steam iron instead.

Suddenly, the office door flew open, and Cassie spun towards the noise. Looking like Sherman making his march on Atlanta, Curt Farchmin moved to his desk and promptly sat. He twisted to peel away his black jacket, carelessly tossing it over the back of his chair. "Okay let's get this show on the . . ." He paused to stare at Cassie, hunched in a distant corner chair. "Up front, now, Ms. Callahan. This meeting *is* for your benefit after all."

Telling her legs to stand past her weak knees, Cassie walked to the desk, her terror directed on the youthful, frowning face with eyes slitted as they moved up and down her like they had a will of their own.

"Too provocative!" he snapped. "And that hair . . ."

"Pro . . . vocative?" She looked down at her suit. *Where did the provocative lie?*

"That skirt barely covers your skinny thighs and nonexistent butt!" he said bluntly. "And that hair . . ."

"Greenwich Village, huh? And Via Condotti or Soho, that too?"

"More like Harlem Streetwalker!"

That one I got, she thought, wanting to crawl into a ditch.

"You're too rustic, too guileless, to wear such revealing clothes, Ms. Callahan."

"Bib overalls . . . I understand, loud and clear."

"Good! Then get your credit cards out, and be prepared to do a little shopping with Geoffrey, my assistant."

Credit cards? What the hell are those?

"And that hair . . . he'll also deal with that little mess!" he barked.

"Who's he?" She rotated her head until spotting the bright smile again. He lifted his hand to her, and this time she forced her lips to return the smile.

"I want you looking like Cassie Callahan before you return in another six weeks for the interviews, radio shows, local television shows, book signing, breakfasts, lunches, dinners, drinks, and parties."

Her head bobbed monotonously while trying to follow the constant 'click' of his drill master's tone.

"And you *will* go to each one, without tantrum." Curt ground a glare into her.

She cowered with the look. *Tantrum? As if I would dare.*

"Now, I will review the pre-publicity with you, Ms. Callahan." His taut cheek twitched as he glanced at papers on his desk. "We plan to inundate the market with cheap publicity to spark curiosity in you; although the company has agreed to a running sign in Times Square."

"Running sign?"

"Who is Cassie Callahan? No pictures, no clues, just a question, in newspapers, flyers, on a couple highly-visible billboards, on radio stations, so your name gets out into the public a few weeks before the book is released."

"What makes you think people will care?" she stammered out.

He replied instantly. "Curiosity . . . the ace in the hole for publicity. I'm going to make sure the curiosity about Cassie Callahan makes the public salivate to the point that they toss down hard cash for your book."

"I believe you." She thought that people wouldn't dare not to salivate with him conducting the show.

"Any questions before Geoffrey takes you on your spree, Ms. Callahan?"

"Yes," she peeped. "Can I use a phone to call the Twin Cities? And then, if Geoffrey wouldn't mind, I gotta find a Fed-Ex office, pronto . . ."

****

The Designer Clothes department at *Saks Fifth Avenue* was fairly quiet of customers, but loaded with pesky sales people. Cassie shuffled through the clothes rack that Geoffrey Haines had asked her, ever-so-politely in his New England accent, to shuffle through.

"I take it that this is the 'farm look'." She lifted up clothes and checked prices that made her sway.

His hazel eyes crinkled with amusement. "If I may be so bold, Ms. Callahan, I think your clothes and hair look just fine."

"Really . . ." She couldn't mask the cynicism that sat like a rising lump inside her. "Well then, why doesn't 'General Pompass Arse' think so?"

He gave a low chuckle. "Curt's only following orders, Ms. Callahan. I hear your book is very good, and they want to capitalize on 'good', and make it better. Cheerfully fitting their image is a small price to pay for the possible better. Don't you agree?"

Frustrated by the prices, she flung the clothes along the rack. "I don't know how I feel, Geoffrey. I feel drenched by all of it. A body can take only so much 'better' at one time."

"Geoff," he said, and she made a question with her brow. "Call me Geoff. I hear enough 'Geoffrey' from 'General Pompous Arse'."

The answer tickled her. "Call me Cassie. I too have heard enough Ms. Callahan in the last few days to want to undoubtedly and forcefully barf."

His rich, mellow laugh gently rocked her ears. "So now that we've settled that, have you found any clothes that interest you?"

She focused on his kindly, if not distinctively handsome face. "If I could be truthful, Geoff, I can't afford this stuff. My grandfather only send me another two thousand dollars and . . . I refuse to ask him for more. I owe him plenty already."

"Hmmm . . ." Geoff's brow made a deep wrinkle of contemplation. "I know of a few shops which sell designer copies, Cassie. Perhaps . . ." He grasped her arms and pulled her along.

"Okay, Geoff, but no limo. I wanna experience Manhattan for the first time . . ."

****

As the light of day sunk below the skyscrapers, the Manhattan delicatessen was loud with racket, every booth was occupied, and waiters and waitresses raced up and down the aisles like they wore roller blades. At least, that's what it looked like to Cassie as she excitedly watched their every movement like a starving person.

"Aren't you going to eat your sandwich, Cassie?" Geoff Haines asked, three-quarters of his own sandwich gone. "I've never seen servers move so fast in my entire life, Geoff. The way they do-si-do around each other carrying full trays is amazing."

"Just go to any halfway decent restaurant in Manhattan, Cassie . . ."

She wondrously widened her eyes at him. "And I would still love it, no matter how many restaurants I went too. After all, I've lived in boring Anoka, Minnesota all my life."

He studied her closely while taking ginger bites of his sandwich. "You have a glow in your eyes that seems to cover your whole face, since . . ." He let out a low laugh. "Your eyes seem like they cover your whole face."

"I've heard that all my life." She plucked up a quarter of her chicken salad sandwich and bit daintily into it. "I got my eyes from leprechauns, if you believe my grandfather. He's got the same eyes."

"They're beautiful," he said suddenly.

"Thanks." She mumbled, uneasy by the words and his probing gaze, so felt the need to get off the topic of 'her eyes'. "Are you sure 'the General' *really* wants me to look like Pollyanna without the bloomers?" she quipped, drifting her gaze to the stacked store garment bags containing her new 'image' clothes.

"Simple, unpretentious lines to your clothing was the order, and I think we got that covered, and . . . did my compliment make you nervous?" His lips danced with an amused smile.

"Of course not." She speeded up her sandwich eating.

"Then I'll also say your hair is beautiful. I've never seen a real color like that before. I think 'the General' is raving mad."

She froze a smile on her face. "Well if you don't mind, I won't tell you where I got my beautiful hair."

He lightly jiggled the iced tea glass between his fingers. "Sounds like a quite a mystery."

"That's me . . . Cassie Callahan, mystery woman." Her skirt bottom fidgeted against the plastic booth.

"A mystery, I'd like to crack. So how about dinner tomorrow night?"

What specifically does 'crack' mean?

"I'll even make reservations at a busy restaurant so you can look at the waiters and waitresses do-si-doing."

Unaccustomed to such male forthrightness, she felt a surge of intense jitters."I don't know, Geoff. I'll have to pack tomorrow night, and probably wash my new hairdo, and watch Italian TV, and talk to the four walls that I've grossly neglected today, and . . .

"Just dinner, Cassie," he cut in. "I enjoy your company and I like looking at you. 'The General' would have my hide if I got any other ideas. So . . . ?"

She lingered her gaze across the booth and studied the mid-thirty-something face bearing hazel eyes that were almost hang-dog, and then the tousled, longish, silky brown hair that looked like it belonged to a schoolboy. He looks harmless enough, she finally decided. "Okay Geoff, but make it Italian if you can. I'm kinda homesick . . ."

****

Much frantic, weary activity ensued for Cassie the following day. Not only did she get her hair tamed down in an expensive New York salon, but she also had a manicure, pedicure, and makeup lesson at Geoff's insistence.

"Who's going to see my toes?" she had asked him.

"You never know," was his reply.

So she conceded to all of it, even the trip to *Bloomingdale's* where Geoff had her try makeup after makeup and innocent perfume after innocent perfume. "But I don't like gardenias," she moaned. He said he didn't either, but 'the General' did, and that's what counted. By the time Geoff quieted his insistence, she found she had only fifty dollars left to carry her until she left for home tomorrow. Suddenly, she was glad she had a supper invitation.

"I made reservations at a nice Italian restaurant, but I don't think you're going to see much activity by the waiters," Geoff told her while they stood by a hotdog street vendor, eating loaded-with-everything hot dogs.

She relished the divine taste of her hot dog, thinking she could live on them for three meals a day. "Maybe just a quick hot dog would do, instead," she said back to him.

He laughed in a way that said she was jesting. "Seven-thirty sound okay?"

"Only if I can look like Cassie Callahan," she replied, taking another big bite and silently swearing she had a new passion.

"I wouldn't want Cassie Callahan any other way . . . so tell me about 'Harry'. I've only heard bits and pieces," Geoff asked out of the blue.

She felt the choke of her hot dog as it coursed down her gullet. "Harry? I. . .don't talk much about 'Harry'. Pretty personal, if you know what I mean."

He gave a lift of his eyebrows. "He's not going to be personal for very much longer."

Cassie tossed the rest of her hot dog into her mouth and chewed while thinking of the best way to answer him. "I know. But for now, I'd like to keep him personal for as long as I can."

"That's unique. An author who doesn't want to talk about his book until one's head is in a spinning headache."

A nervous laugh erupted from her. "Don't get me wrong, I've spun a few heads with my first few books, but 'Harry' is totally different from any other male character I've created."

"Sounds like a pretty special guy."

"He is," she replied evasively, then shifted part ways to toss her napkin in the trash bin. *My ideal man, like no other in the universe.* And the familiar longing gripped her.

He placed a curious look on her, but said nothing and merely glanced at his watch. "I better get you back to Starburst. 'The General' wants you to meet with the 'bio' man. Mind if I hang around and listen?"

"No . . ." She cascaded her lips into a bright smile. "In fact, I insist on it. I need to see at least one non-hostile face so my nerves don't run amuck."

"I'm at your service, Cassie."

She drifted a pleading look towards the hot dog vendor. "Well in that case . . ."

****

Later on that evening, after the plates of succulent pasta had been devoured at a quaint, loaded with atmosphere Italian restaurant on Park Avenue, and a carafe of Asti Spumante had been drunk, and much talk and laughter had passed between Geoff and Cassie, the two stood outside her hotel room.

"So, the next time I see you, all of New York will be asking, *Who is Cassie Callahan,*" Geoff said, lingering over her.

Feeling edgy at his close proximity, she merely nodded.

"I guess this is goodbye, for now." He lowered his face to her, and instinctively she thrust back. "It's only a kiss, Cassie," he whispered.

"But . . ." She had no idea how to handle this. It had been twelve years, after all. "Aren't you worried about 'the General' having your hide?"

Geoff pulled back. "He should talk."

"What do you mean?"

"He doesn't exactly have a sterling reputation with women, is what I mean." Geoff laughed a little. "And LaLiberte doesn't mince on the ladies either."

"Really?" Sparked by the juice, she forgot about her high anxiety. "Publishing house intrigue . . . sex and the two stickmen . . . it should be a book."

"So do I get that kiss? A kiss between friends?" he popped out.

She felt uncertain, especially with the strange look in his eyes. *Although*, she reminded herself, Geoff had been very helpful, a dolphin in a sea of sharks. And he *had* shown her a bit of Manhattan plus a good, laugh-filled time as well. His attention had done much to lessen her loneliness. "Okay, a kiss that two friends would share," she gave in.

Smile expanding, Geoff bent his head and his lips lightly touched hers. And she thought, *That's it*. But he didn't remove his lips. She felt a more pressure, then more, until she stepped back and broke the lip lock.

"That was a kiss between friends?" she accused.

A smile teased his lips. "I couldn't help myself. Your lips tasted like a fine, sweet wine . . . I suppose I couldn't have another?"

She shook her head and rustled in her small bag for her room card. "I think we've had enough kisses between friends," she said sharply.

"Are you angry?"

With room card firmly in hand, she gazed up at him. This time he wore his innocuous expression, and she thought, perhaps with her inexperience, she had blown the entire incident way out of proportion. "No, I'm not angry, only tired. Thank you, Geoff." She held out her hand and he wrapped his own around it.

"I'll see you in six weeks, Cassie. Think about me, huh?"

"Sure," she replied with a touch of a smile. "How could I forget . . . ?"

****

A couple hours later, freshened from a shower and facial mask, Cassie packed the remains of her clothes and what personal effects she wouldn't need in the morning. While she neatly placed clothes in the expensive leather luggage her grandfather had given her as a 'Congratulations on your Success' gift, her mind wandered with every conceivable topic . . . Kristi, her parents' cruel stubbornness, the frightening unknown of her future, and Geoff Haines.

He's no 'Harry', she had undoubtedly concluded. Although despite this conclusion, she thought Geoff Haines to be different from any man she had ever met. He seemed sensitive to her and his kindness couldn't be denied. And his helpfulness . . . Geoff had faithfully stayed by her side while the man doing her biography had snootily probed her as if her life was unbelievably dull. At one point, Geoff had even told the biographer to "back off," and the man had given Geoff's position as the right hand to the top man in the publicity hierarchy at Starburst. To have him by her side had been very comforting. Yet . . .

Feeling acute longing, she zipped her bags and placed them by the door. Was she a bit touched for her obsession with a fictional character, flawless inside and out regardless of his many problems? She wondered. Certainly, a man like this was rare, *if* he even existed. Even so, she decided to keep the hope burning that her Harry would someday emerge in the flesh.

Cassie gazed out her puny hotel window. She was truly thrilled with the magical city. It tantalized her every sense and sparked her old excitement and wonder that had slowly slipped away since the day she started 'Harry'.

I've sacrificed much for my man, and I've built my hopes around him. So whatever comes, comes, and I have no choice but to take it.

She lifted her fingers to her new conservative hairdo. It wasn't her, she thought. Then, the new clothes came to mind and she thought the same.

Yes, whatever comes, I have to take it.

Suddenly, she felt very homesick for people who loved *her*, Cassie, and she turned from the window, knowing the people walking below her would never know this person. It was a very lonely realization. She looked from wall to wall in her hotel room. Nothing but cold speckle. But she kept shifting her eyes, until they halted on the television set.

Nono . . .

She needed to feel the warmth of the man who had never abandoned her. His strong arms always took the intense hurt away. So she hurried to the television, and tried to locate the Italian station. *What was that channel number?* She aimlessly flicked the remote until a flash of a vision hit her consciousness. Quickly, she flicked to the preceding channel, and just stared wide-eyed, as if she had never seen television before in her life.

A quiver spread through her like molten lava, and she blinked, disbelieving. He was tall and darkly handsome with the most incredible, penetrating eyes she had ever seen. His low, soothing voice was beautifully artistic despite the absurd words he was speaking. *He* spoke them wonderfully. And she sensed something, like a powerful prod, while she watched him play private detective amongst others who couldn't even hold a candle. And suddenly, without warning, the prod urgently jabbed her.

Oh my god . . . Harry . . .

Chapter 13—Jack

"Jack settle down."

Filled with intense fury, Jack Torelli stared at the bugged-out eyes which, he quickly calculated, were loaded with deceit.

"Take a seat next to Harv, Jack. A drink? Or maybe a joint to ease the edges? My office, as usual, is at your disposal," Rud Hanna said while a well-chewed panatella hung from his mouth.

Rather than sitting, Jack pressed closer to Rud's desk. "I saw him, Rud, plain as day on that sound-stage. Now, I wanna know, without any bullshit, what the hell is going on?"

"Nothing's going on, Jack." Rud lazily rolled the panatella around his mouth. "The kid's making movies, big deal. That's what we do around here after all."

Doggedly, Jack pressed closer. "He could be my double, dammit! Except for his smaller size which I noticed you've pumped to the max with steroids."

"Steroids?" Rud gave an harmless laugh.

"Yes! Steroids!" Jack tightly clenched his jaw. "What the hell do you want? Another dead kid? Huh?"

"Shut!" Rud whipped the panatella out of his mouth and gave a forward jerk of his body. "That's a fuckin' taboo subject around here, Jack!"

Consumed with the intense desire to let loose with his fists, Jack made himself slowly back away from angry defiance of Rud's bulging eyes. "Taboo doesn't make it untrue, make you guiltless, make you immune . . ."

Rud rapidly chomped his panatella from one side of his mouth to the other, and back again. Finally, he pulled the slimy panatella from his mouth. "What do you want, Jack? It's been eight months. You may not have enough steam left."

The truth of the words made Jack slowly drop into a chair next to a highly nervous Harv Wellson. He didn't know what he wanted. All he knew was that he was broke, needed to stay in Hollywood, and still had that blistering passion no matter how hard he had tried to deny it in a Caribbean paradise. Mattie had known this all along. She had known every carefully hidden feeling he possessed. And now, he suddenly felt more alone than ever, despite the painting he gazed at for hours while her soothing utterances streamed through his mind, and the tender caresses he gave to the wax doll—his hope, she had said. But he felt little hope, multitudes of painful confusion, but little hope.

"I repeat, Jack . . . What do you want? A few roles? Maybe a couple leads now and then? A comeback film? What?" Rud demanded with a shaky undertone.

The choices he had to feed his passion, he thought cynically. What would Mattie want him to do? He mused. And ultimately, there was only one obvious answer.

"None of the above, Rud."

"What?" Harv Wellson leapt out of his chair. "What are you saying, Jack? It's the best I can do for you. The rest is dried up. I have no more options for you," he jittered in protest.

Ignoring the hyperactivity next to him, Jack made his eyes flare with determination across the desk. "I wanna direct a movie, my own way, on my own sound-stage."

The sound of Rud's deeply inhaled chortle rocked the walls of his office. "That was a good joke, Jack, best one I've heard around here for quite a while."

"It's no joke!" Jack lifted from the chair and again pressed against Rud's desk. "Those are my terms, dammit!"

"Terms?" Rud's laughter slowed. "You have no rights to any terms with me, Torelli."

"The hell I don't!" Jack exploded right at Rud's face. "Maybe a Hollywood psychiatrist who forces out all of my torture about Carly Giraldi, will see it differently!"

"Jack stop it," Harv pleaded.

"No!" Jack rotated hi head to the agent. "He owes me for years of what he's done to me, and what I've taken to make the bastard rich. And . . ." He turned a tense, quavering jaw back across the desk. "Now comes the pay back."

"You wouldn't dare tell a soul," Rud's voice quaked with uncertainty.

Jack laughed with sardonic humor. "Try me . . . it would ruin you, you bastard . . . try me . . . you'd be broke . . . expose' all over Hollywood . . . try me . . . what the hell do I have to lose?"

Rud's eyes widened with incertitude, though he tried to mask it by taking furious chomps on the panatella. "Okay!" he finally burst out. "I s'ppose I can give you a couple films to direct."

Jack shook his head until he felt the hard grit his teeth. "That's not acceptable, Rud. I refuse to work with the *shit*. I wanna a clean operation."

"What?" Rud cracked the panatella onto his desktop. "You know the business I'm in. What's this clean horseshit?"

"A small studio, an extension of EMAX," he replied while wondering from where such a workable solution had so suddenly emerged. "I turn out movies for you."

"Clean and Rud Hanna movies don't go hand in hand. I don't need clean in my life. I have enough to deal with, with the dirt."

"Then ultra-soft, sensitive porn, tastefully done," Jack replied.

Rud snorted. "What makes you think that you, whose never directed even a short, can turn out films that will satisfy Rud Hanna's pocketbook?"

"Because I've worked long enough with the half-assed directors that you got crawling around here to know that I can do a better job," Jack retorted back.

With a quick thrust, the panatella landed back in Rud's mouth, and he chewed in a frenzy while looking contemplative. "All right!" The panatella flew to the desk, and Rud lifted a meaty finger stiff with emphasis. "One film, Torelli, made in rented quarters with a lease, and I gotta see a return to renew that goddamn lease. You understand me?"

Feeling victorious, Jack pressed for the rest of his terms. "And I choose the script, hire the crew, the cast, and I get it in writing that you finance the picture to completion, no reneging."

"You'll get my full cooperation. What choice do I have?" Rud shuffled his *Armani* suit back in his chair. "But this is it, Torelli. One shot, only. And I want to get *that* in writing too."

"You got it," Jack replied, hiding an elation he hadn't experienced since his lips touched Mattie's forehead at the Cayman Brac airport.

"And you get a deadline like everyone else, though . . . I'll make it six

Seeking Out Harry

months to this day, three times longer than usual, to give you time to set up your operation," Rud said grudgingly.

"What about my salary?" Jack questioned.

Rud shook out a hoarse laugh. "You get paid the same as everyone else—fifty grand per picture. Take it or leave it."

Jack's elation deflated. Fifty thousand for six months? It was a pittance by Hollywood standards and would mean a major reduction in lifestyle. Could he so easily cast away the outer image one of the final 'big' in his life? Or should he collapse, deny he had ever said any of it, and return to the sound-stage and the 'big bucks'?

"The easy way, Jacko is not a man's way . . ."

He let his father's words bask his ears with sensibility, and he knew, without a doubt, that no matter how frightening, image-destructing, ridicule-producing, he wouldn't take the easy way out this time.

"The salary's fine, Rud."

"But Jack . . ." Harv cut in. "You'll never survive on that. Why just your car . . ."

Jack sat back down and hung his middle over his knees. "You can terminate my agency contract, Harv, if that's your desire. I won't toss one tantrum your way, I promise."

Though looking like that was just what he wanted to do, Harv shook his head. "No Jack, I don't desire . . . over twelve years . . . I won't turn my back. My bat's still out for you. I'll . . . just represent Jack Torelli, the director."

"Thanks." Jack fastened a smile on the agent.

"Well Torelli . . ." Rud scoffed. "You got six months, let's see what the hell you can do with it . . ."

****

In the next few months, life on the other side of the fence was more strenuous of an undertaking than Jack had ever confronted in his entire life. He acted as producer, director, script consultant, accountant, and Mr. Clean for the cast of youthful performers in the operations set up on the top floor of a dilapidated former hotel turned office building on Crescent Heights Boulevard in West Hollywood. True to Rud's word, he had given Jack complete autonomy, and only balked a little about the bills that the production was accumulating, in the name of quality.

Most of the cast and crew were talented, young, eager, and hopeful, average age about twenty-six. Although, Jack *had* hired a seasoned cinematographer and sound man as well as set designer and editor, so few inexperienced mistakes were made. The six-month time line was like a nudge always pushing at his back. He had to make this work . . . *last chance* . . . Rud's words were always in the forefront of his mind at the studio in Crescent Heights.

By mid-June, by the sheer driving force of Jack Torelli, all was done and the production of *The Last Two-Step* could commence. On that momentous day, Jack was in his makeshift office at his usual six A.M., meticulously going over the script and trying to determine ways to make the scenes as powerful as they could be.

He had solicited soft-porn scripts from several literary agencies in and around L.A., deciding time was too limited to do a wider search. He received hundreds, staying up into the wee hours and perusing through each, immediately tossing aside any that possessed a higher degree of porn than he envisioned. Finally, after three weeks, he read a screenplay written by a young Harvard graduate who was trying to make it as a screenwriter. The script contained a sensitive story about a young Canadian male dancer who comes to New York with high aspirations and is consumed to the point of destruction. Not a new story, yet with a soft porn twist which would satisfy Rud Hanna, and with emotional, gripping scenes that satisfied Jack.

Now he immersed himself in the dialogue, beautifully written in his estimate. He could just feel the young dancer's desperation to make it big, as it was the exact desperation he himself had felt in his early acting days. He just prayed that he could capture that desperation on film. His lack of prior experience gnawed at him, yet he hoped, he could take nearly twenty years of study and observation and make something meaningful . . . his final shot at 'meaningful'.

"Mr. Torelli . . ." The office door flung open and a young man flew through the entrance.

Jack smiled at the sight. None of them ever knocked. "What do you need, kid?" he asked the young actor/dancer playing the male lead.

"I came to practice those four dances you had me choreograph for the movie. I was wondering if you wanted to take a peek at the final result?"

As if I know a tinker's damn about dancing, he thought, wishing he had the nerve to hire a choreographer to stage the few dance scenes he dared put in a Rud Hanna production. But he feared that bill would have sent Rud over the edge. "Sure kid. If it makes you better . . ."

Several minutes later, stereo music blasting in his ear, Jack watched the young man plus tap shoes dynamically twirl and gyrate on the stage. He's damn good, he thought, wondering how Hollywood had avoided such talent. Although, as soon as he wondered, he knew the answer. It was the story of Hollywood. Regardless of the talent, one needed that big break to have that talent showcased. Without it, that talent became a casualty. It was heartbreaking, yet the reality. So why even set up oneself for such heartache? He wondered again, though as he did, he also knew this answer. The passion . . . no amount of heartache can kill it *if* it's real.

The actor did a fast-moving pirouette and fell to the floor just as the music stopped. His smile wide with exhilaration and looking like he had just found a billion dollars, the young man stood and looked at Jack. "So what do you think, Mr. Torelli?"

Jack raised his thumb. "I'll try my damndest, kid, so you make a score with this movie . . ."

****

Although it was a blast of fresh air to work with such hungry, untouched individuals, and a thrill to see a quality script come alive on film, Jack felt the familiar longing. It was tough to sit on the sidelines. He wanted to be up on that stage, in front of that camera himself.

But not in Rud's stable.

He was through with that, he constantly emphasized, so the longing didn't overwhelm and he ended up succumbing to something he truly didn't want. It was the easy way, not the better way Mattie had told him to find. He would do anything for Mattie.

After a long day of filming on location, Jack was in his office gathering the bills that needed to be sent to the main EMAX office and experiencing another longing: turquoise water, bambuzzo palms, ridley turtles, and the artist in the clearing. Although, the film was going exceptionally well and he felt a greater amount of 'decent' than he'd felt in years, he was lonely.

For the first time in his life, there was nobody, not even the stilted sex, parties, and casual acquaintances. Nobody. He had his 'kids' during the day and they helped to fill the void, yet once the cameras shut off, there was nothing, except a cherished painting in his new, less than adequate over priced efficiency apartment. Nothing else.

Was it all worth it, Mattie? Was *better* worth it for *nothing*?

"Jack?"

He jerked his head up and saw the cinematographer standing in the door frame.

"The rushes for today are done, if you wanna take a peek. The ones on the beach with those two young kids is a 'doozy'." The cinematographer shook his head in amazement.

"Beautiful actually. I felt like I was losing my virginity myself."

Jack was touched with pride by the words of the experienced man. The feeling was the one he wanted all who watched the scene to feel. He had put many hours of thought into that scene, and to hear that he had succeeded with one person, meant a lot.

"I'm on my way, Carl. I'd kinda like to relive that experience myself . . ."

****

Weeks passed. The moderate L.A. summer drifted into an equally moderate September, and Jack had seven days remaining before his six-month deadline was up.

He was more than nervous. Rud Hanna wouldn't extend the contract for even an hour, he knew. In fact, the studio owner had been on his case. The total tab for *The Last Tap-Step* was nearly equivalent to the tab on his grand baby, Rud hotly complained. How unthinkable! Jack thought with growing frustration, mounting desperation, and indescribable fatigue, while he examined reel-after-reel of film with the editor. Despite the lack of time, it *had* to be perfect.

My life . . . that's what it's finally boiled down to.

"If its gotta be at ninety minutes max, Jack, we should cut out one of the dance numbers, and slice a bit of that beach scene which takes forever to culminate," the editor said.

"No," Jack replied immediately. "All those dance numbers stay in as is, and the beach scene . . . I don't want that touched no matter how the fuck long it takes to culminate."

"So what do we slice, huh?"

He tried to make a decision merge through his sleep-deprived mind. "Slice at the end, at the funeral. Just get a quick facial glimpse of each of those extras we hired to portray Daniel's family, then coffin . . . fade-out . . . flick it off. No use prolonging what's inevitable."

The editor carefully examined the film in question. "It might work, Jack. I'll give it a go. Maybe we'll even get it down to eighty-nine minutes."

"Just don't tell me we need any more redoes. I need that film processed within the next few days, in perfect order, no flaws." He ordered, feeling the teeter of his exhaustion.

"I'll do my best. It's a helluva lot of film," the editor replied.

Knowing that not a single word could alter the editor's statement, Jack

Linda Coleman

waved a pat over the man's shoulder, then headed for his office. Once there, he moved to the cot, serving as his bed on most nights lately. He worked triple overtime, subsisting on hit-and-miss meals and almost nil sleep. His life had never been so structured for a full twenty-four hours, he thought, slowly easing his aching body onto the cot. Yet, the structure and mind-consuming activity had repressed his other miserable thoughts . . . *until I lay on the cot again.*

The mattress was lumpy, and if he thought hard enough, he could picture himself in that shack at Las Tortugas. Once back in that dream scape, he imagined himself naked on the cot, hearing the Jamaican words and feeling the tender touch of Mattie's hands, giving him one of the most physically satisfying experiences of his entire life. But it *was* only a dream no matter how vivid, he stressed silently. She had promised him a woman who would make him feel like that time and time again. Where is she, Mattie? He asked, not knowing how long his body could survive could survive without even a hint of female closeness, no matter how vile.

The coke was gone, the rum, the pot, and he had dismantled piece-by-piece, his little plastic friend the day he returned from Caymen Brac.

Where is she?

He tightly pressed his eyelids together, fearful she wasn't anywhere, not anywhere in Hollywood, that's for sure. So how would he find her? Maybe there was nobody, and Mattie was wrong for once in her life. Maybe it would take years, she didn't specify, only that it would be difficult, and it was . . . difficult as hell.

"Jack . . . sorry to disturb you."

He bolted into a sitting position. The editor stood at the door. "What is it, Mitch?"

"I need you out there again, man. Gotta have your input on a few things, so he we can put her away in a few days like you requested," he told Jack.

Jack nodded away the stupor while swinging into a sitting position. He lifted a hand and swiped his eyes before stretching upright. "I'll be out there, Mitch. We'll put it away even if I become a goddamn zombie doing it . . ."

****

The compact viewing room at the main branch of EMAX studios was packed with top brass, directors, assistant directors—all wanting to gawk at Jack Torelli's, first film.

Jack's pants bottom nervously shifted on the padded chair while he studied the faces. Most looked amused—he had heard the talk—the EMAX executives got a big kick out of his movie-making endeavor. A huge joke, they thought. And by the sounds of it, they were joking it up big, he thought with high anxiety.

Suddenly, the door thrust open. With great aplomb, Rud Hanna entered the viewing room, looking like a pregnant ostrich in an *Armani* suit as he made his way to the center seat. After sitting, he shifted his eyes until they landed on Jack.

Oh shit! Jack stared back at the smug, superior face with the message, "My grand baby is better than yours." He hates it, even before he's seen it. Damn you, Rud!

Rud waved a hand. "Okay Chuck, let it roll. I'm ready to be hit with an explosive device," he directed, and a loud titter of laughter spread through the room.

Bomb, my ass. Jack sent a tense, glare in Rud's direction.

The wide screen flickered, and the movie title flashed on the screen. Immediately, a hoot of laughter went up, and Jack's fists tightly clench.

"Clothes? In a Rud Hanna movie? Clothes?" Rud bellowed.

Yeah, guess your cock will have to stay M&M size for this one.

"Is that tap dancing, is it?" Rud shifted his face around in disbelief. "Tap dancing in a Rud Hanna porn flick? Is that what I'm seeing?"

No, it's a new way to fuck, you asshole. Jack felt pure hate surge through him like a roaring river.

Then the film shifted to the beach scene. Soon a total hush fell over the room. Jack watched Rud and saw the bugged eyes locked on the screen. When the scene concluded, Rud quickly turned a stare on Jack.

He read the astonished incredulity on the owner's face. *Don't tell me that even 'you' relived your virginity.* Jack stared back with complacent glee.

A rapid click of heels, made Rud shift back to the screen. "Is that tap dancing again, is it?"

Another silence ensued while the actor/dancer gave everything he had to his passion. The sight of it lit up the entire screen.

"The kid's not bad . . . a tap dancer in a Rud Hanna porn movie . . . I kinda like it."

Chapter 14—Cassie

Where are you?

Taking small sips of white wine, Cassie shifted her eyes among the party guests in the townhouse located in the Tribeca district of Lower Manhattan. Curt Farchmin had told her the party would contain many theater people, so she hoped to spot him, as she had hoped for the past six months since his vision had tattooed her brain.

"Please call me Cedric, Ms. Callahan."

She halted her eyes movements and turned to the fiftieth, puffed-up, gray-haired actor who claimed he had found some success in Broadway plays. He was much too stuffy for her taste, she thought, though she didn't dare walk away. Curt had ordered her to "mingle graciously," and in terms of Cedric Lane, the publicity head had nearly pushed her at him with the terse warning that the "Old man' was a Manhattan social icon. So be particularly nice."

"Please call me Cassie, Cedric."

"If I may say so, your eyes are awe-inspiring." He sipped on a hefty glass of Irish creme'.

So what else is new? Perhaps said a different way, but 'barfarama' regardless. *And next . . .*

"And your hair, an unusual shade. Is it real, if I may ask?"

"Why yes, Cedric. Never a strand has been touched by chemicals," she replied, nearly choking on the standard line she had replied a million times, it seemed.

"And your dress . . ." He raised his bushy eyebrows while appraising her simple black knee-length poly gorgette dress that showed not a hint of her chest. "Quite 'classic', I assess," he finished, looking less that impressed.

Why don't you just say "Victorian" and be done with it, she thought with resentment, feeling like a schoolgirl dressed for her first dance in comparison to other chic women at the party. "I'm glad you approve, Cedric."

"Yes." He harshly cleared his throat, then planted a polite smile on his face. "I've even perused through your book, Ms. Callahan." His eyes held a dash of derision.

"Perused? How kind of you. What did you think of my little book?"

He evasively took a hefty gulp out of his glass. "I find the book quite charming for the masses . . . a million and a half of the masses, thus far, Curt tells me."

"And you personally, Cedric . . . ?"

"To be truthful, my palate is tempted by more outlandish literary works, and the classics of course. You know--material more appropriate for a play."

"So 'Harry' is a play verboten . . . ?"

He briefly tugged on the knot of his silk tie. "Most definitely, Cassie. It is too mass-market to be taken seriously on the stage, if I may be so blunt."

No you can't, but you will anyway. She was sick and tired of hearing time and time again how *non*-literary her book was as if that fact cheapened it. It was just one more put down she could add to a thousand, that never failed to chop another piece away from her vulnerability as a new author. She hated the parties!

Cedric cunningly sipped. "But television on the other hand . . ."

Damn! She took a glance at Curt Farchmin whose face was cracking smile after smile while he entertained a mixed group. Another lackey, huh Curt? Curt Farchmin had them stashed away at every party. Get Cassie Callahan to relinquish the book rights to television at any cost, pressure tactic after pressure tactic, so they could capitalize big, regardless as to how she felt, she inwardly burned.

"The masses would eat it up," he continued on. "They love overdone characters."

She could hardly unclench her teeth. "Overdone? My 'Harry'?"

"Too scourged, too large for plausibility . . . but on television . . ."

"Maybe I think 'Harry' is much too literary for television, Cedric," she quipped, wishing to shriek this out so every lackey in the room got the message, and got off her back.

He laughed humorously. "And that's the scourge of new authors. All think that their works are literary despite the soft covers under which their literary masterpieces sit."

She desired to toss her remaining wine at the self-important face, but she hadn't dared to be impulsive for months now. So instead she took a healthy drink of wine and looked around. In a corner stood Geoff Haines, his eyes, as usual, fastened on her like a watchdog. He smiled at her, and she returned with a disgusted wrinkle of her nose. His lips quirked in amusement. Feeling in no mood to smile, she forced her attention back to the 'social icon'.

"Where were we, Cedric?"

"Television . . . wonderful medium . . ."

****

"Cedric Lane tells me that you're in a bit of denial, Cassie," a tipsy Curt Farchmin commented while he and Cassie sat in the back of a limousine headed for Midtown Manhattan where Cassie's hotel was located.

She contorted her face with disgust. "Denial, Curt? Whatever does that mean?"

He minced no words."It means that you overvalue your book quality."

"Overvalue? The book is making a fortune. What is this overvalue rubbish?"

"Content . . ." His face grew rigid with defiance. "You seem to think the content is as rich as gold, when in actuality it is merely an effective trap for the literary defunct."

Jackass! She wanted to spew at his face, but she lacked nerve. Curt Farchmin still intimidated her, and he well knew it. He seemed to enjoy cutting her down, as if it gave him some perverse pleasure.

"You were just lucky with this book," he continued on with the tirade she had heard more times than her stomach could bear. "Therefore you should milk it for all it's worth, because your next may not have such luck. I can't work miracles time and time again."

"Why isn't Geoff here?" she asked suddenly, feeling a great need to have her security blanket present. Now.

"I sent Geoffrey home is a cab," Curt replied casually.

"Whatever for?"

He gently rubbed a thumb on one of his silver cufflinks while studying her.

"For personal reasons." Like a snake, he coiled closer to her. "I've been wondering what lies below your monk's robe." He lightly scraped a fingernail down her bare arm.

Smelling the heavy stench of bourbon on his breath, Cassie tightened with repugnance at what he was proposing. She hated him—she feared him.

Curt snuck his lips to her ear. "I never screwed 'Mary Poppins'," he said in a low husky tone. Then stuck his tongue in her ear.

Cassie tightly pressed her eyelids together and hoped the assault would soon end. To blur the wet, sickening sensation, she obtained a mind's picture of Kristi. She told herself that her daughter needed the success of this book, and future books. And she needed Curt Farchmin to make that happen. At least, that's what reality he always ground into her head and her, feeling like an aimless raft in shark infested waters, had no defense but to believe him.

"I'll tell the driver to go farther north . . . my apartment . . . your hotel room is quite *bourgeois*," his voice heaved in her ear.

"No," she shook out. "Ah . . . Harry Two! I . . .have to work on the last two chapters. Orders from John." She slowly opened her eyes and saw the uncertainty in his eyes. That excuse was her 'ace in the hole' when Curt tried to overload her day with activities that ten authors couldn't carry out. She could count on his fear of the powerful, influential editor to gain a tad semblance of the upper hand--the only hand she possessed with Curt Farchmin.

"Perhaps you could fib to John this one time. Tell him you were too indisposed to type a word." His lips nuzzled her cheek.

"I couldn't, Curt. He's already completed the edit of the rest of the book, you know, and he's chomping for those last two chapters. It could possibly be big money, John tells me."

His lips retreated from her face, then the rest of him did likewise. "Heavens! Be it for me to mess with John's pocketbook," he snipped.

"I wouldn't. His temper . . . it ain't a pretty sight," she quaked out, knowing the potential temper before he was even less attractive.

"Yes." His face stiffened with its usual character. "And his temper is going to flare more if you don't escape this denial that you're in about your epic."

She made no retort back. It was a futile debate. Curt would only drench her with more innuendos and insults, and her psyche . . . it couldn't accept even one more today.

"You *must* get that head down to earth and be a professional . . ." He went on and on until gratefully, the limo pulled up to her hotel on Fifth Avenue and Fortieth Street. "And this place." Curt thrust a hand at the nondescript structure in front of him. "Why not the Regent? You are, after all, an insular creature of some degree of success."

Having no response to the statement which she discounted as another for "The Thesaurus of the Publicity World," Cassie gathered her purse and quickly scrambled for the door handle. "I'll see you on Monday, Curt."

"Eight sharp so we can make that Bronx book signing by ten," he ordered, his eyes washed with recalcitrance.

"I'll be on time . . . as usual . . ."

****

While riding the elevator to the Ninth Floor where her small suite was located, Cassie felt the filthy sensation of Curt Farchmin linger in her ear and on her cheek. Curt had made subtle moves before, but nothing quite so bold.

Yet, she mentally cast off each remark, each move, as it just seemed easier then facing her fear and sparring

Could he ruin me as he coyly implies?

She was a smidge of a ball, he a magnanimous bat who whacked that smidge farther than it was intended to fly, Curt always told her. She was on her way to becoming a bestselling author only because of his batting efforts, and for *that* she should be utterly grateful. And the fear of a decreased effort had taken much of the dare out of her. After all her striving, her dreams, for the love of her passion, she'd been reduced to a begging dog.

The elevator doors opened, and she flew out, needing a shower, her bed, the sight of her computer, the soothing sounds of the Italian channel, and escape. She pulled her room card from her purse and with quivering fingers, slid the card through the slot. The red light kept flashing. A sudden rustling sound made her jump and turn. "Who's there?" She skirted her eyes down the dim, secluded hallway until she saw a form emerge from the shadows. A scream lodged in her throat as she stared in wide-eyed terror.

When the form moved into the hallway, sudden relief gripped her chest.

"Geoff, what are you doing here?"

"What did he do to you?" His cheek muscles twitched with anger.

Cassie screwed up her face at him.

"For Christ's sakes, Cassie, he didn't . . .

"No," she cut in with a tremble. "I. . .held him off."

Geoff moved closer to her. Seeing her oasis approaching made something snap, and Cassie rushed towards him. She impacted him with a tight hug and buried her face into his lapel.

"Tell me 'Harry's' good. Tell me I have talent. Tell me." Sobs racked her body.

"He's good. You have talent," he murmured into her hair.

"Thank god!" She pressed her face deeper into his jacket and soaked it.

"I'll take care of you, little Cassie," he said in soothing monotone.

The words lulled her and she grasped him more firmly.

"I won't let the sharks get you."

He always knew the right words, Cassie thought as she pressed even deeper.

With a gentle tug to her hair, Geoff pulled her face off his chest and his hazel eyes searched her face. "Tomorrow, Saturday, I'll take you out for the whole day if you like."

"I don't know, Geoff. Harry Two . . . John says . . .

He softly placed a thumb on her lips. " 'Harry' can hold—this can't."

"What can't?"

"You need to be 'Cassie Callahan' again," he said with gentle firmness.

It sounded heavenly. "I think I'd like that," she replied with a teary choke.

"Eight sharp. I'll buy you breakfast, bagels, fruit, and herb tea in Bryant Park."

My favorite breakfast. He bingo'd again. "No eight sharp, please." She thought of Curt's Monday edict. "Eight oh five will suffice."

One edge of his lips curled up. "Eight oh five it is." Then his face drifted closer to hers.

She widened her eyes with uneasiness at the familiar move.

"It's only a kiss, Cassie, a kiss between friends." He lowered his face until their lips met.

Against her intentions, she kissed back, again. What was the harm? It was one way to keep Geoff Haines happy, and she *did* owe him for his diligence.

"Like the sweetest of red wines," he said when his lips lifted. Then raised a finger to her cheek and stroked, his eyes smoldering with an unreadable look. "Get some rest on your ocean raft, Cassie, and know the sharks are at bay for now..."

****

"Watching the pigeons drop their droppings does put a bit of a damper on breakfast," Cassie laughed the next morning when she and Geoff sat on a bench in Bryant Park eating the breakfast stash they had purchased from a street vendor.

He plucked a concord grape off its stalk and popped it into her mouth. "View the droppings as a creative means for the majestic, if not overabundant birds, to leave an artistic impression on the world."

She curiously chewed the grape. "That's quite lovely Geoff. Almost poetic. Have you ever thought of jotting it down? And Ode to Pigeons, maybe?"

"Actually..." He took a large sip of his herb tea. "I did write once."

"Really?" she asked with much interest. "Why didn't you ever mention it?"

"Inconsequential." Geoff preoccupied himself with his tea.

She saw the rigidity of his cheek muscles when the paper cup touched his lips. "What did you write? Was it poetry?" she pressed with growing curiosity.

"In my younger days, but..." His drinking speeded up. "It was fiction that caught my interest... period epics given my history doctorate and aversion to teaching which I *did* tell you."

"You gave it up, you told me."

"Yes--I gave it up to write," he admitted.

"So you had the passion too." She inched closer to him, fascinated by this new information. "What did you write? What?"

He drained the cup then crumpled it in his fist. "I wrote a Victorian novel, my penchant period, over two thousand pages, six years of near steady work to complete."

"Two thousand?" she breathed out. *"Six years? For one book?"*

Geoff compressed his lips together. "It was a complicated, highly researched book, an epic, not..." He paused and shifted his face from her.

"It was literary, right? You can say it. I'm immune. Really," she told him.

"Yes." His voice sizzled. "It was literary, damn literary."

"So what was the title?" She excitedly ground her shoulder against his. "I've been an avid reader all my life, perhaps..."

"No, you didn't read it!" he flared, irritated. "It never got published."

"But why after six years?"

"Don't you get it?" He furiously rubbed a hand over his brown hair. "I wasn't one of the fortunate few. An editor told me it was crap! He cut it down to bits."

Cassie shook her head in misunderstanding. "So? Go to another editor, or another, or another... if you had the passion..."

"No--I'm content on the sidelines." His voice gave a tortured heave.

"I don't understand, Geoff. If you burn to write, why..."

He suddenly touched his nose to hers. "I feel your passion, Cassie, and that satisfies me."

Though her curiosity blistered, she figured it best to stop pushing. It made her more than uncomfortable to see Geoff Haines so intense. "Maybe we should abandon the pigeon droppings and take our hike," she suggested.

Geoff gave a crook of a smile."Lead on, Cassie, and as usual, I'll follow . . ."

****

Cassie decided that if she walked around Rockefeller Center every day of her life, still her eyes would pick up something that she had missed the day before. It was a microcosm of sensory-stimulating wonder. She loved it!

"There's *Bergdorf's*," Geoff pointed out. "Let's go inside and take a peek."

She looked at the store that screamed 'high-ticket', and crinkled her nose down at her faded jean shorts, white T-shirt that read **I Luv the Big Apple**, white crew socks, white *Asics*, then she patted the white cap on her head, bearing the words **I Luv the Miniapple**. She smiled weakly. "I don't think that place will allow me through the front door."

Geoff laughed. "I'll just tell them that this, in the flesh, is the *who* of *Who is Cassie Callahan*, and they'll fall all over you with the smell of money their experienced noses can 'whiff' a mile away." He grabbed her arm and steered her through the store entrance.

Several minutes later, she was trying on hats, some with elitist flair and others on the fringes of outlandish. She was having great fun despite the dubious looks the salesclerks were giving her. "I don't think they're whiffing money, Geoff . . . more like peasantry, don't you think?" Under the wide brim of the heavily netted hat, she tipped her chin at the rigid female figures.

"Maybe their 'whiffs' need a nudge, Cassie."

Crooking arm to hip, she gave a dramatic lift of her chin. "Are they whiffing Geoff? This damn brim makes me blind."

He laughed with amusement. "I can't tell. I think they're too busy trying to get a hold of the little white men from Bellevue."

She dropped her pose and whipped off the hat. "It's no use. Must be my thin legs. They can't see anything else."

"Well then, maybe we should look at attire which cover those thin legs," he suggested, pulling her out of the millinery department and quickly into another . . .

Cassie crinkled her brow while gazing at the lush, flowing negligees on one mannequin after another. Why here? She wanted to ask him, feeling unnerved. But Geoff seemed occupied with his languid fingering of the satin and lace.

"Look at this, Cassie. Lovely, isn't it?" He held up a padded hanger bearing a short green satin charmeuse chemise with matching wrap.

Fastening her gaze on the fine lace peek-a-boo bodice, she let out all her nerves in a laugh. "It won't cover my thin legs. So . . ."

"Your legs are beautiful," he murmured out of the blue.

Stop Geoff. She hated his abrupt outbursts that placed her off guard.

"Why not try it on for the fun of it," he urged.

"But Geoff . . . I'm more of the light thermal pajama type and . . ."

"Please . . . for me," he interjected in a whispered plea.

Damn! That hangdog look again! It brought out her maternal tendencies, and thus, her rapid concession. "All right. One slip on, then one slip off." She grabbed the hanger, and waved it at the salesclerk . . .

****

Swaying rhythmically, Cassie gazed at herself in the full length mirror. *My god! Now I really feel like a Harlem streetwalker. Well . . . that's it.*

"Cassie . . ."

She heard a low hiss at the door. "Geoff?" she asked cautiously.

"Let me in, the salesclerk . . ."

She quickly pulled the wrap around her and opened the door a crack to see the hazel eyes peering back at her. "I'll be out in a moment."

"No--I have to see you in that beautiful gown," he insisted in a whisper.

"Are you kidding?" she breathed out.

He pushed the door open, thrust through and bolted it behind him. Once inside the dressing room, his eyes locked onto the negligee wrap, and they squinted in scrutinizing fashion.

She crossed herself tighter. "This is crazy, Geoff. Please leave. Frankly, I'm embarrassed."

A slight lift of his hand indicated her to be quiet. "Lower the wrap, Cassie . . . please," he said in a bare whisper while his eyes never left her.

"Lower it?" she asked in hushed disbelief. "Are you mad?"

"Am I? I think not. Maybe hungry, but not mad." He took a few steps closer. "Give me this at least, Cassie, please . . . just this."

She saw the begging droop of his eyes and couldn't stand it. He was her protectorate who stood by her all these months without falter, and she knew that he wanted more, but he hardly ever took it. Didn't she owe him at least one peek? Between friends? She loosened her arms and the wrap fell from her shoulders.

A gulp slowly coursed down his throat and strongly hit his Adam's Apple. Then a perceptible tremor shook his face. "You're incredible, like I knew you would be."

She jittered under his strange gaze. "Can I get dressed, now? I wanna hike some more."

In a wink, he deftly reached into the pocket of his casual jacket, extracting his small 35mm camera. He stepped back and hoisted the lens to his eyes. "One picture, Cassie. Smile." And the bulb flashed in her eyes before she could stop him.

"What are you doing?" she asked in a soft hiss.

"Just one picture, Cassie. Something for my wallet, under my pillow, don't deny me. No one will ever see, I swear. Just me. Mine."

She saw his eyes cascade into intense pleading, and soon thereafter she nodded. "As long as you keep it under wraps. I don't think the General would appreciate it one iota," she told him, then adding bitterly, "He'd have a bird to see his Mary Poppins come of age; although she came of age more than a decade ago."

The corner of his lip curled up. "She sure did."

"Now go!" She pushed him at the door. "That salesclerk didn't seem the tolerant type . . ."

****

A couple hours later, Cassie deliciously twirled her lips around a hot dog with the works while her and Geoff sat on a Central Park Bench listening to a group of musicians playing mestizo music. Hot dog consumed, she lifted her arms then wildly clapped and swung her body in time to the strophic, highly-percussioned sound.

"Give 'em hell, Cassie," Geoff laughed.

Impulses surging, Cassie rose from the bench and danced closer to the band until she was in front of them. The musicians loved her antics and urged her on. So she languidly swayed to the music while the crowds clapped. "I'm Cassie! Cassie!" she yelled with glee.

Geoff squatted at a distance, snapping picture after picture, and she posed seductively for him. A wide smile spread on his face, and he clicked more.

"It's me!" she twirled around and around until dizziness hit and she nearly toppled. Geoff rushed forward to catch her.

"Whoa, Cassie. These people may think that you're a little inebriated."

"I am!" She dramatically collapsed over his arm. "I'm inebriated with happiness!"

He pulled her up and placed a tight arm around her shoulders. "That's wonderful, Cassie, but perhaps we should expel that happiness in a less public place. The General, you know . . . you wouldn't want him to happen to get wind."

"Who the cares about the old windbag today? It's Cassie's free day!" she yelled at the top of her lungs.

Geoff nervously glanced around then hurried her off, not stopping until they found a fairly quiet grass patch shaded by a huge oak tree.

"Why did you do that?" she demanded the moment he plopped her down into a sitting position. "You promised that I could be Cassie Callahan today."

He sat on the ground next to her, risking grass stain to his expensive slacks. "With me you can, you know that. It's important for me to know, that you know that," he pleaded.

"I wanna believe it, Geoff, but . . ." She suddenly felt confused. Was he really on her side? The question had plagued her off and on over the past months. After all, he too was a slave to Curt Farchmin. What exactly did that mean to Geoff Haines? She wondered now.

"Believe it." He urged closer to her. "I was wrong, I admit it. I should have let you dance to your heart's content. Don't be mad at my misguided impulses, Cassie. Please."

She drifted her eyes to his face and studied it. *Oh*, she wanted to believe him. In fact, she had a vital need to believe him. "I'm not mad," she finally said.

Geoff stroked away the hair strands from her cheeks. "My perfect Cassie. I'd never blemish that, no matter how many times she wanted to dance on Saturday."

Touched with spookiness, she brushed his fingers away and stood up. "I wanna leave the park. I. . .wanna be somewhere else . . ."

****

Spent from the excessive walking, the pair stretched out in a booth in a fairly empty grill in the Grand Central District. Looking thoughtful, Cassie slowly massaged the back of her neck.

"You looked bushed," Geoff observed while his fork played with the romaine leaves of his Caesar salad.

She plucked a french fry and rotated it in catsup. "Did I tell you that my parents put Kristi in a boarding school?" she suddenly cracked out.

He placed down his fork, and quietly shook his head.

"Well they did. A fancy place outside of Chicago. She hates it. It's all girls, and she's nearly thirteen and noticing boys. I. . .don't know what to do for her."

"Can't your grandfather intervene?" he questioned.

"I called him." A strong pressure formed behind her eyes. "But he has no control over those two anymore. Their business is exploding. You know . . . parents of Cassie Callahan. Clients are flocking in droves. He has no more threats to hang over the two hot shots' heads."

"But they've given you visitation rights now."

Tears dripped from her eyes. "Yeah--they had to give me some reward for feathering their financial and social nest. Only, it seems to be a little too late."

He encircled her hand. "What's going on, Cassie?"

"Kristi." She felt the choking build up of her tears. "I told her I was coming to Chicago and I didn't give a damn what Curt said. But Kristi said, 'Don't bother . . . Cassie'." And the tears burst from her eyes.

Geoff's hand pressure increased. "All kids go through that stage where they call their parents by their first name. I did--didn't you?"

"Yeah," she whispered, "But with me it wasn't a stage, rather a lifelong habit."

His eyes grew sympathetic. "She'll come around. You're her mother, after all. That will never change no matter the distance."

She helplessly shook her head. "I've done it all for her as much as for myself to save her from such a fate. But I let her down, and now she's getting older. Older means more cynical."

"What about her father? Couldn't he do something?" Geoff offered.

"No," she replied quietly. "My Nono says, Art and June have easily shot down every attempt he's made to see his daughter. Kyle doesn't have the money to fight them in court."

"But you do, and getting more all the time."

She turned her wet face from him. "There's extenuating circumstances, Geoff, and my parents won't get the judge to cancel them, unless . . ." She felt the hard bite of indecision.

"Unless what, Cassie?" He pressed closer.

"Unless I turn over my investments to them-- if you can believe such garbage coming from parents."

"No, I don't believe. They sound like sick parents to me," he murmured. "Parents who don't deserve you."

"Should I do it?" She suddenly shifted to him. "Even if it makes me vomit every day of my life to say 'uncle' to them, should I do it?"

Tightness descended on his face. "No, Cassie. Forget them. They have no feeling for you, and don't deserve a penny of your fortune."

"But Kristi . . ."

"She'll come around--I know this. You have to hold on to that belief," he replied firmly.

"What if she hates me, Geoff?"

A crooked smile dangled on his lips. "Who could ever hate you, Cassie? Only a fool, and from your descriptions of Kristi, I'd say the child is no fool."

"I'm so confused, Geoff." She broke down into tears.

He quickly moved to the other side of the booth and scooted in next to her. "Let me take the confusion away, Cassie." He placed an arm around her shoulder and pulled her close to him. "Trust me, Cassie. I'd never steer you wrong or hurt you," he lulled.

She lavished in his warm, comfortable arm crook. "Thank you, Geoff, for listening all these months. If I had no one to talk to, I don't know what I . . .

His lips made a quiet hushing sound. "My ears are at your disposal, day or night. I've told you that over and over. It's me that thanks you for your faith in our friendship to let me in on your deepest thoughts, Cassie. I'd do anything for you, Cassie."

"I needed to hear that, Geoff. You always seem to know. Always."

"And now . . ." He jogged her head from his arm. "You have to eat, keep your strength up so you can tackle those chapters tomorrow. John, you know . . ."

****

The next week was a usual maze of activity day and night for Cassie. Book signing, interviews, lunches with bland to exotic food, and the unbearable parties where her book was matched against more literary endeavors--her the firm loser in the self-worth department. She longed to escape the trap and return to the attic where she only had her fertile mind for company. But she could see no way out of a trap, twisting tighter by the day. It was the price for her passion, she kept telling herself. It had to culminate at some point. It couldn't reach an inferno without some effect ultimately occurring. And for her . . . this was it.

"Mr. LaLiberte is ready to see you, Ms. Callahan," the editor's secretary said crisply.

"Thanks," Cassie muttered. To add insult to injury, she had been summoned to John LaLiberte's office, and she feared a major chewing out. She had only turned in part of the second to the last chapter of 'Harry Two' after he had dictated one chapter by the end of the week. The writing had come tough despite her thrill with the second book. She had been too emotional to be creative and much of her old spark was zapped. It had lost a bit of its sheer joy, she thought.

She startled when seeing a small smile crack on John's face. Then she shifted her eyes. A strange dark haired man sat comfortably in a chair, his fine linen shirt molded across his chest.

"Sit down, Cassie," John invited in more pleasant tones than normal.

While peeking at the man whose dark eyes were fixed on her, she made her way to a chair by the editor's desk.

"I'd like you to meet Michael Isle, Cassie. He's from Los Angeles," John introduced.

Michael Isle stood and graciously offered his hand. "It's a pleasure, Ms. Callahan. I found your book absolutely wonderful, a sea of powerful emotions."

"You did?" She took the hand, surprised by the compliment. It had been a long time--except from the excited book-buying public, that is. "Thank you for the kind words, Mr. Isle."

"And I heartily congratulate you for surpassing the million mark in sales," he continued on, his hand lingering on hers.

She studied his aristocratic air, and wondered if he was British like John. *But no.* She hadn't detected an English tone, rather a haughty one. Yet, he was a good-looking fox despite his artificial attempts to mask his age. "Thank you again, Mr. Isle." Feeling uncomfortable with his moist hand glued on hers, she lifted her hand and sat down.

"Yes Cassie." John let out a huffy laugh. "Mike is quite taken with your book. He's talked of little else since entering this office."

"That's right, Ms. Callahan," Michael substantiated. "John and I have been analyzing the fabulous 'Harry'."

"Analyzing?" she questioned.

"You know . . . an interpretative debate. What is the true essence of the character? Those sorts of questions."

Fascinated by the answer, she moved closer to Michael. "And what did you decide?"

Michael too leaned closer. "He has many of life's flaws, yet seems perfect nonetheless—a *real* grabber. Magnetizing, actually."

The answer greatly pleased her. It was refreshing, to have such positive feedback and appreciation of a character that contained so much of herself in him. She found herself drawn to the affirmation like a starving person. "That's the essence I tried to convey with the story."

"And you did it so magnificently, Ms. Callahan." He gave a slight bow of his head.

She flashed a bright smile at him.

"And the setting, Ms. Callahan . . ."

"Have you been to Minnesota, Mr. Isle?"

"Minneapolis on one or two occasions. It's a very interesting state. Many a fine films have come out of there," he replied.

"I wouldn't know," she said briefly.

Michael frowned slightly."You're not much of a movie buff, Ms. Callahan?"

She emphatically shook her head. "There's only a rare film that I've liked in all my thirty-three years. I'm more of a reading buff. I've read most of the fine books."

He creased his brow to show great astonishment. "In this age of movies, Ms. Callahan? That's barely believable."

"That's the way I've always been." She gave an unconcerned lift of her shoulders.

"I suppose television is more your cup of tea," he said graciously.

She made a disgusted noise. "That's even worse. It's trite and insults the intellect of the American population."

Michael loudly cleared his throat and directed a hasty glance at John. "Oh come now, Ms. Callahan." He turned back to her. "Aren't you being a little harsh on the medium which has revolutionized society?"

"For the worse, sir," she replied firmly.

"Take Desert Storm, for instance." He folded his hands. "Wasn't that a miraculous sight to view on television?"

"I was writing my fourth novel at the time, so I wouldn't know," she replied pertly, then thoughtfully added, "But I do recall my daughter telling me about it. She did say that it would sit in her memory forever."

"See?" He inched closer. "It made an impact on your daughter. That's what television has the capacity to do . . . make an impact on a thirsty public."

She swallowed her disgust, wishing he would get off the hated subject and back to her book. "Maybe. But try to justify something like soap operas in the same context."

Confusion settled on his face. "I. . .guess one could say that soaps impact on a bored female population, spurning deeper emotions. Always a worthwhile activity. Don't you agree?"

"A way to get their jollies, don't you mean?" she challenged.

His mouth collapsed into a slight scowl. "Perhaps. But don't you also agree that there are different degrees of television? Say news versus cartoons, sports versus game shows, low quality movies versus movies based on literary masterpieces . . . like 'Harry' for example."

Literary? She felt great surprise. "You think 'Harry's' literary, Mr. Isle?"

"Of course, Ms. Callahan," he enthused. "A literary novel like 'Harry' would make a huge impact on television."

Instantly, she sparked with suspicion. "Television? My 'Harry'? What are you exactly saying, Mr. Isle?"

He pulled back in his chair and resumed a relaxed pose. "Why nothing, Ms. Callahan. It was just a comparison. Exceptional television versus the trite, as you termed it."

"Good. Because my 'Harry' will never be defiled on a little screen," she said decisively.

"Defiled?" Michael exploded into amused laughter. "But how could that ever happen with you consulting on the teleplay . . . I mean hypothetically."

"It wouldn't even be hypothetical, Mr. Isle. I don't write such rubbish as teleplays."

"But Cassie . . ." John interjected. "Writing is writing no matter the medium, and to bring 'Harry' to life so millions can feel such a wonderful character . . . Wouldn't that be wonderful?"

Wrinkling her nose, she thought about this. It *would* be wonderful to see 'Harry' in the flesh. Although, the wonder quickly evaporated with thoughts of how such a medium would portray him to amuse a public, rather than do what was best for her beloved character. "I'm afraid, John, that I can't see the 'wonderful'. Television could never live up to my vision of 'Harry'."

"But of course it could," Michael Isle cut in. "It would be your vision as you write it on the teleplay."

"With some actor mucking it up." She sniffed.

"Come on, Ms. Callahan," Michael said in a reasonable voice. "Only the best actor would portray 'Harry', not any old Joe. You could even be part of the selection . . . if the situation ever confronted you, that is."

"Well, since it will never confront me . . ." She stood up. "I have a party to attend."

"Party?" Michael stood too. "And where would that be, Ms. Callahan?"

"Trump Towers . . . should prove quite interesting."

"Not . . ." Michael looked astonished. "The Sondra Abbey party?"

She nodded. "That's the name Curt gave me. Seems she *loves* literary writers, so I should get quite a mental workout defending my mass-market book." She couldn't help the bitterness that exuded from her voice.

"Why . . ." A bright smile broke out on his face. "I'm going to the same party. Perhaps? Do you think? I could possibly escort you to the affair?"

"No," she replied immediately. "Geoff is escorting me."

"Forget it." John stood too. "Haines can stay home for one night. I think you should graciously accept Mr. Isle's invitation, Cassie." He bore blue eyes into her face.

"But . . ." She felt panic grip. "I feel better with Geoff along, John."

"He's indisposed," John replied tensely. "Per my order, he stays put."

She wanted to sob. Trump Towers? Without Geoff? They'll eat her alive.

"Jot down your address, Ms. Callahan. Me and my limo will be there at seven." Michael held out notebook and pen.

Feeling numb with resignation, she grabbed the two items and scribbled out the information he requested. "Seven's fine, Mr. Isle. Thank you for the invitation."

He brandished a broad smile. "Perhaps we can resume our debate, Ms. Callahan . . ."

****

"Who are you, sir?" Cassie demanded after an hour of being in a hot clinch of debate with Michael Isle in the midst of the most luxurious abode that she had ever seen.

"Easy, Ms. Callahan . . . your image," Michael hushed while leisurely gazing around at the hundred guests who were present.

"My image, my foot!" And she stomped her high heel for emphasis.

"Okay!" he hissed. "I'm a studio owner, and . . . a television producer. Miniseries and television movies are my specialty."

"I knew it!" she angered. "You have some nerve, knowing specifically how I feel. Desert Storm . . . how dare you!"

He stiffly held up a halting hand. "Do you blame me? I thought your book was great. Prime miniseries material. And the public . . . they already love 'Harry'. A maniacal bestseller. I'd kill to get rights to that book. There! I admitted it."

"Humph! You can admit all you want, but television will never touch *my* Harry."

"Stubborn!"

"So be it!"

"And selfish too. To deny the world such a wonderful character . . ."

"Selfish!" she flared hotly. "He's *my* character. I have every right to be selfish!"

"The hell he is!" he flared right back. "The day you placed him up for publication, you gave up sole ownership. Now, he belongs to the world. To share!"

"Says you!"

"Damn!" His facial muscles rippled with an angry tremor. "Why couldn't you be like ninety-nine point nine percent of authors and sign a contract that includes movie and television rights. Why? Why this book? Why?"

"I'll never sign such a contract, for this book, or 'Harry Two'!"

"Oh shit!" His mouth twisted with dread. "You have another one?"

She gave a brash toss of her blonde head. "That's none of your business, Mr. Isle."

"Michael . . . or Mike if you insist."

"As if familiarity will get me to change my mind!"

"Do you know that you're beautiful when you're angry?"

"*Oooh . . .*" She flashed her eyes at him. "Now that's really low! What do you think, I was born yesterday?"

"People . . ." A female voice interjected into the argument.

Both pair of eyes flew upward to see the party hostess.

She gave an amused laugh. "I didn't invite you both, to be the party entertainment. Now Mike . . ." she drawled. "There's a group to the right who's *dying* to talk to you. And, Ms. Callahan, our literary person, there's a group to the left who want to discuss a few points about your book. So scoot. Mingle."

Michael started walking to the right. "I'll be in John's office at ten a.m. tomorrow, and I ask you to come and further discuss this point."

Cassie moved to the left. "Maybe--and I mean *maybe* . . ."

****

Hmmm . . . it was fun to spar with Michael. I almost felt like my old self.

She lazily slid her room card in the slot. The green light flashed, then a click, then she placed a hand on the door knob.

Suddenly, she felt someone push against her back and a silent scream emerged.

"Are you all right, Cassie," came a whisper in her ear?

"Geoff! You scared me half to death." She let out a heavy breath.

"I was very worried, Cassie."

She felt his lips moving against her hair. "I'm fine, Geoff, really."

"Michael Isle is an animal. I was so scared that . . ."

"An animal?" She twisted around to face him and saw the desperation in his eyes. "Him?"

"Wise up, Cassie. He's a big Hollywood producer. What do you think?"

"He's got a sly mouth all right," she replied.

"No!" He clutched her shoulders and shook. "He's dangerous. He comes across as one thing, but . . . he's not."

"Oh Geoff . . ." She laughed at the over-dramatization. "That's ridiculous."

"It isn't!" His hands tightened around her. "Stay away from him, promise me. You don't need someone like that in your life. Please. Promise me."

She felt burning in her shoulders. "Let me go, Geoff. That hurts."

He ignored her and pressed tighter. "Not until you promise me."

The continued pain made her angry and she struggled to break free. "How can I promise when I don't know what I'm promising?" she gritted out.

"It's like a hierarchy of sharks, Cassie, don't you see?"

"No!" she shrieked. "Take your hands off me now, Geoff."

His hold grew more restricting and she felt her body pushed against the door frame. "Your agent is a small shark who get fed from bigger sharks like Curt and John who get fed from great white sharks like Michael Isle. You're at the bottom, their mouths open wide above you, waiting to take bite after bite after . . ."

"Fed? Great white shark? What is this nonsense?" she jittered out

His eyes turned wild as he bore more pressure on her shoulders. "Money! It's the shark's game, and they'll do anything, *anything*, to that shark's bait at the bottom. Bait Cassie! You!"

The words terrified her. And his eyes . . . they looked insane, she thought. That was the worst. Geoff! Her protector! How could he scare her like this?

"Please stop it, Geoff."

"It's not talent, you nearsighted woman." His face shook with intense anger. "Do you know how many talented authors there are out there? Thousands, maybe a million, who never get a shot at the gold ring, because they may have a flaw or two that make them unacceptable shark bait. But you . . . you were the perfect bait, and you even had a halfway decent book that had the potential of making it to the great white shark. That's all the hell a bestseller is. But you're too poufed on the fantasy to see it!"

"How can you say this to me?" she trembled out. "You said I had talent. You said 'Harry' was good. You *swore* to me."

His crazed look rescinded, replaced by intensity. "I worship you, Cassie. I would never say anything to hurt you." He drifted his face down to hers. "I need to taste the passion."

She felt the bittersweet touch of his lips grow deeper, and deeper, and then she felt the thrust of his tongue in her mouth. Repulsed, she flailed her head, trying to break her lips free, but his tongue only became more persistent while his hands molded over her breasts. Her flailing grew frenetic. And then, as suddenly as it started, his assault ceased cold.

"Let me make love to you, Cassie. It will bind us so the sharks will never get you," he said in low desperate whisper.

"Go away." Tears ran down her cheeks while concurrently the nausea rose from his lingering taste in her mouth.

"Please Cassie . . ." His eyes grew pleading.

"No." She stared at the hangdog eyes and for the first time, felt nothing but loathing laced with immense desolation. "I don't trust you any more."

"You have to," he insisted. "How can I care for my little Cassie if she doesn't trust me?"

"I'm not your little Cassie anymore, Geoff. I'm . . ." She filled with more terror than she ever thought possible. "Not anyone's little Cassie any more." The panic of her words propelled her to spin around, push open the door and fly through, snapping the lock just as Geoff was about to throw his weight against the wood.

Tears flooded her face while his pounds and pleas came through the door. *He had deserted her . . . truly.* He just wanted the sex. *Passion's kiss . . .* as he had sickly inferred. He, was no better than the other sharks he touted about. *He had baited her too. Geoff? It was incredible!*

She rushed to the television. *Italian channel.* She had to tune out the noise, tune out the hurt that was devouring her more so with each passing second. She needed that secure feeling.

I'm really alone now.

Cassie shook her fingers over the remote, trying to find the sound of the healing voice. *Why can't I ever remember that number?* Face after face flicked before her eyes. *But not his face.* His show was gone and had been ever since she returned to New York. Still, she longed for a dual vision—those eyes and the soft low voice that had lulled away her ills for her whole life.

Where is that channel? Where?

"You're shark bait, Lady!"

Geoff's word and a final slam at the wood door penetrated her panic-ridden mind.

She flicked feverishly until . . . *the Italian voice* . . . and she let it bathe her ears. Such a solacing Romance language. Don't stop . . . don't ever stop. The sound drifted around her. The only true oasis of her life.

Nono, I'm scared. What do I do next, huh Nono? What . . . ?

****

Friday, the next day, New York was New York. The temperature was a basking seventy degrees, deafening noise and congestion were in the streets, and hordes of people moved along the pavement at a constant clip. Hidden behind black sunglasses to hide the facial erosion from her troubled night, Cassie stood outside Starburst Publishing, staring up at the skyscraper and only seeing an ocean filled with wide mouths and flesh-ripping teeth.

Resignation drenched her. This is the reality. Geoff was right. And she didn't grieve for the deflation of her bubble, nor even hesitate in nodding acceptance to what was, rather, she walked towards the ocean, feeling like a minnow on a hook.

I've made a decision, she thought while making her way up to John LaLiberte's office. *But only if Michael can answer a question followed by a concession.*

Sunglasses still over her eyes, she opened the door to John's office and walked determinedly to his desk, ignoring the 'Great White Shark' to her left.

"Cassie. Do you have something in your eye, my dear?" John frowned up at her.

She responded with the void she felt. "Only the ravishes of a dream."

"What in the world?" John's brow pleated into a question.

Slighting his look, she turned to Michael Isle whose dark eyes keenly stared at her.

"Do you want "Harry'?" she asked point blank.

"Ms. Callahan, you know that I do and . . ."

"Cassie," she said in a hiss. "My name is *Cassie*."

His eyes narrowed with confusion. "Okay Cassie."

"How bad do you want 'Harry'?"

"I can make it a hit--I know I can. So, I want it damn bad. I admit it."

"Who's *Clay Slade*?" she asked suddenly.

His eyelids lifted upward. "*Clay Slade*? Torelli's *Clay Slade*?" Dumbstruck, he stared at her. "Jack Torelli? That *Clay Slade*? Why Cassie?"

Torelli . . . He is Italian. I sensed it. A sudden warmth coursed through her. She thrust off the sunglasses and placed a steadfast look on Michael. "Torelli *will* play Harry, and I *will* mold my 'Harry' for that dredge of a communication medium, and I *will* come to Los Angeles to do it." And for a brief moment, she lavished in the wonderful feeling of the tables being turned.

"Cassie!" John flared like an irate father.

She turned to see the blue eyes flashing with angry disapproval. "Or I go back to my attic and kill Ms. Callahan."

"What the hell is this crazy carousal talk, Cassie?" John demanded.

"I'm building a wall around my raft," she whispered.

"What? There you go again!" John yelled.

She pounded her elbows to his desk. "Do you want Cassie Callahan?"

"Want you?" John shook his head, not understanding.

"Me!" she cried out, telling herself she no longer had anything to lose. It was gone anyway, except for her Nono and he would take care of her, she had no doubt. "Me! The author Cassie Callahan, turning out book after book to feed you. *That* Cassie Callahan."

"If book after book is as good as 'Harry', yes," John replied.

"They will be!" she said with quiet determination. "They'll surpass 'Harry', and I'll work like hell to make that so."

John nodded. "Then I want that Cassie Callahan."

One wall up, she told herself while lifting from the desk and facing Michael Isle square-on. "Do you get 'Harry' or not, huh?"

"No Torelli," he heaved with defiance. "I wouldn't touch that sleaze with a ten-foot pole."

"Sleaze!" She charged right up to him. "How dare you call my 'Harry' a sleaze!"

"Cassie, you have no idea," John tried to cut in, but she backed a hand at him.

"He is a sleaze!" Michael shouted. "How does a movie called *Jungle Love* strike you and your high movie morals?"

"How would I know? I haven't been to a movie house since I was eighteen!"

Michael planted his hands on the chair arms and shoved forward. "He wore *nothing*, quite convenient with all the sex going on. And he bit a slimy fish in half until his mouth was caked with blood, may I add. *That's* the 'Harry' that you propose!"

"You mean . . . ?" A cautious distress touched her.

"It's called hard porn, Cassie. Although you probably remember them with the term X-rated movies," Michael replied smugly.

Oh no! Her bottom hit the nearest chair. It couldn't be. Not him. Those eyes . . .

"And then add his sterling reputation in the Hollywood community," Michael spoke on with biting sarcasm. "How do drugs and sexual perversion sit with you? Then, there's his flaunting like he's so damn proud of all of it."

Stop. I can't hear anymore. 'Harry' . . . no more 'Harry'.

"He's no longer an actor, he's a sex machine!" Michael spat out in disdain.

"I could tell he was an actor once. He spoke so beautifully," she murmured.

"In *Clay Slade*? Is that where you're professing he spoke beautifully?" Michael asked with utter disbelief. She fixed a look of defiance on him. "Yes! That's what I'm professing."

"Your inexperienced television watching is showing on that one," Michael muttered under his breath.

"I heard that! I do have ears, you know. And also, an opinion for that matter!"

"Well your opinion stinks! He sounded like a bumbling idiot on that show! And after . . ."

"After what?" Cassie insisted.

He squeezed his lips together and stared at her.

"Stubborn huh?" She drifted closer to him. "You're not telling me everything, are you?"

Michael's lips pursed tighter.

"Was Torelli a good actor once, was he?" she urged.

His lips opened into a snarl. "Okay! He was good once. Does that satisfy you?"

No. She pulled back. It was *now* that counted. Disappointment raged through her. What next? She had no clue. So . . . for the heck of it, she decided to ask, "What's his latest movie? Another fish? Or maybe he wore a fig leaf this time?"

No answer.

She saw his lips pursed so tightly, they were nearly white. *You snake!*

"I didn't get a name. Perhaps I'll break down and enter a movie theater after fifteen years," she said through clenched teeth.

Michael's lips turned stark white.

"I wanna name!"

His face pained, Michael turned to John. "Can't you control your temperamental authors?"

Temperamental author, huh? Another wall for you, Cass.

"Cassie, stop this inappropriateness! You have no cause to challenge a man whose been in the movie-making business all his adult life," John sternly admonished.

"Appease the 'Great White', huh John?"

"There you go again with that symbolic gibberish!" John fisted his desktop.

"I'm an author. I specialize in symbolic gibberish!" She spun back to Michael Isle. "Do you want 'Harry'? Perhaps 'Harry Two' while we're at it. I didn't sign away any television/movie rights for that one either, nor will I ever sign for any of my books!"

"Damn female!" Michael raged.

"The written word . . . it does have a bit of supremacy in the ocean, doesn't it?"

"Ocean? Cassie have you gone mad?" John interjected.

"Yes! I want that bestseller," Michael hissed through his teeth. "It has the potential to make a fortune for my studio with the right handling. *Yes*--I want it."

"Harry feeds that roaring mouth, huh Mike?"

"Oh Cassie . . ." John flung back into his chair in total frustration.

"So . . ." She ambled up to Michael chair. "If you wanna be fed, I wanna movie name . . . Torelli's latest flick to be specific."

Dread soaked his face. "How does *The Last Two-Step* grab you?"

She backed her bottom into the chair. "It grabs my curiosity. The title . . . kind of lilting. Does he wear clothes in this one?" Immediately, she saw the hard chomp of his lips. "So he *does* wear a spot of clothes?" And the chomp grew more resolute. "Maybe more than a spot . . . ?" His lips fastened in an ironclad grip. "Perhaps he was hardly nude at all, *if* at all. Maybe if I call a newspaper in Los Angeles, they would graciously give Cassie Callahan the scoop on the sleaze."

"All right!" Michael gave a forward jerk of his body. "He didn't star in it. He . . . produced and directed it. Now are you satisfied?"

"Was it good?"

Again he pressed his lips to stark whiteness.

Feeling her tolerance at its end, she shook her head. "No more bullshit or sneaky ploys. If you want me to come to Los Angeles and work with you, it's with a clean slate of understanding, including your stubborn honesty. I don't need that in my life."

Michael grudgingly opened his lips. "It was critically acclaimed, actually. Although, how that ever happened has eluded many winks of sleep."

A smile lit up her face. "So he's not a porn star anymore. He's a critically-acclaimed producer/director. Is that what you're actually saying?"

"Of soft-porn, Cassie. It's not legitimate by any means," he argued.

"Soft porn?"

"Well . . . to be completely honest, it's called ultra-soft porn . . . but it's all the same."

"Specifically define ultra-soft porn, Michael." She inched closer to him.

"Damn!" Michael directed his frustration at the ceiling. "Very little nudity . . . more artistic sex with an actual story behind it." He lowered a sneering face to her. "Why did *you* have to write 'Harry'? Why?"

"Please calm down, Mike," John implored.

"Oh, shut up, John!" Michael flared angrily.

"You want 'Harry', and I want a critically acclaimed director/producer to portray him, so . . ." She locked her gaze onto Michael's face.

"I refuse to work with that man!"

"Well I refuse anyone but that man to portray him!"

"I don't need this!" He glared at John LaLiberte.

"Cassie." John spoke strictly. "It means a great deal of money for you, if you cooperate, but this dictating . . . it's not customary and I refuse such behavior to occur in these offices."

"I can see the headlines now . . ." she drawled. "New best-selling author, Cassie Callahan, turns to her nunnery of an attic and hangs up her pen for life—the sharks go hungry—and Michael Isle pulls out all his hair from wondering *what if.*"

"Why you impertinent . . ." Michael sneered.

Impertinent? Wall Number Three, Cass.

"Okay!" She stood up. "Let's just forget it. I don't want any of my books on the boob tube. It's no skin off my nose. I'll just keep writing and make a little less money. Who cares!" Then she started walking out of the office. At least now she had a name for the face, if nothing else, she bravely told herself.

"Stop!"

Feeling hopeful, she shifted around and saw the pure defiance in Michael Isle's eyes.

"What if he won't do it, huh?"

"Then 'Harry' will never be in the flesh, so a little fast talking may be in order."

"I'll be the laughing stock of Hollywood. Torelli? I'll be a joke, Cassie. Your 'Harry' may be nothing but a joke. I want you to know that."

"No, he won't," she disputed quietly. "Torelli *is* Harry Hannigan, and . . . I'll defy anyone who jokes about that fact."

"You can defy all you want, Cassie, but I promise, Hollywood isn't going to listen to you. They'll grind you into mincemeat. Mark my word."

"So be it." She let out an unconcerned sigh. "Torelli plays Harry Hannigan, and I ask you to place that in any contract that I sign, or . . . I just can't sign, Michael. Let my agent know what you decide, huh?" She turned for the door.

"Cassie . . ." Once more she shifted around. "Nothing--I'll let your agent know my decision." Michael's eyes drifted across her face. "If I may say it, I hope to be working with you in L.A., regardless. So if you could you think about that too . . . ?"

She shook her head. "You have my only terms, a great sacrifice for me in lieu of
my strong beliefs, if *I* may say it, so the next move is yours, and yours alone . . ."

Chapter 15—Jack

If a person obtained a bit of success that week, all of Hollywood knew about it--if one read the trades, that is, which was all of Hollywood. Including restauranteurs, proprietors of trendy power boutiques that the shining crust of Hollywood frequented to see and to be seen. At a studied glance, the Byzantine seating ranking in these restaurants indicated who had made it big that week. The others, acquiring a little less success, embarrassingly made do with inferior seats, hoping that by next week things would improve to the point that their seat was more of a showcase or not sink to the point that their seat was even further in Siberia.

"This political shit is enough to totally screw up one's head, Harv," Jack Torelli said, gazing around Martin's, a gathering place for the Hollywood lunchtime crowd. He saw several polite, furtive peeks tossed in his direction, a few even bearing stiff smiles with underlying envy. At one time he would have smugly accepted it all. But was it really that important? He wondered more and more. A year ago, he would have given a resounding *Yes*. To be placed in more than a hidden corner at Martin's would have been prime. But now, was it *really* all that his mind had cracked it up to be?

"Enjoy Jack, because as for next week . . ." Harv Wellson chuckled while he sawed his rib eye steak.

While easy listening music and loud, obnoxious voices filtered through his ears, Jack stared down at his own steak and wished it were pizza from his favorite spot on Sunset. The week had been grueling and he would have preferred to peacefully eat in a restaurant instead of act in one. Yet, it was a free meal, he told himself, picking up his fork and steak knife.

"So how's the new movie going, Jack?"

He popped a piece of steak into his mouth while studying the calculated eagerness in Harv's eyes. How is it going? He bitterly asked himself as he chewed. With Rud Hanna suddenly sticking his big paw into things, trying to gain control of his newest 'grand baby', and zapping his, Jack's, autonomy, it was going like *horseshit*. His steak reduced to a mushy pulp, he swallowed.

"Fine Harv," he muttered, giving the agent the answer he wanted to hear. Harv was thrilled with the success of *The Last Toe-Step* and concurrently, he was intentionally, or not so intentionally, blind to the mighty Rud Hanna.

"When are you going on location?"

"A couple days," Jack replied without specifics. From his mouth, to Harv's ears to Rud's ears. It would never change, he thought as the meat juice coated his mouth. Rud Hanna had Harv Wellson by the tail. *Money* . . . Harv would slice up his mother for it. And now, with the sudden success of the EMAX subsidiary, came the dire need to keep the unpredictable Jack Torelli in line. Jack figured that Harv's pockets were overflowing with moola.

"So what kind of time frame are you looking at for this film?" Harv asked, seemingly preoccupied with his steak.

Why doesn't Rud just ask me? Or to be more specific, hound me? He silently questioned, recalling that lately, Harv's lunch invitations had been nothing more than sneaky interrogations that Harv played badly. "Perhaps a few months. I have no set date."

Harv gave a couple nervous shifts of his shoulders as if he was suddenly warm. "A few more months? Kinda long for a Rud Hanna production, don't you think?"

"For a Rud Hanna production, maybe." Jack picked up his glass of Dom Perignon that Harv insisted he order, and teased it to his lips. "But not for a Jack Torelli production." Then he closely studied Harv while he sipped, assessing that Harv was suddenly roasting hot in his expensive navy pin-striped suit. *Rud would love that comment.*

"Those critics didn't make you a little cocky, did they Jack?"

He popped a piece of steak in his mouth. *Am I cocky?* He wanted to vomit! The hard-fought-for film was worth every word the critics had written. But there had been plenty of skeptics. Few could believe that Jack Torelli *actually* directed such a film. Negative, back-stabbing comments abounded to soothe the shock. It was only an illusion, folks. Or better yet, a lucky shot that could *never* be repeated by a person like him. After all, he was a Hollywood slime ball, overtly so, and these individuals were to be mocked not heralded. Heavens no! It took a bit away from them, the true wonder of Hollywood. And he didn't mask his disgust as his eyes took a swipe around the restaurant. The sneaky distant bites at Martin's . . . a prime example.

"What's 'cocky', Harv? No *comprende*."

Looking a bit cooler, Harv returned to his steak. "So how's Cheryl Lynn?" he asked casually while his knife released a burst of red liquid.

Tenseness twisted Jack's insides. "I'm not seeing her anymore," he replied, hating Harv's probing on this matter. Get Jack back into the mainstream, Rud ordered . . . parties, restaurants, women to go with them . . . because he *did* have a new film out after all, so promotion, promotion, promotion . . .

Yet, the latter had posed a problem. Though the females' outside appearance had cleaned up, their insides were just as filthy as the lowest slut whoever inhabited Rud Hanna's sound-stage. He felt colder than ever, and as a result, a new plastic friend had to be purchased. The soothing sense of Mattie's hands was disappearing more and more. And he hated himself for succumbing, once again. But no drugs . . . he made do.

"And Delia . . . that actress on the television show . . ."

"History, Harv. And so is Trina, Diana, and any of the other so-called legit actresses whose names are sitting like coals on your tongue."

Harv shot a look of disgust across the table. "What's wrong with you, Jack? Legit is good. It makes *you* look good. Brings you up a notch, which can't hurt."

Yeah--Rud loves legit now that he's had a taste of it.

Rud got off on the foreign image, like it somehow made *him* legit, when he was more gutter-like than ever, he thought. The EMAX subsidiary had breathed decency into Rud Hanna-- or so he believed--so of course his director of decency must have a likewise image to maintain Rud's fantasy. It was just another use for Jack Torelli, a new use granted, yet a use nonetheless. *And Rud like to milk the usefulness out of people.*

"I don't want more steady relationships, if that's what you're implying, Harv."

Harv nervously toyed with his navy silk tie. "But Jack, you're forty with a bad rep, if I can be blunt, and jumping from woman to woman isn't going to help your new endeavor."

Help Rud's delusions, don't you mean, Harv? Shit! He wished the man would say it like it was, rather than perpetuate his half-assed coy efforts. "It seems I can't do anything in my life that doesn't require jumping," he said, unable to stop the bite to his tone.

"What are you saying, Jack? Why always the rebellion? Does nothing satisfy you?"

He tossed a large piece of steak between the wry curve of his lips. *No!* He wanted to shout from wall-to-wall of the restaurant. *No satisfaction!* But why? Why when things in his life were more preferable? Why when he had a titch of respect? What did he expect? What *could* Jack Torelli expect? He was nonplused. What's next? That was the question that sat on his mind from the moment he woke up until the time he went to bed. *I'm almost forty for Christ's sakes. Forty! Satisfaction?* He wanted to say *no comprende* to that too.

"Sure Harv--I'm satisfied. I'm just too busy to care about the rest of the game."

Harv nodded his relief. "Rud says he's gonna get you more help, Jack. You do too much yourself, he thinks." He picked up his double scotch and took a hefty drink.

Yeah--Rud does have that effect on people, Jack thought while watching Harv his drink like he was drinking Kool-aid.

The empty scotch glass hit the white-covered table with a slam. "He says a few more experienced people, assistant directors, cameramen, an accountant . . ."

Go to hell, Rud! The last thing he needed was 'Rud's spies' around him day in and day out, reporting his every move. He had fast-talked like hell to prevent this eventuality. He picked up the champagne glass and let it run across his lips before taking a sip. "Tell Rud that's not necessary. I like the people I got," he replied.

"Sure Jack." The empty glass jiggled in Harv's hand. "If I see him, I'll tell him."

You're slipping, Harv. Rud has that effect on people too.

Unable to take any more of the overly-enacted ruse, he placed down his glass and stood. "Gotta make a pit-stop," he told Harv, then turned, walking with forthright steps past the tables, feeling anger and jealousy soak right through him.

Jack hoped the Men's Room was clear. He had to dispose every morsel of his dissatisfaction, rage, rancor, and pain, down a swirling toilet . . .

****

What the hell . . . ?

Jack stopped in his tracks only a few feet from the rest rooms. He stared at Harv Wellson and the man who stood talking to him. Escape, his mind told him, and he shot a glance at the entrance door. It was packed with tourist types who weren't even being given a nod by the employees. *Shit!* He returned his eyes to the table and felt his desperation rise. Should he run back into the can? He wondered. Maybe if he waited it out, the horror would vanish when he came back out again. So, he made a brief turn of his shoulder then froze. Those scoffing eyes . . . they had spotted him. Now he had no choice.

Feeling like the guillotine was only a few paces ahead, Jack made his way back to the table, ignoring every puncturing gaze along the way.

"Well Jack . . . long time, no see."

Jack tossed a glance at Harv and saw the agent's expression. 'Behave', it said. He flicked his eyes forward. "How are you, Mike?" he replied between the tenseness of his jaw.

"I came to congratulate you on your film, Jack."

He couldn't help the cynical laugh that escaped him. "Don't tell me that the Michael Isle went to see *The Last Tap-Step*."

"Of course," Michael replied with aristocratic flair. "It's the chic thing to do, after all."

The response figured! *Thanks a lot you pompous asshole.*

"Of course, how stupid of me. My neurons musta been rose-colored for a moment." Jack let out a laugh to cover his urge to choke the thick neck in front of him.

"Still the same Jack Torelli. *Orifizio fresco*, like I always said."

Fresh mouth! *I just say it like it is, you asino!*

"What can I say? Some habits are unbreakable in certain situations. You know, Mike . . ."

"Explicitly." Michael's cheek rippled with tenseness. "What's your next endeavor, Jack?"

A smile toyed on Jack's lips. "A secret. Guess your next 'chic' will have to be a surprise."

"Really . . ." Michael nervously jerked on his shiny gold bow tie like he wanted to rip it. "Will it take long to complete, if I may ask?"

"A few months, maybe a year, depending on which way my creative juices flow," Jack replied vaguely.

"A year?" Michael gave a subtle shift to Harv who stared, peeved, at Jack. "Does it have to be a year? Couldn't you speed up those juices? If you had, I mean?"

"Huh?" Jack creased his face in confusion at the odd inquiry, and he wanted to retort, *What the fuck do you care?* But he willed restraint on his mouth.

"Well anyway . . ." Michael reached into his pocket and extracted a paperback book. He held it out to Jack. "I'm passing these out to a few of the tables, and I ask you to read it, Jack."

He grabbed the thick book and twisted it around. *"The Life and Times of Harry Hannigan,"* he read out loud, then he tossed the book back at Michael. "I haven't read a book for years, and I have no time to do so. Maybe you should go to another table."

Michael clenched his teeth while he pushed the book back at Jack. "I'm looking for input from a variety of sources, and . . . I ask you to call me with your opinion of the book."

You ask, you asshole? How dare Michael Isle ask him anything, he thought, wishing he had to nerve to tear the book in two, then fourths, then toss the pieces over the producer's dyed black head. Yet, he plucked the book and studied it again.

"Minnesota, huh?" he commented on the outline of the state on the book cover. "Sounds like a setting for a miniseries." He hooded taunting eyes. "Is that what this is? One of your new miniseries?"

"Perhaps. I haven't decided yet, thus the need for input," Michael replied with a slight flinch of his cheek.

Jack flipped the book around in his hand and looked at the black and white back cover. "Oh this is cute," he said with mocking disdain. "Bib overalls and a designer ponytail." Laughter bubbled out of him. "I s'ppose this is Harry Hannigan, right?"

Michael's lips pursed into a tremble of rage. "I guarantee you, Torelli, that is *not* Harry Hannigan."

With a glee-filled dramatic flair, Jack thrust the book out and took another brief study of the black and white photo and could barely contain his amusement at such a highly contrived scene of nature's child against of backdrop of oversized pines trees, bushes, and dirt. "Looks like a 'Harry' to me," he finally said.

Michael pulled the book out of Jack's clutches. "What's your problem, Torelli? Are you so far down on the social order of humanity, that you can't recognize a decent female when you see one!" His dark *Armani* suit rippling in his rage, Michael stormed away from the table.

"Fuck you," Jack sizzled, slamming his bottom back down on the chair. He felt the tight tremble of his jaw as he fixed his gaze on the fine white linen tablecloth.

"What's up with you, huh Jack?" Harv demanded in a hushed voice. "Didja have to act like a jerk? That man is no one to mess with in this town, and you damn well know it."

But he barely heard Harv's admonishments. Michael Isle's final words bit him deeper than he would ever admit to a soul. *I knew Mattie was decent. Doesn't that count for something?*

". . .You royally pissed him off, Jack. You better than anyone knows how he feels about his miniseries. And they're damn successful, may I add. He's always had that knack to sniff out the right properties. So what's the harm in reading that god damn book, huh? You know it would have probably been hot, so why not humor the man?"

Jack pushed his body out of the chair and straightened up. "Thanks for lunch, Harv. I gotta go. I have a film to make . . ."

****

On Monday of the next week, EMAX Subsidiary packed seven rented Winnebagos with cast, crew, equipment, props, and other essentials so they could travel up, then down, the California coast--Santa Cruz, Big Sur, San Luis Obispo--and complete the outside shooting for *Marabella*.

The script, which Jack Torelli acquired from another new writer, centered around a beautiful, free-spiriting artist, who travels the California Coast, painting people so distinctively, she reveals entities about the individual that they aren't even aware exist. Though ultimately, she does so to a murderer, thus discovers his secret. He disposes of her off a peak at Big Sur, then he eventually goes mad by the continued sight of the painting and suffers the same demise as Marabella.

Jack stood by the Winnebagos, directing people and equipment so they could get going. He had only weaseled a week of funding out of Rud Hanna, and much needed to be completed in that short time span.

"Where do you want me, Jack?"

He stopped the barks of his orders to answer the voice. It was Haley Shears, the twenty-two-year-old actress hired to play Marabella. She was dark with long luxurious black hair and had delicate artist's fingers, and he was fully cognizant why he had hired her. The beautiful memory of the artist in the clearing blazed brightly in his mind every day that they filmed. It had been soothing, he recalled now, and it had eased his continued dissatisfaction at being a peripheral stage player by lulling the burning passion. So he couldn't help the small smile he gave her.

"In the second Winnebago with the rest of the cast, Haley," he replied.

"Will you be in that Winnebago?" She played with her long fingernails.

"Nope--I'll be in the first one." Jack turned back to the activity and shouted orders again.

She made no move towards her Winnebago and quietly lingered next to him.

Sensing her continued presence, Jack looked down at her short figure. "Do you need something else, Haley?" he asked, perturbed.

"Why can't I ride in your Winnebago? I have some script questions that I needed to discuss on the way to Santa Cruz." She widened her slanted blue eyes at him.

He heaved out his annoyance. Going over the script with him was turning into a daily affair. She would question a scene, he would explain it, she would argue a little, then end up with his viewpoint anyway. The tedium, in lieu of his schedule, wasn't appreciated. "Can't it hold until Santa Cruz? I planned on getting a little rest during the trip."

"But you *can* rest, Jack. I can flop anywhere."

"I don't know . . ."

"Please," she jumped in. "I really need help. Marabella is the most complicated character I even portrayed, and I want to do an admirable job . . . for you."

Feeling the over fatigue of his body, he wanted to shout *No*. But as usual, he couldn't deny her pleading face that was so much like the one he could never deny. "Okay. Board the first Winnebago, and I'll be there shortly . . ."

****

"Now take this scene for instance, Jack . . ."

Jack felt the droop of his eyes while he laid, propped up, on one of the single beds in the back of the Winnebago as it sped up the California coast.

Haley lifted up from the floor and moved closer to him. "She paints the hidden passion in this sullen, solitary surfer type and he walks away, instead of being drawn to her." She widely opened her eyes. "Don't you think that if the man was lonely with nothing but the ocean waves for comfort, that he would at least reach out a hand and want to touch such a mindful person?"

I'm too fuckin' tired for this, he thought, turning half-mast eyes to her. "But he returns the next day. A guy like that needs time to absorb. His response isn't gonna be immediate."

She lifted up until sitting on the bed's edge. "Wouldn't you be a little immediate?"

A groan rose from his throat. "We're not talking about me, and get off the bed. You're making it jerk and my head is killing me."

Stilling her body, she made no move back to the floor. "So you wouldn't be immediate at all. Is that what you're saying?" she pressed.

"Yeah--that's what I'm saying," he said, irritated. "He falls in love with her, and things like that are rare at best. So of course he's gonna need time to sort things out. There's no such fucking thing as love at first sight. The concept's even too far-fetched for fairy tales."

"I believe in it." She inched her jean bottom closer.

He let out a disgusted snort. "You would. You're not old enough to know any better. Live in Hollywood a few more years and your bubble will burst quick enough."

"I'm almost twenty-three," she said defiantly. "I wasn't born yesterday. I know the score."

"The score . . ." He let out a cynical laugh. "Where the hell did you learn the score? I found you in a stock company that traveled around the circumference of L.A. Dwell in the middle of it for a while, and then you learn the score. Now get off the bed. I need some shut-eye."

"But the scenes . . ."

"Now! Or I'll toss you off." He wished she and her fantasies would evaporate into thin air. He didn't need such rubbish in his life. The reality was enough garbage for him to stomach.

The bed bounce when she hopped off onto the floor.

"Thanks kid . . ." He finger stroked his brow.

Haley raised on her knees elongating her thin body then boldly tossed her long black hair. "I'm going to be a star." She boasted.

He felt his body float in the surrender of his fatigue. "One step at a time, kid. Maybe this flick will get you something legit like it did for my tap dancer," he mumbled.

"He just got a bit part, you told me. I want big roles, center stage."

"Another fairy tale, kid . . ."

"No, it isn't. There's some people who think I know the score already."

"Who? Kids in high school?" he barely moved his lips in a mutter.

Sulking, she kneed herself to the bed's edge. "No--worldly adults like you. They told me I could be a big star if I made an impact in this movie. What do you think about that?"

He dragged his slitted eyes to the side and saw her pouty face nearly in his. "I think you should get off your cloud and wise up, kid. There's no such people."

"Yes, there is!" she stubbornly yelled into his ear.

"Dammit!" He jerked up, startled. "Scat!" And she jumped back, her eyes as huge as silver dollars. "Go tell your fairy tales to the wall! Torelli's too goddamn used for them! He believes in nothing! Do you hear me? Nothing!"

Her head wavered in a nod.

Jack loosened up, now sorry he had been so harsh. He hadn't meant to be.

"Just stick around, kid." He stretched his body back onto the bed. "If you don't play your cards right, you'll believe in nothing too."

"I'll study my lines," she told him.

"You do that. And I'll try my damndest to make a real score for you . . ."

****

The first day of filming ended in Santa Cruz. Feeling restless and in need of some solitude, Jack took brisk strides and headed for the city. Perhaps a quiet drink or even a low-key movie, he thought while he walked. The scenes had been difficult. And Haley! She argued about every little thing, he recalled.

"But Jack . . ."

He must have heard that a thousand times this day alone.

"For Christ's sakes, this is soft porn, not method acting. Just do it, Haley!"

This was the last time he was going to hire a "teeny-bopper" for one of his movies, he told himself. She acted so mature when he first met her, but he figured the key word was *acting*. She was damn good at it.

The late November day had rapidly settled into night when he reached an area with a variety of establishments. He spotted a small, half way decent looking bar, and he walked inside. Immediately, his ears rocked with loud noise. All he saw was young people, mostly in their twenties, and the sight blinded him. He had forgotten that Santa Cruz was a college town. With haste, he closed the door and moved quickly down the street.

Jack slowed his pace when coming to a line of shops. He leisurely peered into the windows, feeling like that child who longingly peeked at all the goodies on Mulberry Street. And if he thought hard enough, he could smell the strong cheeses and fragrant salami. It had been a long time since he window shopped. The activity was strangely enjoyable, he decided. It made him feel like a real person again.

Lingering to the next window, he peered through the glass and felt as if someone had punched him. The window case was filled with books, one to be specific, and behind it a big poster of nature's child in all her ponytail'd glory. Isle's decent female? She's just a kid for Christ's sake. How blemished could she be? He silently laughed out all his cynicism. *It really took brains to call that one, Mike.* He lifted his foot to walk away, then stopped.

Again, he turned to look through the window. Should he? For Harv? *Oh what the hell.* He strode into the bookshop.

The book, front and center, the word 'bestseller' smeared all over the ads, wasn't difficult to locate. He walked up to the display and plucked a copy. *Bestseller . . . Sure you're still thinking about it, Mike.* He flipped the book in his hand, figuring that the producer had probably stolen the book right out from under the kid's nose. That was his usual ploy, he recalled. Michael Isle had big connections in the New York publishing world, a well-known fact in Hollywood.

He started for the checkout, then decided that since he was there he might as well wander around. After all, it had been eons since he had been in a bookstore, and at one time in his life, he very much enjoyed reading. So, he took his time, slowly perusing the shelves.

"What a coincidence, huh Jack?"

He shut his eyes and told himself that this wasn't happening to his relaxed evening.

"Whose book are you buying, Jack?"

Jack turned and saw the young, questioning face peering up at him. "Ah . . ." He read the book cover. "Ever hear of Cassie Callahan, Haley?"

She gave a dull nod. "Many of the actresses I used to work with in the company, read that book. I remember them saying that the main character was loaded with problems but he ended up great. It's a story of triumph, they said."

"Really . . ." He shifted his eyes across the book cover, suddenly a little more than curious about what lie under it. "You haven't read it, I take it . . . ?"

"Heavens no. I don't read such trash. My reading tastes are much more sophisticated. I nearly suck up Anne Rice and Dean Koontz."

Having no comment about either author, he returned his gaze to the book cover. "Triumph over adversity. Should sell well on the boob tube," he muttered to himself. Then he flipped the book in his hand and began to move past Haley. "Well, hope you find a good book you can suck up, kid. As for me, I'm gonna do some heavy-duty reading."

"But Jack . . ." She chased after him.

Cringing at the words, he stopped cold. "What now, kid?"

Haley widened her blue eyes innocuously. "Since we've, by chance, run into each other, I have a few questions about a scene that we're doing tomorrow." She gave a slight bend to her head. "Could you spare some time for me, Jack?"

He wanted to yell out a negative, but figured that he had to walk back to the Winnebagos anyway. *Kill two birds with a three-mile hike, then peace and quiet.* "Okay, kid. Let me just pay for my book . . ."

****

"You know . . . I lived in Santa Cruz for a time, in my younger days." Haley said as she lazily walked by Jack's side.

Jack caught a nighttime view of the Municipal Wharf. The preponderance of white sails set a stark contrast to the clear sky and black-blue shimmering water of Monterey Bay. "In your younger days, huh?" He was quite amused by her statement. Despite her great attempts to be grown-up, he thought her to be more childlike than most twenty-two year olds; although he hoped to capture such a treasured quality on film and didn't wish her any different for now. "So I guess the obvious question is why Santa Cruz? College maybe?"

"Ugh!" She made a dramatic wrinkle of her nose. "I'm not one for structured learning. I'm into more spontaneous learning, like learning in the real world."

"That's for sure," Jack laughed, swallowing the cynical response he wanted to add to it. He figured he had been enough cynical with Haley on that day they rode up to Santa Cruz and now felt plenty sorry for taking all his bitterness out on her.

"I did Shakespeare here, at their famous theater. I once even got the lead role of Kate in *Taming of the Shrew*. Shakespeare's big in Santa Cruz ."

He barely heard her. His eyes were humorously fastened on a group of passing teenage girls with shaved heads and rings exuding out of every orifice. "Looks worse than West Hollywood," he commented.

She drifted her gaze to the sight in question, then shrugged, unconcerned. "That's not an uncommon thing in Santa Cruz—you see all types. Tolerance is big in Santa Cruz . . . so . . . do you have a girlfriend?"

The sudden question took him aback. "Yeah--I have girls. But I wouldn't call any of them friends," he replied.

"Why?"

He stared at the glistening waves of the ocean, nearing with each pace. How should explain his odd response? Did he even know the answer? He wondered. "I guess I haven't found any girls that I want for friends. It's a mind thing. To be friends, minds have to click."

"I'll be your friend," she jumped in.

"No kid, you don't want me for a friend." Jack pick up his pace. Her incessant probing had made him uncomfortable.

"But I do." She jogged to keep up with him. "Our minds click."

He braked the balls of his feet. "It's not the same. We're acquaintances, brought together by a common goal, and not any situations that would preclude a true clicking of minds. Capisce?" Feeling the burn of the book in his leather jacket pocket, Jack resumed his long strides.

She immediately raced after him. "What specific situations are you talking about, Jack? I don't fully capisce."

"Damn Haley!" His feet grudgingly came to a skid. "Situations that a kid like you, shouldn't even contemplate. Just be a kid, huh? For as long as Hollywood will allow, relish your youth. You have talent. Let that keep you high. Now do you capisce?"

She flipped back her long black hair. "You didn't answer my question, Jack."

"Yeah, I did. You're just still too much of a bubbled headed kid to ever be able to capisce." Jamming his hands into his jean pockets, he walked towards the water. His mind felt exhausted, from everything. The confusion constantly gnawed, and his dissatisfaction compounded daily. Would nothing help? His life was one gigantic mess. In many ways it had been easier when he was just a porn star with a well-controlled sex life and no commitments, not even to himself. Now things twisted with more complexity.

Was this the difficult you told me about, Mattie?

"Slow down, Jack, or I'll never catch up to you," Haley huffed, jogging at his side.

He peeked at the flushed face and begrudgingly slowed down. But he said nothing—he suddenly felt dried up of words.

"Do you want to sit on the beach for a while, Jack? That was always one of my favorite activities in Santa Cruz."

He kept walking and tried to tune out Haley's chatter.

"Maybe a reggae band will be on the beach. Reggae is big in Santa Cruz."

Be quiet! He wanted no intrusion into his private prison. He just desired to dwell alone in it, like he always had.

She suddenly jumped in front of him and he grinded his step to a halt. He felt the slow boil of his anger at her bold action. "What? What do you want from me?" he yelled.

Undaunted by his anger, her face shone with a big smile. "I want to discuss that problem scene while we sit on the beach and look at the kelp. Kelp is big in Santa Cruz."

"Jeez!" He wanted to throttle her for her peskiness. "Is nothing small in Santa Cruz?"

Fingering her chin, Hannah thought about this. "A few of the sharks are small, but people in Santa Cruz are big on ignoring them. As you can guess, water sports are big in Santa Cruz, some of the biggest waves in the world."

"Stop!" he commanded. "I'll sit on the beach if you promise to stop saying 'big'."

"But Jack . . ."

"And that too!"

"Can I use those words in the context of my problem scene, it the need arises?"

"That you can do." He forced a smile down at her. "Let's get that scene unconfused for you. Delays from excessive questions are prohibited. My clock on this film is ticking . . ."

****

On the last full day of filming in Santa Cruz, EMAX took over the Santa Cruz Beach Boardwalk for a few hours so they could film the roller coaster scene between Marabella and the lone surfer who falls in love with her. The area was barricaded off, and only extras hired by pre-production crews were allowed beyond it.

The camera work was tricky, and from the time he arrived at the roller coaster, Jack silently cursed Rud Hanna for putting him on such a strict time frame with the location shooting. This particular scene involved not only filming a convincing roller coaster ride, but the need to stop and slow the car in the process to get the total effect of the couple's fumbling romantic activities. It would be a miracle if the cinematographers were able to capture such in the length of time Rud had paid the park to close their doors, Jack thought frustrated.

"Get those cameras to the top of the coaster!" he yelled to an assistant cinematographer. "And I want someone by that carnival operator's side so he knows how to move his crank!"

"Jack . . . when I'm up in that car . . ."

He veered around smack into Haley Shears, dressed in her costume, white shorts, buttoned down white tank top, and white cap with paint splatters. "What Haley?" he demanded.

"I just wondered if I should wear a strapless bra under this skimpy top?"

He felt his patience snap. "Now that's the height of stupidity! You know Marabella is too free to wear a bra!"

"Kind of like me." She lifted with a short gleeful laugh. "I never wear one either. Did you know that?"

"As it I give a shit now!" he raged with all the desperation he felt. "Now get into that car! We went over that scene until fuckin' midnight last night! And I expect you to do it, explicitly how I told you to do it without one, *But Jack!*"

She backed away from him and made a mad dash for the roller coaster car . . .

****

A couple hours later, after acquiring rolls of film of Haley and her male co-star taking one rollercoaster ride after another, the car was now stopped at the top of the track. Jack hoisted up with one of the cameraman and looked through the lens, trying to figure out the quickest way to do the anticlimactic scene.

"Haley! Put your head in the crook of Cameron's arm and place your fingers on his shirt buttons."

"My stomach is sick, Jack," she whined.

Jack lifted his eye from the camera and glared at her. "Just do it, Haley. Be a professional, willya?" He thrust his eye back to the camera lens, cursing the day he hired a child for this all-important role.

Looking like a sulky little girl, Haley did as he asked.

"Now Cameron, place your hands on her thighs and get ready to move them up to her shirt when I tell you. And both of you are to stumble with those buttons. I wanna see the quaver of your hands on this film, and subtle intakes of breath and the innocent smolder of your eyes as if you've just discovered gold. And Cameron, the barely moving lips when you say 'I love you' and Hannah, you whisper the words."

"What if I puke when I whisper the words?" she cried out.

Feeling the shake of his rage, he whipped his head upward. "If you puke, I leap off this hoist into that car and spank you!"

Haley buried her face deeper into the actor's arm crook and didn't make a reply.

"Okay. Let's get this in one take. Everybody . . . positions. And you, Haley . . . quit looking like you're gonna eat Cameron's armpit!"

She let out a whimper and lifted her head.
"All looks ready . . . Action . . . !"

****

"Damn you, Haley!"
"I tried to warn you, Jack," she wailed.
"Get that car and her cleaned up!" Jack shouted, slamming a hand against the camera. "And we almost had it!"
"We can use what we have, Jack, and start at the point when the kid upchucks," the cinematographer reasoned.
"Shit," Jack muttered, flinging his arm up to check the time. "Double shit! Get that car down to the bottom, then back up. Now!"

Haley's loud miserable sobs racked the crew's ears as the roller coaster car slowly moved down the steep track.

The sound only added to Jack's irritation, and he swore, triple swore, that after this film was done, never would Haley Shears grace his sound-stage again . . .

****

The dusk settled over the horizon of Monterey Bay, and Jack was again sitting on beach, this time alone. He was totally engrossed in *The Life and Times of Harry Hannigan* after a quick supper of sashimi, with a few of the film's crew, in a Japanese restaurant near the Silicon Valley.

His eyes glided over the words. He thought they were beautiful and felt himself grabbed into the life of the unusual 'Harry'. It seemed much too sensitive for a Michael Isle film, not his customary taste. The producer liked a lot of action, he remembered, and the main action in the book appeared to be the man's own struggle with his emotions as he dealt with life. Trash Haley? He had read trash in his life, and this, was far from it, he thought.

At one point, he flipped the book around and stared at the image. He could barely believe that nature's child, so young and innocent, could have so much insight. She looked no older than Haley, he thought, yet her words indicated a maturity beyond her years. Maybe it's Minnesota, he reasoned. Perhaps the harsher environment lent to more rapid growth. Having no definitive answer to this point, he flipped the book around and continued reading.

"Jack?"

He spun around. One jean leg crisscrossed over the other and arms clasped behind her back, Haley cautiously raised her eyes to him. "What now, Haley?" He tried to keep his cool.

Her ankle-length boot gently kicked up sand. "I just wanted to apologize for today. I'm sorry the scene went over-budget."

She would have to remind him! He thought. And he was feeling somewhat tranquil. Now worries about explanations to Rud Hanna suddenly filtered through his mind again. "Just go back to the Winnebago or wherever, and forget about it." H quickly turned back to his book.

"I should have admitted to you that roller coasters have never sat well with me," she said to his back. "I'd like to make it up to you."

He kept his eyes on the page. "Leave me be. That's the best way to make it up to me."

"But Jack . . . I got tickets. It was tough, but I got them for you."

Wishing someone would put a gun to his head, he turned around and saw that Haley was waving something. "Tickets for what, kid?"

"Shakespeare!" she replied brightly. *"The Merry Widows of Windsor,* my favorite."

He gave a slight laugh of remembrance. "I played Ford in that play when I was in acting school in New York." He told her.

"Really?" she enthused. "I played Page in high school. A local Bay area newspaper said I brought an enchantment to Windsor."

Feeling sudden deja vu, Jack closed the book and stuck it in his pocket. "I guess I could stand to see a play tonight." He brushed the sand from his jeans and cast a slight smile down at her. "Lead on, Page."

"My pleasure, Ford . . ."

****

I remember it well . . .

Jack closely watched the stage actors and it was like nearly twenty years vanished.

It was him, so eager, so hungry, so thrilled to be on that platform, giving all the passion he had inside him. It was such a freeing feeling! The challenge to recreate a character with one's own unique style was indescribable. There was no greater wonder, he thought.

And I miss it like hell.

There! He had finally put it all into words, the suppressed emotions of the last several months. They hadn't culminated until now, this moment, when he was experiencing the passion from afar. Only he didn't want to experience it from afar. He was jealous, near to tearing his hair out with frustration and restlessness. He was Ford! Him!

"So what do you think of my old theater?" Haley whispered in his ear.

"I like it," he whispered back, silently adding he adored it, desired it, needed it. By Christ, he wanted it.

The curtain went down, and clasping hands, the actors triumphantly walked onto the stage to take their bows. The applause was clamorous and Jack wanted to shout, Encore! He yearned for the glorious feeling to continue, and fill him with the warmth that was stifling in its intensity.

"Sadly, Shakespeare won't be my claim to fame." Haley popped out of her seat.

"How do you know?" He creased his brow up at her. "You may be back here after *Marabella,"* he said, thinking it was the best place for her. She had a lot of growing up to do before she was set adrift in Hollywood.

"You're joking, Jack. Right?" She gave an amused toss of her hair.

"No kid." He stood and stretched a bit. "I'm dead serious."

She huffed out her disgust. "I'm going to be a star, I told you. There's people giving me the eye and they think I can go far."

"And I told you there's no such people!" he raised his hands in impatience. "Either they're feeding you a line, or they're invisible people. It isn't that easy, kid, no matter how many movie magazines you've read. If you don't smarten up, you have no business in this business!"

A piqued expression emerged on her face. "You'll see. It *will* be easy for me!" She marched past him and her small form blended into the exiting crowd.

A Hollywood Dreamer, he thought. Just what Hollywood needs, is another . . .

He sidled out of the row and into the aisle. Tomorrow involved a half day of shooting in Santa Cruz and then they headed South . . .

****

With the view of breathtaking forests, cragged peaks, and midnight blue waters reminiscent of Mattie Claret's eyes, Jack sat on the high bluff at Big Sur, the following late afternoon, immersed in *The Life and Times of Harry Hannigan.*

His eyes ran across each sentence, feeling dragged into the truly desolate yet miraculous life of a fictional man whom he felt he knew well. 'Harry Hannigan' was a man for all men, and a man of all men, he thought, finding it incredible how the author had accomplished this fact in light of more problems than one person should have to endure in ten lifetimes. It was like the tallest of tales, yet so realistic. "Harry's not only the story protagonist, he's the story antagonist. Weird," he muttered, wondering how Michael Isle planned to pull off such a conflict in his miniseries.

Maybe I'll even break down and watch the asshole's production for once.

Struck with the familiar bitterness with just the thought, he placed down the book to gain control his sudden emotions. He settled his concentration on the midnight blue softly swaying water and let each hostile feeling expel one at a time.

Michael Isle had been instrumental in ruining him, after being so absolutely insistent that Jack Torelli leave the safe, comfortable confines of New York and come to Hollywood.

"You have a bright future here, Jack," the producer had convincingly said. "And the environment is perfect for a good-looking guy like you. I predict that you'll like Hollywood as much as Hollywood will like you."

Like the green kid he was, he bought it lock, stock, and eagerly.

****

"The network received many letters about you after the airing of Wind and Fire, Jack. I dare say that you, singlehandedly, quadrupled attendance at stock car races, nationwide."

"Really, Mr. Isle? Wow . . . I just did what I love to do."

"Got a plum role for you, son. A stockbroker on Wall Street, young, brilliant and hungry who claws to mini-barracuda status. How does that sound?"

"Sounds like a challenge, my kind of role."

"I'll contact your agent, and . . . call me Michael, Mike if you insist . . ."

And his role as Noah in The Green Game, brought him a bit closer to the gold ring.

"The females loved you, Jack. I bet brokerage firms all over the country are seeing a hike in sales, if all the correspondence is any indication."

"Just did my best, Mike."

"I'm eyeballing this new novel that's just reached its millionth sale, a medical drama that spans a year. There's a great role for a surgical resident, brilliant, but cocky as hell, and oh those nurses . . . think you could play that one, Jack?"

"No sweat, Mike, and . . . my family should love it . . . inside joke."

The role of Cristoff in The Human Oath, brought him a nomination at the People's Choice Awards. He didn't win, but he was flying high. And the offers poured in for three solid years. He never garnered the lead, but always had juicy roles that he could sink his acting ability into.

Then came married life, and his personal existence quickly plummeted into one problem after another. The action had been a mistake from the onset, and the behavior that followed was a result of his overwhelming unhappiness and guilt.

"What's wrong with you, Jack? You look sluggish up there. I swear that on film, you've aged ten years."

"A lot of shit going on, Mike."

"So I've heard. Sowing a few more wild oats than usual."

"I can't seem to help it now. You'll just have to bear with me. I'll snap out of it sooner or later. I just need a little time."

But he couldn't snap out of it very quickly, and Michael Isle refused to accept that.

"Forget it, Jack. I can't take any chances with this role."

"It's just a minor role, Mike. I can handle it."

"To be honest, you've lost it, Jack. That charismatic, money making quality is gone. I must think of my reputation as a producer."

Not only did Michael Isle wash his hands of him, but the producer got others to do likewise, like he had a personal vendetta of unknown reason. The action prevented him from obtaining any meaningful roles, and he was left with crumbs. This was compounded with a troubled personal life which seemed to have no escape. He finally found himself in a position that he never even dreamed, in his wildest imaginings would occur: A Hollywood casualty, washed-up before he even had a chance to sniff his passion.

****

Or achieve stardom . . .

That was the bitterest pills to swallow, he thought, watching the tamed white water caress the tiny expanse of golden beach. He had worked like hell for Michael Isle and made the producer plenty of money--this he knew as fact--yet when the chips were down, he got the shaft regardless. As a result was denied his destiny, his greatest dream since he had played Romeo at age ten.

"Jack Torelli is such a has-been he should pack it up and move it out," Michael Isle said to Harv Wellson when Harv had desperately tried to get the producer to reconsider.

"He has talent, and you know it, Mike. Why the snub?" Harv had questioned repeatedly, but the only got evasive answers or no answers at all.

What the hell! Jack raged inwardly. He was the great Michael Isle, he didn't have to explain himself. Taking a human toll was an every day occurrence. Big deal!

He slammed the book down on the ground, and for a moment thought about flinging it off the bluff and letting it fall hundreds of feet into Pacific Ocean where some shark would hopefully shred it to bits. But the picture of nature's child stared up at him, and he decided that it wasn't her fault. So he picked up the book then rustled through the pages until he found his place. How would 'Harry' have handled Michael Isle? He wondered, until the answer was clear as the sky rising above the jagged peaks.

He would have said 'fuck you' and reached stardom anyway.

How?

Never say 'uncle'—his philosophy for attaining life's victories.

"And I said 'uncle'," he muttered as his eyes drifted to a distant peak. It was the site of tomorrow's location shoot—a confrontation, then struggle between Hannah and the murderer, then a dummy of Hannah was thrust off the peak. Next scene, the murderer, studying his portrait, goes insane, and finally his dummy, clutching the painting, also goes off the cliff. Then goodbye Big Sur, hello San Luis Obispo for the remainder of the filming.

"Why the hell did you say 'uncle', Torelli?" he questioned to the majestic peaks, and suddenly all the disappointing bitterness overtook his insides. He clutched the book to his chest and leapt up. "Why?" he yelled repeatedly at the peaks until all his emotions gathered into one final thrust. "Never again! *Never* 'uncle' again! Do you hear me!"

Telling himself that he felt infinitely better, Jack flopped back down on the ground and resumed reading. He wanted to finish the book while he had the chance, knowing once he was back at EMAX, life would be hectic hell again.

****

Another Christmas came and went, a new year slipped past, and soon thereafter, the final day of shooting for *Marabella* ended in a champagne feast.

Jack clinked his glass upon the glass of every crew and cast member as he made the rounds thanking them for a fine job. When he came to Haley, she looked sullen and begrudgingly let him touch her glass.

"Back to Shakespeare, huh kid?" he said to her.

"That's what you think!" She tossed up of her chin.

A laugh tickled his throat. "Still in the clouds, I see."

"No--I'll show you! My name will be on a theater marquee, top and center," she yelled, then flounced away in a swirl of huffiness.

He watched the childish behavior and told himself, no way would he give her a recommendation. "Top and center . . . an illusion, kid!" he called after her. "You don't got the right stuff in you to make that happen . . . !"

****

The champagne bottles were empty and the studio, clear of people and noise. At his desk, with one lamp lighting the desktop, Jack was doing the final accounting for the film, so he could hand it all to Rud Hanna in the morning and absorb all the yells about overspending at one time. He felt exhausted and couldn't wait to crash on his office bed, having decided that he was much too tired to make it home that night.

The last of the accounting done, Jack stuck the papers in several file folders, piling them at a corner of his desk. Then slowly, he protracted his body until he was upright. He dragged to the bed and flopped onto it. Within moments he closed his eyes and felt himself drift off.

"Jack?"

He slitted his eyes open and saw a hazy figure next to his bed. "Who's there?"

"Marabella," a soft whispered voice said.

He forced his eyes open wider and Haley's face came into view. "I thought I sent you back to Santa Cruz," he mumbled.

She made no comment and laid on top of him.

"Get off me, Haley," he groaned, then tried to throw her off, only to discover that she was butt naked. In a split-second, his eyes flew open. "What the hell do you think you're doing?"

"I brought you a present, Jack." Between her fingers, she twisted a small vial containing the unmistakable white powder.

He jerked into a sitting position, tossing her onto the floor. "Where did you get that shit?"

"From a friend," she replied snottily.

"Give it to me!" Jack made a grab for her hand.

She thrust the vial behind her back. "Not until you make love to me."

"In your continuing dreams," he sneered, then made another grab, this time wrestling the vial away from her amid her loud squeals. He undid the vial and put a touch on his tongue. "You have some wealthy friend. This is first-rate stuff." He slammed the vial to the floor, crushing it with his shoe until the while powder was ground into the rutted wood floor.

"How dare you do that to a gift!" Her lips pinched into a deep pout.

"Who gave you that prime stuff?"

She climbed on her knees and screamed."I'm not telling you until you fuck me!"

"Get dressed, and then you and me are gonna have a little talk," he said sternly.

"You can't fuck! I know all about it! Maybe if we go to your apartment where you have all your little toys, then maybe, you'll do me, huh?"

A jolt rocked him. He had never . . . how the hell did she . . . ? It was like a horrible nightmare. *How?*

"I can tell by your face that I'm right. Some big stud!"

Trembling from head to toe, he turned his face, unable view her, frightened he would attack if the sight of her provoked his vision. "Get out," he said in a barely controlled hiss.

"My friend was right! He told me you couldn't raise it anymore, that you were washed up in that department. He told me . . .

"Who?" Jack roared until the walls shook.

Wide eyed, Hannah thrust back until she was sitting in the middle of the floor. Her poise was regained almost immediately. "The invisible man, according to you!"

Suddenly, as if pieces of a puzzle floated down from the sky and landed in perfect cognitive order, Jack knew, and the sickness he felt was all-consuming. "How did you meet Rud Hanna?" He turned to face her. "How dammit!"

She lifted her chin high in the air. "He's my new boyfriend. So there!"

"Boyfriend? Are you crazy?"

"He says I'm gorgeous and that I can be a big star if I play my cards right. So I did. I told him about *Marabella* and how you went over-budget. He's going to bitch you out in the morning. You deserve it for trying to make me go back to Santa Cruz!"

"Why you little--"

"That's what you get for not letting me be your friend. I would have been a good one—a friend and a girl--even if you couldn't do it."

The bile rose slowly as the full scope of the degradation pounded into his head. And he gazed around the ramshackle office, not much, but his nevertheless--or so he thought. The realization of the latter made something explode inside him, and he made a mad lurch for his desk, scooping up the pile of folders he had just completed then, with all his might, he tossed them at the naked girl who wore a thoroughly complacent expression.

"You can give these to your boyfriend! Tell him Torelli is through! Capisce?"

Then he grabbed his jacket and his paperback book, and without looking back, he took long, determined-filled strides to his Corvette. He had to get away, his numb mind managed to convey. But where? No answer would come, so he hopped into his car and started the ignition. He would go somewhere far away from Hollywood. He felt too humiliated to stay. *They knew.* Maybe they all knew. With Rud Hanna, one never could tell.

Without hesitation, he zoomed the Corvette in the first direction he spotted . . .

Chapter 16—Cassie

Sporting dark glasses and bearing a stance that said she wanted to be left alone, Cassie sat in the waiting area of the Northwest terminal at La Guardia Airport in New York, killing time with a paper pad and pen, until her plane to Los Angeles was ready to board.

She doodled on the paper while attempting to complete an outline for her next book, *A Season of Sorrow*, as she had titled it. The story's basic premise focused on the tenuous relationships between mothers and daughters, spanning three generations. She could do an admirable job in the emotions department, she thought. Yet she hated doing an outline—she was a more spontaneous writer. But it would speed up the process. She had essentially promised John LaLiberte that she would be a book factory to get him off her back about every minute thing, and this had seemed to satisfy him for the moment.

"I expect a complete outline of your new book, chapter-by-chapter, in four week's time, Cassie," he sternly said, upon grabbing her final revised chapters of 'Harry Two' into his eager little hands. She could just see the dollar signs shining in his eyes. The second book was much better than the first, he had told her.

"Aren't you going to hound me about television and movie rights one more time?" she asked him.

"No." His eye gleam brightened. "I've come to the conclusion that your free-agency theory is correct. A million point five for 'Harry' the first. We could make even a bigger kill with the second, if you allow Ferris and I to push it our way."

Taking on the great white shark, eh John, she wanted to say, but held her tongue. He would just berate her for being 'symbolic' again, she figured.

And then there was Curt Farchmin . . . the final wall of her raft that she couldn't seem to find the moxie to erect. His formidable nature still intimidated her, made her 'jump to' no matter how much she wanted to be temperamental and rebellious.

"Hollywood or not, you *will* return to New York for publicity appearances. You're merely a teleplay consultant, a figurehead, of no real necessity, so you'll barely be missed when the need for you to return to New York arises," Curt had said with his usual shark bite.

Again, merely absorbing the sting, she hadn't disputed him. "Why the lecture, Curt? You know I'm always here, as sure as there are muggers in New York."

"Well you make sure it stays that way." She could still see the acid-seeping glare of his eyes. "Don't you dare get sucked into Hollywood's lackadaisical nature. I still expect the New York work ethic despite your unsavory residence. Don't you dare."

She had wanted to stiffen up, click her heels, and throw a salute as wide as his mammoth office. But she restrained the response and opted for a quick escape, so she could rid her eyes of the look which sat in her brain like an anatomical part. No, she wouldn't dare.

Unable to impossibly doodle another moment, she lifted her head to gaze through her dark glasses. She saw windowed advertising everywhere. **New York! New York!** She was happy to leave, regardless of her immense love for the city. She desperately needed a reprieve from reality. Anything was preferable at this time in her life, even unsavory.

She lazily moved her eyes back and forth amongst the awaiting passengers and was unable to pinpoint an interesting one who sparked her creative curiosity—it was a bland sight. So she focused her glasses across into the next waiting area. Suddenly, she felt the hard thud of her heart. She blinked under her glasses, unable to believe her eyes were picking up the vision that her brain was telling her she was seeing. Yet he sat there plain as day—her eyes *weren't* deceiving her--and she dropped her darkened gaze to the carpeted floor. Damn him!

"Cassie talk to me."

She felt his oppressive presence as keenly as if his body was grounding into hers. "Go away, Geoff. I've warned you not to come near me."

"You still have a half-hour until boarding. I checked with the attendant. Please . . . let me buy you a drink, maybe a sandwich, chicken salad, your favorite."

"I'll tell Curt. I will."

"No you won't," he replied with total surety. Then came the familiar pleading. "I'm going nuts without you and I'm so worried about you without any protection . . ."

"I'm fine. Leave me be," she cut in with tense restraint.

"No--I'll create a scene if I have to, to get you alone."

She heard the underlying rage which left no doubt about his threat. She slowly raised her glasses until they fastened on his face. His eyes wore the customary droop. "One glass of wine in a public place. That's all, Geoff."

He grasped her arm and promptly pulled her up in a possessively. She jerked her arm away and began walking to the bar around the corner, not caring if he was coming or not . . .

****

"You can't leave me." Geoff leaned over the small table in the semi-crowded lounge, trying to get close to her. "Not L.A. . . . you have no idea . . . the sharks. Oh god!"

Cassie inched her chair back. His attempts at closeness were making skin crawl. "I'm going, no debate," she replied with a sip of her wine.

"They'll eat you alive, and lot less graciously than they did in New York." Geoff's face creased with desperation. "You're too innocent, too trusting, to ever survive there and emerge as 'My Cassie'. It's impossible. You have to see that." He made a frantic grab for her hand.

"I'm not your Cassie," she fizzled out, tearing her hand away from his grasp. "I'm *my* Cassie, on *my* terms. That's how I'll survive, dammit."

"There are no *your* terms, you fool. It's *their* terms, letting you think its your terms so you're riper for the kill. If you can't see that . . ."

"No! The terms are mine. I made sure of that no matter what you think!"

"You're so naive—you *need* me," he breathed out urgently. "You'll never survive without me padding the way. You won't Cassie. Please see that."

The acrimony was so pungent it burned. "How can I need you when I don't trust you?"

"You *have* to trust me." Helplessness shifted in his eyes. "I worked so hard, did everything for you, kept up my vigilance at all times." A shudder rocked him. "I earned that trust. I *deserve* that trust."

"You *lied* to me all those months to feed yourself. A mini-shark, but a shark nonetheless."

"No--I worship you." His upper body pressed across the table. "I'd never, Cassie. You have to believe that. Please believe that. I need you too."

"You need my passion." The words stung her lips. "To feed your lack, thereof . . ."

His eyes wildly crazy, he flopped back into the chair. "How can you be so cruel? My writing . . . I told you in confidence, between friends. How could you bring up the biggest . . ."

Cassie saw the face and pose, hungry for sympathy. Perhaps a morsel of passion to feed his cowardly dreams? She thought with gall. It was so horribly sick!

"*That's* your 'biggest'? A lack of fortitude hidden under the term 'passion'? You're grieving for *that?*" A roll of ironic humor escaped her. "If that's the case, you're sucking up compassion from the wrong person. I have no *compredere* of such gutless behavior."

At that moment, Cassie's plane was announced through the lounge's PA system.

She drained her glass of the white zinfandel and scooted her chair back until she was upright. "Goodbye Geoff," she said flatly.

"Cassie." His bodily droop suddenly converted into spasmodic thrusts as he tried to touch her. "Please don't leave me. I'll kill myself. I will." He leapt forward, taking her off-guard and firmly clasping her arm. "I can't let you go. Are you unable to see that? You're part of me . . . the major part of me. Let me love you and I'll show you."

Repulsed, she gave a mighty tug of her arm, but his grasp grew tighter. Another announcement came through the intercom. They were boarding her plane, it said. "Let me go. Or I scream 'Police' here and now, and then you won't even have your great flunky job—not even Starburst Publishing to give you that bit of passion."

Rage rippled his cheek, and he flung her arm away from him. "Go! Get eaten! Go ahead! You're prime shark bait, anyway. You're just sitting by that shark's mouth, waiting for it!"

"You're wrong, Geoff." She skirted around him and made a mad dash for her gate, telling herself not to look back . . .

****

The jet had been in the air for an hour, and Cassie accepted the iced cola that the flight attendant handed her. "Are we near Chicago?" she asked the polite, well-groomed woman.

"Soon, Ms. Callahan."

"Thank you." She sipped her cola and drifted her sunglasses to the window, eager to glimpse the city where her daughter sat as an imperceptible speck.

She had tried, even inviting Kristi to New York for Christmas after securing her parent's permission. A hundred thousand dollars worth of permission, she thought, letting the rancor roll inside her. They had agreed--Kristi didn't. Kristi insisted on going to Anoka for Christmas, and with her publicity schedule, she couldn't do likewise.

It had been the worse Christmas of her entire life—a turkey dinner alone in the hotel restaurant, surrounded by tables of laughing groups all ignoring her. Then she returned to her room, sat by her computer, and cleaned up 'Harry Two' for publication. And there she stayed with her two only friends in the world, wondering what her daughter was thinking, until Christmas passed for another year.

"Would you like to transfer to a boarding school in New York, Kristi? I could buy an apartment or even townhouse . . ."

"No I wouldn't, Cassie. I prefer the centralized location," Kristi had replied in the new uptight, snotty tone that she used whenever talking to her mother on the phone.

"Do you have to call me, Cassie?"

"Why pretend you're anything *but* Cassie," Kristi spat bitterly?

"I'm your mama, honey," she pleaded.

"An 'abandoning mama' maybe, but it's nothing new. Most of the girls around her have *those* types of mothers, so I'm not alone."

"Don't you wanna see me, Kristi?"

"Why?" She made a thoroughly tedious sound. "Why, when I would see you and then not see you for two years again. At least I see Grandma four times in the year and all summer—the consistency is a bit more preferable, Cassie."

"I can be more consistent, Kristi, I swear to you."

She made a noise drenched with cynicism. "Why start when I'm thirteen years old? Why not from day one, huh . . . ?"

Now, the words plunged through her like they had after Kristi spoke them. She had tried to be good mother and friend to her daughter, despite the marital problems, her great need to write, the near-poverty level of their existence, and her own lack of role model.

She *had* tried her damndest.

But none of it mattered. All the quality time, in reality, *stunk*.

It was a major blow.

And the shock had insulated her further. Now, she was more thickly padding the walls of her raft. Otherwise, it would be impossible to bear.

"You can't give up on her, Cassina."

In her mind, she heard her grandfather's phone voice, the only voice she trusted in the entire world to soothe the ills that had grown to humongous proportions.

"Kristi's angry, Cassina. I told you that doctor was *importante* to see. But you were *ostinato*," he said gently. "You were stubborn."

"I couldn't, Nono. I couldn't risk the only thing that could give me some hope."

"So instead you risk your daughter's love," he said with blunt wisdom. "There's no trade off for that, Cassina. I hope you see that one day . . ."

I'm beginning to see it, Nono.

Cassie shifted her eyes down at a miniature Windy City.

But I'm afraid my insight came too late.

The air's view of Chicago faded, and she collapsed her head against the first-class seat. She felt too weakened for any meaningful action where Kristi was concerned. To win her daughter back would take more that a hit-and-miss effort, and she feared her life would allow no more than that. So why even start? It would only lend more to Kristi's disenchantment.

You've lost your little girl. You screwed up royally, Cass. Accept it.

****

Python Studios, located in Century City, was a forty-year institution in Hollywood. A major pioneer in television, in the area of made-for-TV movies, novelizations for television, and the mini-series based on best-selling books, Python had one of the leading edges in the television medium in Hollywood.

Spread across several acres, Python boasted ten sound-stages, seven outdoor lots, a ten-story glass tower of offices, enough equipment to film the world, and even a complex of suites for out-of-town business guests and actors.

The studio was dually owned. Founder Hank Wade, now in his late eighties, was merely a figurehead, while second owner, Michael Isle ran the operations along with a large group of varied professionals. On occasion, when a particular movie or miniseries struck his fancy, he directed and produced. Although whether or not he had a direct hand in a Python production, his indirect hand was in every product that exited the Python lot. Python was Michael Isle, and he never let a soul to lose sight of that fact.

And one of the proofs of this was his offices. They were located on the entire tenth floor of the office building and possessed a splendid view of the entire studio grounds. He loved to raise his high-powered binoculars, stand at the expanse of window and make a slow rotating view of his empire in plain sight of every Python employee. 'Big Brother' was always watching. He was around whether physically there or not. If an employee put the stamp of Michael Isle on a film, it was expected they do so the way he dictated it be done. Autonomy was a dirty word in his book. *Subtly paternalistic* . . . he liked those words much better.

Although, sometimes he ran into a few people who didn't fit the groove he expected, Michael now thought while sitting behind his solid mahogany desk that was half the length of the room. One such person was Cassie Callahan, an intriguing yet irritating woman. Then there's Torelli, he reminded himself and renewed panic hit like a bomb. He lunged forward, grabbing one of the four desk phones between one hand and with the other, he punched in the number he now knew by rote.

"Any word, Harv?" he asked the moment he heard the familiar voice.

"None, Mike, and I'm plenty worried. He's been acting strange lately."

Michael felt the slow drift of his eyes to the ceiling. That's all he needed was a crazy Torelli again, he thought, while nightmarish past memories filled his head. "You have to find him, Harv, nutsy or not. I got a contract resting on it, like I told you. And I don't know how long I can hold off the other party."

"Shit Mike, I know. Jack will freak when he hears the news. I know he wouldn't miss this opportunity for the world."

"Yes--I can imagine," Michael muttered, thinking not even Stallone would miss this opportunity. He had heard from John LaLiberte in New York, that the book had reached three point five million in sales as of last week, and was still climbing like mercury. The time was hot to capitalize on the 'Harry' wave, and he told himself nothing would stop that. "You have to beef up your search efforts, Harv," he said with urgency.

"I've sent investigators North, South, East, and one is combing L.A. I don't know what else I can do, except to stay by the phone and hope he calls me."

"That other party is arriving today, Harv, and I'm getting pretty nervous. If she ever catches wind . . ."

"I'll keep it hushed at this end, Mike. But it's gonna be tough once his new film hits the houses. Rud Hanna already had a preview for critics and they're raving more than they were for *The Last Two-Step*. They're gonna be all wondering, Where is Torelli? I'll tell you, Rud Hanna is plenty nervous too."

Michael raised a disgusted lip. He hated that 'pompous ass of porn' and was glad he was worried too. It was the only bright spot in this whole mess, he thought. "Give Rud my regards when you talk to him next, and keep me posted, huh Harv?"

"Will do both, Mike . . ."

"And I hate that slimy snake of an agent too," he muttered, replacing the receiver.

"Mike . . ."

He popped his head up. Claire Gibson, his personal assistant, stood at his open office door. She wore her usual sly smile, as if she knew every one of his dirty little secrets--which she did. "What now?" he asked with irritation.

"I just got word from the limo driver. Ms. Cassie Callahan is on her way to Python." She raised gleeful eyebrows at him.

He looked at the sleekly elegant thirty-five year old woman and wanted to rip out her every eyebrow. "Is her suite ready?" he asked.

"Ready and full of every conceivable distraction to ward off the wiseness," she laughed.

"Ha-Ha." He slapped a pile of papers onto his desk.

"Little touchy, eh Mike? I don't blame you. I just got a couple calls from the trades and it seems they found out that you're producing *The Life and Times of Harry Hannigan.*"

"Oh hell!" Dread settled on his face. "Tell me you're bullshitting?"

"Nope--by tomorrow all of Hollywood will know and by the next day, the entire country. You'll have women tossing rose petals at your feet."

"They don't know about . . ."

"Torelli?" she promptly jumped in.

Michael nodded.

"No—not that they would believe it anyway, even if I had shouted it from the rooftops."

"Good. It gives me some time," he mumbled to himself.

"It sure does," she mocked. "You have two choices as I see it—either get her to change her mind, or lie through your teeth. I opt for the former first, considering how the maggots will grind you to bits with your choice of actors."

"Out!" He had his fill of her truthful retorts for one day.

"My pleasure. I have to find my maggot scraper anyway, because by tomorrow . . ." She strutted away, her loud chortles filling his ears.

"Smart-ass woman!" he shouted after her. Then feeling a combination of anger, distress and desperation, he flung back in his chair and thought carefully. As usual, he realized, Claire was absolutely right . . .

****

The long streamlined black limousine had just left the Bel-Air area and now was in the Westwood district near UCLA.

"Quite a contrast," Cassie commented to the driver who seemed fairly friendly. "From exclusively decadent to delightful." She watched collegiate types, skateboarding, rollerblading, and wearing some of the strangest attires

Seeking Out Harry

she had ever seen.

"That's L.A. for you," he laughed courteously. "Many contrasts just a hop or skip over a boundary, or I daresay over some streets."

"Hmmm . . ." She thought the area could provide much creative stimulus if she found the courage to venture out. "My goodness what's that?"

"Westwood Village, many shops and even more movie theaters, so if you ever want to combine both . . ."

"If I can find a ride," she quipped, then added in a low mutter, "And a guard dog, Doberman preferably." Then she let her sunglasses shift back and forth, trying not to miss anything while the limousine maneuvered through heavy traffic. Unusually interesting, she thought, hoping she would find a bit of nerve over time.

"And this is famous Santa Monica Boulevard, Ms. Callahan, if you're interested."

"Interested?" she peered at the thoroughfare. "What's there to see? Looks like a Minneapolis freeway during rush hour to me."

"High-rises and movie studios," he told her.

"I've seen plenty of the former in New York and no thank you to the second," she said decisively, then comfortably wiggled back into her seat.

"There's Python Studio, Ms. Callahan."

"Where?" She popped forward, and moved her sunglasses from left to right.

He pointed a finger to the right.

She tracked his finger and her eyes widened under the black lenses. There was a huge sign on a triangle of thick steel poles that seemed to reach the sky. Quite appropriate for a Great White, she thought, able to see the likes of Michael Isle perched at the top of the world, sitting cross-kneed like King Midas. The mind's picture made her smile deviously while she turned to the driver. "Well I guess that's my new home away from home away from home . . ."

****

The Great White Midas must live here.

Cassie wandered through the tenth floor of the office building at Python Studios where the limousine driver had directed her to go. She couldn't believe the luxurious surroundings. The paintings looked real, if she knew anything about paintings--which she didn't. And the furniture looked like it came from the most prized antique store in the country. Is that a Ming vase? And another? She moved closer to study the large urns. My god, that statue! She walked up to the white sculpted nude female form stuck in the middle of a fountain. The sight amazed her. She had never seen such a large fountain in someone's office before, or even a small one for that matter.

"Can I help you?"

She spun around. An immaculately groomed woman appraised her up and down. "I'm here to see Michael Isle." She flashed a bright smile. "My name is Cassie Callahan." She thrust out her hand to the woman.

"Ms. Callahan." The woman took her hand and shook warmly. "Traffic must have been light. We didn't expect you for another hour. I'm Claire Gibson, Mr. Isle's assistant."

"Traffic didn't seem light, Ms. Gibson, but who am I to know."

"Call me Claire since you'll be around here for a while."

"Cassie," she reciprocated, already liking the personable young woman with a distinct twinkle in her eyes. She wondered what someone like this saw in the uppity Michael Isle. "So where is he?" She saw the distinct twinkle grow brighter.

"In his office. You came at a very opportune time, and if we hurry, we can catch the opportunity." Claire grabbed Cassie's arm and pulled her along . . .

****

"What?" Michael Isle quickly pulled out the huge pastrami and Swiss cheese sandwich that he had stuck in his mouth.

Cassie doubled over in gleeful laughter while she pointed at him.

He slapped down the sandwich and focused a glare on an equally laughing Claire. "Why the hell didn't you just invite the entire press corps while you were at it!"

"Well if you want to reenact it, I'll be glad to . . ."

"Out! Now!" he roared.

Rolling with laughter, Claire slunk out of the office and closed the door.

"Why doesn't one ever have a camera when one needs one," Cassie said with great delight. "Please eat. Who am I to disturb such obvious heaven for you."

"I suppose you won't forget this little incident." His cheeks flushed with embarrassment.

She sauntered up to his desk. "I will, except when I eat a pastrami sandwich, then I'll probably choke from the remembrance," she quipped.

"Wonderful." He stuck the sandwich in his mouth. While he chewed, he studied her. "You look different," he said after he swallowed, moving his eyes up the black hosed legs to her short stretch knit black dress covered with a sleek cropped leather jacket. Then he looked at her face, lightly tanned and freckled with little makeup, and her blonde hair was wildly freer looking.

"I'm not in New York any more so I decided to shed the caricature, Cassie Callahan, and be the real Cassie Callahan. Are you gonna tell Curt Farchmin that I've been a naughty girl?"

A slow smile formed on his lips. "No--my mouth stays closed. I thought the asexual caricature was a bit overdone." His smile widened. "I like the real very much, if I may say so."

A bit of discomfited by his lingering look, Cassie flopped into a chair without being invited. "You can say it all you want, Michael. What harm can words do?"

His smile rapidly faded, and he pushed the sandwich between his teeth.

"So . . . was Torelli pleased to get the 'Harry' role?" she questioned, and heard a hoarse sound emit from behind the desk. "Do you want me to slap your back, Michael?"

"No," he gasped, his cheeks flushing again. "I swallowed wrong. So sorry."

"Has he read the book? What does he think about 'Harry'? Does he think that he can play him convincingly?" she asked in eager rapid order.

He lowered the sandwich to the desk, and with a serious face folded his hands in front of him. "There's something I need to tell you that I was leery to mention in New York. But I've thought and thought, and decided you had every right to know about this, Cassie."

She instantly panicked. "Is he ill? Injured? Not . . ."

"No Cassie, nothing like that." He paused for a moment. "It's an incident that happened about eighteen months ago, involving a sixteen-year-old girl."

"Torelli has a sixteen-year-old child?" she asked, astounded, wondering how he could ever explain his wild lifestyle to a sixteen-year-old daughter.

Michael's throat tugged with amused laughter. "Now that's humorous, Cassie. Torelli with a child. If you ever see such an oddity against nature, that's the picture for your camera."

"What about a sixteen-year-old girl?" she pressed, not interested in Michael's assessment of Jack Torelli's parental skills.

He stopped his noise and resumed a severe pose. "He had a sixteen-year-old girl in his apartment, and . . . she died of a heroin overdose."

"What?" she breathed out, barely able to believe such a horror. "Poor man must have been beside himself. Is that it? He's still too upset to play my 'Harry'?"

"No Cassie. You don't understand." He hesitated while studying her. "To put it gently, Cassie . . . the girl was found unclothed in his bathroom and speculation points to—"

"No!" she yelled across the desk. "You made a mistake."

"It's no mistake. You can check the L.A. County court records. Torelli was charged with corruption of a minor," he said with a face that could convincingly, sit at any poker table.

"Oh that scum. I have a teenage daughter myself. And . . . you're . . . Ugh! . . . telling me that he had sex with her?" Cassie felt her nausea rise with each word. Her gaze drifted to Michael, then held. His lips were squashed like a crowbar couldn't pry them loose. "Isn't that what you're saying to me, Michael?" she asked with caution.

His lips mashed together until they were nearly imperceptible.

She sprang out of her chair and pressed against his desk. "You're lying! I thought we were past that, Michael!"

"All right!" He jerked forward and a few black hair strands tumbled onto his brow. "I'm only implying the speculation . . . naked female and Jack Torelli . . . it only adds up to one thing."

"Fooey!" she challenged. "I wasn't born under a rock! He would have been charged with rape if that was the case. I'm a well-researched author. *I know* there are medical tests to determine such a heinous crime."

"Smart woman. You should write detective stories." Michael gnashed his teeth together in frustration. "Okay—I admit it. He didn't screw her according to the medical tests they performed. But the question remains, why was a sixteen-year-old there in the first place?"

"Perhaps she was a neighbor or the child of a friend paying a visit . . ."

"None of the above. She was a runaway from Nevada, a heroin addict for many years, and perhaps Torelli took advantage of that fact, though . . .

"What?" she asked shortly.

He started to compress his lips together, but thought otherwise. "According to his studio—if you can believe a word—he was helping the girl, and they even went as far to say that Torelli planned to take her to the hospital."

"And that's not plausible?" She prodded.

"A well-contrived fairy tale, Cassie, an attempt to cover up his true intentions."

"Which were . . . ?"

He spread his hands in a conclusion. "He planned to have sex with her, but she died before he could screw her."

She pulled back to think about this. If true, she would want to claw out those alluring eyes and maim the rest of him too for such a prohibitive crime. And the thought of her 'Harry' being portrayed by such a man . . . It was unspeakable. Yet . . . if his studio spoke the truth . . .

"I can see by your face, that you're quite incensed, Cassie," Michael commented, trying to hide the glee from his voice. "So I assume another actor . . . ?"

"Another actor?" That was even more unspeakable! "There will be no other actor to portray 'Harry'. If it's not Torelli, it will be no one. I thought I made that clear to you."

The tan of his face slowly faded into paleness. "Are you saying the miniseries is off if Torelli isn't in it?"

She gave a resigned nod. "I'll have Ferris Mitchell, my agent, void the contract since the primary condition can't be met." Her eyes drifted around his office, an effort in overdone superabundancy. "Well L.A. was fun while it lasted." And she asked herself, *What next?*

"Please Cassie . . ." He thrust himself across the desk. "I was probably mistaken. Torelli's intentions *could* have been honorable. We'll just never know for certain, that's all."

"You're right." She saw the frantic look on his face, but she felt no disappointment for him. If he just hadn't brought it up, she would have been none the wiser. *Stupid move, Mike.* "I just don't think I could live with such uncertainty. Did he intend? Or didn't he? It would rest heavy on my mind every time I glimpsed him."

"Are you going to condemn a man on a presupposition?"

"Seems so, doesn't it."

"And it's *Hollywood* presupposition. Those get blown up into gigantic proportions."

With a heavy sigh, she contemplated further. Torelli *could* be innocent, she reasoned.

"Cassie you have to be logical. Yes, Torelli's reputation is less than wonderful. And you accepted that. And yes, the man has problems. I'll admit that too. But . . ." He hedged, then hedged some more. "He's a good actor, a very good actor."

"Okay, Michael," she replied with the firmness of conviction. "I'll give Torelli the benefit of the doubt, for now. But, if I learn otherwise about his intentions towards that child, I'll yank my book away, and I want that as an addendum to my contract, or else I leave right now. I just can't take the chance with 'Harry'. He means more to me than you or anyone else could ever know. We've been through a lot together, Harry and I."

A helpless look formed on his face. "That won't fly, Cassie. I badly want your book, but my studio . . . I can't spend millions of dollars on a production then have it pulled because you discover a horror about the star. I need some protection, a firm contract before I spend a dime. That's only rational—you have to agree."

"I do see it, Michael." She started to stand, having every intention of leaving, when she was hit with a mind's vision of those riveting eyes. Her legs collapsed a bit. They were the eyes of 'her Harry', she told herself, the eyes she had envisioned hour upon hour in the confines of her attic when she poured all

Seeking Out Harry

her inner emotions into her beloved character. The mere thought had made her close her mind to the scummy lifestyle Jack Torelli led. Could those eyes make her mind close a bit on this matter too? She suddenly felt the curse of indecision. Could his studio be telling the truth? *Did* Torelli have enough good in him to help a troubled child? Did he have any good in him at all with the kind of life he led? She shuddered. How could one live in such depravity? She wondered. It was beyond her comfort level, even though she did feel more broad-minded after experiencing life outside of Anoka, Minnesota. Actually, it had opened her eyes to a greedy, cunning, and less than beautiful world.

Yet, this was downright ugly.

She began to move her hand forward so she could give a final handshake to Michael Isle, then suddenly, her hand stopped. He was her 'Harry' in the flesh, and wouldn't she give 'Harry' the benefit of the doubt until she could determine otherwise? Perhaps insinuations *weren't* enough to convict, and she would have to see the truth for herself. Torelli couldn't lie to her. She had a keen sense for people and would spot it in a moment. If he could convince her of his honor . . .

She saw the sweat on Michael's brow. He *had* been accommodating down to the limousine and suite he provided, even though she knew his motions reeked of 'Great White feeding frenzy'. But that was the reality. She had accepted that, and concurrently insulated herself from it. "I want to talk to Torelli myself. I won't walk away until I do. I'll give you that much, Michael. So if you would set up an appointment . . ."

"Certainly." He huffed out all his panic. "As soon as he's done directing his new film, Cassie. He's committed to finishing that first, and from what I hear, he's much too busy to talk to you for a while. But I'll give him your message."

"How long do you think? Not weeks, I hope."

"Possibly," Michael replied. "He's very picky, I guess . . . functions on creative bursts, or so he's told me."

Detecting a little more quaver to his tone, Cassie moved closer to his desk. "Are you telling me the truth?"

"Yes—ask anyone. The film is called *Marabella*. It's a widely known fact."

She closely studied his face. Did that twitch in his cheek signal deception? She wondered. Otherwise, his face was as unreadable as a toddler's writings. "Okay Michael--I'll accept your word. I have a new book outline to compose anyway, so I might as well do it here."

"Since you're here . . ." His lips shook into a pleasant smile. " I took the liberty of hiring a team of teleplay writers to start on the 'Harry' script. Do you think you could do some consulting on the side? I'll pay you of course, the fee we agreed upon in the contract."

Posing a hand on his desk, she mentally diddled with the notion. She had never experienced such writing. A new adventure? Perhaps it might be fun to see how the dredge of the writing establishment earned their keep. And 'Harry', if there was a 'Harry', wouldn't get messed up to the point of dramatic psychosis with her watching every move of their pen. She directed a smile on him. "I'll do it. In fact, I insist upon it."

Michael relaxed back in his chair. "So . . . how about dinner tonight? Wouldn't hurt for Hollywood to get a peek at you . . . just in case 'Harry' is a go, I mean."

Dinner with him? She had to restrain her laughter at such an outrageous idea. They would kill each other, she figured.

Yet... She took a narrow peek at him. He was good-looking, devilishly so, which he tried to mask with sophisticated flair, but devilish nonetheless. And a little publicity couldn't hurt. Curt Farchmin had made a jack hammer point of that, she thought with disgust. Perhaps, if she kept the talk light and non-controversial...

"I think I'd like that *if* I can be the real Cassie Callahan not some Curt Farchmin creation for once. Do you think I could get away with that in public?"

He tugged his plain conservative bow tie. He had sworn to Starburst Publishing that he would preserve the sanctity of Cassie Callahan while she was in Los Angeles. And he was uneasy about challenging that. That Limey, John LaLiberte, held the strings on 'Harry Two', and he just knew the editor would jerk those strings to his advantage without the added provocation of a ruined million-dollar image.

"Why not humor them, Cassie? I thought your New York clothes were charming."

"You said they were asexual," she immediately debated, wondering why the sudden nervousness. He could never be an attorney with that face, she thought.

"Charmingly asexual. Didn't I say that?" He moved his hands across some desk papers, pretending preoccupation.

What are you up to? She willed the answer to pop out of him, but he wouldn't even look at her. You snake! I'll show you. You're gonna get Cassie Callahan whether you like it or not! She smiled sweetly. "Of course, Michael. What time...?"

****

"My... aren't we getting a little daring and a titch rebellious, eh Cassie?"

She filled with dread at the voice on the other end of the phone line. It had been ten days since she had arrived in Los Angeles, and she suddenly realized her luck had ended.

"I have at least twenty Los Angeles papers of various rag status in front of me, Cassie. I must say your picture whooping it up in that West Hollywood club in that black spangled number made something snap in me."

"Perhaps your pants button, Curt?" she replied, trying to make 'light' supersede vomit-stimulating anxiety.

"Shut!" he flared angrily. "How dare you, joke about this serious subject."

"Sorry... must be the gallon of California Rose' that I consumed last night."

"And that will stop! I don't need a drunk 'wood nymph' on my hands. How in the hell would I explain such corruption to a public who loves the innocent, unpretentious Cassie Callahan, everybody's true blue friend," he sneered.

"Is that the way you see me, Curt?" She tried to be casual despite the bitter irony. With the exception of her grandfather, she had no true blue friends.

"Just be grateful none of these papers enter the Midwest—your greatest fans, may I remind you—and knowing those types, they would have little tolerance for your wild activities!"

Some wild! If she wore a carved-out gunny sack with a bit of a neckline and a spangle or two sewed onto it, he would think she was living the high life, she thought caustically.

"You *will* fly to New York today and so I may review, *in person*, my expectations for you. This company has spent a bundle on promoting you. I expect compliance in return, if you want my continued efforts!"

"I won't," she disputed without one ounce of bravery.

"May I remind you that 'Harry Two' is looming . . ."

****

Damn him! Cassie seethed while heading back to L.A. from New York on a DC 747.

Her head was spinning in circles. First had come Publicity 101 with Professor Curt Farchimin while Geoff Haines, with dramatic hangdog look, stared at her the entire time. Then came Responsibilities of a Book Machine courtesy of more mild professor, John LaLiberte.

If mild had any bit of a punch.

"How far can you be on your outline, Cassie, with these Hollywood antics that are highly unbecoming to a woman of your type?" John spoke in his highly cultured, superior British tone.

"Ten chapters outlined," she replied, wondering what type of woman he saw her as. But she was too exhausted from Curt's harangue to explore this topic.

"Not acceptable!" He dictated. "You have only two weeks left!"

"Two weeks and four days," she corrected.

"Well!" he huffed. "It doesn't hurt for a responsible professional to be a little early. You, remember that, Cassie!" His voice sounded like the thunder of God.

"You'll have it, John. Don't you always?" She couldn't help the bite to her tone. "I'll fax it to you in two weeks and three days, if you insist . . ."

And then came the clincher, she now thought, shuddering at the memory.

"Geoffry *will* escort you to the airport. He suggests that may be a prudent move to keep you out of trouble," Curt commanded.

"No! I won't get into trouble, I promise, Curt."

But Curt wouldn't listen, and she was forced to ride in a limo with Geoff who didn't dare be too insistent with the chauffeur so close. Yet he hissed in her ear the whole way to La Guardia, pleading with her to come back to him while she sat as rigid as Michael Isle's fountain statue.

The experience had been terrifying. So when the limousine hit the curb at the Northwest terminal, she dashed out of the limo and rapidly moved to her gate while Geoff's desperate yells trailed her. Once in the waiting area, she plunked herself between two solid looking citizens and chatted like a magpie, noticing out of the corner of her eye that a wrathful Geoff kept his distance. Although, Geoff *did* made one forward move when her plane was announced. But she grabbed the arm of the man next to her, making it seem like he was most fascinating when he talked about his Wisconsin cheese business. The move helped her board the plane without incident.

Never again, she told herself. She *would* tell Curt if need be. *She would!*

"Would you like something to drink, Ms. Callahan?"

She flipped her head up and directed her sunglasses at the friendly looking male flight attendant. "How about California Rose'? I feel a bit daring . . . a little rebellious."

"I may have a reasonable facsimile," he replied with amusement, then shuffled through his liquor stash and filled a wine glass for her. "Your 'daring' drink, Ms. Callahan."

With a gracious 'thanks', she took the glass and sipped. It wasn't the real thing, but tasty nonetheless. She laughed silently as memories of her first ten days in L.A. flooded her head.

Michael Isle was more jittery than suave about her appearance and cast-to-the-wild-wind behavior. She loved it! It was the most fun she'd had in a long time. She could just hear his insistence whenever a reporter came near. No one was allowed to photograph, Ms. Callahan, he said sharply. But she posed dramatically just to get his public-poker-up-the-ass goat.

"Take me to Whiskey AU Go Go, Michael. I've heard of that place."

"Are you out of your mind?" he rumbled like an earthquake fault. "I refuse to socialize with orange and purple-headed people, people tattooed up to their eyeballs, and voidoids!"

"Voidoids? It sounds like book material. Take me there . . . Take me there . . ."

Now she couldn't help the giggle that escaped with the recollection of her dancing with a voidoid while Michael, hunched at a corner table, wore an African straw hat and black opaque glasses the entire time.

Yet . . . She let the wine glass gently touch her lips. There was an attractive aspect to him, despite his immutable public persona which seemed to disappear in the confines of his office. There, he could be amusing, even funny, and he never hid his admiration of her book. 'Prime miniseries material', he always called it. 'Harry' was the most important production at his studio so *he* would personally produce and direct it. She rather liked that notion. It was a thrill to get the best of everything for her book, even the writers, skilled at their brand of writing despite her earlier misguided assessment. They had graciously accepted her into their fold and picked her brain like a nut pick scraping a walnut shell. She knew Minnesota and most definitely, she knew 'Harry' well enough to get into his head. It made their job easier, the writers said.

She lightly rubbed the glass rim across her lips. Although, whenever she gave input, verified dialogue, or clarified confusions about her character in the teleplay department, she wondered, *Was it all for not?* A scorching question always rested in her brain.

Where are you Jack Torelli . . . ?

Chapter 17—Jack

"Be a man, Jacko."
Too late, Pop. My castration's complete.

A desolate Jack Torelli sat in a worn webbed lawn chair outside his low-priced motel room in Carson City, Nevada, staring at the jagged, white-capped Sierra Nevada Mountains.

His final destination had chosen him rather than the other way around.

After leaving EMAX subsidiary that night two weeks ago, in his shock, he drove on the first highway he found and his Corvette ran out of gas in Nevada's state capital. So here he stayed. And here he planned to stay even if he ended up a bum or homeless on the street. He could never face Hollywood again. They all knew his shame—he was sure.

He felt the dirt in his tangled overgrowth of hair, the gristle and grime on his face, and smelled the stink of his body odor. But he felt too weary to be concerned about personal hygiene or any type of care. Every time he tried to place anything between his lips, the nausea commenced, so his clothes hung on him like they were two sizes too large. Plus he felt intense over-exhaustion, a result of Hannah's tormenting words invading his light reposes, making him wake up in a chilling sweat that penetrated to his bones.

I wanna die. What the hell's taking so long?

Several times, he thought about putting a gun to his head to end the agony. But every time the notion became serious, the long-ago Irish brogue of his childhood filled his head, and he just couldn't. So he was stuck with a slow death, wasting away bit-by-bit until there was nothing left. He wished at least his brain would die so the misery of his entire existence would be erased. All he could think about was his wasted life, leaving no meaningful mark on this world, and leaving it with a legacy of hurt and pain for the people he loved the most. He had nothing else to give them, and the realization, like always, made his body rack with tears that had dried up days ago.

The sudden crack of footsteps on dirt and rocks, made him flip up his head. He was still vigilant enough to detect intruders, as he wanted none. He peeked between the slim tree branch posts, two of several holding up the ramshackle roof over the wooden planked veranda outside the line of twelve motel rooms. His eyes moved back and forth as he tried to detect a human form, but none came into view. Thinking his lack of sleep was creating hallucinations, he pulled back onto his chair and refocused on the distant blue-gray mountains, numbing his mind with the sight.

"Hi there."

He veered his head to the side. There stood a middle-aged man, dressed in jeans, cropped leather jacket, cowboy boots, and rawhide cowboy hat that looked new.

"You look pretty lonely," the man commented in a friendly Nevada-twanged voice. "Thought I'd come over and give you some company."

"Go away," Jack said in a low hiss.

"Not very friendly, huh?" The man moved closer to the veranda. "I'm just being neighborly. You don't have to bite my head off. Name's Bobby. What's yours?"

"Fucked up," Jack replied in a menacingly whisper.

"Yeah." The man gave a hearty laugh. "I feel that way too sometimes."

Jack gritted his teeth at the knotted wood planks, willing the stranger to leave as he had no strength to evict him bodily.

"I got a ranch near Virginia City 'bout ten miles from here, but every Saturday night I hit the big city for a little food, booze, and gamblin'. I always stay at this motel—the owner thinks I'm family."

"Bully for you," Jack sneered.

"You look like hell, boy." The man cautiously stepped closer. "You need food in the worst way, and . . ." He made a bold wrinkle of his nose. " A bath, for sure."

"I don't want food and I don't give a shit about a bath."

The man spoke sympathetically. "A little down in the dumps, huh? Maybe lost your girl and you think the world's done for? Somethin' like that, maybe?"

"Yeah--I wish," Jack muttered at a knot in the wood.

"Wanna talk about it? My horses think I'm a pretty good listener. I take care of all their problems every time they whinny."

Tossing to his greasy snarled hair, Jack bent at his middle and squarely fastened his hazy feeling eyes at the wood plank. "You can't help me, Mister. No one can."

"You got an accent. Eastern, I bet . . ."

"None of your business." He winced, feeling a stomach cramp.

The man quickly moved up to the veranda. "You need a doctor, boy?"

"No!" Jack cried weakly. Then needing to get away from the insistent intruder, he tried to stand, but another cramp stabbed him and he clutched his stomach and doubled over. A strong pair of arms encircled him. "Just let me be," he pleaded in a low hoarse voice.

"I'll help you to your room, boy. You need some tendin', and old Bobby has all the time in the world . . ."

****

"Drink this juice I got you from the machine out front," Bobby urged, lifting the bottle to Jack's mouth.

"I'll puke it I drink it," he moaned, thrashing on the bed. His middle was now experiencing near continuous cramping.

Bobby placed the bottle on the night stand then hung over Jack. "You need a hospital, boy. You'll starve otherwise."

Jack feebly shook his head. "Just let me die. Maybe now's the time."

"I can't do that, boy. I'm a Christian man. I gotta help those in need."

"Oh shit!" Jack moaned loudly. "Why the hell me? I can't even die right."

His eyes full of compassion, Bobby spread his hands to each side of Jack. "Why do you wanna die, boy, when you still got lots of livin' to do?"

Jack's torture escaped his parched throat. "I burned out all my living a long time ago, Bobby. I have nothing left."

"Your heart is tickin' and your lungs are still spittin' out air. That's life in my book," Bobby said with gentle insistence. "You're just waylaid, boy, at a crossroads. Life's full of 'em, believe me. I've hit many in my fifty-eight years."

Jack tried to digest the wise, prudent words, but he could see no future. What was left? He wanted to find the courage to face it all. But he had lost his manhood, the last semblance of his self-image, *gone*. There was *nothing* left of Jack Torelli.

"What can I do to comfort you, boy?"

He felt gentle finger strokes on his face, and he wanted to sob at the genuine kindness he hadn't felt since crying in Mattie's arms. *Mattie!* He needed her so much. She would protect him.

"My book on the night table. Read 'Harry' to me," he whispered.

Bobby grabbed the book and a smile crossed his face. "Never say 'uncle'. I read this book." He turned to Jack. "You like this Harry Hannigan guy, huh?"

"Yeah—I like plenty. I just wish I had one-tenth of his superhuman guts."

"Naw, not superhuman no matter how it seems. It's just an amazin' fightin' spirit, a great unfalterin' persistence to reach something higher, better, no matter the odds or heartache—the measure of a true man, the way I see it." Bobby flipped the book over and laughed. "Or in this case, the measure of a true woman."

"Woman?"

Bobby flashed black and white photo at Jack. "The way I see it, a lot of Harry Hannigan is in this little lady. The emotions aren't all masculine by a long shot. Harry Hannigan is definitely a female creation."

Jack moved his blurry eyes over the picture of nature's child, and he wondered how one so young could have the amount of courage Bobby was implying. Yet, it made perfect sense, he thought. 'Harry' was so complex it would be unavoidable for the author to omit her own self from him. Sudden shame filled him. She was far braver than him, *and her* so much younger.

"Yup--I think she was trying to tell us that the true measure of a man is what's inside him. Harry sat in the gutter, uglier than sin, yet he found that courage to rise regardless, and that made him beautiful to her. I could just feel that beauty. How about you?"

Wetness exploded from Jack's eyes. Tears that must have been hidden for all these days, he thought of the display. "Yeah--I could feel it. I could feel every word, and I grabbed them because I'm that ugly man, aren't I?"

Bobby flipped the book in his hand. "Are you Harry Hannigan? What if I said, yes?"

Jack rolled his knuckles over his drenched eyes. "I'd say bullshit with a capital 'B' and plenty of exclamation points after it. I'm not even close."

"Well . . ." A wide smile spread across Bobby's lips. "A man in Hollywood named Michael Isle says you are, and he's been pretty frantic to find you."

"Isle?" His eyes filled with desperation, Jack tried to push his pain-ridden woozy body upward. "Who the hell are you? Who?"

Bobby extracted a black packet and flashed it open at Jack. "Bob Grayson, Private Investigator from L.A., one of many who've been looking for you, Mr. Torelli."

"How did you find me?" Jack collapsed back on the bed in teary resignation.

Bobby gave a low chuckle. "You didn't cover your tracks very well. How many Corvettes does one see parked at a dive like this?"

Jack groaned at his stupidity.

"Amateur time Mr. Torelli, *or* subconsciously you wanted someone to find you."

"No! I didn't want anyone from Hollywood to find me. I can never go back." Panicked, Jack tried with all his grunting strength to lift up.

Bobby gently grasped Jack's shoulders and wrestled them back down on the bed. "Settle down, Mr. Torelli. Everything will be okay—I promise you. Just relax and listen to me."

"Oh shit!" Jack fell spread-eagled on the bed, his stamina totally spent. He had never felt so helpless or desperate in his entire life, knowing he would be forced to face it all. He possessed no more strength. *Let me die now.*

"A lot of Hollywood bigwigs have been crazy to find you," Bobby said, reaching under his jacket. "And I got messages from every one of them."

"No," Jack moaned. He was destroyed. Didn't anyone realize that? Why did they want him back in Hollywood when there was nothing left to kill? There was no more blood to take--he was exsanguinated. What the hell else did they want from Jack Torelli?

Whipping out a notebook from his pocket, Bobby began to read. "Rud Hanna . . . says the bitch is gone from EMAX and no one else knows, he swears on his mother's grave. P.S. . . . even though my mother is alive, Jack. And P.S. again . . . *Marabella* is *tres* wonderful."

Thinking he had heard wrong, Jack lifted a wobbly hand to reach for the notebook. "Let me see that," he heaved out, and Bobby held the message in front of his face so he could read. He shook with relief when seeing the familiar handwriting of the EMAX studio owner and a convulsion of feeble sobs racked him.

Bobby pulled the notebook back and flipped the page. "Harv Wellson . . . get your ass back here, Jack, or you'll be damn sorry."

"I don't have to see that one. That's Harv all right." He tried to laugh through his tears.

"Now for Michael Isle . . .

"Isle?" Jack felt the stiff anger of his body. What the hell did that bastard want with him? Hadn't he done enough to Jack Torelli? Did he want to gloat? "Why the hell would he ever, in a trillion years, send me a note? Huh?"

Bobby lifted his eyebrows in frustration. "I told you, Mr. Torelli . . . Mr. Isle says that you're Harry Hannigan."

"What kinda fucking sick message is that?"

"He says . . . there's a girl who wants you to portray Harry Hannigan in one of the biggest miniseries to ever come out of Python Studios and . . . there's a pause here . . . he agrees."

"What?" He shook his head back and forth to clear the sudden shock. "G. . .Girl? What girl? Am I hallucinating?"

"The girl's name is Cassie Callahan, Mr. Torelli, and according to Mr. Isle, she's in Hollywood waiting to talk to you."

Jack felt total disbelief. "You mean *nature's child? That* Cassie Callahan?"

"Nature's child?" Bobby started laughing.

"Well that's what she looks like to me." Jack too found his laugh, wishing he had the energy to yell out all his exultation. *Harry Hannigan* . . . it was a career dream come true. He couldn't believe it. After all the shit, it was incredulous!

"Do you want to hear Mr. Isle's P. S.?" Bobby asked.

Jack waved a limp hand. "Might as well be polite to the sonofabitch now."

"He says . . . Hurry, Torelli. I'm worn out. Whiskey AU Go Go nearly killed me. She's like a untamed stallion. Help . . . !"

****

Seeking Out Harry

The proceeding days were strongly-willed rebuilding efforts. After being medically airlifted out of Carson City, Nevada to UCLA Medical Center in Los Angeles, Jack began the process of body and mind rejuvenation so he was prepared for the biggest acting role of his life.

Without a balk, he followed every order that the hospital staff gave him, including forcing down the bland food and pushing himself beyond capacity with the physical therapists, assigned to strengthen his body. In between, he read *The Life and Times of Harry Hannigan*, refusing to look at any other literature or even watch television, for he knew the portrayal would be a high magnitude challenge; it had to be in lieu of Harry's complexity. Therefore, he wanted to absorb himself with the man, Harry Hannigan, and not distract himself with other things.

Despite that his transfer out of Nevada had been done under total secrecy, the Hollywood press picked up his hospitalization and were clamoring for details--especially since EMAX Studios had released *Marabella* to several theaters in the L.A. area and critics had acclaimed it "an artistic masterpiece by new director Torelli." Plus, Haley Shears was proclaimed, "sensitively talented," a "new star" on the Hollywood horizon whom people should watch closely.

Just what you wanted, Haley, Jack thought bitterly as he sat in a comfortable chair, tasteless breakfast in front of him, in his hospital room.

Although he had avoided reading Hollywood trade papers, he couldn't help shuffling through the one a nurse had brought him with his breakfast. He spotted an article about his hospitalization. A severe case of the flu, Harv Wellson fed the press and his primary physician substantiated. Security personnel had even being hired to keep the press away from Jack.

A small laugh tickled him while he jellied his whole grain toast. He could just imagine the three-way payoff—Michael Isle paying off Rud Hanna to "steal" the studio owner's "star director" so Rud's pocketbook was eased a bit, and Rud Hanna paying off Harv Wellson to keep Jack firmly in the EMAX mode despite his temporary hiatus, and Harv paying-off everybody else to do the bidding of the two "big piranhas." Must be some sight, he thought, amused, envisioning the gracious circle, though each man hated the others' guts.

Masters at the Hollywood game, all three.

And all three had been the height of graciousness to him too . . .

He crammed a whole half-piece of toast into his mouth and remembered Rud Hanna's hospital visit. He had never seen the studio owner so humble and figured 'something big' had taken a bite out of Rud's pocketbook.

"I was drunk and pissed off at you, Jack, when I told the slut about your little problem. I never thought she'd dare shoot off her mouth. When she told me what she'd done, I almost killed her. She'll never work at EMAX again . . . and I don't give a flying fuck what the critics say about her performance."

"What if she shoots off her mouth to other people?" Jack asked, trying to hold back his rage at Rud's confession.

"*That* she wouldn't dare, Jack. I threatened to ruin her, and she knows I will, if she doesn't forget about it entirely. She's cocky as hell, but she's not stupid . . ."

Rud had even promised him an updated, remodeled studio when he returned, he recalled, shoving another piece of toast into his mouth. In fact, Rud had said "when he returned" so many times, it wasn't difficult to figure out what primarily was on the man's mind. He had no contract with Jack Torelli, having refused to give him one and only agreeing to a per picture contract. *Dumb move, Rud.* Now Rud had no guarantees. For once it was Jack Torelli with a throat hold on Rud Hanna and the feeling was *sooo great.*

Then there was Michael Isle, he thought, leisurely scooping bland scrambled eggs into his mouth. Even *he* had emerged from the throne in his glass tower to pay a visit, and now Jack recalled the demeanor. It was totally out of sink with the producer's usual "high self-control."

"Are you getting better, Jack? You look pretty fit," Michael said with an undertone of shake to his voice.

"I'm working like hell to get there, Mike."

"So . . ." Michael stiffened like he was bearing up. "I suppose you got my message . . . ?"

"Yeah--the kid sounds like a handful," he laughed with great amusement, thinking he had never before seen Michael Isle's face flush so much, not even when he was angry.

"Well 'the kid' would like to talk to you. She's driving me nuts with her pestering. 'Where's Torelli?', She always asks. So I told her you were in the hospital sick with the flu, and she looks at me, like she can see right through me. 'Are you lying?', She questions in this . . . this probing manner, and I spend half my day trying like hell to look legit so she believes me. I swear Torelli . . . I've never come across such an infuriating female. I'm losing my frickin' sensibilities. You gotta get well and get her off my back . . ."

He laughed as the eggs slid down his throat. What he'd give to be a bug on Michael Isle's office wall. The icon must project a fortune with this miniseries to even put up with such shit, he laughingly told himself.

Michael Isle meets nature's "wild" child . . . *I love it!*

A knock on the door halted his humor and he called out a "Come in." Harv Wellson slid through the door like a rattled snake, his eyes instantly shifting appraising Jack.

"You look better. Are you?" Harv 's face pleaded with Jack to give him the answer his panic-ridden brain needed to hear.

Both icons had put Harv through hell, Jack figured, watching his agent's hyperactive state as he approached the chair. "I'm coming along, Harv, slow but sure."

The heave of relief that Harv let out sounded like a wind blast. "Good. Just keep improving, Jack. I'm losing my fuckin' mind with all the politics going on. I feel like each of those assholes has a hold on my arms and they're constantly pulling in opposite directions."

"Money's a powerful pull, Harv." Jack sipped his herb tea.

"Yeah--don't I know." His hand trembling, Harv grabbed a nearby chair and scooted it close to Jack. "And it's only gonna get worse," Harv continued on. "EMAX is releasing *Marabella* to a few select theaters in New York today, and the pre-publicity Rud's done there would make *Jungle Love* look like a half-assed attempt."

"So he's finally got another grand baby . . ."

"*You're* his grand baby, Jack," Harv replied tensely."The sonofabitch has already solicited nationwide, for top notch scripts so you're set to go after you get the 'acting bug' outa you."

"Acting bug?" Jack asked humorously.

"Rud views it as a healthy endeavor so you can get your shit together for bigger and better things. You know Rud . . . he insists on creating his own reality."

"And I s'ppose he's pushing for a long-term contract . . . ?"

Harv extracted a well-used white handkerchief and dotted away the fine patina of sweat on his brow. "He's driving me fuckin' loony, Jack. He's already had a lawyer draw up the contract. *Five years*. Do you believe it? That cheap asshole actually went for *five years*--at an exorbitant salary, may I add."

Jack let out a low whistle of astonishment.

"And then there's Isle . . . he's even worse." Harv more vigorously moved the white linen square. "You have to be 'Harry', he always says to me in that pompous voice of his. And if you have to be 'Harry' for this miniseries, you most certainly have to be 'Harry' for the sequel which he'd slit his mother's throat to get, he says. Shit! It's like listening to the merry-go-round at the Santa Monica Pier."

"Sequel?" Jack put down his tea, propelled with sudden curiosity. "What sequel?"

Harv absently stuffed the handkerchief back into his pocket. "It seems the dame has written a book two and it's going to press as we speak. Isle says that New York says that this book may be hotter than the first. And you know Mike . . . he can sniff out money from a minute crack in a perfectly-laid sidewalk."

"So he plans on weaseling that book out of her too, huh?" Jack questioned.

"Weasel?" Harv gave a furious shake of his head. "He paid one point five mil for that first book, and he mutters to me that he'll pay double, even triple, for the second."

"One . . . point five . . . *million?*" Jack sat back in his chair to absorb this impossibility. *Twenty thousand* . . . that's what Michael Isle had paid for the highly successful Wind and Fire, Jack recalled. And even though that had been a decade ago, one point five million from Michael Isle was beyond comprehension.

"I swear Isle is going as nuts as Rud, and him 'Mr. Cool'."

"I can't believe Mike's generosity, Harv." Jack nibbled on a bacon strip. "You remember that writer who wrote The Green Game? Middle-aged, writing for eons and this was his first successful book?"

"Very vaguely, Jack. After all, it's been a while . . ."

"Well I remember. It gave me my first insight into Mike's dirty dealings with authors."

"How so?"

Jack placed down his bacon and looked closely at Harv. "The guy was so crazy to get his book on the boob tube, a craziness Mike fed with his 'cool indifference', that he nearly gave the book away. Fifteen grand, Harv . . . and The Green Game made millions for Python. So why the hell so much? She's a green kid for Christ's sakes. He could have probably twisted the book out of her for ten grand."

"No Jack, you don't understand . . ." Again, Harv extracted his handkerchief and dabbed his brow. "The book has four million in domestic sales, the sequel's released right on top of it, fueled by a miniseries that Mike's prepared to spend mega-millions to get produced . . . it's a fuckin' money machine, Jack . . . and I can tell you, no 'kid' is running it."

With nature's child smack in the middle, he added silently. *Everything was clearer*. They were twisting the 'green kid', thus Mike's sudden tolerance of a 'pest'. He burst out laughing at the irony. Michael Isle needed *him*, Jack Torelli to keep the machine running.

"So I see your great dilemma, Harv. I'm Mike's grand baby too."

"To some degree, Jack." Harv nervously lowered the white cloth to his lap. "He . . . oh what the hell . . . he feels forced to hire you for the Harry Hannigan part, I heard through the Python grapevine. The dame insists, and for some reason, which I couldn't discover in my wildest imaginings, he's kowtowing to her. So it's gonna be rough going, Jack, if you accept this role."

"If?" Jack questioned, unable to believe that Harv Wellson dared breathe such a word. "I don't care how rough, Harv. I'm taking this role, and I don't give a fuck how I got it. It's my second chance. You have to see that."

"Yeah." Harv reached a shaky hand to Jack's back and patted. "I figured you missed acting, thus the reason for your less than sane behavior. I know it's been damn tough, so what the hell, huh? My bat is still out, rough or not."

"Thanks Harv. I may need a powerful bat before this is all over." Jack reciprocated the pat, the first time he had ever done so, he decided.

"Now you just needa get better, Jack. You got an important meeting to attend . . ."

Chapter 18—Cassie and Jack

Feeling healed, minus the nerves, Jack Torelli, attired in the epitome of conservatism— black suit, white shirt attached at the cuffs with smooth silver links, wide tie of no eye-catching print—sat sentry-stiff at a long table in a meeting room at Python Studios.

At his side sat Harv Wellson, no less nervous. Jack could feel the shake of Harv's shoulders from a good two feet away. He wished he could find the voice to tell Harv to "Calm down." The agent's jitters were only adding to his own. Where the hell is she? She had demanded his presence then she was fifteen minutes late.

Hurry and eat your popsicle kid, willya.

"I apologize for the delay, Jack."

Bored and perturbed, Michael tapped a gold pen on the tabletop. "With Cassie, one never knows," Michael continued on. "She could be playing in the teleplay department or at her computer, lost in time. She foils structure every chance she gets." He sneered out the last remark.

"I'm cool, Mike." Jack wanted to sneer too. *Spoiled brat!* He fastened his stare on the table and tried to settle himself with the sound of the ticking wall clock.

Suddenly the door flung open, followed by a quick click of footsteps.

"I'm so sorry, Mike. I was talking to my Nono and I couldn't seem to hang up."

Nono? Jack lifted his eyes in the direction of the soft, yet most determined voice. He saw a head of wildly tousled pale blonde hair and a pair of thin arms swinging in explanation to Michael Isle who appeared to have a raging headache.

"All right Cassie! I get the point! You *had* to hear him sing that Italian lullaby!" Michael flared with total irritation, then he waved a hand at the table. "Well there he is, Cassie. Go meet Jack Torelli. Scoot!"

She veered her head and looked around, fixing her eyes on his face.

That's nature's child? He stared back, barely able to believe it. She was no *kid*, far from it. *She was* ... Seeing her move towards him, Jack quickly rose to his feet. A ripple of rigidity ran the length of his cheek while he watched her approach, finding impossible to remove his gaze from those incredible eyes. *My god!* He felt the tense shake of his shoulders and willed them to calm down. But it was impossible. He had never ... *Cool it, Torelli. She's almost here.* And then her slim form, clad in a severe black business suit, stopped in front of him.

He gulped as his eyes raced across her light tawny skin with a sprinkling of freckles that held no makeup except for a hint of blush and touch of lipstick. Then he fastened his gaze on the green eyes that seemed take up her whole face, adorned with nothing except for thickly fringed black lashes. They were gorgeous, yet sad like something deeper lie beyond the green brilliance.

Cassie thrust out her hand. "How do you do, Mr. Torelli. I'm Cassie Callahan," she said distinctively, then thought that Jack Torelli had ripened since his television show. Although it had done nothing to disturb his looks, on the contrary, he seemed better than ever. And those eyes ... they possessed even more sparks of intensity while they stared at her. It was unnerving! And she stiffened her stance in defense.

"It's nice to meet you, Ms. Callahan." After barely getting the words past his dry, immobile tongue, he encircled her hand with his, and a tremor shot through him when he felt the velvety softness of her skin against his. *Say something!* He commanded himself, refusing to look like a bumbling fool in front of her. "So . . . how did you ever get a Nono with that color hair?"

"My mother is Swedish," she quipped. "You have to be at least half Scandinavian to cross the borders of Minnesota, Mr. Torelli."

"Then I guess I could never cross the borders," he said back, feeling the slight shake of his voice. *She was so beautiful.* And to curb his anxiety, he dropped his gaze, then per custom, eyed her from the feet up, wondering what lie behind the shapeless suit that gave him no indication.

Cassie watched the slow upward motion of his eyes and felt enraged. How dare he treat her like one of his cheap dames! She slightly jutted her chin forward. "Not a Hollywood bod, I'm afraid, Mr. Torelli," she said with tense restraint.

Jack jerked his eyes upward, feeling truly horrified at what she thought. "No--I didn't mean that," he stammered.

"Yes you did," she replied with surety. "But don't despair because it bothers me none in the least. I want the biggest muscle in my body to be my brain, after all."

Realizing that she knew all about him, Jack silently pleaded for the floor to turn into quicksand. Mike must have given her an earful, he figured. How the hell did he deal with this? *She's like an alien for Christ's sakes. Never in my life* . . . And he had not a word of justification. None. "This is my agent, Harv Wellson, Ms. Callahan," was all he could think of to say.

Harv peeked up suspiciously at Jack before he took Cassie's hand and said a few words in greeting. Jack watched the handshake, yearning for his own hand to be the one touching those slim, graceful fingers that felt as cool as a Spring rain.

Michael let out a prolonged sigh of fatigue. "Well now that the introductions have been so graciously made, perhaps it's time we all sit down and talk about the miniseries."

Cassie pulled her hand out of Harv Wellson's grasp and spun around. "No miniseries, Michael, until I talk to Mr. Torelli. Alone! And you know what I'm talking about, so don't pretend everything is *prodigioso!*"

What isn't wonderful? Jack felt his legs grow jellylike at the prospect of talking alone with her. He wanted to and he didn't want to. How the hell was he supposed to talk to her no matter how desperately he wanted to talk to her? How did one talk to such a fabulous creature and still make an impression? He wondered, racking his brain already.

"All right Cassie!" Michael leapt from his chair, his hair angrily flying in all directions. "Cm'on Harv--I'll buy you a drink. Double for me!"

****

What does she want from me?

Stiff with trepidation, Jack watched Cassie slowly pace as if she was composing some sort of grave thought from the look on her face. Suddenly she halted, glanced at him, then paced some more. *She looks like she's a funeral for Christ's sakes,* he thought with a blast of anxiety. *Say Something! Say something so I don't have to say something.*

"Mr. Torelli." Cassie said at last, sitting in a chair next to him and feeling her heart flutter at his close male presence. She lifted her eyes square into his, and for a moment her resolve melted. He was so gorgeous. Too bad that he was such a . . . She couldn't think about it. Never in a million years would she believe that this well-groomed man would . . .

"Do you hurt somewhere? I mean your face, Ms. Callahan," Jack stammered.

"No." She shook her head until her eyes were fixed on the oak table. "I just have something very difficult to discuss with you."

"You look pale. What is it?" he urged, greatly affected the by her real emotions.

"I'm a mother, you see. I have a thirteen-year-old daughter, and . . . I love her very much." She paused to rid her throat of the choke. *Firm Cassie.* She made her body brick rigid. It was the only way she could feel comfortable around this *very* disarming man.

"She sounds like a lucky kid," he replied, having no other response for such genuineness.

His misguided words made a choke penetrate her solid wall of defense. "I need to discuss a serious matter with you, Mr. Torelli." Cassie folded her hands in front of her until they were knuckle white. "It's about a matter of another kid."

He noticed her sudden starchiness as if daring him to come closer. *Don't touch,* he interpreted, and instinctively sat back in his chair and tightly gripped the chair arms, willing them to stay that way. "A kid, Ms. Callahan?"

Oh! How could she say this when he looked like a big teddy bear if one got past the face? "It's so horrible, I just can't say it, Mr. Torelli. You . . ." She stopped, unable to go on.

"Me what, Ms. Callahan?"

And his gentle voice, she thought. It could be her Nono's voice.

"Why don't you just say it, Ms. Callahan, whatever it is? I have a pretty tough skin, believe me," he lied, knowing his skin was paper thin in her presence.

She nodded her assent. She *had* to know unless she wanted it eating away at her conscience. *But be gentle.*

"It's about a heart-wrenching situation which I'm sure you'll agree was very tragic for you. I. . .learned about it by accident, and I was hoping you'd clarify a couple things."

Jack's insides painfully collapsed. "Carly Ribaldi. Right?" As he said it, his face crumpled with all his inner emotions. "I don't know what to say. I. . .never talk about it."

Moistness filled Cassie's eyes at his very obvious distress. This was a child corruptor? "I'm so sorry, Mr. Torelli. I didn't mean to dredge up painful memories, believe me. It's just that there were a few questions, and I am a mother."

Her honest compassion warmed him, and he felt drawn to her. "I swear on every family grave that I was going to take her to the hospital. She was a sick kid, I knew that But she didn't wanna go, and killed herself before I could get her help."

By his face and voice, she knew he was being truthful. "I believe you, Mr. Torelli. Point one closed. Point two . . . What was she doing there in the first place?"

Oh Christ. He stared into her eyes and saw a trusting, pleading quality reflected back at him. The sight was so lovely that he never wanted it to disappear. How could he lie to such eyes? How could he ever tell the truth? She may never speak to him again. *No*, she wouldn't speak to him again, and he *had* to speak to her--Jesus, something undefinable was coming over him—he just *had* to speak to her.

"She was my neighbor." He willed his facial muscles into a ironclad impassivity. "She was a messed up kid and I befriended her. That night she ended up on my doorstep strung out on heroin, and when I told her I was taking her to the hospital, she ripped off her clothes, locked herself in my bathroom, and that's . . ." He shuddered at the memory. "Where I found her."

With a narrowed look, Cassie studied him. "Are you telling me the truth?"

Don't move a muscle, he commanded himself. "Of course Ms. Callahan. I . . . wouldn't lie to you." He felt a guilt-filled lump painfully go down his throat. And then a second lump when her face broke out in a breathtaking smile that made his whole body weaken with helplessness.

"Call me Cassie . . . Harry."

His own face exploded in a smile. He hadn't fucked up with her yet.

"Jack—I insist."

She thrust her hand out to him again.

Trembling at the sight, Jack gently encircled her hand like he was reaching for a delicate piece of crystal. He wanted his fingers to linger on the glorious sensation, but he feared such a bold move. So he made his fingers release much too soon for him to be satisfied, if he could ever be satisfied. "I'll look forward to working with you, Cassie."

"Me too, Jack." She still felt the touch of his strong fingers though they had unclasped hers moments ago. "Well . . ." She stood abruptly, suddenly uneasy. *Remember who he really is, Cass.* Despite his well-groomed appearance, he had an altar life. And *that* made her skin crawl. "I must get back to my new book, chapter one . . . a real task . . . I'm on a deadline, you know."

Jack too stood quickly. "No, I didn't know." He wondered why the sudden change in her demeanor; she looked stricter than some of the nuns from his youth. What had he done wrong? He quickly asked himself, then retraced the conversation from the point their hands fell apart. He couldn't determine anything incriminating. "Deadlines are hell. I've had a few in my life."

"Yeah." She laughed lightly. "Another existence of take out pizza and 'tap-tap'."

He gave her a curious look. "Tap-tap?"

"Just another term for the Cassie Callahan thesaurus," she quipped nervously, wishing her tongue had fallen off before she said such an asinine thing. "I'm afraid there's many terms, Jack, too many to explain . . . writers you know . . . live in a world and vocabulary of their own."

Finding her manner of expression totally delightful, Jack smiled broadly. He yearned to hear more. "I understood take out pizza, my favorite food. I know a great place. We could talk about 'Harry'."

"Oh no . . . my book," Cassie quickly replied, her insides quaking at his invitation, thus her need to escape fast.

He took pause. Where had such bravery emerged to ask her for a date? Yet, since it had emerged . . . "One pizza and home again. Two hours at the most, I promise. I...have a few questions about 'Harry' that only you the author can answer."

Oh god. How do I get out of this?

"My clothes!" she burst out. "They aren't suitable for a pizza place and you . . . Mr. Model of the year . . ."

"I think you look wonderful," he murmured before he could stop himself, then he loudly cleared his dry throat to cover the daring voice tone. "I mean . . . I don't care, if you don't."

Damn . . . no matter how sleazy, I just can't be rude to him, she thought in a panic. Now, he looked like a teddy bear from the neck up too. "I only eat cheese—"

The thrill of her acceptance coursed his lips. "I love cheese—"

****

"My goodness . . . I haven't seen so many voidoids since Whiskey Au Go Go," Cassie commented, looking at all the leather, tattoos, and body rings in the pizza parlor in West Hollywood where Jack had taken her.

He laughed while inching ever-so-closer across the booth. "Another term from your personal thesaurus?"

"To be honest, I got the term from Michael's thesaurus," she replied, leaning a bit closer to Jack. "I love to bug him, you know. He needs someone to pull the poker out once in a while."

"So I've heard, on both counts."

His words sparked her curiosity. "What have you heard about me?"

"Just that you're a little too wild for the likes of Michael Isle," he replied, then gathered his courage. "I could ask you the same question. And . . . I guess I am." He held his breath while he watched settle back into the booth, obviously repulsed, although making facial contortions to hide this. "Cm'on Cassie—I can take it."

She sunk into her baggy suit. *How could I ever . . . ugh! . . .talk about that?*

"Should I start you off?"

Rapidly, she shook her head.

"Women?"

"I don't want to talk about that, Jack."

"Drugs?"

"Negative."

"Skin flicks?"

"No . . . definitely not that!"

"Then what do you want to talk about, Cassie?"

"You forgot sexual perversions."

"You don't wanna talk about that, do you?"

"No," she breathed out. "I was just completing your list for you."

Frustrated, Jack pulled back. *What exactly had Mike told her?* He could imagine, but he wanted to know, exactly. "What if I told you that I'm none of the above anymore, and haven't been for a very long time?"

She raised her eyes to view his face. She saw the determined jut of his jaw, the tense twitches in his cheekbones, eyebrows high with expectation, and those eyes . . . they were nearly burning right through her with his desire that she believe him. "I *do* know that you're not in skin flicks anymore. You're a director," she squeaked out.

"But you don't believe me about the rest. Is that what you're saying?"

"Well . . . to be honest . . ."

"No drugs, Cassie. No sexual perversions, though I will admit there have been a couple women. But they meant nothing to me." He mesmerized his eyes with her green ones, wishing he could tell her about the feelings that he scarce understood, except they were there and had been from the moment he laid eyes on her, making it imperative that he be with her. "Please believe me, Cassie."

How in the world did they ever get on this on this subject when they merely were going to talk about 'Harry'? She wondered in desperation, wanting to race out the restaurant entrance and scream 'Help'. He was so dashing, so dangerous, and she was terrified of him. "I. . .want to believe you, Jack, truly I do, but . . ."

"You can't. Right?"

"Well, based on your past history—"

His face shook with raw emotion. "So, I'm not entitled make a new history? There's no hope for Torelli, because he was a stupid bastard? Is that what you're telling me, Cassie?"

The words made her body surrender with compassion. He looked so sad, so lost, yet . . . he scared the hell out of her. "I don't know, Jack," she mumbled.

"Hypocrite," he dared to say.

"What?"

Jack thrust his upper body over the table. "It's okay for 'Harry' to be a stupid bastard and have a new life. But not me, huh?"

"Harry? My Harry?"

"Yes your Harry," he replied through the grit of his teeth. "I read that book four times! Four! So four times I saw Harry climb out of the gutter, the same gutter I was in! And I started my ascent months ago! Give me some credit, willya?"

Tears stung her eyes. Oh god. She *was* a hypocrite. "I'm sorry," she whispered. "Please feel free to discuss your vices if it makes you feel better, Jack. I'm listening . . ."

****

"Theoretically, I should have been hooked on coke, but I never used it for addictive purposes, but more . . . let's say . . . medicinal purposes." Jack lingered over his fourth mint iced tea.

Her compassion heightening with each word he spoke, Cassie listened avidly. "Harry was hooked on cocaine but his purposes weren't medicinal, merely a Minnesota kid who went wild with his freedom when out in the bigger world and became addicted. I never heard of 'medicinal' except in hospitals."

He wished he had the courage to fully explain. She was so wonderful, he thought. Listening to him and being nonjudgmental . . . he could feel her warmth. He never wanted to let her go. "Sometimes Cassie, a person needs 'medicinal' to cure what he lacks in 'real'."

"Like loneliness? Because that's what I sense in you, Jack," she said softly, reaching across the table and placing her hand over his.

Jack slowly lowered his eyes to her silky hand and wanted to smother it in kisses for her tender words. But instead, he lifted his own hand and grabbed her long sleek fingers into his. "Your senses are right on, Cassie. It's been a hell of a lonely life."

She trembled at the feel of his fingers. Most of her fear had disappeared.

Jack Torelli was a much deeper man than a mere sleazy life style could define. "I guess I'm more insightful because I know the feeling well."

"You?" He was astounded. "You're so vital, talented . . . beautiful," His voice said the last word almost reverently. "I'd never imagine you being lonely. I'd imagine a hoard of people drawn to you."

Pain gripped her. "Hoards of people don't make you any less lonely, Jack. In fact, depending on the hoard, you can be lonely as hell."

Jack acutely sensed her high emotions, and wanted so badly to ease her distress. "If you wanna talk about it, I'll listen, Cassie, I swear . . ."

****

". . .So essentially my passion ruined my life." Tears flooded onto Cassie's cheeks."I lost everyone except my grandparents and my Nona's so quiet, I never know what she's really thinking." She broke down in racking sobs.

"Oh Cassie . . ." Without second thought, Jack whipped out of his side of the booth and slid next to her. He wrapped a shaking arm around her back.

"And then there was New York . . ." she sobbed on, telling Jack about the image-building efforts and how no one liked her real self. ". . .And they put me down so much, I never knew if I really had talent or not, until I had to show my claws and force it out of my editor. I showed him that I wasn't shark bait like they all thought."

"Shark bait?" He pulled his arm tighter and felt her vincible smallness as her upper body shook against his arm. "You'll never be shark bait, Cassie. I dare anyone to try," he muttered, then without a thought, brushed his lips against her silky blonde hair. The sensation was so superb, he did it again. How long had it been since his lips had kissed anything human? He wondered. Then the kiss to Mattie's forehead came to mind.

It had been a helluva long time.

Cassie sunk into the crook of his arm, basking in a strength identical to her grandfather's embrace. "You're so understanding, Jack, but I guess you would be. From what you told me, your passion resulted in a lot of bad things too."

"You mean the skin flicks and what went along with it."

"And *Clay Slade*."

"*Clay Slade?* You even know about that disaster?"

"It's where I first saw you, by accident, on a television station in New York. I just knew that you were 'my Harry'."

He shot a disbelieving look down at her. "You picked me, based on *Clay Slade?*"

"Not on *Clay Slade*, per say. I thought it must have written by brain dead writers."

"You got their number, Cassie." He smiled down at her. It actually felt good to find some humor in one of the darkest periods of his life, he thought.

"You were very good . . . or at least tried to be . . . and I thought that was very admirable."

His insides quaked with warmth as he stared down at her. She made him feel so good with just a few words, even about *Clay Slade* one of the worst embarrassments of his career. "Thank you," he murmured, desiring to plant his lips into her hair until they drowned. But he didn't. Those big green eyes . . . they held somewhat of a trusting quality and he didn't want to change that with impulsiveness. "I appreciate the . . . appreciation."

"It was actually a fluke," she continued on. "I've barely viewed a television for years—I hate it, if the truth be known—but I was trying to find the Italian station. Homesick, you know. And I saw you instead."

He crinkled his brow in deep confusion. "You hate television?"

"An affliction that's zapped the intelligence of the American society."

"A diehard, huh?"

"Most definitely!"

"Then why . . ."

"Why 'Harry'?" she finished for him.

Jack nodded.

She paused to think about this. The answer was far from easy to explain, she thought.

"I was unhappy in New York. I. . .had a bitter disappointment." She left it at that. Never could she tell a soul about Geoff Haines and the terror-filled humiliation she had suffered at his hands. "Something snapped with all the pressure to bring 'Harry' to Hollywood. In a nutshell, I cried 'uncle', something I've fought against doing all my life. Weird huh?"

"Cry 'uncle'?" He looked closely at her. "Like Harry's cry uncle?"

She laughed to cover her nerves. He was fishing too deep below the surface, she agitated, and no way did she trust him *that* much. "It's my philosophy too. End of topic," she quipped.

He felt her stiffen under his arm and sensed she was concealing much from him. *Who are you Cassie Callahan? Are you Harry Hannigan?*

He had his suspicions. However he didn't press because she looked like she didn't want him to. "It's a damn good philosophy, although tough to maintain in this world. The outside forces seem to play against such an idyllic."

"Don't I know," she replied with a hint of sadness. "It somehow seemed easier in Anoka, in the confines of my attic."

"Where you created a world where you could say 'uncle' to your heart's content." Jack took a stab in the dark.

She couldn't hide her panic. "But it's not the real world, is it Jack? Case closed."

Shut out again, Jack thought. *Was she Harry, or a major or minor part of him? What?* He wished he had the nerve to hold her tight and tell her it was okay. He would understand any deep dark secret she possessed as she had understood his secrets--even though he glazed over the details and sugar coated the rest. *The rest?* She never needed to know, he firmly decided.

"Fair enough, Cassie. Case closed."

Jack drifted his eyes around the area and saw only a couple patrons which was unusual for that particular restaurant. So he briefly glanced at his wristwatch, then startled. "I better get you home, Cassie. I know I said two hours, but how does nine strike you?"

Cassie thrust her wrist to her face and widened her eyes. *Three A.M.?* She wanted to lift up, but his arm felt so good she thought she never wanted to leave it. Still, she had blown away the entire night and part of the morning. She had a book deadline, she reminded herself. She *had to* keep her raft on calm waters and keep all the walls erect. She couldn't let missed deadlines tumble them down. So she slowly freed herself from his arm.

"Nine hours were fine, Jack. I think I needed nine hours . . ."

****

The March ocean wind had turned cooly brisk when Jack and Cassie stepped outside the restaurant and walked towards Jack's Corvette. He opened her car door, somewhat surprised that his long lost gentlemanly actions had so easily reemerged with her. He hadn't opened a car door for a woman since . . . when? . . .maybe for his mother? He figured.

The moment he slipped into the driver's seat he began to lift the roof to the convertible. The air felt unusually chilly to him.

"Do you have to do that, Jack?" she asked.

He stopped the ascent of the roof. "You won't be too cold?"

"I think it feels warm actually, and I do like the free feeling of your convertible."

He lowered the roof while peeking at her. Her blonde hair glistened against the jet black sky, and her green eyes sparkled like emeralds. "I'm glad you like my convertible. I hope you ride in it often," he gathered the nerve to say, even though it seemed like the most natural thing to say. Then he forced his eyes from the beautiful sight and started the ignition.

Cassie turned to him and saw his intense gaze fastened forward. His hair looked so thick and silky, she thought, resisting the urge to reach out and touch the lush waves. And his shoulders . . . so powerful and full of strength attached to appendages with like attributes. She could still feel those attributes around her own shoulders. Suddenly, it was if that lingering feeling presided over her discomfiture. "Do you mind if I sit closer?"

Just about to shift into drive, Jack halted his action and trembled as he turned to her. "No—No, I don't mind at all." Then came the rapid transit of her body next to his. Although it seemed to be the normal progression, his arm shook when he lifted it to place around her. She immediately snuggled her head in his arm crook. He could hardly bear the splendid sensation.

Pressing her eyelids together, Cassie lavished in his strength and buried herself deeper. "Can you kiss my head again, Jack? I rather liked the feel of your lips on my hair."

"Cassie," he whispered, submerging his whole mouth into the top of her head, moving his lips more tenderly than he ever had in his entire life.

She gently bit down on her lip and sucked in a soft breath. "That feels so good, Jack."

With her affirming words, he kept moving his lips until they slowly careened down her forehead, her cheek, until they reached the corner of her lips. Feeling like his mouth was electrically charged, he reached for her lips and released all his emotions, that had built over the last nine plus hours. *How long since I've kissed a woman's lips?* And he let the sweetness of her lips wash over him.

Why did you let him, Cass, after swearing that you wouldn't? And she could provide herself with no answer, except that it had seemed to be the perfect next step. So she kissed back, loving every moment—soft, gentle, with just the right push against her mouth—he had wonderful kissing lips!

When he felt her ardor, a warmth spread in his groin, and he almost cried out at elusive feeling--and it was getting stronger. He pressed his lips tighter against hers to express his utter joy. *Jesus.* All he had to do was feel her lips! He ran his hand up and down her silky soft arm, desperately wanting to touch more of her, but not daring to break the miraculous spell with any improper activity.

Don't stop. For the first time in my life I'm really thrashing. Cassie moaned with pleasurable, unable to deny the ripples of desire shooting through her like rockets.

Jack felt the growing tightness in his pants, and thought he would die from sheer joy. Could this woman help him find his manhood again? All indications pointed to this, and he raised his free hand to stroke her hair, his movements growing frenzied to correspond to the heat that was spreading in his groin like hot lava.

Lifting her hand, Cassie let her finger lose themselves in the black hair strands which she had desired to touch earlier. Now she touched to her heart's content.

The sensation of her gentle fingers on his head, made him feel like he would burst to the point of either crossing his legs or raising his lips. So he opted for the latter and immediately shifted his mouth to her ear. "Please Cassie . . . I want you . . . Please," he pleaded in a whisper, unable to restrain the words that he knew were so wrong, yet so right at the same time.

"Please Cassie . . . Please . . . Please . . . Please . . ."

Her body grew rigid. Those familiar words. That familiar whisper . . .

"No." She let out a soft whimper.

He flipped his head up and stared at her. She wore a wide-eyed frightened look on her face. "I'm sorry, Cassie. I. . .didn't mean to." If his foot was close to his behind, he would have given it a hard kick, he thought with rising self-anger. What in the hell had possessed him? He had known she was far different from the usual fare, didn't he? Yet, he had stupidly . . .

"Just take me home, Jack." She scooted to the passenger door and hung by it. "And if you would, put the top up. I suddenly feel a little cold."

Damn you, Torelli. He could see the shake of her thin body as it curled into a tiny ball. He had scared the hell out of her. "Give me another chance, Cassie. I was an ass—I admit it. I need to have another chance . . . please."

"No pleases," she said in a desperate whisper. "I just need to go home."

With ultra-cautious motions he leaned closer to her. "Can I see you again? Maybe pizza?"

"I don't know . . . my book."

"I won't interfere with your book." He dared to move closer. "Two hours max next time." His desperation escalated at the sight of her cowering. After what he had told her tonight about himself, she had to be tentative, he reasoned. Then he followed this with every self-directed curse that came to mind. He had blown it royally when this was the last thing in his life he needed to blow! Fuck-up Torelli! Perpetual Fuck-up!

"I'll think about it," she trembled while burying her face into the seat.

He pulled back, afraid to press anymore, lest he didn't want her to even think about it. So he swung towards the steering wheel and shifted the car. Then, remembering her request, he began to elevate the car roof.

"Forget it, Jack. I. . .need to feel a little bit free."

Chapter 19—Jack

Had six weeks ago even happened?

Jack watched Cassie quickly go through the food line at the Python Studio commissary. He burned his eyes into her. Look at me! He willed like he willed every time he saw her. Just one look, Cassie. Give me some semblance of a day. Just a glance. He trembled. She looks so natural and beautiful, like a breath of fresh air that could ease the loneliest of souls. Just a peek, Cassie, one lousy peek.

But she never drifted her eyes in his direction, and the burn slowly left his eyes while watching her retreat until she disappeared out of the commissary. He perched his elbows on the table and collapsed forward. He had done nothing for the past six weeks except study the parts of the script that were done, get hassled by a frenzied press, and think of her. He felt her without touching her and felt her touch without her fingers being in close proximity. He felt so wretched! But how to change it? With a woman like Cassie Callahan, he had no clue.

He stuck his cheeseburger into his mouth and chewed miserably. Imagine what would happen if you showed up at her suite. Would she be gracious or slam the door in your bold face? Could he accept the rejection or would it just make life worse? She was decent. Had he no chance with a decent woman? Had he no chance with her specifically? Was he doomed forever?

And Jack kept chewing . . .

Did any of this matter when his insides scorched with just the sight of her? Did it when he had a rumble of feelings so foreign yet so wonderful, and an intense desire to hear that funny, compassionate voice that warmed him? Shouldn't he claim what was his from the moment he set eyes on her?

Be a man, Torelli!

He knew if he found the courage, she may be in his arms again. Easier said than done. Add *fuck-up* into the equation, he thought. That makes the word *man* take on a more tedious property. *So what do I do?* A fucked-up man who desires a perfect woman. The hope seemed more remote by the moment.

Feeling a presence next to him, he jerked his head up. An expensively attired Michael Isle stood above him. He wanted to scream *fuck you* in the worst way. It was him! Mike hadn't helped matters one iota by prejudicing her before they had even met.

"I wanted to remind you about the television interview today, Jack," Michael said in a less-than-enthusiastic manner.

"KDLA . . . how could I forget?" Jack replied, barely controlled.

"It's no party for me either." Michael glared down at Jack. "How would you like to be called certifiably committable in five major Hollywood trade papers?"

He didn't give a rat's ass. In fact with the way he was feeling about the producer, he would gladly drive the 'nutmobile' to the insane asylum.

"Trying to make you smell like a rose has been no picnic, you know." Michael continued on, miffed. "I feel like I should win an Emmy for the season's best 'crap-blower.'"

The hypocrisy made Jack snap. "This shit's sickening! On one hand they sing the praises of *Marabella*—Torelli is brilliant. Then Torelli's been chosen to play Harry Hannigan and the proverbial horseshit hits the fan. What the fuck's their problem?"

Looking like a thundercloud, Michael slammed his high-priced slack bottom onto the chair next to Jack. "Are you dense? It's the medium! Your medium is just fine for the artistic perverts, but television means family—Middle-America. And the two don't mix!"

"That's bullshit! *Marabella* could be viewed by anyone in Middle America. Well... anyone eighteen or over in Middle-America. Artistic perverts, my ass!"

Michael's lips curved into a deep sneer. "If you don't believe me, ask Cassie!"

A tremor rattled him. "Cassie?"

"Yes," Michael sizzled. "Ask her about her radio interview last week where they chopped her to bits because she chose you to play her book character. The limousine seat was soaked with her tears by the time we got back to Python."

Oh god! He tried to hide his pain from the despicable man. "How did they chop her?"

"Unrelenting pressure by a radio team who shot her down from two directions. And her, bravely trying to stand up to them, never faltering once in her choice of you, even though I could just feel the shake of her body from the control booth," Michael replied with disgust.

He couldn't stand the picture. *My poor Cassie.* And never faltering... he wished he could properly show his appreciation for that move.

"It doesn't help her, you know." Michael tightly pursed his lips. "Just six weeks ago, Hollywood saw her as 'Little Red Riding Hood', lovely, child like wonder, too damn innocent to dwell here, and now they think her hormones have been activated by a wolf's picture on TV!"

Shit! This was Hollywood. He knew Michael was putting it *very* mildly. "That bad, huh? Horny woman who gets her sexual jollies from the boob tube?"

"*Much* worse, believe me," Michael replied. "And her editor isn't happy about these perceptions. He's spent plenty to project 'The Little Red Riding Hood' image!"

Jack tipped his head in curiosity. "How the hell can they project such an image for a woman who's thirty-four years old? What the hell do they think? She's lived in a box all her life? Minneapolis isn't exactly a backwoods hovel."

Michael shrugged, not knowing. "She doesn't look thirty-four. That was probably the major attraction the way I see it. They figured she had the maturity to handle it, yet the quality of being younger, something they could play around with to their advantage."

Jack pressed closer. "Who's they?"

In a split-second Michael stiffened.

I know all about it, you sonofabitch, Jack thought in a rage. And the bastard dared to complain about what *he* was doing to Cassie.

"No one you know, Torelli," Michael answered vaguely, then promptly changed the subject. "The majority of the script should be done in another three weeks, but I want to start rehearsals on what we have, so filming can commence shortly thereafter."

"Wow... sounds like you're in a hurry, Mike," he commented tightly.

Michael angrily stood up. "Your contract says that you merely do, not question, Torelli. You just show up for that interview and let me do the majority of talking like always." Looking like a pigeon poufed with rage, Michael stormed away.

Yes sir, asshole. Angrily, Jack shifted back to his cheeseburger and ate despite its lukewarm state. *I'm so damn sorry I've added to it, Cassie.*

The food choked as it moved past his throat. Should he quit so she got some relief? He pondered. But even after he posed the question, he knew that solution would worsen matters. If he wasn't 'Harry', no one would be, and she would leave for who knows where. Plus the pressure on her from who knows who would probably intensify with such a revenue loss.

Furthermore, he thought on, he had an inkling about the dirty dealings going on and with this knowledge, he could keep an eagle eye on the situation so she wasn't hurt. For all her thirty-four years, she was so innocent about the workings of such a soul-killing business. *A babe in arms.* That's what made her so endearing. She was so untouched by anything ugly, yet had enough compassion to find the tears for another's ugliness. She was so beautiful . . . an exquisite female specimen, as rare as the rarest bird on earth. And she needed him, he finally decided. At least the notion gave him a touch of hope that he could capture the lovely rare bird.

Jack crammed down the rest of his burger, then with script in tow, he stood, deciding that he might as well pull together his flawless ultraconservative, I'm-the-solidest-of-citizens, porn-is-filthier-than-sin, I'm-kissing-Python's-ass-for-this-magnanimous-chance, look for Mike's big show . . .

****

"Why the hell doesn't he just put a muzzle on me and be done with it," Jack angrily muttered four hours later after the exiting the limousine and heading for his Corvette, parked in the Python Studio parking lot.

He hated the interviews! They were so contrived and full of traps. Anything to get the *juice.* "Why the switch to legitimate entertainment, Jack? Ha-Ha." He could just hear that wily female who had the nerve to put a make on him after the interview. He almost leveled her. "How about a drink in my office, Jack, to celebrate such an enlightening interview. Ha-Ha . . ."

He wanted to puke!

And then the bastard in a two thousand-dollar producer suit . . .

While furiously digging in his pocket for his car keys, he seethed with recollections of how Michael Isle had treated him like a mute without a brain.

"After being out of legitimate acting for so long, Jack, how do you perceive to handle such a complex role like Harry Hannigan? Ha-Ha," the woman asked. And he opened his mouth to speak, when he felt a jab to the arm.

"Jack has a great acting ability which has been submerged, granted, but he's proved to us he can handle such a role and do so well—our only concern at Python," Michael Isle had hastily jumped in.

"Is this a new trend, Mike? Recruiting porn stars for your miniseries? Ha-Ha."

"Jack Torelli is a director, as am I, so maybe I'm a bit prejudiced. Ha-Ha."

"How do you explain a woman like Cassie Callahan choosing you to play her highly popular character? Animal magnetism, Jack? Ha-Ha?"

"I can assure you," Michael interjected. "Cassie Callahan isn't affected by such trite things. She's an intelligent woman and recognizes Jack Torelli's acting qualifications."

"Oh cm'on Mike . . . Ha-Ha . . . she's a female, isn't she . . . ?"

The best . . . Jack sighed deeply as he tossed his shades over his eyes. He squealed out of the parking spot and gunned his accelerator. Suddenly his foot smashed down on the brakes. He stared, watching the slim familiar form, sunglasses cast to the ground, feet shuffling, and blonde hair pulled back in a ponytail. She headed directly towards him.

Should he stay and risk a snub? Instinctively, his foot shifted to the accelerator and the car lurched forward. Again, he braked. So be it if it's a snub, he decided.

Upon noticing his car, Cassie halted cold and fastened her sunglasses on him. He held his breath, willing her not to run away. Finally she resumed her step, and Jack exhaled his relief.

Calm down, Torelli.
No fuck-ups.
Take it easy . . .

"Hi Jack," Cassie said quietly when reaching the Corvette.

"How are you, Cassie?"

"Maintaining," she replied in a less-than-convincing voice.

"How's the book coming?"

She fixed her sunglasses at the ground and didn't respond immediately. "Slow going. Only four usable chapters. The words seem clogged. Maybe I need to build an attic onto my suite."

"Sorry—that must be tough." Jack moved his sunglasses up and down her person. She had lost weight, and her spirit too, it seemed, he thought with great concern.

"It kinda loses its luster with a deadline, that's for sure," she said.

He watched the lingering movement of her foot against the pavement. It looked so sluggish, so lifeless.

"And its plain dull," she added in a whisper.

She looked so sad and vulnerable, it took every bit of restraint he had not to jump out of the car, grab her to him, and let her know he cared . . . *very much.* "Where are you headed? Need a lift?" He crossed his second and third finger, then tightened them rock hard.

"I don't have anywhere to go in particular. I'm just walking." She lingered some more.

He closely watched her for some sign that it was safe to perhaps make a move. "Do . . . you need something? I mean, you look . . ."

"Maybe pizza? I think I may need some of that." She raised her sunglasses to him.

Despite the turmoil inside his body, Jack managed to give a cool nod. "Just what I was craving too. Jump in . . ."

****

"You know, you don't always have to eat cheese pizza, Jack. You could have ordered a little meat . . ."

Jack held a piece of pizza to his lips while watching her pick at the stringy mozzarella without eating any of it. "Cheese is fine, Cassie. Love it." To make his point, he took a big bite then chewed, watching her drizzle some of the cheese into her mouth. "Aren't you gonna eat? You're . . . looking a little thin." He finally found the courage to voice his concern.

She shrugged her shoulders and picked some more. "It's my typical symptom."

"Typical symptom?"

"When I write and I'm emotional at the same time, I concentrate so hard on the writing to block out the emotional, I forget little niceties like eating."

He noticed her green eyes droop like 'emotional' was plaguing her at that moment.

"Still . . . you should set an alarm clock or something. It's not healthy. You may get sick."

"Maybe that's my salvation," her voice shook. "A month in a hospital bed."

Frightened by her tone and words, he slapped down his pizza and leaned over the table. "What does that mean? Huh?"

She raised her eyes and met his square-on. "An escape," she quipped. "A high-priced attic, so to speak, with a sign on the door that says 'No visitors allowed except God'."

Her answer chilled him with terror. "Is it that bad, Cassie?" He urgently pressed closer. "I wanna help it's that bad."

Her face screwed up. "I've missed you, Jack," her lips quavered.

He fixed his eyes on her while his insides exploded with joy. "I've missed you too, Cassie," he whispered back to her, and then he couldn't help adding, "Very much."

"You know tomorrow's Saturday . . ." She hedged a bit.

He managed a nod at her.

"Saturday's my day to be Cassie Callahan. Did I ever tell you that?"

"No," he replied. "I don't recall."

She plucked a piece of cheese off her pizza and pulled it apart. "It was my special day in Manhattan. I miss Manhattan. One can walk and enjoy in Manhattan."

He intensely watched her behavior, and thought he was starting to get the gist of something. "And you can't walk and enjoy in L.A. . . . ?"

She let out a humorless laugh. "Not without a pair of guard dogs, or so I've heard, and heard, and . . ."

He couldn't stop the smile that spread from one cheek to the other. "Would a guard dog named Torelli do?"

Her eyes squeezed out a couple tears. "I wouldn't want any other guard dog except one named Torelli, if the truth be known."

So badly, he wanted to fly over the table and take her in his arms. But would she pull away again? He couldn't risk that now that he had a second chance. "Do you know where you wanna go tomorrow, or . . . should we just play it by ear?"

"Westwood Village," she replied promptly.

He laughed, amused. "Westwood Village? Collegeville? Why in the world there?"

She popped a piece of cheese in her mouth and shrugged. "It looked interesting when I passed it in a limo. I'm curious, I guess. You know . . . writer and all."

"It'll be crowded, Cassie," he warned.

"That's okay," she replied immediately. "I used to like people very much."

He gave a sad nod. "Westwood Village it is. Nine o'clock all right?"

"Could you make it eight oh five? No! Eight ten? Breakfast maybe?"

Her sudden anxiety lent to much curiosity, but he didn't press. She seemed ready to snap. "I'll buy you the biggest breakfast in Westwood Village . . . fatten you up a little."

Cassie let out a laugh that shook with nerves. "Anything, but a bagel, fruit, and herb tea. It's . . . my least favorite breakfast."

"Sure." His curiosity rose like a barometer in a jungle. "How do Spanish omelets sound?"

"Like heaven." She hiked the piece of pizza to her mouth and took a large bite, then another. "You know, Jack . . . suddenly the pizza tastes like heaven too . . ."

****

Next morning, Jack arrived at Cassie's suite at nine minutes after eight and was greeted with quite a surprise. She looked like a carefree kid—faded jean shorts, plain white tank top covered by an equally faded denim shirt, white socks, *ASIC* sneakers, only a hint of makeup, and her blonde hair under a white **Hello Minnesota** cap. He thought he had never seen anything so gorgeous, and suddenly he felt overdressed in his designer jeans and silk shirt.

"You look wonderful, Cassie. Like a breath of spring."

She looked him down and up, meeting his face with a smile. "You look pretty wonderful too, Jack," she said softly.

His entire body shake with pleasure at her closeness, Jack felt the need to divert before he did something impulsive. "So . . ." He fixed on a thoroughly messy corner of her suite. "That's your computer."

"My tap-tap." She flounced to a table to get her purse.

One definition clarified, he thought with great amusement. Then he shifted his eyes around the rest of her suite. It was more utilitarian than luxurious, a place to just hang one's hat. Jack stopped his eyes at her queen-size bed, without a wrinkle and covered with a homey looking colorful quilt. A quaver rocked him. "Pretty quilt," he commented.

Cassie went up the bed and lovingly stroked the fabric. "My Nona made this. She's quite a quilter, knitter, crochet'r, and gourmet maker of Italian food." Her face suddenly screwed up.

"And you miss that," he observed, longing to take her in his arms and tell her that he too felt the same. But he didn't dare. He never wanted her to learn what he had done to his family. She would probably spit in his face, he figured. He was a closed subject with the Torelli family so they were also a closed subject with him.

"I do miss my grandparents and . . . Kristi . . . but as for the rest . . ."

He nodded. In bits and pieces, she had sobbed out about her strained family relationship that first night they had pizza. He understood her and her parents weren't close and it had something to do with her daughter. But she had given no details.

"This is Kristi . . ." She handed a picture to him. "She's twelve in this photo. I . . . haven't received a new picture for this year yet."

Jack carefully examined the face of the very pretty child, but saw little, if any, of Cassie in her. "No blonde hair or green eyes, and light skin too."

"Yeah--she's Kyle's daughter on the outside, but mine on the inside."

"Inside?"

"People say she's a lot like me when I was her age. You know . . . inquisitive, barely ever shuts up, uses words that word make a dictionary groan

Seeking Out Harry

. . . that type."

"A smart kid," he interpreted.

She snatched the photo and placed it back on the night stand. "I had my moments."

"So . . . does she live with her father and . . ." He braked his tongue, wanting to bite it off. She had cried about her best friend for a solid hour, he remembered.

"My former best friend in all the world, Sarie?" she crisply finished for him.

Hanging his head, Jack nodded.

"No," she replied. "Kristi won't have anything to do with that situation. It's embarrassing for her . . . her age, you know."

"Yeah--must have been a shock for the kid."

"She goes to a private school in Chicago, *very* extravagant. She . . . loves it."

He heard the anxious shake of her voice and didn't believe a word. Something was up. She seemed to always make light of things that were deeply touching to her, he was noticing more and more. It was a defense mechanism that he knew well.

"That must put your mind at ease, her loving her school, I mean," he couldn't help fishing.

"Yeah," She made a dash for the door.

While drifting his eyes back to Kristi's photograph, Jack spotted something else out of the corner of his eye. He elevated his gaze to get a better view, and saw a floral arrangement, of what looked like black orchids, compacted in a trash basket. They looked fresh, he determined, and immediately wondered who had sent her such an expensive, yet unusual arrangement. And why the destruction of it? It was odder than odd, he thought, his tongue sparking with curiosity.

"Are you ready to go, Jack? My stomach's rumbling," she said with a small lilting laugh.

He forced his eyes away from the bizarre sight and he firmly told his tongue to 'cool it'. It was none of his business unless she wanted to make it so. Though, as he moved next to her, his self-proclamations didn't satisfy him. He viewed Cassie Callahan *as* his business, the most important business in his life, and he hated the fact that he didn't know about every morsel about her. She belonged to him, he admitted to himself while he gazing down at the fresh, freckled face. And he had to make her see that this meant something to him. *But how?* That was the question he held in his head while he walked through the door with her . . .

****

She's like a little kid, Jack thought with high amusement while watching Cassie romp from shop window to shop window in Westwood Village, pulling him along with her. "Hold my hand, Jack. I rather like the feel of your hand in mine," she said, and of course, he promptly obliged. So now he had the supreme pleasure of her skin next to his for as long as she allowed it.

He insisted that both of them be hidden under dark glasses, and he purchased a cap right away. The crowds were oppressive, nearly dancing in the streets, and he feared recognition, especially with both of them in the frequent spotlight as of late. He refused to have anything disturb her happy mood. It thrilled him to see such a sight.

She had consumed an entire Spanish omelet, an order of wheat toast, a massive plateful of red and green pepper potatoes, a giant glass of orange juice, and at least a pot of minted green tea. He had watched in astonishment, barely able to eat his own breakfast. She was excited to be 'Cassie Callahan', she said, and this always lent to a hearty appetite. He told himself that he adored 'Cassie Callahan' and wanted her no other way, but . . .

"Don't you wanna go into any of the shops, Cassie?" he questioned.

"No!" she shouted with exuberance. "Why ruin a good thing with price-tags and indecision? I love to window shop and dream instead."

Delighted with her behavior, Jack let out a long laugh. "I see your point. I'm not much for shopping either . . . too pushy to be enjoyable."

"But oh!" She suddenly pulled him to another window. "I love to try on hats." She raised her brows innocently. "It's a fetish with me . . . the only type of shopping which prolongs the dream thus the fun." Without warning, she dragged him into the hat shop, and immediately popped hats onto her head and his too.

He peeked in a mirror and doubled over with laughter at the hat she had chosen for him.

"So . . ." She stepped back and looked at him closely. "That's what a sexy Aussie looks like—I've always wondered."

Shifting a smiling face from the mirror, he turned to examine her. "So that's what a beautiful Southern plantation owner's daughter looks like—I've always wondered that too."

With a coy smile, she picked up another hat and flapped it at him. "How about a sexy African safari hunter. I've never seen that." And they spent a good hour trying on hat after hat, immersing in their own little world, and ultimately leaving the shop empty-handed.

"Now what?" he asked her, feeling superb after his plunge into Cassie's dream-scape. Had he ever in his entire life smiled or laughed so much? He wondered. He decided that he loved Cassie's world. It was so freeing from everything else.

"Any New York hot dogs around here?" she asked with a look of desperation.

"I don't know." He shifted his sunglasses around and spotted a lone hot dog stand. "Maybe that place has a reasonable facsimile." Jack tipped his chin up at the distant cart with a plump hot dog silhouette at the top.

"Oh I hope so." She fretted while pulling him towards the cart. "I'm in a near withdrawal state. The taste almost sits in my mouth constantly now."

He chuckled merrily. She was so marvelously funny! "Well if not, Cassie, we could go back to the shop, purchase a New York top hat for you, and you could chomp on the Los Angeles hot dog and pretend . . ."

****

"That didn't quite settle the taste in my mouth," Cassie said with disappointment after consuming her third 'dog'.

"Do you wanna fly to New York?" Jack raised his brows . "Because if you do, there's a kiddy helicopter over there." He laughed while pointing to a children's ride, rocking back and forth to a small child's delight.

"No thank you." She rubbed her full stomach. "I'll probably upchuck all those pseudo-New York hot dogs if I go on that thing."

"So what's next, besides fighting the crowds?"

She let out an indecisive sigh. "Let's just walk and see what hits, okay?"

Jack grabbed her hand and let his fingers sink into her cushiony palm. Then they spent the next several minutes dodging assorted groups of people whom Cassie found fascinating.

"Oh!" Her mouth cascaded into disgust. "How can anyone pierce their nipples? It hurts me just to think about it," she said, gaping at a long-haired shirtless male.

Jack looked in her direction and he nearly tripped with laughter. "Is that what you would term a voidoid, Cassie?"

"A voidoid with absence of pain sensation, I think," she decisively quipped.

And he laughed more fully. "You're so wonderful, Cassie," he blurted, before he could pull back the 'iffy' words. He stopped his noise and sucked in a breath. How would she interpret that? He felt the increased pressure of her fingers over his and he dared to release the breath.

"And you are an absolutely wonderful fantasy game player, Jack. I may play with you often," she replied with pure delight.

Though the expression was round about at best, Jack interpreted it to mean that she would spend more time with him. The thought filled him with total joy. He *hadn't* fucked-up with her. And he gently squeezed her hand to show his appreciation.

"Jack!" She bounced up and down on the balls of her feet to see above the heads of the crowd. "I see where I wanna go next!"

Dread rained over him as he looked up at the theater marquee.

"*Marabella*, your movie," she whispered in awe. "I've got to see it, despite that I haven't been in a movie house for fifteen years. This will be my first. How appropriate."

Jack shot a disbelieving look down at her. "You haven't seen a movie for fifteen years?"

"*On Golden Pond*. I just had to see the Hepburn/Fonda duo in their later years. And, I do admit I saw *Schindler's List* on video in the interim. That's my all time favorite movie. I cried like a babe at both."

Oh shit. I'm doomed.

"Shall we get in line. It's pretty long. Must be a good movie," she said with excitement.

He helplessly shifted his sunglasses around the area. "Cassie, there's *Sleepless in Seattle*. Why don't we go to that movie instead? The line's not quite so long."

"Are you crazy, Jack?" She pulled his arm along. "I don't let down my resolve for any old movie. This is *your* movie so I'm making a magnanimous exception."

Wonderful. He wanted to cry as they walked to the back of the line, especially when viewing the other patrons—they screamed out 'artistic perverts'. And likewise the word *Fuck-up* screamed and echoed in his mind .

****

"Thanks for the *Juicy Fruits*, Jack. I remember I used to love to eat these when I watched movies," Cassie whispered in his ear while they sat in the back row, at his insistence, in the large darkened theater.

"Don't mention it," he replied in more than a groan than voice.

"I feel like a high schooler sitting in the back row," she giggled into his ear.

He wanted to slither down his chair and dissolve into the floor. *On Golden Pond?* He wanted to wail.

"Since we're in the back row . . . would you mind putting your arm around me? That's the way I always sat in the back row of movie theaters," she requested with thorough delight.

Without a moment's delay, he placed an arm around her and dared to pull her close to him. *Maybe I can obliterate her face*, he thought, his panic rising with every tick of his watch.

"You're choking me, Jack," her muffled voice protested.

He quickly loosened up on her head, and she emerged with a loud pant. *Can't anything work out?* His inner voice cried out.

"My goodness, Jack," she laughed, snuggling her head in his arm crook. "You've given me an idea as to how you used to behave in the back row of theaters."

Jack miserably peered down at her smiling face. *You haven't seen nothin' yet, Cassie.*

"Oh . . . it's starting." She whispered like she was in a beautiful dream. *And the start of my nightmare . . .*

****

Jack had nearly gnawed his lips to bits by the time they walked back out into the glaring California sun. She hadn't said a word during the entire movie, and now he was terrified to look at her, certain she would hail the nearest cab, and go back to her suite and hide. "I'm afraid it was no *On Golden Pond*, Cassie," he found the courage to say.

No answer.

"Or even close to *Schindler's List*," he continued on.

She made no reply.

"And as for *Sleepless in Seattle* . . ."

Finally Jack couldn't take not another minute of her silence and he looked down. Then he stared, stunned. Her sunglasses were off, and her eyes were closed while she gloriously sucked in the air around her.

"It was absolutely beautiful, Jack, a masterpiece of sensitivity. I can still feel it. Why oh why are you an actor when you can create such resplendence on film? Oh . . . it's my new favorite movie of all times."

His heart burst with elation, and without thinking, he lifted her up in the air and madly kissed her lips. Then, he pressed harder when her arms tangled around his neck and her lips molded tightly against his. Suddenly, his fear evaporated, his reservations smashed, and his insides were as warm as the sun beating down on them. He raised his lips off hers. "I love you, Cassie," he whispered feverishly.

She crushed her lips against his and they kissed like two wild people, ignoring the gawking stares as crowds of people skirted around them . . .

****

Entwined in each other's arms, Jack and Cassie entered the Python complex where her suite was located. Jack agitated with emotions. He wanted her so badly. But with his first-time error clearly in his head, he didn't dare state his desires. He felt the heat in his groin with just her closeness, and knew that loving her would be a transforming experience for him. Yet, he firmly told himself, *No fuck-ups.* Not now. Not when he had found the guts to say the words that had broiled inside him from his first glimpse of her.

"You feel so good, Jack." Cassie tightened her hold around his waist.

Good enough to love, Cassie? She hadn't reciprocated the words, and that hurt. But he tried to convince himself that his outburst had been so sudden, she perhaps was taken off guard and needed time. Maybe she wasn't the impulsive type about something like that, although she seemed impulsive about everything else. But neither was he impulsive about things like that. Yet he had spilled his feelings, as foreign as they were. *Though real as hell.*

"Ms. Callahan . . ."

Both jerked their heads up to see the uniformed attendant for the suites standing in front of them. He held a huge flower arrangement of black orchids.

"More flowers, Ms. Callahan. Someone gets off on black orchids."

"No," Cassie whimpered.

She quickly disentangled herself from Jack, then slowly backed away.

"What is it, Cassie?" Jack started to walk towards her, but she flung out her hand.

"Get those away from me. Now," she trembled out.

He looked at the arrangement, then back at her. She looked absolutely terrified.

"Who are they from? Do you know?"

Her face screwed up and she nodded.

"Who?" he demanded then rushed forward and snatched off the accompanying card. "Is someone bothering you? Is that it, Cassie?"

"Yes," she squeaked out.

"Call the police, kid," Jack said to the attendant.

Cassie lunged forward. "No police, I beg you, Jack. It will make things worse."

Having heard of such craziness, he didn't want to heed her pleas. He knew the nuttiness of the world and viewed trust as an elusive thing, unlike her who seemed to need to trust the world around her. "If you know who this guy is, Cassie, you have to tell me, so I can stop it now," he begged. "If anything happened to you . . ."

"He wouldn't dare," she sizzled under her breath. "He's a coward."

Not reassured one iota by her words, Jack ripped open the envelope.

"He never signs his name, Jack. I can tell you what the card says already."

Ignoring her, Jack pulled out the card and read. The message only contained two large case words with several exclamation points after it.

PLEASE CASSIE!!!!!!!!!

"Please Cassie," she sneered. "I can just hear the liar's hiss."

Stuffing the card into his pocket, Jack charged up to her. "This is nonsense! You have to tell me *who* so I can stop this insanity. You're defenseless for Christ's sakes, just a little thing."

She gave a hasty shake of her head. "He won't touch me. He'd be worse shark bait than me, and he damn well knows it."

"Is he from New York?" Jack pushed himself nearer. "Is he?"

She gave a stiff nod. "From the other side of the world and he wouldn't dare stray. So don't worry, Jack. He'll never come to L.A."

Although feeling more than uncomfortable, Jack shifted part ways to the attendant. "Toss the flowers out and any others that should happen to come. But save every single one of those cards. I want them."

"Yes, Mr. Torelli," the attendant said, then rushed off with the arrangement.

Jack turned back to Cassie. Her shoulders trembled and her face looked ready to burst into tears. "Cassie . . ." He gathered her in a hug and her arms clung tightly around his waist.

"Just hold me, Jack. I need to feel your arms holding me . . ."

****

In the ensuing weeks, filming of *The Life and Times of Harry Hannigan* began, and Jack felt like he was working in a cloud of hostility. Most of the cast and crew were tensely polite, the general belief being that he was merely a woman's whim, a wart on the prestigious production, despite the daily rushes, showing he *did* have talent.

But he tried to be indifferent to the attitudes no matter how tough.

This was his chance, he kept telling himself, and thus, he gave two hundred percent to every scene. Of course, the fact that he was playing Harry Hannigan helped greatly. Bringing to life the character created by the woman he loved was an added incentive. He wanted to do an admirable job for 'his Cassie, the saving miracle of his life.

Every break he had from the set, he wandered over to the suites, always toting food from the commissary so she wasn't negligent about eating in the midst of her writing cloud. Once there, she melted into his arms and tearfully told him about her writer's blocks which seemed to ail her more and more.

"I've lost it, Jack," she cried.

"You need a break from it, honey," he soothed.

"I can't," she replied desperately. "I have a deadline, and he'll chew me up if I'm late."

"Who'll chew you up, huh? I dare anyone to try."

"You can't help me, Jack. It's bigger than you, and getting bigger."

"How is that, Cassie?"

"Harry Two. It's coming out next week already. Oh god! I can't face it all again."

"What do you have to face? What?"

"Curt's little show, and him."

"The orchid guy?" he demanded, and she gave a fearful nod. He firmed up his jaw. "You aren't facing that guy. I won't let you, Cassie."

"I have no choice, Jack. But you're so wonderful to worry about me, thank you—"

Of course I worry about you. I love you for Christ's sakes.

Jack sat off in a corner of the sound stage, studying his lines for the next scene, and trying to put Cassie out of his mind for the time being. It was damn tough. He loved her more than he'd loved anything in his entire life. And he desperately wanted her. But did she love him? She never said, despite that he had cautiously fished on several occasions.

It was so ironic!

At one time, he had all the sex he wanted when he really didn't want it, and now, when he finally wanted all of a woman, he couldn't get it. So damn unfair! He never thought in a trillion years that he would find such a woman in Hollywood. *It was a fuckin' miracle.* So why? Why the hell the tortuous denial?

His body was ready. He was raring to go. The long suppressed male senses rumbled whenever he held her, when he kissed her . . . he felt like he would burst right out of his pants. She was the one! Cassie Callahan was the woman he had needed all his life. They clicked like magic. So why the hell didn't she make a move? *He* couldn't risk making a move. It was she who would had to give the signal so he didn't *fuck-up* the best thing that ever happened to him.

"You look pensive, Jack."

Upon hearing the familiar smart-aleck voice, he jerked his head upward. Instantly, he wanted to kill. "What the hell are you doing here, Haley?" he gritted out.

Haley Shears gave a brash toss of her long black hair. "I landed a part in this miniseries, a small role, but one I can make great. You know me."

"The hell you did." Jack stood and began to charge off, fully intending to get her fired.

"Michael says I'm a natural for the role," she quickly touted.

Damn him! Jack veered around and his eyes shot dagger looks at her. "Up to your old tricks, huh Haley? Using the old tired and true method of getting a bit part. Is that right?"

A smug smile crossed her face. "He's my new boyfriend, actually."

"Bullshit! Is that some kind of a joke? He wouldn't give you anything but a tumble or two then a boot in the ass. You're still a dumb shit kid."

"Well maybe you could wise me up a little, Jack. Michael has an important party to attend so I'm free tonight." She twirled a smile on her lips.

"Go to hell!"

"Still can't do it, huh Jack?" Her smile filled with pure glee.

Rage bubbled inside him. "I could choke you for that," he said in a barely controlled tone.

"Don't worry, Jack. It's our little secret. I've been duly warned, believe me. Can't defame the big star, you know."

"Get out of my sight, and stay out," he warned.

"My pleasure," she replied in a sassy voice. "You never did appreciate me anyway. Too spontaneous for you. Mechanical is more your cup of tea. Capisce?" With a mocking smile, she sauntered away.

He wanted to pounce on her. Rud had guaranteed she would keep quiet, and what does she do? Perhaps a call to Rud was in order. Maybe he could put some pressure on Michael Isle's over age hormones and get rid of her. But on second thought . . .

Perhaps Mike would get suspicious and ask questions, he worried. Michael Isle was the last person he wanted to know about his past problem. Mike would *sure shit* find some no good way to use the dirt. Now with the important role he played in the machine, he had an upper hand with the producer and he preferred it that way so he wasn't totally scathed after the miniseries. No . . . it was best to leave things be and hope Rud's threat made an impact on Haley Shears.

"Get to Wardrobe, Jack," one of the assistant directors called out. "Scene in an hour."

He placed the script under his arm and nodded to the man who stood twenty feet away as if he, Jack, had a major case of cooties. He tried to tell himself that it didn't matter as he raised to a standing position. "I'll be there, Brett," he called back.

And after that, I get to see Cassie. The warming thought helped propel him to Wardrobe where he told himself to bear up for another batch of cold shoulders . . .

****

"You look as delicious as 'Harry', Jack," a slyly smiling Cassie commented the moment Jack walked through the door to her suite.

Jack glanced down. He hadn't taken the time to change out of the expensive suit in his anticipation to see her. "Thought I'd dress for lunch today." He grinned as he held up a paper bag to her. "L.A. hot dogs that are hoping they taste like they came from New York."

"Let the expert be the judge." She held out her hand for the bag.

He made no move to give her the bag, instead let his eyes take in every inch of her. The blonde hair was tousled about and the clothes rumpled, but her eyes were lit up like huge green lights on a Christmas tree. He wanted to bury himself with the sight.

"Well? I'm waiting for my mouth to experience total satisfaction."

Jack tossed the bag on a nearby chair and rushed over to her, lifting her up in his arms and holding her face close to his. "I'll give you total satisfaction." He powerfully moved his lips on top of hers, trying to show her every speck of feeling he had for her. "I love you, Cassie," he whispered the moment he released her lips.

"I know, Jack. I can feel it," she whispered back.

"What do you feel, Cassie?"

"Like I'm floating on a the fluffiest of clouds in the middle of heaven," she replied.

Disappointment washed over him, but he tried to hide this from her. "I'm glad, honey," he managed to get out, then he lowered her to the ground and went to get her lunch.

"You're getting closer, Jack," Cassie said minutes later while she munched on the hot dog.

Barely able to get his own hot dog past the misery-filled lump in his throat, Jack made no reply, rather remained suspended in his own thoughts. *Do you love me, Cassie? What am I to you? Am I something temporary to amuse you? Or do you see me as something deeper? What?* He yearned to point blank ask her these questions. But he loved her so much, he owned no such courage. He had to have her in his life no matter the type of relationship.

Do what you want with me, Cassie. I'm your slave, and I damn well know it.

"Hard day on the set today, Jack?" she inquired closely.

He flipped up his head. "It went okay," he mumbled.

"You seem down. Do you wanna talk about it?" Cassie leaned forward, her eyes full of compassion. "I'm listening, Jack."

Pain creased his face, although he tried like mad to *un*-crease it. Her look was so warming, so inviting, he wanted so badly to tell her what was on his mind. The words were blistering his lips. "I. . ." He couldn't do it. All he could see in his mind was the picture of her cowering by his car door because he dared to be bold. "I'm just tired, Cassie. I stayed up late last night studying the script." Then he forced a smile on his face.

"Tomorrow's Saturday," she said brightly.

He widened his smile. "What do you wanna do?"

Her eyes dropped. "Write my book," she mumbled.

"What?" he asked with distress.

"I have to, Jack. He's on my case majorly. I got chewed out on the phone this morning, because I'm so many chapters behind."

He shook his head with angry disgust. "How the hell can somebody force an artistic endeavor? That's what *whoever*, is doing, you know. It's a wonder you can write at all with 'Big Brother' loading the pressure on you."

"Wow, Jack. You just summed up my entire writing career in three short sentences," she said bitterly while tears misted her eyes.

"Honey . . ." He moved forward and knelt in front of her. "I didn't mean to be so blunt. I know you're having a tough time." Then he reached up and furiously kissed her face, groveling for forgiveness. But she pushed him away.

"You promised you wouldn't interfere with my writing, Jack," she accused tearfully. " I don't need the added pressure of the cruel truth compounding everything else. Writing is so high pressure in itself. You just don't understand. It's a high-intensity mental game that needs clear mental processes. And I just don't need the added stress of this right now."

Jack filled with terror. "What are you saying?"

"Maybe I should get a better handle on this book before we see each other again."

"No, Cassie . . ." He reached up and gently stroked her hair. "I won't say another word, I swear. Write tomorrow. I have things to do anyway. Okay?"

"But this isn't fair to you, Jack." She glided her fingers through his hair. "Writers are selfish people. The only relationship they're entitled to, is with their tap-taps. I know this . . . firsthand. A person involved with a writer will only get hurt in the long run. I. . .know this too."

"It doesn't have to be that way, Cassie, no matter what you've experienced," he pleaded. "I love you so much, I'll take you any way I can get you. I won't turn my back, I promise."

She wound her arms around his neck and hugged tight. "I just don't wanna hurt you, Jack. I love you so much too."

He ground her body into his while his eyes misted with tears.

I didn't fuck up . . .

Chapter 20—Jack

Saturday was a bright, baking seventy nine degrees, and Jack, feeling the bite of loneliness, tried to combat it by getting some sun on his new enclosed patio.

He had moved from his cheap apartment a couple months ago, per nervous suggestion of Harv Wellson who said it "wasn't fitting" for a man of his upcoming status to live so lowly. "It didn't look good," Harv, indoctrinated in the Hollywood perception, intimidated. So feeling a bit of the old indoctrination himself, he had taken his less than adequate funds plus a substantial loan from Harv, and bought a small furnished walled-in two bedroom home with lap pool on the southern border of Beverly Hills.

It wasn't extravagant, a mere upper-middle class abode that could be the home of any American family. But it was the first home he'd owned for a long time, and he did feel some pride in ownership. He even had a gardener, housekeeper, and pool man twice a week, three entities that had been long deprived as he hadn't wanted any strangers messing his life and discovering his secrets. Now he possessed few secrets except that he wildly loved Cassie Callahan.

And that secret was the only one that seemed to occupy his brain.

While spreading the coconut oil over his naked body, Jack felt the burning need of her. To deny himself of her was pure agony, a feeling completely new, as women had been aplenty from day one, it seemed. But he hadn't truly loved any, and that fact led to most of his suffering. He wanted to love her as freely as he had felt since the day he met her. To have no restraints on himself, to just let himself go, *whatever*, was such a blistering desire, he ached. He *needed* to feel like a whole man. This was his first step in finding himself, he strongly sensed.

It would make me a Torelli again in the defining sense.

And even though he had accepted, months ago, the fact that he would never be a Torelli in the familial sense, at least the defining sense greatly soothed his conscience. It was something, he told himself, something to bind him with the men he had once so reverently looked up to, and in his heart and occasional memory excursion, still did.

I'm trying to clean up, Pop, so I'm worthy.
But when?

Jack buried the back of his head into the padded lounger. She had to write. He had sworn to accept that fact. How long? He clenched his teeth. He hated *whoever* for ruining her spontaneity, her happiness, her talent, *them*. If *whoever* hadn't meddled, he would, right this moment, have that 'Cassie Callahan' that he had every Saturday. It was the one day she had to be that Cassie Callahan, and not some uptight, anguished caricature who was in tears more than not.

Fucking money machine!

They were sacrificing the woman he loved for a lousy buck, he thought in a fury. He wanted to throw a bomb right on top of it and watch all the cogs, nuts, and bolts fly in all directions so the woman he loved was set free. But could he?

He wondered. Could he when Cassie was smack in the middle of that machine, helping it run smoothly by her own agreement? She had fed into all the shit, by virtue of what? Fame? Money? They seemed to mean little to her, he thought. She wasn't some prima donna who flounced around like she was the hottest thing in literature to hit this country--which she was, if one believed the media. So why get sucked in, Cassie? It was a puzzling question with a more puzzling answer.

Could he solve it? Should he meddle and risk upsetting what little balance she seemed to have? Or should he just love her and hope Saturday came for him? He had promised her he would do that, and she said she loved him because of it. Could he even dare to upset that apple cart?

No, he finally concluded. No matter how tough, he would stick by his promise and keep himself secure in her life. If he lost the rare bird, he figured that they might as well put him in a deep hole and toss dirt over him.

So he pressed his eyelids together and baked, so he looked good for what? He didn't even know anymore—it suddenly seemed so inconsequential when he put it in his larger life. What only seemed to matter was her. Even the coveted role, which he was paying hell to play, held no color in comparison to her. An image? Forget it! He was only a shell of an image without her. She had destroyed every ounce of his pretense, because there could be no pretense with her. One couldn't be pretentious and love her.

Yet he baked, perhaps out of habit, something to occupy his time, exposure to a warming entity as warm as her. The reason didn't matter, he decided. He was without her, that's all that mattered. *Sleep Torelli. Put yourself out of your misery, and perhaps Saturday will pass.* . . .

****

The ten-story office building at Python Studios was quiet of activity after the usual maniacal work week. There was, as a rule, no work on weekends by Michael Isle's edict. He wanted his executives rested and stress-free so he could work the hell out of them Monday through Friday. Only severe work overloads necessitated a break in the rule, and only by his agreement. Otherwise, he expected to see his executives on Newport Beach on Saturdays and brunching in Malibu on Sundays.

However, he could work seven days a week if he chose--and he chose on more occasions that not. His highly desired single life, marred by three divorces, had no personal commitments except for select parties when the need arose, and a sporadic jaunt to an exclusive restaurant for lunch or dinner so people wouldn't forget who he was. Otherwise he lived his life on his own terms, taking when he wanted, casting off when he also wanted, and having to answer to no one.

And *no one* dared tamper with his pocketbook, Michael thought in a rage while studying possible location shoots for *The Life and Times of Harry Hannigan*, his baby, the miniseries and sequel that would seal his supremacy in the television medium. In fact, he had decided that he and Cassie Callahan clicked as a team—her type of writing and his tastes—they meshed like fresh warm bread and creamy butter. As long as the writing was good enough for New York to promote to the maximum, he reminded himself, and that seemed to be the rub.

"What the hell are you doing to her, Mike? She's slipping," John LaLiberte raged in a phone call a couple weeks ago. "You're cutting your own throat if you don't find some way to get her ass in gear, Mike. Or maybe I should just come out there and get her ass going myself!"

Thankfully some fast talking prevented this eventuality. He knew what was going on, and if the 'Limey' ever found out, Michael feared he would never get 'Harry Two'.

And Michael *craved* 'Harry Two'.

The manuscript was wonderful, better than part one, and destined to make television history. But John LaLiberte and Ferris Mitchell from Chicago had deliberately slowed negotiations for vaguely given reasons. He knew well their ploy was a stand-off with a definite message: Do your job with Cassie Callahan or we find a producer who will.

"Michael . . ." a sing-song voice said.

He gazed upward to see Claire Gibson, grinning like a Cheshire and leaning on his door frame. "What do you and that look want?" he asked tightly.

She gave a lofty lift of her eyebrows. "The bearer of sexual intrigue has arrived, looking like a teeny canary about to be devoured by the King of the Beasts."

"Ha-Ha." He swiped a stiff hand at her. "Send him in, and make it quick. I'm busy."

"Do you want me to scope out the location information, darling?" she purred.

His jaw rippled with anger. "How dare you intimidate that one unfortunate night."

Claire tossed an innocent look at him. "You mean that night you got roaring drunk at the Python Christmas party at the Beverly Wilshire? Is that the night you mean?"

"Yes--that unfortunate night!" he snapped.

She moved in leisurely seductive fashion. "I thought it was wonderful, darling. I never had Godiva chocolates fed to me or my toes massaged in such *luscious* fashion."

"Out!" He partially stood up in his chair, hating that Claire Gibson, scheming seductress *extraordinaire* had one more dirty tidbit on him--and this one, he would never live down.

"Of course, darling. I don't want to upset you." She blew him a light kiss before exiting.

"Damn woman," he muttered, wishing she was neither his right hand nor his left hand so he could boot her ass out the front door. Michael threw down his pen and sat back in his chair when seeing a nervous form slink through his office door.

"Hello, Mr. Isle."

"Well . . . ?" Michael blazed his dark eyes on the young man making his way up to his desk. "Spill it! I don't have all day to watch you grovel!"

"Ah . . . he came all week for short spurts during the day, never at night."

"And today, his usual day with her?"

"He never showed up and I haven't seen her leave her suite."

Michael narrowed tight eyes. "You sure, never at night? It doesn't sound like him."

"No, none of us have seen him at night, I swear, Mr. Isle."

"But you've seen him kiss her, you told me," Michael pressed.

"Yes, every Saturday he does. He can't seem to keep his lips off her."

"Damn him!" Michael fisted his desk. That animal was luring her into his carefully-laid trap, he seethed inwardly. And her! She was so damn raw, she had no clue what he was doing to her. No wonder she couldn't write! He had put some sort of ga-ga spell over her! She probably thought it was romantic for a good-looking Hollywood actor to pursue her. He could just read her flighty, dream-laced mind!

No way in hell!

He locked an intense glare on the young man. "I want her watched like a hawk. Any intrusions by him are to be reported to me immediately. Do you understand?"

"Yes sir, Mr. Isle. I'll pass the word . . ."

Michael twisted a wry smile on his face while looking the young man up and down. "And if you do a good job for me, I may have a bit part for you in one of my television productions."

The young man's face lit up. "Really? I'm . . . taking acting classes at UCLA and my teachers say I'm pretty good and . . .

Holding up his hand, Michael moved forward in his chair. "Cut the bullshit, kid. I don't give a rat's ass about your credentials. I only care that you do what I ask you to do. Those are the only credentials I need. Understand?"

The young man gave a jittery nod.

"Now go do your job. Pronto! Scat!" Michael commanded, and the young man scampered away like a frightened bird.

Michael stared down at the papers scattered across his desk, and he wanted to fling them away in his anger. He was ruining her! Sure as day, he was hardening the creamy butter. He was ruining everything!

"What did you do to him, darling?" a laughing Claire asked. "The kid ran out of the office like a tornado was on his heels."

"Fantasy-based incentive. Works every time," he sneered. "And as for tornados, you ain't seen nuthin' yet. I plan on whipping up a storm that will pulp-crush a slime ball to liquid status . . ."

****

A little after five p.m., Jack stepped out of the shower and briskly toweled off his newly bronzed skin. He glanced in the mirror, ran a hand over the fine gristle over each cheek and thought, *why the hell for?* However, he did run a brush then comb through his hair. For what reason? For something to do, he decided.

He was just dressing when he heard the phone ring. Immediately, he tightened his jaw. "No damn parties, Harv. I've told you, and told you," he muttered, charging to the phone and snatching it up.

"What?" he answered shortly.

There was a long pause. "Jack?"

He felt a strong pound hit his chest. "Cassie," he whispered. "I'm sorry. I thought . . . How are you, honey?"

He heard her suck in a sob. "Lonely. Could you come over, Jack? Maybe bring a hot dog or two?"

The pound rippled through his chest. "Of course, honey. I'll just finish getting ready, grab my keys, and stop at a hot dog place on Santa Monica Boulevard, then I'll be there."

"Thank you, Jack. I knew I could count on you . . ."

After hanging up the phone, Jack raced into the bathroom, pulled out his electric razor and felt the tremor in his hand as the blades ran up and down his cheeks and chin. Then he clicked it off and hastily ran the brush then comb over his hair again. He took pause, staring into the mirror and panting out all his anticipatory nerves. When relatively calm, he hurried back into his bedroom, whipped off his underwear and replaced them with a brand new pair. Then after several moments of indecision, he put on a pair of well-worn faded jeans and a Los Angeles Dodger sweatshirt with partially cut off sleeves. He wanted to look as non-threatening as possible.

Once dressed, he anxiously searched for his car keys, never where they were supposed to be. He found them carelessly tossed on a living room chair. Before turning for the door, he caught glance of the ridley turtle painting which hung center stage above his living room couch, even though the decor was purely art deco.

"Wish me luck, Mattie," he whispered. "If you hear me, give me a potent charm."

And then he spun around, jogging as fast as he could to his Corvette . . .

****

"Mr. Torelli . . ."

Jack impatiently looked up. He had just spent and hour and a half cussing his way through oppressive Saturday traffic, then in a line as long as Cuba at the hot dog stand. Now his insides were in a fevered uproar. "Did you want something, kid?" he asked the attendant at the Python suite complex.

"Um . . ."

Perturbed, Jack stared at the young man who looked like he had ants crawling all over him. "You got more cards for me? Is that it?"

"Cards! Yes, sir!" the young man exclaimed, then hurried behind the desk and pulled out a manila folder. He held it out to Jack.

Jack grabbed the envelope and shook it. "Goddamn asshole," he muttered. He raised his eyes to the attendant. "And I assume Ms. Callahan isn't catching sight of those orchids . . ."

"No sir."

With an grateful half-smile, Jack pulled out his wallet, extracted a fifty-dollar bill, and slapped it on the counter. "Thanks kid." He folded the envelope in two and jammed it in his pocket while making his way to the elevator.

Jack felt the heated pitch of his body while he rode the elevator. He flew out of the car then pounded his sneakers to her door while the hot dog bag flagged.

"Hi Jack."

Oh Cassie . . .

She looked beautiful, all fresh and perfect, with her hair shining and slightly damp from a shower. All he seemed to have the muscle power to do was hold up the bag to her.

She read the bag and her face broke into a smile. "My favorite place. You're so thoughtful, Jack. It's always so crowded, poor man."

"No problem, honey," he replied, wanting to add that he would wait in ten thousand lines to see that smile on her face. "Might as well eat them while they're warm . . ."

Jack tried to swallow his hot dog while he watched her chew thoughtfully. Just the sight of her . . . His insides roared. "Book going okay?"

Her head drifted down and she gave a small shake. "I miss 'Harry'. I never had trouble writing about 'Harry', but this . . ."

He placed down his hot dog and leaned closer to her. "What are you trying to write about? Maybe I could help."

She closely studied him before answering. *"Season of Sorrow* is about mothers and daughters, and . . . their relationships."

Curiosity instantly filled him. "Why are you writing about that? It seems a far-cry from 'Harry'. *A far-cry.* Why not just stick with male protagonists until you get a better handle on your writing style. I mean . . . I'm no expert, but wouldn't that be a little easier?"

She nervously shifted in her chair. "I don't know why I picked that topic. It just seemed appropriate."

"Why?" he pressed a little.

"Expertise?" she answered vaguely.

"Expertise?" he asked with caution, sensing a little more of Cassie Callahan was soon to be revealed to him.

She shrugged with indifference that was too shaky to truly be indifferent. "My relationship with my mother was a little interesting, that's all. And I thought that I could create a fictional world around it."

"But you can't? Is that what you're saying?" he pressed a little more.

"Maybe one can't create fiction out of glaring reality. It's too hard on the psyche."

"You mean it dredges up too many painful memories that get in the way of the writing."

"No!" Her body twitched like a nervous cat. "It never bothered me. I kept a stiff, obstinate upper lip, and never said 'uncle', not once."

"Uncle?" He moved closer, now definitely intrigued. "Like Harry's 'uncle'?"

"No big deal, Jack," she began to quip. "Of course, I'd use a term that I used all the time. It's only natural that a piece of the author meld with the character."

Her defensive tone, didn't he know it well, he thought. "So what was your relationship like with your mother. Specifically, if I may ask?"

"No, you may not ask," she promptly replied.

"Why? Why wait 'til *Season of Sorrow* comes out? Why not just save me the wait?" he asked casually.

She jittered her eyes back and forth. "What makes you think that you'll find out about my relationship with my mother in *Season of Sorrow?"*

Should I push farther? He wondered. Already she looked to be in a high agitated state.

He decided to take the chance and make one more point. "But honey . . . you told me that it was inevitable that the author meld with her characters," he said as gently as he could. "So I just assume that a big part of the relationship would have to be revealed in the book."

Tears slowly glided down her cheeks. "But I'm trying so hard not to do that, Jack. It . . . makes me vulnerable, and I can't be vulnerable. In the area of June Scarpelli, vulnerability kills."

Jack took her in his arms. "And in the case of June Scarpelli, 'uncle' is the operative term. Right?" he asked with resignation, gaining a little more insight into what was going on. Although he had a long way until complete comprehension came to him, he told himself.

Suddenly she flung forward and fixed her big pleading green eyes on him.

"I need you, Jack," she whispered. "I need all of you."

"Cassie . . ." Jack crushed his lips on top of hers and his hands grew maniacal in their exploration of her clothes body.

"Undress me, Jack." She dreamily closed her eyes. "I wanna glory in your lips touching every inch of my body . . ."

****

Feeling the throb of his groin, Jack lowered a naked Cassie onto the top of the quilt, then lowered his naked body onto the top of her. He felt the churning of so much love as he smoothed the hair back from her face. "I love you, Cassie," he said in a bare whisper.

"I love you too, Jack. You're so gorgeous," she whispered back.

With a low moan, he buried his face in her neck, running his lips down her gently curved throat to her breasts. His tongue traced around each rose-colored nipple cast against the slightly dark skin, and he savored the swell of their erection in his mouth.

"Yes, that . . ." Cassie's voice drifted in total pleasure.

One by one, he drew a supple breast into his mouth and felt the growing fever in his groin fueled by the taste of her hot flesh and the sound of her soft ragged breaths. His lips and tongue gently moved down her flat stomach. The growing sensation in his groin felt large and unnatural, yet more throbbing and pleasurable than he had ever felt in his entire life, and he knew it wouldn't be long.

"I need to touch you, Jack," she half-cried, half-moaned.

He scooted to her face and brushed away the sweaty hair strands from her brow. "It's too late, Cassie," he panted. Then he gave her a powerful kiss before easing into her, rocking gently while his eyes burned into her face, needing to see her own fulfillment. Her breaths grew more urgent, her moans guttural, and finally he felt a gentle shuddering beneath him while her mouth opened in a loud, shameless cry.

Her satisfaction complete, he thrust deeper with hard, forceful strokes while feeling the silkiness of her legs tangle around him. The trembling heat of his body escalated at the most glorious sensation he had ever felt—two bodies in perfect rhythm. So natural and spontaneous, just two people in love, freely expressing every bit of it. It was so beautiful . . . and tears bit his eyes when he felt the pound of his own splendid release.

"Oh Cassie . . ." His lips gently caressed hers. "I love you madly, honey."

Her response was a pleasure filled moan while her back gently arched from the bed.

Jack tenderly stroked her face to settle her throbbing body. *She's mine*. He had made his indelible mark on her, and she him. There was no turning back. He needed Cassie Callahan over and over, and screw exhaustion. No way could he live without her warm, unadulterated body pressed into his. "Let me hold you, Cassie. I need to be as close to you as I can . . ."

****

"Can I touch you now, Jack?" Cassie whispered while tightly snuggled next to his body.

"Not yet, honey. I need to cool down." His lips gently grazed the top of her head.

She stroked his abundant black chest hair. "I've never felt so much like a woman."

Jack gazed down, and a slight smile spread on his lips. "I can say the same, honey, except substitute the word 'man'."

"Can it always be this wonderful?"

Tipping up her chin, Jack lightly touched her lips with his. "I'll make sure it is."

She speeded up her finger movements. "Will you get tired of me? You know . . . want a more beautiful body like you're used to?" she blurted out.

The question smacked his very core, and Jack lifted her up so he had direct eye contact. "I love you, Cassie. *Love you.* And that makes me worship your body like I've never worshiped another body. Capisce?"

Her face shook with tears. "I had to ask, Jack. It was heavy on my mind."

"Oh Cassie . . ." He pulled her to him so her cheek rested in his neck. "That life's been over a long time, honey. I was *never* satisfied. It was one of the darkest periods of my life and I saw very little brightness until I met you. Now my life glows, and you're the reason for it. I wouldn't trade what I have with you for *nothing."*

"Really, Jack?"

Lack of trust . . . you shouldn't be surprised, Torelli. You brought it on yourself with all your contrived, reckless sex. And now you ask, Why did I even do it?

And the answer is: Because it was there.

Stupid fuck, Torelli. Stu--pid.

"It *is* a concern, Jack. I'm pretty wounded already and I don't think I could take . . .

"No!" Again he pulled her up to him. "It's *love*, Cassie. That invalidates every past relationship. You gotta believe that I only want you, honey." He lightly touched his nose to hers. "It may have taken me longer than most man, but I know damn well not to be a fool about this. I know what I have to the point of utter appreciation. *I swear,* Torelli's finally matured."

She paused to look closely at him. "I believe you, Jack. I love you so much . . . darling."

Greatly stirred by her words, Jack tenderly gazed into her eyes. "And I love you more than anything, Cassie Callahan." He crashed his lips onto hers and kissed as he pushed her back onto the bed, wanting her again, and again, until he croaked from sheer joy.

"Can I touch you now, Jack?"

"By all means . . ."

****

On Monday morning, feeling exhausted but elated, Jack pulled his Corvette into the Python Studio parking lot at exactly eight a.m. He shifted his sunglasses to the suite complex where he had left only four hours ago so he could go home for a fresh clothes. He figured that Cassie was dead to the world after their weekend frenzy of discovery which hadn't let up except for short bursts to cool down and eat the take out food they had sporadically ordered. He had never had back-to-back sex in his entire life, even in either of his marriages, and his body still bathed in total satisfaction. A warm, giving, compassionate love had miraculously healed it as if it had never betrayed him in the first place.

He tapped a finger on the steering wheel and smiled. "You were right Mattie," he whispered at the suite complex. "All I had to do was find a woman to make me feel good time and time again. Why the hell was I so stupid all of my life?" "Hey there, Jack . . . ?"

Jack gazed up to see George, the old white haired Python Studio security guard, as much an institution as the buildings. "Morning George. Great day, huh?"

"Yup." George squinted his eyes at the smoggy sky. "But it's gonna get pretty monotonous for the next few months. Would be nice to see some rain so the sky gets cleaned up."

"Well you know what they say, George . . ."

"It never rains in Southern California. I've heard it, Jack, and heard it, and . . ."

"Monotonous," Jack laughed.

"I came to tell you that the big Honcho has ordered you into his office before you go to the sound-stage." George imitated Michael Isle's pompous flair.

Jack glanced at his watch. He wondered *why* when he had a nine o'clock call and the 'Big Honcho' screamed like a banshee at any delays in the production schedule. "Do you know why, George?" he asked, as it seemed like George knew everything that went on at the studio. The old guy was better than the National Enquirer, Jack thought.

"Ah . . ." George looked tentative. "Maybe Mr. Isle better tell you."

Jack wrinkled his brow at the behavior. "Sound serious."

"You know Isle . . . he blows up everything. Alarmist since I've known him." George smiled mildly. "I wouldn't worry, boy. He's just got some steam to spout. Let him spout, and then do the what the hell you want. That's my advice."

Now curious, Jack grabbed his keys and exited the car. "Maybe I'll catch up on my z's while he spouts . . ."

****

"Well Jack . . ."

Jack tried to hide his disgust when seeing Claire Gibson sitting queenly behind her desk. She had been at Python since she was twenty, starting as a secretary then rapidly moving up the ranks until she reached the tenth floor. There had always been speculation as to how she made such a rapid ascent, but the woman was too sneaky to give any definite clues. "How you doin', Claire," he said without enthusiasm

"Fine Jack, and you? Or is that a loaded question?"

"What the hell does that mean?" he demanded, hating her perpetually sly look.

"It's just that . . ." She gleefully eyed him up and down. "you look like a new man . . . fully rejuvenated . . . or something like that."

Jack clenched his teeth. "Well maybe I am."

"Oh . . ." she said pleasurably. "To be able to float on a cloud like you must be pure heaven on earth, Jack."

His jaw muscles taut, he moved closer to her. "Now what the hell does that mean?"

Claire let out a low cunning laugh. "Mike has finished sharpening his claws, so he's all ready to see you, Jack. I'll let his Highness tell you 'what the hell'."

After sending an intense glare in her direction, Jack stormed into Michael's office and slammed the door behind him. "How the hell can you stand that woman, Mike?"

Ignoring the question, Michael waved a hand at the chair in front of him. "Sit down, Torelli," he said with tight restraint.

Jack curiously stared at Michael while making his way to the chair. "What the hell's this about 'claws', huh?"

"Shut!" Michael leaned across the desk and stiffly thrust out his finger. "You just shut up and listen, Torelli, if you know what's good for you!"

Jack fastened on the crimson face, and decided it had been a long time since he had seen that shade of red on Michael Isle. "Okay—I'm listening."

"How dare you, sleazeball! Diddling with a decent woman and bringing her down to your sordid level! What? Is it a novelty? A new perversion of yours? Transform 'Little Red Riding Hood' into one of your common sluts?"

"Fuck you!" Jack exploded right out of his seat. "I love her for Christ's sakes, if it's any of your business. Which it isn't!"

"Damn you! It *is* my business when she can't write and maintain her image *because of you!*" Michael exploded right back. Then he let out a sneering laugh. "And what's this about *love*? *You* Torelli? What kind of fairy tale are you trying to feed me, huh?"

He didn't care what Michael Isle thought. He had answered to the most important person, and that's all he cared about. Mike could be damned! "I'm not gonna stay here and listen to this shit. *I repeat,* it's none of your goddamn business, Mike!" Jack strode to the office door.

"If you don't stop this today, you'll be sorry, Torelli—I warn you."

Jack shifted around and let out a cynical laugh. "Oh, what will you do? Ground a thirty-four-year-old woman or put her in a corner? Or put *me* in a corner? In which case, your face would be mashed into the corner first!" Jack stormed out of the office, slamming the door so hard the frame shuddered.

"He got you a little testy, hey Jack?" Claire laughed.

Panting like a raging bull, Jack spun towards her. "Do the world a favor and put a clamp on that goddamn mouth, Claire!" Badly shaken, he stormed the rest of the way out of the office, needing to hold Cassie in the worst way.

****

From behind his office window drape, Michael Isle watched as Jack stormed to the sound-stage. *Damn you, Torelli. Still the troublemaker, aren't you?*

He clenched the drapes between his hand and squeezed. *Her image . . . carefully groomed at a great expense and effort for a carefully groomed end . . . he* would contaminate it. *And her compulsive work habits . . . his* obsessive sexual appetite would kill it. And perhaps he would drag her into the booze, drugs, perversions, so she couldn't write at all. Damn! *Why Torelli?*

Could he use threats on Cassie? He wondered. But he quickly discarded the idea. The woman had his number and would quip him to death, giving him a raging headache in the process. She knew she had him by the tail, so his threats wouldn't work. *He* had no power over her. But . . .

With a quick check of his watch, he made a lunge for his private phone and told himself to be on guard so he didn't give anything away. He knew his goose would be royally cooked if the truth was made public. *That* had to be avoided at any cost.

"John . . . Mike Isle . . . Our girl is feeling some pressure out here and I feel that a trip to New York is exactly what she needs . . ."

Chapter 21—Cassie

Where's the passion?

Gnawing on a pencil eraser and staring out the window at the Python buildings reflected in the blinding sun, Cassie sat at her computer and wondered about this question, like she had spent her days wondering for the past several weeks.

Season of Sorrow was an emotional mess, fragmented with a poor flow, and she wanted to dump the whole thing in the trash can and write a 'Harry Three'. *But no.* John LaLiberte wouldn't hear of it. He loved her chapter-by-chapter outline, and insisted she complete it per contract. The book would make her mature as a writer, he said, and perhaps help her bridge the gap to more literary works. 'Harry' was used up, he told her. He didn't want literary critics to call her an author with just one book idea. That wouldn't do for her image. *Oh no!*

Perhaps he did love her chapter outline, but she couldn't seem to fill-in those chapters with anything meaningful. There was no-good feeling, only darkness, as dark as her own soul. If the truth be known, the book frightened her. It hit too close to home, churning up more than she wanted it to churn.

"Come to Anoka, Cassina. I will fix up my attic for you," her grandfather always offered whenever she cried out her woes to him over the phone. "You need to get out of that *inferno*," he said. "You need to get out of that hell."

But it isn't hell, Nono. Jack has turned it into heaven for me.

Now she ached for her 'teddy bear'. She couldn't stand being parted from him for even a few hours. He was the only person in the world besides her grandfather who made her feel secure and warm, and she needed him. She had let him climb up on her raft through that one *un*-erected wall, and now her raft felt steadier and safer. She trusted him and knew, without a shadow of a doubt, that he loved her.

That part of her life was perfect.

But her book . . .

She chewed deeper into her pencil. *Where is it?* She always asked herself. Once she had an unsatiable thirst, an unshakable obsession, a desire to drown in her words and the fictional fantasy for twenty-four hours a day if she could. But somewhere along the line it had grown tedious, lost its luster and fulfillment; although she would admit this truth to no one. It was a humiliation, like spitting on all those years that she had yearned, worked like hell night and day, sacrificed and lost, and never said 'uncle' to make her greatest dream a reality.

Why?

It wasn't supposed to be this way. Her passion should only grow.

Shouldn't it?

Her writing should only get better with all the affirmation that she *had* talent.

Didn't she?

Cassie shook frightfully.

Do I really? Or am I a talent created in men's minds?

To be a talented writer had been her burning desire, her reason for breathing.

Was it all a sham?

If I don't have talent, how long can they create out of nothing?

Will I be a sham as well?

It was all a joke, folks. Sorry. Cassie Callahan doesn't exist. She's only been a figment of your imagination. She's sucked dry. Forget about her and go on to truly talented authors who don't need a *they* to be great. After all those years—after what she's lost in the process— Cassie Callahan was truly nothing. *In fact . . .* it had all been for nothing.

Oh, I can't bear it!

She flung the pencil out of her mouth and turned back to her computer. *Concentrate!* She cursed up then slowly down, rereading the last scene she had written in Chapter Six. Where's the feeling? Her mind half-cried, half-screamed. Nothing but cold fact, unable to arouse even the most vibrant creature. And *this* was her protagonist. She felt no sympathy—she felt *nothing*.

Quickly, she deleted the entire scene, then went to the preceding one. *This is absolutely awful. Sandy is so wooden.* She deleted this scene too, then kept reading back. *No life, no spark . . .* And she continued to delete. *She doesn't face life, rather cowers to it like a mongrel beaten into submission by a cruel master.* And she deleted. *I wanna slap her, tell her to wake up instead of feeling sorry for her mealy ways. Wise up, Sandy. You're turning into a clone.* In a frenzy, she deleted. *Where's your fight?* She deleted and deleted. *You're such a coward. Take 'Harry' for example . . .* And soon the entire chapter was a blank page.

"I hate her!" Cassie pounded her fists on the keys, then kept pounding while tears of rage moistened her eyes.

I've truly lost it. 'Harry' is my last hurrah, the only passion I can cling onto.

Unable to stand the sight of 'no words', Cassie leapt from her chair and rushed to the window, needing to see something, *anything,* to distract her from her 'sham' of a life.

She skirted her eyes over the buildings, the people, then back again, then again, trying to get her head into perspective, but the fear and panic held tight.

What do I do? What next? Oh god! I feel so alone . . . not even my fantasy world . . . not even 'Harry' to comfort me.

No 'Harry Three', *they* had said.

And I have to heed that.

Suddenly her heart lurched and the fear slowly dissolved. He's coming! The large, muscled form, swinging a paper bag, headed for the suites. *Oh thank god . . .*

She hastily unlocked the door then haphazardly tossed off her clothes and dove between the quilt. Placing two pillows behind her, she propped up, finger tousled her hair, pulled the quilt under her arms, and smiled languidly . . .

****

Jack walked through the door and stopped. Slowly, his mouth curved into a devious smile. "How'd you know I had a three-hour break? Must be telepathy."

"Our minds are bonded. I admit it." She smiled brightly. "I heard your voice drift into my head and it said, 'I'm horny as hell so get ready, Cassie'."

Never taking his intense piercing eyes off her, he locked the door, tossed the paper bag on a nearby table, and began peeling off his clothes until he stood naked by the bed. "I am horny as hell," he murmured. "I'm always horny as hell for you, honey." He reached down, pulled away the quilt, then slowly lowered himself on top of her.

The heat of his body and smell of his maleness made her shut her eyes as a pleasurable shudder rocked her insides. His lips covered hers and his moist urgent tongue moved inside her mouth. The ample hair on his chest crushed into her breasts while his magnificent penis compressed into her crotch, and she felt every trace of despondency melt away.

Oh . . . her mind echoed with the moan that she couldn't get past his insistent lips.

"I love you, Cassie . . . I love you . . ." Jack kept whispering while his lips moved down her neck to her chest where he attacked her breasts with his mouth and tongue. She felt the exquisite sting as each of her nipples firmed and raised into his mouth, and he grasped his lips around each and sucked upward until a scream consumed her mind.

"I need to touch you, Jack," she shook out in a soft cry.

Immediately, he lifted and covered her mouth with his while he rolled onto his back with her on top of him. "Please touch . . . please do," he begged while his eyes burned into her face.

With a loud moan she moved down his chest, burying her face in his soft curly hair while her lips gently touched his skin.

"Don't stop the lips," he groaned pleasurably, and she pushed her face deeper into his chest, moving her lips more avidly and rolling her tongue around his nipples perched on firm muscled pectorals. "More, Cassie . . . I love your lips."

She traced her lips down his solid stomach while her trembling hand went to his crotch. Her fingertips lightly touched the tip of his penis and she felt the thrust of it into her hand. Delicately, she moved her fingers around the head, then she gently enclosed the shaft in her hand and let it slide up and down her hand, her fevered senses rapt with the velvety touch. She felt his thighs tense beneath her and then he let out a loud moan.

"Don't quit the fingers . . . they're drivin' me frickin' nuts."

His words increased the near-orgasmic pound of her body as well as her insensibilities, and she thrust her mouth over his cock, a forbidden pleasure she had never attempted in her life. But her desire of all of him blew apart the ingrained barriers. The satiny feel inside her mouth knocked out any other thought from her mind and she let her tongue roll, feeling him expand between her cheeks while his heightened moans rang through her ears.

Suddenly, she felt herself being lifted forward and she nearly screamed in protest. She wanted more! But his lips firmly pushed against hers, then moved wildly while he entered her from the front. His strong arms smashed her down on top of him while she tried to release her climactic yells from his tight grip on her mouth. Her body rocked in tune with his as she sensed his growing pressure and force inside her. Finally he let go of her lips, and she screamed out all her unreleased ecstasy a split-second before he exploded inside her.

Feeling the intense quake of his body which also shook her in its power, Cassie stared down at the tight grimace of his face. He was so beautiful, she thought, her eyes tracing his firm jaw, smooth bronze skin, straight, well-defined nose, and his eyes, so gorgeously boring in their intensity. "I love you so much, Jack," she said softly.

"Oh Cassie, my love . . ." He tenderly flipped her on her back, wrapped his arms around her, then gently toyed his lips over hers. "I'm addicted to you," he murmured over and over.

"And now I'm addicted to you too . . . darling . . ."

****

An hour later, Jack was propped up in bed with Cassie tangled in his arms. She shut her eyes and pressed closer, and closer, unable to get as close to him as she wanted. He felt so wonderful . . . her 'teddy bear'.

"Cassie we need to talk," Jack said suddenly.

She let out a mischievous laugh while softly pinching his chest. "I bet I know . . . the day after tomorrow is Saturday and you're wondering where Cassie wants to play. Right?"

He smiled down at her. "I know already where I wanna play."

"Oh Jack! We can't live in bed. We have to come up for air sometime."

"Who the hell needs air?" He gently touched his lips to her hair.

"I do." She snuggled deeper into his arm. "I have to be Cassie Callahan, you know. It's the highlight of my week."

"How would you like to be Cassie Callahan seven days a week?"

"Is that our new fantasy, Jack?"

He lifted her up so his face was close to his. "No--it's glaring reality. I want you to get out of this suite and move in with me."

"What?" She flopped back down into his arms and the dread descended. Live with someone? How would it look? And her writing . . . How could she concentrate with gorgeous him around to tantalize her? She could just envision herself getting on a rare roll, and him rearing that magnificent penis at her so any train of thought was impossible.

"I love you, honey, and I wanna be with you without all these *eyes* around us. My house is private. We can make our own world and not have any interruptions."

Cassie gazed up and saw the immense pleading in his eyes. *Oh those eyes, my teddy bear's eyes. How can I?*

"I have a spare bedroom," Jack quickly spoke on. "I'll turn it into an office for you. It's facing the back yard so it's perfectly quiet and if you want, there's a patio where you could write. And a pool too. You'd like that wouldn't you?"

He's thought of everything. What in the world do I do?

"Think about it, honey . . . a new environment may help you get your writing back, and *we do* love each other. We should be together. I need you with me, Cassie."

She thought about this point and wondered . . . *Could he be right?* Maybe, his spare bedroom would remind her of her attic. *Maybe . . .*

"And I promise to let you write. I'm satisfied just knowing that you're close by. I'd never disturb that, I swear to you."

"Really Jack?" She looked up in frank disbelief. "I mean, you'll really understand about the writing and not hassle me? Like . . . determine certain times when I have to be with you, or something like that?"

His brow deeply furrowed. "Of course not. Why would I do something asinine like that? When you need a break, you let me know."

"Oh, it sounds wonderful," she breathed out hugging him tightly. He was such a throughly sensitive and cognitive man, so much like her 'Harry' more and more.

"Then you'll do it?" he asked with baited eagerness.

Feeling a great impulse, she reached up and wildly moved her lips across his. "Looks like you got a new roommate, Jack."

Laughing, he pressed his lips into hers until she was flat on her back. "We'll move you on Saturday morning, so get packed," he murmured. "But as for now, I have an hour and a half left, and a lot more satisfaction to feed..."

****

Still feeling the broil of her and Jack's lovemaking of yesterday afternoon, Cassie packed her suitcases and garment bags. She had already covered the computer and packed her disks, deciding she wouldn't attempt another word until she was in that back bedroom where she just knew, the words would flow. Why torture herself now? She reasoned. *And I'll have my Adonis too.* Her body tingled with pleasure at the mere thought.

The phone on her bedside table rang. Certain it was Jack, she nearly attacked the receiver. "I'm panting for that back bedroom," she breathed into the phone.

"What back bedroom?" a demanding voice asked.

She raised a shaky hand to her brow and rubbed. "John... I just had some dialogue running through my head. You know writers... they have dialogue running through their minds even when they sleep. I do at least."

"Uh-huh," he said abruptly.

"So... did you call me to tell me how 'Harry Two' is doing in sales." Her stomach fluttered with anxiety.

"Good," he replied without elaborating. "Thus the reason for my phone call. We need you in New York to promote the book. Curt's set up several parties, book signing, a couple interviews, and he even weaseled a gig on Letterman."

"David Letterman?"

"Of course, Cassie," he replied with impatience. "I reserved a room for you at the Regent and put a computer in there for you. You *do* have a book to complete for me, may I remind you... Well... how far are we this week?"

"Ah..." She felt the bite of raw nerves while scanning her luggage. "Nearing Chapter Seven, actually."

"Chapter seven?" he said tightly. "Chapter Twelve was supposed to be done by now."

"I know--but to be honest, I'm having a tough time grasping the main character."

He let out an exasperated sigh. "What the hell is there to grasp? Your chapter outline reads her loud and clear... Sandy is a sick woman, hiding in one life to cover up her past life and this unreality falls onto her daughter. The basic premise is self-deceit—Sandy's struggle to conceal the mental torture. Juicy stuff if you get your damn act together."

"No, she isn't," Cassie disputed, churning with the familiar rage. "Sandy's a coward who says 'uncle' to that past life and is unable move onto something more... comfortable. I'm a 'no 'uncle' person, so I'm having trouble identifying with her, that's all, John."

"Fooey! Who the hell says an author has to identify with a protagonist? It's a fictional character which you create, for Christ's sakes. It doesn't have to be a relative, or even someone that you can stand. Just make the reader cry buckets over her like you did with 'Harry'."

Cry buckets? When I wanna spit on her, rip out her perfect hair, yank her tongue out for her politically correct statements, and shake her for her 'Yes, M'am' attitude?

"I'll have our research department do a literature search at the New York Public Library on split-personality disorders. You may want to go that route with Sandy. Maybe a little serious reading will help you dredge up some compassion for the character."

"Split . . . Split-personality? Like a lot of people in one body?" A continuous tremor assailed her body.

"Not *a lot* of people, Cassie," John said with irritation. "Two will do nicely, one obviously the protagonist, the other the antagonist, *which* you indicated on your chapters outline. Interesting as hell."

"I did?" She cowered, not remembering that she had indicated anything of the sort. Then her eyes drifted to her luggage. *Oh god, I need him. I need some comfortable . . .*

"Your plane leaves at three p.m. from LAX, and I'll get that literature to your hotel room so you can study it over the weekend and hopefully get some work done."

She kept her eyes fastened on the suitcases and a quaking pain rocked her. "How long, John? I don't wanna be away from L.A. too long. I. . .like it here."

"About three weeks, maybe four, Curt says."

Three, four weeks? Tears blinded her. *My teddy bear.* But she dared not refuse--she couldn't. Her passion . . . *they* were her only salvation.

After hanging up, Cassie let the sobs flow freely. How would she survive without those arms soothing all her ills? He loved her! He loved *Cassie!* She no longer cared about his past or his deep dark secrets. He was what she needed--he made no demands.

He just loves me.

And she trusted that love, she thought fiercely, almost as much as she trusted the love of Angelo Scarpelli.

My passion . . . that was the trade off.

Was three, four weeks worth such a trade off?

Without her passion what would she have?

My god, what would I be?

Without even an attic to shield her, she'd be a . . .

Noooo . . . !

She hurried to her suitcases, flipped out clothes onto the bed and replaced them with her asexual clothes. Then she did likewise to her garment bags.

****

Shortly after noon, Cassie was packed and dressed to leave for New York. She stood by her window, peeking behind the curtain, waiting. After another twenty minutes passed, she saw the familiar form, dressed in jeans and T-shirt, carrying a white bag, and heading in her direction. Was he whistling? Oh Lord! She had never seen Jack whistle before. He looked so happy—even behind the dark glasses, she could tell. Or maybe she could just feel it by his lilting gait. She wanted to dissolve. How would she ever tell him? How?

"Hot dogs!" he announced the moment he walked through the door. "Thought I'd get something special to celebrate our new connubial existence."

"Just what I was craving, Jack," she managed to get out. He looked so wonderful, almost glowing, and so inviting with that bit of black hair tousled on his forehead.

He looked around and his face exploded in a smile. "I see you're pretty much packed and . . ." He paused to look at her, his brow furrowing. "Why the hell are you dressed like that?" Then he gave an amused laugh. "Kinda reminds me of the first day we met, then had pizza, then . . . I'll never forget how sweet your lips tasted to me that night."

"Jack . . ."

"So I thought I'd pick you up early tomorrow, say . . . eight-ten, maybe eight oh nine if traffic is light," he said with a flash of a gorgeous smile.

Deep grooves of pain formed on her face. "Please Jack . . . I need to . . ."

"Cassie?" He hurried forward and gathered her in his arms. "Is that too early or too late? Do you wanna come tonight, instead? Whatever you want, honey."

"What . . ." She paused to gather her creaking nerves. "What if I said I wanted to go to New York, instead?"

"Huh?" He stepped back, his eyes bearing cautious fear. "What are you saying?"

Shakily, she told him about the phone call.

"Three or four weeks?" he flared angrily. "Hell! I had the maid come in an extra day to give the house a good cleaning, I spent all last night getting your office ready, I even went grocery shopping to fill the refrigerator, and . . . I put clean sheets on the bed for Christ's sakes! I'll go fuckin' crazy for three or four weeks in that bed!"

"I have no choice, Jack. It's my career," she pleaded, wishing she had the bravery to run to his house and hide from them all. She couldn't stand the look on his face. He looked more like a wild grizzly bear, and she wanted her teddy bear back.

"You could say, no." Jack pressed closer to her. "I need you more than they do, Cassie. Please don't leave me." He frantically touched his lips to her face. "We're just starting out. It's like a honeymoon with you, Cassie. I'm not ready to let go of that yet. Are you?"

"No . . . But . . ." She turned her face. "I have to go, Jack, even if I go crazy in my bed for three or four weeks, I have to."

"Bullshit!" His eyes blazed with fury. "Why are you letting them sucker you into their little game? Three or four weeks for a book promotion? That's asinine! A few days, a week maybe, but three or four weeks? That's nuts, Cassie!"

"It isn't with Curt running the show, Jack," she said in a small voice.

"Speaking of Curt . . . that orchid man is also there, may I remind you, and I have a hunch he works for that company! Am I right?"

"No!" she burst out, knowing it was much too quick for 'Eagle-eyed Torelli'.

Slowly, with a look that said 'liar', Jack shook his head. "It only makes sense, Cassie. Why would the guy not dare, huh? You're just a little thing. There must be someone bigger scaring the bastard. Like some 'big bazoo' at Starburst who could crush him if it's found out that he's bothering their 'star' author?"

How in the world . . . ? He was like an ace detective. "Nice theory, Jack, but save it for your first novel *Pervert in the Publishing House*," she quipped with a light laugh.

"Won't work, Cass. I *know* he's a Starburst employee which means that you're not going anywhere near that place," Jack said definitively.

"You have no right . . ."

"*I have every right,*" He disputed with a roar, then he sucked in his anger and quickly calmed down. "I'm the guy who loves you. Remember?"

"How could I ever forget?" She reached up and tenderly kissed his lips. "Will you wait for me, Jack?"

Another roar. *"Wait for you?"* He took several deep breaths before speaking again. "What the hell does that mean?"

"Well . . ." She felt tentative to bring it up. "You're a man with a healthy sexual drive . . ."

This roar shook the walls. *"Are you mad?"*

She stared at him and kept silent.

Jack huffed and panted as he stared back. "Who the hell else would I wait for, huh? Any damn animal can mate and end up with a minute or so of satisfaction. But why even the effort then? A hundred women? Less than ninety minutes of satisfaction. A thousand? Less that a fuckin' day's worth. Is it worth it to blow years of satisfaction with you for seventeen fuckin' hours of *nothing*? Hell no! I'm not a stupid shit!"

"Wow . . . You've been really thinking about this, haven't you, Jack?"

"Damn straight!" He pulled her close and his eyes pierced into hers. "I love you. Only you in the whole wide world. Capisce?"

"I capisce." Cassie melted into his arms. "Will you call me, Jack? I'll be at the Regent."

"Yeah," He gave her shoulders a dispirited shake. "In between cold showers, I will."

"And I'll drown in your voice while I'm taking my cold, cold, bubble bath."

He lifted a stiff finger and stuck it up to her face. "You be careful! Only hotel to limo."

"Even on Park Avenue?"

"Yes! Even on Fifth Avenue."

"What if I need a hot dog?"

"No way, Cass. Your mouth will just have to suffer. Now promise me!"

"Even . . ."

"Yes! Promise now."

"I promise, and . . . I love you very much, Jack."

"Call me darling . . . please . . ."

"Darling . . ."

His mouth plunged on top of hers while his fingers artfully unbuttoned her asexual dress.

****

Gazing down onto Park Avenue from a window in Curt Farchmin's office, Cassie saw rapidly moving heads and pampered, ridiculously decadent, pooches making deposits for their owners' 'poop bags'. Planet of the Apes with dogs, she thought humorously, watching an expensively attired man pluck a turd.

It had been twelve days since she had come to Manhattan, and she was starting to believe that Jack was right. The light publicity schedule didn't merit a three, four week stay. But when she tried to bring up this point to Curt Farchmin, he shot her down like a cannon.

"You *will* stay for the prescribed time, Cassie. You have appearances and a book to finish, so live with it!"

She wished she could tell him to *go to hell*, but he still scared her half to death. *Why?* She had no clue, except that his cold, calculated manner sent shivers up her spine and made her back down every time.

"Forget the window, Cassie! I need your full concentration."

The voice soaked through her like acid as she spun around. Curt's face was rigid and his eyes, like two fireballs. Without delay, she shuffled to a chair, carefully ignoring Geoff Haines who sat leisurely draped in a corner. His eyes constantly bore into her even when he wasn't around, giving her a worse spine-tingle than Curt Farchmin's look.

"Now for tomorrow . . ." Curt began in his dictatorial tone. "You have a half-hour interview at a Manhattan radio station. Cal Davies in the disc jockey's name and he's known to be quite crude with his guests. So stay on guard. Act shocked if he gets a little lewd. Don't forget your homespun persona for a moment."

"Cal Davies?" She had heard the name at a couple parties and people said that the disc jockey was schemingly ruthless. "Why would you deliberately toss me into such a situation? I see no benefit to my book promotion."

"Exposure," Curt replied abruptly. "Millions of people listen to him."

"And millions of people will hear him chew up my book."

"No, you alarmist woman!" Curt's cheek twitched impatiently. "He's been told that 'bashing 'Harry' is out, and he's only to concentrate on you."

"Me?"

"He's going to try to break down your inhibitions, I assume. You know . . . try to gross you out a little, see if you're really as innocent as we claim. That's what he gets off on . . . expose'."

"And what if she does . . . expose me, I mean?" Cassie panicked. Her book image . . . it was all she had left and it could be gone, *pouf,* in a mere half-hour. How crass of Curt!

"How can he do that, Cassie?" Curt looked her square in the eye. " Your unworldliness makes you full of inhibitions that he could never break down. Therefore you'll come out smelling like a rose and respected by all for not succumbing to 'The Butcher', as he's so lovingly called."

Her panic rose. *Curt can't really believe the bullshit he's been peddling, can he?*

"Geoffrey will escort you. He'll be right there in the control booth, giving you support," Curt said as if it wasn't going to be any other way.

"Why can't you be in that control booth?" She could feel the mocking pair of eyes as they stared at her from the corner.

"I have a meeting with an important author. You aren't the only author in our stable, you know," Curt replied in biting tones. "At least this one *produces!*"

She sunk into her basic white oversize linen jacket. Curt was starting to turn his back, she just knew it. She *had to* concentrate on that book. *Produce!*

"One p.m. sharp tomorrow, so you *will* meet Geoffrey here at eleven. If traffic is light, you two may want to get a bite to eat before the show. There's an outdoor cafe next door. The food is blase' but edible."

She wanted to wail out her terror at Curt's words. But instead, she merely nodded and ached like hell for *him*. His warm, safe arms, beautiful sensitivity, and his unconditional love . . . She missed him horribly. And to hear his voice night after night had only made things worse; even though she would have died without hearing that voice trying to convince her that he was "making do" when she could tell that he wasn't at all. He would protect her. He would *kill* Geoff Haines if he dared lay a hand on her. Should she call him now? Tell him the whole truth so he could put a stop to it? He would—he said he would. *But do I dare?*

"And perhaps after the radio show, Geoffrey would take you for a haircut. That hair! It's starting to look shaggy again. Do you understand, Cassie?"

Bobbing her quaking head upward, she saw the defiant look registered on Curt Farchmin's face. The sight made her melt between her shoulders. *I need you so much, Jack. Help me . . .*

At precisely three minutes after eleven the next morning, the a long black limousine with **Starburst Publications, Inc.** written on the side, pulled from the Park Avenue curb. The uniformed chauffeur, familiar with both occupants, chatted about every conceivable subject from the weather to presidential politics as the vehicle headed towards West Lower Manhattan where WWNY, one of the largest radio stations in New York was located.

Wearing in a warm, black, buttoned-to-the-throat dress despite the high humidity of the late May day, Cassie hung close to the passenger door and kept her black opaque sunglasses focused out the window. Her body rattled with a continuous shake. Geoff had acted with the coolest of deference from the company entrance to the car; although now, she sensed him cautiously inching closer.

"Turn down this street, Errol. We want to make quick time. Ms. Callahan and I need to have some lunch," Geoff Haines directed in a cultured New England accent that could comfortably grace any Ivy League campus.

Cassie shuddered at the sound.

"Don't we, Cassie?" She keenly felt his stare on the back of her head as if his eyes were buried into her scalp. "No," she replied in a stiff whisper.

"Come on, Cassie. We *must* do as Curt ordered," he hissed in a tone that froze her blood.

"Go away," she said, unable to hide the tremble from her voice.

"Never Cassie. You should know that by now."

"Why are you doing this?" She felt the gathering of tears behind her sunglasses.

His hot, moist breath covered her neck. "I made you. You're mine, Cassie, and you're going to know that someday."

"I'm not yours." She flung from the door and leaned forward. "Tell me about the Yankees game last night, Errol," she quickly requested.

More that happy to oblige, the chauffeur began recapping the baseball game in vivid detail while Cassie kept her eyes fastened on him.

"It won't help you . . ."

She felt his lips softly graze her ear and nausea rose to her throat.

"I worship my perfect Cassie."

Having every intention of letting loose, she flung towards him, then stopped cold in terror. Geoff held a photograph curled in his palm. It was her, wearing a short, revealing green negligee. His thumb gently traced the outline of her breasts, then it pressed when directly over them. Next his thumb moved down to where the negligee cut to the groin, and with slow, circular motions, his finger caressed that area.

Her eyes felt paralyzed.

"My passionate Cassie . . . it's slipping. Where oh where has it gone?" His thumb languidly moved back and forth across the negligee panties. "She needs to come back so she can find her passion again."

"Errol!" she suddenly cried out.

Geoff slickly slid the picture into his pocket.

"Tell me what happened on Wall Street today and don't leave out anything . . ."

****

"You're quite a driver, Errol. Eleven forty eight on the dot. We now have time for a bite." Geoff Haines exited the limousine stopped on Twentieth Street near the Hudson River. He held the door wide and teased his lips with a smile while he looked down at Cassie. "Time to go, Cassie. There's no turning back, now."

Knowing her options were few, Cassie flew out of the passenger door and with terror propelling her, began quickly walking down the street towards the building with a large WWNY letters on the top.

"No good, Cassie."

She felt a pair of arms encircle her waist and bring her to a rapid halt. A loud whimper escaped from her throat. "Let me go or I'll scream."

"You won't scream." His eyes darted around. "Now come along nicely. Curt's blase' cafe is over there." He tightened his hold and shuffled her up the street . . .

The open-air cafe was only fairly busy and Geoff insisted that the waiter place them in a quiet, hidden corner, far from any other human activity.

"So . . ." Geoff sipped on an illegal vodka martini. "Is Kristi talking to you yet, or are you still groveling?"

"How dare you." The glass of ice water shook to her mouth.

"June still has her by the tail, eh?"

"Shut up." She fizzled.

He ran the martini glass across his lips. "Perhaps you should grovel to June too."

"Damn you!" She wished she could control her emotions. She knew they were egging him on, and she hated herself for them.

Geoff emitted a low laugh. "I've got the goods on you, Cassie, every little dirty one. There's no escape for you."

"Escape?" she shook out.

After skirting his eyes in all directions, he moved his mouth to her ear. "You can't escape me. You're in my blood and soul, the lover who tantalizes my mind when I lie naked at night in my bed. I can feel you, Cassie. Your passionate heat makes me wild." He deftly plunged his tongue into her ear.

"No!" She jumped away and looked around helplessly. He was insane! Now she could never tell, her mind spit out frantically. If he lost his job at Starburst because of her, she would have no protection, no leverage. A madman would be set free to . . . *Oh god!* . . . She could barely think about *what*.

"I saw you at the Regent last night in your bathtub, covered in a *fluff* of bubbles. And when you lifted a leg and placed a sponge to it, I couldn't hold my response. I can still feel the burn in my pants." A leering smile danced on his lips.

Was I in a bubble bath last night? I was! How did he know? How could he see? *It's the Regent for god's sakes!*

"And when you stepped out of the tub, I could just taste you. Perfect pussy." The words slid smoothly off his lips.

Cassie bolted upright. "I wanna go," She felt like a million slime-covered points were sticking into her.

"Sit!" he ordered up at her. "You must have lunch. Curt says."

Terrified by the rage in his hazel eyes and not wanting to set him off, Cassie sat.

"That's a good girl. We *must* do what the General says, you know." He wore an ugly sneer. Then in a heartbeat, his face shifted into a pleasant pose. "Ah . . . here comes our food. Chicken salad, your favorite, Cassie."

The young waiter graciously placed down their plates. When he straightened back up, his hand accidentally brushed against Cassie's bare wrist.

"Don't you touch her," Geoff said in a tight controlled tone to the young man. "I'm the only one who touches her, lad."

"I'm sorry, sir," the waiter replied, looking confused.

Also, confused was Cassie. "Just drop it, Geoff. The kid didn't mean, *whatever.*"

A smile flashed on Geoff's face. "I'll defer to my lady's wishes," he said to the waiter.

With a slight bow, the young man left their table.

When alone again, Geoff whipped out a spotless white handkerchief from the pocket of his expensive dark suit and quickly patted Cassie's wrist with the cloth. "No contamination to my perfect Cassie," he said in low, reverent tones.

She stared at the up and down motions of the handkerchief and wanted to shriek in fright at the demented behavior. But her vocal cords felt frostbit as did the rest of her. "Let . . . me eat, Geoff. The interview . . . one sharp . . . Curt says," she managed to quake.

Immediately the cloth raised, and Geoff's face sculpted into tenseness. "Yes--whatever Curt says." He pulled back the rest of the way into his chair. "And if she performs well with 'The Butcher', Geoff will buy her some exquisite black orchids . . ."

****

The quarter of the chicken salad sandwich Cassie had forced herself to swallow, sat like a lump in her gullet ready to burst forth any moment, as she sat in Cal Davies's 'hot seat'-- or so the flamboyant, long-haired, *voidoid extraordinaire* disc jockey had called it when he wiped his hand on his filthy jeans before shaking hers.

"Anoka, Minnesota, huh? Cow udders, horse testicles, moose shit . . . all that crud, I bet," Cal laughed.

She felt the lump move up a bit further. "I've never even seen any of those things except a cow udder in a schoolbook, Mr. Davies."

"And what did it do to you . . . the picture I mean? Did it make some sort of hidden raw female emotion burst forth so you just had to run those silky fingers up and down an udder . . . ?"

"Heavens no! I thought it was so droopingly disgusting," she replied in a huff.

"Oh . . . a dark emotion like an irritant which has plagued on your mind for years so you're adverse to anything anatomically drooping, huh Ms. Callahan?"

"No! That's not one bit true . . ."

He quickly cut in. "So you *do* like a few anatomically drooping things. Which ones specifically?" He leaned closer and raised his eyebrows at her.

"Ah . . ." She willed herself to turn to Geoff Haines who stood behind the glassed-in control booth, his lips fixed in an amused, sick smile. Quickly, she shifted back to Cal Davies. "I'm not adverse to drooping eyes, ears . . ."

"Lower, Ms. Callahan. I can just feel your unexpressed tension."

"Okay! Mouths too!" she flared with exasperation.

"Mouths . . . sensually drooping mouths where moist, delicious tongues hang out. I do see your point, Ms. Callahan. Makes me want to see a drooping mouth myself," he laughed. "So I bet you *looove* the feel of a drooping mouth. Am I right?"

Now she the lump sat directly in the back of her throat. He was ruining her!

"I can see by your face that you do. So . . . where specifically do like these drooping mouths to hang out, if I may be so bold--which I am . . ."

****

"I'm afraid the orchids are out and Curt's bitching is in," Geoff said matter-of-fact as the limousine cruised back to Upper Manhattan.

Unable to stop the sobs that had started after she disposed of her chicken sandwich in the radio station restroom, Cassie again hung by the car door. It had been awful! Her fragile career was in jeopardy, she just knew. And Geoff had been making derogatory cracks since the limo merged into traffic. He said, "Forget the haircut." Curt would want to see her immediately'.

"I wanna go back to the Regent," she cried.

"No such luck, I'm afraid." Geoff nonchalantly brushed a speck of lint off his suit coat. "You *must* face the music like Curt expects of all his *bad* little girls."

"What do you mean?" She turned and directed her dark glasses on him.

"There's a price when you screw up, and *you* have *definitely* screwed up. So now he holds all the cards."

"What cards?" Sheer panic gripped her.

Geoff lingered a mocking look at her. "It's the name of the game."

"Game?" she stammered.

"You are such a naive fool," he snickered. "The Shark Takes a Big Bite . . . that's the name of the game. You'll see . . ."

****

Trembling in fear from toe to eyelid, Cassie sat in a chair in Curt Farchmin's office, waiting for the Publicity Head to arrive from a meeting. Perched against a wall, Geoff Haines stared at her with gleeful malice. She could hardly bear the inferences of his look.

Jack . . . He was all she could think about.

He would crush both of them between his big fists if he knew about her predicament. Although that thought gave her little comfort now, she thought with utter resignation.

Jack could never know about any of it. She had to keep her career separate--the ugly and dark separated from the beautiful and bright--or else she would lose her mind. There could be no intermingling. She needed some lovely fantasy world in which to dwell, *somewhere* where she could be 'Cassie Callahan'.

The office door flew open, and looking like a mad hornet, Curt Farchmin stormed into the office. He immediately shifted to Geoff Haines. "Leave us,

Geoffrey!" he commanded.

With a highly amused look, Geoff pulled himself from the wall.

"Sure Curt," he replied, focusing his look on Cassie. "I've got some pressing work to do anyhow." Then he strolled out of the office.

Curt moved right up to Cassie and hung a glare over her. "You stupid woman! Why couldn't you have chosen moose shit? What the hell could he have done with that?"

She stiffened up her body and held on tightly.

"You've destroyed all my efforts! Do you realize that? He made you look like a frustrated, panting female. *And that* makes me and this whole company appear to be pack of liars! Millions of people for Christ's sakes!"

She could feel his rage while he half-circled around her chair.

"All that time that I spent on promoting you, down the drain because you couldn't control that simpleton mouth of yours! So where the hell do I go from here? Huh? Maybe I'll just wash my hands of you and let you float into nothingness!"

"No Curt," she begged. "I'll do anything. I promise to make it up to you, even another interview with Cal Davies to rectify myself."

And he kept circling while she felt the bore of his eyes on her head.

"Maybe," he replied vaguely. "Maybe I can make something out of 'Harry Two' after this debacle . . . and maybe not."

"But you'll try hard won't you . . ." And she stopped cold when feeling his fingers lightly stroking her hair.

"Perhaps . . ."

Ever-so-slowly she felt her dress zipper being pulled down. She froze, too immobile to stop it. His hands twined to her chest to pull down her bra. Next she felt his slimy, moist hands squeezing her breasts.

Let me die . . . just let me die . . .

****

Filth . . .

Choking on her sobs, Cassie raced to the bathroom in her room at the Regent and quickly peeled off her clothes. She thrust herself under a steamy shower then scrubbed her body raw while her tears co-mingled with the hot stream and her mind screamed out for the man she loved.

But would he even want her now that she'd been so horribly defiled?

A voice pounded inside her head. Jack could never know. *You need Jack Torelli.*

God help me!

She could still feel Curt Farchmin's snaky hands crawling over her body and his lips slobbering like a pig. She crossed her legs to try to squelch the pain of his cruel assault. Was it her punishment? She cowered in a corner of the shower, holding herself so tightly, her arms ached.

Was this the fantasy world I dreamed about in my attic, day in and day out?

It was supposed to beautiful, fulfilling, *so* perfect, *so* freeing. She could be *Cassie* in its purest sense without interruption, doing what loved to do--create fictional world, after fictional world and never have to come up for air. Never even having to live in reality if she chose not to.

An idyllic world . . .

And I fought like hell for it.

But now she wanted to burn it to ashes, crush it between her fingers, toss

TNT onto it.
It wasn't even close to idyllic
She could never be *Cassie* in it.
And sobs racked her body.
Stupidly, she had tossed her precious 'Harry' smack in the middle of that false idyllic world, and no way could she desert him. They would both swim in filth until, perhaps, both of them drowned.

"No!" Her scream pierced through the air.

She had to play the game for 'Harry's' sake, she agitated with overwhelming fear. 'Harry' needed to be preserved at any cost! *It's self-preservation.*

'Harry' had to be her contribution to the world or else her life was a sham. He defined the entire existence of Cassie Callahan. When people read 'Harry', they would see *Cassie*. It may be the only defining factor she had left, she thought, jittering her eyes around the stall.

I'm losing the rest of me, slowly but surely.

And as for *Season of Sorrow* . . .

Cassie stuck her face under the steamy spray and let the water trickle down her body.

She would write anything, any disjointed thought that came to mind, just to fill John's precious chapters. After all, 'Harry' *would* be her final hurrah, and *Season of Sorrow* . . .

The end to my pseudo-idyllic world.

She had fucked Curt Farchmin for 'Harry', but only for 'Harry'. She would walk on hot coals, on glass splinters, and destroy her body bit-by-bit for 'Harry'. But no one else.

Then after . . . she would shrivel up.

No more passion.

Fini.

Stoically, she stepped out of the shower and toweled herself as briskly as she had scrubbed, trying to remove the last trace of the bastard from her body. Suddenly she stopped, gazed forward and her hands gently touched her breasts, then outlined her flat belly, and finally traced around the light brown triangular fluff.

I need him!

She needed *his* touch, not her own.

Now.

Twirling a bath sheet around her, Cassie took quick steps to the phone on the night stand. She began to punch, but after a quick check to her watch she threw down the receiver. Damn! It was only a little after three p.m. in Los Angeles and that meant that Jack would still be at the studio. Should I try? She wondered. Maybe she could disguise her voice somehow. After thinking about this for a moment or two longer, she snatched up the receiver and quickly punched in the general number for Python Studios.

"Python Studios . . . where may I connect you?" a rushed sounding voice answered.

Her hand muffled the receiver. "I'm trying to get a hold of Jack Torelli, the actor."

"I'm sorry M'am, but we cannot forward calls to any of the actors."

"It's an emergency!" Cassie cried out.

"I'm sorry M'am, my instructions are not to bother the actors."

"It's life and death. He'll be mad if he doesn't get this call!" Her voice rose with hysteria.

"All right M'am. I'll get a name and see if Mr. Torelli will take the call. That's the best I can do. Who may I say is calling?"

Cassie gazed around as she racked her brain. "Tell him its Harry's mother. He'll know."

"It may take a while M'am. Please hold . . ."

Cassie jittered on the bed while listening to the soft piano music on the other end of the line. *Please answer, Jack, please.* Feeling ice cold, she wrapped the towel more tightly around her. Her mind couldn't seem to settle. Curt Farchmin's glacial face as he hung over her seemed to be a permanently fixed. *Make it go away.* But the vision of the Publicity Head pounding into her like an animal, quickly followed, and fresh tears ran down her face.

Then she heard a loud click. "This better not be some crank . . ." a tight voice warned.

Her heart gave an immediate thud. "Jack," she trembled out.

"Cassie," his whispered, and she heard him shuffle the phone. "What's the matter, honey? You sound like hell."

"I need you, Jack, here in New York. Now." Sobs racked her body.

"What did they do to you?" he demanded in a hushed voice. "Was it that orchid guy? Was it? I swear if it was . . ."

"No, Jack," she tearfully cut in. "He's . . . been behaving. Really. It's me. I miss you so much, darling, I can't function. I'm just away from you too long and I feel as tense as a board."

There came a long pause. "Can't you come back to L.A.? I. . .don't like New York, Cass."

"I thought you were born here. You told me . . ."

"I was, honey. But . . . I haven't gone back in years, for a reason, and . . . I'd like that reason to hold. So just come home, Cass. I'll pick you up at the airport. Anything but New York."

The firmness of his words made her hysteria escalate. "I can't come home, Jack. They'll never let me. Why won't you come? I. . .thought you loved me."

"Honey, I do," he whispered in a tortured voice. "I do so much. But . . . I just can't. My psyche can't take it. I'm not mentally prepared to just fly to New York."

"Why?" she screeched into the phone, unable to believe his stubbornness when he implied that he would be there for her. Had he been lying like all the others?

Then there was another long pause, and it enraged her.

He isn't going to be there for me. I can tell.

"Forget it, Jack! I'll make do!" She slammed down the phone. Then her rage peaking, she called the front desk of the hotel.

"This is Ms. Callahan in room 808. I want no calls sent to my room . . ."

And then she let all her fears, revulsion, and anger explode in a storm of wild sobbing.

Chapter 22—Jack

"What do you mean you can't put any calls through?" Phone to ear, a panic-ridden Jack yelled at the desk clerk, at the Regent Hotel in Manhattan.

"I'm sorry, sir. Ms. Callahan said no calls, so I cannot ring her room."

"Damn!" Jack flung down the receiver and a pained look rapidly fell onto his face.

Feigning illness, he had left the Python Studio sound stage early and drove ninety miles an hour home, so he could talk to Cassie in private and try to make her understand why he could never set foot in New York. But now he felt terrified. She had sounded so final. Would she forgive his cowardice or . . .

Jesus. He couldn't make it without her.

Now he plopped down on the living room couch, shivering in the fairly warm room, trying to determine his next move. Him here—her there. He felt so damn helpless. And what if something horrible had happened to her? She had sounded so agitated and out of control.

How can you deny that Torelli, no matter what?

But could he do it?

He admitted to himself that he did feel cleaner, much more together, perhaps even a little more worthier. Yet, he was a far-cry from that innocent Italian boy who romped on Mulberry Street, and he had always vowed to himself that he wouldn't return to his origins until he wasn't such a far-cry.

Which he had assumed would be never.

So he had accepted the fact that he would never return to New York.

But was that vow possible now?

She needed him.

Did his intense discomfort justify such disregard?

Envision, he told himself, envision yourself in the middle of Manhattan, looking left and right, back and forward, at all the once familiar buildings and landmarks that had been part of your young adulthood when you had stars in your eyes, a burning passion to make it on that stage and stay there. It was a time of wonder, loving acting for acting's sake without any outside forces blurring those bright stars. You jumped on the stage, performed your craft, and got better and better with each attempt. You could see a future, as bright as your eyes. There were no hostile reporters, vindictive producers, pressure to conform, pressure to perform . . . it all came naturally without a care except to be as spectacular as your will would allow.

Innocence . . .

But could that ever last?

If he had stayed in New York instead of coming to Hollywood, would that innocence, torturing him with envy and longing for the past several years, even have survived?

When his career had started going downhill, he had always blamed Hollywood.

If only I would have stayed in New York . . .

But New York had all the same vices if one wanted to find them. If he had stayed, starred in Broadway play after play like he had always visualized with his yearning, would he have eventually succumbed anyway? Would there have been another Gloria or Sheeny to thoroughly screw up his life? Drugs and excessive booze? Different women every night so ultimately his sex life was wasted? Now he wondered, for the first time since he crossed the gates of Hollywood, he truly wondered . . .

Why had he succumbed in the first place? He asked of himself. Why did he get so easily sucked up in the Hollywood scene, when supposedly, he had merely come to Hollywood to further his career, practice the craft he loved, and nothing else?

Because it was there?

It was so damn easy?

Easy . . . the word pounded his mind like a tom-tom.

Yeah, envision your past life . . .

He wanted to act, but took the easy way out and went to Fordham University where he took the easy way out and deliberately flunked, then took the easy way out and didn't admit this to his family, then took the easy way out and stayed away for over a year, and then, it wasn't even him who made amends. His father made it easy, so he never had to face anything.

And then envision Hollywood . . . He came to act and got suckered into the scene from day one, ripe for the picking, an easy mark. It was just too much effort to say, no, to do what was right for him based on his solid upbringing. He should have seen the ultimate devastation that such a life would bring to him. But once started, it was too tough to stop--so naturally he didn't.

The swirl down the gutter was inevitable, totally predictable.

That life could have never worked for him.

For Jack . . . *Torelli.*

He constantly bemoaned the fact that he came from a family of real, decent men, and he wasn't one of them. *Poor me* . . . Hollywood had snatched it away. Hollywood had fed him drugs, the booze, provided free and easy sex on demand, made him marry women that were far from respectable, destroyed his promising career, then made him turn to a repulsive alter-career that nearly ruined his life.

It's bullshit!

It's easy to blame, Torelli.

Jacko, the bambino, still isn't taking an ounce of responsibility.

It was you, Torelli!

You dammit!

Not New York, Hollywood, Michael Isle, Gloria, Sheeny, Rud Hanna, Harv Wellson, an unforgiving family, or the multitudes of others that he blamed, and blamed, for his failed life.

It was you and your god damn easy way from day one.

Feeling the slow trickle of tears, Jack flung his face into his hands. And just imagine now, he thought, imagine your life now when suddenly a less than 'easy life' had been thrust on him. To make a comeback had been damn hard, yet rewarding as hell to see his renewed acting talent shine on the daily rushes. Then most importantly and most difficult . . . *Cassie.* He had wanted her so badly, and against all odds, he had gotten her, traumatized as she was. It had been very tough—he had suffered much and was still doing so—yet he hung in there, faced every hardship, because he loved her. He would face anything, including suffering like hell, to make his very precious relationship work.

Cognizant or not, he hadn't taken the easy way out lately, and despite that, he was happier than he had ever been.

He wanted to be happy, he silently emphasized. He had needed to be happy for so long, and he had craved it for so long. Yet, he would have never had it with the 'easy way', he finally admitted to himself. He could have whined until hell froze, but until he was a man, in the true sense of the word, which wasn't prowess or raising it on demand, rather his ability to give love, he would never had even a bit of happiness.

Was it tough?

Damn straight!

But he, Jack Torelli, *had* given love to a woman, nonetheless. And now, he finally felt like a man for the effort. He *was* 'Jacko the man' in his heart and in his soul and regardless what anyone else thought.

He knew that he was.

Lifting his face from his hands, he sunk back into the couch. Jack Torelli had fucked-up his own life. Alone, he admitted without a shred of doubt. And he paused to digest this indisputable truth while he cursed his blind stupidity.

It wasn't New York--it never had been. It was his own cowardice to face up to what he had done, *as usual*. It had been easy to blame the loss of innocence as the reason—sorry folks, that's Hollywood for you—instead of examining the why of the loss, an activity that would have been damn tough to stomach--or to try to rectify. And if the truth be known, it hadn't even been him who started that process. Mattie Claret had been the catalyst to get him to act. Without ever having known her, now he wondered . . .

Would he even have still even been alive, or taken the easy way out one final time?

He would never know.

It was hard to tell with cowards—would they find a few guts? Or wouldn't they?

With a true man, there should be no question.

Jack bounded up from the couch and made a lunge for the phone. His fingers raced over the number panel and then he waited, feeling the jump of his nerves.

"Regent Hotel . . ."

"Room 808, please." He tightly crossed one finger over the other.

"I'm sorry, sir. That room is taking no calls."

"Okay! But could you at least get a note up to her?"

There was a short pause. "I could send someone to her room, I suppose."

Jack felt the joyful pound of his heart. "Tell her Jack's coming. As soon as he can manage, he's on the first jet . . ."

****

"What do you mean you need a few days off?"

Jack nervously eyed Michael Isle while he sat in the producer's office first thing the next morning. *Should I tell him the truth, knowing his probable reaction?*

"I need to finish these interior shots so we can head for Utah and then a couple days in Minneapolis to get those outdoors done. And then the outdoors here . . . there's no god damn time for production delays, Torelli!"

"It's . . . my father," he blurted out. "He's ill, very ill, and I have to go home." He placed a sad look on his face. "Can't you film around me for two lousy days?"

"New York?" Michael asked with much caution.

"Lower Manhattan . . . *way* lower Manhattan . . . by the Bowery," Jack replied, never taking his gaze off Michael. *Does he believe me?*

"I don't know . . ."

Jack hung over his knees, acting as miserable as he could. "But it's my father, Mike. How can you be so cruel to deny me maybe my last shot at seeing my own father?" He kept his eyes to the floor while feeling Michael Isle's close appraisal. *Keep acting like hell Torelli.*

"I never knew that you were even close to your father, Jack. I mean . . . I guess I assumed. They were a decent lot from what I remember, so . . ."

"But an Italian lot," Jack quickly jumped in. "They forgive as a way of life. I'm . . . their bambino, after all. I . . .could commit mass murder and never be black in their eyes." He tried to hide the mournful choke of his lie.

Thrusting back in his chair, one leg over a knee, Michael thought about this. Finally, he let out a loud exasperating noise. "All right, Torelli. I suppose we can shoot around you for a couple days, maybe get a few of those outdoor shots completed around the lot. But! I want you back here on Monday morning, and be prepared to put in a long day."

"You got it!" Jack leapt out of his chair and stuck his hand across the desk. "Thanks a helluva lot, Mike."

Michael looked at the hand like it was some shocking specimen, but eventually he took it and shook firmly. "Don't mention it, Torelli."

"Well . . ." Jack abruptly let go of the hand and turned. "Gotta catch my plane. I got the last first-class seat, so . . ." And he began walking away, trying to conceal his hand-wiping motions on his designer jeans . . .

****

A little after six p.m., Eastern Standard Time, Jack stood outside the American Airline terminal at La Guardia Airport in Queens, studying the long line of yellow New York City cabs. He needed a plan. *How do I sneak into that Regent undetected?*

He had started with attire, carefully put together in a men's room stall at the airport— expensive jeans with holes in the knees, designedly so, a T-shirt he had purchased in Chicago on the shot stopover that indicated he could be from the 'Windy City', white *Nike* Airs that looked fairly new, and a jet black Chicago White Sox cap, also purchased in an O'Hare gift shop. He decided he looked more "rock star" than "movie star," so told himself to act, "rock star," even though he hadn't played an instrument in his life, and didn't know a bass guitar from a bass drum.

Tossing on his sunglasses and hoisting his large shoulder bag, he began to walk towards the taxicabs. He would figure out the rest of his plan on the hour drive to the Regent, he decided. No more time could be wasted on indecision. His Cassie needed him and his body . . . it was roaring with anticipation.

Leisurely, he walked down the line, peeking into each cab. *Think foreign.* No barely speakay English, he told himself while he peered. Finally he saw a little dark man behind the wheel who looked like he came directly off the boat and into the driver's seat. Quickly, he opened the back door and slid through to the man's startlement.

"Where you headed, Buddy?" the man asked in a purely New York accent.

Shit! Jack melted into the back seat. *So you fucked up already?* Big deal?

279

Stay cool! He gave a nonchalant toss of his head. "The Regent, man, and make it snappy, huh? I gotta gig in three hours."

"Musician, right?" the driver asked while pulling away from the curb.

"King of the Chicago hard rock circuit," Jack boasted.

"King huh? Well why a cab? Don't they usually send limos for kings?"

"Anonymity, man," Jack replied in secretive tones. "Saves my clothes from all those female hands. I always sneak into Manhattan. Limos are too obvious."

"I see your point," the driver said. "But don't the kings usually have bodyguards to prevent that from happening?"

"Bodyguards? I'm no wuss, man. I take care of my own problems. I'm my own heavy-hand," Jack sneered.

"Independent type, huh?"

"Totally." Jack gave a genuine swagger to his head. "And proud of it . . ."

****

Now what?

Jack stood in front of the Regent silently cursing the chatty cab driver. The guy had barely let up the entire trip, and as a result, he possessed no concrete plan. *Think!* He commanded himself, drifting his eyes to the eighth floor. How to get up there . . . ?

He walked forward, wondering if he could just slip onto an elevator. How tough could it be with people walking back and forth? He reasoned. Certainly, all the eagle-eyes couldn't be fastened on everyone at one time. But he had to be very careful. If Michael Isle ever found out, he'd be dead meat and then some, he figured. And then the media . . .

No, he firmly told himself, neither he or Cassie could afford to take any chances.

Upon entering the expansive, I'm-exclusive-as-hell, lobby, he boosted the bag onto his shoulder, straightened his stance, then strolled to the elevators like he lived there.

"Hold it, sir!"

Jack froze with the sound of the low insistent voice. Carefully, he lifted his sunglasses and saw a uniformed man with thick glasses heading towards him. He pulled the brim of the cap deeper over her brow. *Loosen up, dammit. You look guilty as hell.*

"Where are you going, sir?"

"On the elevator." He made a face that said, *What the hell do you care?*

"Are you a guest?" The man pulled out what appeared to be a roster.

"Ut-huh. I'm delivering something to a friend." Jack patted his bag.

"Who?" the man demanded, still eyeing his roster.

"Ms. Cassie Callahan. She's expecting me for an expresso and a little literary talk. I came from Chicago to promote my new book . . . ah . . . *Pervert in a Publishing House.*"

"So what are you delivering, if I may ask?" the man raised his eyes over his glasses.

"My new book of course, an autographed copy with a special message for my dear literary friend." Jack closely watched the man through his sunglasses. "Call her if you don't believe me. Tell her that Harry is downstairs. She's waiting for her copy, man. Told me she was nearly jumping out of her pants in anticipation of me walking through her door . . . with my book, of course . . . and some literary talk, of course . . . and a great thirst for expresso, *of course.*"

"Come with me," the man directed. Then he quickly moved towards a wall phone.

Jack watched the man's calculating gaze drift up and down his person while he waited for the phone to ring. It was plainly evident that the man didn't like what he saw. *Perhaps I should have been a fag instead.*

Suddenly, the man thrust the phone from his ear and Jack plainly heard Cassie's squeal come out through the phone line. He smiled gleefully.

"Yes Ms. Callahan. Certainly, Ms. Callahan. I'll send him up by rocket." The man hung up the phone, then motioned Jack to follow him. "That must be some book . . ."

Minutes later, the door to room 808 was flung open and Cassie flew into his arms, nearly knocking him over. "Oh Jack . . ." She kissed his face and lips like a wild woman.

He held onto her lips with his own while moving through the room entrance, then he lifted a sneaker to shut the door. After loosening the bag from his arm, he madly attacked her body with his hands, trying, in his great heated anticipation, not to rip her clothes while her hands did likewise to his clothes.

In very short order, they flung naked onto the bed, acting like they hadn't seen each other for a year. Touching . . . they couldn't get enough of it. And when his lips touched her groin and hers his, he thought he was floating on a glorious cloud in the middle of heaven. This is all that mattered, he thought through the senselessness of his overwhelming emotions.

Screw the rest.

He was her man even in Timbuktu.

"I love you, Cassie," he whispered down into her green eyes, simmering with desire for him. "I'm sorry, I ever lost sight of that for even a split-second. Never again, honey, I swear . . ."

****

"Jack!" Cassie giggled while playfully smacking him. "Enough already."

It had been thirty-four hours since his arrival, and they had spent close to thirty-two of those hours in bed, in the bathroom, on the floor, anywhere, where he could show her how desperately he loved her.

And still, it hadn't been enough.

"I'm just making up for lost time, Cass," he murmured into her ear, then sensually moved his tongue around it while feeling the firm hardness in his groin. His cock had been working overtime, he thought with much amusement and a great deal of pleasure.

He felt like a twenty-year-old again! She made him feel so damn free! He was so much in love he felt like he would explode with the feeling!

"But today's Saturday, Jack."

"So?" His lips coursed behind her ear and down the nape of her neck.

"It's my day to be Cassie Callahan. *Please, Jack . . . ?*"

He abruptly lifted his lips. "We can't, Cass. What if someone sees us?" He pressed his lips into her chest. "Anyway, who the hell wants to be around people?" He kept pressing. "Just you is the only people I wanna see in New York."

"But I love to romp around Manhattan, and I've never done it with you. I bet it would be wonderful," she pestered.

"This is more wonderful." He devoured one of her breasts with his mouth.

"Jack . . ." She gently pushed his head off her chest.

He let out a loud, frustrated groan.

"Let's compromise . . . four hours maximum. You certainly can contain yourself for four little hours, can't you?"

He wanted to yell, No! But her face looked so eager and he loved her so damn much, he couldn't refuse her. "Okay." He lifted up on his elbows. "But we gotta disguise ourselves, and I mean *really* disguise ourselves. Nothing to indicate who we really are. And I'm holding you to four hours, so you better have an idea where you wanna go," he said decisively.

"I already know," Cassie enthused. "I'd love to go to Washington Square with you. Quiet, collegiate, artsy . . . we'll meld right in."

"Sounds safe enough," Jack agreed, then he dove under the covers and emerged on top of Cassie to her squealing delight. "But first, honey . . . I got some baggage I just have to unload . . ."

****

Entwined in each other's arms Jack and Cassie walked along the cracked pavement of Washington Square Park, well-worn from much pedestrian use. A melange of atmosphere permeated the park, conservatives and Bohemian-types, young and old, enough leashed dogs padding their paws on the dog run to fill a few large pounds, and a lone trumpeter belting out jazz stood in the middle of it.

After so much quietude for the past couple days, they found the combined noise nerve-racking and decided to find a solitary place to sit down and share some togetherness in the beautiful, though humid, May day. They finally located a spot near New York University under a leafy oak tree. Jack stretched out, back against the tree, and he pulled Cassie close to him. He hated the intrusion of New York and only desired to return, separately, to the Regent where they could shut out the world. But he *had* promised her four hours, he grudgingly reminded himself.

"So how's the miniseries going? You've kept me so busy. I haven't had time to even ask," Cassie questioned, snuggling into his arms.

"The script is great. You did good, kid," he replied with a low laugh.

"I didn't do much, except say that'll work, that won't work, 'Harry' would do that, say that, react like that, and yes, Minnesota really does have crappy weather twelve months out of the year. *Really.*"

"Well it pulls off as realistic, so . . ." He nuzzled the top of her blonde head with his lips. "I still say you did good, kid. I'm proud of you. How's that?"

She flashed a smile that lit up her whole face. "You really are, Jack? I mean . . . you really think I have talent for such a thing?"

"Writing?" He kissed the tip of her nose. "How can you even ask such an obvious question? You're a brilliant writer, Cass. I read 'Harry' four times didn't I? And I can't wait to get my hands on book two."

"I'll give you one, Jack, your own personal copy, signed with much love from Cassie Callahan. And I may even toss a big red kiss on it," she excitedly told him.

He moved his mouth down to her lips. "How about the real thing now? No red, just beautiful naturally pink, moist lips that taste like honey." He pressed his lips into hers. When Jack released her mouth, he slid his hands onto her cheeks. "You're the most important thing in the world to me, Cass. Nothing else even comes close."

"You're important to me too, Jack. I feel so emancipated with you," she replied softly, then buried her head in the crook of his arm.

She looks so content, he thought, looking down at her. Had that hysteria he heard on the phone the other night really happened? It was odd. She never even mentioned *why*, though he knew that something was horribly wrong. Should I probe? He wondered. He finally decided that perhaps a little nudge wouldn't upset the apple cart. "How's *Season of Sorrow* coming along?"

Cassie shifted uneasily. "It's coming, but I have a feeling it will go faster from now on."

"That's great, Cass. You got it together with that tough character, I take it."

Her lips drew into a stiff smile. "Let's just say that Sandy can be as wooden as she wants and I won't fight it."

"Wooden? *Your protagonist?*" Jack was blankly incredulous. "That doesn't sound like you, Cass. Take 'Harry' . . . he was loaded with real emotion."

She spoke abruptly. "I can't make Sandy anything but wooden. Point closed."

He intently studied the stubborn face, and sensed that something strange was going on, like he'd sensed many of times when they talked about her third book. *Season of Sorrow* was such a total antipathy from *The Life and Times of Harry Hannigan*, this led him to many curious questions. Something wasn't right. But what could he do? She always clammed up when he delved into the subject.

"Anyway, John's putting the pressure on me so I have to go purely on instincts and just do it, get it over with, and then . . ." She paused with an unreadable expression. "I'll just float on a cloud in the world of no pretense. I'll be *Cassie* forever."

Not sure he was interpreting her right, he tread cautiously. "You mean you'll give up the image bullshit that New York is feeding you?"

She smiled up at him. "Yeah, Jack. That's exactly what I'm saying."

Thrilled at this news, he returned a broad smile. "I'm glad, Cass. You can write in peace and at the whim of your creative streaks like it should be."

"Yeah . . ." She buried her face deeper into his arm crook. "Like it should be."

"That calls for a celebration, Cass. Since we're out anyway, we might as well split a little wine and grab a sandwich. Man can't live on love alone, no matter how much he wants to . . ."

****

"Eclectically Continental. Not a hot dog or chicken salad in sight." Cassie flipped down the menu at the open-air restaurant on Bleeker Street.

"Hmmm . . ." Jack had his sunglasses firmly pointed in a southeast direction. *I wonder what they're doing right at this moment?* Maybe the whole family's over for some celebration. How many now? Knowing his brothers, the whole upper level was probably exploding with Torelli's. And his sisters . . . baby factories, every one. *Bet the garden's in full bloom.* He could just see those little kids and those blueberries. His mom must be really spewing out the Italiano . . .

"Jack!"

He saw a hand waving in front of his face, and the sight jarred him. He turned and stared. Her large pair of shades seemed to cover her whole face and not a strand of blonde hair was evident from beneath her *Coors* cap.

"Sorry. I was just daydreaming. Did you say something?"

"I'll have the penna pasta with marinara sauce and some Asti Spumante. How about you?"

He studied the menu, but found his mind still drifting to Mott Street, uncomfortably close to where they sat. "I'll have the same. A carafe of wine okay?"

"Sure . . ." She leaned forward and fastened her dark glasses on him. "Are you okay, Jack? Even with those sunglasses, you look funny."

"Yeah, honey." He the slapped his menu down on the table, wondering if perhaps he should say something to her. She loved him, and It felt funny to be so evasive with someone that he loved. "You know . . . I was born just a few miles away from here in a place called Little Italy. You ever hear of that place, Cass?" Jack began haltingly.

"Really?" She moved closer to him until nearly on his lap. "It's East of Soho. I've been there. Best Italian food in Manhattan. Tastes as close to my Nona's cooking as one can ever get outside her kitchen."

"You're right. The food's great," he stammered, wishing he hadn't opened up his mouth. She looked more than interested. "It was just on my mind so . . . I'll get the waiter over here."

"Do you want to go and see your family? Is that what you're trying to tell me, darling?" Cassie pressed closer to him. "I'm game . . . unless . . . you would rather go alone. I'm okay with that, I guess." She lowered her sunglasses to the table.

"No Cassie." Jack picked up her hand and touched it to his lips. "I don't wanna go. And if I did, I'd certainly take you. You're the woman I love, honey. Please . . . let's just drop it, all right?"

But to his chagrin, she wouldn't drop it. "Do you have a big family, Jack? A lot of brothers and sisters and cousins, uncles . . ."

"Nine brothers and sisters. I'm the youngest," he quickly answered, then drifted his eyes around, hoping she would get the message that he wanted off of the subject.

She let out a low whistle. "Nine? You must have a Christmas list a mile long."

"Yeah, Cassie, at least," he muttered. "Where the hell's that waiter . . ."

"I love big families. They're so cozy. Was your family cozy, Jack?"

"Cozy as hell . . ." He finally succumbed to the misery, knowing he had stupidly sparked an unquenchable curiosity. "Very close family, lots of love."

"You're so lucky, Jack. I. . .always wanted to live in a big family. Lots of brothers and sisters, sharing things, laughing, there for each other, even sibling fights. Oh . . ." She let out a deep sigh. "A family that size could have shielded so much."

Shielded? Now his curiosity was sparked as well. "So . . . you were an only child?"

Cassie suddenly pulled back and turned her face. "I have a sister eight years older than me, so with the age difference, we weren't exactly close. I had some hope for her at one time in her life, but not any more."

Sensing another puzzle piece was about to slip, Jack now moved closer to her. "Hope? What exactly does that mean?"

She spun around with a bright smile on her face. "It's just that Meg was more spontaneous as a youth, a bit more interesting. Now she's rather *blah*, stiff as an old granny. I don't like her."

Jack gave a puzzling shake of his head. "What changed her?"

"An witch tossed her into a cauldron of snobs and Voila'," she quipped with great delight.

That voice, a dead giveaway, he thought with frustration. Why the god damn talking in circles, Cassie? "In other words, she's not your kind of person, right?"

"Heavens no! I can't stand the clone."

"Clone?" he asked closely.

"Did I say 'clone'?" She laughed lightly. "I meant 'clown'. Meg belongs in the center ring of a three-ring-circus and her stuff of a husband Todd, belongs right beside her. He gives me the absolute creeps."

Jack picked up his water glass and guzzled while watching her. *Clown, my ass. You said 'clone' and meant it.* Clone of whom? He wondered while the iced liquid drizzled down his throat. He tossed the glass down and again moved closer. "And Kristi . . . you didn't tell me how the kid's doing? You musta heard from her lately."

In a split-second, he saw a ripple of pain shoot across her face. "She's fine, Jack. Loves school, her classes, her teachers, the other girls, and . . . she misses of me, of course."

Pulling back, he slumped in his chair, not believing her for a moment. He wished that she would trust him enough to spill her guts.

Who are you Cassie Callahan?

"Although she forgets to write like she should. You know kids, Jack . . ."

"No," he replied truthfully. "I can't say that I do, never having much contact with them. I never really wanted kids. I'd probably be a lousy father. Anyway, I'm forty . . . too late to change my views on that subject."

"Kids are tough all right," she agreed, and left it at that.

Sensing her sadness, Jack quickly motioned for the waiter. All the talk had left a bitter taste in his mouth and now he just wanted to end their outing. Anyhow, her four hours were nearly over . . .

****

"Oh! I just love the Washington Arch, Jack." Cassie gazed up at the majestic wooden structure at the entrance to Washington Square Park.

"You know . . ." he laughed while looking up as well. "When I was a kid, me and my friends used to walk through, pretending we were an army. We always fought about who was gonna be the general. I got quite a few black eyes under that arch."

Cassie laughed gleefully. "Oh Jack, tell me more—that was a wonderful story!"

Feeling discomfiture set in, he gazed down at her, wondering why he had told the story in the first place. It had just slipped out, though he had no intention to let it slip out. But Cassie seemed to bring out something out in him that he thought was long suppressed. "No more stories, honey. Your four hours are almost up."

"I concede, Jack. A deal's a deal." She grabbed his arm. "We'll just walk through the arch then hail separate cabs."

When they were just below the Washington Arch, Cassie came to a grinding halt and suddenly hugged him close. "Now kiss me, right under the arch, and make it deadly so I have something to hold me while I ride in that cab alone."

Laughing, he lowered his face and planted his lips over hers. Suddenly, he felt a bright flash of light. *What the hell?* He quickly released her to look around. A smiling man, dangling a camera in his hand, caught Jack's eye. His fear shot up like fireworks. "Who are you?"

"I'm from the New York Times, Mr. Torelli, and . . . Ms. Callahan." The man gave a loud hoot. "Author and 'Harry'." He hooted again. "Little House on the Prairie meets *Jungle Love*. I didn't believe it. But I saw it, sure as the sun rises, I saw it with my own camera lens."

Jack rapidly moved towards the man, having every intension of ripping his camera lens into a million pieces. "How in the hell did you find out? How?" he yelled at the top of his lungs. "No way could you have discovered our true identities. I the hell don't even recognize us!"

The reporter backed away. "Calm down, Torelli. We got an anonymous tip, low male voice, telling us exactly where you were and how you were dressed. I thought it was a crazy prank. But followed up on it for the hell of it. In fact . . ." He backed up quicker. "I've followed up on it for the last two hours, so my camera's full."

"Low male voice?" Cassie hurried up to Jack's side and she slumped in terror. "What exactly did he say?" she trembled out.

"Do I dare repeat it?" The man cautiously looked at Jack who looked ready to pounce.

"Please tell me," Cassie quavered.

"He said . . . Cassie Callahan's been fuckin' Jack Torelli at the Regent for the past two days . . ."

****

"Who the hell is he, Cass? Now, I swear I'll break his neck with my bare hands!" Jack roared when they were back in their hotel room. With the gig being up, they had arrived in the same taxi, and made no secret about riding up on the same elevator.

Near hysterics, Cassie sobbed face-down on the bed and didn't answer.

"We're in deep-shit trouble, honey. And I'm in even worse trouble," Jack said in a panic. "Mike Isle will kill me. He already knows about us, Cass. I . . . didn't tell you."

"My image . . ." she sobbed over and over, beating the bed with her fists. "How could that sick animal do this? How could he?"

Jack charged up to the bed. "I wanna a name, Cass. Now!"

"I can't, Jack," she wailed. "If he loses his job, there's no telling what he'll do. It's the only thing that's protecting me. Otherwise . . ." She flung her face back on the bed.

"That's ridiculous! I'll get him arrested, so he can't bother anyone!"

"He'll get out of jail. He's sly and oily. And then he'll come after me."

He sat on the bed's edge and pulled her close to him. "I'll make sure he doesn't get out of jail. I have all those cards and I'll be by your side when you file a complaint. You won't be alone, Cass, I promise you."

"He's insane, Jack," she squeaked in a terror-filled voice.

Suddenly alarmed, he pulled her out in front of him. "He did do something to you, didn't he?" He searched her wet face. "Is that why you were upset when you called me at the studio?"

"No!" She shrieked. 'I . . .was just stressed-out and I missed you so. The combination made me very emotional. That's all, Jack."

He stared into her eyes and wanted to shout 'Liar', but she looked totally unglued and he refused to add to that. So instead he grabbed her close to him and spoke in tender tones. "Let me hold you, Cass, then hold on tight. I'm afraid we're in for quite a ride . . ."

****

At ten p.m. the next evening, Jack arrived back at his Beverly Hills home. Quickly, he locked his door, tightly pressed his eyelids together, and hung his back on the wooden frame.

It had been an absolute nightmare . . .

Reporters greeted him in the Regent Hotel lobby the moment he stepped off the elevator, even though the hotel staff was trying their best to control the chaos. Several hotel security personnel had to escort him to his limousine, then the mob followed him to La Guardia Airport and airline staff had to help him onto the plane. He had been an emotional mess all the way back to Los Angeles, polishing off three scotch on the rocks to try to get a hold of his nerves, only to be greeted by even a larger mob at LAX that airport security had a hell of a time controlling. Finally came the last insult—a mob outside his home, and no security people in sight.

It had been a near battle to make it to his front door, and now, he could still hear them outside.

He slowly rubbed his head, trying to erase all the comments that wouldn't seem to erase.

"A total Hollywood mismatch," they had called it.

"How the hell did you ever seduce *her*, Jack?" was the most frequently asked question.

"A love-nest at the Regent? *The* Regent? Are you kidding, Jack?"

"A little *Jungle Love* in a million-dollar canoe, huh Jack?"

"Torelli's two day affair. Kinda long for you, isn't it, Jack?"

"Affair under the Arch . . . cute kiss, Jack."

Affair . . . Affair . . . Affair . . . He wanted to smash that word in two. He loved her for Christ's sakes. But he desperately feared that no one would believe this, and make his so very precious love something filthy.

He couldn't stand the thought.

She would be hurt . . . that was an even more unbearable. Cassie was so fragile already, he greatly feared the assault would put her over the edge. It wouldn't take much, he figured. So he would absorb the bulk of the dirt and protect her as much as he could, he decided then and there.

He hadn't wanted to leave her in New York. In fact, he had begged her to come home so they could weather the storm together. But she refused, saying that it was more important than ever that she stay in New York and try to smooth the edges no matter how unpleasant. "It was for 'Harry'," she said at one point.

"What the hell does that mean, Cass? Harry's a fictitious character and needs no safeguarding. It's you, a flesh and blood human being, that needs shelter," he argued.

"To shelter 'Harry' is to shelter myself, Jack . . ."

Now her words pealed through his head. She had believed them. The words spoken so decisively, though so ascetic at the same time despite her high emotional state, had been stunning, he recalled. Why? Why the need to protect a book character that has already been a proven success—millions of copies sold worldwide—making her a very wealthy woman? Harry Hannigan was the last person on earth, real or otherwise, that needed protection, he thought with intense curiosity. It made no sense

What for god's sakes is going through your mind, Cassie?

He feared it was something horrible. The woman he loved was in deep trouble, he could sense. But what? *How can I save her when she won't 'fess up?"*

Jack pulled himself from the door, dropped his shoulder bag, and made a beeline for the antique desk in a corner of the living room. Maybe if he wrote down all the clues she's given him . . .

Grabbing paper and pen, he jotted down every remembrance, even those insignificant. When done, he studied the information, twisting it back and forth in his head, then twisting it again, until his head was spinning.

"Damn!" He flung the paper on the floor. Puzzle pieces without an interlock! There had to be an interlock, he told himself. But what? *What?*

Finally, he decided it was too late to solve anything. He would have hell to pay tomorrow, so he might as well rest up for it . . .

Chapter 23—Cassie and Jack

Dwelling in Pacific Standard Time, was more than a nuisance early Monday morning, when the phones on the tenth floor of the Python Office Building, specifically Claire Gibson's phones, were ringing off the hook by five a.m. She had been at the studio since three, as had Michael Isle and members of the Python publicity staff, mapping out a strategy so disaster was averted with the highly important miniseries *The Life and Times of Harry Hannigan* only six weeks into production. Now just two remained, Michael and Claire, flopped in two chairs in Michael's office, sipping on coffee, and sifting through the ruins of an explosion.

"The affair's being blown way out of proportion, Mike, no matter how many times I say 'big deal', it's another Hollywood romance. No one is buying that."

"Damn him!" Mike replied with the two words he had said at least a thousand since yesterday when the whole debacle had detonated in New York.

"It's got all the juicy ingredients, Mike . . . innocent, much-respected woman lured and ravished by an ex-porn star--and no matter his accomplishments in the interim, *Jungle Love* burns brightly, believe me. Then add the Regent, one of the most exclusive hostels in New York, and one not quite so copacetic to such depravities, plus the triumphal arch which celebrates George Washington, the Father of Our Country, and I'd say that Jack Torelli muddied many more shrines than just Cassie Callahan, the creator of one of the most popular book characters to ever hit United States soil who, may I remind you, has fan clubs all over the country that espouse the concept 'never say 'uncle'—goddamn motivational seminars from what I hear," Claire concluded, exhaling out a big breath.

"And in essence, Cassie said 'uncle'," Michael said between the grit of his teeth.

"To her animalistic tendencies, the ones she should be able to morally control, yes."

"So the miniseries will be a sham and also the book, right?"

"Hell no, Mike. It makes both hotter than ever. Everybody will turn on their televisions to view the rapist, and curiosity about the book contents should skyrocket. But only once. You'll never repeat the phenomena with 'Harry Two' unless major reconstructive surgery is done."

Michael tried to rub away the thoroughly annoying headache which had plagued him for hours. "What a hell of a mess."

"What a hell of a mess in New York. I bet Starburst is having stroke after stroke."

"And I'll hear everyone from that pompous Limey," Michael groaned.

"But for now, they're hotter than hot. Everybody wants to get a glance at Jack and Cassie. Where do they hang out, Claire? Do you know their favorite foods, Claire? Is Cassie getting implants to please Torelli, Claire? I have a hunch that they're going to make Donald and Marla look like Hansel and Gretel."

Michael increased his brow stroking. "Believe me, Starburst won't see it that way. They spent a fortune on that image which I had the responsibility to maintain, and they planned for their initial investment to last and reap for years to come, as did I."

"Major reconstruction, Mike. It has to be played as a fleeting affair, one which Cassie was sucked into by a dashing movie star, not porn star. The handsome and exciting Jack Torelli who is so much so, he cracked the toughest of chastity belts. And boom, it ends. Cassie reclasps her belt, Starburst plays that to the hilt, and Torelli is seen around Hollywood with only the most beautiful and talented actresses to perpetuate his gorgeous Italian stud status which will entice the American public to the boob tube."

"Oh Claire . . ." Michael pounded his head with his fist. "There's a major complication . . . Torelli's in love with her."

"Rubbish!"

"No, Claire. He told me, and . . . I think I believed him."

Claire baited an utterly amused smile. "And did you have rose-colored spots in front of your eyes that day, Mike?" she retorted. "*That*, no one will believe. Not Torelli, proprietor of the sex-factory in Hollywood, owner of two marriages that lasted a total of fourteen months, and a man who flounced his body stark naked, at will, in front of any movie camera that was pointed at him . . . it won't fly for a moment."

Michael limply dropped his hand to his desk. "But what about recently, Claire? The last two years to be specific. Things . . . changed with the guy. He's been pretty quiet except for his two directorial attempts. I've heard this, Claire. He hasn't been the same Torelli."

"Doesn't matter," she quickly jumped in. "All those media bozos can see is his unsavory, flamboyant past. *That's* the defining factor of Jack Torelli. And if the media sees it that way, the public will see it that way, and what you think, makes no difference."

Opening an aspirin bottle, Michael popped two in his mouth and swallowed them dry. "And what if that willful woman is in love with him, huh? What do we do then? Won't her defining factor neutralize his a bit? I mean . . . the guy must have something for a woman like Cassie Callahan to fall in love with him. No way, could I imagine *her* plunging into a sordid lifestyle. It's not that cut and dried, Claire, believe me."

"You mean that Torelli's playing it straight?"

"Of course!" Michael flared, then winced deeply. "You know Cassie. She may be a little eccentric, but could you ever imagine her participating in such corruption? I'd say it was *she* who corrupted him, sucked him into *her* lifestyle. She . . . has a way of doing that, Claire . . . a highly persuasive woman."

Claire rapidly clicked her long nails on the chair arm. "If that's the case, I'm afraid that Starburst will have a major bird, with you being bombarded by most of the bird droppings."

"And I can kiss 'Harry Two' goodbye, as well as any other book that Cassie Callahan should write."

"I'm afraid so, Mike." Claire gave a sly lift of her eyebrows. "Therefore your only recourse is to snatch those stars out of Cassie's eyes with a major dose of reality." She curled her body like a cobra ready to attack. "Don't worry, darling. Claire will put her brain on spin cycle and once again save your beautiful ass."

****

Seeking Out Harry

On the northbound side of the street outside of the Regent Hotel in Manhattan, there was a traffic jam of sleek town cars and stretch limousines waiting for their wealthy wards to emerge from the hotel, well-known for being a watering-hole of power during the breakfast hours, drawing like a magnet, some of the richest and most influential minds in the country.

Shrouded in black despite the climbing heat, Cassie directed her sunglasses at the luxury vehicles and stared impassively. The sight was dizzying, almost intrusive. She hated the clog of oversized cars greeting her every morning. And today they were particularly bothersome, she thought, trying to gain hold of the hysteria that had barely abated since Saturday.

What will they do to me? Her mind cried out.

The clock registered five minutes to seven in the morning, and John LaLiberte was already on the phone, ordering her not even to turn on her computer. Her presence was demanded in his office at nine-thirty sharp, and she better be there if she knew what was good for her.

Not turn on her computer? She viewed the inference with ominous dread. They were going to drop their effort, she just knew it. She had blackened her image beyond repair--and after shedding blood for Curt Farchmin on Wednesday to save her hide. Now even that degradation had been for not.

No! Her mind shrieked as she quickly walked onto the sidewalk and took brisk paces.

Sandy fucked Curt. Sandy! The good little girl who would do anything to please.

Not Cassie!

Cassie fucks Jack, a free and lovely man. Don't forget that Cassie.

IT WASN'T YOU!

"Ms. Callahan!"

She spun around. Errol, the chauffeur from Starburst stood outside the company limo and waved at her. "I wanna walk the five blocks, Errol! Forget about me!" She rapidly shifted around and walked as fast as she could, dodging bodies while fastening her eyes to the ground, trying to control the preponderance of voices that had suddenly invaded her head.

Go away! I've kept you away for a long time. Just leave me alone!

"You will wear that pink ruffly taffetta with you black strap shoes, Cassandra!"

"No! I hate it. It's not Cassie. It's not!"

"Nonsense, Cassandra. I took time out from the office and bought it specifically for this important affair. And you will wear it, even it I have to put you in it!"

"What'll I do at the affair? Sit in a corner and twiddle my thumbs because I won't be Cassie in that thing!"

"Yes, Cassandra! You sit in a corner and keep that fresh mouth closed. No one wants to hear your ridiculous poems or your silly jokes that only make you laugh. You will sit like a little lady and smile!"

"No! I'll puke instead! I'll put my finger down my throat, just watch me, and then let's see what your friends say, Mother!"

"If you dare, Cassandra, I'll lock you in the attic without a speck of books or paper and pencils. Nothing but your naughtiness, Cassandra . . ."

Stop! She commanded her mind upon seeing a twelve-year girl, looking more like an overgrown seven, with pink taffeta in her hair and on her person, shuffling black patent leathers covering white ruffly anklets and sitting in a corner, forcing a big smile at everyone who passed.

That was Sandy! Sandy said 'uncle'. Not you, Cass.
NOT YOU!

Filled with angry rancor, Cassie briefly raised her sunglasses. The words **Starburst Publishing, Inc.** glistened in all their glory at a short distance. She lifted her wristwatch. *Ten oh nine*. Plenty of time, she soothed herself. And she collapsed onto the first set of steps she saw, sinking into the concrete like it was wet cement.

Get a hold of yourself. You can't let her loose. For Harry's sake you gotta play the game and hold on tight to Sandy . . . !

****

By the time that Jack Torelli entered Sound-stage C at Python Studios on Monday morning, he felt as limp as a mushy rag after fighting hoards of media outside his home, then their car pursuit of him while he drove west on the Santa Monica Boulevard, culminating in even more wild media outside Python Studios, held back by security personnel and a few Los Angeles police officers. And the worst, he thought, was that they all seemed to be yelling the same message.

"You sly, filthy fox Torelli, sticking your poker into a 'Prim Miss' and ruthlessly deflowering her."

Bullshit! His mind yelled out. How the hell could it have eluded the idiots that Cassie had been married for over a decade and had been deflowered many times before he got his hands on her! Like a virgin . . . that's what they were all implying! It was crazy! Why the hell didn't someone stop it, now? Why couldn't they be just left alone? Why the hell them?

Sunglasses focused forward, Jack walked into the sound-stage. The area was like a tomb, people everywhere, standing as stiff as post sentries, staring at him, and not uttering one word.

He could just read their minds: You horribly marred this production, Torelli . . . our big chance, our place to shine, our coveted roles . . . you blew that royally for us, by not being able to control your perverse pleasures. Why her Torelli? Why not your usual fare, then we would have still been politely cool?

If he thought it had been bad before . . . now he figured it would take a miracle to emerge out of this production without being completely flayed. And, he hadn't even faced Michael Isle yet. After that, he wondered if there would be anything left to flay.

He suddenly felt the old urge to cower in a corner or flee to parts unknown and hide out until it all blew over. *Easy way,* he firmly told himself, the way of a coward, not a man, and he desperately wanted to be a man even while swimming in this muck. Cassie, the woman he loved more than anything in the world, counted on him to do just that, and he vowed, here and now, not to desert that responsibility.

He would fuck up no more.

"Jack!"

The sound of a human voice made him jar. Jack shifted his sunglasses around until seeing Brett Jonah, Michael Isle's assistant director, motioning him. He purposefully picked up his pace, refusing to show even a hint of remorse for loving Cassie Callahan. Even if the rest made it less in their minds, he would never do it in his own, he told himself.

Seeking Out Harry

"What do you need, Brett?" He walked directly up to the man.

"Get to Wardrobe, Jack. We're behind schedule. Michael is tied up today, so I'll be running the show," he said with an undertone of accusation. "After all, we were delayed for two days last week, if you remember."

"Yeah--I remember." Jack bit down the retort he wanted to make at Michael Isle's chief lackey. "I'll get right to Wardrobe, and feel free to work my ass off today. I need the distraction." He shifted to the left and began to walk, already able to hear the subtle snips from the chatty Wardrobe people.

****

John LaLiberte's office was like dark hole with no escape, Cassie thought while sitting directly in front of the editor's desk. His cold glare made her feel a very bad child, possessing no defenses whatsoever. He had commanded that she sit still until the others arrived. What others? Her mind had cried out. *Was it the other she feared most in the world?* The mere thought made her bones feel like ice. When the door opened, she nearly jumped out of her skin in fear.

She managed to find the courage to turn. The trio of Ferris Mitchell, Curt Farchmin, and Geoff Haines walked through the door. Immediately, she felt the precarious rock of her raft while the walls slowly crumbled around her. And her mind screamed for Jack Torelli, followed by screams for, *Nono!*

Curt's eyes were so fiery, she felt her skin burn with his mere gaze, and Geoff shot her a jeering look. The expression infuriated her after what he had so boldly done, and she found the courage to sneer at him. Only her literary agent, Ferris Mitchell, looked somewhat normal, although she could see he too was perturbed.

"Everybody take a seat," John directed, and to her horror all three circled around her. She nervously glanced at each one, imagining their mouths open and huge white incisors, gleaming. When all were seated, John leaned across his desk and folded his hands in front of him. "Now for the damage control . . ." He bore his blue eyes into her.

"We get her out of New York until things cool down and then bring her back as a wood nymph, tarnished perhaps, but willing to do anything it takes to live that down." Curt ground his gaze into her with the message that she better cooperate.

"Our agency will stand by anything that you gentlemen decide," Ferris cut in. Then he disgustedly shook his head at her. "We of course desire your continued business despite this recklessness from one of our clients."

"Where do we send her? Back to Anoka, maybe?" John posed.

"No!" she suddenly piped in. "Not Anoka. I. . .won't step foot in Anoka. I'll go home to Los Angeles, today."

"The hell you will!" both Curt and John roared in near unison.

"Los Angeles is the last place you will go, Cassie!" Curt seethed in a fury.

"But the miniseries . . . there may be script rewrites and they need my input," she protested weakly.

"Forget it!" John exploded. "Mike Isle will just have to manage!" And then he muttered under his breath, "It's the least the bastard can do."

"What about Chicago?" Ferris offered. "We could keep an eye on her there."

Cassie churned with terror and the only word that screeched in her mind was *rejection*. "I can't go to Chicago. I . . .don't like Chicago, too cold."

"Maybe a suburb like Oak Park. It's shielded from Lake Michigan," Geoff said with a hint of deference and much malice.

Damn you! She wanted to claw at his eyes and the rest of him.

"No suburbs, Geoffrey. Too open to provide obscurity," Curt replied.

Cassie felt her growing panic. "L.A. has obscurity. That's where I wanna go, regardless as to what you say. I. . .need to go to L.A."

"Why?" Curt's eyes blazing like red-hot coals. "So you can let Jack Torelli lure you into another sick trap? You stupid woman! I could shake you!"

The sound of Curt's searing voice triggered a mind's picture of his unclothed frame hanging over her, and she could feel his hands plundering her body mercilessly until she was coated with filth. "You should talk about sick traps!" she shrieked at the top of her lungs, wildly flailing her arms. "Now you send me to Los Angeles. Or else!"

Curt's face cascaded into a nervousness as he took sneak peeks at John.

The sight startled her. It was obvious that John was ignorant of Curt's well-practiced tactics. It gave her some leverage against the man, she told herself. And then the fact that perhaps she could use that leverage to protect 'her Harry' began to drain into her head.

"Los Angeles is the only place I'll go, Curt!" she said with finality.

"How dare you dictate after what you've done!" John flared angrily.

Cassie ignored her editor. "Well do I go, Curt? Or do I merely let loose here and now. And Cassie will . . . in descriptive Technicolor."

"Let her go, John, if she's so inclined," Curt jumped in quickly. "Perhaps a second chance will make Mike more conscientious."

"What?" John yelled at Curt. "Do you know what you're saying? All that revenue . . . 'Harry Two' . . . and the subsequent miniseries which will have to star Torelli. A stupid move like this has the high potential of backfiring."

"I agree with, John," Ferris Mitchell piped in. "It's too big of a chance to take. Both of them have to come out in the wash like Ivory Snow no matter how tough that will be with Torelli. Remember . . . we agreed to suck every last dollar dry . . . once in a rare lifetime, Curt . . . the golden ring in one swoop."

As if spattered by a glue gun, the roundabout words fearfully sealed in Cassie's head. "What do you mean, Ferris? What is this Ivory Snow and one swoop about?"

"Nothing, Cassie. Just write and keep your image squeaky clean," Ferris said in a firm tone. "Leave the rest to the people who know, and have known, for many years."

"So L.A. is a *no go!*" John sharply said to her.

"Yes, Los Angeles!" she challenged back. "I'll stay in my suite and write *Season of Sorrow* in four months max, if you let me return, John."

"Mike could post a few extra security guards around that suite complex." Curt hurled a nervous expression at Cassie.

Oh god! She thought with ripples of trepidation. She just couldn't be without her teddy bear. She would *die* without him. *Think Cass!*

"Are you serious about four months, Cassie?" John asked, unable to hide his eagerness.

"Yeah--four months, and you'll have it." She replied with surety. "But no guards. I. . .can't write with such a restriction around me. They would make me too paranoid."

"*Season of Sorrow* does have high miniseries potential, John, if she pulls it off," Ferris pointed out. "Could be another 'Harry' for all you know."

That's what you think. Cassie filled with resentment at the comparison. In fact it made her blood boil. She would show them! Sandy's story would be *nothing* except for sweet revenge. And 'Harry' . . . *even sweeter revenge.*

"All right!" John conceded. "You'll stay for a few more days so Mike can get his crap together, and in that time, I want you to get a good handle on your book. You'll leave Thursday morning. Haines will escort you to the airport in case the press should happen to catch wind."

"No!" She glanced at Geoff Haines who wore a sanguinary expression. "I prefer to go by myself. Errol can escort me to my gate, if need be."

"That's ridiculous!" John shouted. "Haines here is experienced in handling . . . "

"I said no!" she screeched, bolting up from her chair. "I just wanna be by myself! Leave me alone, all of you!" Cassie backed away from her chair, while watching all the shocked stares on her. Except for Geoff Haines. He was halfway out of his seat, looking ready to attack her. "I'll leave for L.A. on Thursday and get my book to you in four months, John. That's . . . all I have left to offer. I'm so tired . . . that's all."

"What in the hell is the matter with you, Cassie?" John heaved in mortification.

She felt the heavy pants of her breath. "It's Sandy . . . she's making me lose my grip. It's just too much."

In an instant, John leapt up from his chair. "I told you to just write about Sandy and not get so involved with her like she was an extension. Did you read that material I sent to you?"

Desperately, she tried to swallow her accelerating emotions that seemed to have a will of their own. "I'll read it, John. Just dismiss me please. I have to leave. Your . . . office is stifling and I need to get back to my book . . . only four months, you know."

John glared at her. "One word of warning . . . stay away from Torelli or you won't even have a third book. We can probably salvage 'Harry Two' because of the popularity factor. But *Season of Sorrow* will be another story, if you don't change your ways."

The news thrilled her, and she felt a sudden, miraculous calm. "Of course, John. I'll do what's best for my career, as usual," she quipped lightly and even fastened a smile on him while waiting for his magic word.

"Okay Cassie. Dismissed!"

****

Again foregoing the limousine, Cassie, feeling lighter than she had in days, took lilting steps down Park Avenue, heading back to the Regent. Perhaps she would even have a bite to eat in that snooty hotel restaurant, she thought with a bit of a twirl to her purse.

I feel like Holly Go-Lightly.

And she thought, perhaps a window-shopping trip to Tiffany's would be appropriate. The notion made her giggle with delight, having no care about the looks she was getting. 'Her Harry was safe, and she was going home to her teddy bear. At that very moment, she felt his strong arms around her, and she stopped dead in the middle of the sidewalk to relish the sensation.

Warm up the bed, Jack. I'm coming home, darling. What . . . ?

She felt her body moved along quickly from the rear, and her mouth gaped in a silent scream. Then suddenly, she was thrust against a building, face down, while a moist breath muffed her ear. "You think you're pretty smart, don't you, Cassie. Damn Curt, that fool! He lost his hold and now you can run amuck, even back to Los Angeles to that sleazeball who'll spread his dirt all over you. I saw his hands. I could just see the filth between his fingernails. I had to save you from total ruination."

"Get away from me, Geoff, or I swear I'll scream," Cassie trembled out in total terror.

He pushed her face deeper into the wall. "I saw him fuck you that day in his office. I watched every moment and pretended it was me. I told myself I could do much better. But I couldn't tell Curt. You know Curt . . . always has to be a cut above everyone else. But I could have been better, and right now, if I chose, I could show you how much better I am than him."

Cassie felt the slobber of his lips on her neck, and nausea wound its way up to the back of her throat. "This time I'll tell Curt if you don't leave right now," she whimpered.

Geoff flung his lips from her neck and pushed them tightly against her ear. "Curt," he sneered. "What good is he now? He lost his hold. He's worthless!"

She shifted her eyes left and right, trying to spy some help for herself.

"And he dirtied you for nothing. That's unforgivable."

"You're scaring me--let me go." Cassie squirmed wildly against his hold.

"Your passion is mine, Cassie. I'll never let you go."

"Ms. Callahan!"

"Errol." Cassie desperately tried to turn her face in the direction of the sound.

"Keep quiet or that near naked picture of you from *Bergdorf's* goes in the New York Times. Remember . . . I have connections there." Geoff jumped away from her back and planted a smile on his face as the chauffeur headed in their direction.

"Oh, it's you, Mr. Haines," Errol said cheerily, then he smiled at Cassie. "I'm afraid my eyes were deceiving me a little. I thought you looked to be in trouble, Ms Callahan."

"No, Errol." She rapidly moved up to him and grabbed his arm. "Mr. Haines and I were just sharing a joke, a big joke, and now I'm a teensy tired, so I think I'll take that ride after all."

"Can I drop you anywhere, Mr. Haines?" Errol asked pleasantly.

"Gracious no!" Cassie tugged on the old man's arm. "Geoff was telling me that he needed to get in shape so that he's a cut above . . . if that's possible. Therefore, I think we should help him with that effort and let him walk."

"That's fine, Errol." Geoff's jaw rippled with rage as he stared at Cassie. "Take Ms. Callahan to the Regent. I'll see her there later."

Cassie shivered despite the black attire and humid high eighty degree temperature. "Just take me back to the hotel, Errol. I. . .need my teddy bear. Now . . ."

****

"Cassie where are you?" Jack muttered in desperation from a pay phone at Python. He had stood there for a half hour, trying to connect to Cassie's room at the Regent. His worry of her had grown so immense he could barely concentrate and only by sheer will had he made it through his scenes that morning.

"I'm sorry sir—Room 808 still doesn't answer," the voice at the other end said.

"Shit!" Jack slammed down the receiver and quickly glanced at his watch. His time was up, he told himself. He had an outside shoot in ten minutes that would occupy most of the afternoon. And he wouldn't be anywhere near a private phone.

Jack exited the phone booth and cussed himself. Why the hell did he leave her there instead of bodily dragging her home? Now, he was helpless.

"You doin' okay, Jack?"

Jack shifted his sunglasses to the side. George, the white-haired security guard, stood a short distance from him. "Yeah George, relatively okay," he replied in quiet tones.

George walked forward and with comforting motions, placed an arm around Jack's shoulders. "You've been through hell, haven't you, boy?"

Jack gave a jerky nod of his head.

"Best advice I can give you is from one of my favorite people: Never say uncle'," George said kindly. "Cassie's a good person, a little nutty sometimes, but a good person nevertheless, and someone worth holding onto with two tight fists."

Jack was startled. "You telling me that you don't believe that I'm using her for some diabolical sexual purpose like everybody else?"

George let out a hearty laugh. "No Jack—you're in love all right. I've never seen anyone suffer so much over these last several weeks or be so happy at the same time. That's the definition of love in my book and I got thirty-three years of married life to prove it."

Jack let out a low whistle of astonishment. "Thirty-three? *Years?*"

"What can I say?" George replied with a squeeze to Jack's shoulder. "Once I met Dorie, not another woman on Earth looked good to me. So I was stuck."

"I guess I could see that," Jack said. "Once in love, always in love? Something like that?"

"I'll tell you all about it while we walk to the shoot, Jack."

"Say George, speaking of the shoot . . . you got a spare cellular I can use?"

****

At Cassie's insistence, Errol escorted her past a pesky mob of reporters waiting like vultures outside the Regent despite angry attempts by management to rid the place of the loud group. And then, she had further insisted that he walk her to her room. She still keenly felt the cold shake of her body from Geoff Haines's assault and well knew things could have turned out worse if Errol hadn't shown up.

"Thank you, Errol." She placed a twenty-dollar bill in his hand when standing in front of her open room door. "Just a little appreciation to you."

"I'm glad to help, Ms. Callahan," he replied graciously, then with a tip of his hat, headed back for the elevators.

Cassie quickly bolted her door, then lunged for the phone. She snatched up the receiver and in rapid succession, her fingers pounded out the numbers. Then her legs jittered up and down while she listened to the phone ring.

"Python Studios. Where may I connect you?"

She ground the phone against her mouth. "I'd like to speak to Jack Torelli, please."

"I'm sorry. Absolutely no calls are to go through to Mr. Torelli."

"But this is highly important," Cassie cried out. "I need to talk to him."

"No calls M'am. Those orders come from the top."

"I'm . . . his girlfriend and I have to talk to him, Lady!"

An exasperated noise came through the line. "Listen M'am. I get about fifty calls a day that say the same thing, and today, maybe a hundred. Mr. Torelli cannot be disturbed. Period!"

"But I am his girlfriend! I am!" she yelled, her hysteria rising. Then she heard a loud click.

"Witch!" Cassie screeched, letting the phone drop out of her hand. "I need some peace. I need my teddy bear's voice!" She sobbed where she stood. Her mind spun with turmoil and the pressure was so oppressive, she felt it pushing down on her.

I'm losing Cassie. Bit-by-bit, she's being crushed.

STOP HER!

She *couldn't* become that little girl in the corner at the party.

She *had to* hold on until help arrived.

Nono!

Cassie retrieved the dangling phone then punched in the Anoka number. She settled somewhat. There was no witch at the other end of her grandfather's phone, she told herself.

"Hallo?"

"Oh, Nono."

"Cassina! I try to call you for hours. What is happening to you? I hear the TV. Who is this Torelli man?"

"My friend, Nono."

"Friend? But Cassina what they say. Are you having a love affair with this Torelli?"

"Yeah--I love him, Nono. He's a wonderful person," she choked out.

"Wonderful?" he breathed out. "They say he take his clothes off for dirty movies, Cassina. Your Mama and Papa are in a *fracasso.*"

"Good! I'm glad the Ice Queen and her elf are in an uproar." She let out a rippling laugh of amusement. "You tell June that I had him for two straight days and didn't come up for air until Saturday and I let the world know just for her. Tell her it's an early birthday present from her precious Sandy. That should throw her for a loop."

"What's the matter with you, Cassina?" He asked with urgency. "You make no sense. Reporters are beating down the doors of your parents' businesses and things aren't good. *E un uomo di cattiva fama,"* he concluded in a hushed tone.

"He doesn't have a bad reputation, Nono! He's a film director and has been for a year and a half. He's not that man who took off his clothes. He's not!"

Angelo spewed out a string of Italian words, most of them obscenities. "You come home, Cassina. This has not been good for you. I can tell. You write in Anoka and we try to persuade Kristi to come back. It will be hard, but she may come back it you're settled. You need your family, Cassina, not some *un adicione."*

"He's not a dirty man!" she flared. "And I *do* need him, Nono. I tell you, he's kind and sensitive and he loves me. He's a good Italian boy. You should like that."

A loud sniff came through the phone line. "Good Italian boy! Good Italian boys don't hang out their *Pene* like it was wash!"

"How can you say that about him, Nono? He's playing 'my Harry'."

"Humph! How can you let such a man play your 'Harry'? I thought you and 'Harry' were *Amore*."

"I do love 'Harry', and I love Jack too. You'll all just have to accept that, especially June. I'm not saying 'uncle' to her on this one. Her enamored friends will just have to be shocked!" And then she let out a wild glee-filled laugh.

"Cassina! Something is not right. I can hear it. You must come at least for a visit, or else I worry terribly about you. You sound *logorato*."

"Crazy?" she screeched. "How can you say that to me, Nono? You better than anyone should understand!"

"Yes Cassina." He let out a weighted sigh of sadness. "You create your own world with bricks around it so the hurt cannot touch you. That I understand. It has made you miss out on much. But I'm always afraid to tamper. You're happy only in that world."

She felt her body shake with tears. "Oh Nono . . . the bricks are tumbling down and Sandy is sneaking in."

"You don't have to tell me about the bricks, Cassina. I can hear them falling. You need to see that doctor, honey."

"No! He'll make all the bricks tumble and then I'll be Sandy forever. I just can't say 'uncle' all my life, Nono. All of me will die," she cried in a small voice. "But Jack . . . he keeps the bricks sturdy. He loves *Cassie*. *Me!*"

"All right, Cassina." He exhaled with sheer weariness. "I will turn the bricklaying over to this Torelli. I am tired, Cassina. Old. I can barely lift a brick any more."

"Then you're not mad at me, Nono?" she pleaded.

"How could I ever be mad at you, Cassina? It would be like being mad at a rare, delicate flower growing hidden behind a rock out of fear that a larger world will crush it and destroy its rareness. Pure innocence is not compatible with anger, Cassina, only *compassione* . . ."

****

For the next couple hours, while propped up between two pillows on her bed, Cassie stared into space, basking in the gentle words her grandfather had spoken. Yet, despite the soothing remembrance, she still felt the slow descent of brick-after-brick. They had done this to her. They had so easily peeled away each brick to make her into something that she abhorred . . . a perfect little 'Sandy'.

Wind her up and she dresses right, has manageable hair, is witty in social situations . . .

A blah.

And now she knew, or perhaps knew from the onset, regardless how tight she had tried to hold on, that she could never truly weather such a world.

It was so ironic . . .

She had balked about seeing a psychiatrist, even at the sacrifice of her daughter, just so 'Harry' could culminate without interruption, and maybe, just maybe, he would succeed and plunge her into the much-coveted world of publishing.

And he had.

But once in that much-coveted world, an even more insulated world--or so she had thought--they had did a number on her worse than any psychiatrist could do, and she had lost herself anyway.

So in essence . . . she had sacrificed Kristi Anne-Marie Callahan for nothing but the truth: She was a crummy mother, too mortared between her bricks, to even have been anything *but*. She was aware that the undesirable marriage had made the brick wall higher so her world was more secure. Though in the final analysis, Kristi had no desire to dwell in that world, and she had been too needy to dwell out of it. Unfortunately, Kristi had been the product of a brick-building marriage that shut out, rather than let in, thus they all had been doomed from the start. If only she could have raised Kristi alone, things may have been different.

She had succumbed, cried 'uncle', played 'Sandy', for that walk down the aisle. And then, 'Cassie' had fought against that activity for eleven years. It was the most devastating 'uncle' of her life, and now she would pay for it all of her life.

Kristi . . . she had lost her forever.

Her child refused to scale the wall, and instead, preferred to turn her back on it. While she, more than ever, couldn't escape the confines, rather try with all her waning strength to make those bricks even sturdier.

So ultimately, all we have between us after thirteen years is a brick wall.
The notion was unbearable!

Sensing a rapid crumble of the mortar between her bricks, Cassie rolled towards the night stand, plucked up the phone, and punched in the familiar number. She felt the rise of her desperation while listening to the ring of the phone, twelve times to be exact, before she flung down the receiver. Where was he? It was past six in L.A. He should be home from the studio.

So again she called the studio, and this time got a different witch who told her Mr. Torelli was still on the lot filming and under no circumstances could he be disturbed.

Damn!

She slammed the receiver against the cradle. What now? She needed to feel her teddy bear's love and embrace, if only through words.

Her desperation quickly converted into a panic, and she agitated on the bed until a thought struck, bizarre as it was, bold as it could be, it still was comforting.

Where's that Manhattan directory?

She rustled through every drawer until finding the thick book, then located the name. My god! There were so many. So she began the process of elimination. *Close to Bleeker Street.* Finally, she had narrowed it down to four addresses, all in fairly close proximity.

Less than twenty minutes later, she picked up her purse and was off like a flash . . .

****

By the time the cameras shutdown on the filming of *The Life and Times of Harry Hannigan*, Jack felt achy in his lower back, calves, and shoulder muscles. He figured the punishment had been intentional. Michael Isle had chosen the most physically grueling scenes to be placed in one day to torture him in indirect fashion, wearing him down before doling out the *real* punishment. It was coming, he knew. He could taste it as acutely, as if someone had compressed the word "punishment" into a sourball and placed it on his tongue.

Seeking Out Harry

But what could Mike really do? Jack lifted slowly to straighten his spine. Slap his hand? Give him lecture 101 on the "no-no's" of production delays? Play God and preach the immoralities of lying and screwing? *Ha-Ha.* He couldn't fire him with a production dependent on Jack Torelli starring in it. And, if the truth be known, there was nothing Mike could do about Cassie. She was a grown woman and could do as she pleased, regardless of how different Mike envisioned the way things would be—how any of them envisioned it for that matter.

They needed each other, and no one in the world could deny that.

George, the old security guard, had said, "No one can fight true love and come out the victor. So just hang in there, boy. You'll be the victor eventually."

The prudent words had strengthened his resolve. Someone *had* understood, despite his fucked up past, and that meant a helluva lot.

Wearing his first smile since Saturday, Jack began to swiftly walk off the lot, meeting eyes with all the people who had contributed heavily to his body's discomfort. They returned no smiles, rather hung gazes as if he was even too filthy to view. Yet, he kept smiling—it felt good like he was thumbing his nose at the snubs and even disputing them.

I've been bathed a bit, and if you can't see it, I at least, can feel it.

And wasn't that the important thing in the larger picture of life?

He kicked up the last bit of dust on the lot, then stepped up his pace to the pay phone. Cassie would talk to a "new man," a "tougher man," who'd leave no doubt in her mind that he'd make everything all right for her. He'd put a beautiful cage around his rare bird, the most safe and beautiful he could to create, so she could freely and happily extend her wings and fly as high as she desired. And he'd place a sign on the cage.

Cassie Callahan, the one and only. Do not disturb.

It's a great idyllic, he thought, boosting the phone to his mouth and feeling the tremble of his body while waiting to hear her voice.

Cm'on Cassie, make my insides explode . . .

"I'm sorry sir. There's no answer from room 808," a cold voice told him.

Jack slumped, all good feelings replaced by renewed terror.

"Where the hell is she?" He absently hung up the phone. "Have they done something to her? Is her punishment worse than mine?" Then terror struck. "Is Cassie, still Cassie?"

Jack flew out of the booth and beat his feet like a marathon runner to his Corvette. Where to? Home? Maybe the airport? A private plane? Helicopter? Anything to get him cross-country pronto? *Where do I go? What do I do?*

Hanging his upper body over his car door, Jack paused to pant out his sudden anxiety and determine his best recourse. If only he knew she was all right, then he could drive home at a safe speed, make a triple decker sandwich with all the trimmings, stretch out on his patio, sip on a cold *Michelob*, place cellular in lap, and keep trying the number until he heard her voice.

But he didn't know, and New York was too big to search.

Perhaps the police? But what could he say? How could he ever explain her delightful and mysterious complexities that even he was yet to fully comprehend; even though he loved her, so was more than willing to make the effort. What in the hell could he ever say to make another care about her, rather than condemn her for her eccentricities?

Officer . . . she grasps tightly onto life like a constantly drowning person does to a buoy, trying to climb higher despite the whirlpool below that tries to pull her down. And the struggle is getting tougher. The world in which she's chosen to dwell is difficult for the heartiest of souls. *I know, I dwell there myself.* But for her? She's much too guileless, too idealistic, to *ever* weather such a monstrous storm. So why did she ever try? Well . . . *That's still a puzzle to me too.*

Jack kicked the car door.

Why the hell did I ever take that plane out of La Guardia on Sunday?

If he only knew that she was unscathed by those greedy, hungry cats who could *never* be concerned about the rarity of a bird, rather view it for its "meal quality."

He hated them, Jack seethed, veering his head up to the tenth floor of the office building. He was one of them!

Impelled by his sudden rage, Jack hurled himself from the car and resumed his marathon running. He would force it out of the bastard if he had to . . .

****

"Oh dear." Cassie said to the wearied taxicab driver. "That place looks too small to ever hold ten children without bodies hanging out the windows."

"Are you for real?" The driver rubbed his hat from his head.

Cassie gladly ignored his unfriendly tone and gazed down at the ripped out page from the phone directory. "I have one more on . . . Mott Street. Do you know where that is?" she asked.

"Depends Lady. It's a long street, goes clear down to Chinatown."

"Ah . . ." Cassie checked again. "Looks like East First."

"By Old Saint Pat's." He replied then shifted the cab into drive. "Should be only a few bumper-to-bumper miles..."

****

"Where is he?" Jack demanded of Claire Gibson the moment he reached the tenth floor of the Python office building.

"Well . . . the plunderer of 'Little Miss Muffet's' tuffet has finally shown himself," Claire said in highly amused fashion while she leisurely perched at the edge of her desk.

"Not one more word, Claire. I'm warning you . . ."

"A little testy about your 'tuffet' snatching, I see," she said with great glee.

"I swear I'll level that mouth of yours, Claire . . ."

Smiling like a kid who secretly ate all the cookie dough, Claire boosted off the desk. "Well in that case, for the sake of my ten thousand dollar teeth caps, I'll very gladly escort you into the wolf's den." She gave Jack a low throaty growl before motioning him to follow . . .

****

"Is this place big enough for you, Lady? It looks like it could hold twenty kids," the cab driver said irritably.

Raising her sunglasses, Cassie gazed at the big two-story rectangular building with the words **Torelli Bros.** on the darkened window below and lights burning above. A porch was in the front with a swing and pots of tomatoes. She sucked in a gasp. It could be a smaller version of her Nono's porch, she thought with intense longing. This had to be Jack's home. She could feel the coziness and love already. "We're here," she breathed out in awe, hardly able to wait until she felt such love up close. It would be the next best thing to her teddy bear's love—she just knew.

"You want me to wait, Lady, so you can make sure this is the place?" the driver asked, looking like it was the last thing he wanted to do.

"This is the place," she said with surety, handing the driver a hundred-dollar bill. "Please keep the change with my appreciation for you helping me to locate my teddy bear's' family."

Eyes wide and lips smacking, the driver grabbed the money, and flashed a wide smile that was missing a few teeth. "My pleasure, Lady. And if the mood strikes you tomorrow, maybe we can look for your Barbie doll's family. Here's my card."

Forcing a stiff smile despite his insolence, Cassie took the card then promptly tore it while walking to the porch, letting the pieces flutter to the soft warm breeze. She paused on the porch. *What should I say?* After all, this was New York and she was a stranger . . . and she wondered . . .

****

"Dammit, Mike! You are to tell me right now that my lady's okay, or I turn your eyes from black to blue!" Jack yelled across the producer's desk.

Looking more angry than frightened, Michael bobbed forward in his maroon leather chair. "You have a lot of nerve, Torelli! It should be me that gets first crack at your eyes for holding up my production and costing this studio a fortune!"

"Just try . . ." Jack thrust his face closer. "You wanna do it—I know you do—so go ahead. Get out all that frustration that's been building inside you ever since I fucked up my life and ruined your great plans for me seven years ago. I did it to myself! There I said it! I admit it!"

Michael wore a look of frank disbelief.

"Now I just wanna hear about my Cassie and then I'll leave," Jack said, more subdued. The humbling hadn't been comfortable despite the ease of the words. Now he only wanted the information then a rapid exit so he could eat his humble pie in the privacy of his car.

"Stay away from her, Torelli, that's the wisest information I can give you," Michael said with tight restraint.

Jack rocked his head back and forth with the emphasis of an exclamation point. "No can ever do—not even an option. In fact, I resent the fact that you were bold enough to whisper such an absurdity. She's mine. And Torelli *would never* give up his most prized possession."

Michael suddenly looked uneasy. "Who the hell are you? I don't know you anymore, Torelli. You used to be so readable. Make a defaming comment and Torelli pops a cork. Subtly refer to his past moment of glory and Torelli sinks into himself until he's invisible. You were as predictable as a crystal ball, but now . . ."

Jack angrily slapped his elbows onto the desk and lunged forward, determined to make this point so there was never any doubt or question in Michael Isle's mind from hence forward. "Because I'm not that man! I've taken responsibility for all of it. I absorb every ounce of blame. Torelli fucked-up! And he isn't, no matter what happens to him, good or bad, fame or obscurity, disappointment or acquisition, *ever* going to fuck up like that again! Capisce?"

Michael was jarred, dumbstruck.

"Now I can read your mind." Jack pulled back, shaking with anger. "You don't the hell believe me. Actions speak louder than words, huh? Well then I gotta say that you've been blinded to my actions. Perhaps an unalterable prejudice. But I tell you now, I haven't been that man who starred in *Jungle Love* for quite awhile. I know it, and more importantly, Cassie knows it!"

"Regardless . . ." Michael began with nervous evasiveness. "To continue this relationship is destructive for her and dangerous for you."

"Are you threatening me?" Jack shot a look of incredulity across the desk. "Because you can threaten until you run out of breath, and I'm still not gonna give her up. She needs me dammit! She had no one else to pave the way for her. She's been sucked of all her mobility, thanks to you and *whoever* in New York. You're using her, man, and I know it!"

"How dare you utter such a thing, Torelli. . ."

Jack's rage gathered in his eyes. "But it's gonna stop, and I'll make sure it does."

A glint of uncertainty crossed Michael's face.

"Now I wanna know if my Cassie's all right, or else you can bet you'll have more production delays in the next few days because I'm gonna be in New York!"

"She's okay. She's . . . coming back on Thursday in my charge," Michael replied grudgingly.

A smile of sheer pleasure teased on Jack's lips as he raised up. "You got that wrong, Mike. She's gonna be in my charge . . ."

****

"Who are you?" the Italian-fringed voice demanded while its owner stood ten feet from the door.

Cassie peeked around the body to study as much as the interior as she could see. Her eyes gloriously bathed in the homey atmosphere while her nose gained whiff of the delicious, rich smells that drifted towards her. So badly she wanted to move deeper into such a magnetizing world. "I'm Cassie . . . Callahan. The writer?"

The abundant graying woman clasped her chest and yelled at the top of her lungs.

"Carlo!"

Soon a sturdy gray-haired man took excited strides into the foyer and spoke in rapid Italian. Then the woman indicated to Cassie while speaking rapid Italian back. Cassie cocked a careful ear towards the noise trying to grasp of gist of the conversation.

"Yeah--that's right. I'm the woman you read about in the New York Times, but I'm no *prostituta*," she said with indignance.

Both Torelli's clamped there mouths and stared, until finally Carlo Torelli charged forward. "Why you come to my house and bother my *famiglia?*"

Cassie looked at the wrathful face and let out a little cry. "Oh! You look so much like him." Tears misted her eyes. "I miss him so much and I needed to be close to him, so I came here. He told me it was cozy and had lots of love and I need some of both."

Marianna Torelli loudly choked with a sob and stunned, Carlo slowly backed away from her. "My Jacko say that?" he shook out with great caution.

"Uh-huh. He misses home, I can tell." Cassie boldly took a few more forward steps and looked around again. "Oh my . . . I can just see him growing up here, and it makes me miss him more. I love him so much." Her face screwed up with more tears. "He's such a wonderful, kind man. You should be so proud of him."

Now Marianna Torelli openly sobbed while Carlo stood frozen, unable to comfort her.

Thinking that perhaps she had been a little too 'soul felt', Cassie curved her wet cheeks into the brightest smile she owned.

"He told me he was the bambino. My Nono always said that the bambino was special— and Jack is. I've never known such a brave, sensitive man. He's had a tough life, but he faces it so admirably. You must have given him a lot of good stuff Mr. and Mrs. Torelli."

"And you even have a Nono too, eh?" Carlo said, his lips smiling also.

Cassie fluffed her blonde hair. "Half of me has a Nono, and the other half . . . well, you can probably guess."

"Come in, Cassie." Marianna Torelli nearly attacked her with her arm. "I make you some spaghetti. You look a little skinny. And you can tell me all about my Jacko."

"I'd love that, Mrs. Torelli!" Cassie leapt into the rest of the house, savoring every sight and smell. *"Jacko . . ."* she said dreamily. "I love that name. I'm gonna have to remember that."

****

By ten p.m., Jack was a basket case as he paced his living room. Nearly continuously for the past three hours, he had tried to get an answer in Cassie's hotel room and now wanted to rent a pair of wings and fly to New York. *One a.m.?* Where the hell could she be?

He fretted about every conceivable mishap, especially that orchid guy. Had he somehow gotten his hands on her? *Shit!* Should he call the NYPD? If anything happened to her . . .

Jack lunged for the phone and decided to call the Regent one more time. But it she wasn't there, he *would* call the police.

"Hello," a thoroughly cheery voice answered.

"Cassie?" He breathed out all his anxiety.

'Jack!' She squealed at the top of her lungs.

"Where were you, Honey? I tried to call for hours," he asked shakily.

"*Oh Jack,* I had the best time. The food was superb and the ambience . . . it was so wonderful, I swear I had tears in my eyes the entire night."

"I repeat . . . where--were you?" he demanded.

"At a spaghetti feed with a bunch of people," she replied with great delight. "Steve drove me home."

"Steve? Who the hell is Steve?"

". . .Or was it Jimmy driving and Steve was in the back seat with the rest. Oh well! They all look alike to me."

"What?" he roared.

"They look like quintuplets and they all kiss alike too, so it was tough to tell them apart."

"WHAT?"

"And I didn't feel so homesick for you, darling, with their lips all over me. They could have been your lips--they *were* your lips. In fact . . . you could have made it a sextuplet."

He fisted his forehead in frustration. He may as well be connected to a Japanese geisha, he figured. "Is this some sort of new world, Cass, a far-far-far-out world?"

"Why yes it is, darling. It's a whole fifteen miles from the Regent and it *was* a beautiful new world, one I plan on visiting often--with you of course."

He finally nodded his understanding, figuring her mind was on overdrive tonight and she had been off in a corner, somewhere, dreaming. "I better let you hit the sack, Cass."

"I'm coming home on, Thursday, so pack up my stuff. I can't wait to see that back bedroom." She gave a soft giggle. "And your bedroom too, darling."

His body churned with heated desire at her words. "I can't wait either, Cass. I'll get out the fresh sheets," he murmured. "And fill the refrigerator, get the pool cleaned, the lawn mowed, the house spotless . . . I love you so damn much."

"And I love you so damn much too . . . Jacko . . ."

Chapter 24— Jack

In the ensuing weeks, Jack and Cassie tried to settle down to a quiet life in Jack's Beverly Hills home, despite that their living together had leaked to the Hollywood media and reporters plus cameras were always lurking around the premises. On several occasions, Jack even was forced to call the police to intervene. He tried to tell himself that soon it would pass when a hotter romance or juicier scandal befell the highly inquiring community of voyeurs. In the Hollywood press, "temporarily famous" was the usual fare, so besides the highly elusive nature of their relationship, he was puzzled as to why 'temporary' was so prolonged with he and Cassie.

'Harry Two' had sold a million copies after only two months in circulation, Jack figured this accounted for some of the mania. Radio and television shows and magazines were always bothering Cassie's pushy Chicago agent for interviews. But for the most part, she refused, and that sat fine with Jack. He seethed with the notion that some less than ethical interviewer would gain hold of her for the sole purpose of probing about their relationship--*very* likely in lieu of their highly secretive life.

Everybody seemed to want the scoop on Jack and Cassie.

"Stay in the back yard, Cass, unless I'm with you," he had sharply told her, fearful a sneaky reporter from some rag would nab her and make mincemeat out of Cassie in his or her publication. Cassie had already been hurt by the preponderance of gossip blowing around them and he refused for any more hurt to touch her.

"Don't worry, darling. I'm busy in my back bedroom," she replied as content as a baby in a bunting--and for that he was horribly grateful. Gone were the hysterical moments and terror-filled crying jags, replaced by a serene and happiness that was as innocent as a child's smile. She wanted no world outside of the Beverly Hills house, and Jack, having had his fill of Hollywood himself, made no balk about that. He was as content in his new world as she was.

The only regret for both were their Saturday jaunts, impossible now lest they wanted to get mobbed. So they spent their free time alone, providing each other warmth and soothing the intense loneliness that had plagued both in their adult lives. It was all he wanted, Jack told himself. The rest, once so paramount, had suddenly lost its glitter in the more glittering sparkle of a pair of huge green eyes. Nothing, he firmly believed, not parties, restaurants, "being seen" and "seeing," meant even a hundredth as much as Cassie. He loved her more each day and only lived to hold her in his arms, kiss her, fondle her on the couch, in the shower, in bed, and feel her heated body close to him. Without that, he figured he'd be a goner. She was suddenly his entire universe.

On their sixth Saturday in the Beverly Hills house, Jack stared at the closed door of the back bedroom. If he listened carefully, he could hear the constant tap of her computer. It was like the story had suddenly burst forth, he thought. She never complained of "blocks" anymore and constantly raved about the book's progress.

"Can I read some of it?" he had asked lately out of curiosity.

"When it's done, Jack," she'd respond vaguely, even evasively if he really wanted to analyze. Although he never pushed and for the most part, left her alone when she was on one of her creative streaks. He wanted no disturbance of any world which kept her on an even keel.

As for his time spent when she was occupied, Jack relaxed in the pool with the 'Harry' script, refurbished his tan on the enclosed patio, and read 'Harry Two' to the degree he read the first 'Harry'. He thought the sequel was wonderful, far better than the first in terms of its emotional impact. She told him that she had written the second book during a 'highly insulated' time of her life thus all her emotions had burst forth onto 'Harry'. So he intently studied the book, trying to accrue more pieces to the continuing puzzle of Cassie Callahan. Because, despite her tranquility, Jack still sensed something disturbing about her. The clues continued to come out in odd ways and roundabout talk, yet he just felt like she was trying to give him some sort of message to decipher, like she *wanted* him to find the meaning to the words.

Was it a cry for help? He always questioned after one of her riddles, and this made him feel desperate. So he would return to 'Harry Two', studying it like one would a textbook, telling himself to grab *anything* that could save the woman he loved more than his own life. But so far he could determine nothing concrete. The emotions were so woven tightly into a riveting story that microscopic dissection was difficult with his inexperienced eye.

Perhaps, he thought, once the second book was made into a teleplay the experience of the writers could do a better job of dissection and provide the much coveted clues. It wouldn't be long. The writers were working on the teleplay now, Jack reminded himself as he lay stretched out on the living room couch, basking in the coolness of the central air and leafing through the paperback with a worn cover from his constant thumbing.

"I want to start filming of Harry Two shortly after the first miniseries hits the airwaves," Michael Isle had told him in a barely controlled tone, his usual tone since the day Cassie had moved out of the suite upon returning to Los Angeles.

Mike had acted like a raving madman. He tried to coerce Cassie with anger and threats, including the threat that he would call New York and, in essence, 'tattle' on her.

"Tell Curt," she quipped in all her glory. "I dare him to make a peep. It is *I* with the upper hand now. He screwed up once too often."

"But Cassie . . ." Mike protested in a panic. "Your image will be blemished beyond repair if you live with a . . . with a . . ." He stopped to glance at Jack, and in that split-second Jack saw the discomfort as well as the truth behind the eyes. Michael Isle had believed him that night in his office, all right, but just was too pigheaded to admit it.

"With a wonderful man who has a lovely back bedroom which I am very anxious to get a gander at," Cassie finished for him, then motioned Jack, carrying her computer, to follow.

Then looking like a beautiful, exultant queen, Cassie strutted past Michael and with merry steps, walked to Jack's Corvette and perched herself in the passenger seat like it was a decorous throne. "Take me to my bedroom," she had commanded like a tragic actress.

Now he laughed as heartily at the remembrance as he had at the actual event. He wished he had caught the moment on film, especially the expression that hung on Michael Isle's face. It was prime to see such shell-shock in the usual formidable demeanor. Though his laughter came to an abrupt halt when he also recollected that the demeanor was back to status quo the next morning when, to his aching joints, he discovered that Michael Isle had changed the production schedule to include every gut-busting scene that could be found in the script—his punishment for not heeding the warning.

A taste of things to come.
And I've tasted like a sonofabitch.

Not only did heavy production schedules besiege him but also forced publicity to promote the miniseries—interviews from all mediums including *People* which photographed him in a thousand dollar 'Harry' suit for next month's cover plus a stint on *The Tonight Show*. And with each query, Mike let the interviewers loose on him, not stopping the sly questions about Cassie; in which case he gave an emphatic "No comment." Then add the siege of reporters at the front gates of Python on most mornings, which Michael had ordered the security people to leave "as is" without interference. Append to this, the atmosphere on the sound stage which was becoming frostier upon Michael Isle's edict. And finally were the constrained lunches at some of the most popular haunts in Hollywood and beyond, including Mike's favorite the *Polo Lounge*, where the producer displayed him more like a "Hollywood peacock" than Rud Hanna had ever done.

"Just go with the flow, Jack," Harv Wellson said when he had bitterly complained about the excessive treatment doled out to him. "You know Mike. He's as vindictive as hell when he's pissed off . . . seven years and counting for you, Jack."

"But why so tough, huh? He's gotta know by now that Cassie and I are gonna stay together no matter what he does," he reasoned back.

"Yeah Jack--but you messed up their little machine. Her image, regardless how asinine, was a big part of that machine. They created her Jack, as sure as Trudeau created *Doonesbury*, and they did so for a purpose."

"Greed and money . . . yeah . . . I got that much sitting in my craw."

"That's the reality, Jack, and you better than most should understand that."

"Oh, I understand all right. It's just tougher than hell to accept when if involves the woman you love. Then it supersedes acceptance, Harv . . ."

****

Later on that afternoon, Jack popped two rib-eye steaks on the Hibachi and threw together a reasonable facsimile of a Caesar salad. Once done he softly knocked on the door of the back bedroom. Not getting an immediate answer, he placed an ear to the door and heard a steady stream of tapping which would make even the most capable secretary groan. Should he disturb her? He wondered, and quickly decided that he would. She had barely eaten all day.

"Cass!" he called out and pounded on the door a little bit harder.

The tapping abruptly stopped and footsteps rapidly padded to the door.

"Darling!" She flung the door open and flew into his arms. "Is my day done already?"

Jack hugged her tightly and his lips made frenzied motions across her silky blonde hair. "If you want it to be, Cass," he murmured into her head.

She disentangled herself from his arms and made great drama about shutting off her computer. "My day is done. The rest of my day belongs to my sexy Jacko."

Immediately, he stiffened. "*Where* did you say you got that new name for me?" he asked like he asked every time she called him that. He hated it. In fact, it made his skin crawl with every emotion under the sun.

"From my beautiful world in New York," she replied unconcerned.

"So," he probed. "You just happened to think up that name. Is that it, Cass?"

"I heard it, loved it, and decided I had to call you that. It makes my body tingle just thinking about that lovely name."

He gave her a leery look. "You mean someone named 'Jacko' was at that spaghetti feed you went to with all those Italian guys? Is that where you heard it?"

"Exactly!" she enthused. "I must have heard it at least a thousand times."

He nodded resignedly, knowing that Cassie wasn't going to be more specific. "Must be a popular name in New York."

"It is . . ." She brightly walked past him. "On Mott Street it is . . ."

****

"Where the hell did you get Mott Street from?" Jack demanded with much inner anxiety, slapping down a steak in front of her as she perched daintily on the kitchen chair.

She plucked up her steak knife and fork then began to saw off tiny pieces of meat. "From the phone book. That's where Jacko was from, so of course the name stuck in my head like someone pasted it there."

He put his plate down and slid into the chair next to her. "So what part of Mott Street is this Jacko from?" he asked, telling himself it was all a horrible nightmare of a coincidence. "I mean, Mott Street is pretty long."

"Yeah--it goes all the way down to Chinatown, doesn't it?" she replied thoughtfully. "But this Jacko lived in the other direction, by someone named Saint Pat."

"What?" Jack held a shaky stare on her. "You mean Old Saint Pat's Cathedral?"

"Oh yeah . . . I think Steve or Jimmy did pass a church and they told me that was where Jacko had his First Communion." She popped a morsel of steak into her mouth. "And they also said he tripped on his altar boy robe, tumbled into the aisle, then cried like a baby. I told them it wasn't funny, and I wanted to cry myself."

"Are you telling me . . . !" Jack exploded out of his chair, his insides quaking with so many emotions, he couldn't separate a single one. "Where did you have that spaghetti feed, Cassie?"

She shook her head like he had asked the dumbest of questions. "At my new Mom and Pop's house, of course . . . and Mom let me eat all the blueberries I wanted."

Jack felt total shock descend on him.

"And everybody wanted to kiss me. I swear my cheeks had diaper rash when I walked out that door. Then those Italian men . . . they had lips all over me, especially that Steve or Jimmy. But they tasted so much like *your* lips, Jacko, that I let them kiss me all they wanted. My quintuplets of Jackos, that's what I called them. And they told me 'Ah, just forget about the bambino, he has nothing on us'."

"Oh Cassie . . ." Tears slowly ran down his cheeks. "Whatever possessed you, honey?"

"I missed you, Jack, and those witches at the studio wouldn't let me talk to you. So I decided to find that cozy house with lots of love. It made me feel closer to you."

"I can't believe it."

"Mom was crying in her spaghetti whenever I talked about you, and *those girls* . . . they were full of 'Jacko' stories. Then all those little kids . . . I thought I was in a grade school. But those men . . . *animales* every single one."

"And . . . what about my Pop?" Jack managed to ask.

Cassie brandished a beautiful smile. "He sat with me on the porch swing, placed an arm around me, and told me that Jacko is a lucky man. And he told me to bring him around sometime. So I said I would."

Overwhelmed with emotions and a flood of tears, Jack began to walk out of the kitchen, needing time alone to grasp this miracle and only cognizant of one thing—more than ever, he loved the woman who had created such a miracle, innocently or not.

"I'll save you some salad, darling. The ranch dressing is yummy . . ."

****

It took Jack four full days to come to terms with what Cassie had done, and while she wrote, he did much soul-searching. Where would he find the courage to walk through that door? He wondered, even though she had smoothed the path for him. After all he'd done to them, he found it incredulous that he was forgiven so easily. The revelation made shame consume him, and he didn't know how he could ever raise his eyes to a single one of them.

Playing interference with his thoughts was Cassie. It was "Mom this" and "Pop that" like she had readily adopted his parents. It was gratifying and bizarre at the same time. Then add to this his brothers and sisters, all of whom thrilled her, and he couldn't help asking *why*. Sure she was innocently demonstrative, he reasoned. Yet, she let so few people into her world and too suddenly glop onto so many at one time was *very* curious.

In the worst way, he wanted to probe further, but he didn't dare. Despite her seemingly constant happiness, her fragility had increased. More and more she was sinking into her own world and out of the realm of reality, and many times he would shake with terror at the thought that he was losing her. *It was something.* But he couldn't seem to find that missing piece.

Starburst Publishing frequently called, badgering her to fly to New York so she could promote 'Harry Two'. Jack wouldn't hear of it, and had personally told *whoever*, that Cassie wasn't leaving L.A., point blank, no debate. It made no sense anyway. Harry Two had rapid-fire sales and needed no promotion. He refused to have anything upset her apple-cart, especially for the sole reason of sucking a few more bucks out of her. That was over.

No way, could Cassie handle New York anymore.

For this reason, he couldn't wait until *Season of Sorrow* was completed. It would mean the end of her association with all of them, as she had expounded to him many times. She wanted peace, she said. And after the book was completed, she told him that her peace would be made on both spectrums of the scale. *Whatever that meant.*

"Darling . . ."

He looked up from his script and saw Cassie drag her feet towards the couch. "Are you done for the night, honey?"

"I'm so tired, I can hardly keep my eyes awake." She flopped down on the couch and wriggled into his arms. "You feel so good, Jack. I could make a bed out of you."

Sadly, he looked down at her. She had so little energy lately, he thought. "Maybe we both should call it a night, huh?"

She buried her cheek into chest hairs and rubbed. "I feel happy like this."

Tears of desperation misted his eyes while his finger tangled through her hair. "Then that's where I insist you stay," he replied gently.

"Tell me the story about the turtle picture again, Jack. I love the sound of your voice when you talk about it."

Without hesitation, he spoke low while describing, in great detail, the island of Cayman Brac, the ridley turtle, and the fifty-year-old artist who had greatly changed his life.

"Were you in love with her, Jack?" Cassie questioned.

He paused to think about this. His feelings for Mattie had always seemed so complicated, he had never really taken the time to sort them out and merely accepted the fact that they were there. "I guess I loved her like a friend. At that time in my life, I very much needed a friend, and Mattie was a friend in the truest sense. "

She smiled up at him. "Then I love her as a friend too."

Jack lifted her up and pressed her face into his, longing for the soft feel of her skin. "Mattie would love you," he murmured, wanting to devour her beautiful sweetness. "I love and need you so much, Cassie. Please don't ever forget that."

"How could I ever forget my Jacko," she murmured back? "Tell me more about the turtles. I can tell that you loved them too."

He smiled down at her. "Do you notice the big fins on the turtle, like fish fins?" he asked. Cassie gave an eager nod.

"Well . . . they have those fins so they can migrate hundreds of miles . . ." And he kept talking, using the same spiel he had once used on the paying tourists who visited the farm. When he concluded, he gazed down and saw Cassie softly snoring on his chest, her blonde hair tousled around the heart-shaped face.

Instinctively, Jack raised his fingers to brush the hair away, but he stopped the impulse. Instead, he stared just down at her, letting his love of her flood through him until he felt a torrent of emotions build.

What is it, honey? I wish you would tell me, or I could discover the truth. I wanna help you fight the hurt. I yearn so much for you to realize that. I'm not one of them, honey. I could never be one of them. Can't you see that?

With the sudden sense that time was running out, Jack had overwhelming desire to be as close to her as he could. He hoisted Cassie up into his arms and headed for the bedroom. He would carefully undress her then hold her close to him, so maybe, *just maybe,* the intensity of his love of would somehow penetrate her tortured world.

As he moved with her, he felt one consolation. She must be eating well, he thought. Her lanky bulk seemed a slight bit heavier. Perhaps, she did have a few bright moments when he wasn't around to watch her. At least, he could hope this was the case.

****

Over the next two weeks, production wound down on *The Life and Times of Harry Hannigan.* Jack had to leave for a grueling three day jaunt in the snow-capped mountains of Utah, which were used to simulate several outdoor Minnesota scenes that couldn't be filmed on the lot. Worried about leaving Cassie for so long, he begged her to come with him. However, she refused, insisting that she was going to meet John LaLiberte's four month deadline and couldn't lose a day of writing. So he ended up having the housekeeper live-in until he returned, paying her handsomely to make sure that Cassie was well-taken care of.

"She had a touch of the flu when you were gone," the housekeeper informed when he returned home. "I made her rest and drink plenty of fluids, and she's better today."

"And she didn't put up a stink about resting?" he asked, startled.

"No Mr. Torelli. She was too weak and tired to make a fuss."

He immediately rushed to the bedroom. Cassie was spread out on the bed whimpering into a stack of three pillows. "Are you worse, Honey?" He nearly flew onto the bed and landed to the side of her, lifting her face to check her condition himself.

"Jacko, where were you? I missed you," she sobbed into his shoulder.

"I was in Utah--you knew that. I told you several times, Cassie," he said helplessly, hating the fact that she was crying. He hadn't seen her cry for weeks.

"I thought you were with someone else, a big-busted sexy-looking girl. I had nightmares."

"Oh Cassie . . ." He felt more helpless, without a speck of defense after the life he had led. And the fact that such fears still plagued her mind, filled him with intense pain. "I would never, honey—I couldn't. The thought sickens me. I love you so much—how could I ever? You gotta believe that and put those nasty nightmares to rest."

"Could we lie in the warm bathtub? I wanna love you in the bathtub, Jacko"

Desperate to dispute her fear, he repeatedly made love to her in the bathtub and then in bed. It was gloriously reminiscent of their two-day love-a-thon at the Regent Hotel.

And after, he had heard no more comments about big-busted, sexy-looking girls.

****

Three days after returning from Utah, Jack came home from the studio and was surprised to find Cassie in the kitchen, looking like a chipper hostess and cooking dinner. She wore a white dishtowel around her waist and told him to pretend it was chiffon and covered in ruffles.

Unable to hide his great amusement he told her that his vision was blurred with "ruffles," and then he dramatically sniffed the air. "What are you cooking, Cass?"

"Tuna casserole, your favorite," she said brightly.

He turned his face, trying to convince himself he had to eat the "gunk" one more time. And briefly, he had a strong craving for fresh pasta from Hugho's in West Hollywood. "Sounds great, Cass." He turned back to her, smiling.

"Perhaps we should invite Harv over for supper. He's such a witty, if not a bit crude, little guy. I made extra—with him in mind, of course," she said with much delight.

"I don't think so, Cass," he laughed, entertained by the way Cassie saw his agent. "This, for certain, isn't Harv's thing. Maybe if you serve the meal in your ruffled chiffon apron, *only*, or spoon-fed Harv the casserole in the pool, then he may come."

"Ugh," she shuddered. "I don't think cream of mushroom soup and chlorine would mix too well. So . . ." She flounced like a blithe fairy. "I guess Harv misses out on a gourmet meal."

Just the sight of her filled Jack with intense love and he moved up to the stove. In a split second, he grabbed her and kissed wildly, his tongue playing havoc inside her mouth.

She giggled while pushing his away from her. "None of that, Jacko. You have to eat first."

He groaned inwardly, having hoped he could preoccupy her so that he didn't have to eat.

"Now take your shower and when you come back bare chested, barefooted, and wearing a pair of shorts, if you must, I'll have dinner on the table."

Upon returning to the kitchen after his shower, dressed in a pair of athletic shorts, he stopped dead in his tracks. Cassie languished against the kitchen counter in nothing but her white dishtowel. He wanted to tackle her to the floor.

"Dinner's ready, Jack." She eased her lips into a seductive smile.

A gulp hit the back of his throat. Now he'd never make it through dinner, he agitated silently. Nevertheless, he forced himself to sit in front of the plateful of casserole, and he stared at it while trying to gather his nerves. Suddenly, she leapt on his lap and he started to attack her with his lips when he felt a mushy noodle thrust between his teeth.

"Open wide, Jacko," she breathed out loftily, and soon he saw her willowy fingers slide another noodle into his mouth. "Now isn't this better than the pool?"

"I love this shit. Gimme more." He opened his mouth like a baby bird. By the time his plate was clean, he felt like his body was a furnace and his groin was straining against the shorts. "Why the hell did 'I must' wear these," he groaned, afraid he would burst where he sat. Jack boosted her in his arms, ruffled apron and all and scooted her to the bedroom, panting into her ear that he wanted tuna casserole tomorrow night too . . .

****

"Now for dessert," Cassie said with a merry giggle as she dove under the covers, laid her head on Jack's thigh and took him into her mouth while her sleek fingers stroked him with tender motions. Groaning stiffly, he drove his tongue into her most intimate spot, and mouthed her until he tasted her orgasm. She twisted around until her face was over his and their tastes and scents blended as they rolled around in each others' arms, kissing madly.

A ringing phone brought their motions to a slow halt.

"Let it ring, Cass," Jack moaned, then thrust his lips over hers.

She gently shoved his face from hers. "But it might be Harv, reconsidering on dinner."

With a louder moan, Jack let her go and stretched an arm out to the phone.

"Hullo," he barely said, then he heard a long pause. He repeated a louder "Hullo."

"May I please speak to Cassie Callahan," a stiff formal male voice said?

Suspicious that the caller was *whoever* from New York, Jack thrust the phone at her with the warning, "You tell them 'no way'. Cass."

She placed the phone to her and spoke with emphasis. "No way." And then her face paled. "What do you want?"

Jack moved closer to her, fearful it was the 'orchid guy' from New York. He was just about to snatch the phone from her when she let out with a blood curdling scream that rocked the walls of the bedroom, and phone flew across the bed.

Stunned, Jack didn't know whether to comfort her or grab the phone, so with one hand he tried to restrain her while with the other he made a grab for the phone. "Who the hell is this?" he demanded loudly, and another pause ensued.

"Art Scarpelli, Cassie's father," he said with a choke of indignation. "I called, Mr. Torelli, to inform Cassie that her grandfather has suffered a fatal heart attack . . ."

****

"Honey, please let me go with you. I don't give a shit what Mike says," Jack pleaded while watching a sobbing Cassie haphazardly toss clothes into a suitcase.

"No, Jack—I just can't. They'll eat you alive."

"Who's gonna eat me alive? And even if they do, I don't care," he tried to persuade, terrified about her traveling alone in her much deteriorated state of mind. He knew how much her grandfather meant to her. It was always "Nono" whenever she happened to talk about her past life, and he feared his death would push her over the cliff. "Cassie, Honey . . ." He made frantic motions to pull her close to him. "You're in no shape to go by yourself. You need me with you."

"I can't do that to you, Jacko. I love you too much to place you in their clutches."

"What exactly does that mean, huh? No one can do anything to me, Cass. That's a lame excuse. I insist on going to Minneapolis with you."

"No!" she suddenly screamed and flailed back and forth in his arms.

Dumbstruck, Jack released her and watched her hysterical gyrations. *What is it, Cassie?* What was it about home that always made her relative calm go sour? He feverishly wondered.

"Just be 'Harry', Jack. That's the best way you can console me," she quavered out to the point her teeth clattered.

"What's frightening you, tell me, honey?" He pressed closer to her. "I won't be able to *be* anything with you in such a state. I won't even be able to function, dammit. You gotta trust me. I'll . . . understand and accept anything you tell me. Please Cassie . . ."

Her face scrunched tightly, Cassie stared at him, looking like she wanted to say something. But ultimately, she turned back to her suitcase and began tossing again. "Nothing is frightening me, Jack. I just miss my Nono." And she collapsed into fresh tears. "He always took care of me, even when I was little, did I tell you that, Jack?"

"Yeah Honey—you told me." Jack slumped with resignation, wondering if she would ever open up to him or just let him float in a cloud of disjointed ignorance forever.

"When I was little he would sit me on his strong lap and sing Italian lullabies . . ."

"You told me, Honey."

"And he used to tell me stories about Roman leprechauns and life in the Italian countryside when he was a boy."

"I heard that too . . ."

"He used to weave beautiful, colorful worlds for little Sandy . . ."

Sandy? Jack deeply grooved his brow. "Who's Sandy?" he asked closely.

"Sandy?" Her tossing grew more frenzied. "Did I say Sandy?"

"Yeah, like Sandy your book character." He moved behind her and solidly placed his hands on her shaking shoulders. "What's going on, Cass? Please tell me."

She choked nervously. "I'm so upset that I must be saying things that I don't mean. I meant little Cassie . . . *Cassie.*" *The hell you did.* Jack wanted to yell at her, but instead he stroked her hair. "Finish your packing, Cass. We have to leave soon to catch that flight . . ."

****

Jack watched the jet until it was a lighted dot in the night sky. A sudden shudder made him press his eyelids together. Already he was horribly concerned about her and figured by the time Cassie got back, she would have to peel him off the walls.

"Mr. Torelli, we're ready to go."

Slowly turning, he opened his eyes to see several airport security personnel. They had been a necessary accompaniment ever since he and Cassie arrived at LAX. Somehow, and he never knew how, the press got wind that they had emerged as a couple and the response had been like a nightmare. Cassie grew hysterical upon sight of all the confronting faces yelling questions, and he had alternated between trying to shield her from view and shouting at the press to leave them alone. Now the mob was still lurking off to the side, held back by airport employees and he could hear a constant stream of "Jack" being yelled, followed by the most asinine queries he had ever heard. He wished he could throw a bomb right in the middle of them.

"I'm more that ready, to get the hell out of here." Jack sneered at the maniacal group before charging in front o the security people and taking long strides out of the terminal . . .

****

Suffering from insomnia, Jack slowly paced up the bedroom carpeting. He could still taste her lips when she had kissed him before boarding the plane, and his fingertips burned with the feel of her velvety skin. But would he even have those things when she returned? He wondered over and over. Or would she be crushed by some unnamed force that sent her into spasms of terror?

What? What? Sandy . . . Sandy . . . Sandy . . .

The name poked his brain like a pick.

What? Sandy . . . What?

Jack suddenly stopped cold and just stared into space. Could it be possible? He weighed the ethical pros and cons, finally deciding he couldn't question this when his Cassie was in trouble.

Allowing himself no further vacillation, he hurried to the back bedroom and his dark eyes zeroed in on the computer. Pushing back a loose strand of hair, he tried to orientate himself to the screen. He found the *on* switch and a menu appeared at the top. Where next? Darting his eyes around he found the computer mouse. This he had watched her use a couple times. Clumsily, he moved the mouse around until it was on *file*. His finger gave a click and a listing

Seeking Out Harry

appeared. Carefully, he scanned each title, finding several for *Season of Sorrow* numbered one through twenty. He clicked on the first file and Chapter One popped up on the screen.

He read the first sentence which was placed in italics.

"The iceberg has frozen us into two . . ."

Highly confused, yet intrigued, he kept reading, cursing down with the mouse and trying to make sense of the fragmented writing with enough symbolism to sound Greek. By the time he finished Chapter Three, Jack had no idea where the story was leading. 'Sandy' wasn't even real, rather a stiff caricature of stilted behavior and unexpressed emotions.

"This isn't her writing," he muttered to himself repeatedly. It was the writing of some stranger, not Cassie Callahan. He knew her style by rote, and this wasn't it.

However, he kept reading, Chapter Four, Five, Six . . . until he got to Seven and then he widened his eyes with each word he read. The story had stopped, replaced by scenes written in primarily dialogue with sentences more fragmented than ever.

"Sandy always stood like a predator outside the brick wall, waiting for the bricks to slip so she could sneak in. Therefore, the mortar *had* to be of the finest quality."

He paused to let the confusion soak him, then he read on.

"Cheap mortar! Cheap mortar! Ha-Ha, Cassie!"

Now, he thought he was really confused.

"No Sandy! I'm making the wall impermeable. *He'll* stop you! A male to beat all males who'll 'never cry uncle' to you!"

Jack slowly lifted his eyes from the screen. "Harry . . . her unbeatable male," he mumbled. "To fight what?" Feeling on the fringe of something, he feverishly read on.

"Hardy-har-har, Cassie. There's no more attic to make him strong. I'll beat him, I will. Uncle—Uncle—Uncle——"

"My back bedroom is my new attic, SANDY! You'll never beat him now!"

"You can't stay there forever, CASSIE ! *I'll* get you to New York again."

"No! My teddy bear says I'm not to go to New York. And I won't!"

"If MOTHER says YOU WILL, you will, Cassie."

"NO UNCLE!"

"YES UNCLE!"

"NO UNCLE"

"Yes Uncle."

"NO! I win."

"But not next time, Cassie . . ."

After reading the bizarre dialogue one more time, Jack sat back in the chair and contemplated while dread washed over him. "Who the hell she talking to?" he mused out loud, and then immediately answered. "Sandy. But who is Sandy, really? A friend? No, obviously an enemy. Someone, that she created 'Harry' to fight. But why? What did this 'Sandy' do to her?" Jarring forward, he locked his eyes onto the screen and continued reading.

"Mother will never get me back to New York, SANDY! Mother fucked up on the office couch and now his 'I WILL' sounds like 'I will'."

"What?" Jack breathed out, and he read the line repeatedly until he felt his nausea rise. "I'll kill him . . . I'LL KILL HIM!" He flung out of the chair and began

317

to pace, feeling more like a madman with each step. "Who is it?" he panted while his body shook with wild rage. Now, he knew why she had been so upset in New York and desperately needed him. And he wanted to strangle, choke . . .

Who is it? His mind's voice roared through his ears.

That orchid guy? Did he finally find his guts?

He tried to allow reason to soak through the intense anger. He had no idea, he finally decided. He knew very little about *whoever. Keep reading.* Jack forced himself back to the chair, curious and terrified at the same time. What the hell had they done to her? He didn't know if he could bear finding out.

"But I got the baby, CASSIE!"

The chapter abruptly ended and Jack scrambled for the mouse, carefully saved the file, then quickly clicked on Chapter Eight.

The baby was pink, squishy with softness, and possessed a shock of dark blonde hair on the top of her head. Cassie loved to snuggle her up to her neck. She smelled so delicious with baby smells, powder, spit-up, and was so utterly helpless and innocent. *She* belonged to Cassie, a blank piece of paper that CASSIE could fill to her heart's content.

". . .And Cassie did, bringing the precious little bundle up to the attic, keeping her warm from the ice-covered window by wrapping her, with much love and concern, in the beautiful yellow and white crocheted blanket that her Nona had made. There, she would speak out loud while she wrote and in between feel the tiny lips against her breasts. It was one of the most lovely times of her life, despite the big, hulking spoiler who lurked in the house below. But he wasn't allowed in their world. She had placed a Do Not Disturb sign on the outside of the brick wall and he heeded, fussing only a wee bit."

"SHAME ON YOU, CASSIE! HE was your husband, AND YOU an Italian girl who knew better. SHAME—SHAME!"

"He made me sick! Our minds were as far apart as Minneapolis and Afghanistan. He trapped me! He purposely put a hole in that condom, to hold Cassie forever! HE WAS VILE!"

"But Mother said, Cassie. MOTHER said YOU WILL marry him, Italian girl. YOU WILL marry him for the enamored friends so they never know HER disgrace. Sit pretty, Cassie in your white, lacy wedding dress and SMILE at all the guests."

"Oh god . . . I'm only nineteen, my whole life, a wonderful mystery yet to be explored. My writing . . . NO UNCLE!"

"Even Nono says YES UNCLE. What do you think about that, HUH CASSIE?"

"I don't love him, Nono, he'll NEVER be allowed in, Nono. So why . . . "

"For the bambino you silly girl. Nono is a mighty 'bambino-lover'. And MOTHER will tolerate for the enamored friends. So there's NO UNCLE to this CASSIE. Ha—Ha."

Feeling a weighty understanding, Jack paused in his reading. It was her mother, he told himself with total certainty. He could just feel Cassie's hostility. This, was the person that Cassie needed to fight, say 'uncle' to, and in the case of 'Harry', say a strong 'uncle'. An indefinite uncle? Maybe the uncle that she had sought all her life, but couldn't bring it forth herself. So she created one. Why? Maybe her desperation was growing? Her life was peaking with misery? The frantic need for escape, before . . .

Before what?

And Jack anxiously kept reading.

"Ho-Ho-Ho. The baby escaped from the brick wall as soon as she could walk, Cassie. She felt stifled, restless with a child's wonder, and HE WANTED HER TOO!"

"No! THEY lured her away with candy, cookies, and things that tantalized a baby. THEY wrote on her piece of paper and scribbled out MY writings. THEY ruined it . . . SANDY!"

"She hates you, CASSIE! She hates you for that attic!"

"Nooooo! THEY made her hate that attic. THEM . . . !"

He read on, Chapter Eight through Eleven, all detailing the destruction of Cassie's relationship which her daughter, which he had figured out wasn't as rosy as she painted. She hadn't received any letters from Chicago in all the weeks she had lived with him. He knew that something was wrong. But this? It sounded so devastating when told from Cassie's perspective.

She had tried with all her fragile strength to lure that baby back into the attic. But with all the outside forces playing against her, especially Mother, she could never do it. If she wanted her daughter back, she would be forced to live in their world. And from the sounds of it, Cassie didn't have a stable enough psyche to be able to do that.

Jack felt a stinging moistness in his eyes.

It was horribly sad.

Tousling the mouse in his hand, he saved the file and moved on the Chapter Twelve, while feeling the pressure of responsibility bear down on him. He had never in a million years dreamed just how brittle Cassie Callahan truly was.

"THAT MAN on the bench said YOU WILL go to the penetrator of brick walls if you want that baby back. OR ELSE she stays with MOTHER!"

"No! I couldn't go. He's evil! A devil who wants me for his laboratory rat, so he could tell the whole world, INCLUDING MOTHER!"

"But his Honor says, and YOU MUST DO! Mother says. Father says. AND EVEN Nono says. 'EVEN' . . . CASSIE!"

"I can't Nono. I NEED to be 'Cassie', now more than ever. I feel the *verge*. The book is good Nono. It is! If the devil gets his hands on me now . . ."

"Your MAN would be a ninety-pound-weakling and MOTHER could blow him over with a puff of her frosty breath, and THEN your brick wall would follow like the last of the 'Three Little Pigs'. Ai-yi-yi! You'll be captured to hell, CASSIE."

"No Uncle!"

"You're getting weaker, Cassie. I can hear . . ."

"Stay out of New York—Stay out of New York—"

"New York—New York, it's a helluva town . . ."

"Hold on tight to your teddy bear. NO New York!"

"Glorious Manhattan, a sensory paradise . . . your kind of place, Cassie."

"No, a crumbler of bricks except for Mom and Pop. They provide some mortar."

Jack collapsed back in his chair and carefully fingered the tears out of his eyes. She had lost custody of Kristi . . . that much blared clearly. But why? That he couldn't discern. Who was this devil? Someone in her mind, or someone real? It was a missing puzzle piece at the moment, but one that he could just sense was vitally important.

And then his parents . . . he finally understood the immediate attraction. He supposed that it was Cassie comparing his mom to Mother and his Pop to Father, who curiously was never mentioned. Then he recalled the conversation that they had at the restaurant on Bleeker Street. She had called her sister a clone. *Of mother?* Cassie had intimated that she hated her sister, and conversely had taken to his brothers and sisters without hesitation. It all must be connected somehow, he desperately told himself.

But how?
And who the hell was Sandy?
So he read on . . .

" SEE—I did it, Sandy. I'm on the ferris wheel. AND NOW, mother can never touch me. YOU lost Sandy!"

"THAT MAN will never stay strong, CASSIE. I'll sneak the bricks out, you'll see."

"No, YOU WON'T. I'll make him stronger, and stronger. I WILL, SANDY and my mortar will be as tough as irreversible glue. YOU won't even loosen a brick."

"But the pervert can, CASSIE. He'll break the bricks with his hisssss . . ."
"Shut up, Sandy!"
"Ha-Ha-Ha—the bricks are falling. I can see them. HISSSSSSS . . . !"
"NOOOOO!!!!!!!!"

"He betrayed you with his HISSSSS . . . He took pictures of you. He'll tell, he will."

"He wouldn't dare, Sandy. HE WOULDN'T DARE!"

"Yes he would, CASSIE. He'll find a way to put it in Times Square with a black orchid and note that says Pleeeeease Casseeeee! He'll tell MOTHER on you."

"Mother can't do anything. He hung over that couch with those fire-breathing eyes. He can't tear away another brick. And if he tries . . . I SET FLAMES TO 'THAT' COUCH!"

"Cassie won't do that, would she? After all IT IS mother."
"I WILL!"
"You won't."
"Yes . . . I will, Sandy."
"No, YOU WON'T!"

Oh god . . . Jack flung his face into his hands. Rape? Blackmail? Coercion? Stalking? What else, dear God? She's an innocent little girl for Christ's sakes! And who the hell was 'Sandy'? He kept asking himself. She sounded like the worst of the bunch. Can I go on? His insides shook with overwhelming fear at what he may learn next. *You have to Torelli. For her, you gotta go on.*

Shivering from wrist to fingertips, he picked up the mouse and went to the next chapter.

"And then I saw him . . . rolling on the ground with a gun in his hand while those dark, piercing eyes nearly punctured the screen. IT WAS HIM! MY STRENGTH!"

"I looked for him all over New York, at every BORING party and MUNDANE book signing. I moved my eyes across every face, hoping to find him. But I didn't. I didn't until The Great While Shark told me, and then I DID!"

"But the shark scared me, took a big chomp out of my strength. "He's a frightening creature, Cassie. He lives in a dark, dark, DARK world like a slithering snake that attacks little girls willy-nilly. HE'LL DEVOUR YOU, CASSIE!"

"But is he REALLY that dark, Mr. Hollywood Shark?"

"Well . . ." And I found out he had stretched the truth a bit.

"So I weighed back and forth in my head, until I said to Cassie that you'll just have to make your mortar tougher in his presence. IT HAD TO BE HIM!"

"But the moment I saw him, the mortar crumbled like dust. THOSE EYES . . . they didn't lie. He was dark, MY FOOT!"

"He IS dark, Cassie . . . MOTHER says . . . BEWARE!"

"No Sandy, he's my teddy bear. He is!"

"He'll feed you drugs then defile your body over and over like a debasing maniac until the bricks are scattered all around you and then EVEN I won't want to touch you, CASSIE!"

"Nooooo! He loves me—he loves me—"

"HE LOVES SEX!"

"No Cassie!" Jack leapt up from the chair. He flung himself into an empty wall and sobbed into it. *What else can I do to prove it to you?* His mind cried out over and over until it was numb. Would she condemn him forever? Would she condemn him even more than he condemned himself. *I thought she loved me . . .*

And his body racked with ragged sobs.

Jack sobbed at the wall for, he didn't know how long, but when the tears were dried up, all he felt was apathy and hopelessness. *What the hell . . .*

Swathed in insensibility, he dragged back to the computer. But as he continued to read, Chapter Thirteen, Fourteen, Fifteen, clear to Sixteen, he grew progressively relieved. Her words expressed her deepest emotions for him, and there was not one interruption by Sandy.

She does love me.

And this time he sobbed for sheer joy.

"My teddy bear owns my heart and soul. He's so wonderful, the perfect man for *Cassie*. He loves my world and participates lustily without a protest or admonition. HE LOVES 'CASSIE'!!!! I need my teddy so much. Nothing can ever pull out his stuffing. NOTHING!"

"Nothing will, Cass," he tearfully said to the screen. "I'll always be there for you, Baby. Jacko will love you 'til the day he dies."

Feeling the pounding intensity of his emotions, he read the rest, trying to make sense out of the sea of befuddlement created by the exchanges between Cassie and Sandy.

"DESERTER CASSIE . . . you're a clone of MOTHER!"

"No! I swore I wouldn't be. I took her into the attic with my papers and pencils. Nah-Nah mother I'm in the attic with my papers and pencils and BOOKS hundreds of them. NO UNCLE! I didn't desert the baby. NEVER!"

"You did as sure as JUNE. Ha-Ha-Ha. I said her name. YES UNCLE!"

"go away . . ."

"JUNE—JUNE—JUNE!"

"go away . . ."

"UNCLE JUNE—UNCLE SANDY!"

Shifting his eyebrows back and forth, he thought about the peculiar sentence he had just read. He peeked up and saw only traces of dusk remaining below the blue sky and remnants of a rising sun. Quickly, he turned back to the computer screen, knowing he couldn't go to the studio until he knew.

Then as he read the last paragraph of the last chapter, he froze with shock when it all came crashing down around him.

"...And Nono sang little Sandy a lullaby, then he sang it to Cassie/Sandy, but only Cassie was listening..."

Chapter 25—Cassie and Jack

Swaddled in monastic black from head to toe despite the high August humidity and her eyes hidden under large black sunglasses, Cassie walked out the back entrance of the Minneapolis *Sheraton*. Flanked by hotel security guards, she hurried to her awaiting limousine and quickly slid into the back seat. Soon thereafter, it pulled out of the hotel parking lot.

Cassie fastened her glasses at the mobs of reporters at the hotel's front entrance. They looked like predators ready to pounce, and the sight terrified her.

I want my teddy bear's arms.

Her mind kept screaming out this desire. Now she wished she had relented and let Jack come with her. She had to get back to L.A. She couldn't deal with any of this.

None of her family had called nor offered her a place in their limousine or cars to the funeral. She had never felt so alone and unprotected in the Twin Cities. And now she would have to feel this way in Anoka, the one place where she *couldn't* feel this way.

Oh Jack, why didn't I listen to you?

To make matters worse, she felt sick with the familiar churning in her stomach that had afflicted her several days ago and she didn't even have the housekeeper to take care of her.

There's no one to take care of me. Not even my Nono . . .

Tears ran down in streams beneath her sunglasses. She was *really* alone for the first time in her life. She was facing the hostile hoard without a bricklayer to rebuild when the mortar began to melt in the 'heat', she panicked. How would she ever survive?

My bricks . . . oh god, my bricks . . . I can feel them crumbling now.

What would they do to her? She agitated with near hysteria; although her fertile mind could vividly imagine, and she heard her 'uncle' coming out like a peep.

Oh the horror!

Maybe she should have the limo exit off the freeway and head back south, she suddenly thought, leaning forward to talk to the chauffeur. *But* . . . she slowly pulled back.

This was her Nono! The man who had supported her no matter his agreement. He *always* stood by her. She owed him at least a nip of courage to say goodbye.

"I'll save you, Cassie."

Go away, Sandy! You're the last thing I need.

"No the first thing. Remember June? You'll never last a minute."

"Yes I will, Sandy. I'll be as spiteful as I can be."

"Baloney! I can just see that spite seeping out of you. You'll be like a meek little mouse by the time you reach that church."

Stop it! Go back to your prim, accommodating world, Sandy. You never knew my Nono, and he never knew you. You have no business at that funeral.

"He was 'my' Nono for twelve years. I have as much right as you, Cassie. And I'm going. June would looove to see me."

"June will never see you. Never!"
"That's what you think. I'll just toss off the black and smile."
You'll do no such thing! Now leave me alone!
"Ha-Ha-Ha, Cassie. You'll see . . ."
"No," Cassie trembled as she felt the pop of the mortar from between the bricks. She had to kill her, once and for all. Sandy was gaining strength.
And If I ever have to go back to New York . . .
Her body quavered. She would never be Mother's girl. With everything, she had left inside her, *she wouldn't*.

The limousine came to a grinding halt, and Cassie's spun her sunglasses to the passenger window. She saw the familiar church that had held every Scarpelli family celebration since she was a young child. Expensive cars and a couple limousines lined the street. Then her sunglasses fell onto the morgue limousine and she felt the rise of her hysteria.

Oh Nono . . . This isn't really happening. Tell me it's a fanciful tale that you've woven or sing me a lullaby. I just can't lose my Nono.

When the passenger door opened, she startled to see the driver standing there in all his graciousness. She shivered a hand to smooth out her knee-length skirt and suit jacket, adjusted her black straw wide-brimmed hat and veil, then slipped her black strap high heels to the tar road, clutched her small black bag under her arm, and stood.

"Thank you, sir." She reached into her purse and extracted a fifty-dollar bill, then held it out with her black gloved hand. "Please wait. I'll need a ride to the cemetery as well," she requested flatly. Then she stiffened her stance while turning towards the church. Her body rumbled with terror, and it took all of her will to make her right shoe step forward . . .

****

Low, humming organ music greeted Cassie's ears when she entered the church narthex and a crowd of dark-suited people bearing solemn expressions stood at the entrance to the church interior. The whole place whiffed of death, she thought with high anxiety.

She hesitated in her approach, seeing long time friends and neighbors and people who held no familiarity. Her Nono was friendly and popular, she reminded herself, and he'd probably acquired a parcel of new friends after she left Anoka sixteen months ago.

So trying to be gracious, she walked up to the group and tossed sad smiles at those she knew. Her responses were stiff nods and straight mouths coated with hostility. Paranoia instantly struck. Why the looks when these people weren't even her family? She wondered. But she didn't ask, rather she swept past the large ogling group and walked into the church.

Immediately, she was stopped by the sight of the coffin, huge and bronzed, sitting at the front of the altar, wide-open with her immediate and expanded family surrounding it. Some wailed and others dotted their eyes with handkerchiefs and tissues. The sight numbed her. They looked like a pack of wolves ready to leap on her and chew away each brick the moment she approached, she jittered. Could she approach?

It's your Nono, Cass! You have to pay your final respects. You have to no matter how many bricks you should lose in the process.

With a shaky nod of acceptance to her inner voice, Cassie placed a heel on the shiny wood floor. Her shoes hollowly echoed over the wood as she moved forward. She tried to keep her covered eyes directed on the coffin, but saw the turn of several heads of family members, their gazes penetrating through her like molten lava.

Perpetual Black Sheep, their expressions said.

No matter what you do, what you've accomplished, you never merged properly so this is your lifelong designation. Accept it. Now!

"How are you, Cassandra?"

A rolling tremble went through her, as she turned to see the ice-blue glare of June Scarpelli directly fixed on her.

"I'm . . . well Mother," she managed to reciprocate.

"Come and see your Nono, Cassie. They're about to close the casket," Art Scarpelli directed like he was talking to a brief acquaintance.

Giving a nod, Cassie moved forward, only to spot a tall, slim Krisi standing between two of her uncles. She paused and stared at the hardened face bearing too much makeup and could just feel her daughter's intense resentment. The sight made her insides crumple like tissue paper and she could barely find the mobility to make it to the casket. There she saw her Nona, looking frailer than ever. She must be so lost, Cassie thought sadly, making a move towards the old woman. But she was rebuffed when the wrinkled face turned into her son's black suit coat.

Not you too, Nona, she wanted to scream, suddenly whelmed with the sensation that she, without any defense, had been coaxed into the middle of a wolf pack that would attack her mercilessly. Still, she mustered all her near nonexistent courage, moved up to the casket, and forced herself to look inside.

She saw the shiny black shoes sticking at the end of the immaculate gray suit, always her Nono's favorite, and then the pure white shirt with the silk maroon and gray tie that he would proudly wear. Convulsions bombarding every inch of her, Cassie slowly raised her eyes to the face. She cringed back in horror.

The face looked molded in gray clay, the mustache and hair brittle as if it had been made in a costume factory, and his once firm, decisive nose looked like putty that could be bent into any shape she chose. His eyelids were pressed closed as if someone had hot glued them together, and the lips looking like pale pink wax without a hint of the curved sensuality she remembered.

This wasn't her Nono!

Suddenly she let out with a rippling scream and tears flowed in sheets from her eyes. "It's not him! You liars! It's not him!" She lifted a fist and repeatedly pounded the rim of the casket.

"Cassie!" Her father rushed forward and tried to restrain her, but she turned her fists on him and pounded as hard a she could on his custom-made suit coat.

"You lackey! Why couldn't you have been like him? Why?" she screeched like a madwoman. "You're a joke! A joke of a father! I want my Nono!"

And then her uncles hurried forward to help their brother.

She felt what seemed like a hundred hands on her, and she flailed mightily to break their hold on her. "Your hands feel like slime to me!" she sobbed, wielding her fists in the air. "I want my Nono's hands."

"He's gone, Cassandra. Nono can't save you anymore!" June Scarpelli said sharply.

Seeing the cold, calculated face in front of her made Cassie sink with more terror than she had ever felt. "I want my teddy bear," she whimpered, and then the room began to twirl and she felt the back of her head touch the cold bronze of the casket.

****

Drenched with immense worry, Jack Torelli was at a barely functioning level by the time the last scene of the day had been cut and printed. How he made it through this day, he had no clue. He must have been on autopilot, he figured, because the only picture in his mind was the face bearing the biggest green eyes he had ever seen.

"Torelli, I want to remind you that we finish shooting for two days in Minneapolis, at the end of next week." Michael Isle looked like an angry windbag as he moved in Jack's direction.

"Yeah—I got it," Jack replied absently, only wanting to go home in case Cassie called.

"Oh Torelli . . ." Michael placed a restraining hand in front of him.

Feeling the rise of his impatience, Jack halted his step.

"If you should happen to hear from Cassie, please offer her my condolences. I heard the sorrowful news on an L.A. radio station this morning. I hope she's faring well . . . ?"

"What do you think?" Jack muttered, not trusting any question Michael Isle asked about Cassie, no matter how innocent. He was one of them! And now, more than ever, that fact made him seethe with fury.

"When do you expect her return, Torelli . . . if I may ask?"

"None of your damn business, Mike." Jack batted the carefully manicured hand away from him and began walking to the sound stage entrance.

"It's not out of nosiness, Torelli." Michael quickly followed and fell in step with him. "The writers need her input on a few scenes that are to be shot in Minnesota."

Jack braked and turned with a clenched jaw. "Cassie can't come to the studio. That mob you allow to run loose at the gate will crush her, and I won't allow it. Capisce?"

Michael spoke with a nervous undertone. "She doesn't have to come here. The writers can call her at your house. So . . . when is she returning?"

Detecting the urgency in 'Mr. Cool's voice, Jack wondered if he should answer. Maybe *there were* crucial scenes needing Cassie's input. Now that he knew *exactly* how much 'Harry' meant to her, he decided to be cooperative, this once. "Tomorrow evening," he replied, then resumed moving to the entrance. But he stopped again when seeing one of the security guards making frantic waving motions at him.

"Mr. Torelli!" The guard held up a cellular phone.

Knowing only one person would call him at the studio, Jack broke out in a run and snatched the phone out of the man's hand. "Cassie?" he asked in desperate tones.

"No, Mr. Torelli. This is a Doctor Sandstrom from Anoka-Ramsey Medical Center in the Twin Cities. I called to let you know that Ms. Cassie Callahan has had a small accident, and she's asked us to contact you. She says to tell you that she needs you here."

"What accident?" Jack shouted.

"A slight head injury at her grandfather's funeral, but she's in quite a high emotional state and she's begged me to call you."

Quickly, Jack pulled out a small notebook from his shirt pocket, then got a pen from the security guard. "What's the name of the hospital again, and you're. . ."

The doctor repeated the information.

Jack closed the notebook and pressed the phone close to his mouth. "Tell her that I'm on the next plane out, and . . . tell her I love her so to hold on . . ."

****

Cassie scrunched below the covers of her hospital bed, feeling the smarting throb in the back of her head. Everything had been so scary, she thought. They made a big hullabaloo in the Emergency Room when she was brought in and what seemed like a million people surrounded her from the moment she arrived. Then they had placed an oxygen mask on her face, stuck her with an intravenous needle, and drew tube after tube of blood. After being poked and prodded by Dr. Sandstrom who had been her physician since she was a little girl, they sent her to X-ray, followed by a special X-ray where they stuck her whole head under a massive hood where she felt like a turkey being microwaved. And to compound things, her family skulked outside her hospital door. Their antipathy percolated through the wooden rectangle like a putrid odor that burned her nostrils with fear of an imminent invasion.

I want my Jacko . . .

A fresh stream of tears rolled from her eyes and down her cheeks while she silently prayed that he would rescue her before every single solitary brick blew apart like a tornado-struck house.

A sudden soft knock at the door made her push farther under the covers until all that was visible was the quivering between the creases in her forehead. "Go away," she cried out.

"It's Dr. Sandstrom, Cassie," the gentle, familiar voice called out.

Cautiously she raised until her mouth hung above the white cotton mesh blanket. "Are you alone?" she shook out.

"Yes Cassie. I need to talk to you," he said in a soft yet serious tone.

"Okay—come in." She pulled up until she was propped up in bed. The door opened and a combination of English and Italian voices filtered through. Her body grew rigid. "Hurry—close the door," she pleaded.

The stately physician with thinning salt and pepper hair strode through the door and closed it firmly behind him. He moved up to the bed and looked down at her over thick bifocals which Cassie thought made his eyes look like oversized fish eyes.

"May I pull up a chair, Cassie?"

She cautiously bobbed her head.

Promptly he pulled a utility chair to the edge of her bed and sat, crossing one leg over his knee and wearily tipping back. "Your X-rays and CAT scan were clear and . . ."

"Is my Jacko coming?" she cut in.

With a weighty sigh, the physician nodded. "He's coming immediately, Cassie, but I don't know if that's such a good . . ."

"Oh thank god!" she breathed out, a slow calm descending on her. "You were saying Dr. Sandstrom . . . ?"

The physician gave a frustrated head shake. "For the most part, your blood tests were fine, including the drug screen. Your parents were quite worried that . . .

"Drugs? Why?"

"Cassie," he said sharply. "Your lifestyle *does* bring up a few questions."

"I don't take drugs," she heaved with indignation. "I've never in my life taken drugs. Why in the world would my parents ever assume such a thing?"

He ignored the question and continued on. "And you also cleared for hepatitis, venereal diseases, HIV and . . ."

"What?" she demanded. "Why did you check those things when I just bumped my head?"

"And your blood alcohol came back negative."

"Alcohol! I haven't had a drink except for a single glass of wine!"

"And except for being a little bit anemic, all your blood indices are normal."

"How *dare* you violate my arms with needles!" she flared angrily.

"And . . . you're pregnant," he concluded with a raise of his eyebrows. "I want to do an ultrasound immediately to determine how far along you are."

"Pregnant?" The word slammed into her head like a hammer driving a nail in one healthy pound. "I. . .can't be . . . or . . . , can I? Oh no!" She jolted when remembering Jack's words in New York. He never wanted to be a father, and now he would be furious at her. She couldn't have this baby. But . . . could she ever? The mere thought sickened her. And then she thought, *A new baby . . . a new piece of paper.*

"I also need to do a vaginal exam, of course, and as for Mr. Torelli . . ."

"No! No one is to know, my family included," she interjected with hysterical undertones.

"But Cassie, your parents and their concern about you."

"They should win an Oscar, Doctor," Cassie said bitterly. "Although I suppose you travel in their social circle, thus explains their Broadway production." She fastened a firm look on him. "But I demand you respect my right to privacy. Or . . . I'll sue you with every penny I've got . . . and that's a helluva lot of pennies. Capisce?"

****

After a quick vaginal exam, Cassie found herself in the ultrasound room with her belly exposed. She lowered her chin to look at her middle. Surprise! Had she been so preoccupied that she hadn't even noticed the small bulge where a flat stomach used to be? Now she understood the nature of her virus— she remembered the nausea well. Though the revelation caused no elation, rather severe apprehension.

What in the world would she do?

"This will feel cold, Cassie." Dr. Sandstrom squeezed blue jelly atop her belly.

Cassie watched the ripple of blue when he thrust a probe over the jelly and her anxiety. Heightened. Was there really a bambino in there? Jacko's bambino?

"Now look at the screen, Cassie. My guess is four months."

Four months? Cassie did a quick mental calculation and she widened her eyes. That would mean that it happened on that first weekend they were together. *Damn.* That's what Jacko gets for being such an *animale.*

"There he is . . ."

"He?" She looked at the picture and gave a gasp of wonderment. It *was* a bambino! And a *boy* bambino . . . *a little Jacko.* Prompt tears came to her eyes.

"Close to four months all right. The sex is obvious. He looks healthy so far, Cassie."

"Oh, my baby." She breathed out her awe. She had another chance, a new blank piece of paper. Suddenly, she felt thrilled! It *was* really a baby.

"I'd say that you're looking at a New Year's baby, Cassie."

By New Years she would be smelling the baby smells again, she thought joyously. And feel those tiny lips nipping her breasts, she added pleasurably. She couldn't wait!

"Next Cassie, we'll get you a picture . . ."

****

By eight the next morning, after directly hopping into a limousine parked on the airstrip so he could enter the Twin Cities unnoticed, Jack took long urgent strides down the fifth floor hallway at Anoka-Ramsey Medical Center. He was attired in an tan linen suit complete with cufflinks and tie and the perpetual black sunglasses covered his eyes. He slowed his gait upon approaching Cassie's room. Stationed in front were several people who suddenly stopped talking to stare at him. Their eyes glaringly appraised his person. Cautiously, he walked forward, not sure what the delegation meant.

"Mr. Torelli, I presume."A tall, graying man of stiff demeanor stepped in front of Jack.

"Yeah--I'm Torelli. Who are you?"

"Art Scarpelli . . . I believe that we . . ." He gave a raspy clear of his throat. "Spoke on the phone once."

"Cassie's father . . ." Jack immediately shoved his hand forward and saw the man's eyes fill with revulsion. Tightening up, Jack pulled his hand back. "If you don't mind, I'm a little anxious to see, Cassie, Mr. Scarpelli." Jack moved towards the room when suddenly he found himself surrounded by a group of gray-haired males. "What the hell's going on?" he demanded.

"Mr. Torelli . . ." A blonde woman with a regal demeanor and chilling blue eyes stepped in the middle of the group.

Jack studied her face, and his teeth clenched tighter. *Mother, sure shit.*

"Cassandra is too ill to see you."

"Cassandra?" Jack asked cautiously. "Who's that?"

"My daughter. Didn't she tell you that her real name was Cassandra?"

Cassandra . . . The name flowed through his head until the significance struck. *A combination of Cassie and Sandy.* He couldn't help the boring gaze he leveled at her. *And the witch seems to be the only one using that name.*

"Sure she did Mrs. Scarpelli. Just forgot," Jack replied at last, wanting to attack the cold witch for what she had done to the woman he loved.

"She's a very sick woman, Mr. Torelli," June continued on. "She's been sick for eons and should have seen a psychiatrist long ago, but the stubborn girl refused, a thorn in my side with her stubbornness, Mr. Torelli. You've most likely discovered that yourself."

"I've discovered no such thing, Mrs. Scarpelli." Jack stepped forward with his own stubbornness. "No shrinks. I won't allow it."

"*You* won't." June let out a tinkling laugh. "*You* have no say, Mr. Torelli, that's what I'm here to tell you. Cassandra is our daughter, our responsibility, and we plan to take it. Cassandra is too sick to handle her own affairs. She needs guidance from her mother and father, and you *will* leave her alone."

"The hell I will!" Jack roared right at her and June sucked in a gasp. "You *especially* aren't getting your hands on her--or her money, which I assume is the *gist* of your responsibility!"

"How dare you!"

Jack sauntered directly up to her. "Didn't you make her pay to see her daughter? A cool hundred grand if I remember correctly. I'm not sure, but from what I can figure, Cassie's handed an even cooler half a mil over to your business, even though the goddamn thing ruined her life!"

"The money is being invested, Mr. Torelli," Art Scarpelli interjected sharply.

"Oh really . . ." Jack turned to Art. "Then why hasn't Cassie gotten any financial statements from you, huh? Before I boarded the plane late last night, I went through her records and found not one statement from your company. Not one. Isn't that customary for an investment business, or is that just an L.A. thing?"

Art stepped back and tossed a nervous glance to his wife.

June fixed her icy blue look on Jack. "It's all in the family, Mr. Torelli, so why bother with statements? We're a close knit clan, you don't understand that."

"And I say liar." Jack sneered at her. "I know exactly what you did to Cassie, *Mother*. Your desertion screwed her up plenty and now you act like it's her fault when you're as guilty as hell. My Cassie can't even function in the real world because of you. But I don't give a shit. I love her, and I'll take her no matter what world she's living in!"

"Mr. Torelli! Are you implying that I wasn't a good mother?" June stiffened her stance and her lips quaked.

Jack blazed his eyes at her. "You shoulda never been a mother, you monster!"

June wove slightly and Art quickly moved to her side, steading her stance. "Leave, Mr. Torelli. You don't belong here. Cassie was a decent girl once," Art said in a voice that lacked authority or conviction.

"I'm not going anywhere without my Cassie." Jack twirled an amused smile on his lips. "And if you put up a stink, I go to press with the unfortunate story of Cassie Callahan's life in the Scarpelli family."

"You wouldn't dare," Art disputed like an unsure schoolboy.

"Furthermore, I'll self-publish Cassie's latest book *Season of Sorrow*, the vividly detailed account of life with Mother from the standpoint of a dueled personality woman who didn't get that way by being *stubborn*, Mrs. Scarpelli. Interesting reading. Should uphold my 'monster theory'. And I'll pass them out free-of-charge to every major newspaper in this country, including the one from the Twin Cities. That should impress your *enamored* friends."

"What do you want from my daughter, Mr. Torelli?" Art questioned with clear anxiety. "Money? Decency for yourself? A pad to your crummy image . . . ?"

Jack let out a low, cynical laugh. "No, Mr. Scarpelli. This may sound strange to you, but I only want 'Cassie' for herself. Capisce?"

****

Still burning with rage a couple hours later, Jack lay stretched out on the hospital bed with an arm tightly encircled around Cassie, beautifully content even though she was describing her horrendous experience at the funeral and the Anoka-Ramsey Emergency Room.

"Don't worry, honey. You'll never have to see them again, I promise you,"

Jack said gently, feeling a greater need for closeness after the heart-ripping information he had learned from her computer disks. But he wouldn't tell her, he decided, rather, he would carefully probe bit by tiny bit so as not to upset her. Understanding was enough at this point, he figured. It gave him an edge, a route for his next steps in life, surer feet with Cassie Callahan.

"I wanna go home, Jacko." She stroked the fabric of his suit coat. "I hate Anoka. And now with Nono gone--if that really was my Nono--I'm never coming back. They all hate me here, except for Dr. Sandstrom. He took *especially* good care of me."

He tenderly kissed the top of her head. "We're leaving at eight tonight, Cass. That's the earliest I could get plane reservations. But I won't leave you. No one will ever hurt you again."

She fastened her big green eyes up at him. "I hate asking." Her lips danced with a curvaceous smile. "But I'm craving an ice cream sundae, chocolate and strawberry toppings, tons of nuts, filled to the brim with whipped cream, and a plump cherry on top, of course . . . and a cheeseburger on the side with the works, a chocolate chip cookie with a packet of sugar to sprinkle over it, and milk naturally, maybe two milks so I can catch up. I think that's it, if memory serves me."

Jack stared blankly at her. "You're kidding," he dead panned.

"*Pleeese* . . . Jacko. I'll die if I don't have those things. Right my tongue is salivating for those greasy onions dripping out of that cheeseburger."

Utterly confusion, Jack nodded. "Is there a place around her to get those things?"

She nodded eagerly. "The hospital cafeteria. They have everything, even tuna casserole, if you're hungry too, Jacko."

"No thanks." He wrinkled his nose while he stood. "No one can make tuna casserole like you, Cass. I'm too spoiled to eat anybody else's tuna casserole . . ."

****

Feeling like an ass of a waitress, Jack carried a tray brimmed with Cassie's order. He looked left and right before exiting the elevator on Fifth Floor. Even him, who didn't give a shit, refused to have some sneaky reporter photograph him in such a state. The stares in the cafeteria were bad enough.

"Isn't that Jack Torelli? Torelli . . . Torelli . . . Torelli . . ."

He had heard the whisper of his name the whole length of the cafeteria that seemed to have no end. Now all he desired was a quick undetected scoot into Cassie's room and total obscurity until they reached the confines of the Beverly Hills house. So, he quickly paced his steps, his sunglasses focused forward. However, his gait suddenly slowed when he saw two young girls lingering by Cassie's door. As he moved closer, one of the girls grew familiar to him.

It's Kristi.

His heart thudded with anxiety. What the hell would he say to her? He had no inkling how to talk to any kids let alone a young teenager.

Yet, he could see no escape. Each was draped leisurely to the side of the door although making no attempt to go through it. What was going on? He curiously wondered. The scene looked highly bizarre to him.

He was composing a conversation in was his head when he saw Kristi's friend jerk her head up to spot him. She quickly slammed an arm into Kristi. Soon, the indignant stare of two pair of eyes fastened on him. Immediately, it was obvious that he held little esteem with Cassie's daughter. In fact Kristi's look chilled him more than *Mother*.

Had Cassie *really* hurt her that bad? He asked himself as he neared the pair. Or perhaps, *Mother* had exaggerated the whole affair, influencing Cassie's precious baby--although she didn't look precious now, just pissed.

"I know you." Kristi pushed herself from the wall and strolled up to Jack. "You're using my mother. I had a friend rent the video *Jungle Love*, and I know exactly what you're about. But of course, she's too up-in-the-clouds to see it." The words spoken by one so young-made helplessness engulf him. Although at the same time he wanted to dispute the sulky, defiant face in front of him. "You shouldn't be watching videos like that, kid. They take you away from better things that a kid like you should be doing, for instance soccer. I...hear you're quite a player."

In perturbed fashion, Kristi raised her eyes to the ceiling. "That's all my mother knows. I wouldn't be caught dead on a soccer field. I have more important things to do than kick around a stupid ball. I'm nearly fourteen, after all."

"Yeah, that's old kid," he muttered while getting a better hand grip on the tray. "Well . . . I gotta get this food to your mother. So are you coming in?"

"Not a chance, Tarzan," she snottily retorted. "I came to talk to you. And this is my friend Heather. She just wanted to eyeball you, so I brought her along."

Jack turned to the other girl who flashed a mouth full of hardware when she smiled. "Hi there, Heather," he mumbled, then shifted his face back to Kristi. "Just get it out, kid. I don't want the hot food ice cold or the ice-cold food warm."

Kristi gave a brash toss of her long light brown hair and Jack could have sworn that Haley Shears had just made that move. "You ruined my life, you know. Grandpa had to pull me out of my school in Chicago because the harassment was so bad. It's not easy having a mother whose shacking up with a hard porn star."

"I haven't been a porn star for a long time so the harassment was for nothing, kid." He replied decisively. "So if that's your only beef . . ." He began to move towards the door.

"She's crazy, you know. Everybody says that. But she won't get help, not even to get custody of her daughter. Did you know that?" Kristi retorted with unmasked hurt.

"No," Jack creased his brow at her with the sense that another puzzle piece was just about to fall into his lap. "Tell me what you mean, kid."

Without hesitation, Kristi bitingly told him the story of the judge and the psychiatrist.

"...She promised to rescue me without going to the shrink, but true to form, she never did. She didn't want a daughter, just her damn attic and computer."

Immediately, Jack repudiated her. "I know she loves you. And that should be the most important thing that you know, kid."

Kristi paused and for a brief moment her face screwed up with pain. "It doesn't matter," she said with strained flippancy. "I'm not allowed to see her anymore as long as she's with you. Grandpa took out a restraining order. Me and Heather snuck over here today for the hell of it."

Sadness gripped his insides. Clearly, Kristi was unsure. And Cassie—he never wanted her know about such parental cruelty. To intentionally separate mother and child . . . he didn't know what to feel.

"I can't see my father either. He and his slut moved to Montana anyway. So . . . instant orphan," Kristi said with so much bitterness, Jack could taste it. "Some pair of parents, huh?"

"You know when you're eighteen, kid, you don't have to listen to any restraining order," he said in the gentlest of tones. She was just a very scared kid, he decided. "You're always welcome in L.A., Kristi, and if you wanna keep in touch, we won't rip up any letters."

"Maybe." Kristi was noncommittal, but he could see a trace of longing in her eyes.

Life must be hell with *Mother*, he figured.

"Do you wanna come in and say goodbye?" Jack tipped a head at Cassie's hospital room door, then he smiled at her. "I won't tell *grandpapa* so don't worry. Your mother would love it. She misses you a lot."

Kristi twirled her head towards the closed door, then back at Jack, then back to the closed door, though ultimately she grabbed Heather's arm and started to drag her friend away. "No--I can't. You tell her for me," she choked out painfully. "I'll see you, Mr. Torelli." And he watched the two girls scurry down the hall looking side-to-side as they did.

"I'm Jack!" he called after her. "Don't forget that, Kristi . . . !"

****

Jack watched in awe while Cassie ate like she was starving. He had never seen her consume so much food in a single day, let alone at one sitting. Was she making up for lost time or did she have a secret penchant for the awful-looking hospital food? He pondered.

Cassie slowly swirled her spoon in the ice cream sundae then brought it up to his lips. "We could pretend this is tuna casserole," she said with a devious crook of her mouth.

With an equally devious smile, he took the ice cream into his mouth. "Not here, Cass, unless I triple padlock plus barricade the door with a ton of steel. The last thing I need in this town is a rumor circulating, believe me."

"In that case, we'll have to make super-duper sundaes at home," she enthused. Then her face grew thoughtful while she toyed with the ice cream. "I wish you could have known my Nono, Jack. I'm quite sure that eventually, you two would have gotten along."

"If you loved him, Cass, I woulda loved him too." He softly fingered her hair. "But he lived a full life, honey. Eighty-two years is quite a piece. I guess I could say that you should be thankful that you had him for that long."

"And now I have you." She said with a combination of desperation and pleading.

He studied her and immediately understood her fears. She needed a strong male in her life, one who would care for her without condition. That much he knew with certainty about Cassie Callahan. "You got me all right, Honey." He replied, touching her gooey lips with his own. Then on impulse, he grabbed her close to him. He could leave her no more easily than he could leave himself. She was irrevocably part of his heart and soul. To lose her would be the equivalent of every part of him disintegrating. He wouldn't be Jack Torelli . . . he would be nothing. "Just hold on tight, honey. Jacko's here for you no matter what . . ."

****

Anoka, Minnesota out of their minds, Jack and Cassie returned to life in the Beverly Hills house. Jack hadn't said a word about Kristi, nor about the restraining order. Cassie didn't need the added stress with her book, which would never be a book, he knew, though she treated it as such so he left it at that.

Now home from another rough, snub-ridden day at the studio, Jack stared at the closed back bedroom door. Hearing no tap of the computer, he moved closer, placing an ear to the solid oak. Perfect quiet greeted his hearing. Curious, he lifted his ear and stared down at the doorknob. Should he interrupt her, he wondered. Maybe she fell asleep. She had been unusually tired lately.

Or . . .

Jack suddenly panicked. Perhaps her writings had sparked something destructive. Without hesitation, he crashed his shoulder at the door, then kept crashing until he tripped into the middle of the room. While he righted himself, he stared straight ahead. Cassie sat with a dreamlike loveliness about her while she gazed at something in her hand.

"Oh hi, darling," Cassie greeted almost mystically, without raising her eyes.

Filled with sudden curiosity, Jack inched closer to her. "What do you got there, Cass?"

"The most wonderful picture in the world. I can't stop looking at it," she replied vaguely. "It's a very special person close to my heart. Mom and Pop will absolutely love this picture."

Now he was *really* curious. "Why would my parents love that picture?"

"They can see their future in this picture." She flashed a luminescent smile. "Mom will cry in her spaghetti, and Pop will take this picture on his porch swing and just stare."

"What?" He asked totally baffled. Per usual, his head was spinning in circles. "Just let me see the picture, Cass." He held out his hand but she pulled hers back.

"I don't know, Jacko," she said with a slow tone. "I'm worried that you won't view this picture in the same way as Mom and Pop."

He groaned. "Cm'on Cass. You got my gut jumping to see that picture."

"Well . . ." She paused to contemplate before giving a hesitant thrust of the picture.

He snatched the black and white photo and looked. His brow wrinkled more by the second at what looked like a fluff of white clouds to him.

"Isn't he beautiful, Jacko?"

"He?" Jack held the picture closer to his face until he thought he discerned a distinct outline. A rumble of trepidation shot through him. "Where did you get this picture, honey?" he could barely ask.

"It popped out of a machine at the hospital and Dr. Sandstrom said 'Happy New Years'!"

Now the trepidation made him shake. "Is this what I think it is, Cass?"

"It is . . ." Her face burst into a shining smile. "If you think that's your son."

"Jesus H. Christ." The picture drizzled from his finger to the floor. "Its gotta be a mistake. I mean, its just gotta. Tell me you're joshing with me, Cass."

Cassie's face screwed up with tears. "You *don't* think like Mom and Pop, do you?" she accused. Quickly, she skirted around the picture and ran crying out of the room, leaving a shocked Jack in a haze of emotions . . .

Seeking Out Harry

"Please let me in, Cassie. We gotta talk about this," Jack pleaded an hour later while pounding on the locked door of their bedroom where he could hear Cassie's loud wails through the door. The sound made him frantic. He couldn't remember ever hearing such a heart-wrenching sound come out of Cassie. "Cassie! Open this door now!" Jack yelled in a panic.

"You don't want my bambino!" she shrieked. "You don't love your *own* child! And I do!"

"That isn't it, Cassie! I'm . . . just shocked. I don't know what to think. I'm forty after all. I never expected this in my life. It's never been in my scheme of things. We gotta talk about that."

"What's there to talk about Jacko? It's coming on New Years no matter how much you talk. Take it or leave it!"

He smashed his fist into the oak. "What the hell does that mean?" he shouted at the top of his lungs. "I'm the father for Christ's sakes! Don't I have any say?"

"You're no father! You're . . . You're a good actor!"

"Actor?' He hollered. "You call this acting?"

"Yes!" She tearfully flung open the door. With a suitcase in hand, she marched past him, a petulant, but determined look on her face. "Me and the bambino are leaving for a new attic where we'll be safe from predators who don't really love us!"

All his terror came out in a roar. "The hell you are!" He frantically clasped her arm. "You gotta know I love you, Cassie."

"The heck you do, Jacko! Me and the bambino are one! How can you love one without the other?" She fastened an accusing glare on him.

He tightened his grasp, desperately wanting her to understand his position. "I'm forty, Cassie, set in my ways, and I never, if I may be blunt, wanted kids. I just don't know anything about kids, and if the truth being, I don't wanna start learning about them. I'm . . . just not cut out to be a father, you gotta see that."

With a mean look on her face, she jerked her arm out of his grasp. "Coward!" she spat in denouncement. "You'd kill your child to save what you consider a comfortable existence, and then what? I guarantee you Jacko *Torelli* will never be comfortable again, knowing his son is in heaven because he selfishly couldn't find the guts!" She broke into choking sobs while heading for the front door.

The words made him feel like a Mack truck had impacted him and found his mobility burdensome while he tried to go after her. "Don't leave me, Cassie. Maybe I just need some time. If you stay, I'll promise to think about it. How's that?"

"*That's* even worse! Find a way to sugarcoat your selfish cowardice and ultimately minimize what's *really* going on. I want no part of it. I have a child to protect, a blank piece of paper to fill someday, and I thought this time around would be so glorious because I'd have my Jacko, the only man I've ever truly loved, helping me fill up that sheet. It was supposed to be so different . . ." She broke down in fitful sobs which made her whole thin body quake.

The sight of her wretched sadness compounded with her words made Jack's own eyes cloud with wetness. "Please Cassie . . . give me a little time. Please . . ."

Her face painfully pleated. "If it's really love, and not merely something else masked under the name, acceptance should be automatic with no need to dwell. And perhaps as simplistically romantic as that may sound, it's the way I see things."

So utterly confused, Jack could hardly look at her. Only the sound of a car's horn penetrated his muddled mind. "Who's that?" He hurried to the door and pulled it open. Parked at the curb was a Python Studio limousine, and his insides twisted with fright. "What's that limo doing here, Cass?"

Lifting her suitcase, Cassie headed for the door. "I'm going back to the studio suites until I decide where to raise my little Jacko so he'll never be hurt. I called Claire and she kindly sent the limo for me."

"Yeah--I bet she did!" he yelled out all his panic at what she was implying. "Don't do this, Cass." He made a frenzied grab at her arm. "We'll work it out. I'll . . . figure out something. I'll die if you leave me, I will!"

She turned with a stiff pout on her lips. "I won't be far, Jacko, and you know where to find me--for a while, that is. So I suggest you use your time away from me in a productive manner before your son, *your bambino*, is lost to you forever!"

And then, feeling as helpless as a newborn bird, he merely watched her charge to the limousine. When the vehicle turned the corner and out of his sight, he felt the warm stickiness of his tears coat his cheeks. God . . . he was feeling so alone . . . already.

****

Wearing a grin as wide as Texas, Claire Gibson strolled into Michael Isle's office without knocking. Once in front of his desk, she snaked across it. "Guess who we're getting back?"

Perturbed at the interruption, Michael kept shuffling papers, never lifting his eyes. "I'm in no mood for goddamn guessing games, Claire. That Limey is so pissed at me now, he's barely civil when I call to beg for 'Harry Two'. He tells me that Spelling and Turner are both interested in the book. I have to find a way to get the edge even if it means making under the table reparations for a ruined image, which I can't seem to stop no matter what I do to Torelli. That Stubborn Dago! He nixes anything he can, even a dangerous game such as this!"

Claire jerked out a laugh of pure delight. "What if I tell you that I can knock the 'stubborn' out of Dago, darling?"

"I'd say bullshit." Michael raised a steely glare to her. "None of our plans have worked out. Something always throws a wrench. Take for example Cassie's trip to Minneapolis, she was supposed to be home at a certain time so we could execute that marvelous plan you thought up, and as fate has it, she ends up in the hospital and Torelli chases after her. We had to crush the plan and notify the participants. It was thought out down to a 'T', and what happens?"

"What would you say, darling, if I could turn that jinx around in an hour?"

He narrowed a look at her. "I'd take you out for a week of lunches at Chazen's for that jalapéno chili you snarf down like it was mineral water."

Claire smiled pleasurably while leisurely glancing at her watch. "Well in about an hour, a limo should pull through the gate bearing a teary Cassie Callahan who tells me that she had a big fight with her Jacko."

Michael's eyes brightened with sudden gratitude.

She reached a hand to his bow tie and played. "I can keep her here for twenty-four hours if you can keep Torelli away from her suite, to prevent any undo pressure on her."

Michael thrust out of her reach and a hearty laugh escaped him. "This is perfect. I'll gather the particulars tonight so the plan comes off without a hitch. And I'll make sure Torelli is too busy to think about any suites. That Limey has to be impressed. I can taste that sequel now."

"And me . . ." Claire replaced her hand on his tie. "I can already taste that 'spicy hot', inhibition-cracking, chili, darling . . ."

****

Unable to calm himself, Jack quickly moved from one room to the other, seeing traces of Cassie everywhere. What was he to do? His brain was impotent with the numbed confusion.

You gottta settle down, Torelli.

She was nearby, he tried to reassure himself. Cassie wouldn't do anything desperate with her bambino to think about. Once these reassurances sunk into his head, he felt a bit more composed and fell onto the living room couch, tightly pressing his face into his hands.

Her condemning words kept moving through his head like a running sign. Coward! Selfish! Attic! Filling the paper in together! Her little Jacko! She had never truly loved a man until him! Murderer! Son-killer! . . .He couldn't bear any of them.

Maybe because she's right, Torelli?

He pressed deeper into his face. Why the first two, the coward and the selfish? Or is it just the first and the second an excuse for it?

No, he tried to tell himself. He just didn't care for kids. Even with all his nieces and nephews he had been cooly indifferent. Why? He didn't exactly know, except that the lives his brothers and sisters lived seemed so surreal, so hokey, in comparison to the life he chose to live, and kids were part of that. Nobody he knew in Hollywood had kids, not even a few casually married couples that had once been acquaintances. It certainly wasn't a popular activity in the circles where he once traveled. He himself would have never, *ever*, contemplated such a thing in either of his two marriages. In fact, he would have dragged his ex-wives to an abortion clinic himself if a pregnancy, by chance, had occurred. Neither had been permanent entities, he had painfully discovered very shortly after saying, "I do."

Bullshit, Torelli! Bullshit to all of it!

This is Cassie!

He dug his fingers into his forehead. How could he even place Cassie within the context of his past life? She was like a fresh breath of air in comparison to his smelly former existence. To even compare was like placing a slap on the precious relationship that *he* had fought like hell to have for himself.

Stupid, asinine fool, Torelli!

Why did he have to react before he gave himself a chance to think this through?

No kids! No!

Why?

What does it boil down to?

That's your task . . .

He was hit with a shock, granted, and that prevented any meaningful response or action on his part. H reacted, as he would have in his past life, like a gut-reaction rather than rational thought. That's where he screwed up with Cassie, he told himself with surety. He should have just smiled, excused himself, then drifted in the pool until his wildly confused thoughts were placed into perspective. That was his first fuck up. Although he emphatically told himself that he wouldn't make the same fuck up again. Now it was total perspective for this very important dilemma—no gut reactions allowed.

Jack slowly raised his face. His mind did seem a little more relaxed now that he had forged a course, rather than let his anxiety run willy-nilly. And to coincide with his more tranquil state, he settled back against the couch and tried to fight against the remaining tension.

Is it selfish?

He analyzed his life in its present state. It was quiet, relatively stable despite an eccentric and sometimes unpredictable Cassie. Although her behavior was certainly the 'spice of his life'. Her antics made Cassie, Cassie, and he loved that Cassie, shrink-bait or not. They had a nil social life; although neither wanted one at this point in their relationship. They were still in the honeymoon phase and desired no intrusion.

Would a baby intrude?
Is that your beef, Torelli?
Are you worried you won't have Cassie all to yourself?

Sinking his back farther into the couch, Jack thought about this. He wanted to say *Yes* if he was to be totally honest. But it sounded lame, even to him. Could he really kill his son conceived out of the greatest love he had ever expected to have in his life? *Cassie's child?* Could he, for the simple reason that he, a forty-year-old adult man, lusted after the baby's mother like a horny teenager? Did that lust have to die if a child was added to the equation? Or was he just imagining that it would? Fearful that it would? Without any concrete proof that it would? Could he dispose of a child on such a floppy supposition? And if he were to be completely frank with himself, could he ever dispose of Cassie's child on any supposition, strongly verifiable or not?

Do you want a baby by Cassie? Ask yourself.

However, it took little thought when he pictured a son, part of him, part of her, a joint expression that bonded them forever without one doubt. A physical reminder day in and day out of how much they truly loved each other. He decided the picture highly attractive.

But was it highly desirable as well?

He let his mind fill with passages from Cassie's book. He recalled the lovely, almost idyllic world she had created with her firstborn infant. It was obvious she was thrilled to be a mother, and if not for so many outside influences wrecking this experience, the end result may have been different. So he could see her desire. Cassie most likely viewed this as a second chance, not easily acquired, as he well knew, thus the reason she was holding on so tight.

She *would* have this baby with or without him . . .

Listen to your thoughts, Torelli. Listen!

This was *Cassie* he was talking about! With, or more specifically *without* him and him *without* he. How could he ever, *ever*, contemplate the latter in a trillion years?

Picture it! Her, who knows where, scared, alone, carrying your child, and

where are you? In Hollywood back to your carefree life which you couldn't stomach?
No Cassie in your in life.
That's what it all boils down to. They came as a package like it or not.
He *couldn't* live without her, so he told himself, naturally he would take the package and cope the best he could once his son was born. Perhaps he may even come around a little by New Years. *Perhaps . . .*
He flung off the couch and paced. Could he guarantee that 'perhaps' would ever come? A child's life lasted decades after all. Would *mere coping* be fair to a child?
Having a sudden remembrance, Jack stopped his movements and walked to the back bedroom. There lay the photograph tossed carelessly on the floor. A definite message to Cassie right on the carpet, he thought with self-anger, scooping up the picture into his hand. He lifted a finger to trace the silhouette of his son. It already looked like a baby, he thought, then he wondered, What color hair and eyes? Would they be a lovely shade of green like Cassie's? Or would he, maybe, even be a miniature of him? The thought was intriguing as well as awesome.
Jesus . . .
It was growing inside her.
Her.
The woman I love.
My--son
Mine.
Jack's eyes exploded in tears and he thrust the picture to his chest, daring anyone to touch it. How could he have been so *blind?* When he had first looked at the picture all he had seen a *no-no* in his broader scheme things, therefore disposable so his scheme of things wasn't messed to the point he couldn't maintain his careful hold.
Coward!
Cassie had been right. *That's* what it really boiled down to.
He was so scared of fucking up again, he would dispose of anything, *even his son,* that may cause him to fuck up again.
Pulling the picture from his chest, Jack held it in front of him and his tears fell onto it.
This was his flesh and blood! A *Torelli.*
And my future.
And his future was growing inside the woman he loved in his entirety. He should be kissing her feet for giving him such a wondrous gift, *and triple damn him,* he had denied that gift in the most horrible of responses.
She wasn't Gloria or a Sheeny—he never in a million years wanted children by them.
But he wanted this child, no matter the fear. Normal for first-time fathers, so not to despair, he told himself. He *would* cope like his father, brothers, and a million other men who found the guts to create their future.
It was noble.
And by damn, Jack Torelli is going to be one of the noble ones.
Jack scanned every inch of the photo, letting the true wonder of Cassie's gift fill him, and he ultimately came to once irrevocable conclusion:
I love you already, Little Jacko . . .

Chapter 26—Cassie and Jack

By seven the next morning, the shades on the tenth floor of the Python Studio Office Building were already lifted. Shifting around his binoculars while standing in the middle of the open-air simulated windows, Michael Isle scanned the grounds for any infractions which he did every day upon arriving at his office.

Finding nothing out-of-the-ordinary, he was about to replace the binoculars on the ledge when his lenses happened to pick up a white-haired form, head down, slowly walking towards the office building. Michael lowered his binoculars and smiled. Right on time, he thought, happy the old man had learned not to dawdle when he had been summoned. It saved him his five thousandth chewing out, he laughed silently, then rid his hands of the binoculars and sat down, posing in his stern executive stance while he waited . . .

"You wanted to see me, Mr. Isle?" a gruff voice questioned from the door.

"Get in here, George, and take a chair, quick. I need the information that I told you to collect." Michael waved up a hand at the uniformed man.

Looking hesitant, George cleared his throat several times before speaking. "The kid over at the suites said he called several times, wanting to be connected to her room."

"No one connected him, right?"

George hung his head and shook. "The kid said that she was refusing all calls, and he didn't take that well, so . . . he showed up in the lobby at three in the morning demanding entrance to her room."

"That crazy sonofabitch," Michael muttered angrily. "The kid didn't let him go up to her room, did he?"

"No, but the kid said he was plenty scared. He said Jack yelled for a half-hour straight saying that him, more than any more in the world, had a right to see her. Then Jack nearly attacked the kid for the elevator key."

"The kid should have had him arrested and let him cool off with a few low life L.A. scum for a few hours." Michael rapidly tapped his gold pen on his desk. "So how did it end, George?"

"The kid said he just gave up and stormed off, muttering that he would come back later, that she needed her sleep anyway." George laboriously spoke each word.

Michael lunged forward and stabbed his pen into the air. "You are to keep Torelli away from those suites. Inform all your men. If he tries, physically inject him, per my order. He is not to go near Ms. Callahan under any circumstances."

"But Mr. Isle . . ." George's face grew stiff with distress. "What if she wants to see him? Maybe they just needed a night apart to come to their senses and both wanna get back together. What do we do then, huh? You can't stop nuthin' like that."

"Yes I can, and that's exactly what I plan on doing. So just do it, George."

George shook his head until his eyes were fastened on the ground.

"I take it that you don't agree with me, George?" Michael said, unconcerned.

"Does it matter?" George shot his gaze upward. "Are you gonna listen when I tell you that those two are in love and that you have no cause to tamper with that? Why make them miserable for whatever. Is whatever really that important, Mr. Isle?"

Michael twisted his lips into an amused smile. "Damn straight it is, and I'll thank you to keep your big mouth shut if you want to keep your job, George. If I find out that Torelli has somehow snuck up to her room. I kick your old ass out the front gate. Dismissed . . ."

****

Driving his Corvette at top speed heading west on Santa Monica Boulevard, Jack Torelli could feel the sleep deprivation of his body. He hadn't slept a wink with his worry about Cassie and his horribly insensitive treatment of her when she was in such a fragile state. It wasn't good for the baby, he figured, and now he felt guilty as hell for maybe having caused harm to his child because of his utter stupidity and blindness. He had to beg for her forgiveness and make her see how much he loved her and the child she carried. They were his family . . . and he shook with just the awesome thought. He, Jack Torelli, finally had permanency in his life.

When he reached the Python Studio gate, there were a few reporters, but Jack noticed that they had thinned out considerably. Maybe he and Cassie could resume their Saturday jaunts soon, he started to think. They yelled their usual questions at him, all of which he ignored and nearly plowed his Corvette through them in his anticipation to see Cassie. He squealed his car into a parking spot, not caring that he was parked cockeyed.

He jogged towards the studio suites complex. He had a little under two hours, not an ideal amount of time to make up like he wanted to do, but enough time to glean a bit of forgiveness, maybe total forgiveness if he chose the right words. Anything to get him to the lunch hour when he would bring her hot dogs like he used to do. Otherwise, he figured his day would be crap, and with his lack of sleep, not even his autopilot would kick in to save him.

As he ran, he told himself that was too emotionally spent to take the gruel or the rebuffs today. It was hard enough after a full eight hours. There was only a certain amount that a body could absorb and he was close to his maximum capacity. No one was making his comeback easy, no matter that he worked like hell and gave two hundred percent to that role, for that comeback. He made 'Harry' shine on film, he damn well knew, even if no one else acknowledged that fact.

"Stop Jack!"

Braking his feet, he looked around and saw a group of security guards massed at the entrance of the suite complex. Rapidly moving towards him was George, the old security guard.

"What the hell's going on?" Jack demanded, then he filled with sudden fear. "Is someone hurt?" And then he took off at a clip. "Cassie!" he yelled, skirting past George who caught him around the waist. "What the hell, George?" Jack twisted his body in a struggle.

"Cool it, Jack," George hushed insistently.

Jack stopped his struggling.

"You can't see her, boy, orders from the top."

"What?" Jack raged. "I'll smash that fucker's teeth down his throat and he'll be spitting caps with his goddamn orders." Jack pulled out of George's arms and began to take long angry paces towards the office building.

"Don't be a crazy fool, Jack," George said in desperate tones, trying to wrestle Jack to a halt. "You're playing with fire, boy. Somethin' big is up."

Jack jerked his arm away and faced the old man. "What big something?"

"Sh, sh . . ." George grabbed his arm and pulled him off to the side. "I don't know exactly, but I aim to find out. Just go with the flow for the time being. That's one desperate fucker up there." George looked up to the tenth floor of the office building. "He's been acting stranger than usual and secretive as all get out."

"I don't give a shit," Jack whispered insistently. "You gotta get me in that suite, George."

"I can't Jack. My job . . ."

Jack pressed closer to George and him looked square in the eye. "She needs me, George. She's pregnant, so I'm not just fetching Cassie, but my kid too. I gotta get them back to my house and out of the fucker's clutches. If he's planning something, she's sure to get hurt. He doesn't give a shit who he hurts. Do you wanna see a pregnant Cassie hurt?"

George's face filled with painful indecision. "Of course not . . . but . . . there's nothing
I can do, Jack. I need this job. I'm close to my pension. I can't risk that. I'm so damn sorry . . . a baby, huh? . . . that's wonderful, Jack. Congratulations."

Jack felt a resigned panic, knowing that Michael Isle had won this round. "Isn't there anything you can do, George?"

"Keep my ears and eyes open, Jack, and I promise to duly warn you . . ."

****

Suite Five at the Python complex had a spooky quality. The shades were tightly drawn, and the room had a sterile, freshly cleaned appearance as it waiting for a new inhabitant.

Shriveled and scrunched in a corner, Cassie tried with all her rapidly draining resources to envision a high four-sided brick wall around her.

Where is he? Her mind again screamed in a panic.

No phone calls, no visits, when she had expected both. That was her reason for going to the suites. She was in close proximity to the Beverly Hills house and Jack spent his days here. The sight she had chosen for her defiant show had been perfect.

So where was he when she needed him?

He had promised to take care of her and love her no matter what, and now he had so handily forgotten about her. Maybe he *was* going to turn his back on his child, despite her total disbelief about this. She had sensed something different in him from nearly the first moment she had met him——Jacko was a nurturer. He wouldn't hurt easily, and with all the hurt she had sustained, she yearned for someone like this in her life.

But he's hurting me now.
How can that be?

Jerky, terror-filled whimpers came out of her.

The brick wall was shrinking—she could feel it, And the voices in her mind were growing stronger to coincide with her heightening sensations of defenselessness. Without her Jacko she felt like one paralyzed from the neck down, possessing no strength of mobility to fight even though her brain kept torturing her. She was sinking fast.

Oh god, Jacko. Where are you?

Seeking Out Harry

"Get out of that corner, Cassie. I'll help you."
Go away, Sandy
"You're getting closer to 'uncle'. I can see your spirit ready to burst. Boom!"
Stay away from my wall, Sandy.
"Ha-Ha-Ha. I'm peeking over your wall. A few more bricks, and I can lift my foot and . . ."
"No!" Cassie's scream rang through the room. She held herself tighter. She had to hide so Sandy couldn't see her vulnerability. Sandy fed off Cassie's vulnerability with cold calculation, freezing her more and more into an impotent piece of ice that could never melt into another more fluid form. She couldn't freeze and kill Cassie.
Jacko!
She needed his strong arms now, to protect her and her son from the she-devil.
Oh god!
Maybe Sandy wanted this child too!
"No!" she sobbed over and over. Not her precious Little Jacko. He was hers, and of no concern to any of them. They wouldn't invade her attic this time. Her Jacko promised that she would never have to see them again.
But . . . without Jacko . . .
Feeling the heightening sensation of icy pokes to her skin, she moved back and forth, trying to dodge the punctuate blows, to little avail. She was freezing little by little.
Soon I'll be her!
"I can see the dripping icicles, Cassie. I can see then hanging on your very soul."
"Leave us alone!" a wildly sobbing Cassie screeched, thrashing from side-to-side to block the chilling pick that was chipping away at her bricks.
"My eyes are growing cooly refreshed by the sight, Cassie."
"I'll claw those blue eyes, Sandy, if you come any closer!"
"My eyes are frozen on you, and you won't claw . . . Uncle, Cassie."
"No Uncle! Never Uncle! Harry!"
"Harry doesn't belong to you anymore, Cassie. They *took him away from you* and *won't let you write about him so he can get stronger.* Nah-Nah-Nah. Only *they* can make him stronger. You're at their mercy. New York--New York, it's a helluva town . . ."
"He's mine, Sandy! He'll always be mine. I made him! "
"He's putty! Molded like clay to *their* specifications. He's not your Harry!"
"He's my salvation!" Cassie screeched
"Har-dee-Har-Har. He can't save you anymore, Cassie. Uncle-Uncle-Uncle."
"Jacko!"
"And he can't save you any more either, Cassie. Mother hates him!"
"Jacko . . ."
The sudden ring of the phone made her heart gave a leap. It's Jacko! And she started to untangle her body from the floor.
"Don't leave your brick wall, Cassie. It may be Mother."
The taunt of the mind's voice made her hesitate, but only for a moment, and she made a mad dash for the phone. "Jacko?" she asked breathlessly.
"Sorry Cassie—it's Claire."

"Claire?" She jittered in place while staring at the unprotected corner.

"Mike gave me the day off for the specific purpose of taking your mind off that stubborn man. So let's have fun shopping and stuffing our faces on Melrose."

"I can't Claire. I. . .have things to do," Cassie replied shakily.

"You sound like you need a Valium too," Claire retorted. "And you definitely need to get out of that stuffy room. Now, I won't take no for an answer. I'll even get you a hot dog at Pīk's, closest to New York that you can get."

The persuasive voice was tempting. Cassie thought, her eyes still glued to the corner. Claire was a tough woman, and Sandy wouldn't dare intrude. It would buy her a little time, she told herself.

"Okay, Claire, but no New York anything. I wanna dwell only in L.A."

Claire laughed with delight. "That's my kind of shopping partner. I'll pick you up in the limo in a hour. Might as well let those Melrose peasants eat their envious little hearts out . . ."

****

"Now you *must* try that on, Cassie," Claire said, pointing through a store window.

Cassie raised her dark glasses to look. She already felt tired. Her and Claire had been walking between La Brea Avenue and San Vincente Boulevard for the past three hours, and she swore that Claire dragged her into every trendy boutique along the way.

"So what do you think?" Claire pressed.

"I think I saw a nun in that once." Cassie wrinkled her nose at the long black stretch velvet dress with wrist-length sleeves and a high, round scoop neck. "Or maybe it was Morticia Adams."

"But Cassie . . ." Claire inched close and casually brushed a strand of blonde hair from her shoulder. "It's absolutely marvy for your image, perfect in fact."

Feeling uncomfortable with the conversation, Cassie stepped away from Claire. "I don't care about my image, which isn't 'my' image anyway. Living with Jacko is my image. It's . . . the only image I want from now on."

"After what he did to you?" Claire questioned with plainspoken incredulity. "I say let him suffer a bit. A few weeks alone will change his tune and temper, if I may be so forthright."

The words made apprehension prod her. "A few weeks? I can't be away from my Jacko for that long, Claire. And . . . he doesn't have a temper with me. He's a kind, wonderful man."

"Oh pooh! What's a few weeks? You get your book done, send it off to New York, maybe attend a few wild parties there, get a handle on your next book and by the time you're done, your few weeks will be up and . . .

"I don't wanna talk about that." Cassie arm-wrapped herself to stem the panic she felt about such a suggestion. New York? She would never go back without her Jacko. "Why don't we eat? I'm tired of shopping." She walked in an easterly direction, her arms still encircling her.

"But you didn't buy a thing, Cassie!" Claire called after her. "Wait up . . . !"

****

A little past one in the afternoon, after the morning filming on *The Life and Times of Harry Hannigan* was completed, Jack took long determined paces towards the Python suites. He *was* going to see her, even if he had to run over a couple security guards and sail in a suite attendant or two.

"Hold it, Jack," George said upon spotting the raging form. "I said, hold it!" With a firm arm slap to Jack's chest he halted him.

"Let me pass!" Jack yelled in a fury. "I have every right in the world to see her!"

"Calm down, Jack!" With a firm grasp to Jack's arm, George pulled him off to a less public spot a few feet away. "She's not here, boy, I'll tell you that much."

"Where is she?"

"With Claire Gibson. Isle's shadow picked Cassie up in a studio limo."

"That bitch!" Jack yelled angrily. Claire Gibson? She was the last person he wanted near Cassie. The cunning woman may find a way to brainwash a defenseless Cassie against him, he fretted. He could just hear Claire repeating every filthy lie that came out of Michael Isle's mouth. "Where did they go?" he asked with sheer desperation.

George shook his head. "I don't know. But believe me, I tried to find out. That Claire is a sly one. She wouldn't even give me a clue."

Frantically gazing around the immediate vicinity, Jack tried to coax his weary mind to think. But it was tough. His rationality seemed zapped. "What the hell do I do, George?" He turned a plea to the kindly security guard.

George firmly grasped Jack's shoulders. "Finish your scenes, get the damn miniseries done, then get her the hell away from that bastard in a highfalutin suit. Something stinks bad. He's maniacal about Cassie Callahan."

"Money," Jack shook out.

George nodded emphatically. "Maybe billions to make him act this way. Something's up his sleeve and I fear Cassie's smack dab in the middle. I mean . . . what he's done to you . . ."

"Real asshole," Jack agreed.

"You're blowing something big for him, Jack. I've never seen him so crazy where you're concerned. Just watch your back around here." George released Jack's shoulders. "Now get to that sound stage. Act like you don't give a crap, and he'll make a slip one of these days."

"If she comes back, you'll watch out for her?" Jack implored.

George nodded sadly. "I'll watch her like a hawk for you, Jack."

****

"So what do you think of this place, Cassie? Radical on the opposite end of the spectrum, wouldn't you say?" Claire questioned with delight. She and Cassie sat in a long red leather banquette in a strategic location, obtained at Claire's loud insistence, at Le Bohemè, a cooly elegant restaurant on La Brea.

Cassie glanced all the tables of women sounding like flocks of canaries. She had never seen so many odd hats perched atop perfectly coiffed hair. And their clothes were matronly yet screaming, one-of-a-kind design; although she had no clue *which* designer as she possessed no such clothes herself. She gazed down at her own jeans and T-shirt, and she wanted to laugh out loud at the contrast. "Looks like a fun place for a mashed potato fight," she replied at last.

Claire let out a low underhanded laugh. "Now that I'd love to see. But not instigated by the mild mannered Cassie Callahan, of course. Your image, dear—it wasn't geared towards slapstick or surrender to such delicious impulses."

"So . . ." Cassie dangled a long-stemmed crystal water glass between her fingers. "What *is* my image as you see it, Claire?"

Taking a sip of her Bloody Mary to which she had added extra Tabasco, Claire studied Cassie for a few moments before answering. "A down-home girl, unspoiled by a broader world, whose impulses explode passionately on her computer. That's you precisely, Cassie."

"And when you add Jacko into that equation . . . ?"

Never altering her eye contact, Claire teased the drink glass on her lips. "He doesn't fit into the equation—the numbers just don't add up. Maybe a distinguished doctor, an up-and-up lawyer, a beyond reproach businessman. But an ex-porn star with a smelly Hollywood reputation? Two and two make five."

Cassie stiffened with resentment over the blunt, misguided words. "Then I guess your image of me is shot to hell, huh Claire? A fantasy that was never really Cassie Callahan if she could so easily fall into the arms of such disreputable man."

"The persuasive arms . . ." Claire pointed out.

"No! Cassie slammed her water glass on the white linen tablecloth. "Jacko didn't lure me, if that's what you're implying. If anything it was the other way around. Jacko was a perfect gentleman until I gave him the go ahead. It was love that sent us to the sack not some animalistic mating ritual. And whether you can imagine it or not, Claire, it *was* love! It *is* love!" She miserably stuck the water glass to her lips and guzzled, fed up with the insinuations, the need to defend, the sacred image, all of it.

"No need to get testy," Claire drawled. "So? For once in his life Jack Torelli played the gentleman. He probably knew that was the only way to get you into the sack. I said his reputation stunk, not that he was stupid."

"Interpretation . . . He's using me, right?" Cassie said with tight anger, and Claire spread her hands in assent. "For what purpose? Huh?"

"My guess is that it's his chance to look good. In Hollywood impression is everything."

"How dare you?"

Claire made not a flinch. "I dare, because I consider you somewhat of a friend, Cassie, despite our all too infrequent meetings. *Someone* has to set you straight."

Cassie quivered the water glass to her lips and took a hefty sip to cool the sudden heat. Could Claire be right? No—she isn't. She can't be. But Jacko *is* a good actor. *Could he have* lured her for a definite purpose? *Oh god!* She was so confused. All that had happened in the last twenty or so hours had taken their toll on her thought processes, and nothing of the reasonable nature would touch her mind. "Let's just order, Claire. Despite my sudden lack of appetite, I find myself in a position where I must force down a bite."

"Sounds like a luscious secret, Cassie. Perhaps you could tell me about it when we play tourists on Hollywood Boulevard . . ."

****

When the cameras shut down on the final interior scene of *The Life and Times of Harry Hannigan*, a lusty cheer went up among the crew. Now all that was left was a few outdoor scenes and two days in Minneapolis to film the rest. A Python crew and applicable cast had been in Northeastern Minnesota for the past four weeks filming 'Harry's' early life and this group would latch onto the incoming group early next week.

Feeling no elation, only relief, that his imposed torture was soon ending, Jack ignored all the noise and walked to Wardrobe to shed his warm suit. He reemerged a few minutes later in faded jeans and T-shirt. He planned on heading for the suites with the hope that George had some new information for him.

"Hey Jack, hold it! We got a celebration here!"

Jack shifted around. The cast and crew mingled in front of a table bearing a cake and bottles of liquor. Quickly gazing at all the reticent faces, who had done little to ease his way back into legitimate Hollywood, he decided, no thanks. "Count me out—I got things to do." He turned to leave when another voice stopped him.

"Cm'on, Jack--you're our star. The least you could do is toast a glass of champagne."

Again, Jack turned. Brett, the assistant director, stood in a challenging pose—legs slightly spread, hand on hip, head tipped precariously, and a dare blazed in his slitty eyes. *Why the hell the look?* Jack stared back at the man. What did the tight-assed little pisser care if he had a glass champagne or not?

"One drink, one piece of cake, Jack, so we can pay our accolades to a wonderful performance by our star."

The words were stunning. It was the affirmation he had been yearning to hear since April. And he told himself that he should ask, *why now,* or more closely assess the sincerity of the words. But in the final analysis he discovered that he still had enough ego left to eat it up. "One piece and one glass can't hurt, I guess." And he made his way to the table.

Immediately, a glass of champagne and plate with large piece of marble cake was thrust into his hands. He downed the champagne in one gulp, then in hurried fashion stuffed the cake into his mouth while glancing around. A few of the crew gave him pleasant looks, while the remaining crew members and all of the cast still reflected distant facades.

"Here Jack . . ." Brett held up the champagne bottle and refilled Jack's glass, uninvited. "You need some more of the bubbly for my toast."

"Just one more." Jack downed half the glass before Brett even stood in front of the group.

"To Jack Torelli, a marvelous Harry Hannigan, and the other cast who brought a tough, but highly gratifying book to life."

"Here-Here!" came a chorus.

Jack drained his glass and was about to leave when yet a third time, Brett filled his glass. "One for the road, Jack. Someone's gotta drink this shit."

Shit is right, he thought, never acquiring a taste for moderately-priced champagne. Yet ever-so-politely, he cracked a small smile and emptied the glass in one gulp. "Thanks," he said to Brett, then placed the glass and plate on the table, turned, and took rapid strides out of the sound stage before anyone else could stop him.

As the blazing sun beat down on him, Jack jogged to the suite complex. By the time he stood in front of George, he was huffing and his brow sweated heavily. A slight dizziness made him whirl. The sun had affected him a little, he figured. "Is she back, George?"

"No Jack—no limo in sight," George replied with a pitied look.

"Damn that Claire," Jack muttered, deathly terrified about Cassie's state.

One never knew what would happen when she was provoked, and he knew Claire Gibson could provoke like no other. But none of them knew this, only him. And only him, knew how to keep her brick wall securely blanketed around her. "I gotta find her, try to comb L.A. the best I can," he told George, then felt another whirl of dizziness.

"What's wrong, Jack? You're sweatin' buckets." George steadied Jack's arm with his hand.

"I don't know. The sun must be getting to me." Jack felt the unstable weave of his head.

"You're getting too stressed out, boy. Claire's a tigress with long claws, but you know that she's not gonna place Cassie in harm's way. Cassie's okay, that I can tell you for certain."

"You don't understand . . ." Now Jack felt the weave of his entire body.

George raised his other hand and held Jack under his arms. "Jack! What did you take? Drugs? Is that it? Did you do something foolish?"

The words resounded through his head, but his mouth felt too fuzzy to respond. Although when he got a blurry flash of champagne and a piece of cake, he violently tried to form these words on his lips.

"Help!" George gave a frantic yell. "What did you take, Jack? Dammit, what?"

A groan gurgled out of him, and the last thing to strike his consciousness was a pair of strong arms and the yell of several voices . . .

****

"Pregnant? Is that what you said, Cassie? My god girl! Are you mad?" Claire heaved with much distress when she and Cassie exited the Lingerie Museum at Frederick's of Hollywood. "What a thing to spring on a body in front of Mae West's peignoir!"

Cassie jammed her hands into the pockets of her navy shell jacket. "I don't know why I said it. He was just on my mind, and . . . maybe I just had to tell someone."

"Does Jack know?"

"Sure he does." Cassie kept her sunglasses directed on the pavement.

Promptly, Claire threw a halting arm in front of Cassie. "And what pray tell was his response? Though I can imagine. Torelli and a child—Rod Serling would have loved it."

"He . . ." Unable to hold in her emotions, Cassie exploded in tears.

"Oh that beast!" Claire flared hotly. She wrapped an arm around Cassie and hurried her to the awaiting limousine. Once there, Claire shoved Cassie inside and ordered the chauffeur to "Take a hike." When settled in the back seat, Claire quickly turned to Cassie. "Is that what you two fought about?" she urged.

Unable to get any words past her chokes, Cassie gave a nod.

"He wants you to get rid of it, I suppose."

Cassie gave a noncommittal shrug. "He didn't *actually* say that, only hinted without saying it. I don't think Jacko knows what he wants. So I left him to think about what he wants."

"But has he even called you? Made any attempt to see you?" Claire demanded with an air of superiority that said she was right about Jack Torelli.

Cassie crumpled against the car door. At that moment, she felt a horrible ache that only her Jacko could soothe. "No," she whispered, then broke down in convulsive sobs.

"Well that proves it! He doesn't want a baby messing up his life," Claire said with blunt cruelty. "How could he ever bring a child into *his* lifestyle? My god woman! That child would be traumatized from birth."

"Jacko's not like that anymore, he isn't!" Cassie cried out.

"How in the world could *that man* change so drastically, Cassie?"

"He has!" Cassie said inexorably. "You don't know him . . . maybe you don't wanna know him . . . maybe you're just too prejudice to ever know him. He loves me!" But even as she spoke it, she wondered if her inexhaustible defense was purely a way to convince herself. Claire's words from lunch were like weights pressing down on her security. Yet, she should be sure by now.

Shouldn't she?

"And your image . . . what in world will the public think? A Cassie Callahan knocked up by a former porn star? They'll turn their backs in droves. I can just see it. You'll look like a liar of high magnitude. And with Hollywood sniffing around you . . . you need to get *un*-pregnant quick before this leaks out," Claire said with the insistence of a scolding mother.

Cassie turned a disbelieving expression on Claire. "Are you out of your mind? I'm an Italian girl and a Catholic to boot. And this is my son! He's not dispensable, no matter how many turn away in droves!"

"But . . . your career, Cassie." Claire sputtered. "Certainly after all your hard work and desire . . ."

Her career! She thought disdainfully. She had crushed it, placed it out of *their* reach forever. They had stolen her only reason for writing—Milton, Rufus, Anson, Gregor, Cyrano, and finally her triumph, 'Harry', her means to an end. They had snatched that hard-fought end right from under her, and now she was dry. She could never duplicate 'Harry'—he was one of a kind. Her contrived 'uncles' were over, she told herself without an ounce of bravery but plenty of resignation. She had created 'ultimate', and still . . . *I lost.*

"I don't care about my career, Claire, and my so-called image can be damned too. This time, my child *will* take precedence over anything else," Cassie said without flounder.

Making no response, Claire glanced at her watch. "So where to?" she cast out casually, though he stance carried the stiffness of anger. "A snack perhaps?"

"No--I better get back to the suite in case Jacko . . ." Cassie couldn't finish. What if there were no messages? She doubted she could face such terror. "I have nowhere else in the world to go." And the pain of her words made her crumple against the limo door.

"What about home?" Claire kicked out.

Cassie abruptly pulled herself up. "You mean home in Beverly Hills? That home?"

"Sure . . . have it out with the big lunk. He *is* the father after all, and even if it is *Torelli,* the man has to take some degree of responsibility. If he won't, you'll just have to make him whether he likes it or not. It won't you do any good, moping around the suite--that will get you nothing. If he loves you as you claim, use that to your advantage. *Make* him respond."

Cassie felt more than tentative. "I don't wanna force Jacko to respond. I want him to come to his own conclusions."

Claire made an exasperated noise. "That may take forever, considering the man and his well-ingrained ways. I say go for it, and if he balks or flares, I'll be waiting outside in the limousine so you have a ride back to the suites."

"You really think so, Claire?" she asked eagerly, needing to believe the words. She would see her Jacko! He would make everything all right like he always did, she just knew he would. Now she couldn't wait. "And you'll be outside if he should get stubborn again?"

"I'll be right outside, Cassie, holding your hand at a distance . . ."

****

During the entire drive to Beverly Hills, Cassie silently chafed about the intelligence of Claire's plan. Fearful it would dilute her position, she didn't want to look like a beggar, even though in terms of Jack Torelli she was the biggest beggar on the face of the earth. Nor did she desire to be pushy, figuring Jack had enough to swallow without her hysterical two bits. And then, he may entice her to bed which always weakened her, left her wanting more, making her firm stance a joke. It was a risky venture all right.

Add to this her nerves, which had yet settle after her disastrous trip to Anoka, compounded with the anxiety of her pregnancy and her worry about how the man she loved would deal with such a drastic change in his life. The combination set her up for a vulnerable state when she was trying, with every scant ounce of courage, to fight for this child. If he rejected their baby or dare mention the word 'abortion', she had no idea how she would respond.

"Bear up, Cassie—we're here," Claire announced with a hint of derision.

Cassie peered out the window. The high stone fence and tall palms beyond obliterated the house's view. Suddenly a realization struck, and she knitted her eyebrows in confusion. "Where's those awful reporters? There's usually a couple always hanging around."

Claire jerked out a tinkly laugh. "Perhaps they're on a coffee break. I happen to know there's a quaint bistro a few miles down the road."

Making no comment, Cassie stared for several moments longer before opening her car door. "Well, here goes for broke," she said with a quaver to her voice.

"Be brave, dear. Remember, even Torelli, is only a man . . ."

****

When standing at the front door of the darkened house, Cassie heard the distant thud of hard rock. *That's strange.* Jack always listened to classical. His hard rock tapes were stashed deep in a closet and he told her he was thinking of giving them away. The sound more than curious, Cassie placed an ear to the door to make sure she was really hearing *Aerosmith.*

"Cassie . . ."

The low hissing voice made her jump from the door. Suddenly apprehensive, she darted her eyes around. "Who is it?" Her voice shook in a question. She saw the rustle of the perfectly manicured cedar bushes, hazy under a dusky sky rapidly turning to night. Terrified, she made a grab for the door handle. *Maybe New York finally found the cheekiness to catch up with me.*

A shadow eased around the corner, and the cold metal handle jiggled in her hand.

"It's me, Cassie," the voice whispered.

She quickly discerned that the whisper wasn't the one that frightfully clouded her thoughts at rare moments. So she gathered the courage to stretch her neck and look while her hand tightened, knuckle-white around the handle.

"Who's me?" she jittered, feeling her nerves climb into her throat.
"Can the 'Lady Piranha' see the house from the street?"
"Lady . . ." Cassie anxiously bobbed her head until she saw a small square of the black limousine between two palm trees. "No." She turned back to the shadow. "Why?" With slow caution, the shadow stepped out the rest of the way and Cassie exhaled a loud gasp. "George? What in the world . . .
"Be quiet, and listen," he cut in urgently. "Do not go in that house."
Feeling total bewilderment, Cassie scanned the shadow that fell over halfways over his face. "What's going on, George, specifically. I'm too emotionally spent for games. I. . .just need to have it out with Jacko, once and for all."
"I can't say specifically. Frankly, I'm scared." His voice gave credence to his words, and Cassie loosened her hand from the door handle. "All I can tell you is that it's a cruel ruse, brought about by sick desperation, and she's in on it." His white head tipped towards the street.
"What cruel ruse?" She forced her head to shift partway towards the shiny black square. "I have to know." She turned back to fix her gaze square onto the shadowed face. "Is it my Jacko? Is he part of it? Is he?"
"He's the central part of this, but you're the central part of the other," he replied in nebulous fashion. "Just don't go inside that house and fall into their trap. What you see *isn't*, and I repeat *isn't*, the truth."
"Is my Jacko in trouble? You have to tell me." She made a soft pleading cry.
"Yeah--he's in trouble, Cassie, but not the type that will cause major harm. He . . . should be himself in the morning, or relatively so, and you have to leave it at that. Trust me. Please."
"Oh god." She whimpered while looking at the door. What did it all mean? And why was George so frightened? It wasn't like the man. He was always so laid-back and warmly gracious. But her Jacko . . . he may need her. Maybe he was sick or hurt worse than George knew, and the mere thought scared the wits out of her. She couldn't exist without her Jacko. If anything happened to him because of her inaction . . .
Propelled by panic, she thrust her hand to the door handle. She just couldn't walk away because of some baneful warning.
"Cassie you can't—I beg you. Jack . . . he told me about your condition. Think about that baby and walk away. Then come home tomorrow and just stay there. Jack loves you. He's been going nuts without you. That much I'll tell you." Pain was written all across his face.
"No!" She pushed through the door and slammed it on the voice that was muddling her . . .

****

The air pounded with hard rock and reeked of pungent odors that stung Cassie's nostrils.
"Jacko?" she cried out as loud as her terror would allow.
A strongly familiar stink greeted her nose and she jolted back. *Pot* . . . Cassie knew instantly, having experimented a few times in high school. She quickly flicked on a lamp and moved her head around until spotting an ashtray. It was brimmed with stubbed out joints.
"*Jackooo* . . . What have you done?"
She trembled with panic. Had he actually smoked such a quantity? Then

she panicked even more. What could such a quantity do to one's body? *I have no idea.*

"Jacko! Where are you?" she shrieked in terror. Had he done something foolish because of the shock she handed him? *Follow the music, Cass,* her brain tried to calmly tell her. She forced her feet to shuffle forward. A stronger odor mixed with the pot smell blasted her nostrils.

Weaving through the darkened house, letting her ears be her guide, a shaky Cassie finally stood in front of their closed bedroom door. The smell was so oppressive, she pressed a hand over her nose and mouth, fearful her child would inhale the drug if she did likewise. The bronze doorknob felt icy cold as she turned it. What she would do if he was . . . *My god!* She loved him, so totally, so trustingly—the only man she could ever love in this way.

He was her *whole* life.

What would she find?

The music pounded in time with her thudding heart. She cracked open the door and was smacked with malodorous air. Cassie gagged and pressed tighter against her nose and mouth. She took a step inside the bedroom and her foot knocked against something. Her gaze plummeted. She saw an empty pint bottle that said *Bacardi,* then a trail of like bottles along the carpeting. The sight made her reel. She had never seen so many empty booze bottles in her entire life.

"Well look who's here. Are we making it a threesome, Ms. Callahan?"

Startled, Cassie shot her gaze upward. A nude female form, made hazy by the drug cloud, languished atop her bed. The light on the night stand suddenly flicked on, illuminating the haze. Cassie widened her eyes in horror while a continuous painful whimper shook past her lips.

The woman swung her long black hair and crawled seductively across the bed, so her naked person was nearer to Cassie. "He's my boyfriend. What can I say? We took advantage of your absence. It's tough for us to find private time, if you know what I mean."

With all her remaining will, Cassie looked at the woman--the perfect little body, the firm, large-rounded breasts, the small curve of her waist, her firm shoulders, thighs, and legs--firm— firm—firm. Her will completely drained, she gazed at woman's face and assessed her to be beautiful--clear, luminous skin without a freckle in sight and lips full and moist.

The perfect Hollywood bod . . .

"Perhaps, I should get dressed and leave Jack to you." The woman giggled with delight. "As you can see, I wore him out a bit."

Unable to turn her head to view the inevitable, Cassie kept her gaze locked on the woman, watching her jump off the bed and pick up her strewn clothes. Then a bolt of realization struck. "You're . . . You're Marabella."

"Why yes I am. I see you've watched my great triumph. It was a wonderful film, not only the thrill of acting, but . . ." She gazed at the bed. "Jack couldn't keep his hands off me. I had him every night and on some days too." She turned a malicious grin on Cassie. "And he still can't keep his hands off me. I'm forever in his blood. *His Marabella."*

"No . . ." Cassie backed away from her. As if to torture her, scenes from the beautifully sensitive movie filled her head. She could tell from the first moment that Jack had put much of his own emotions into the film. Now she wondered, *Was she the reason?* The mere possibility curled her insides with agony. "No!" she repeated, and repeated, and . . . Her voice elevating into a scream.

Haley Shears pealed out with a victorious laugh. "I'm his 'bad girl' and you're his smokescreen so he can cross the line to legitimate films. He needed a 'good little girl' to do that, you must realize. Once he does, it's *Adios* 'Miss Minnesota' and *Hola* to Marabella. Didn't you really know?"

The words precisely stabbed her in the chest, and Cassie couldn't halt the scream, endless in its resonance.

"I must thank you for one thing, though," Haley tossed out while zipping her expensive tight white slacks. "Because of you, he can raise it again. No longer do I have to use his little mechanical toys to get a response out of that masterpiece of a cock."

"You liar!" Cassie screamed over and over, jumping wildly, trying to ward off such perverted filth from penetrating her brain. She couldn't believe it. Not her passionate Jacko.

Nooooo . . . !

A loud moan from the bed, jolted Cassie and she twirled her hysteria towards the noise. Jack was on his stomach naked, his head and body thrashing back and forth like he was trying to arouse herself. She saw the shiny tousle of his black hair, then the fluffy black down on his firmly curved back and buttocks, and the backs of his muscled legs, and her insides rumbled with even more hysteria.

"Why Jacko!" she screamed at the top of her lungs, then she rushed to the bed's edge, beating her fists on the back, the buttocks, the thighs, unable to stop the assault. "You promised! How could you do this to me!"

Jack thrust up his head and it whirled while he squinted his eyes at her. "Cassie?" he groaned, then pressed his eyelids together and in repetitive fashion, shook his head back and forth. "Whassa matter?" he asked in a stupor.

Her body consumed in convulsive sobs, Cassie lifted her fists and stepped back from the bed. "You *did* use me. All those words and actions, so well-contrived and *practiced*, for your own gain! You lousy bastard!"

Twirling upward, Jack made uncoordinated shakes of his head. "What the hell's going on? My head . . . what the hell . . . ?" his voice slurred. Then he lifted higher, whipping his head back and forth while his fingers made furious rubs over his eyes.

Wearily slumping from the scream she couldn't seem to control, Cassie grabbed onto on the tall bedposts and hung on.

"What a sight!" Haley laughed while buttoning her snug fitting jacket. "I'd love to get it on film, especially you Jack! It would be sweet revenge to circulate such amusement, my man."

Giving a violent upward bob of his head, Jack tried to focus his eyes towards the voice while the sounds of Cassie's screams echoed through his ears, arousing him more and more with each passing second.

"Is that you, Haley?" he groaned, although his face bore up like he was trying to speak stronger. "What the hell are you doing in my house? I. . .told you never to come near me."

"So sorry, darling. I know that your house is off limits for now. But you know us . . . whenever we can," Haley replied with convincing delight. "I'm afraid you just got carried away with the rum, pot, and a couple snorts on board."

"You filth!" Cassie screamed at the white form, looking blurry to her panic-stricken vision. *Her walls . . . the bricks were popping out in all directions.*

Suddenly, as if it had all hit him, Jack lunged his upper body towards the bedpost. "No Cassie, you can't believe . . ." He lunged closer, stretching an arm, trying to reach her. "It's a set up . . . set up . . . cake . . . cheap . . . cheap champagne. They did it . . . I . . . hate her . . ." He breathed out the last statement repeatedly.

"But I love you, darling," Haley jumped in with great aplomb. "What's love to you anyway? A wild romp in the hay, that's what. So in that context, you *do* love me, Jack."

"No . . ." He made furious grabs at Cassie. "I never touched her. She makes me sick. I despise her, Cass. You gotta believe that."

Cassie jerked her wet face to Jack, then to Haley, and then back to Jack, her eyes lingering across his. *Oh . . .* she so wanted to believe him. In fact, she would spend every last cent she owned if her mind could muster just a flicker of doubt. But the sights, sounds, and smells, had collapsed on her brain and made rubble of it. She could muster no type of flicker past the destruction. "I gotta leave." She numbly clutched her middle with one hand while her other pressed against her mouth and nose. "Goodbye, Jack."

"Cassie!" He scrambled off the bed as quickly as his drugged-up body would let him. He clumsily gathered the comforter around him and dragged after a slow-moving Cassie. He felt the cool touch of glass on his bare feet and tripped to the floor. Empty bottle after bottle caught his hazy gaze and more desperation filled him.

"You're sunk, Jack," Haley Shears retorted above him. Then like a triumphant queen, she stepped over him, swung past Cassie, and made her way out of the bedroom.

Jack let out a tortured yell at the retreating form. "You're a bitch, Shears. *Bitch!*" Helplessly, he switched his gaze to a dazed-looking Cassie shuffling in front of him. He grunted into a partial lift and staggered after her. "Cassie stop, please. Set up . . . set up, I tell you."

The words briefly penetrated Cassie's brain, but she couldn't think, not here, not now—all she felt was her utter vulnerability, walking unprotected with only a couple loosely attached rows of bricks surrounding her. *How did it ever come to this?* Her mind screeched in absolute terror.

It had once been so unshakable in another time, another place only illuminated with one small bright white light. There my fortress had grown to invincibility. This wasn't supposed to happen. Never!

Jack tightened the comforter around him and tried to lift higher. At some point, the remembrance of his child struck his consciousness, and the panic knocked him like a flung boulder. "Please Cassie. I love him and want him as much as you. I want him. I want him . . ."

He broke down into tears, cursing the impulsive fuck up that had made them prime for the rest. If only he had kept his damn mouth shut last night, none of this would have happened. And the hurt she must be suffering . . . he was glad his brain was numb so he didn't have to feel that too.

"I want him . . ." The words touched her brain, but she could make no response. *How could the wall fall like Humpty Dumpty?* And she sensed another brick slipping away while she walked into the living room. Two more steps, and another sped across the carpet, and another . . . until she sensed a single shaky row around her feet. *Snort? Rum? Pot? Boyfriend? Mechanical*

toys . . . ? Is that what she said? Mechanical?

"Talk to me, honey. I can make it right. It was a set up, you gotta believe that. I would never . . . I *love* you . . . *I would never.*" Blinded by tears, Jack tripped into a faster pace.

Cassie sensed one of the bricks crack with unstableness. *Oh Harry, don't desert me too.* She felt the rocky shake as if it would burst from excessive pressure at any moment. *Keep moving,* she told herself, even though the cracking intensified with each step she took. She placed a hand on the front doorknob and turned. Like a bullet fired at close range, a loud crack hit her mind, and everything went blank. A split-second later she felt the gentle twirl of her body.

"*Casseee . . . !*" Jack gathered all his strength to make it to the fallen form. The front door swung open in tune to the balmy breeze. For a brief second, as he hung over a pale-looking Cassie, he glanced outside. The area swarmed with media, and in all her glory, Haley Shears was in the thick of them, her mouth going a mile a minute. In a total panic, he returned his attention to Cassie, wanting to take her in his arms, but too frightened to move her much too still form.

"Oh God! My babies!" he sobbed out with a myriad of emotions, including an intense degree of self-hate. He securely wrapped the blanket around him, and stumbled to the door. In a split-second, he heard the squeal of a car and saw a shiny black flash move down the street, though he took no time to investigate further.

"Someone call 911!" he cried out into the milling crowd. "Hurry . . . !"

Chapter 27—Cassie and Jack

Nono, Kristi, and nearly 'Harry' too . . . the remaining bricks feel so loose that I'm afraid to breathe. But that God not the baby . . . almost though.

Not moving a muscle, Cassie laid atop her hospital in a secure, private room at UCLA Medical Center. She had some spotting, the obstetrician told her. So she needed to remain quiet to avert disaster. Although the pregnancy seemed healthy, he also said, thus the chance of miscarriage was small in his estimate. Yet she couldn't take any risks. Her child was all she had left and it was vital she rebuild her wall, brick-by-brick if need be, for his sake--which, in reality, was for her sake.

How? By writing? She had asked herself. But she found the notion less than appealing, almost obscene. She had already tried this route and lost miserably. If she made another attempt, she figured that it wouldn't be long before the woman, Cassie Callahan was reduced to the obedient, ruffled created caricature, smiling in a corner. Not a single solitary aspect of *Cassie* would remain—*death.*

She could never do that to her son.

He *would* have *Cassie* for a mother, never June.

Never!

. . .And then there was Jack.

She had never heard him sob so hard or plead so mightily to be allowed to see her. He had posted himself like a sentry at her door. Even now she could hear his sobs which hadn't abated for the three hours since she had been brought to her room. The sound tore at her heart. She still loved him despite what he had done; although trusting him was another matter. She couldn't bring herself to face him with such an uncertainty inside her.

It was so hard to think.

Her mind was so swamped with all the different voices and sensory stimuli that no logical thought processes would seep through the muck.

A nurse entered her room, and briefly, she heard the noises outside the door. Jack's loud sobs mingled with a variety of voices. The only familiar one was the fast-talking voice of Harv Wellson who was obviously comforting Jack.

"Who are all those people out there?" she asked the nurse.

The nurse moved up the bed and grabbed the blood pressure cuff from its holder on the wall. "Python Studio executives, publicity types, here to control all the reporters downstairs. You know, Ms. Callahan . . . they always have to cover-up."

"Cover-up?" Cassie asked with confusion. "Cover-up what?"

Her look tentative, the nurse wrapped the cuff around Cassie's arm and took her blood pressure without answering.

"What did you mean?" Cassie cried out, her paranoia sparked by the evasiveness.

"Nothing, Ms. Callahan. It's only an assumption." The nurse took her pulse and stuck a thermometer probe in her ear.

"I wanna know what you meant!" Cassie shrieked.

The nurse ignored the outburst. "All your vital sign appear to be fine, Mr.

Seeking Out Harry

Callahan. Can I get you anything?"

"Tell me!" Cassie screamed.

The nurse quickly leaned forward to firmly grasp her shoulders. "Calm down, Ms. Callahan. Your baby, remember?"

The hands felt frigid, and Cassie perceived the woman's eyes as likewise. "Take your hands off me!" She swatted the hands away. "I don't want your hands on me!" She was gripped with terror at the unknown and vague inferences. "I want my Jacko's hands! *Jackooo . . . !* She screamed at the top of her lungs.

Within moments a panicked Jack rushed into the room.

She screamed for Jack again while frantically trying to push away the nurse.

Jack quickly moved to the bedside and pulled Cassie into his arm, holding her as tightly as he could. "It's okay, Baby. Settle down. Jacko's got you . . ."

****

Weary and carrying a heavy emotional weight, Jack walked out of Cassie's hospital room a little past seven-thirty the next morning after the most terror-filled evening and early morning of his entire life. Harv Wellson, who had also acquired very little sleep, greeted Jack when he stepped out the door.

"How is she, Jack?" Harv asked with much concern.

"She's finally asleep." Jack plopped down on the couch outside her room where he had shed so much of his terror the night before. He pressed his face into his hands. "I just don't know if she'll ever forgive me, Harv," he choked.

"Sure she will, Jack." Harv sat down on the couch as well. "It'll just be a little sticky, that's all."

"She'll barely talk to me. When I try to explain, she turns her face from me and says she doesn't know if she can trust me anymore." Jack shook with fear at her words. "What if I lose my son over this, huh, Harv?" And the mere possibility made his eyes flood with tears, especially after all the painstaking conclusions he had come to. They were his whole life, his future hope, and without them, *I have no future.* Never again would he find such a wondrous love that he shared with Cassie. If wasn't her, it would be no one, he vowed to himself.

How could I . . . after burning the candle at both ends for the last twelve years and still ending up with a brightly burning glow, despite . . . how the hell could I?

"There's just no proof, Jack, no matter how many times you scream, set up. And that Shears dame really did a number with the reporters. But of course she's nowhere to be found. Someone stashed her away but good."

"You can bet that's there a few people involved, so someone's bound to slip. And all those people at that trumped-up celebration saw me drink the champagne, Harv."

"Cm'on, Jack . . . you don't think that spiked juice is still hanging around, do you?"

"But I *did* insist on those blood tests when I came to the hospital last night."

"Smart move, Jack. This way you can prove to Cassie that you didn't have any pot, coke, and booze on board, and it also let's us know what they fed you." Harv patted Jack's thigh. "You were using your head on that one, Jack."

"It's still a fucking mess, regardless," Jack moaned.

"Yeah, with those reporters going manic with the 'trouble in paradise' and 'see Cassie we told you so' crap, it is, Jack."

"What?" Jack raised his face and pleated his brow with perplexity. "How can that be? You saw those Python execs last night? They were fretting like a flock of hens about hiding this mess."

"Well they didn't try very hard on a few things . . ." Harv reached into his back pocket then dangled a trade paper in front of Jack's nose. "Looks like in the case of you and Shears, they let the reporters' imaginations run wild."

Jack grabbed the paper and groaned. The story was front and center . . .
And Marabella Makes it a Threesome.

Tight with rage, Jack read every word, discovering that Harv was right. Haley *had* really done a number, implying drugs, perversions, and wild sex that had been an ongoing thing between her and him. Next to the article was a perfectly manicured picture of Haley, an older one of him, and Cassie, to his near gag, as nature's child. The combined messages were *very* damaging.

"Shit!" Jack yelled with angry disbelief. "What the hell good were those suited assholes, pretending all that concern, when they let them massacre me!"

"If you noticed, they *did* hide one big thing—Cassie's pregnancy. Maybe that was enough to ruffle a few hens' feathers," Harv said with suspicion.

"Why the hell did they hide it?" Jack slapped down the paper. "Why not make Torelli look like a total degenerate, knocking up an American phenomena while screwing another woman at the same time?"

"Yeah--why?" Harv questioned slowly. "Why not let the maggots in on the whole scoop when they would pounce on and devour such news. It would ruin you, Jack. So why not, when the purpose of this plan was to ruin you. Or . . . was it really?"

"You mean ruin up to a point, and then put the brakes on?"

"Or they don't care if you get muddied a little. What the hell . . . it's Torelli after all. But they care a helluva lot if Cassie is muddied in the process."

The theory striking him as curious, Jack settled back into the couch and tried to place all he knew into perspective. He was well aware that Michael Isle had an agenda for Cassie that was in cahoots with *whoever* in New York, involving big money. Even Harv knew about it. He too was part of the machine, but only because of Cassie. Without his agreement to play Harry Hannigan, Michael Isle wouldn't have his miniseries. So he was part of the machine under duress—*their* duress. Otherwise, Mike would rather slit his throat than offer Jack Torelli anything. In fact, he figured *him* in the role of Harry Hannigan was the first rotten cog in the machine.

But then there had been more . . .

Knowing Mike, he thought, knowing Mike, he had the mechanical function all tied up in a neat package, no loose ends, no glitches, plowing straight ahead, not caring who he ran over in the process, his usual mode of operation. But again, Torelli was an unexpected glitch. His relationship with Cassie had thrown them all for a loop and Mike had fought against it ever since he found out. Why? Was it actually Cassie's image as they all so strongly claimed? By now, he reasoned, her image must be tarnished so what the hell did it matter if a baby was thrown into the equation? After all, at the end of five months the world would know anyway. And in reality, who in the world gave a shit? Famous, unmarried women had babies all the time. So why the big stink with Cassie? He posed this exact question to Harv.

Seeking Out Harry

"I don't know, Jack," Harv sighed. "Things are getting strange. All I know is that Cassie is smack in the middle of their plan, like the hub of a wheel, the part that keeps the rest of the machine working."

"You mean with 'Harry Two', don't you?" Jack questioned, enraged that the woman he loved, with delicate mental workings, was the wheel hub, surrounded by greedy spokes with enough morals to hardly fill a thimble. *Season of Sorrow* would blast the wheel to bits, he told himself, and he couldn't wait for the holocaust.

"Well . . ." Harv bent over his knees and tightly folded his hands. "Grapevine has it that Isle hasn't acquired 'Harry Two' yet, although he's in heated negotiations with Starburst Publishing in New York. That's the rumor anyway."

Jack assumed the identical pose as Harv. "The rumor's crap, Harv. I happen to know that those writers are doing the teleplay as we speak, and Mike told me he plans on filming the sequel shortly after the miniseries is aired. He has to have acquired that book."

"Have you seen that fact in any of the trades, Jack?"

"Huh?"

Harv leaned closer to him. "If that was true, wouldn't the press would have jumped on that fact? I read the trades every day. *Nada* in terms of Isle and those book rights."

Jack admitted that he rarely read the trades anymore.

"My question is *why?*" Harv spoke on with calculation. "Why when we know the machine is Isle plus Starburst plus Cassie plus you. Why muddy you and cut out Isle when all the money hasn't been sucked out yet? And . . . why intentionally hurt Cassie with that ploy last night. It can't be productive to be messin' up the hub's mind."

"Intentional?" Jack filled with fearful caution. "Are you saying that Cassie was lured into that situation last night, on purpose?"

"Haven't you figured that out, Jack?"

Jack pulled back, stunned. No, he hadn't thought that. He assumed that Cassie happened to come home. He would never have believed that even Mike would be so cruel to do such a thing to an innocent woman when mere publicity of the trumped up event would have sufficed in the damage department. But now he wondered . . .

Who had sent her into that house. And why for Christ's sakes . . . ?

"I see that you're seriously considering my theory, Jack," Harv cut into his thoughts.

"Damn him!" Jack flared in a fury. "She could have lost the baby! And if she had, I can assure you, he would have been the *Late, Great* Michael Isle!"

"Calm down, Jack," Harv said nervously. "Cassie and the baby are okay, so my advice is to blow it off. He's no one to mess with. You have to think of your career and he could ruin you with a snap of his fingers--as you well know. You got a kid to think about now, Jack."

"So he gets away with it all, is that what you're saying, Harv?" Jack asked tightly. "Just blow it off, you say? He can defame me with lies, ruin my relationship with Cassie, cause her great pain, and threaten the well-being of my unborn child, and I just go on as if nothing has happened? Is that what you're telling me?"

"You got to, Jack," Harv firmly replied. "You have a contract, and if you screw it up, I can guarantee you that you'll never act again and end up at EMAX subsidiary for the rest of your Hollywood life. It's your choice, Jack."

"Okay," Jack conceded grudgingly, as the latter option curled his insides with disgust. Cassie, a child, and Rud Hanna were far from compatible. "I'll restrain myself for them, but that's the only reason. After 'Harry Two', I find an alternative."

Harv gave a jovial pat to Jack's back. "That won't be tough, Jack. I've already got a few legitimate inquiries about you. 'Harry' should cinch it if your performance is as good as the grapevine tells me. But as for now . . ." Harv stood up and lowered his gaze to Jack. "You stay here. Python can do without you for one day since they caused the fiasco in the first place. Although, I will be gracious for you and send Mike Isle your apologies . . ."

"Sure, Harv," Jack replied cynically. "Play the game 'til it chokes all of us . . ."

****

Enough Valium to lay out a Brahma bull . . .

Jack thought this for the umpteenth time since noon when the doctor had given him the results of his toxicology screen and blood alcohol level. "It could have killed you, Mr. Torelli," the doctor said. "And mixed with alcohol, no matter how benign, potentiated the effect. It's fortunate that you're a large person or the results could have been tragic . . ."

He sat at Cassie's bedside staring down at her. *What would have become of her and my son if?*

A soft choke escaped his throat.

Her delicate mental balance was one of the best kept secrets about Cassie Callahan, a secret that only he understood well enough to keep the scale centered so it didn't sway from one extreme to the other. Without him, she would aimlessly swim in a sea full of physical and mental threats and his child with her. The thought was so chilling, he could barely look at the two lab report copies that sat in his hands. He wanted to tear Michael Isle from limb to limb for what he had done without little thought to consequence . . . the only aim on his mind being his ultimate aim.

So typical, Jack thought in a rage.

Nothing stood in Mike's way . . . *not even murder.*

A soft moan and the rustling of bed covers made Jack leap up from the chair and hang over the bed. He wanted Cassie to see him first thing when she awoke so she knew that she was safe. He lifted a hand and gently stroked away the blonde hair that tousled around her face. Soon, he saw her green eyes grow larger and larger.

"What time is it, Jacko?" she asked softly.

Jack briefly glanced at his wrist. "A little after four. You had a good sleep, honey. I'm glad. You needed it."

Groggily, Cassie pulled herself up until she was propped against two pillows. "It wasn't a good sleep. I had nightmares, horrible nightmares," she told him.

Jack pulled her close to him and held tightly. "I'm sorry, Cassie. I never want you to have anything but beautiful dreams." He was unable to keep the choking sadness out of his voice.

Promptly, she pulled away from him and turned her face away. "Then why did you create the horrible nightmare, Jacko? Why, when I trusted you to never do that to me?"

Seeing the flat expression on a woman who usually teemed with emotions, alarmed him. He *had* to make her see the truth. "It was a set up, I tell you, Cassie, a way to ruin us. I was intentionally drugged and placed in that bedroom. Here look . . ." Jack pushed the lab reports in front of her face. "This proves I didn't snort coke, smoke pot, or empty all those booze bottles you saw. I was given Valium. Look!" He frantically pointed his finger across the lab reports.

To his relief, she took the papers and read them herself. Then she paused, wrinkling her brow in contemplation. "How do I know that you didn't intentionally take that Valium?"

He firmly grasped her shoulders and made her face him. "That's asinine. Why in the hell would I take something to knock me out if I was supposedly gonna have wild sex, huh?"

Her brow scrunched deeper, and she lowered a lost look to the bed. "It's all just so confusing, Jacko. My mind . . . it can't think," she whimpered. "That scene in the bedroom . . . I never felt so helpless or exposed."

"Oh Cassie . . ." He again held her close. "You're still in shock, honey. That was quite a mouthful for a woman like you, but I wanna help *un*-confuse you. I *can un*-confuse you, if you give me a chance. I love you so much, Cass. Only you."

Again, she pulled away and turned her face. "She was beautiful . . . Marabella I mean, almost perfect . . . a perfect Hollywood bod, I noticed."

Jack's insides shook with pure misery. "Cassie . . ." He reached his arms out, but she moved farther from his reach and he was afraid to push her. "I said I love you, all of you, every inch, inside and out, and that's more important to me than all the perfect bods in the world. I hate Haley Shears, I admit to you. She . . . caused me a lot of problems on the set of *Marabella*, and I'll also admit that she went after me. But nothing happened between us, I swear. That pissed her off, and she's wanted revenge ever since. And she would anything to be a star, including doing the bidding of every producer in town to get there."

"But she sounded so convincing, especially when she told me that you and her . . ." Cassie broke down into soft injurious sobs.

"Haley *is* a good actress, and that makes her a good liar as well." He pressed closer to her whether she liked it or not. "I go to the studio in the morning and drive ninety miles an hour on Santa Monica Boulevard to get home to you when I'm done filming. Now tell me when I have time to be with Haley Shears?"

Cassie pushed her cheek into the pillow and didn't answer right away. "Maybe when you went to Utah and . . . maybe when I went to Minneapolis and New York. Maybe . . . Oh Jacko, how can I really know?"

Jack drew back and slowly massaged his forehead. He wanted to say, *Because you're supposed to trust me,* but her answer to that was obvious. Perhaps she would always have that doubt about former *sleaze,* Jack Torelli.

He pulled back a little farther and let desolation wash over him. Her trust of him was so sacred, almost like a prayer. It had come despite his past which would bely any degree of trust to form. Yet, he *did* have her trust at one time after fighting like hell to acquire it.

But now . . . I wanna tear Mike apart for one more unforgivable thing.

He turned to her and replied the only way he could reply. "Because I tell you, Cass, and I'd never lie to you about this."

She gave a small nod. "I'll think about that, Jacko, if I can ever sort it all out. Right now I feel buried under a ton of destruction, and it's taking all my energy to keep my baby safe and protected."

"Our baby, Cassie." He desperately tried to get close to her. "I wanna help you keep our son safe and protected. I love him, and I'm so damn sorry for not realizing that the moment I found out. I. . .needed to get unconfused too."

"I believe you, Jacko. Your voice didn't lie that time." She curved her face into the pillow and kept it there.

Jack drew away from the bed and back to the chair. At least she hadn't asked him to leave, he comforted himself. She still needed to feel him close by despite her feelings.

But it would never be the same, he thought sadly.

How can I ever make her see the truth to the point that I'd garner her complete forgiveness for today and past I can't change . . . ?

****

"A limo will pick you up at eight-thirty in the morning tomorrow. Here's our production schedule for Minneapolis, Jack."

Barely able to look at Brett, the Assistant Director, Jack snatched the schedule, scanned it quickly, and felt his anxiety rise. It had been four days since the event at his house. Still confined to a hospital bed under doctor's orders, Cassie hadn't come around much in terms of forgiving him; although she never sent him away and even welcomed his arrival.

As he stared at the sheet, he fretted about leaving her. Granted, it was only two days to complete filming of the miniseries and after, he would be home for a long while, able to make it all up to her.

But those two days . . .

They felt uncomfortable to him even though they were yet to occur. She seemed much more fragile in the midst of her great confusion which didn't seem to be sorting out rather intensifying. Cassie said that all the excessive stimuli from that night was so bombarding, it was better to block it out rather than think about it.

And she won't allow me to help her sort it,

Jack wanted to crumple the schedule in his fist. Every time he tried to intervene, she cut him off by stuffing her face into the pillow. It wasn't a good time to leave, pure and simple, regardless of the short time frame.

Later that morning, he brought up his concerns to Harv Wellson during a phone call between a couple scene redoes.

"You can't hold up Isle's production, Jack. He'll destroy you. I'll keep an eye on Cassie, maybe get her a private nurse to keep her company. But *you* need to go."

"That's *really* fair, Harv," he had disputed back. "Isle ruins my public and personal life, and I still have to kowtow to the fucking bastard. I fail to see the equality."

"Equality? With Michael Isle?" Harv gave a diverting chuckle. "I think all the stress has clogged your reality base. You know damn well that he speaks in a whisper and people in Hollywood jump a hundred feet. Just go to any restaurant in town and watch the Maitre'D when they catch sight of his flashy bow tie. You'd think that God was coming."

"Perhaps His Highness needs to be jostled on his thrown a little," Jack snarled.

"You ain't gonna do it, Jack. Maybe Starburst will. But I'll tackle you before I allow you near that throne. Two fucking more days, Jack, and then a few months to give you time to cool off so you can face the bastard again."

Jack gave his reluctant assent. "What's behind all this, Harv? I've tossed it in my mind for hours, and even stooped so low as to pump information from Cassie so I could fill the holes. But it just upset her, so I stopped. What the hell is it?"

"Forget it, I tell you! Just play your part in the machine and let the big boys do whatever. It's too dangerous to probe when you have a future to think about." Harv replied. "You have a big enough job picking up the pieces. Put the rest out of your mind . . ."

But I can't . . . He hung up the phone and gazed into the sound stage. People moved around like bullets and the noise sounded like the spectator section at a Dodger game.

Not one of them had acknowledged their part in that night. In fact, they believed it their right to turn even a colder shoulder in lieu of the further shame that Jack Torelli brought upon the production with his illicit sexual antics.

It was so hard to take.

Despite him knowing he had a reason to take it--Cassie and his unborn son--it was still so damn hard on the psyche. He was dwelling in a world of constant hostility—the media too had been scalding—and he seemed to only find relief and comfort in a hospital room with a woman who would hardly talk to him, let alone listen to his desolation. It was a horribly lonely existence.

Yet with Cassie, it was never supposed to be that way again.

None of it was supposed to be this way.

Break into a legitimate role, he thought with bitterness. Do that, and all his troubles were over. He would give it a thousand percent and show the world that he still had it.

The snub would be kaput.

Jungle Love would be forgotten.

Bullshit!

A *cruel, cruel* fantasy.

Jack turned and took long paces to Wardrobe so they could doll him up for his final redo.

He felt more like a beggar than he ever did—even though he knew he had performed brilliantly in the most prestigious of productions, and he dared anyone to dispute that if asked straight on. Yet he still felt like a bigger beggar than he had ever felt with Rud Hanna.

At least Rud had been up front, never once coy, letting Jack know what he expected point blank. Now he had no clue, only nagging gut feelings. What the hell did they want from Jack Torelli? A complete gutting of mind and spirit? What the fuck had he ever done to them to deserve *this*? He wished, with every working cell of his body that he could find out.

And he kept walking towards Wardrobe where he'd be gutted some more . . .

****

Three hours later Jack reached UCLA Medical Center. Pacing determinedly, Jack told himself he would forge through the reporters, the curious gawks, the loud whispered comments, to get to his only sanctuary in the entire world.

The reporters outside the hospital pounced like they had been expecting him, firing questions about his affair with Haley Shears and probing like scientists with an eye to a microscope, about Cassie's response.

"Shears can go to hell and no comment to the rest," he muttered angrily.

When Jack stood inside Cassie's room, his heart immediately swelled with love upon sight of the wildly tossed blonde head peacefully reposing on a pillow. He walked to the bedside and just stared down, resisting the urge to crush her against him and place his lips to every exposed patch of bare skin. She looked so peaceful and content, he thought, taking in her lightly freckled face and the long-fringed black lashes sealing her eyes shut. He always wanted such peace and contentment for her, he decided then and there.

Or was that just a pipe dream of high impossibility?

Could they ever live such a life with him being him and her being her? Would anybody ever accept the fact that they combined beautifully despite the fact that were rancid oil and crystal clear water?

Needing to think until his brain couldn't think anymore, Jack collapsed into a chair and pulled it as close to the bed's edge as possible. What *is* most important? What's paramount to *your* life, here, now, ten years from now, twenty . . . ? And he thought, through all Cassie's quiet moments, as day became night, night became dawn, right up to the point he kissed her lips, and begged her to "hold on." He would be back in two days . . .

****

Not even half of twenty-four hours had elapsed since Jack left, and Cassie felt a horrible terror descend. What if Haley Shears was in Minneapolis? She let her imagination run wild with scenario after scenario, all identical to the one that was fire-branded on her brain He loved her, she had no doubt about that after all the hours he spent at her side, soothing her into tranquility.

Yet was she enough for his plainly evident healthy sexual appetite?

Her stomach churned with nausea at the mere thought. No way could she share Jacko with anyone and keep her sanity, she frightfully told herself. If that was the life he envisioned for her . . .

"No!" She pressed her face into the pillow. She couldn't allow such a notion into her mind on top of everything else that was turning her brain into a high-powered egg beater.

It was just too much!

Although she had to admit her brick wall *did* feel more stable. His voice and actions in relation to her and the baby, had gone a long way to secure that wall. Just the knowledge that he wouldn't abandon either of them for the likes of a young actress had added several bricks.

But was if a forced move? She couldn't stop asking herself. Did Jacko *really* want to chuck his infamous lifestyle to be trapped at home with her and an infant?

It just didn't jive!

How? She asked herself. How could he so readily change his stripes, or even more importantly maintain those stripes over the long run, when his life had been so totally different from what it was now? The contrast was almost preposterous, she thought. To go from plenty to nothing . . . she thought it must be horribly hard for him. He *had* to be restless, maybe maniacally so, but he was too afraid to tell her after his proclamations about his great love. He didn't want to be a hypocrite, that's it. If there was one thing that Jacko was, it was stubborn, she told herself.

The door swung open and she caught a glimpse of white moving through it.

"More flowers, Ms. Callahan," the nurse said in a cheery tone, then she spun around to face Cassie.

"No!" Cassie screeched, backing away from the nurse.

"Ms. Callahan!" The nurse placed the arrangement on the bedside stand then rushed forward. "It's only orchids, an exquisite bouquet. What's the matter?"

"Take them away! Now!" Cassie yelled while dodging the nurse's grabby hands.

Not heeding Cassie's request, the nurse pulled the card off the arrangement and held it out. "At least see who it's from in case you need to make a 'Thank you' note, Ms. Callahan." She took a healthy whiff of the fragrant black bouquet.

"I can't." Cassie melted under the covers. She needed her Jacko. Now!

Without invitation, the nurse tore open the envelope, pulled out the card and read. "Now that super stud's out of the way . . . Please, Cassie." The nurse let out a small laugh. "Sounds like a comedian or an admirer. Strange message."

"Toss them out. No! Keep the card. Jacko saves them. Put it in my purse, out of sight."

With a shrug of confusion, the nurse did as Cassie asked. Then, turning back to the bed, she held out a white envelope. "This came for you too, a card it looks like." She gave the envelope to Cassie and lingered expectantly by the bed.

Cassie looked at the envelope, then at the nurse. "Is it time for my blood pressure? Or a pill perhaps . . . ?"

"Just curious," the nurse replied in a friendly tone. "You know . . . the lives of the rich and famous holds a fascination for us peons."

That's odd, Cassie thought, wondering how a professional could make such a statement. She felt a sudden chill of uneasiness followed by gobs of paranoia. "Please leave. I don't care to quench your fascination. Ms. . . ." She intended to make a complaint about the nurse's gall.

"Ms. Browning, Delores," the nurse replied with a wide grin.

"I wanna be alone Ms. Browning, so . . ." Cassie flashed her eyes directly on the woman.

"Certainly, Ms. Callahan. I'll just take the flowers before I leave . . ."

As soon as the door closed, Cassie picked up her phone and reached the hospital administrator. She hotly made her complaint against the nurse, adding that she refused to have the woman near her.

"We'll check up on this immediately, Ms. Callahan. And please accept our utmost apology," the administrator said in all graciousness.

After hanging up, Cassie tossed the envelope in her hand for a few moments before opening it. Like the nurse had predicted, it was a get-well card. She read the front then opened it. A note fluttered out in front of her. Curious, she plucked up the note and read.

"Get out of that hospital, Cassie, I warn you. He's got spies everywhere, and with Jack gone . . . Go to your house in Beverly Hills and I'll contact you.

We need to talk as soon as possible. Rip up this note it you care a fig about me . . . George from Python Studios."

George? She read the note again and her panic rose. *Spies? George?*

Cassie raised her eyes from the note. He was such a meek old guy, she thought. *And who was 'He'?* As she tried to compose her thoughts, a vision flashed in her head, one that she had completely obliterated in the shock of what she had found in their bedroom.

My God, George had warned her that night!

"Don't go inside, Cassie. She's in on it too . . .'"

How could I have forgotten?

Had George been implying a set up like Jack claimed to her repeatedly over the last few days? She had to know! *Stay calm, Cass . . . the baby.*

Gently, she eased from the bed and headed for her closet. The doctor said her pregnancy was healthy, she firmly reminded while she pulled down the shoulder bag that Jack had packed for her. Ever-so-carefully, she walked to the bathroom to dress. She put on the clothes she wore the day she and Claire went out.

Claire!

What was her part? She wondered, stuffing her hair under her favorite *Coors* cap that Jack had thoughtfully placed in the bag. Could Claire have set up her too? Could she have done something so tricky under the name of concerned friendship?

What do I 'really' know about her?

After placing the large black opaque sunglasses over her eyes, Cassie slowly walked out of the bathroom. *If I can only get to those elevators undetected . . .* She cautiously moved towards the door. When she was halfway, the phone jangled, halting her cold. Cassie stared at it for a moment, wondering what to do. Then she made a mad lunge for the ringing instrument.

"Jacko?" she asked breathlessly.

It was a female member of the hospital administration.

"Ms. Callahan, could you have perhaps gotten the name wrong? There's no Delores Browning employed on your floor or in this entire hospital, and her name doesn't appear on any of our nurse registries."

"Really?" Cassie's eyes shook to the get-well card. "Thank . . . Thank you." The phone drizzled out of her hand. Again a look at the card. Without delay, she plucked up George's note, ripping it into tiny pieces and sticking the bits in her purse. Then with shaky hand motions, she did likewise to the card.

Feeling the sheer terror of her paranoia, Cassie cracked open the door and peered into the hall. When the thoroughfare looked fairly clear of hospital personnel, she sidled through the door crack and melded into a group of visitors . . .

****

Drenched from the high Twin Cities humidity, reminiscent of summer days in New York, Jack dragged into his hotel suite at the Minneapolis Raedisson after the first day of filming was completed. Feeling near exhaustive collapse, he fell stomach down on the king-size bed. Not only had the scenes been physically and emotionally grueling, but the place had been like a circus atmosphere from the moment he exited the terminal at the Minneapolis/St. Paul Airport.

He recalled the unbelievable crowds, mainly females held back by at least thirty police officers, all screaming "Harry" at him. The combined noise nearly burst his eardrums.

"Smile pretty, Torelli," Michael Isle sneered gleefully into his throbbing ear.

Despite his urge to gag, he brandished his most gorgeous smile and lifted his hand now and then, feeling like Bill Clinton as he made his way to the awaiting line of limousines.

And the crowds hadn't let up. They seemed to be everywhere, especially female screaming meemies of every shape and size at the front of the hotel being patrolled by Minneapolis P.D. He thought he couldn't hear another scream of "Harry" and stay standing to talk about it.

He lightly pounded his face into the pillow to stem the dizziness he felt from such long exposure in the hot, wet air that he was no longer acclimated to.

Once his head stopped spinning, he headed for the bathroom to take an icy-cold shower. When he felt the heat seep from his body, Jack turned off the showerhead and headed back into the bedroom to get fresh clothes. As he dressed in ripped faded jeans and a white tank top, he thought about Cassie. Only for short spurts had she left his mind since he walked out of that hospital room. He lightly brushed his fingers over his lips, still able to feel that last kiss, more perfunctory than passionate, and the memory made intense sadness grip him.

Will she ever abandon herself to me again, or would all their future encounter be perfunctory with the mistrust standing between this and passionate?

After what they shared, the idea was unbearably inconceivable, he told himself. Thus he wouldn't think of such grievous things and instead, decided to call Los Angeles to hear her voice and pretend everything was all right so he could make it through one more day of filming without cracking up. Once the miniseries was done, he kept reminding himself, he could began the reparation of their lives into that meaningful, trusting entity that it had once been. He would show her how much he loved her every moment of the day, if need be.

He was comforted by this final thought while he waited for the phone connection to Cassie's room. Ten rings passed before a strange female voice answered. She spoke quickly to him when he identified himself.

"What do you mean she's missing?" Jack shouted while looking around with helplessly. "The doctor said she needed to stay in bed for Christ's sakes!"

"All her personal effects are gone, Mr. Torelli."

"Weren't you people watching her? You all knew how emotional she was, couldn't you have kept a closer eye out for her?" he raged out all his panic.

"She's an adult, Mr. Torelli, and bottom line is that if she wants to leave a hospital, she had every right to do so, with or without a doctor's consent."

What the hell do I do? More than a thousand miles away. What do I do?

His panic exploded with the horror that she had left him. Maybe he would never find her. The world wasn't a small place after all, and if Cassie really wanted to hide . . .

"Dr. Morris has tried to call around and locate Ms. Callahan. Her pregnancy may be jeopardized with this move and he thought she should be warned. But as far as anything else, there's nothing we can do, Mr. Torelli. Like I said, she has every right to leave . . ."

He slammed down the phone, knowing *damn well* he couldn't stay in Minneapolis now. He wouldn't be able to speak a line, or perform a stunt. Every moment counted, he told himself as he jogged out the door of his hotel room.

****

Cassie sat stiffly on the couch in the living room of the Beverly Hills home, worried her frantic flight from the hospital had injured her pregnancy. She dared not twitch a muscle until her heart stopped pounding and her breathing normalized.

Thinking back, she deemed herself lucky. She had gotten past the hoard of reporters stationed outside the hospital by pretending she was with a man and his abundant family. Italians most likely, she figured. And then, not one reporter was outside her home when the taxi pulled up to the curb. But she well knew, it all would reverse once her disappearance from the hospital was made public. So she would have to get out before then, she told herself.

Oh, where was George?

As dusk settled, she still sat, exhaling and inhaling slowly, despite the jitters in her stomach and the paranoia blooming like a California poppy field. During the interim, the phone rang several times, but she forced herself not to answer even though it may be her Jacko. On the flip side, maybe it was *He* . . . or someone who would tell *He* where she was. And now the thought of *He* filled her with sheer terror. *He* had planted spies who brought black orchids and opened her cards and she wondered how much *He* knew about her.

It was nearing nine p.m. when she heard a window tap coming from the back of the house. She widened her eyes then shifted them. *Did she dare?* It might be George or . . . It might be *He*.

But it might be George and I have to know.

She propelled upward and moved slowly, gearing her ears towards the sound. Finally she ended up in her back bedroom office. She turned an ear and determined the sound was coming from the far left shaded window. Cautiously, she made her way to the window and lifted a single slat, then peering through it.

She saw the thick white mustache and her heart jumped with excitement. Quickly she lifted the shade up and yelled for George to go to the back door. Minutes later, he stood in her kitchen with his hand around her arm, leading her back to her bedroom office. He closed the door, bolted it, then with frenzied eyes motions, looked around at the windows before speaking.

"News got out that you left the hospital. The Lady Piranha has been on the phone to Minneapolis for the last two hours," he panted out.

"Claire? Why should she care so much?" Cassie asked with utter confusion.

George's jaw grew rigid. "Because she'd go to hell and back for him. How do you think she made so high up at such a young age? For every dirty deal he's been in for the past ten years, Claire Gibson's fingernails are just as dirty, maybe even dirtier. She's after his tail. She likes the idea of being hitched to a multi-rich studio owner, and that bitch will do anything to get it."

"Are you saying that her and Michael . . . ?"

"It's one-sided. He likes to play around with the not-so-nice girls. You know . . . boobs, no brains . . . though she puts up with it to stay on his good side. But you can bet, if she could, she'd claw the eyes out of every one of them."

Cassie shook her head with greater confusion. "So what does this have to do with me? It's juicy and all, but I don't get it. Who's *He* and those spies? And I need to know about Jacko."

"First sit down," he said in a serious tone.

A fearful shudder ran up and down her back as she sat down in her desk chair. Never had she seen the out going, amicable George, in such a state. "I'm listening," she told him.

"Jack was set up, as plain as the nose on your face," George began. "Isle's been determined to make life hell for him, and he's damn well succeeded."

"How?" Cassie breathed out in distress. "Jacko never said a word to me."

So George went on the describe the treatment that Jack Torelli had received at Python Studios long before production of the *Life and Times of Harry Hannigan* began.

Cassie broke down in sobs.

Oh god! He put up with the torture for me, knowing what 'Harry' meant to me. And at that moment, a warm explosion of love spread through her.

"The plan was to drug Jack, place him in a compromising situation with that Shears woman who, may I add, is thick with Isle herself, and then get the press there to catch it."

"Why in the world for?"Cassie tearfully burst out.

"Because of you,' George replied. "Isle's been acting like a maniac about your relationship with Jack, and this was a sure way to split you up."

Cassie slowly shook her head in disbelief.

"He's tried on several occasions including recently at the Python suites," George continued on. "Jack was like a wild man, calling and trying to see you after you left him, and Isle gave us all orders that he wasn't to come near you."

"That bastard," Cassie sneered softly.

"And that trip you took to New York . . . that was his doing too. I heard the Lady Piranha laugh about it on the phone."

"Why?" Cassie leaned closer to him. "Why would he ever intrude so horribly?"

George grabbed a wooden high-back chair, placed it front of her and straddled it. "For the usual reason . . . money. Your second book to be specific."

"Harry Two?" She tightly screwed up her face, trying to make sense of this. "What does 'Harry Two' have to do with any of this? That's ridiculous. How could a book cause all this? This sheer vindictiveness?"

"He wants it badly and they won't give it to him. This makes him crazy. The more they say, no, the crazier he gets. Nobody says, no to Michael Isle without someone paying the price. Its equal measures of ego and greed, and Claire is the primary ego-feeder. That's why she's his right hand, and not for any reasons of competence. Bottom line . . . you fuck up Michael Isle, you pay a severe penalty."

Cassie gave a slow nod of understanding. "And he views Jack as fucking him up."

"Not only now, but several years ago. He never forgets, Cassie. One fuck up and you're screwed for life." He focused his kindly face on her. "Torelli was a rapidly rising star and Isle could see dollar signs clouding his vision. He had big plans of mega-stardom for Jack. Jack had the look and his talent was awesome. But Jack started having severe problems with his personal life that couldn't be resolved just because Michael Isle commanded it. And the hopes for mega- stardom disintegrated . . . no money . . . plans shot . . . and Isle ruined him. No one in Hollywood would touch him on Isle's say."

"My poor Jacko," she whispered sadly.

"That's Hollywood, Cassie. Piss off an egotistical big shot, and that's it. It soothes *his* ego, and to hell what it does to his victims. *He's* all-important."

"He?" Cassie asked with a fearful shake. "You mean, Michael is the *He* who sent spies to the hospital?"

"And she . . . Isle and Claire are of one devilish mind."

"Why?" Cassie pressed. "I doesn't jive. I understand he's desperate to get the book, but why be desperate at all? He and my publisher are sharks swimming in the same vicinity."

"It took awhile to piece together." George sighed heavily. "Again, it boils down to you."

"Why me?" she cried out with traces of hysteria. It was unimaginable as to what lengths Michael would go to for a few hundred pages plastered between two pieces of cardboard, she thought. It was *sooo* . . . sick.

"He's being blamed for your ruined image. After all, you got hooked up with a no-no like Torelli right under his nose and he's been unable to break it up. But now, with all the publicity about you and Jack busting up, that's got to be a feather in his cap, right? So theoretically, he should have that book in his hands any day now. In other words, he made the necessary repairs."

"John LaLiberte, Father in a shark suit. He's the one behind this, with Mother egging him on." Cassie muttered to herself.

"Huh, Cassie?"

Ignoring him, she kept muttering. "They have great plans for me, book-after-book and I suppose miniseries-after-miniseries, even though I hate television. But they'll find some persuasive means even if they have to chip away small chunks of bricks at a time. They have my number . . . or to be more specific, my number's been *hissed* to them all along. They're gonna dig and claw until they have their perfect 'Sandy', the ideal author, prime bullshit material, who they can twist and turn like a Barbie Doll." She abruptly stopped her noise and lifted her eyes to George. "It's getting clearer by the moment. And it may boil down to *me* as the means, but in the final analysis, the almighty dollar, the main scourge on society, the stuff men kill for—is the predictable end."

"But there's a rub, and that's *your* rub, Cassie," George said solemnly.

"What pray tell? What more could those scums do to me and the man I love?"

"I ask you to stay calm, Cassie." George placed his large wrinkled hands over her dainty ones. "It's your pregnancy. It can't happen for Isle to get that book. Having Jack Torelli's child will kill your image, and thus his last chance at redemption."

Horror coursed through her like a stream of ice. "What are you saying for God's sakes?"

"You weren't supposed to come into this house that night. That wasn't part of the original plan. I figure that Claire lured you away from Python, not to ultimately bring you home, but because Jack was getting more insistent and they were afraid you two would get back together before they could execute their plan with Haley Shears."

"So why did she convince me to go home and have it out with Jack if she was trying to keep me away from him?" Cassie cried out.

"You told her that you were pregnant, right?" he asked closely.

Cassie returned with a barely perceptible nod.

"What better way to induce a miscarriage than for you to receive such a shock."

"Oh my god."

George placed a tighter hold on her hands. "She decided to inject you into the plan on her own volition. For Isle. Remember . . . she would go to hell and back for Isle and the moment you told her about your pregnancy, she knew that his plan was foiled."

Her voice fearfully agitated with each word. "So he's still foiled. I didn't quite have a miscarriage. That's why I had to leave the hospital—his spies, right?"

"I've been hanging around this business for thirty years, and it never ceases to amaze me what hungry actors and actresses will do to get a break in an Isle production. Hundreds. . .maybe thousands . . . hungry enough to even pull some sort of stunt to make a woman have a miscarriage, by accident, of course. No one would be able to prove it."

Cassie pulled her hands away from him and pushed them into her face. Now her terror was beyond description, and she wondered how she could ever protect her child. She wouldn't be safe at the Beverly Hills home, not without Jacko around. So where?

As if reading her thoughts, George spoke with quick urgency. "You have to get out of L.A. as soon as possible. When Jack comes back, I'll tell him where you are and let him know what's happening. But you can't stay here. Things are getting more desperately crazy, and even if Isle's not here, his lackeys are."

"Shouldn't I go to Minneapolis, to Jacko?" she trembled out. But as she did, she felt the bricks shaking in tune with her body. The Twin Cities was the last place on earth she wanted to go, but . . .

"No! That's the worst place with Isle around. No telling what he'll do."

While contemplating, she turned to her computer and gently tapped on the buttons.

She couldn't help thinking back to where it all began—her attic, her selling of the book, her plane trip to the 'Big Red Delicious Apple', her limousine rides around New York one day, and to Starburst Publishing the next . . . then everything went downhill from there. And she came to a conclusion and a question: It wasn't supposed to be this way; *although* wasn't this part of the price all authors, to some degree, had to pay for that glittering world?

"Uncle!" she cried out with total decisiveness.

"What Cassie?" The corners of his eyes crinkled in befuddlement.

Cassie flipped on her computer and began cursing like mad. "It means that I'm going to New York. But I need your help, starting with my third book. I have to get three hundred eleven pages printed before I leave and a new title page typed up. I've . . . decided to add a few words."

"There's no time, Cassie . . ." George began to protest.

"We *have* to make time. You see . . . I'm gonna kill all my birds with a bogus stone . . . then find some peace . . ."

****

The Presidential Suite at the Minneapolis Raedisson, had been the center of a heated debate for the past hour, ever since Michael Isle had returned from his leisurely two-and-a-half hour supper in the downstairs dining room. Surrounded like a king by his production crew, he made cracks about the *bourgeois* food and lack of fine imported wines, while cooly ignoring the parcel of admiring stares from the *simpletons*, as he minced no soft words calling the other patrons.

"I gotta catch that early morning flight, Mike. Why are you being such a hardass?" Jack demanded angrily while watching the producer sit perched on a velveteen couch like he had not one care in the world.

"Because you can sweat it out in this Hades reincarnate for one more day like the rest of us," Michael replied with a steady terse look at Jack. "And may I remind you that your contract says that you finish this miniseries? I don't think you can afford to ignore terms of a contract again, Torelli, unless you want history to repeat itself, a hundredfold this time."

Rage rippled through Jack. "You just can't let me forget that can you. Mike? Is that what this is all about? You can't hold off for one lousy day because I fucked up all those years ago?"

Mike raised his eyes to the ceiling and nonchalantly bobbed his head. "The fuck up that reverberated all across Hollywood and is still reverberating. What can I say?" He lowered his eyes and grinned broadly. "And it doesn't stop reverberating until I tell it to stop. Capisce, you stubborn Dago who doesn't know when to quit until someone flattens you? Capisce, finally?"

The words sparked thoughts about the near-lethal dose of Valium, and it took all of Jack's will not to attack the smug-looking man who thought the world was molding clay sitting in his palm. "I capisce loud and clear, Mike, and it's getting clearer all the time," he replied through the grit of his jaw, knowing once again Michael Isle had won.

But never again, he thought, coming to an irrevocable decision in his life. *Next time, I toss him outa the ring . . . right on his ass.*

"Anyway, why worry?" Michael continued on with a look of pure hatred. "Cassie's probably snug in some Los Angeles luxury hotel suite which makes this one look like the Watts, sitting in a chair, preferably the oak rocking kind, knitting baby booties, one after the other, instead of following her forte which is writing. Sound like a fair trade to you, Torelli?"

"Yeah—it sounds fair to me," Jack replied, this time the smug looking one. "In fact I think I'll encourage her to knit sweaters, rompers, nighties, and enough blankets for a hundred babies. That sounds like an even fairer trade to me. Capisce?" With a slight salute, more mock than deferent, Jack took long strides out of the suite.

Once in the hallway, Jack's complacency rapidly disintegrated into renewed panic and helplessness. He paused to contemplate his next step. Finally, he decided that he had no choice but to try to contact Harv Wellson. Perhaps his agent could put a secret posse out for her . . .

****

"The last file is almost printed, Cassie," George said while Cassie hastily filled a large shoulder bag. "Hurry with that packing. We have to figure out a way to get you out of here and to the airport. You need to get somewhere safe in New York and stay there until Jack comes."

Cassie kept packing and made no comment. No use upsetting George with the fact that her hiding place wouldn't be 'hiding' anymore once she deposited her book one month early at Starburst. In fact, she thought with vengeful delight, the crap should fly all the way to Python Studios and smack Michael Isle right in the face. It would be her way of taking care of her Jacko for once rather than the other way around.

A delicious payback for everything that happened after that second limo deposited me on Park Avenue that fine April day, seemingly eons ago . . .

"It's done, Cassie," George announced indicating to a stack of white paper.

"Place it in that box that you just emptied of computer paper and I'll stick it in my bag," she directed. Placing her traveling gear aside, Cassie turned to her computer, found the file for her title page and typed in her addition. She printed it, then stuck it on top of the other papers.

Now I'm ready for my final journey before the peace sets in.

"Let's get moving, George. My plane leaves in two-and-three-quarters hours and Marina Del Ray isn't exactly a hop and a jump, especially on that San Diego Freeway which no man, *or* pregnant female, should travel."

"First, I'm making one anonymous phone call to the L.A. Times so we can get rid of a few pesky reporters outside your wall," George said with a sly smile, then he picked up the phone. "I think we'll put you at the Æmbassador."

"Now that's synergy," she laughed lightly. "I'm staying at the Plæza in New York . . ."

Chapter 28—Cassie and Jack

Next morning, suffering from jet-lag although feeling freer than she had in two years, Cassie browsed through a rummage shop on Fifth Avenue in New York, looking for a proper attire. She *was* Cassie Callahan, she repeatedly told herself as she browsed. The outfit had to possess no degree of Via Condotti, plenty of Soho, and a dab of pregnant Harlem streetwalker.

After much debate and plenty of silent laughter, she chose skin tight black pants with a front maternity panel that was stuff-*able* and a glittery, loud top of Indian fabric bearing only one arm strap. She topped this off with a pair of long beaded earrings that nearly hung to her shoulders and black platform shoes with gaudy diamond buckles. After paying for the items, she hoisted her shoulder bag, empty except for her manuscript box and her 'stuffing', and snuck into one of the dressing rooms.

There, she felt like a costume designer, creating that special look for her starring role. She even put on a little eye makeup and red-red lipstick, then debated about perhaps going braless, but decided her *finally* big bust couldn't take the strain. She pulled out the small white hand towel that she filched from the hotel and stuffed it into the panel of her maternity pants, which in actuality looked like tights, she decided while turning from side-to-side to get the total effect.

Perfect, she silently proclaimed, daring 'Sandy to even come close when she was dressed in such attire. *If only June's enamored friends could see me now . . .* and she let out a rip-roaring laugh full of gleeful victory.

And soon I'll see my Jacko!

She couldn't wait to forgive him!

And with this totally delicious thought, Cassie strutted all the stuff she could muster and made her triumphant exit out of the dressing room . . .

****

"Cut! Print!"

Christ Almighty! This place is like a combination Death Valley and the Everglades in July, Jack thought, dragging his body attired in a warm thousand-dollar suit to a shady area outside the Metrodome in downtown Minneapolis where the cameras had just filmed Harry Hannigan acquiring part ownership in the Minnesota Vikings with a small handshake and a big threat. Why the hell so dramatic, Cassie? He thought with frustration while gurgling down ice cold mineral water. Couldn't she have written some of these Minneapolis scenes indoors?

He felt much more calmed this morning and could even smile a bit. Harv Wellson had called him a little after four in the morning, Minneapolis time, to tell him that Cassie was at the Æmbassador Hotel in Los Angeles, a tidbit he had learned from a drinking buddy who reported for one of the Hollywood trade papers.

Briefly, he thought about calling her. But in lieu of the hour and her need for sleep, he restrained himself, deciding to make his call after filming was done and before his plane to L.A. took off at eight-thirty that night. He couldn't wait to see her, he thought, gulping down another bottle of mineral water. And he couldn't wait to return to the moderate L.A. climate either.

"Jack!"

Jack raised his eyes above the bottle. Brett, the Assistant Director stood at a distance, a taunting smile playing on his lips. He held his stare, having a strong desire to stuff those lips into the bottle he held. But he told himself, *A few hours longer. Calm down, Torelli. The little pisser will get his comeuppance soon enough*

"Whatcha need, Brett?" he asked as pleasantly as he could force past his clenched teeth.

"Time to hit the road," Brett said with a haughty superiority so reminiscent of Michael Isle, that Jack now felt the urge to vomit in his bottle. "It's time for 'Harry' to acquire part ownership of the IDS Building . . . on the window washer's scaffold . . ."

****

Starving writer, who hooks on the side.

Cassie loved it! It was the title she had dubbed her character, and she played it to the hilt as she sashayed past the receptionist's desk at Starburst, big black sunglasses covering her eyes. She ignored the receptionist's loud protests for her to "Stop!", and made it to the elevators before two familiar security guards halted her step. With a gleeful look, she lifted her sunglasses over her head and produced her most brilliant smile. Both pair of eyes bulged, but they pulled away and let her pass. She lowered her sunglasses back to her eyes and wildly fluffed out her hair, hoping that 'Mother' was around to appreciate it.

A few minutes later, she stood in front of John LaLiberte's secretary who looked like she was in the throes of a grand mal seizure. Utterly pleased, Cassie silently patted her back for finally 'yanking the stick out'.

"He's in a meeting with Mr. Farchmin, Ms. Callahan. Shouldn't be long. will you wait?" the secretary stammered, her eyes squarely on Cassie's middle.

"Absolutely. I *must* deliver my book," she replied lightly, then walked into John's office without being invited to do so. She didn't have long to wait. The office door flew open and charging footsteps came through less than five minutes after she had sat down. *You're Cassie*, she reinforced, before turning to see the usual trio, John, Curt, and Geoff. The sight of the latter sent a brief cold tremor up her spine, but she told herself that it was almost over, and Geoff Haines could go to the devil!

"Cassie?" John asked cautiously as if scared to come near her.

Feeling in her absolute glory and silently telling her Jacko that his was for him, she stood up and stuck out her stomach. "Hello John. How are you?"

John inhaled a sharp gasp as he eyed her up and down.

"To answer your question . . . Yeah—it's Torelli's illegitimate kid." She said.

"How could you do this?" Curt Farchmin's eyes darted as if unable to even look at her. "And those clothes . . ."

"And *that* hair . . . What do you think, Mother?"

"*My God!* You've gone totally West Hollywood and then some," Curt said, revulsion dripping from his lips.

"Like it?" Cassie clicked her platform shoes around in a circle. "I got it on Sunset at 'Sluts R Us'. Wonderful store for the expectant mother who likes to go wild in Hollywood with her maniac of an 'old man'. I'm thinking of getting a leather tunic with chains draped across my burgeoning bust for when Jack and I zoom around Brentwood on his Harley, spraying water bottles at all the straw hats."

John blazed his fiery blue eyes at her. "You mean you're still with him? After that illicit situation with that cheap actress? I was assured . . ." He paused and just glared at her.

She wanted to smack him for his pressure role in creating so many problems with her and Jack, but she told herself, *Cool it, the best was yet to come.*

"Of course I'm with him. Do you think I'm a fool? What red-blooded American girl could ever turn down the likes of Jack Torelli, no matter what he did. Such an obtuse question!"

"I'll kill him," John muttered under his breath while making his way to his desk chair. "He's out of it," he added in another mutter.

"Oh, I meant to tell you, John. I would like Darling Michael to produce Harry Two." She pretended to play with her fingernails. "For six . . . no seven million dollars . . . contingent of course on my Jacko repeating his stunning performance."

"What?" John breathed out angrily. "You have no cause to make such a request. We have the book rights."

"Okay John," she said, unconcerned. "But don't come sniffing around me when you want the television/movie rights to *Season of Sorrow*. I'll very nicely, or not so nicely, tell you to 'stuff it' . . . or have my Jacko tell you. Have you ever run into a Mack truck, John?"

A looked of discomfort froze on his face. "Speaking of *Season of Sorrow*, Cassie—"

She patted her hand across the black leather shoulder bag. "It's in my bag, John, a month early. So . . . I thought I'd stroll around New York for a month . . ."

His gaze fixed on the shoulder bag. "Can I have it since you're done anyway?"

"Only if Michael gets the book rights to 'Harry Two', contingent of course on Jack Torelli playing 'Harry'. You know . . . same as last time. And a sizable chunk of the seven million in my pocket, minus yours and Ferris's percentage cut, *naturally*. Then you can have book and rights in one swoop, and you make a good piece of money too. So . . . what the heck do you have to lose, except a little vindictiveness?"

"I have to discuss this with our attorneys," John told her.

"So discuss . . ." She flopped back into the chair. "I have all day." And her hand made gentle, circular motions on the black leather.

"This is obscene!" Curt Farchmin suddenly flared. "Where do you get off dictating to us!" His icy eyes locked right onto her.

You're Cassie! Cassie! She forced herself to meet the blood-chilling look.

"Where do you get off dictating to me when I've made all you guys rich with my little creative burst called 'Harry Hannigan'? I'm a best-selling author. I've earned the right to be obscene. And while we're on the subject of obscene . . ." Cassie promptly tipped her head towards John's office couch.

Curt quaked with rage, but he made no further comment.

Cassie smiled inwardly as she sensed that remaining unprotected wall on her raft slowly erect. Next, telling herself it was inevitable, she peeked at Geoff

Haines. His eyes had a wild, demonic quality as they locked onto the center of her maternity top. She twisted her gaze forward and instinctively gathered her arms around her middle and held tight.

Don't look anymore, her mind shrieked.

"So do we have a deal, John?" she managed to ask.

His gaze glued on the black leather bag, John's paused to contemplate. "You say it's done? Up to your usual standards?" he finally questioned.

She forced her cheeks to curve into brightness. "I'd say it's way beyond my usual standards. A new level and dimension for Cassie Callahan," she replied without a falter to her cheek muscles.

"All right! What does it matter if I give Isle this book? He'll never get another and I can soothe my satisfaction by watching the sonofabitch beg for a few years to come."

"Sounds good to me," Cassie piped up. "I'd like to watch that myself."

"Luckily, the contracts have already been drawn and only require Isle's signature," John admitted hesitantly. "And the seven million . . . I'm going for seven-five . . . if you agree of course, Cassie."

"Why not eight . . . if you think he's eager enough?" she tossed out in reply.

"Yes--why not?" John snarled softly.

"And you can fax them to his office. He's not there, but Claire is. I have no doubt she'll make sure that he gets the contracts in Minneapolis, pronto. She's plenty worried about a bun that's ready to explode in the media's oven."

"What?" John demanded. "Are we speaking merry-go-round again?"

"No." She smiled glowingly, feeling victory blaze like an inner torch. "From this point on, I promise there won't be anymore merry-go-round talk . . ."

****

"Why the hell did 'Harry' have to buy *this* bar?" Jack whispered to Brett as they stood in the famous Carolina Club on Hennepin Avenue in downtown Minneapolis. He turned his face, trying not to watch the topless waitresses strut back and forth while production crew members positioned the extras at the tables and booths.

"Harry loves women, and this place satisfies that little pocket of depravity that he can't quite rid himself of. You should approve of that, Jack," Brett replied with the glee of malice.

Telling himself to *un*-ball his fists—this was the last of it—Jack made no comment to the comment. "But this is television for Christ's sakes. Couldn't Mike have nixed *real* this one time?"

"I don't know, he's not around to ask," Brett replied. "He took off like a bat in hell with the studio attorney and I haven't heard from him since. Anyway, the scene is brief . . . You ogle a bit while leaning on the bar, coercing the owner into giving you part ownership and we only film bare female backs. Mike will push it through the censors, have no fear."

"You could have reproduced this on Sunset in L.A.," Jack groused. "Why drag us to a tropical jungle to film this when we could have been done by now?"

"But that's the *real*, Jack. Why produce a lousy imitation when the television viewer can have the pleasure of its true ambience. That's what makes Michael Isle so great. He always gives the viewer the pleasure, any time he can," Brett replied in a well-practiced spiel.

"Yeah great . . . ten percent pleasure and ninety percent self-touted," he couldn't help muttering, not caring if Mike's 'lackey premiere' heard or not.

Brett responded with a low jeering chuckle. "He can self-tout all he wants. He's Michael Isle after all. He even has a stack of nut brancakes named after him in the pink coffee shop at the Beverly Hills Hostèl. You can't get any better than that." He briefly toss of his head, then walked off yelling orders.

Better than that . . . Jack let the words disgustedly roll in his head while wondering if getting a stack of raisin wheatcakes named after him would make him great—wheat flour, eggs, milk, and a handful of raisins. Great? Was that truly the measure he had measured himself against all these years? He seriously asked himself as he stared down at the surface of the old antique bar, so polished it clearly mirrored his reflection.

If he really took the time to peel all the pretense away, what would remain? Passion . . . *perhaps?* Would the bar ripple into a picture of a twenty-year-old who had the world by the tail? Or . . . would it ripple with nothing but wood grain? Was he as self-touted as well? He wondered, as he thought back to the first time he had stepped off that plane at LAX and into the glittering world . . .

He had learned to play the game with sureness and rapidity. His looks hadn't hurt. People liked "to see" him and he loved "to be seen." The latter had seemed to be his only mission in life between his acting. So when he lost that, after his futile struggle to remain a big shot in the midst of all his problems, it had hit him hard, knocked him on his back, making him feel desperate to get it back anyway he could.

And Rud Hanna was a sure way.

Notoriety . . . In the public's eye at any cost even self-respect . . . Is that what he had really been reduced to? He asked himself with frank shock.

For what?

What had he truly ended up with after nearly forty-one years of living? Even if he had ended up with, *oh my,* his name on a stack of raisin wheat cakes at a prestigious hotel that Hollywood had dubbed *the* chic place, he would still ask, *What?* And keep asking. Although now the answer seemed as clear as the smooth surface below him.

He had truly been one of the lucky ones, if compared to several others in his vast, former social sphere. He had good stuff in him from the day he was born, rich stuff that money could never buy or imitate, stuff that stuck no matter what cheap reproductions one tried to toss on top, a privileged world that was an absolute antipathy to the one which he coveted to dwell in, then fought like hell to dwell in.

But I never could have won no matter the weapons I used. Because in reality, I had no armor.

Jack pressed his eyelids shut as the truth rained over him. He had no strength of armor without Mott Street guiding the way for him like it had in his youth when he knew with certainty what was right, what was moral, *what* he was about. Mott Street had been like an anguished mind's tattoo, torturing him at his most sordid moments when he knew full well, without a single star blurring his vision, that this was wrong for the man named Jack . . . *Torelli.* Now he could see clearly that his rapid downfall and failure in life was so predictable, *so* inevitable, that he was a total imbecile for not realizing the truth long ago and wasting his energy with a hopeless climb.

So what was left . . . ?

He pried open his eyes, fastened them on the bar top, and looked. Then he smiled.

Seeking Out Harry

It was Jacko Torelli, youngest son and bambino of the Torelli family on Mott Street.

. . .And Jacko was their shining hope.

Unfortunately Jacko had taken these words to heart, maniacally so, and created an impossible dream. And now, after all that mania, he thought with nearly laughable irony, *I'm back to where I started* . . .

"Brett! Get over here!"

Jack lifted his eyes when hearing the imperious voice. Michael Isle stood in the club entrance, smiling wider than a New York block while standing next to the studio attorney whose smile was equally huge.

"I got it, Brett!" Michael yelled joyously, grabbing his Assistant Director in a bear hug. "Can you believe it? *They* contacted me! I guess they *do* know who's the 'King of Television' after all."

Jack turned his eyes from the nauseating sight and fastened them back on the bar, trying to conjure up a picture of the most *real* in his life—silky-to-touch pale blonde hair, huge, brilliant with excitement, green eyes, and the woman who owned such glorious entities as well as carried inside her 'the true shining hope' of the Torelli family. He couldn't wait to grab both of them and hold on as tight as he could. Never again would Jacko let go of *real*.

"Another feather in my Hollywood cap, eh Brett?" Michael crowed loud enough for the entire avenue to hear.

Jack sneered while glancing at the producer. *What pray tell is it this time, to make you so uncharacteristically jovial, Mike? Perhaps an Isle omelet filled with hot air and the turds of bulls at Spägo* . . . ?

****

"What are you up to, Cassie?"

Cassie stiffened when the hiss touched her ear.

She still sat in John LaLiberte's office waiting for him to return while Curt Farchmin, looking like he wanted to throttle her, and Geoff Haines who had abandoned his usual watchdog stance and was pacing the office, waited also.

Feeling the words burn on her lips, she wanted, in the worst way, to make a retort about his dash of sudden bravery to make such a bold move in Curt's presence. But she decided to diffuse the response and concentrate on her lap until John returned, hopefully with the signed contract. It had been close to three hours, and now she worried that perhaps she misjudged everything. Maybe complications had arisen.

Her insides jiggled with apprehension at the mere possibility. It was imperative, in her mind, that she close the chapter today. The chance had been taken, in the name of vengeance, granted, and not exactly on the up-and-up which was a little bothersome. Although she kept reminding herself that John would lose nothing except a future perhaps, and that most of the muck would fall on that tenth floor office building at Python Studio where it belonged.

"You won't get away with this, Cassie."

Another hiss, and she sunk deeper into the chair, protectively shielding her abdomen with her arms. Hold on, she told herself. It was almost over and soon she would see her Jacko-- and Jacko would crush Geoff Haines between his hands if he dared harass her again.

When the office door flew open, she jumped and flung around. A cleverly smiling John LaLiberte entered with a manila envelope swinging in his hand.

"It's done, Cassie. All the papers are signed and the eight point five million is being transferred as we speak." John gave a gleeful raise of his eyebrows. "Quite a chunk. What are you going to do with your share of all that money?"

"Ah . . ." She told herself the time had come, her final hurrah was upon her, her passion, if it ever was ever passion, was spent. It was time, in grown-up fashion of her nearly thirty-five years, to start dealing with June rather than trying to fight her. The task would be far from easy, she knew, and she envisioned some regression along the way. But with her son and her Jacko, her course would be less bumpy.

Cassie willed her body upright, then she lifted the bag to John's desk. Feeling the majority of nerves in her fingertips she lifted the box and placed it directly on John's brown leather blotter. Like a wolf pouncing on a baby rabbit, John grabbed the box and opened it. He looked down and then just stared, his brow pleating more by the moment.

"An autobiography?" he suddenly thundered. His eyes flew up to Cassie.

"No John," she began quietly. *"Season of Sorrow*, an Autobiography by Cassie Callahan, who fought all her life against one personality so her true self would gain supremacy. That material you got me from the New York Public Library was right on." And then she tightened her jaw at Geoff Haines. "Which I assume you knew all along."

Geoff's eyes became like a brown inferno as his stare pasted onto her. And although he made no remark, Cassie saw murderous thoughts lurking behind the blaze. Raw terror gripped her, and she swung her eyes from the sight to John. She only desired to get back to the Plæza and hide out until Jacko showed up.

"I admit that Geoffrey provided us with much insight, Cassie," John told her in a matter-of-fact tone. "But you must understand that we needed some leverage. A great expense was spent on your development and we could afford no rebellion. We chose you, and for that you should be eternally grateful. We made you out of nothing, and you've become richer for it as well as quite famous, more famous actually, than any of us could have imagined that first day you walked through my door, green as hell."

"And you've become richer too," she said with sheer boldness. "That fact always seems to get ignored. Without me or 'Harry', you'd never be padding your pocket with a chunk of eight-point-five million. So it wasn't just you . . ." And she spun her head towards Curt. "Or you, like you tried to indoctrinate into me." With a huff, she turned back to John. "It was me too, admit it!"

John deliberately ran a finger across his cheek while he took careful note of her. "Certainly I'll admit it. Is that so God awful important? You have the fame, the money, so how God awful important can that be?"

"Believe it or not, it *is* the most God awful important," she whispered. She *did* have talent once, she told herself, contented.

"Cassie" had made a mark on the world.

It all hadn't been for nothing.

But now it was over.

She had been seeking one thing and had found a wonderful other, and that other, would help put her at peace, *finally*.

"So what do we do about her image, John? It can't stay as is, *obviously*," Curt said acidly. "I suggest something like Minnesota meets L.A., a wood nymph is enlightened concept."

John shook his head while looking at her. "No more images, Curt. I have a hunch that this book isn't for sale. Right Cassie?"

She coursed her lips into a shaky smile. "Well, to refute the words of Harry Hannigan... "Uncle'... 'Uncle' to all of it. Cassie's words are finally as dried up as her passion, one of the hugest deceits of her life." And she dared to glance at Geoff Haines, then had to gain a grip on the mighty shudder that rocked her. He looked like a crazed-eyed panther ready to jump on her with his claws. "So..." she breathed out, turning back to John. "You can do what you want with *Season of Sorrow*, even commission an established author to muddle through the mind games and create something viable, if you wish. I just ask you to please not use my name. I'm... not quite that strong yet."

With gentlemanly graciousness and not even a trace of anger, John LaLiberte stood and thrust out his hand. "It was a pleasure to know you, Cassie, and I wish you luck. If you should ever get the writing bug again..."

Just as graciously, Cassie took his hand and shook. "Thank you for launching 'Harry'. I'll never forget you for that. It gave me some hope... for a little while."

"No!" A sudden noise from the corner broke the hand lock and both turned. Geoff Haines stood, trembling against a wall looking like he wanted to cut off his tongue. "Sorry, John," he mumbled, refusing to raise his eyes, though Cassie's could see the familiar intense rage.

John ignored the outburst and smiling, he turned back to Cassie. "So what's next, Cassie, besides Motherhood?"

Her gaze shook with terror when again facing the editor. "Return to the Regent, of course, pack, and take a fast boat back to L.A."

****

When Jack walked into his hotel suite at the Minneapolis Rædisson, leaving the illustrious cast and crew to celebrate in the hotel's downstairs lounge and bathed in sweat from head to toe, he yelled out a wild *Yipeeee*... and flew onto the bed in total joy.

It's over... Shouldn't I be a little sad?

"NO!" he promptly shouted at the top of his lungs, telling himself that he was too relieved to ever be sad. He was finally his own man, like he was meant to be all along. The rebellion's over! And silently but firmly, he pounded into his head that despite everything, including *Jungle Love*, he had won! What was left of him, after all the dust was cleared, the dirt swept away, the muck drained, and filth peeled off, made him the victor over all of it.

Damn it was great to be plain old Jack Torelli again, he thought with sheer exhilaration.

A ringing phone jostled his euphoria and he lunged at it. Could it possibly be...?

"The *real* Jack Torelli," he couldn't help answering.

"The... *real?*"

It was Harv Wellson.

"Yeah Harv, just what I said," Jack replied brightly. "Or the one and only, if you prefer that designation instead."

"Whoa Jack... a little too much post-production celebration, I hear."

"I don't need a pint, or quart, or gallon of booze to celebrate. My natural high is more potent than all of those things," he disputed. "And why I thought I ever needed those things to be happy, now eludes me. I'm so fuckin' happy I could fly!"

"Well hold that thought, Jack."

"Why?"

Harv exhaled a heavy sigh. "Cassie's not at the Æmbassador, never was, according to my reporter friend. It was a hoax brought about by an anonymous tip to the Times. Sorry Jack. I truly thought the information was correct."

"Oh shit!" Jack hollered in a total panic. "Where is she? Where the hell . . .?"

"I have a few people combing L.A., even Grayson that investigator who found you in Nevada. But there's been no word as of yet," Harv replied.

"Did someone check at Python? Maybe someone there knows like the bitch on the tenth floor." Jack spoke in frantic tones, hoping-beyond-hope that Claire Gibson hadn't somehow gotten her hands on Cassie again. He well knew that Claire would go out of her way to confuse Cassie even more, perhaps, turn Cassie against him completely.

"The bitch is probably celebrating just as wildly as you people are," Harv told him. "Word just got out that Isle obtained the rights to 'Harry Two' for . . . hang onto your hat . . . a whopping eight-point-five million."

"Eight . . . point five . . . *what?*"

"Cassie made a major kill," Harv continued on. "Of course, according to the Hollywood Associated Press, the deal is contingent on you playing 'Harry'. So this time, we too can make a major kill and keep killing for years to come, Jack."

"Yeah, kill," Jack snickered, deciding to let Harv bask in his Jacuzzi full of moola for a while yet. There was plenty of time to unclog the jets, he told himself.

"Now all we have to do is find Cassie for you . . ."

Jack squashed the phone against his ear. "I'm packing and going out to the airport now. Maybe I can find a flight that lands at the Burbank Airport, or John Wayne in Orange County. I don't know how the hell I'll be able to wait until eight-thirty for that LAX flight. I'll . . . figure out something, Harv. Just keep looking . . . please . . ."

****

Sitting on the edge of her hotel room bed, aimlessly swinging her legs and staring at the wall directly in her gaze, Cassie felt too terrified to even breath. All she could see in her mind was the final expression that Geoff Haines gave her when she exited John LaLiberte's office. It was so full of menacing threat that a two-month-old could have interpreted his facial message.

Perhaps I had been a little too blunt, she thought now, especially when knowing about the truly insane mind that was listening in the background. Even if no one else in the entire world knew this, she had. And therefore, she should have exerted greater caution and not spouted off willy-nilly. *Especially about my passion, or my lack thereof—his obsession.*

And since she *had* so thoughtlessly threatened a madman's obsession, she wondered if it was time to tell Jacko everything so he could take action, legal or otherwise. It may be the only way to stop Geoff Haines once and for all, she reasoned. Or else . . . she may be forced to look over her shoulder forever.

Feeling the rumbling hunger of her stomach, Cassie gazed down at her middle. Her eyes caught sight of the black tight pants and colorful far-out maternity top. She hadn't changed, and furthermore refused to. The outlandish costume still stuffed with the towel gave her a secure feeling, as if warding off the evil Sandy until Jack arrived to place a firmer foundation on her wall. It would be a challenge, she thought now. To get rid of the wall, until she was left exposed would be no easy proposition.

But at least I'm raring to try.

And that she viewed as a magnanimous future hope to hold onto.

Feeling the stomach rumble expand into discomfort, Cassie decided, like it or not, she would have to call Room Service so her baby could be fed. She really craved a couple vendor hot dogs, but she possessed no such nerve to step onto the street. So she located the menu, groaned loudly at the preposterous prices, and decided to have a full course dinner that would hold her until Jacko arrived to get her the hot dogs that she *really* wanted.

"This is Room 423, and I'd like to order a T-bone steak, medium, the six butterfly shrimp, Texas fries, a salad with ranch dressing, a Baked Alaska, a basket of onion rolls, and a triple order of milk, and . . . if someone should just happen, for some reason or the other, to step out the front door, two vendor hot dogs with the works . . ."

****

A little after seven p.m. Pacific Standard Time, Jack's plane landed at the Santa Monica Airport. He had been fortunate to find a charter pilot that was willing to fly to Los Angeles--at an exorbitant rate--and the man had done so in record time despite two short refueling stops in Denver and Las Vegas. Now he would take the fastest means possible to get to Beverly Hills where he could jump into his Corvette and search like a madman.

Despite the churn in his stomach from the rocky ride, Jack jogged across the runway, wildly looked around, trying to locate some sort of shuttle, limousine, or taxicab, anything to get him to Beverly Hills. Finally he spotted a couple cabs and hurried towards them, jumping into the first one he approached.

"Palm Drive off Sunset," he quickly told the driver.

"May take awhile." The driver placed the cab in gear. "Traffic's no picnic tonight."

"Is it ever?" Jack muttered.

The taxi exited east onto the Santa Monica Parkway and traffic was backed up shortly thereafter. Growing more frenzied by the moment, Jack cussed repeatedly.

"Say . . . aren't you Jack Torelli, the movie star?" The driver peered into his rearview mirror. "I saw you on the cover of *People* last week, looking like the 'Man from Forbes'."

"Yeah—I'm Torelli. But I ain't no star except in my own home," he retorted in irritation. "Just step on it, willya. I'm in a helluva hurry."

"As you can see, Mr. Torelli, I'm trying my best, but . . ."

"Damn!" he muttered under his breath. "For the price that I paid for that plane, I should of told that pilot land on Palm Drive and to hell with what the neighbors said . . ."

****

The last spoonful of Baked Alaska slid down Cassie's throat, and she told herself that despite the horrendous prices, her one hundred eight dollar plus gratuity meal had been delicious. She decided to save a small remaining piece of steak, the two shrimp, and three onion rolls in case she desired a snack later. Never did she want to go through the terror of room service again.

For the entire time the young waiter was in her room, all that had coursed through her mind was the question, *Is he a spy?* She couldn't take such a chance with her baby, she firmly told herself.

After placing her small stash of food in the small refrigerator, Cassie moved her gaze to the tiny table which held the dirty supper dishes. The waiter had instructed her to call when she was done or place the table outside her room, she recalled. She thought about this for a moment and decided that she didn't want the waiter anywhere near her, no matter how innocent and benign he seemed; therefore, it was most prudent to wheel the table outside her door.

With much difficulty, Cassie pushed the table to the door. A stubborn wheel kept sticking and she was forced to kick her platform shoe against it the entire way. Once at the door, she removed each lock and opened the door a crack, moving her eye left and right down the hall. Determining it to be clear, she glided the table out the door, again thrusting her shoe at the sticky wheel. Damn! The thing wouldn't steer! Finally, feeling frustrated, she gave the wheel a strong boot so it landed with a crash against the wall. There! She again glanced left and right, then grabbed the door frame and her mouth opened wide into a silent scream.

She felt her body being pressed to the wall while a sweaty palm pushed against her mouth. Soon she heard the hiss in her ear, and she widened her eyes in sheer terror.

"I'm going to fuck you until that baby and all your rebellion is gone, Cassie."

Her rock hard body was inched along the wall to the open room door. She felt the moistness of Geoff's clothes and his body heat as he pushed flush against her back. When they reached the door opening, he paused to place his lips on her neck and slobbered all over it while his free hand roughly caressed one breast then the other. She popped open her eyes above his hand, and they fell onto the bed. *Noooo . . .* her mind screamed out like a surge and she chomped her open mouth down onto his hand and sunk her teeth into his skin. Gag after gag rose into her throat when tasting his sticky blood mixed with her saliva.

Geoff yelped loudly and jumped away slightly. Propelled by the worst terror she had ever felt, Cassie lifted one of her platform shoes and smashed it into Geoff's groin. He pulled back, doubled over, groaning with inhuman sounds.

With a loud continuous scream, she ran down the hall to the elevators and jabbed her finger on the down button while keeping an eye at the end of the hall. Seeing Geoff begin to limp and drag towards her, she jabbed faster while nervously bouncing of her knees. When he was merely ten feet away, the doors slid open and she leapt onto the car, seeing his form lunge at the doors just as they closed.

Oh god! Where to? She jittered as the car descended to the lobby. Her only thought was that her hiding place was blown and she had to leave the hotel. Nothing else, neither reason nor logic seemed to penetrate her brain. Near rape! Her mind screamed like an echo, driving her panic and terror to even higher levels.

The elevator doors flew open in the luxurious lobby. Ignoring all the stares and helpful hands thrust out, she raced out the entrance into the black night still hot and humid. What time is it? She looked around not knowing the answer. Regardless, she rapidly clicked her platform heels to the avenue, jumped off

Seeking Out Harry

the curb, then wildly waved her hands while springing up and down.

Briefly, she glanced at the hotel entrance. Geoff Haines stood outside looking around. Panicked, she carefully stepped to conceal herself between two cars and then wildly shifted her eyes into the street hoping a taxi would emerge. Finally, she saw a blaze of yellow barreling towards her and she bounded upward, flailing her arms like a madwoman.

"Cassie!"

In desperation, she spun her head to see Geoff heading towards the avenue. "Stop!" she screamed to the taxis that were nearing her. One of the yellow vehicles came to a screeching halt, and she jogged towards it, sliding in and locking the door just at Geoff made it to the avenue. He made a grab for the door as the cab took off and his back smacked square into a parked car.

"What's with that guy?" the driver asked, looking in his rearview mirror.

Cassie bent over, heaving out all her hysteria. "Maybe . . . he wanted . . . this cab too . . . who knows?"

"Where you headed?" he asked her.

"Ah . . ." Cassie looked around, having no clue. "Where . . . do you suggest?"

The driver turned and spoke dryly. "I'd suggest my house, but I don't think the old lady would appreciate me bringing home a pregnant hooker."

Cassie nervously gazed back at him while telling herself, *Think!*

"Cm'on Miss, East, West, South, or North?"

"What's in the North?" she asked, her orientation dissolved in her panic.

"Too ritzy for you," he replied.

"East?"

"Queens may be your thing. Wanna take a ride through the Midtown Tunnel?"

"Towards La Guardia?" she verified, and he nodded at her. She thought about hiding in the airport, but quickly tossed out this idea. At this time of night, she would be more than vulnerable to attack. "No thank you. Run the West options by me."

"Garment District, Theater District, Clinton, and if we go farther south, Chelsea, the Village, Washington Square, Soho, TriBeCa . . ."

"Stop!" she rapidly cut in. "Washington Square!"

"Hey Miss, that park ain't no place to be at night."

"No! What's below it? Below it, you know . . ."

"South?" he asked.

She bobbed her head in a nod.

"Well, we have Little Italy, Chinatown . . ."

"The first one! That's where I'm going," she said quickly.

He scratched his head. "Do you know where in Little Italy or do we play the North, South, East, and West game again?"

"Ah . . . starts with an 'M'! Long street, long . . ."

"Mulberry Street? Is that it?"

"No!" She tried to think despite the sheer terror that plugged her neurons. "It's by some Saint's house. That's it!"

"Only other long 'M' street that I know of, is Mott Street," he said with irritation.

"Mott! It's Mott by some Saint's house. Ah . . . Saint . . . big house . . . *huge.*"

"I'd guess it's south Mott Street then . . . because unless the name ended in an 'a', 'o', or 'i', I doubt they live on the North end and . . .

"Torelli! That ends in 'i'. That's where I'm going," she said with much relief.

He slightly shifted his face around. "You mean like in Torelli the actor? Like that Torelli?" he asked in total disbelief.

"My Jacko, that's right. I have to get to my Mom and Pop's house . . . and his Mom and Pop's house too," she said, feeling much more calmed with just the thought of the warm, inviting home and Marianna Torelli's abundant arms holding her.

"Are . . . you his sister or somethin'?" he asked with suspicion.

"Do I look like his sister?" she retorted back all her anxiety. "I'm the mother of his child. Who do you think the father is?"

"What's your name?" he asked cautiously.

Think of a name. Think!

"You're not that author he hangs around with, are you?" he asked again.

"Of course not! I can't write a word, my mind is devoid of words. Ah . . . my name is Pat-- Pat Saint!"

"Like the cathedral?"

"Cathedral! Where Jacko tripped when he was an altar boy. That's it! Mott Street by the cathedral. Do you know where it is? Huh?"

He made a left turn and let out a low snicker. "Should be there in an hour . . . Miss Lady Author. . ."

****

Nearly two hours after entering the taxicab, Jack unlocked the door to the Beverly Hills home. He heard the persistent ring of the phone the moment he stepped into the stone floored foyer. Quickly depositing his bags on the floor, he jogged to the ringing instrument and prayed that it was Cassie.

He heart sunk upon recognizing Harv Wellson's voice.

"Thank God you're home, Jack. I called Minneapolis but Mike said that you had left already, so I've been calling for the past hour. Bob Grayson picked up some vital information. He's on his way over to your house . . ."

****

"So you're telling me that 'Harry' didn't really find any satisfaction in acquiring all those businesses, Cassie?" The cab driver drove past Old Saint Patrick's Cathedral and turned onto Mott Street.

"Absolutely not, Sam. All his acquisitions were a cover-up for what he really needed in his life . . . love that wasn't purely sexual," she replied, leaning into the front seat.

He glanced in his rearview mirror and shook his head. "I hate saying this, but I could swear there's someone tailing me. I've noticed it for the last seven or so miles."

Heart pounding, Cassie spun around to see a pair of blinding headlights directly behind them. "Maybe it's just a coincidence," she mumbled in a less than convincing manner. It was incredible the way he could find her, she jittered. He was like a 'super bloodhound'.

"Just get me to the Torelli's and all will be okay," her voice shook over the front seat.

Minutes later, she spotted the large familiar building with a light burning above. She stared at the homey porch with the creaking swing, and an immediate sense of comfort washed over her.

"That'll be thirty-two bucks." He stuck his hand over the seat.

Seeking Out Harry

Cassie instinctively reached down and sucked in a loud gasp. "I don't have my purse, Sam! I left so fast and under rather odd circumstances, that I forgot it. Can I give you an IOU with a big tip attached to it?"

"Cassie . . ." He scratched his head with uncertainty.

"Maybe Pop will pay you!" she rapidly cut in. "Come with me and we'll ask him."

"Well . . . it might be kinda nice to say that I talked to the father of Jack Torelli . . ."

Before he had second thoughts, Cassie threw open the door and slid her platform shoes to the tar surface. But she pulled them back into the cab when a set of headlights glared directly in her face from behind. "It's him!" she cried out, quickly closing then locking the door.

"Who's him?" The driver craned his neck to the rear.

"Ah . . . one of those stalker fans. You know . . . the nuts that follow a person wherever he or she goes," she quaked out, her eyes fastened on the headlights.

He picked up his radio. "I'm calling the dispatcher and have her notify the police. Those stalker nuts aren't someone to take lightly, Cassie."

"No!" she cried out. "Just walk me to the house. He's . . . basically a wimp of a stalker. He wouldn't dare show his face when someone's with me."

"Are you nuts yourself? There's no such thing as a wimp of a stalker." He placed the radio to his mouth. "Maybe a few police sirens will make him think twice about stalking a pregnant woman. Don't worry. This vicinity has more than a few good Italian cops the size of Amazons." And ignoring her protests, he made his call.

Oh god! She sunk down in the seat. It would only get worse if the police got their hands on crazy Geoff, she silently bemoaned. Not only *didn't* she have the proof, *he* had the pictures and had threatened to make them public. What would Jacko say? And what would the media do? Weren't they notorious enough already?

The noise of distant sirens filled her ears. It sounded like the whole NYPD was coming, she thought miserably. If Mom and Pop weren't up, they would be in short order, she figured. Suddenly she jumped. There was a loud tire squeal then a blaze of yellow flashed by her window.

"That was a cab!" The driver leapt outside to get a better look. "The only number I saw was a two and possible eight or zero. Damn! I wish I woulda known that was a cab behind me. We coulda caught him, Cassie."

Thank God he didn't know that was a cab. She let out a weighty sigh of relief.

"Here they come. Looks like a dozen or so cop cars," the driver informed, looking up the street. "He went that way!" he yelled at the top of his lungs, jumping up and down at the nearing police cars. "Boy . . . I think we woke up all of Mott Street, Cassie, from the looks of all those building lights."

The squeal of police sirens blocked out any other sounds, and Cassie sunk deeper into her seat, wishing it would devour her. What in the world could she tell the police about Geoff Haines? *And worse yet*, how would she explain all the noise to Mom and Pop?

"I think your Mom and Pop are coming, Cassie, along with at least hundred other people from the looks of it," the driver informed. "He went that way! That way!" he said to a police car that stopped flush with the cab. "New York City cab with a number two and an eight or zero with damn good headlights. The nut is a passenger."

Two squealing police cars sped past the taxi and down the street. Soon thereafter, Cassie saw a dark, handsome face peering in her window. He tipped up his police hat and flashed a smile at her. Then he hand motioned for her to come out.

She slowly pulled up in the seat then wanted to sink back down when seeing a crowd of people, some in nightwear, surrounding the cab. In the center was a glaring Carlo Torelli donned in a bathrobe, slippers, and his gray hair tousled in all directions. *She had no choice.* The young cop was tapping on the window now.

With as much nonchalance as she could muster, Cassie swung her legs out of the cab and wobbled to an upright position. She brandished her brightest smile on Carlo. "Hi Pop. I thought I'd come for a visit."

Marianna Torelli rushed to her husband's side and whimpered while her eyes fastened on Cassie's middle.

"Gravidanza?" Carlo thundered in disbelief.

"Yeah pregnant." She smiled weakly. "Jacko's gonna be a daddy around New Years."

Stunned, Carlo eyed her up and down. "Why you look like *prostituta*, eh?"

She scanned all the faces staring at her like she had two heads. Then she looked to the side of her. At least twenty cops smiled and laughed. Suddenly everything, all the terror, hysteria, and hormones caved in on her, and she broke down into tears.

"Can't you just take care of me, Mom? I need a warm bed and a bowl of blueberries . . ."

****

After pacing up and down the living room carpet like a maniac for over an hour, Jack finally heard the chime of the doorbell. He pounded his feet to the door and pulled it open to see Bob Grayson, the private investigator who had rescued him in Carson City.

Jack thrust his hand out and greeted him as warmly as his nerves would allow.

"Harv said you had some information on Cassie," Jack said as he widened the door for Bob. "Do you know where she is? Is it Los Angeles?"

Bob pulled off his cowboy hat and briefly wiped the bottoms of his leather boots on the entry rug. "She's in New York, Jack."

"What?" Jack breathed out in distress. "That's impossible. That's the last place Cassie would go. She . . . can't handle New York, Bob."

"Regardless, Jack, that's where she is," Bob Grayson said with certainty.

"How do you know this?"

"An informant, a frightened one, who's scared to make himself visible."

"Who is it?" Jack pressed fearfully, not liking the sudden secrecy surrounding Cassie.

"I coaxed him to come with me. But he won't leave my Cadillac," Bob replied solemnly. "I think you better come out and talk to him. He's got quite a piece to tell you, Jack."

"Let's go . . ." Jack raced out of the door to the sleek black car that looked top-of-the-line. He thrust open the door then paused, widening his eyes as he stared into the interior. "George? Is that you?"

Seeking Out Harry

"Get in Jack," George said anxiously. Then shifting his gaze to Bob, "You drive around. That was the deal. I'm not gonna be a sitting duck. They're already suspicious about me . . ."

****

As the Cadillac cruised around southern Beverly Hills, George told Jack the exact same story he had told Cassie the night before. By the time he concluded, Bob had to quickly pull to a curb to help the elderly George restrain a raging Jack Torelli.

"I'll kill him!" Jack exploded into the interior of the car while his fists flew in all directions. "And her! That Bitch!"

"Calm down, Jack. Isle's got 'Harry Two' so he should settle down a little," George pleaded. "He'll hopefully leave you and Cassie alone now--just be happy about that. You can't do anything about the rest anyway."

"The hell I can't!"

"They covered all their tracks, including sending Haley Shears to Australia to play a part in some movie produced by an Aussie who's good friends with Isle," George explained on. "And I can guarantee you that all those young performers who invaded that hospital and took part in that plan to ruin you, are also gone to places unknown. He's got movie and television connections all over the world."

"That bastard!" Jack angrily flared with an underlying sob. "To kill an unborn child for a goddamn book right!"

"He craves that edge, always has," George replied with much disdain. "He'd slit his own mother's throat for that edge. To be the 'King' in Hollywood is his only mission in life. And it's getting tougher to maintain, the competition fiercer with the rise of producers as big or *bigger* than him, then all the cable channels . . . so likewise, his tactics are getting more desperate. Python Studios used to be a place of high regard, but it's turning into a smelly garbage dump more each day and the future is damn frightening."

Jack allowed himself to calm down enough to map out his next step. He wouldn't allow Michael Isle to get away with this horror. *His son!* He wanted to break the producer into a million pieces. It was sooner than he had planned and sooner, perhaps, than he was mentally ready for, but he told himself that none of that mattered now. No way could he ever, *ever*, contribute to the bastard's 'King' status. It was a matter of pride, morals, sheer conscience, and more love than he could have ever conceived would come into his life. Those were his priorities, which he had painfully, though with much resolve, placed in order. And he *would* exercise those priorities despite it was months sooner than planned, he firmly told himself. They all would just have to understand . . . Cassie, Harv Wellson, Rud Hanna . . . and accept the fact that he *was* a changed man and that he liked the man he was changing into.

"What time is it?" he asked to neither man in particular.

"A little after one in the morning," Bob replied.

"I wanna find a way to get to New York now, this moment, but . . . as long as I know Cassie is snug in the Plæza, I'll be content for now. First I need to knock a 'King' off his throne or I'll go frickin' crazy with the need. It's the woman I love and my son after all. I refuse to have that bastard bask in his triumph one more second than necessary."

"Don't try, Jack." George begged. "He'll really ruin you next time."

Jack turned to the security guard and a slow bittersweet smile coursed on his lips. "He ruined me in Hollywood long ago, George, and I helped him, believe me. So even though I hate him with my very soul, I don't fully blame him. And if the truth be known, I blame him very little, maybe not even at all. It was me who fucked up and gave Mike and everyone else the ammunition to fuck me up more. They took advantage of that. But that's Hollywood . . . loves to take advantage then pick and feed on the remains like vultures. It's a lifestyle, a survival mode, as sick as that may sound. But it's the reality and I'm not gonna change it. Although I can put a damper on it at least, before . . ." He smiler broader. "I say 'uncle'."

"What are you saying, Jack?" George asked in distress.

"I think you know, George, and I know Bob knows."

George's face sunk into a sad, thoughtful look and Bob slowly nodded his head. "As soon as the sun rises, I'll drive you over to Python, Jack. And don't worry about a ride to New York. I've already got my private plane on standby and ready to go."

"You got a plane, Bob? On a PI's salary?" Jack asked to total amazement.

Bob curled an amused smile on his lips. "I just do this as a sideline. Satisfies a repressed desire, I think. Otherwise, I spend the rest of my time on my ranch."

"You mean you really gotta ranch near Carson City?"

"Well not quite, Jack. That was a fib, I'm afraid," Bob replied. "My ranch is located in a crest above Malibu. Old, old money. I'm the maverick. No Pasadena for me."

"Malibu?" Jack found the first laugh he'd had for several hours.

"But for now . . ." Bob started his car and pulled away from the curb. "I better get George home. Then you and me can sit down and plan your strategy . . ."

****

After dropping off a shaky George and reassuring him that all would work out, Jack and Bob returned to the Beverly Hills house. They positioned themselves at the kitchen table where they wolfed down cotto salami and Swiss cheese sandwiches and drank coffee while sorting through all they knew so Jack could be as damaging as possible.

Jack only paused to pack a fresh bag for New York, shower, change, and gather up his evidence. Then he was back at the table, drinking cup after cup of coffee so his faculties were perfectly clear.

Precisely at five a.m., the wall phone in the kitchen jangled. Jack sprang to answer it certain it was Cassie as she had no concern for things like time zones when she needed him. He smiled joyfully when plucking up the receiver.

"Cassie?" he breathlessly asked.

There came a long pause. "It's me, Jacko."

Momentarily muted, Jack widened his eyes at the number panel on the phone while a surge of emotions roared through him. "Pop?" he managed to shake out.

"Cassie is here, Jacko. She come late last night, crying and scared."

"What happened, Pop?" Jack asked in frantic tones.

"The taxi driver tell *Polizia* that a man follow her, and Cassie she just cry and say nothing except to tell your Mama that he come to her hotel room."

"Damn him!" Jack raged. "I'll break him in two, Pop!"

"You know him, Jacko? The *Polizia* need to find out. The bambino . . ."

"I know, Pop." His eyes moistened with tears. "I'll find who he is this time. Cassie has to tell me. I can't take any more chances with her."

"She is safe here, Jacko. Your brothers . . . they all go to the hotel to get her things and dare that man to come near them."

Jack felt the pressure behind his eyes build. "Thank them, Pop."

"And your sisters all come too so they can help. Cassie no sleep well. She has nightmares. They stay with her while your Mama cook."

With these words, his eyes exploded in tears and he couldn't stop the flow no matter how hard he gulped to swallow them.

"Come home, Jacko." Carlo urged gently. "We love you, son. And even with *imbrogliare arrufflar le cose*, even with the mess of things, we never stop loving you. All we could do was pray every chance we get. And now God answers. Everybody is crazy to see you, Jacko. Your Mama is cooking spaghetti and baking bread, and she makes your favorite blueberry pie."

Gulping ferociously, Jack could only get a few words past his tears. "I'll be there, Pop. I don't know when for sure. But I'm really coming . . ."

Jack hung up the phone and the tears flowed freely. *It was a miracle.* Not only was Cassie in the safest place in New York, in his mind, but he was truly going to be a *Torelli* again, in every sense of the word. He had earned the right. *Him!* And now he thanked God for answering his family's prayers as well as his, despite that he had barely prayed at all.

"God is forgiving, Jack, even when you go astray . . . He loves you more."

The long-ago Irish brogue hummed through his head like a lullaby, and he experienced a greater convulse of his tears. *Why now in my head?* It was like an affirmation that all would be okay no matter what he had to do, how much he had to give up—all would be well, despite. He had been forgiven, and now in one swoop, he suddenly forgave himself as well. Today and beyond . . . that's all that would matter from now on. And then he thought with the purest of joy,

My life is finally complete. Jack Torelli is content . . .

Slowly he turned from the phone and looked at Bob who wore a multitude of questions on his face. Jack felt so overcome, he couldn't muster a single response to Bob's expression.

"I'm ready to get this done with. I need to get on with my life and live it rather than act it. I was never cut out to have it both ways."

"I understand more than you think, Jack," Bob replied with a quiet smile. "I think I understood it in Carson City. You desperately were seeking something in your life that you couldn't seem to find, or more precisely didn't know how to find. But you learned, boy, tough as it was, you sure as hell learned your lessons well. And when all is said and done, that's the most important thing—no learning, no meaning."

He quaked a smile through the wetness. "Let's go add to my meaning big time . . . as big as your ranch, in fact . . ."

****

Cassie felt like a pampered queen, as well as a stuffed one, while lounging in the Torelli living room. "She was to stay calm for the bambino," she had heard so many times, she didn't dare move a muscle lest she wanted one of Jack's sisters to cluck at her. Now all four sat around the couch, watching her like gray-haired hawks while the five male Torelli watchdogs plus a few neighbors stood on the porch waiting to pounce on Geoff Haines. She couldn't believe the neighborhood effort in a city such as Manhattan. Had she ever seen such an effort in a city even the size of Anoka? She wondered.

Suddenly the room exploded in loud noise. "Jacko! He come home!" Marianna Torelli screeched and sobbed as she rushed into the living room. Soon the place detonated into deafening noise and earsplitting wails, not only inside but outside as well. Cassie held onto the couch, sensing that the entire room was rocking.

"Debbie, call . . ." And then in quick succession, Marianna rattled off at least fifty names to her daughter.

While Cassie bobbed her head in time with Marianna's mouth movements, she wondered, *Why all the fuss for Jacko?* So finally she asked the sister who looked the most composed, and suddenly the sister wasn't composed anymore.

"Can someone please help me here?" Cassie said loudly into the noise. "I have a very pressing question." And she kept asking until the noise subsided. When she had relative attention focused back on her, she looked at each face. "Why all the bru-ha-ha for Jacko? It's me, who should be making the bru-ha-ha."

Within moments, a profusion of voices all competing to be heard, floated around her. Scrunching her eyebrows, she listened closely, trying to discern the gist. Most frequently she heard 'naughty boy' and 'lover of loose women' and 'dirty movies where he bared his *natica* which they all had powdered.' It was finally beginning to sink in, she told thought.

Uncanny . . . Jacko's as much as a black sheep as me.

"So the *pecora nera* finally makes an appearance, eh?" Cassie said generally.

"No!" was her shock-filled resounding answer.

"Jack's our baby, Cassie. How can a baby be a black sheep?" one of the sisters responded. "It's almost barbaric no matter how many stupid things he's done."

"He's a *birichino*, and a spoiled one at that. Jack's always been coddled. He could kill a million people and we'd still coddle him," his oldest sister said.

Jacko was a spoiled brat? Cassie thought in astonishment, barely able to believe that 'her Jacko' was such an irritating type at one time in his life. "So . . . what did he do that indicated to you that he was actually . . . spoiled?" And in a split-second, her ears burned with example after example to prove their point.

"He never had to take responsibility, it was always taken for him," one of the sisters replied. "Like Fordham for example . . ." And she went on the tell Cassie about Jack's brief stint at the prestigious university. "I wanted to smack his rear-end but Pop forgave him and let him get away with everything," she concluded.

"Hollywood was the worst possible place for him," another sister began. "There he could be as irresponsible as he wanted, and of course he was. There was no family to smooth the way for him so he took off on a tangent. All of us knew what was happening, Cassie."

"I think that's why he chose acting, if you ask me," another sister piped in. "It gave him cause to be reckless, out of the mold, and avoid taking adult responsibility. He could be this character or that and not have to be Jack Anthony Torelli who deep down, he knew he should be but couldn't face being.

Still, the bambino . . ."

"None of us did him any favors," his oldest sister admitted. "We shoulda belted that responsibility into him long ago, each one of us, taking turns with the belt."

Cassie felt an intense sadness. She finally understood why Jack had gone so awry with his life. It had to be rough, she figured. To come from such an obviously decent, loving family, and his life sinks into a murky gutter. She could just imagine how enormous his guilt must have been. After all, she too had come from an Italian family where "guilt" was a way of life.

"No belt. Jacko's been belted enough by himself," she said quietly, looking at each face. "He *has* taken responsibility. I couldn't love and trust him as much as I do, if he hadn't."

Stillness fell over the group.

"So . . ." Cassie spoke on, directly from the heart. "Maybe we should put all the spoiled brat stories aside and just appreciate the man that he's become." A glow settled on her face. "I for one can't wait to see that man walk through the door . . ."

****

The tenth floor of the Python Studio Office Building was flooded with light when Bob Grayson's Cadillac pulled up in front of it. He turned a sympathetic look on Jack.

"Its still tough no matter how bad you want it, isn't it Jack?"

" Nearly a quarter of a century. It's a big chunk out of one's life," Jack replied with a hint of melancholy. "Once I had big dreams and perhaps a bit of true passion. But none of that was the reason. I covered it all under an umbrella labeled 'passion' when it was *me*, living a lie that grew bigger every year until I couldn't see the truth anymore." He let out a cynical laugh. "But I felt it every day of my life, and that was my downfall until Cassie forced me to face all of it." Tears moistened his eyes. "And that's why I love her so much. She wanted 'Jack Torelli', not some lie. Cassie's the only woman outside of my mother and sisters who was satisfied with just me, and just knowing that set *me* free, Bob."

"She sounds wonderful. You're a lucky man, Jack."

"I am lucky, luckier than a stupid sonofabitch like me deserves." Jack braced up to hold in his emotions. "But despite, I ended up one of the fortunate few . . . a Hollywood casualty resuscitated and made viable again."

"And that's what matters, getting that rare second chance." Bob gave a comforting pat to Jack's shoulder. "I have no doubt that you'll make this one count."

There's no doubt.

Jack opened the passenger door and slid out. He briefly glanced up at the Python office building, then he took long, determined strides . . .

****

Standing just outside Michael Isle's princely office, Jack heard the sounds of male and female laughter, and his body cringed with rage. *Calm down, Torelli*, an inner voice warned, and he heeded it, slowly inhaling and exhaling a few breaths. When relatively calm, Jack walked directly into the office without knocking. *It's for Cassie and Little Jacko*, he kept reminded himself as he moved closer to Michael Isle's desk and past a wide-eyed staring Claire Gibson.

"Well Torelli . . ." Michael laughed with haughty superiority. "Did you come to congratulate me too? I swear this office has been like Grand Central Station. The phones started ringing at five a.m. Eastern Standard Time."

An amused smile danced on Jack's lips. "Congratulate you for *what?*"

Michael startled momentarily, but he quickly recovered. "If you haven't heard, I've acquired the much coveted book rights to 'Harry Two'. I beat out Spelling and Turner, and few other non-*significants.*"

"Really?" Jack held his smile as he sauntered to the desk. "So who's gonna play 'Harry'?"

Michael huffed as if he had asked the most preposterous question in the world. "Why you know that I'm hiring *you* for this miniseries too. It's part of the contract so . . ."

"You're forced to hire me," Jack finished for him.

"Of course," Michael curved back into his chair, looking totally in command. "I don't see anyone else hiring you," he said in a totally conceited voice. "You should kiss my feet for this second legitimate chance, Torelli."

"Izzat so?" Jack moved closer to the desk until he was hanging over it. "Now why is that if you have to hire me to even produce this miniseries? Shouldn't you be kissing my feet instead?"

"Fooey!" Michael spat out as if the notion was incensing. "What else would you do? You have no one else breaking down your door."

"I could always go back to EMAX Subsidiary. Rud Hanna made a whole new studio for me, and Harv Wellson tells me that Rud is still waiting. I could continue to turn out critically acclaimed films."

"Rud Hanna!" Michael snorted. "What is he?"

"He's as powerful as you, maybe even *more* powerful, and I happen to know he's a helluva lot richer," Jack pointed out. "He could keep me financed for years on any quality property I wanted and eventually let the subsidiary slide into legitimate productions that could even be shown on television." He raised his eyes in gleeful thought. "Now I would love that––my Cassie writing book after book that I acquire for nearly nothing and produce high-quality miniseries. I bet Rud would even go for that even sooner than I think. What the hell . . . if me and Cassie as a team could convince him that his pockets would be lined."

"What?" Michael thrust forward in his seat. "I'll bust you in ten directions if you should even suggest . . ."

"Yeah--now that I think about it, Cassie and I will make quite a team. The two Torelli's, forever bound, turning this town on its heel with greatness," Jack said with much inner glee, just able to see the sheer panic before him.

"The *two* Torelli's? *You? Married?*"

"Me, Cassie, the bambino, and more bambinos . . . my dream come true."

"What?" Claire Gibson suddenly interrupted. "You can't make us believe that you . . ."

"Want lots of bambinos?" he concluded for her, wanting to attack the smug looking woman. "Or maybe it was permanency and commitment that you were referring to, Claire."

She gave him a hard glare and didn't respond.

"Affirmative to all three. What do you think about that?"

Her eyebrows lifted a bit, but she kept silent.

"I'll find some way to ruin you, Torelli, if you dare try a stunt like that. And you know I can," Michael threatened.

"Oh yeah--I know." Jack lifted his bottom up to the desk and hung it there. ""You did a number on me and Cassie at my house. You little girlfriend and sack mate, Haley Shears, was pretty convincing."

"Sack mate?" Claire now turned her glare on Michael. "You never told me that. I thought that she was just a little hungry actress you found," she accused.

"Like all the other hungry little actresses, Claire?" Jack stepped in. "The ones that were at the hospital trying to finish the job that you failed that night at my house . . . child murder?" He could barely hold in his cool.

"How dare you!" Claire flared nervously. "I. . .have no idea what you're implying."

"Should we ask Cassie for an interpretation?" He tried to keep the tightness out of his voice. "She knows every detail, and I can guarantee you that Ms. Cassie Callahan will never set foot on this studio lot again. And . . ." He lifted up and gave Michael the most sweet with complacency smile he could force on his lips. "That goes for me too. No way will I be 'Harry'."

"You can't!" Michael roared so loud the window glass shook, "I paid eight point five million on the belief that you would comply!"

"Then I guess you're out of eight-point-five-mil unless you can beg me to reconsider." Jack said with great delight.

"Beg!" Michael thundered. "I don't have to beg. I'll see you dead in Hollywood, I will! Not even the sleaziest of hard porn directors will touch you! You'll be on the sidelines forever! *Forever!* Do you hear me Torelli? I know you! You can't take that!"

"You're right—I can't take it. I can't take any of it anymore, and neither can Cassie. So . . . we're both retiring. Do your worse to me in Hollywood, I don't give a shit!" Jack said with much aplomb, never having imagined how good it would feel to actually say the words. "Then there's the small matter of your security guard, George . . ."

"George?" Michael asked with terse cautiousness.

"He wants to retire a little early, arthritis is acting up and wife wants to travel. So I'm sure you'll give him a *full*, early pension." Jack reached behind his casual jacket, as he could just envision the reaction before it even occurred.

"Are you out of your mind? When did that 'Old Dinosaur' talk to you?" Michael demanded angrily, trembling a hand to his brow to brush away a black hair strand.

"He not only talked to me, but also a private investigator who taped his statement about what happened that night in my house," Jack replied calmly.

"So? The Old Buzzard has no proof!"

"Is this enough proof?" Jack thrust two papers at him. "My blood was loaded with Valium, the action potentiated by the champagne. The doctor told me it was a near lethal dose . . . attempted murder, Mike."

Trying to hide his panic, Michael stared at the lab reports. "How could you ever prove that I fed you Valium?"

"Look at the rest . . . no rum, coke, or pot like Haley Shears swore to the press that I took. Which makes her a liar. I'm sure Rud Hanna can get the truth out of her, even in Australia. He hates the slut and it would be his pleasure. And then all the others. I wonder how long it would take them to crack once the LAPD got a hold of them."

An anxiety-ridden Michael went on a frenzy tearing up the papers until only confetti remained.

"Wimpy move, Mike," Jack laughed. "I got copies all over this town and the hospital has the original. There's not a goddamn thing you can do." And then he turned to Claire. "I can just hear Cassie Callahan, sweetheart of the literary world whom millions respect and love, sitting on that witness stand and tearfully telling a judge and jury how the renowned Claire Gibson who slept and ego-fed her way to the top, tried to kill her baby. Talk about being ruined in this town . . . and I'll make sure it happens."

Claire placed a shaky hand to her forehead and looked like she was going to be sick.

Eyes wild with fury, Michael bolted up from his chair and flew across his desk. "What do you really want, Torelli?" he exploded. "Fame? Okay you got it! A home in Bel-Air? You got that too! A Mercedes-Benz? A lifetime contract? A role as producer or director once in awhile? Your right to select or reject any part? A prime table at any restaurant of your choice? You got it all!"

"You forget wheat cakes named after me," Jack added with casual amusement.

"Okay! That too! Just play 'Harry'! I need you to play 'Harry', dammit!"

Jack let out a long, low chuckle. "If only you would have asked me a year ago, I woulda probably had a coupla strokes, but I would have jumped on it regardless. However now, I can give you only one answer . . ." He wound up his lips into the brightest smile he owned. "Go to hell, Mike." With an exhilarating sense of freedom, he snapped a highly dramatic salute, did an about-face, and took proud strides out of the office, ignoring the screaming protests that fell onto his back . . .

****

Jack didn't halt his triumphant trek until his face basked in the glorious California sun. At that moment, it felt more glorious than it ever had. Extracting his sunglasses from his jacket pocket, he whipped them over his eyes and took one last glance around.

The place where it all started for me.

He saw the familiar buildings and people in various attire rapidly moving back and forth doing various activities that were like rote to him. Then he turned his glasses to the Python suites, and he smiled at the sight. It was the one part of Python Studios that he could never forget, he told himself. It was the place where his life *really* started. On impulse, he touched his fingers lightly to his lips and tossed a minuscule kiss in gratitude.

No more looks, Torelli. There's no more glitter to see.

And with this firmly resigned thought, Jack hurried to the Bob's Cadillac. He pulled open the passenger door and smiled into the interior of the car. "Well that chapter's closed, and now. I'm as excited as hell to start the next one . . ."

****

Riding on Bob Grayson's private plane had been as smooth as riding in a supersonic jet, Jack thought as he stood by the Hértz Car Rental at La Guardia Airport in New York City. He had decided to drive to Manhattan. He hadn't done so for a while and desired to feel the thrill of being back in the city of his birth. Furthermore, he wanted a vehicle to take Cassie around the old neighborhood so they both could relive the unforgettable years of his youth together.

He vacillated about what type of car to rent, finally deciding a convertible was preferable. *Tough to break all old habits at once.* And so he chose a black

Mustang convertible, a more appropriate car for Jack Torelli, *the man*, rather than a 'Vette or a Porsche which now fitted a nonexistent entity. The last thing he would from now on do is put on the dog for anyone, he thought with all the firmness of his new convictions.

He just wanted to be a *Torelli* again.

Before jumping behind the wheel, he wondered if he should maybe call home and tell the folks that he was on his way. But on second thought, he decided it would be more fun to surprise Cassie. Maybe an element of surprise would get a stronger response out of her, he hoped. The thought that maybe she wouldn't respond quite as heartily as he longed for, had rested heavily on his mind during the entire plane trip.

Did her talk with George resolve the trust problem? George hadn't said for certain.

But at least her love was there, he assured himself while starting the ignition. And onto that he could build mountains, even trust.

Traffic was just as bad as L.A., Jack decided ninety minutes later when he finally made it through the clogged Queens Midtown Tunnel into Manhattan. Favoring the accelerating pound of his heart, he resisted the urge to cruise a little and turned left on East Third. He battled traffic the entire distance to East Fourth where familiar sights began to pop up on both sides of the avenue. He slowed a bit and relished the feel of the atmosphere. It felt so clean and decent, he wanted to bathe in the incredible sensation. When he came to Old Saint Patrick's Cathedral, he stopped the convertible, lowered his head and made the sign of the cross, something he hadn't attempted for so long, he astonished that the action had come so naturally.

Yet if *had* come naturally.

Perhaps there was more hope for him than he even realized, he thought.

With growing excitement and a body hot with desire for the woman he loved, Jack gunned the car all the way to Mott Street, deciding to save his reminiscent cruise on Mulberry Street for tomorrow. He and Cassie would walk, if she felt up to it, and window shop like he had done as a child; although this time he planned on sampling every treat that his mouth or nose couldn't resist. And he may even try to find a game of stick ball. He knew Cassie would be thrilled to see him scamper around the bases like a kid. Next, he would find a *very* secluded street where he would kiss her until his lips were blue, then he would just hold her close and let her feel his love while he felt hers, and from there they could start the rebuilding process of their lives. He would give everything he had in him to gain her trust again, he silently vowed.

He slowed the Mustang when his boyhood home came into view. It hadn't changed! It was as if he had never left! His mouth suddenly watered with just the mind's smell of the spaghetti and crusty bread he knew his mom had in her kitchen. And then he saw his brothers! They were a little grayer but always recognizable. All five leaned against the rail of the front porch, and his insides stirred while his eyes filled with tears. Now he picked up speed unable to wait until he could bear hug every one of them.

Quickly he pulled to the curb behind the multitude of cars that lined the street. He smiled with wonder. *I bet every Torelli family member in town is inside to greet the long lost son.*

Thrilled at the thought, Jack hoisted his large shoulder bag over his arm and pulled off his sunglasses, firmly sticking them in his pocket. He would get a new pair tomorrow, ones that reflected a bit of his eyes, he told himself. No longer did he need to hide himself from the world.

"I'm satisfied with me," he joyfully whispered, and the mere words warmed him to the point of even more satisfaction. And he took brisk strides, his excitement escalating with each step. Cassie! His family! *Jesus, my eyes are craving.* He *really, truly* had a second chance!

Now he could see his brothers more clearly. They looked healthy, same loud big lunks. He could hear them already, telling dirty jokes from the sounds of it. Suddenly he couldn't wait to join them. The Six Torelli Brothers . . . they would be all together again. And he picked up his pace until he was jogging.

Finally, after what seemed like forever, though in actuality it had been a few minutes, he stood on the sidewalk in front of the building. Making no sound, he just stared, waiting for them to spot him. It was Jimmy who turned first and Jack flashed a big smile full of exhilaration.

"Torelli!"

He spun around and widened his eyes at the glint of black that pointed at him.

"YOU RUINED HER!"

The roaring voice rang through his ears and in split second he swerved just as he heard an explosion. He felt the impact of something hit the upper part of his body and then came a slow weave to the ground. Next, somewhere in mind, another explosion echoed. And then he heard yells and screams, thousands of them. Finally, one last sound hit his consciousness and he tried to hold on longer, knowing the shrill terror-filled scream belonged to the woman he loved.

Chapter 29—Heart-to-Heart

The shocking news spread from coast-to-coast like wildfire, and national media flooded to New York. Jack Torelli, star of the much awaited miniseries based on the popular bestseller, *The Life and Times of Harry Hannigan*, had been shot outside his parents home in New York City by a crazed executive from Starburst Publishing who had an obsession for author Cassie Callahan.

Geoffrey Haines, thirty-six and second in command in the Publicity Department at Starburst, had a history of mental problems according to his estranged parents, two upper-middle class professionals from New Hampshire. He had seen psychiatrists off and on since age twelve for problems with abnormal rage, although refused any further treatment once he started college at Princeton, and this fact had drawn his family away from him out of fear.

Upon search of his expensive upper Manhattan co-op, the NYPD found blown-up pictures of Cassie Callahan on nearly every wall as well as sexual paraphernalia. There were also at least forty copies of *The Life and Times of Harry Hannigan* and fifteen copies of the sequel. All were marked up with editing symbols and obscenities were written across whole pages. On a wall in a spare bedroom, devoid of any pictures of Cassie Callahan, hung a large photo of Jack Torelli, a graffiti of obscenities, artwork, and a butcher knife stuck in the chest part of the picture.

The self-inflicted bullet to the head had been lethal on impact, and Geoffrey Haines would be buried next to his grandparents in a cemetery in Concord, "Finally at peace," his parents had been quoted as saying by several media. Geoff Haines made only one final request in a note found at his office desk . . . He wanted exquisite, passionate black orchids on his grave.

Starburst Publishing refused any comment.

****

Pandemonium reigned outside of New York University Medical Center. The media mobbed any medical staff that emerged to try to find out the condition of Actor/Director Jack Torelli. Finally the NYPD had to intervene to maintain control.

The Torelli family, a least a hundred in count, remained secluded inside the Medical Center. They kept vigil while waiting for their son, brother, nephew and cousin to get out of surgery to remove a small-caliber bullet from the upper part of the left chest. The bullet, doctors gratefully told them, missed the heart and was lodged to the side of the left lung.

In lieu of her pregnancy, the doctors also tried to admit a hysterical Cassie, but she refused. In her overwhelming terror, she felt the most comfortable in the arms of Marianna and Carlo Torelli. The intense guilt was also overwhelming. *Why didn't I bring Geoff's name to the attention of authorities long ago?* Now all her reasons for not doing so seemed foolish and insignificant when viewed within the larger picture of such a tragic event.

If he didn't make it . . .

Sobs exploded from her deepest inner recesses. She would be hard-pressed to make it as well despite his child inside of her. She couldn't live without her Jacko's strong arms around her. He was the only one who could truly keep her safe, as evidenced by her brick wall. She could sense it trembling like an earthquake climbing the Richter Scale with each moment passed. If the news wasn't good, she quavered to herself, she knew total collapse would be imminent.

Another two hours passed before the cardiothoracic surgeon stepped into the surgical waiting area to talk to the mass of family that had congregated. A sudden sacred hush fell over the room and every face fixed pleadingly on him.

"The surgery went well. None of his vital organs were nicked. The bullet landed in soft tissue between the lung and shoulder and we were able to remove all of it. I anticipate no problems or complications. He's a basically healthy man."

Cassie burst out in wild sobs while dozens of pairs of arms hugged her. Then she gazed around at the flurry of ecstatic family members, thinking that the cumulative noise of cheering, wailing, and squealing was probably waking up the entire hospital morgue.

"When can I see him?" she choked out to the doctor.

"As soon as he gets to his hospital room from Post-Anesthesia, Ms. Callahan."

Feeling words of gratitude on her lips, but too emotionally overpowered to express any, she merely nodded her thanks while the totter of her wall slowly rescinded into a comfortable quietude . . .

****

Two days after the shooting, Jack sat propped up in his hospital bed. His bare chest sported a large thick dressing that extended from the top of his left chest to his shoulder. He ached like hell, but told himself it was bearable. With Cassie still in such a hysterical state, he didn't want to be pumped up with excessive painkillers. He needed all his faculties to keep her secure despite his infirmity.

He felt forced to recover quickly, he thought. And he had. The intravenous needle was gone and he was taking full liquids plus sitting in a chair three times a day. Tomorrow he wanted to walk, he told the doctor, and from there he saw it as only a matter of days before he could just keep her in his arms and let her know that everything was all right.

Jack was aware that many of her emotions stemmed from the flood of pregnancy hormones, as explained to him by the doctor keeping an eye on her. She refused to go home with his parents and glued herself to the hospital. Thus his family took turns staying at the hospital so she had someone with her at all times. Now if he turned a listening ear, he could hear his brother Mark trying to joke her out of her sobs while they sat outside his room.

Visitors had been in and out, mainly family members who gave him teary hugs and said prayers in English and Italian. It had been wonderful to see all of them despite the trying conditions, he thought. And he remembered when he came out of anesthesia and saw his parents and all his brothers and sisters hovering over him with tears in their eyes, he wished for them to never let go of him again.

Held up by his parents, Cassie whimpered like a wounded animal, crying out all her guilt to him. "It's all my fault, Jacko. I'm so sorry, darling. I should have had him locked away. *Stupido! Stupido!*"

He lifted his right hand and motioned her to come nearer which she did with much caution, her eyes on his large bandage the entire time. "I woulda taken a hundred bullets to protect you, Baby," he whispered to her, then he planted his dry lips on hers and briefly brushed his fingers on her hair before his hand dropped in exhaustion.

Shortly after he heard the news, Harv Wellson and a couple of his publicity people had flown to New York in Bob Grayson's private plane which had just landed back in Los Angeles before it took off for to New York again. The publicity people conducted a couple press conferences, instilling some calm into the wild media mobs.

Stretching out on the pillows, Jack recalled yesterday when a tentative Harv had come for a visit. He had heard about Jack's conversation with Michael Isle, he said. The producer had screamed at him on the phone for two hours demanding that Harv get Jack to take the 'Harry' role.

"Did he also tell you that I quit, Harv?"

"Yeah--he said something crazy like that. But I wanted to tell Mike he was full of horseshit."

"What if I tell you that he's not full of horseshit, Harv?"

Harv had to place a hand on the bed to keep from reeling. "What the hell are you saying, Jack? We could make a killing on this miniseries and the future . . . Christ Almighty! Are you a frickin' idiot? I'm already hearing the word 'Emmy' from critics who viewed parts of that miniseries."

"Doesn't matter. Even if I were nominated, I wouldn't go or accept it. Why for Christ's sakes? To sit there in the midst of a flock of Hollywood peacocks all trying like hell to outdo each other while I'm sitting there trying to remember why I'm there in the first place. Let me tell you, the joy of the craft gets obliterated in all the bullshit. No thanks to that fucking ritual."

"Have you finally gone nuts?" Harv hollered in total disbelief. "What the hell did that bullet do? Graze you head too? An Emmy! A culmination! Wear a goddamn blindfold if you must, but this is an *Emmy!*"

"So?" he challenged. "What the hell do I with it? Crack nuts? Toss it through a window when I'm pissed off? Use it as an indoor hydrant for the dog I plan on getting my kid? *What* is the usefulness?"

The question stunned Harv into silence while he thought about this. And to Jack's great amusement, Harv never came up with an answer.

"I'd place it on the same plane as Michael Isle's nut brancakes served in the infamous pink coffee shop, Harv," he laughed.

"He'll massacre me, Jack," Harv moaned.

"No he won't, Harv. All you have to tell him is that you have a copy of the two lab reports, and I guarantee he'll be hiring your clients left and right . . ."

Despite Harv's disappointing loss of 'the green', they parted on a very amicable level. He had been fortunate, Jack thought now. He was probably one of a minute percent in Hollywood who truly *saw* their agent plus felt the strong swing of his bat to boot. He'd never forget Harv Wellson as long as he lived, he figured. The fast-talking agent had taught him much about perseverance in a climate of impossibility.

And then there had been Good 'Ole Bastard, Rud . . .

He grimaced with a laugh he couldn't restrain. The studio owner had flown to New York on his own private plane and charmed his mother so much, she had told Jack that he *must* invite his friend over for spaghetti. He had decided to just tell his mother that Rud had an allergy to Italian food, but *never* the truth.

"So Harv tells me that you're not coming back, Jack," Rud said point blank.

"Nope--I'm sucked dry and I need major refilling," he replied.

"Well . . . I got a few director prospects for that new studio, but if you ever want to come back, the door's open at EMAX," Rud said without a blink and plenty of directness.

"Thanks, but no thanks. I don't care if I ever see another studio. I'm taking another direction with my life, Rud."

"You've been through hell, I know that, Jack. But I plan to ease it a little." Rud said in a no-nonsense tone. "The moment that Shears bitch places her foot on Hollywood soil, I kick her ass back to Santa Cruz, *sure shit* . . ."

And not even the chance to watch that would make him return to Hollywood, he thought humorously. But what next? He had thought carefully over the last couple days and believed he knew what the most prudent move would be. The bullet, and Cassie's reaction to it, had changed many things for him. First priority had to be the woman he loved. And as he saw it, what she needed most was peace--as did he. The rest would have to take care of itself, he thought.

"Stay in New York, Jacko. You could start an acting school. You and Cassie have the money to do that," his father had suggested.

"Might be something that I'd like to do, Pop. But not now. Who knows though, a few years down the line?"

Wrinkling his face with discomfort, he adjusted his back on the pillow. It was time to talk seriously, he thought. He needed to get Cassie settled down because in the worst way, they needed to talk, heart-to-heart . . .

****

The next evening, Jack sent his family home, told the nurses he didn't want to be disturbed, and he pulled Cassie close to him on the bed, ignoring every bit of pain as he held her tightly.

"I think it's time for 'truth and consequences', Cass," he began, then winced.

She winced too. "Is your arm okay, Jacko. Do you need a nurse or a pill or something?"

Seeing the desperation in her eyes, Jack promptly he planted a kiss on top of her head. "I'm fine, honey. I'll be good as new in a couple days. Put that out of your mind."

"I'm trying, Jacko, but it's hard. I feel so damn guilty and I can't help that."

He lifted his right hand to stroke her hair. "You know, an old Irish priest once told my Catechism class that God does things for a purpose, and perhaps this too happened for a purpose, and eye-opener so to speak."

Cassie stared up. The evidences of pain were gone from his face, replaced by a serenity that she had never seen before. "I take it that your eyes have been opened to something . . ."

He saw the inquisitiveness and he couldn't help smiling at the sight. "I have a great desire to start fresh with my life and a big part of that is clearing the air. Both of us. So I have a few confessions to make."

Greatly curious, she lifted her head from his arm crook so her face was closer to his. "I'm listening with both ears and eyes on you."

He took pause to compose his thoughts, not wanting to skip anything. "I read your computer disks for *Season of Sorrow*. I. . .knew something was up with you and I felt helpless because, try as I might, I couldn't figure it out. So I looked."

Apprehension shot through her. *My god, what he must think!*

"I know it was wrong, Cass. But I learned a lot. It made me understand you so I could better love and take care of you. I know how now."

Tears pooled in her eyes. He wasn't holding it against her!

"What did you understand about me, Jacko?" Cassie choked out. "Perhaps if you misinterpreted, I could fill in some holes, be a little honest myself."

"I know about Kristi and how you lost her. But you gotta have faith that the kid will eventually discover the truth for herself. Maturity can be a very profound thing."

"I hope so, Jacko," she whispered, tears cascading down her cheeks.

With his fingertips, he lightly brushed away the wetness. He understood. It must be wonderful for her to have someone truly know her and still accept her.

"I also know about your mother and Sandy, and how you fought so hard to be your own person though you were smaller and younger. And I realize why you wrote in the first place, and specifically why you wrote 'Harry'. Then it all collapsed on top of you when you entered the big time because emotionally, you had never been cut out for any of it. That's why it fell apart. I also know about the abuse . . . the rape too . . . and I still wanna kill because of it, but I realize it would change nothing."

"Are we supposed to be totally honest?" she trembled out, thrilled by his approbation of all of it. She would never have to pretend or hide She could live in her world whenever she chose and know he would readily enter it. "It was Curt Farchmin, the man with the icy eyes like Mother, the man over Geoff Haines who paralyzed me emotionally by bringing out Sandy more and more. I almost lost it after he raped me but you came to New York and saved me."

He nodded, having figured that out long ago. "I'm glad you turned to me, for several reasons, including the fact that it forced me back to New York, because . . .

"I know, Jacko," she cut in quietly. "Your sisters told me. I can just feel the guilt that you must have experienced all those years. One of your sisters said the Hollywood was the worst possible place for you to go, but I disagree. You would have been trying to find that man wherever you went, and most likely would have screwed up horribly until you did."

"Oh Cass . . ." He frantically touched his lips to her hair, grateful that in only a few tender, compassionate words, she had so keenly summed it all up without one ounce of reproach. "But I found that man now, and I swear that I'll try my damndest never to lose sight of him."

"That's what I told your sisters," she said softly. "I said that if Jacko wasn't that man, I wouldn't love and trust him like I do. So no need to swear—I believe you."

He grabbed his lips with his own and kissed passionately while feeling the passion of her lips as well. Her affirming the magic 'trust' word filled him with indescribable joy, and he knew now, that he could even admit more.

"Cassie . . ." He slowly released his mouth. "That first day we met at Python, you asked me that question about Carly Ribaldi . . . well I lied. I did purposely lure her to my apartment--not knowing she was only sixteen, mind you. If I did, I would never have. But I did, because she was young, unblemished, and I guess I felt that I needed that."

Cassie closely studied his face and saw much anguish in his eyes, and something else. She looked deeper until the scattered puzzle pieces flew together into a whole picture, and she knew.

"Does this have to do with the mechanical toys that Haley Shears told me about?" And in a heartbeat, the elusive emotion exploded across his face.

"She told you?" he cried out, wanting to hide in his horror. *Jesus*. This was the woman he loved and desired with every part of his body. *She knew*.

"Oh darling!" Cassie held him as tight as she dared and promptly felt his tears fall onto her neck. "Don't ever be ashamed. You're the sexiest man in the world to me. *No one* can turn my body into flames like you. They were just the wrong kind of women, don't you see? It was your guilt, Jacko. You knew deep down that you shouldn't be with them, and *that* made you impotent, nothing else. Think about it. Not once were you ever that way with me. In fact . . ." She gave a devilish laugh. "You were an absolute *animale*. The proof is growing inside of me."

Jack's shoulders racked with sobs at the awesome and insightful understanding that she had just laid on him. Not one disgusting or pitying look. All he felt was her love, and at that moment, he thought that he had never loved her so much.

"It was all part of the repulsive package, Cass, a downward turn that kept turning and me helpless to stop it until Carly Ribaldi stopped it for me." He lifted his wet face and looked her square in the eye. "Ultimately, I *did* do the right thing that night. I didn't touch her, I tried to help her, even though my efforts failed. From the point I said 'No' to her, that's when the turn started slowly but surely upward, and it was still climbing when I met you. Otherwise, I wouldn't have been able to look someone like you in the eye, let alone find the guts to pursue you like a maniac."

She brushed away a few careless strands of black hair from his brow. "I sensed 'that man' in you almost immediately or else I would have run screaming in the other direction after all the indoctrination Michael did on me. Maybe . . . I even sensed it the moment I accidentally watched *Clay Slade*. I don't know. All I know is that when I saw your face, I knew that you had the strength of character and body to be my 'uncle'. And you did Jacko. I could never feel so secure with any other man."

"Speaking of 'uncle' . . ." Jack lowered his eyes, asking God to make her understand. "I turned down 'Harry Two', Cass. George told me what Mike and Claire had done, and I just couldn't, and . . . if the truth be known, I didn't know if I could anyway. To be honest . . . I'm giving up acting . . . well . . . Hollywood at least and acting for a while, maybe a long while. I just don't know now, Cass."

"I just knew it!" She broke down into gleeful laughter. "That's why I insisted that Starburst sell Michael the book rights at an exorbitant cost. I just knew that once George told you, Michael would probably be lucky to escape with all his capped teeth." She raised her palm. "We got 'em good! Give me five, Partner."

Startled by the unexpected response, Jack didn't raise his hand immediately. But when he finally found the mobility to do so, he smacked her hand with all the intense happiness and relief that suddenly filled him. Now he felt even freer.

"I love you so damn much, Cassie Callahan, and I so gratefully thank the day I signed that *Clay Slade* contract." He wrapped his right arm around her and crashed his lips atop hers, never wanting to stop the soft, moist sensation on his mouth . . .

****

Cassie lay snuggled in the crook of Jack's arm and his fingers gently ran up and down her cheek. "So are we done with 'truth and consequences'?" she asked.

Jack slowed his fingers movements as he carefully thought about his answer. For a few moments he wondered, then vacillated, and ultimately the thinking stopped, replaced by certain resolve. "I think we should talk about passion, Cass."

"Passion?"

Jack gave her gentle nod. "You know, I always prided myself on having the passion of my craft. If nothing else, I had that. And I thought I knew that because I firmly believed that passion could never be crushed by any amount of heartache *if* it was real. With all my heartache, yet my still pursuit of my passion, I thought I had it covered. But it was all bullshit, a mask, an excuse for what was really going on." He looked down at her. "Does that sound familiar to you?"

Bittersweet emotions flooded her. She knew the answer without a moment's thought. "It sounds very familiar. Twelve years worth of struggling to create a 'Harry—that's how familiar. And now it's funny. I *had* to write day in and day out. Physiologically and psychologically, I couldn't stand to be away from that attic. I ruined myself. My body . . . you should have seen me. It's passion, I drilled into myself. So I kept on regardless, under that auspice. I couldn't help it, I thought. It was a must, like an addict's fix. I had to let the words stream, and perfectly so, immaculate. I could sense the power of 'Harry'. I felt that 'verge' and I wasn't gonna stop until I had it."

"Now *that* sounds even more familiar." He let out a low chuckle. "Just substitute stage for the attic, and it's my exact scenario."

"So it was never really passion for either of us."

"It's a rare entity, Cass, perhaps inborn for all I know. But so many people do so many crazy things because of the word 'passion'. 'I have the passion' . . . you hear that all the time in Hollywood. However, it's easy to say and even convince oneself it's there when in actuality it's being forced for some deep-seated need. True passion can't be forced. It's an enigma, yet at the same time so obvious, one can feel it on impact."

"Have you ever felt it?" she questioned.

"Yeah." He smiled at the remembrance. "A tap dancing kid that I once knew had it and now his success is growing. Maybe to find one's true passion leads to the greatest satisfaction in one's success. The true *umph* and unstoppable drive is always there, and to use that productively must be the greatest feeling in the world, I've concluded." She lifted a curious look to him. "So is this leading somewhere?"

He raised his eyebrows in a knowing way. "Maybe I need to find my true passion, and maybe you do too. I'd kinda like to live out the rest of my life with that *umph* and drive. How about you?"

"Sounds like a mighty task." Cassie's insides agitated with sheer terror. To accomplish what he proposed would mean total destruction of her thirty-five-year-old brick wall.

"Take my hand, Cass. I promise to hold on tight, and not peel away a brick until you're ready. I'll be with you every inch of the way, honey. Please trust me," Jack pleaded.

"Where?" Now her voice agitated as well. "Where in the world could we do something so recklessly frightful? I mean the exposure alone would be so . . . difficult . . . with so many eyes. I. . .

He grasped her lips with his to stop all her foolish excuses that held no more water for either of them. They both were filled to the brim with excuses, he thought, and now it was time to shed them one-by-one and try to discover what lie beyond. He wanted not an ounce of pretense with Cassie Callahan.

No brick walls.

No fantasy worlds.

Only *real* would suffice.

And he knew that someday she would see it the same way.

"Jacko!" She pulled away with a terror-stricken look. "We need to discuss this, and not lightly. I'm scared. I admit it. But I also admit that with you . . ." And she tried to force a brave smile. "I'm not quite so scared anymore. If I trust anyone to peel away the bricks, it's you. There! I just surrendered myself."

Feeling his joy explode, he held her tight and damned every ounce of pain. "Then I just have one question for you, lady . . . How would you like being married to a turtle farmer?"

Conclusion—Hand-in-hand

The balmy, mid-October Caribbean Sea breeze blew lazily across the street and gently shook the fronds of the coconut palms that surrounded the variety of shops and buildings. Having emerged from their three confined days in a bungalow, renewing their love in the peace and quiet of the tropical paradise, Jack and Cassie strolled hand-in-hand along the street.

She raised her sunglasses to the clear, cloudless sky, and felt so much tranquility it overwhelmed her. Their lovemaking had been more beautiful than ever, she thought with total satisfaction. They both could be their own abandoning selves without an eye on them. And during the last few days, she could even say that one or two of her firmly mortared bricks had painlessly slipped away without a single urge on her part to retrieve them. Yet, she felt even more like *Cassie* despite the plunge. She knew, without a doubt or further reservation, that this place and this man would be her salvation.

"I need to find a car rental, Cass." Jack gazed left and right, then for a brief moment his gaze fell on Cassie. Her middle was expanding, he thought with the growing expectant thrill of holding his son in his arms. He loved to gently rub her middle and set his palm over it to feel the baby's strong kick. *My future hope.* He told himself that it was a glorious new adventure, the icing on the cake of his new life. *Cassie Torelli* . . . he could run the name through his mind forever and still not believe his wonderful fortune.

"Why not just buy one, Jacko?" she asked playfully. "That International bank on the Grand Caymans must be busting at the seams, so maybe you should give it some relief."

He thought about this for a moment, then wrinkled his nose below his sunglasses. "Naw-- who needs a car? Maybe I'll get an old jeep later on when your due date gets closer."

She giggled with delight. "Suit yourself, Mr. Average Joe-Blow Torelli."

He reached down to kiss her. "My pleasure Mrs. Who the Hell are You Torelli . . ."

****

In a rented jeep that looked circa 1940's, Jack and Cassie headed along the northern coast in a southwest direction. She took in the tropical beauty and breathed in the salty sea air. Soon her fertile mind activated into the creation of another world.

"Me, Jacko, and little Jacko, swimming hand-in-hand in the lushness of the green, blue and brown, day in and day out, without a care. Just loving and touching each other and finding our passion in that before we apply it to a broader world where our true passions will surge for all our basic efforts."

Briefly, Jack took his eyes off the road to look at her. She looked so beautiful at that moment, he thought. The breeze picked up her blonde hair and tousled it while her face below the small sunglasses was bathed in dreamy thoughtfulness. *And her words* . . . they were equally beautiful and warmed his heart. It was *Cassie!* He shifted his eyes back to the road, thoroughly content with the world she had created.

When finally he caught view of the familiar sign through his sunglasses, his heart jumped in anticipation. He and Cassie were home! He raised a finger at the distant sign. "See that Cass? Now that turtle picture you admired will come to life."

He turned into the road and the jeep passed under the colorful sign. Instantly, Cassie raved about the detailed artistic talent that went into it. And he noticed that not once did she complain about the increasing smell of reptile. She merely said that she could picture herself on the bottom of the sea like a turtle princess, grasping the magnificent fins whenever she wanted to take a ride. He wanted to kiss her then and there for making their new life sound so gloriously poetic, he possessed not one doubt about the rightness of bringing her to Cayman Brac.

Although the once grand house appeared even more dilapidated, the turtle pools looked the same, and he felt a mist of nostalgic tears under his sunglasses. When he exited the jeep and stretched out his legs, he darted his sunglasses towards the artist's clearing and memories abounded.

She had been my salvation then. Perhaps . . . for both of us now?

Suddenly, sensing her nearness, he jerked his glasses to the right and held them there. Her back was still stiff with proud determination, although she moved a bit slower and her hair had grayed a little more. Yet her midnight blue eyes set against the rich, mahogany skin tone glowed with incandescence.

"Jack Tyler." Mattie Claret's eyes flashed with knowing. "I've been expecting you. My dolls don't lie." She shifted her look to a brightly smiling Cassie. "And you too . . . Cassie."

He knew that he shouldn't be surprised, rather feel awestruck to be mind-connected to such a treasure of the world. "We're back where it all started, Mattie. I hope you don't mind a couple of instant guests," he said, knowing already that Mattie wouldn't mind at all. She would nurture both of them, and perhaps even capture Cassie's world on canvass so he always had a remembrance once her brick wall was nothing but blowing dust.

"Are those the turtles?" Cassie squealed upon seeing waves of water escaping the sides of the pools. "I have to see them!" She wobbled off as fast as her body would take her.

Mattie raised a devious eyebrow to him. "I see that you need no more manly water, Jack Tyler." She walked forward to grasp his arms between her feathery hands. "I envision it as being wonderful having a child on Los Tortugas. Grandma Mattie can sing Jamaican lullabies and pretend it is the child of Mr. Claret instead."

With a broad smile, Jack pulled her close. "I love you Mattie Claret, if I never told you before." Then he looked down into the sharp, all-knowing eyes. "And now I'd like to see my old turtle pals too."

So they walked, sharing the special bond that would be there no matter the distance between them, and ultimately they stood at the edge of the pool. Cassie was bent over the pool wall, gently stroking the turtle shell while she made loving noises. Jack placed his free arm around Cassie and also pulled her close.

"I love it here, Jacko!" Cassie enthused, hugging him tightly.

He focused his sunglasses down on Mattie, then down at Cassie, touching his lips to hers and telling himself that he'd never let go of his greatest treasure in all the world. Finally he looked down into the pool. The sight of the magnificent ridley turtle made his heart swell. And he wanted to shout out his magnificent thoughts.

Perfetto!

If you enjoyed reading Seeking Out Harry by Linda Coleman, and wish to order additional copies, please send $12.95 plus $4.20 S&H to:
Press-TIGE Publishing Inc.
291 Main Street
Catskill, NY 12414

Look for our other titles in your favorite bookstore.